LITTLE WINGS

Paul Fox

Front Cover Art by Kelsey Beerman

ISBN: 0692327797
ISBN 13: 9780692327791
Library of Congress Control Number: 2014920202
Paul Fox, Leesburg, VA

FOREWORD

Every day another World War II veteran dies. Soon none will remain. I want to thank them all for what they have done for their country and celebrate the families and legacies they left behind.

This book is dedicated to the brave men and women who sacrificed their lives for our freedom during war. For every Joe DiMaggio and Ted Williams, there were a thousand who never had the chance to play the game they loved and show the world their talents. I wanted to give them one last chance to take the field and another opportunity to save the world.

UTOFU GLIDE

God stood on the ledge and stared at the empty black slate of space. He held a thimble of light between his forefinger and thumb. He cast the light into the void.

Nimrod found him by the glacial cliffs of the Utofu Glide, which overlooked the newly created and brilliant Dyollet Lift Nebula.

"God, it's Nimrod," he announced quietly.

"Nimrod. That's a rough name. Makes you sound like a buffoon."

"Yes. However, I was once a brave warrior on Earth and an angel in Heaven."

"I know." God paused and lowered his head. "I can't concentrate."

"Why?"

"The universe is under attack. We are at war."

"These are troubled times."

God turned to Nimrod. "I need your help."

"How can I help you?"

"Michael, the archangel, is piecing together a team, but he is short on angels. They have been sent into the tumultuous war being waged in the Stounfad System. The survival of the Blanco Trollien Archipelago hangs in the balance. The Darkness is striking on all fronts."

"How can I be of service to Heaven?"

"I have spoken to Michael and asked that he include you in Earth's defense."

"Michael took my wings and swore never to return them." Nimrod bowed his head. "I failed horribly on my first assignment."

"I am aware. Michael can be stern. I have spoken with him. He is aware you will visit him."

"And my wings?" Nimrod inquired.

"Your wings will not be returned, but there are other ways to help." God stroked his beard. "There is a new resident in Heaven. He lives near Ghara Serpiana. His name is Jairus. Jairus is a victim of the raging comet that pinballed through the Behorrin Debartik galaxy. The moon-sized projectile ricocheted through the Yarrges Winch solar system and left several civilizations on multiple planets in desperate need of Heaven's help. Jairus's mother survived the carnage and will remain behind to assist the living on Blanco Trollien. I want you to take him under your wing." God coughed lightly. "Sorry. It's just an expression."

"It would be my honor," Nimrod said. He found the courage to ask God a question. "I failed Michael before. I don't want to fail again. Satan is a cunning adversary. Can you share any thoughts that would help me be better prepared?"

"Yes. What would you like to know?"

"May I start with some background questions?" God raised an eyebrow. "How did you create the world in seven days?" Nimrod asked.

"Well, that's a bit of an understatement. It wasn't just seven days." God said.

"What do you mean?" asked Nimrod.

"For eons there was nothing—just the numbness of limbo. In a universe of darkness and nothingness, there is no language or thought. There are no ideas. Deep in my consciousness— or subconsciousness, as the case may be—a frustration wore on my soul. That frustration awoke my soul. I use these words we understand now, but many billions of years ago, a soul with no identity struggled restlessly with this 'feeling' or urge to become something. Concepts are especially difficult to rationalize with no other basis on which to judge. That was where I was at the beginning of what we now call 'time.' Alone. In the dark vastness with nothing but an urge." God gazed with loneliness into the newly filled void.

"How did you manage to break free of this tomb of nothingness?"

"One basic truism. It is a truth now, but it was an incredibly difficult realization at the time. If there was nothing, there must have been something. It's the beauty of math. Nothing is a value equaling zero. In order for zero to exist or have meaning, there must be something to equate it with. I didn't have the first clue what that was, but it was something. That was a start. Do you know how long it took me to create the number one? Ideas and concepts children of all thinking species all over the galaxies grasp at the youngest of ages took me eons to conceptualize. I was a very slow student." God laughed humbly. "But I had plenty of time."

"The concept of the number one from a formless soul is a long way from a universe filled with endless galaxies, billions of stars, planets, and life-forms. How did all this come about from nothing?"

"Remember, if there is nothing, then there is something. Everything you can see, smell, touch, or feel only has to be imagined. I had plenty of time to imagine anything I wanted. The more I imagined and thought, the more things became real. The first thing I imagined was something to hold. I felt alone because

I was. I didn't know myself, so I couldn't create any friends to play with. I imagined something stationary and solid to hold and feel. I created a rock. This rock tested my patience. I flailed trying to reach for something—tangible. The rock was simple, though, compared to light or sound or shapes. Do you have any idea how long it takes to dream up a square?" God smiled wryly.

"No," Nimrod replied.

"It takes a very long time. How long I could not say. I had not yet determined a measure for time." God opened his pocket watch and smiled. "It took quite a while. Creating things takes time and imagination. Once I got through some complicated concepts such as light, space, time, and distance, my mind and I took a trip around the universe. It was a dark place that yearned to be decorated with some of those grand colors and forms I had conceived. This universe is a lovely place. For billions of years, all I did was renovate this bleak, drab universe with astounding places of light, color, shape, and form. I could go visit them anytime I wanted. Then I realized that wasn't quite true." God peeked forlornly past the edge of the Utofu Glide and into the abyss.

"What wasn't true?"

"I couldn't go anywhere I wanted all the time. Not safely anyway."

"What do you mean?"

"From nothing comes something. I had become a creator, and from the creator came a destroyer. The universe's dark force is just as determined to return us to the night as I am to lead us into the light."

"Did you create the universe's dark force?"

"I was; so was the Darkness. I stirred; so did the playing field. In the earliest days, there was the fear a child imagined—loneliness. I am what I am. He is the opposite. He became when I became. My existence woke him from a comfortable slumber. The Darkness is evil, wicked, and angry. He despises the light. He has vowed to extinguish all that is good. He is and has always been a staunch opponent, but he will fail in the end."

"How can you be so certain?"

"For everything that I create—joy, life, the advancement of my imagination—he too must create something that destroys what I have conceived. The Darkness yearns only to defile and destruct. Eventually there will be a crossroads. There will be a moment he has erased all that exists. Only one will remain. Will the Darkness destroy himself? No. He is too vain. It is better to be than not to be."

"What do you think would happen if the dark force was the only thing left in the universe?"

"He would appreciate life. The flavor of existence is a taste far too sweet. Being dormant in the universe is a far cry from being alone. I surmise the Darkness would amend his thinking. He would turn to creation." God held his cane closely to his chest. "But I can't take that chance. We've all come too far. I am not a gambler. The Darkness is."

"Why are souls the keys to living things?"

"They are life's engine. Tissue, muscle, and bone form fascinating vessels that transport the souls. The soul infuses joie de vivre into the inanimate. The soul is my finest opus. By creating the soul and placing it within a species that could think and imagine for themselves, I had a foundation of friends. For the first time in my existence, I was not lonely. I had companions all over the universe."

"Why does the Darkness covet souls?"

"The balance of the universe. The Darkness understands my vulnerability. Friends are the most precious commodity. To love and care. Not to possess and control. Not to infect with material or manipulative ends. The more the love grows, the more the Darkness hates and tempts. He goes to great lengths to destroy souls through seduction, corruption, and violence. He turns good souls against one another. He creates the pain that causes good souls to lose their faith. A society that has lost faith is low-hanging fruit for an annihilator such as the Darkness. The more souls he can condemn, the weaker I become. That is why I have an extraordinary resolve to justify the faith of the souls that believe in me the way I believe in them. The armies of Heaven are ubiquitous and there to protect them. The Darkness thrives on duels. He will pass over millions of tainted souls to corrupt and defile the righteous. He takes particular glee in that pastime. His plan unfolds. He diverts your attention to aid the weak, needy souls. Then we leave the righteous exposed and vulnerable. If the universe's balance ever tips too far one way or the other, then the fate of the souls will be decided."

"Why did you create souls that can be tempted?"

"The ability to think, choose, create, and enjoy are the rights of a living soul. Otherwise the soul is a slave to the master. I cannot be that master. To create a universe of puppets would be a child's game—a game I played with the dinosaurs. I loved the dinosaurs. They didn't have souls, but they were magnificent beings I created. I was young and creating new, disparate undertakings that appealed to me. The beautiful *Brachiosaurus* majestically strode above the treetops, and sauropods, *Diplodocus*, and *Stegosaurus* dined on the underbrush. They laid eggs and regenerated life. This revolution of life helped me define the next level of living being." God's smile turned grim. "Then the Darkness sent in the destroyers. Those assassins he created weren't dinosaurs. They were butchers. Raptors and *Carnotaurus* sank their knifelike teeth into my beautiful creations. Even then my dinosaurs adapted and survived. The Darkness wouldn't be satisfied, though, until all my creation was destroyed. We have battled in every galaxy. It was the first time he attacked Earth. He diverted a comet shower directly to Earth and killed everything." God paused. He prayed. Then he looked at Nimrod and beamed. "Almost everything. Life has an uncanny ability to survive."

"Why do different species worship different gods?"

"There is only one God. I am he. I have sent many messengers too many places with the Word of goodness. Species cling to what they have seen, touched with their fingers, and heard with their ears. My messengers then become idols of worship. To be clear..." He looked at Nimrod sternly. "I become very upset when people worship me. I want them to worship the thoughts of goodness and the idea that goodness begets more goodness. By failing to follow this map to Heaven, the Darkness will take a soul into his hole of pain. The Darkness loves to inflict pain on life before extinguishing it. He is sadistic in more ways than the mind can conceive. He's cruel. He is crafty. He manipulates each species against the very messengers I send with the Word of goodness. He fashions wars among the species. This causes me great pain. All the messengers brought the same Word. The Darkness twists that around with vanity, greed, and lust. 'My God's better than your God.' A masterstroke the Darkness inflicted from my good intentions. I am not perfect. I am good. I am always looking to create a better universe. I can't do it alone. All the thinking species must help and be strong against evil."

"Is Satan the Darkness?"

"No. Satan is the public face for the evil franchise on Earth. He is doing a convincing job," God noted ruefully. "It's too bad. He could have been one of the great angels. I've never seen the Darkness. He manifests in the forms of many things, in many species, and in many ways. He could be in the wind or rain. He hides in the sun or an asteroid bent on destruction. Disease is one of his most beloved measures. He can be a brute or as subtle as a whisper into madness. The Darkness is the will of evil and damnation. Satan has a soul, vanity, and pride. I've seen his soul's beauty, but it has become eroded and bilious. I am afraid the Darkness has no soul. Maybe that is the Darkness's pain."

"What makes you happy?"

"The very simple things. Picking people up when they are down. Finding cures when they are sick. Going to someone's aid after tragedy. Getting to truly know someone. Love. Compassion. Passion. Life. Attempting and achieving the impossible things I revealed in the spirits of all the species I created. The souls in the universe expand the endless possibilities of goodness. The deeds of kindness multiply and inject into the universe the energy needed to defeat the Darkness. For all the defeated souls teetering on the edge of despair, there is a sunburst of kindness that illuminates all the galaxies with acts of honor and glory. These acts show the way to the everlasting light of the Divine Star Vetene." God began to walk away from his ledge. "And I like a warm chocolate chip cookie and a cold glass of milk at bedtime."

"Do you sleep?"

"Sure. A few hours a month."

Nimrod had to try. "Who shot John Kennedy?"

"I could tell you, but it would make you very sad. You'll have to find that one out on your own."

"Thank you for your time. I know you are very busy."

"I am. You seem like a nice boy. You will do a great job with this assignment."

Nimrod could only pray. He had screwed up so badly the last time.

Ghara Serpiana

An immaculate trail lay before Nimrod. He could smell the sea. A brilliant sun rose high above a sky that shifted from orange to yellow to Prussian blue. Different quadrants remained lemon yellow and melted into salmon on the horizon. Four different orbs shared the canopy. A balding cypress as tall as a New York sky-scraper cast shadows on the path. Misty bracelet mushrooms with their white-brown caps played in groups with saffron parasols and tiger sawgills with peach blossoms. They dotted the landscape with blooms of unnatural intensity. Nimrod moved closer to the waters of Ghara Serpiana.

Two men and a youngster folded a handwoven net and threw it into the back of an ancient craft. The intense but never-too-burning light in the sky tanned their strong shoulders. As Nimrod approached, they looked up but were not startled. One of the men, Andrew, stood upright and extended his hand. Nimrod went to shake his hand, and the grasp snared his forearm.

"Hello, Nimrod. I'd like you to meet Jairus," Andrew said while untangling the net.

"Hello, Jairus. What do you have in the net?" Nimrod hadn't dealt much with young teens.

"Oontal."

"What is Oontal?" Nimrod loved Oontal. He just wanted to get the kid talking.

"Oontal is a rare species of fish from the small orbital planet Oshu Land in the Blanco Trollien Archipelago. When captured the Oontal drops its eggs into the ocean and creates its own life cycle. It has to be caught, or its species won't survive. We are very thankful it survives in Ghara Serpiana. It has a wonderful flavor too."

Wow! thought Nimrod. "The sun is really glaring into my eyes."

"That doesn't look like the sun. It's much bigger. The sun is in the Milky Way galaxy and provides the Earth with light and heat," Jairus explained. "That is the Divine Star Vetene. The other three orbs are the moons of Heaven. The biggest is Ondora Place. The second largest is Doyvi Star. The small one is called the Deurutor Bands for obvious reasons. I learned them by their sizes because they are never in the same place the next day."

Nimrod decided to challenge young Jairus. "That's the Ebonea riddle. No one knows why they rise in a different order every day. It drives Galileo mad."

Andrew and Mark chuckled at the thought.

"Where exactly is Heaven?" Jairus asked.

"You're in Heaven," Nimrod said.

"No. Where in the universe?" Jairus continued.

Mark waded knee-deep in the surf and shouted, "We keep it a secret so the Darkness will never find us."

"Nimrod used to be an angel. He knows where Heaven is," Andrew added.

"Used to be?" Jairus asked.

"All I know is we are at the Wiyo docks on Pyrub Cape—a small village outside of Judeah, the main city of Heaven." Nimrod avoided Jairus' question.

Mark jumped into the boat. He was ready to launch. Andrew started pushing through the small waves.

Nimrod and Jairus began the short, pleasant walk into Pyrub Cape. Souls from Earth milled about on their daily routines. Everyone was so very happy. There were no cars, horns, street-lights, or crossing signals. Passersby waved kindly to one another and went about their business. There were several cafés and bistros, and the people serving in them seemed the happiest of all. Nimrod and Jairus ambled down the middle of the cobblestoned path with the others. Towering American elms lined the streets. The windows of the small, well-appointed homes shared their ledges with camellias, chrysanthemums, and yellow mariposas.

"So, why did you used to be an angel?"

Nimrod had hoped Jairus had forgotten that part of the conversation. Nimrod stopped and sat on a bench near the park. Jairus sat with him. "God sees something special in you, Jairus. He has asked me to teach you the cultures of the universe. I will tell you of my failures so you will trust my future teaching. First, you should know who I am." Jairus listened intently to his new mentor. "I am from Earth and was once a mighty king there. I descended from Noah—many generations removed. I led a proud people, and we grew a beautiful world that spoke one language and treated one another with love and dignity. I praised God, and as I aged I yearned to meet him. I devised the plans to build a great tower that would rise into Heaven. It was to be a path we could walk to meet him. I left Earth and the plans with people I thought I could trust. The tower became an obsession of sin. They forsook God's love and enslaved children to build the tower. I watched from a ledge in Heaven as God went down to the tower. He saw the children brutalized in his name. God was furious and destroyed the tower. As a punishment he splintered the universal language."

Jairus hung on every word. "So what happened to your wings?"

"It took me a long time to earn my wings. Michael gave me an assignment on Earth. I was to protect eleven very special people and watch over their families. It was a challenging time. A tremendous war consumed Earth, but I felt I was up to the task."

"Who were they? What happened?"

"Come with me." Nimrod rose, and Jairus followed. They came to a corner surrounded by blooming magnolias and flowering dogwoods. Before them was the Library Basmilla. It stood proud like the Greek Parthenon. "You're going to be spending a lot of time here as well as at the Escuela de Angels."

"I'm going to Angel School?" Jairus displayed his broad smile.

"Yes. You are, and I am going to be your mentor. So pay attention." Nimrod winked at his new student. "First, though, you are going to read about my failure so you can understand the vast responsibility an angel has."

They started up the stairs, and Nimrod waved at Mark Twain. He had just emerged from the grandiose, vault-like doors. The doors loomed over them with their secrets inside. The doors opened with a murmur, and they stepped inside. A kindly gentleman was patiently going about rebinding some books on a small wooden table. He stood to greet them. "Hello, Nimrod."

Nimrod knew so many souls. "Hello, Bartholomew." Nimrod shook the hand of the patron saint of bookbinders, butchers, cobblers, shoemakers, and nervous diseases. "This is Jairus. I ask you to bring him this book." Nimrod handed him a folded piece of paper.

Bartholomew returned. "Here it is."

"Thank you," said Jairus. "It was a pleasure meeting you."

"And you, young man." Bartholomew placed the book in Jairus's hands.

Jairus opened the cover. It read, "On September 1, 1939, on the planet Earth in the Milky Way galaxy, the Darkness unleashed a battle for control of the planet's collective soul. At that very moment in time, in Kwellew years, a similar battle in the Stounfad System on the Blanco Trollien Archipelago began. One war has ended. The other has not."

"Go to the *Book of Souls*," Nimrod told the boy.

Jairus placed the book on the lectern amid every book written on Earth and opened to the pages marked as *The Book of Souls*. Nimrod ran his finger down the page and highlighted eleven names—Carl Broodend, Egan Paal, Shaun Joint, Manny Droad, Chet Skairny, Norm Leymoita, Rat Doovaine, Jason Cenode, Raytel Kigmenis, Dan B. Kerichuck, and Gary Alesse. Jairus began to read his first lesson.

PART ONE: CARL AND RAT

November 1940, Commerce, Oklahoma

Carl Broodend could hear the sounds of the Glenn Miller Orchestra drifting behind the painful wails of his mother's crying. Carl was just returning from his final high-school football game in Commerce, Oklahoma, and a postgame meeting with Oklahoma University head coach Tom Sidham. The coach had just offered him a scholarship to play football for the Sooners. He was so proud, and this news was going to make both his parents gleeful. There was rarely glee in the Broodend household.

Carl swung the front door open and stood paralyzed. Doyle tucked the whiskey bottle under his left arm and smacked his wife, Ida, with the open palm of his right hand. Blood trickled from Ida's right nostril as she held her hand over her face in preparation for the next punch. Doyle hoisted the whiskey bottle, and streams of firewater seeped through his prickly beard. He eyeballed Carl in the doorway and started to remove his belt. The World *War I veteran wrapped the belt leather around his palm so the buckle lay flush over his knuckles. The bottle fell harmlessly to the floor as he refocused his attack on his son. "You want some of this, big boy?"

"No, Doyle!" Ida screeched from her seat at the base of the couch.

Doyle was so drunk he could hardly stand. He could hardly speak, but he could punch and whale on his fragile wife. He reeled back and smashed Ida in the face with a roundhouse right. The buckle's edge sliced into Ida's cheek. Blood seeped down her neck. Carl went for the gun in the bedroom. He had seen enough too many times.

"Where you going, big boy?" Doyle shouted in his whiskey-laden bass. "You going to get a gun to shoot your old man? I ain't good enough for you? Gonna come protect your mama? Your mama ain't nothing but a whore! All women are whores, boy!" Doyle picked Ida up off the floor by her hair and drove his knee into her nose repeatedly. "Whore! Whore! Whore!" He kept slamming her forehead into his knee. He finally grabbed her by her bottom with his other hand and flung her toward the wood-burning stove. Ida lay motionless. "Doyle Broodend isn't man enough for you? You won't ever talk nice to that drugstore fella again. I'll make sure of that."

Carl couldn't find the gun. It was always in the closet in Doyle and Ida's bedroom. Always. His hands were trembling, and his lip quivered. Tears of rage raced down his cheeks as he looked for the gun. Carl wouldn't be beaten again. He had been part of the rampages—the broken bones and bruises. He had tried to fight back so many times, but Doyle was a killer. He was unnaturally cruel. He was stony. Tonight it would end, but he couldn't find the gun.

"You looking for this, boy?" Doyle had the gun. "You wanna shoot your old man, boy? Do you? How are you gonna do that when ol' no-good Doyle has the gun?"

Carl inched slowly into the light from the bedroom. The gun was in Doyle's right hand and pointed directly at his belly.

There was malevolence in Doyle's eyes. That wicked father wasn't there. Someone or something else had gone inside him. It was something more evil than even Doyle could conjure. Carl didn't want to die, and die he would if he waited this one out. He stared straight at the gun and swore to God he'd return and take Mama away from all this. He spun quickly as the gun fired and blasted the doorjamb to splinters. He went through the window head-first and rolled over the bushes as the second shot whistled by his head. Carl ran. He ran as fast and far as he could. He'd come back for his mother—with the army if he had to.

Thanksgiving Night 1940, Madison, Wisconsin
Egan Paal was a handsome young man with a pedigree. His life was laid out before him. His father, Quincy, was a prominent Madison attorney, and his mother, Lois, was a gin-swigging socialite. His ten-year-old sister, Veronica, would surely be the debutante of the decade. He had made the football team as a freshman at the University of Wisconsin. He had also made it through the fraternity hazing and was prepared to call the elite his friends.

Gretchen wondered why all these things in Egan's life were suddenly going to change. She couldn't focus as Egan's tongue roamed across her neck. She had only met him recently at the drugstore where she swept up and Egan's family shopped. When Egan had approached her and asked if she would like to meet sometime, she took the opportunity to see what a boy from way on the other side of the tracks was like.

Egan had said his mother would be ashamed if she knew they were together. He thought she was pretty, though, and didn't care where she lived. It seemed as if his life was just as complicated as hers but with money. His mouth met hers again. It was nice.

"Egan." Gretchen pushed him away gently. "I don't understand why you are going to join the navy. It makes no sense."

"This world I live in is fake. Fake people with fake ideals. I am surrounded by rich college kids being protected from the real world." Egan tried to go back in but was rebuffed. "I am one of those kids. I don't want to be a hypocrite."

"What about football?" Gretchen questioned as Egan fumbled with the buttons on her blouse.

"I will miss football, but there is something more important out there. I can't hide behind a game."

"But, Egan, you could get killed." Gretchen dreaded the idea anyone she knew could be pulled into the crisis.

"Europe has been at war for over a year. America will end up in this war." Egan ignored the "kill" comment. A button snapped, and Egan's hand lay on Gretchen's stomach.

"Did you already sign up?" Gretchen let Egan pet her.

"I have already spoken with the coach about my decision. I have spoken to the fraternity leaders. I leave for basic training in San Diego for basic training tomorrow."

Gretchen held Egan close. "I don't want you to leave. Let someone else fight this stupid war."

"Who? The guys who live in your neighborhood? Guys who don't have the means to hide behind ivy walls? Freedom is for the entire country. We should all fight the Nazis. We should all do our parts."

"Have you told your family?"

"No. No yet. It will create a terrible fight with my mother. Tomorrow will be an awful start to the day." Egan looked at Gretchen. "It is the right thing to do."

She unbuttoned the rest of her blouse. Egan rolled on top of her. Duke Ellington had never sounded so good.

A Few Days after Christmas 1940, Pittsburgh, Pennsylvania
Paige and Shaun walked hand in hand. They stole a kiss every few yards. Wreaths decorated the doors, and lights abounded. It

sure was great to be home for Christmas. Shaun Joint had joined the army after they both graduated from high school. She had been the prom queen. He had been the high-school quarterback. They loved each other. He had not wanted to leave Paige, but work was tough to come by in Pittsburgh. Playing college football hadn't seemed like the right thing at the time. He had rethought that decision several thousand times. He had wanted to stay close to Paige, and now he was going to be as far from her as possible. Basic training at Millfield Airfield in New Jersey had been challenging. Paige noticed Shaun was much more of a man. Maybe it was the military haircut. It was soft and fuzzy, and she kind of liked it. She missed those curls too. He was promptly being shipped to an air base in the Philippines called Iba Field. It would be a while before he and Paige could settle down and be married.

They sat on a bench in the rail station. The riders on the platform fidgeted with their luggage. The train was scheduled to depart. Shaun and Paige pored over the final details for the 308th time.

"Write." Paige put a pen in Shaun's hand and closed his fingers into a fist. "Don't forget to write and send pictures." Paige had sketched a picture of her and Shaun on a swing.

"Stop by and say hi to Mom and Dad." Shaun loosened his grip of Paige as the porter called the riders aboard. "Help out with Sarah if you can. The polio makes it difficult."

Paige's auburn hair fell free in the wintry wind. Ripe, rosy cheeks adorned her soft, pale skin and offset her cobalt eyes. Shaun knelt before Paige. He fumbled through his government-issued coat and produced a small box. Shaun held her hand and opened the box. A simple golden band with a small marquise-cut diamond was nestled in the pillow's groove. He slid the ring on Paige's finger. She began to cry. No one heard her say yes over the porter's bellowing.

The whistle blew, and the stragglers stepped aboard. Paige's heart started to crumble. Shaun edged toward the train. Paige gripped his jacket and refused to let him leave. She reached into her coat pocket. From beneath her copy of *The Grapes of Wrath*, she pulled out two lockets—a silver heart cut into halves. One had her picture for Shaun. The other half had Shaun's picture for her.

"When the two sides of this locket are joined together, we shall be together forever." Paige muttered through her sobbing.

The tears welled, and gravity pulled them to Earth. Soaked cheeks pressed against each other in their embrace, and farewell kisses passed. Neither stare wavered as Shaun walked onto the train backward.

"I love you, Shaun." It was the last thing Paige whispered before the doors closed.

The train chugged slowly out of the station into the Allegheny Mountains. It took him across the fields of Ohio and Indiana, through Illinois, and across the Mississippi River. Everyone was going one way or the other by train. The train stopped every fifty miles or so, and passengers got out to stretch. In North Platte, Nebraska, the train was at a standstill. Shaun transferred at this giant junction to another train that took him to San Francisco. He mailed his first letter to Paige there.

January 1941, Fort Ord, California

Manny Droad was going to move his wife, Anna, and the three small boys, Jaime, Miguel, and Juan, to Fort Ord on the Monterey Peninsula in California. California was stunningly beautiful. The Pacific Ocean was boundless. The climate was cool and comfortable. Seals barked on the rocks, and there were beautiful cypress trees. Monterey was worlds from El Paso, Texas. Texas was dusty and always hot. Manny did not believe Anna would ever leave El Paso. It was her home. So he just sent his paychecks to her and promised to be home soon. The promises had felt empty in recent weeks. There had been increasing activity on the base. Generals and colonels came and went. There were longer meetings in the mess, longer drills for the soldiers, and very serious faces. Manny rinsed his face with the water from the lavatory sink and looked in the mirror. He had put on about five pounds since he and Anna had had Jaime in 1938. It hadn't helped the army had made him a cook. He had signed on to be a soldier, but even a born-and-raised Texan couldn't catch a break in the US Army. Hispanic faces and Hispanic names meant Hispanic jobs. Manny didn't mind too much. He and Anna wanted to open a restaurant when he got out of the army, and this gave him a chance to try out some of his recipes on the more adventuresome staff. People couldn't live on spaghetti and steak all the time. The soldiers loved the tamales.

One enlistee mopped the floor, and another emptied the trash. The mess was always immaculate, which was remarkable considering some twenty-five thousand soldiers were stationed at Fort Ord. The day's work was almost over, and Manny looked forward to listening to the *Grand Ole Opry* back in the barracks. He stepped outside to a marvelous purple and orange sunset. He wondered what was on the other side of that beautiful ocean. A few men were throwing around the football, and Manny got in on a few plays in the parking lot. Manny covered a guy who broke to the right. The pass was late. He intercepted the ball easily and sprinted the other way. The ball felt natural in his hands. It seemed so long ago when he had gotten to carry the ball almost every down on his high-school team. His hopes of playing beyond high school disappeared, though, when Anna got pregnant.

Night fell swiftly, and he meandered back to the barracks. One of the boys had put up a new picture of another Hollywood girl. This one was Katharine Hepburn. *Pretty,* Manny thought. *Nice red hair.* Only Anna's picture and one of the boys adorned his bunk. Anna's superb black hair fell over her shoulders. She had lush red lips. There was no woman as beautiful as Anna. An envelope was on his bunk. It was army official. Manny opened it. They were orders to report for transfer to Iba Field in the Philippines. Manny was going to find out what was on the other side of that beautiful ocean.

March 1941, Jacksonville, Florida

The train ride seemed eternal. Lily Townsend had received a cable from her fiancé, Chet Skairny. He would be shipping out to Manila in the Philippines. Chet wanted Lily to get to Jacksonville, Florida, as quickly as possible so they could be married.

Lily stepped off the train in Clay County, Florida. The stifling heat belted her. Even March was warm in Florida. It was still winter back in Missouri. When she had left, four inches of snow were on the ground. Chet was waiting for her, and he had that gleam in his eye—that enthusiastic gleam he only had when she was around. Chet looked very handsome in his pressed uniform and had lost a little weight. He was a big boy and had been a defensive tackle in high school. He was tall and burly, which was just right for Lily. She was a tall, handsome woman who could take Chet to task, even when he was feeling his oats. She'd often line up on Chet to see if she could stop his energized rushing techniques. Lily never actually stopped the insurgence but often tackled him to the ground so she could roll around with him. Lily was a crackerjack student enrolled at Washington University in Saint Louis where she studied languages. Neither college nor college football was an option for Chet. He was third-generation military, and there was only one road to follow—the US Army.

Chet embraced her and gave her a short kiss. He was never overly affectionate in public, and they slipped into the cab he had hired for the day. They were both nervous, and they fumbled around trying to hold hands in a comfortable fashion. Chet instructed the cabdriver to head to the base chapel at Camp

Blanding. Chaplain Carmody was to marry them as soon as they arrived. Chet had made arrangements for them to spend the following two nights at a beachside hotel east of Jacksonville. Chet was very excited to get there. They arrived at the chapel, and Lily removed only one hanging bag from the taxi. She asked Chet for a few moments alone in the ladies' room to put on her dress. She hadn't had any time to find a proper wedding dress but had found a suitable white gown that did her remarkable justice. If it weren't so hot, she might feel a bit more comfortable. The surging adrenaline didn't help. She took a deep breath before the vanity and slowly opened her eyes. This impulsive behavior was in contradiction to Lily's even-keeled approach to life. She liked adventure, but she did not want this to seem frivolous. The next few minutes would change her life. She would be marrying the man of her dreams. She was positive he felt the same way. She tried to block from her mind her mother's clinically disposed chats of being naked with a boy. She would deal with that part of it when it came.

She stepped from the ladies' room and saw the gleam. She knew Chet was dazzled. She felt about ten degrees cooler. The chapel was quiet and serene. They joined their arms as if the entire world were watching on a newsreel. They strode down the aisle and stepped up to the altar. Chaplain Carmody began the Sacrament of Matrimony. They both would cherish that moment. When they both said, "I do," the pressure slid off their backs, and they left it puddled on the sidewalk. The smiles were grand, and the hugs were tight. They thanked the chaplain and headed back to the taxi, which was waiting patiently for the bride and groom. Chet slipped the cabbie a five for the bucket of ice with two glasses and a bottle of champagne that awaited the newlyweds in the backseat. They popped the top and made a toast to love. Smiles and laughter littered the way. The driver sped them to their sandy destination overlooking the Atlantic—not that they ever saw the sand. The two fairly large people filled the small room and even smaller bed and sewed their oats.

May 1941, McChord Air Force Base, Washington State

Gray clouds hung just out of reach and dropped the rain steadily day after day. That was life at McChord Air Force Base. The glacier-flattened land was the last stretch for the famous explorers Lewis and Clark. McChord Air Force Base was located just north of Fort Lewis, which was named after Meriwether Lewis. General Dwight David Eisenhower had recently been stationed at Fort Lewis near Tacoma. McChord Air Force Base was established in 1937. None of that stopped the rain, and the goddamned rain had gotten Norm Leymoita's letter wet. Norm shook the wet off his lid and shoes. He gently removed his jacket so the gutters of rain would run to the floor. He sat in a corner chair of the communications office and ran his fingernail down the letter's crease. It was from his mother. The penmanship was perfect. Norm was certain French monks had schooled his mother. Each loop curled precisely. The top of each letter plateaued at the perfect height. It was like a forest of letters. Norm noted the letter was not sealed in wax. It would have been so appropriate. Norm held the letter to his forehead and played his game of crystal ball. Like any good magician, he found it entertaining to fool the audience. There was always a trick. Norm's trick was simple. The letter would contain some negative news about his brother, Dominic.

Just before Norm joined the army, he had had to bail Dominic out of jail. Dominic had been in a brawl with some kids from a different part of Boston. Dominic's face was all banged up, but Norm was quite certain the other guy had taken the worst of it. Norm had explained to his younger brother that he wouldn't be around to cover for him. Norm had said he loved him but told him not to make Ma's and Pa's lives miserable. Dominic mumbled something about not being like Norm. "I'm not a big football star that's going to Georgia Tech. Let me lead my own life."

Dominic had been a senior in high school at the time. He had chosen a lonesome path. Dominic was due to graduate about that time. Norm wondered if that meant good news in the letter about Dominic. It didn't.

Dominic had long been a truancy issue with the school district in Boston. Truancy was preventing his graduation, and he was hanging out at that bakery again. The bakery wasn't just a bakery. Vinnie Peloso made good sourdough. Vinnie Peloso made good bread too. There were cards and craps. Rumor had it they even had a wheel. They ran numbers, and Norm had caught Dominic with a roll of cash that could have only come from being a bag man for Vinnie Peloso. Norm prayed for his poor mother. Bostonians loved their sports—especially the Red Sox. Norm was excited about their chances with that new ballplayer, Ted Williams. He could take them back to the World Series. That would be great. Norm and Dominic hated the New York Yankees. He also hated his brother had chosen crime as a business.

The furnace melted the chill, and Norm finished the letter. The more things changed, the more they stayed the same. There would be no high-school graduation for Dominic. He'd continued to have scrapes with the law, and now the military didn't even want him. Ma had enclosed Dominic's draft card. *At least Dominic was patriotic enough to register,* Norm thought. Dominic Leymoita had been rejected for the draft into the US Army on a 4-F: physically, mentally, or morally unfit to serve. Norm knew it was morally. *Damn, Dominic.* Norm said a quick prayer for his brother's safety and his mother's and father's mental health. He secretly thanked God for letting Dominic be rejected. A storm was brewing, and the Japanese were becoming brazen with the Chinese. Hitler was now surging into Africa. What was America's next move? Norm Leymoita knew what he was going to do. He was going to work for General Douglas MacArthur in Manila in the Philippines. His orders had come in yesterday.

June 1941, The Pacific

Rat Doovaine walked the deep cargo space of the transport ship and tried to balance the bowl of water. The ship pitched and rolled over the waves, and the dogs became very thirsty down in the "hole." They were tired of him spilling their water. The cages were inhumane. The poor puppies deserved a lot better than most of the grunts sleeping in the bunks—not that a bunk was any slice of heaven. They were very brave German shepherds. Rat always thought it was ironic he would end up fighting the Germans with German shepherds. He reckoned there weren't that many Germans in the Philippines. All the puppies had eaten, and now they had their water. Rat referred to them as puppies, but each had been trained to clamp their jaws onto an assailant's neck and puncture the jugular vein so the assailant would bleed to death quickly. They were strong, swift, and smart as well. These six dogs had been selected for a special live training environment at Fort Stotsenburg on Luzon in the Philippine Islands. In a melon field back in Georgia, they had planted fifty fake mines to test the dogs. They found forty-nine.

He would take the dogs topside for walks and let them get some fresh air and do their business. He strolled down the six cages and peered into the eyes of these trained tunnel and mine hunters. Which needed to be attended to right away? Which would be the lucky dog? Would it be Madison? Broadway? Hudson looked impassionate about the whole process. Lexie's ears were pointed straight up, and her big pink tongue was dangling about her canines. Harlem had been the last to get his dinner, so he could wait. No. It would be Commander. Sitting straight backed and looking forward, Commander had pride. He also had Rat's respect. He was easily the most talented, well-disciplined dog he had ever been associated with. He would take Commander topside first. He deserved it.

The ship never seemed to roll topside as it did down below. The fresh, salty air felt invigorating and the breeze was a terrific alternative to the stifling heat below. The dogs were patient in the heat. They had been with Rat at Fort Benning, Georgia, and were the first to be trained to hunt mines and tunnels for the army. It was always hot and humid in Muscogee County, southwest of Columbus and crossing into Alabama. Rat didn't do as well as the dogs. A New York City boy had no business in the South, but that was where fate (or the army) had taken him. Luckily it had brought him to the dogs. Rat had convinced his commanding officer he had a knack with dogs, and sure enough he did. Even though that Yankee talked funny, he seemed to speak dog. They reached the bow, and Commander pointed his nose toward the sunset as if he knew where to navigate the ship. He was truly a leader. Rat threw his elbows over the rail and thought about the Big Apple. How he missed home and his family. He wondered how his kid sister, Valerie, was doing. Mom Kay would be working the West Side for the best bargain, going to Mass every day, and saying a Rosary every night. His father, Ronald, would be down on the docks with the big boats loading and unloading goods from all over the world. Rat would have to write them a letter soon. He took Commander back to the hole and took all the other puppies up to the deck.

August 1941, Fort Crook, Nebraska

The B-25 rumbled through the Nebraska morning sky like buffalo across the plains. Fort Crook was a long way from Riverside, California, but that was fine by Jason. That was why he had joined the army—to see the world—and a superior view he had from the machine gunner's nest above and behind the pilot. Private Jason Cenode had originally wanted to fly these birds but had wavered at the heavy academics required. Besides he was far too big for the cockpit as it was. At six feet five inches and almost 250 pounds, the mighty University of Southern California Trojans coveted him as the best offensive tackle in California. He liked his vantage point and felt every bit a part of this team. His superiors considered him by far the best gunner in the squadron.

Aunt Julie thought differently about the entire thing. Julie had raised Jason almost from birth after his mother, Julie's sister, left him on the living room rug and never came back. Julie never did tell Jason the whole story. She never wanted Jason to feel the stigma of being abandoned. Jason was Julie's son, and she didn't like him being too far from home—just like any mother. She also wanted him on the ground and wondered why he couldn't have just worked in the motor pool. She wondered why he had joined the army at all. The whole world had gone mad. Jason had recently sent a letter that Colonel Claire Chennault of the US Army Air Force was recruiting "first group volunteers" to engage the Japanese in the skies over China. He added a bounty of five hundred dollars for each Japanese plane shot down. This was no carnival game. *Wouldn't the Japanese be shooting back?* she thought.

They flew by the tower at Fort Crook, and Jason thought about the story of Colonel Crook, who had risked his military career to help Standing Bear, a Native American chief. His superiors had forced Colonel Crook to arrest Standing Bear in a time of war. Standing Bear was only passing through the territory to fulfill his dying son's wishes to be buried on sacred grounds. At Standing Bear's trial, Colonel Crook testified to the judge that Standing Bear had indeed broken no laws and should be allowed to continue on his journey. The trial was racial profiling at its best, but Colonel Crook's testimony helped return the Indian chief to freedom.

The B-25 made a wide, sweeping turn, and the pilot snickered and recommended buzzing some old folks for fun on the landing path. It sounded good to Jason.

November 1941, The Philippines

Norm had been in Manila over five months, and he was still try-ing to get a handle on the food. A plate of *tosilog* lay before him, and it was OK. It was just different. He was hungry, though, and had to eat. The marinated fried pork was good, and the garlic rice was very good, but he never understood why they threw a fried egg in there. It was also taking quite some time to get used to buko water—coconut juice. He sat at the café and watched the sights of Manila pass by. It teemed with people and energy, but there were only two classes of people—rich and poor. So many people rode on bikes with incredible balance as they carried gro-ceries and packages to every destination while weaving through the untamed streets littered with pedestrians, scooters, and ox-driven carts. Some rode horses or had pack mules to load their produce to the Manila markets. All the locals had their angles and scams, and they all tried to grift a quarter or dime from the unsuspecting tourists or newly arrived American military.

Norm recalled a very drunken night in San Francisco. It was the night before embarkation. He had met a few card players at the hotel, and things had gotten out of hand on pay night. Fortunately the hangover was not all he had taken away from the evening. Dominic had taught him a few lessons along the way. He wondered if Dominic had heeded any of his lessons. During the brief stopover at Pearl Harbor, which occurred just about the time Norm stopped being hungover from San Francisco and seasick from the passage to the westerly island chain, he was able to walk on the sandy beach. He met a nice gal who introduced him to the palmetto tree. Hawaii was heavenly. Everybody was so peaceful and relaxed. Everything about Pearl seemed professional, but it all seemed to go in slow motion. He wished he were stationed at Pearl. That was the place to be—especially now that the Japanese had made inroads into Indochina. He was closer to the action than ever.

More and more soldiers arrived every day. New bombers were being delivered to the bases at Clark and Iba Airfields. The harbor was in constant motion. Supply ships moved in and out, and the naval and army forces trained. Admiral Thomas Hart had a fleet of three cruisers, thirteen destroyers, and twenty-nine submarines. Norm thought that didn't sound like a volume of vessels large enough to monitor an area larger than the entire US coastline. The minesweepers were in and out of the docks. The US Army Thirty-First Infantry Division seemed to be battening down the hatches by installing twelve-inch coastal batteries to protect the beachheads of Luzon. The Japanese were only three hundred miles north on the island of Formosa, but the Nips wouldn't invade the Philippines. General MacArthur had the Philippines built up. They didn't want to see America in the war. Those poor bastards on the Malayan Peninsula—well, that was a different story.

Norm took his last sip of buko water and stared down Roxas Boulevard, which was right in front of the water's edge. The breeze came off the bay—a refreshing delight from the constant humidity that pounced a block inland. The road would lead him past the US Embassy to Malate Church, where he would say a prayer for his mother, father, and Dominic. He thought about playing some cards with the new B-17 fighter pilots staying at one of the slimy downtown hotels while on leave. There was always a way to pay for the *tosilog*. In the morning he would be back to work as a communications specialist, US Army.

December 4, 1941, Pearl Harbor
Seaman Egan Paal shipped out of Pearl Harbor on November 28, along with the other 2,918 crew members of the USS *Enterprise*. The *Yorktown*-class aircraft carrier shredded the peaceful Pacific waters with its 19,800-ton displacement. It was a floating city. More populated than most towns in Wisconsin, it was 827 feet 4

inches in length with a 114-foot beam. It housed eighty-five war-planes, sixty-seven Grumman F6F Hellcats, and eighteen TBM-3 Avenger torpedo bombers. It could maintain thirty-four knots in the open sea. Four giant screws propelled a fortress that had batteries of five-inch guns, forty 40 mm guns, and fifty 20 mm guns. Egan was a gunner. Finished in Newport News, Virginia, the *Big E* was commissioned in 1938. It was the single finest warship the United States had in its navy. Vice Admiral William "Bull" Halsey handled the helm as they delivered twelve F4F Wildcats to the US Marine squadron guarding the airstrip on the little island of Wake due west of Oahu. The clouds were billowy, shaded pink from the setting sun, and raised to the top of the Earth's canopy. Egan stood at his post and looked dutifully around for bogeys in the twilight sky. He adjusted his life jacket and helmet. He wished he could remove the cumbersome helmet and enjoy some of the dusk's breeze. There would be no bogeys tonight. There never were. Alarm after alarm sounded on the carrier and back at Pearl, but there were never any bogeys.

He thought of that great Thanksgiving night. He had written, but she had never written back. He'd have to look her up when he was back in Milwaukee. The *Enterprise* swung softly to the east and into the gloom. They were sailing back to Pearl.

December 7, 1941, 5:30 a.m., Northwest of Oahu

The vessel heaved forward and crashed into the night waters of the Pacific. The gigantic spray washed the entire deck and crew of the Japanese cruiser *Tone. Chikuma* and *Tone* were sister ships of the Imperial Navy, and they awaited Admiral Nagumo's orders to launch predawn reconnaissance flights of Pearl Harbor and Lahaina anchorages. A fleet of six carriers with 350 aircraft, protected by battleships and cruisers, had slipped north of the regular shipping lanes. Under the cover of bad weather, they had crept within two hundred miles of Oahu. Pilots were fed and dressed.

Seaplanes were being fueled on the *Tone*. Short bursts of light came from the aircraft carrier, *Akagi*. Orders were confirmed.

Six hours and a different day away, after seeing Humphrey Bogart in *The Maltese Falcon* on a makeshift screen at the PX at Clark Airfield Base in the Philippines, Carl Broodend lay down for the last good night's sleep he would ever have.

5:45 a.m., Hawaiian Time
The Ninth Indian Army at Kota Bharu was no match for the blasting guns of the Japanese destroyers. The pillboxes at the mouth of the Kelantan River were reduced to rubble, and the five thousand Japanese troops came up the beachhead in the pouring rain. General Yamashita's Fifty-Sixth Regiment split into three different invasion forces, strangled the North Malayan coast, and headed for Singapore. In a brisk two hours, Yamashita's main landing force would storm Singora Beach on the Kra Peninsula of Thailand. No shots would be fired.

6:00 a.m., Hawaiian Time
The lobby of the Manila Hotel was whisper quiet until the doors to the fire escape stairs crashed open and a gaggle of American B-17 bomber pilots fell out on top of each other into a pile on the ornate carpet. Bottles of whiskey and Scotch leaked onto the rug, but the men dexterously held the bottles with great balance and prevented a brown liquor catastrophe. At the bottom of the pile, a stash of bills and a deck of cards slipped out of one of the merry men's jacket. As the group members found their way to their feet, Private Norm Leymoita put the roll and cards neatly back in place. They sang their way back to the barracks.

6:15 a.m., Hawaiian Time
Chopping through the waves north of the big island of Luzon in the Philippines, twenty-seven Japanese transport ships lumbered

through the South China Sea from the Formosan port of Takao. The Forty-Eighth Division of the Imperial Army remained quietly apprehensive as they read inspirational messages from their leaders, General Masaharu Homma and Admiral Takahasi. Homma was not as quietly apprehensive. He demanded weather reports to see if the low-lying clouds and fog would hamper the flight of the Eleventh Air Fleet's bombers. Over four hundred bombers waited on the airfields of Formosa to rain destruction onto the American air bases on Luzon.

At Fort Stotsenburg Private Rat Doovaine was sleeping. So were Lexie, Broadway, Harlem, Hudson, and Madison. Commander, however, remained awake and rigid. He had his nose pointed to the north as if a strong wind was beginning to blow.

At Iba Field Private Manny Droad was sleeping, although he had to get up very soon to start breakfast for the troops at the mess. Private Shaun Joint was one of the sleeping soldiers who would be enjoying Manny's fine fare in a few hours. In Manila Private Norm Leymoita had just passed out drunk and was snoring with a Chicago roll in his pocket. Private Chet Skairny had dutifully gone to bed early. He had a 6:00 a.m. Monday post time. Seaman Egan Paal slumbered with the rolling waves in a tidy bunk on the USS *Enterprise.* Private Jason Cenode was just waking up in Fort Crook, Nebraska, and thinking of shopping for a Christmas present for Aunt Julie. General Douglas MacArthur was sleeping as well as General Jonathan Wainwright. So were General Brereton and his flyers. So were the people on the battleships *Arizona, Oklahoma,* and *West Virginia.*

As the morning sun crept over the horizon, Admiral Halsey was west of Oahu and returning from his excursion to Wake Island to drop off fighter planes. He was less than two hundred miles from Oahu and had been ordered to send in a flight of Dauntless dive bombers. Halsey followed standard procedure and sent a search patrol of fighters to make sure the skies were clear.

7:35 a.m., Hawaiian Time

The green signal lamps they left behind on the carrier in the darkness seemed a dream from a different time. The clouds broke over Kahuku Point, and Commander Mitsuo Fuchida led his 183-plane attack force to the northern tip of Oahu. Forty-nine Val bombers stared into the sunrise. Each of these dive bombers had a two-person crew and a 1,300-horsepower Mitsubishi engine that could carry the plane seven hundred miles round-trip. Beneath each plane were winged armor-piercing shells and fore and aft machine guns. The forty Kates were essential to the success of the Pearl Harbor strike. Each Kate was thirty feet long with a fifty-foot wingspan and could drop one oxygen-powered Long Lance torpedo equipped with specially made fins that stopped the torpedo from diving into the mud. Their escort to the dance of destruction was the quintessential Zero. At 336 miles per hour, it had a great ceiling of nineteen thousand feet, and the one-person crew had a 250-pound bomb, two twenty-millimeter cannons, and a pair of machine guns. The Zeros were by far the head of the class.

Each pilot remembered the lesson learned during practice drills over Kagoshima. The Kates would be coming very low, as they had with the target vessels anchored in Kagoshima Bay. The Vals had practiced very steep dives and pulling up within five hundred feet of the water while dropping their bombs. They had become very accurate. Fuchida led his squadron around the Kodakan peaks from the southwest. With his binoculars he was able to see they had achieved a complete surprise on the enemy. He ordered his operator to apprise Admiral Nagumo of their status.

Hickham Field was just south of Pearl Harbor. It came under attack from eighteen Vals. Fighters and bombers were lined up like bowling pins to prevent sabotage and were easy prey for the highly trained marksmen. Hot metal shards flew through the air, and fuel explosions funneled skyward. The black, choking fumes filled the blue sky. Bombers pounded Ford Island in the middle of Pearl Harbor. The PBY boats exploded like wooden ducks hit with a shotgun. Hangars were emptied rapidly as the flyers moved onto the main prize.

The response was groggy. The rocking explosions of bombs, the jackhammer of the Zeros' machine guns, and the deadly whistling of the torpedoes deafened the church bells and marching bands that started each peaceful morning. It was once said that a person was most vulnerable to attack while sitting on the toilet. Pearl Harbor was being attacked while in the middle of a Sunday-morning crap. Japanese cannon fire systematically chipped away at the decks of the *Iowa*-class USS *Arizona* and USS *Maryland*. The Japanese then made their way up the pond to the *Oklahoma* and *West Virginia*. Sailors jumped overboard as Japanese fire pummeled their fellow seamen. The Kates found their range after a pass or two, and the torpedoes raced through the shallow waters of Pearl like underwater lasers. The torpedoes ripped open huge gashes in the sides of the battleships. The *West Virginia* was listing badly as the crew began counterflooding to prevent the great capital ship from capsizing. More and more waterspouts jetted toward the heavens. More and more torpedoes sliced toward their targets. Fires raged through the ships' passageways as the crews tried to rescue the ships and themselves.

The *Oklahoma* crew paused only for a nanosecond to hear the reverberation of the explosion of the forward magazine of the *Arizona*. Oil had begun to spill into the harbor and had caught fire. This created a slithering snake of flame on the surface. Escaping into the water was not a genuine alternative. Many of the *Oklahoma*'s crew members were below. They were trying to repair damage and correct the list by preventing more water from crashing through the unclipped hatches. The ship kept rolling, and the warm water engulfed more than four hundred crew in briny graves.

The *California* took two torpedoes under the bridge and began to list terribly. The crew managed to bring it upright, but it was taking on water and sinking into the mud. The *Nevada* made an attempt to get away. Its screws rumbled as it built up steam. Antiaircraft fire now peppered the sky but created only token resistance for the bombers, who had inflicted a war's worth of damage in fifteen minutes. Admiral Kimmel watched his fleet burn. The explosion in the forward magazine of the *Arizona* shot a thousand feet in the air. A dense black cloud smothered the entire area. Japanese planes buzzed around the dying ships like green-eyed flies on rotting carrion. The *Arizona* belched its remaining breath from the inferno, cooked, and sank a thousand souls. Fuchida circled overhead and snapped photographs from his bomber's cockpit.

8:30 a.m., Hawaiian Time

Word about Pearl spread through the *Enterprise* like a social disease at a brothel. The Klaxon blared, and sailors scrambled, each trying to find out a little more information and situated themselves for war. Was it really the Japs? Was it really Pearl? Were they going to see any Japs? No one had the answer—not even the president. It was all going down as they discussed what was next. The Dauntlesses had embarked for Pearl and skirted the Zeros. They were low on fuel and unaware, and they landed on golf courses and screeched onto the end of blown-up runways of Hickam and Hilo. The marine pilots did well just to land on the ground with bullet holes decorating their fuselages and wings.

The bombing resumed after a short pause. The second wave of the attack glided around Oahu to the angry clatter of antiaircraft fire. The Japanese bombers made a beeline to the escaping *Nevada*. It chugged down the channel with guns unleashing a determined defense. Bombers headed to the dry dock area where the *Pennsylvania* relaxed and awaited repairs. One Val dropped a bomb that shattered the deck of the *Pennsylvania,* and collateral damage blew the entire bow off the destroyer *Shaw.* In a little over half an hour, four of the main US battleships were destroyed, and three others were badly damaged. Wheeler Field was devastated along with Hickam and Ford Island. Thousands of sailors were injured or burned and later died. These reports sifted through the decks of the *Enterprise.* All sailors were silent with prayers for their fallen brethren. Inside a rage boiled, and the *Enterprise* teetered on the edge of chasing the Japanese fleet. However, it stood down for lack of a better understanding of the enemy's forces.

10:00 a.m., Hawaiian Time
General Brereton was awakened at four in the morning in the Manila Hotel. His chief of staff informed him about Pearl Harbor. He immediately put his flyers on call. Many had been playing cards and drinking with Norm Leymoita only hours ago. Brereton himself was scheduled to fly for Java that morning. Upstairs in the penthouse, MacArthur dressed hurriedly and swore under his breath about how this could possibly happen to Pearl Harbor. Brigadier General Leonard Grew, chief of the army's war division, had warned that an attack on the Philippines might be imminent. MacArthur readied to meet his staff and pondered whether the general might be right.

At five thirty in the morning, the staff had gathered and confusion reigned. General Brereton wanted to get the B-17s in the air for a raid on Formosa. MacArthur received a cable instructing him to initiate Rainbow 5—an Atlantic Ocean–based war strategy that proposed the enemy in the Pacific would instigate nothing but a few flurries. He was to conduct air raids on enemy bases in the most logical tactical radius. McArthur had beefed up the protection of the Philippines with his 227 aircraft and beachhead batteries and felt they could handle themselves.

On Formosa the air armada of the Japanese Eleventh Air Fleet and Fifth Army, which was supposed to provide cover for the soon-to-be-arriving transport, was tied down in a fog as thick as a good New England clam chowder. Homma and Takahasi paced like inmates on death row waiting for the inevitable attack from the B-17s on Luzon. Certainly the Americans knew of Pearl, and the bees would leave the hive. They waited in the mist.

Fuchida dragged behind the rest of the fighters and bombers. They had achieved a glorious victory for the emperor. Landing the plane on an aircraft carrier was a dire enough business. Now the sea was choppy, and some of the younger pilots were intoxicated by victory and careless on their landings. Many crashed into the edge of the bouncing runway or slid hazardously down the flattop like an out-of-control toy. Fuchida navigated the landing and returned to the roar of the vessel. He immediately requested a third attack as the death knell for the wounded military base.

Nagumo pondered the success of the mission and was certain the American carriers had been let loose to find his scent. They had scored a knockout blow, but the carriers weren't there—not any of them. They must be somewhere.

Fuchida pleaded. The oil farm and repair facilities, if destroyed, could open the door to the East without an American presence for many months. Nagumo knew Fuchida was correct. He was also way ahead in this fight. He was farther than anyone had planned or even dared to dream. Nagumo took his foot off the dying dog's neck and left it heaving for breath.

11:30 a.m., Hawaiian Time

In Riverside, California, Julie Cenode sat down to a bowl of mashed potatoes and a leftover piece of chicken. Her neighbor Joyce scurried over and told her to switch on her radio. Her son Jason had just finished dining in the mess at Fort Crook with other crew members when a snappy sergeant silenced them and had them gather orderly to listen to the radio. Doyle and Ida Broodend looked at each other with grave concern for their son, Carl, as the special news bulletin crackled over the airwaves in Oklahoma. Quincy, Lois, and Veronica Paal stopped short their meal when they heard the president was going to speak. Lois even placed her gin martini aside for a moment. Ronald Doovaine and his wife, Kay, and daughter, Valerie, held hands and prayed. They also noted the mean streets of New York's West Side had gone silent as the citizens sat with strangers for the news. Paige held Sarah Joint's polio-ridden hands and worried for Shaun. Lily Skairny started crying before the broadcast even began. Her worst fear was coming true. Anna Droad held her three baby boys close and switched on the dial. This was no time for a war. Vincent and Carl Leymoita stoked the fire and fine-tuned the temperamental dial. They wanted a clear reception for Roosevelt. Dominic had not come home for dinner. The families of Gary Alesse, Dan B. Kerichuck, and Raytel Kigmenis tuned in from various parts of the country, as did the other 120 million Americans. There would be no Billie Holiday on the radio that night.

1:00 p.m., Hawaiian Time

While Roosevelt broke the news of the attack on Pearl Harbor to the American public, the Japanese Imperial Army was just getting started. It was December 8 across the date line in the Pacific and 5:00 a.m. in Singapore when the air raid sirens sounded. Bombers raced through the night sky and let loose on the darkness below. Searchlights began to light the sky and look for the elusive bombers, and antiaircraft fire flailed into the pitch. A thousand miles east, bombers from the close-by Japanese island base of Saipan spanked the tiny island of Guam. Five hundred American marines were expected to repel a four-destroyer invasion fleet with the USS *Penguin* and a couple aged craft floating about in Apia Harbor. The marines were equipped with machine guns and pistols—the equivalent to popguns. The marine barracks were quickly nullified, and the USS *Penguin* was destroyed and sank in Apia Harbor.

Wake Island was being assaulted at the very same time as Guam. Thirty-six Japanese bombers laid waste to seven of the twelve brand-new F4F Wildcats—the only hope the soldiers had of fending off the oncoming invasion. The Japanese bombers left from Roi-Namur in the Marshall Islands and steamed through a rainsquall off the coast of Wake. This gave the empire the ultimate advantage. The gasoline storage tank for the island went up in a furious fireball. A Pan Am commercial plane called the *Philippine Clipper* had enough space left to evacuate the company employees and a few of the wounded. The pilot headed northeast and radioed that a Japanese destroyer and cruiser were steaming to bring more war. The marines on Wake gathered the dozen or so dead and tried to regroup.

1:45 p.m., Hawaiian Time
The phones were ringing like mad. Generals were calling generals who were calling admirals who were talking to Washington. Everyone had some advice for the other person. No one had a game plan. General Brereton tried to get MacArthur to at least send a reconnaissance flight over Formosa to check the feasibility of an attack or grasp an understanding of the Japanese forces. General Arnold called and warned not to get caught with their pants down the way they did at Pearl. He urged to get the bombers in the air and safe.

At Iba Field Private Manny Droad would normally be knee-deep in scrambled eggs and waiting for flyers wanting their breakfasts. Sirens began blaring, and the crews ran toward the planes. The thirty-six P-40 fighters and the B-17s got off the ground quickly because the radar at Iba indicated unidentified aircraft. The news of Pearl had just reached the waking bases of the Philippines, and no one was sure whether this was a drill. MacArthur received news the radar report from Iba was false and ordered the P-40s down. He left the bombers in the air to circle Mount Arayat. MacArthur once again denied General Brereton the chance to send the bombers to Formosa.

Private Shaun Joint sauntered into the mess. He was smiling and hungry. The early-morning drill would not prevent him from eating. "What's for breakfast, Soldier?"

Manny Droad responded with a smile. "Eggs and bacon, and I'll get you some toast if you want."

Shaun grinned bigger, and Manny started making the toast. He also found some fresh eggs for the young soldier. He grabbed a couple for himself and started cooking them both breakfast. Shaun fixed himself some coffee. It was as thick as the mud at the bottom of the Monongahela River back in Pittsburgh. Manny brought the meal over to Shaun and pulled up his own seat.

"You didn't have to bring it to me. I would have come and picked it up." Shaun was genuine. He was just a grunt in this army.

"It's OK. I have my own too. Do you mind?" Manny asked as he bent his knees to sit. "My name is Manuel, but everyone calls me Manny." He extended his hand, and Shaun grasped it like a man. Not all white people shook the hand of a Latino.

"My name is Shaun. I'm from Pittsburgh."

"Texas. A little border town called El Paso." Manny scooped up his eggs with some toast. "Have you ever heard of it?"

"Doesn't the US Army Air Force have a B-17 training base there?"

"No. That Pecos, Texas. You're at least in the right state." They both chuckled. "Do you know what all the commotion is here today?" Manny didn't always get to know about such things.

"Everyone was saying the Japanese attacked Pearl Harbor this morning." Shaun was starting to digest the food as well as what he had just said. Details were hard to come by. Pearl was still burning.

"Oh! That's terrible. That means we are going to war over here. Aye yi."

"I know. It's awful. I've got a beautiful fiancée waiting for me in Pittsburgh. If this is true, she's probably a wreck." Shaun's life never centered on himself. It was always Paige.

"I've got three sons back in El Paso with my wife, Anna." Manny thought a lot about his woman too.

"Three boys." That sounded great to Shaun—the idea of raising a family.

"Yeah. Jaime, Miguel, and Juan." The proud father whipped out the ready pictures of the boys.

Shaun sopped up the glaze of yolk left on the plate with the last of his white bread crust. "They are very handsome. You should be very proud."

"I am," said Manny. "What do you do at Iba?"

"I work on the planes. I am a mechanic. Hoses, belts, wires. Anything that's broken, they come find me. I've actually got to get back to the hangar. They're probably looking for me. Thank you for breakfast. It was a pleasure meeting you. Maybe you'd like to join us for some cards one night?" Shaun heard the whine of P-40 engines and the squeak of rubber tires landing on the airstrip.

"That sounds fun," said Manny. Manny would never play cards. He had too many mouths to feed, but he appreciated the gesture.

Shaun stood and checked his left pocket. That was where he carried the locket from Paige. He tried his best adios and headed for the hangars.

Manny picked up his dish and took it to the sink. He began washing a stack that had piled up. He thought of Anna and her big brown eyes and absorbing smile. He thought of his little boys learning to walk and talk. Anna was teaching them both Spanish and English. She was a good mom. Manny thought maybe he was being a coward. The idea of bombs and guns made him nervous. He didn't want to die in a war—no matter how good the cause.

He took a long gaze at the picture of Anna he had taped to the wall.

Norm thought his bunkmates were having a little fun with him when they rustled him from his bunk and told him Pearl Harbor had been attacked. He was waiting for the punch line or the end of the practical joke. He swiftly realized there was no humor in their voices. The hangover kicked in, and he bolted for the shower. He needed to get to work. There was an urgent need to transmit and receive sound messages by electromagnetic waves of radio frequency. He grabbed a towel and adjusted the water temperature to be cooler. There was never a need to have the water very hot in the Philippines. The island heat would have him sweating like Joe Louis in the sixth round of a title fight. Louis had recently beaten Lou Nova on a technical knockout in the Polo Grounds back in September. This was after a tough thirteen rounds with Billy Conn back in June. He was positive Dominic could have gotten them into the fight. Oh, to see Joe Louis fight just one time.

Norm harked back to just a few hours before at the Manila Hotel. The girls weren't exactly the type you'd take home to Mother, but they were entertaining for sure. He remembered the pilot's face when he had turned over his cards. The pilot had already been sweeping the pot with his pair of aces when Norm turned over the king-high flush draw. Thirty bucks. It was a nice win, but last night was over. He looked out the window. It sure looked like a regular day in Manila.

Private Chet Skairny and the rest of his battalion broke down their M1 carbine rifles. The five-and-a-half-pound .30-caliber rifle held fifteen deadly rounds. They cleaned them and put them back together. Their rifles were their friends. If only the Filipino nationals felt the same way. The Filipinos were an enthusiastic but ragged bunch in dire need of more training and drills. One hundred thousand rough-around-the-edges Filipinos had become part of MacArthur's defense strategy. Their rifles were antiquated Word War I small arms, and most could barely hit the horizon from fifty yards. They were sloppy in formation and struggled with teamwork concepts. They practiced with Browning .50-caliber machine guns. Anyone within a 358-degree perimeter was in mortal danger. The guns shook them to the bones. They were farmers—not warriors. Maybe with sheer numbers they could withstand an invading fleet. *Maybe,* Chet thought. He looked out over the rough waters of the Luzon Strait. The Japanese were out there somewhere. Pillboxes and batteries had been shored up. The Filipinos were on edge. The news of Pearl Harbor had trickled through their poor ranks. Fear glowed in their eyes as they received their daily orders. What had seemed like a decent paycheck for defending the national borders suddenly seemed like suicide.

Chet thought of Lily and how scared she would be. She wrote every day. Chet couldn't keep that pace. He hoped she didn't mind. Lily had written she had thought she was pregnant, but it was a false alarm. Chet looked forward to trying again. He thought of the small hotel room in Florida. A couple days like that could keep a person going for quite a while.

Private Carl Broodend wondered just how long the Japanese would take to attack Clark. He was sure it was not a question of if but when. Clark Field was on alert, and he was ready to take handle of his forty millimeter—an almost four-thousand-pound gun—and fire some two-pound shells at the incoming Japs. The buildup of supplies at Clark had grown exponentially since he had arrived in September. Day after day of unloading supplies had seemed a tireless chore but was now showing its worth. Another convoy of transport ships was en route from Hawaii—seventy more warplanes, six hundred tons of bombs, nine thousand barrels of aviation fuel, forty-eight seventy-five-millimeter guns, and several million pounds of ammunition.

Take that, Japan. Carl thought of his mother, Ida. She always defended and protected Doyle after each night of mayhem. She said the war had screwed up his father's head. He'd like to see how the new seventy-five-millimeter guns would screw up Doyle's head.

3:00 p.m., Hawaiian Time

Rat went through the regular morning drills with the puppies. Lexie was extremely playful, and Rat was having fun grabbing her by the back of the neck and throwing her. She liked to roughhouse. Madison was barking at some birds that had come to rest on one of the phone lines that ran around Fort Stotsenburg. Broadway and Harlem were playing a game of chase around the barracks, and Hudson seemed a tad under the weather. Commander remained at full attention. His eyes never wavered from the north. Manhattan Mike—Kansas—liked to play with the dogs, and he was one of the few soldiers Rat would let horse around with them. He loved Broadway.

"Hey, Rat." Mike threw a stick for Broadway to fetch. "Did you hear about Pearl?"

"Yeah. I heard. Makes my stomach sick."

"They say they sank the *Arizona*." Mike was talking the big news of the day, but Rat knew he was talking himself out of being scared. They were all scared. "You think we could be next? Huh, Rat? Do ya?"

"If they'll attack Pearl, they'll attack anywhere, Mike." Rat knew the kid wanted some consolation, but real New Yorkers only knew how to say it straight.

"What's the matter with Commander, Rat?" Manhattan Mike had noticed it too.

"I don't know, Mike. He's been like that all day. It's like he sees something, but he can't tell me. You know?" Commander was rarely wrong. Rat just couldn't figure out what Commander knew.

The beginning of the day at Fort Stotsenburg was already a long day at the Manila Hotel. Thirty-two Japanese bombers had dared the fog and weather and had gotten under way. They were making their first strafing runs on the small airfields of Baguio and Tuguegarao in northern Luzon. Another 192 planes had just lifted off the now-clear runways of Formosa. General Brereton again begged MacArthur's chief of staff to recall the B-17 bombers that were circling Mount Arayat without bombs and wasting fuel. The Japanese had struck the first blow on Philippine soil. Brereton wanted the planes to attack. MacArthur refused Brereton again. Three-quarters of an hour passed before Brereton received permission to fly the reconnaissance flight, and only if they concurred on a target selection would MacArthur agree to an afternoon strike of Formosa.

The long day at the Manila Hotel had become the longest day at the White House. By all accounts Roosevelt was apoplectic about how the great fortress of Pearl Harbor could be decimated in an hour. All the generals and admirals whom he worked with daily and had strategized with for months or years had known the looming danger of a Japanese attack. He had to go on national radio, however, and tell the country they were going to be asked to fight a war that anyone walking the streets of Tucson knew they weren't ready to fight. Pearl Harbor had made that extremely obvious. The public bought the grand idea that it was an unprovoked sneak attack, but the people gathered in the Oval Office knew all too well this was a very real and dangerous time. They were supposed to be prepared, trained, and ready.

Republican and Democratic leaders gathered in a solemn mood at the White House. Roosevelt declared the meeting the most important since Lincoln assembled his cabinet before the Civil War. After recounting the horrible day's events to any and all who would hear his frustration about Pearl Harbor, Roosevelt covered sensitive issues regarding military installations and factories across America that were about to build the war machine. He grounded all private planes and muted amateur radio operators. The FBI was to round up Japanese aliens. The long day at the White House was about to get a lot longer.

5:30 p.m., Hawaiian Time

The P-40 Warhawks were arriving and being refueled. Shaun checked with the pilots to confirm all systems were functioning normally. He helped to refuel and prepare for takeoff again. Manny was cooking hot dogs and baked beans. The word had come the pilots needed nourishment before going back over the South China Sea. The B-17s at Clark Field were also recalled, and sixteen of the big birds were being equipped with either camera equipment or one-hundred- and three-hundred-pound bombs in anticipation of an attack on Formosa. Those pilots needed a little lunch too.

The single operating radar at Iba Field had previously given a false report and scrambled the air fleet early in the morning. Radar picked up a new blip on the screen just past noon. The radar operator tapped out the alarm for Clark Field. The operators at Iba frantically phoned Clark. A lieutenant answered the phone and promised to detail the report to his commanding officer at the earliest opportunity.

Three of the B-17s with camera equipment readied for the reconnaissance mission taxied out onto the runway. The general alarm crackled through the dense Philippine air. A group of planes approached the runway. One of the pilots pondered how they were going to take off while the navy fighters tried to land. The pilots looked at the planes curiously. They seemed to be dumping trash. The cannons of the Japanese Vals had shredded the fronts of the planes and ignited furious explosions. Two additional B-17s suffered the same fate. The crews in the messes at both Iba and Clark raced for their planes. Japanese bombers, Betties, began delivering their relentless payloads of 2,200-pound bombs. The bombs fell with fury and precision. Soldiers scrambled aimlessly for safety. Carl kept low and helped a Warhawk pilot buckle into his plane. The pilot was terrified but brave as he swerved down the runway in search of a path to take flight. The runway was blocked, aflame, and littered with twisted metal. Shrapnel ricocheted from blasted aircraft and commenced a deadly game of dodgeball. Another Warhawk taxied behind the first and found a launching point. Explosions rocked the earth. The barracks wilted under the immense inferno. Screams of agony emerged through the barrage. People on fire rolled helplessly on the ground and hoped to die to release the pain. Carl saw a few of the men had gotten to the antiaircraft gun, but they were ineffective. Rounds failed to explode and caused no difficulty for the Japanese fighters. A pair of Zeros targeted the turrets and decimated the gunner with cannon fire. The hangars were now ablaze, and the Japanese war machine flattened more and more planes. Carl received a taste of hope as three Warhawks gained altitude and joined others from Iba. They were immediately effective and drew fire away from the crippled airfield.

A mirror scenario ensued at Iba Field. Manny wasn't sure how to help. He grabbed a fire hose and tried to quench the flames that ravaged one of the hangars. The ferocious heat scalded Manny's skin. The bombs landed closer. The explosions were deafening. One officer had taken shrapnel to the abdomen and lay bleeding. His intestines leaked out of his skin, and his spleen was on the grass. Shaun Joint escaped from the hangar with only a moment to spare. The concussion knocked him off his feet. Dazed but undaunted, he raced toward a Warhawk and attempted to escape the pummeling. A wheel block was caught under one of the landing gear wheels. It jammed the plane and prevented a quick escape. Shaun darted under the plane and removed the block. The cannon fire made him dance. Shaun looked at the tower engulfed in flames. An American soldier hung by one foot from the observation window. His carcass sizzled in the blaze. Warhawks returning from the South China Sea fell under siege from the speedy Zeros. They chased one another across the skyline like mad hornets from a disturbed nest. The Warhawks were outnumbered and outgunned. The Zeros trapped the Warhawks and sent them screaming to the soil. The bombs continued to rain, felling the officers' quarters, mess, and PX. There was more fire than water. Manny held the hose taut and caught Shaun out of the corner of his eye. Shaun realized damage control might be better than retaliation. He grabbed the hose and fought the losing battle.

A couple miles away, the dogs howled at the air-raid sirens. Fort Stotsenburg had been spared today. Rat called for Manhattan Mike. They loaded up the dogs in the back of a canvased army truck. Commander jumped in first, and the other dogs filed in behind. Rat was going to Clark Field to lend a hand. Mike drove. Rat sat in the back with his dogs. They didn't seem scared. They seemed confused. Rat knew animals sometimes seemed confused when humans did things animals couldn't understand—such as war.

At Clark Field, Carl moved to the burning pilot's body in the wreckage of the doomed P-40 Warhawk. His plane had been struck earlier in the battle, and he had been left for dead. Carl noticed movement and leaped into the flaming wreckage. The pilot's hands were scalded, and his shoes were burned. The soles reeked of hot rubber and the air of burning flesh. Carl winced as he realized the man's face had melted off his skull. He removed the dog tags and pushed them deep into his pocket. The family would want to know the story of Lieutenant Oscar Davis. Disoriented and feeling incredibly alone, Carl did not hear the whistling of the two-thousand-pound bomb that struck the Clark

Field administration office. Walls of metal and material crashed down upon him and buried him alive.

Norm juggled the thousands of calls on the switchboard at his office in Manila. They were overwhelmed. His team was trying to tackle the incoming communications from the American bases and tap into the Japanese radio output. It was complete chaos. His commanding officer asked for a report. Norm had no answers. People were screaming and shouting orders, but nobody was getting anything tangible done.

The Japanese relented after a debilitating assault. In under an hour, they had clobbered several integral air bases, decommissioned half the fleet of B-17s MacArthur desperately needed, snuffed out fifty-six fighters and dozens of other aircraft, landed the first of thousands of troops on a tiny island north of Luzon called Batan, and opened the front door to the Japanese invasion force that would help the empire bound southward.

Rat Doovaine and Manhattan Mike mourned at the destruction. Scorched bodies lay on the ground, and edifices smoldered in the afternoon sun. Crew members worked to salvage planes, but there was no place to take them. The hangars were burned to the ground. Fire hoses drenched burning structures to no avail. Air-raid sirens droned in the background. The injured were being carted to a makeshift hospital as nurses and doctors screamed for supplies not readily available. The smell of burning flesh twisted in the breeze.

Rat led the dogs to the rubble to search for survivors. The dogs poked tentatively, but the heat hampered their ability to search. Manhattan Mike leashed Hudson, and the dog started barking feverishly. A patchwork crew began digging through the sand and concrete. Electrical wires were coiled, and shards of glass jutted everywhere. Hands lifted chunks of plaster and threw them aside. The work went slowly. The rescuers were careful not to cave the pockets of air that might be protecting the entombed. Tile and flooring mixed together and stirred with pieces of toilet bowls and windowpanes. Twisted metal pipes and copper wrapped together. A two-thousand-pound bomb had fashioned the scrap art. Piece by piece they removed the wreckage. Hudson continued to bark. His scent was keen. They saw a soldier's combat boot. It lay motionless under tons of debris. The weight of the falling building had smashed the fingers and hands flat.

The dogs barked. Each dog identified new locations by the minute and spread the rescue crews thin. Clark Airfield remained in chaos as the wounded kept pouring into the field tent. The dead surfaced in the oddest places. Bullets had pierced the walls of a latrine and slain a soldier while urinating. Many died in the fires. Others lay in the cockpits of their warplanes and waited to be retrieved. The injured suffered from concussions, burns, severe lacerations, and the loss of limbs. A dazed soldier walked around crying and screaming while looking for his arm. Commander sniffed around patiently and then looked up at Rat. Commander had found something. He didn't bark so much as whimper sadly. Rat was frustrated the hits they were making were of the dead. The dead needed to be recovered, but the time to recover a survivor was starting to wane. Rat started removing debris. Every pile seemed to house the same inanimate contents—plaster, metal, wood, wire, and lots of glass. Commander scratched his paws on the softer materials to help. Assistance arrived. Rat and Steven, a young kid from Boise, were able to remove a few larger pieces. Commander had been on the money. A few feet down they spotted US Army fatigues. They worked furiously and carefully to excavate the hole where the soldier lay. Rat reached down and felt the soldier's wrist. He had a pulse. Rat's mood skyrocketed. Commander had found someone alive. The soldier was bruised and battered but alive.

"Stretcher," Rat screamed. "We've found someone! He's alive!"

The dead that surrounded Rat tempered his joy. Gingerly they lifted the body onto the stretcher. Rat pulled the dog tags from the soldier's neck. Broodend, Carl.

Medics carried Carl to the makeshift hospital tent. Rat held Commander firmly as he petted the hero's ears. Commander pulled at the leash. He was ready to search for more survivors.

Shaun and Manny dropped their hoses and fell exhausted to their knees. The building couldn't be saved, but the fire would no longer endanger any other buildings that had survived the attack. Medics with stretchers still hauled the wounded to the hospital at Iba. The first glimpse of body bags appeared. Shaun and Manny wept. They shared tears of lost friends and raw, angry emotion.

"We're alive, Shaun." Manny put his arm around his new friend. "We're lucky."

"We are lucky, Manny. Unlike those brave bastards out there." Shaun's fury boiled over. "They were everywhere! Everywhere!" Shaun ranted at the vacant sky.

"You'll have your chance, Shaun." Manny rose to his feet and extended his hand to Shaun. "We'll all have our chances."

Manny noticed the deep gashes on Shaun's shoulders and arms. Shaun noticed Manny's hair had been singed while combating the fires. Soot and charcoal coated his arms.

"I'll bet you've never have a fire that bad in the kitchen," Shaun said, and he picked at a bullet wound that had grazed his triceps.

"Only when I make fajitas," Manny returned dryly.

Neither laughed out loud, but it was the first time either had smiled since breakfast. The last streams of sunlight bounced off the low clouds over the Luzon Strait near the coastal batteries of the north shore. The surf was thick and choppy. The Filipino cooks had made beef shank in onion broth with cooked rice. Chet moved the food around with his fork. The morning news of Pearl Harbor and the afternoon reports that air strikes had mauled Iba and Clark had removed his appetite. The war had begun. Chet started writing a letter to Lily. He was behind in his correspondence and felt he'd better get a letter to his love in the mail. There was no telling when he'd have the next opportunity.

10:00 p.m., Hawaiian Time
The communications office would never be calm again. Norm was quite sure of that. The communication traffic had subsided to a barely manageable point. Grim casualty reports trickled in over the Teletype. Eighty were dead in the attacks on Iba and Clark. Another 150 were wounded—many severely. The count continued to grow. Over forty fighters had been destroyed, and some estimates said half the coveted B-17 bombers had been as well. Countless additional aircraft were decimated, and the damage to the physical structures at the air bases made them inoperable. Norm looked at his picture of Carole Lombard. She usually cheered him up. This time it didn't work. Norm picked up some chatter on the UHF band. The Malayans and Australians had tried a counterattack at Kota Bharu and had been pushed back. Singapore had given them permission to evacuate 150 warplanes to the relative safety of Kuantan. Civilian evacuees were heading away as the surviving Indian army prepared for a final stand.

The British battleships *Prince of Wales* and *Repulse* were leaving Singapore through the Johore Channel to engage the Japanese navy at sea. Admiral Phillips had already been radioed he would receive no airborne support. They were on their own.

Midway Island was east of the Philippines, and a pair of Japanese destroyers had shelled it before midnight. *A calling card of the future*, Norm thought. The marines on Wake Island girded for more hostilities. Tiny little Guam braced for a rough ride. All were on their own.

The entire West Coast fell under a president-ordered blackout from Seattle to San Diego. The great citizens of San Francisco and Los Angeles patrolled throughout the night and waited for the invasion to breach their own solemn shores. Admirals and generals alike started working around the clock to plan a counter to the swift, organized devastation. The Japanese ruled the Pacific, the Germans controlled the Atlantic, and Satan laughed and laughed.

December 8, Chicago, Illinois

Gary Alesse did things fast. It was Monday morning, and Gary's father, Lawrence, headed off to Chicago's meatpacking plants. Gary skipped down the stairs. Pancakes topped with melting butter and real Vermont maple syrup waited on the table. The syrup steamed as it dripped over the pancakes. The warm syrup was a special touch from his mom, Donna. Donna listened to the news on the radio while Gary devoured the pancakes quickly. She read the paper cover to cover daily. She rarely listened to music, although Gary had tried to get her to sample some Louis Jordan jump blues he had heard thumping at the high-school dance.

Donna watched her son gobble up the pancakes. Gary had always been fast. She couldn't catch Gary by the age of four. Gary ran track and even kept up with the colored boys from downtown. Gary had galloped for 1,300 yards as the high school's star tailback and made three interceptions on defense. Gary wanted to play for the Chicago Bears. He wanted to follow in Tom Harmon's footsteps and go to the University of Michigan. He wanted George Halas and the Bears to draft him—just like Harmon. Gary needed to get his grades up, though, and stop fooling around with that pretty girl, Annette. He spent way too much time with her. Gary quaffed a glass of milk. He had listened to Roosevelt with Larry and Donna last night and seemed concerned. He was going much faster today than normal. Gary showered, ate, ran, and did his homework fast. Donna knew everything about Gary. What she didn't know was Gary was going to sign up for the army. Fast.

Gary leaped down the stairs of his house and hit the sidewalk running. The recruiting office opened the doors. Teen males waiting to sign their names and protect America inundated the room. The attacks on Pearl Harbor had struck a patriotic chord that resonated across the forty-eight states. Gary didn't slow down until he reached the main street of town. He was stunned to see many of his friends were there to sign up as well. It was the first day of school he had ever missed.

"Gary, what are you doing here?" asked his fellow high schoolers.

Most expected Gary to attend Michigan and accept the football scholarship. Gary had expected that to be the case as well—until yesterday morning.

"I'm going to fight some Japs. How about you guys?" Gary spoke loudly and invoked a grand cheer from the people in line.

"What about Annette?" Joel said and blew his breath into his hands.

"We'll be fine. I don't think this should take very long," he said. Gary dreaded breaking the news to his mother and father. He hadn't told Annette either. The line crept slowly, as did the reality of joining the army. "Where do you want to go?" Gary asked Joel.

"I want to go to Europe. My family is from Poland. The Nazis have turned my mother's country into a cemetery. The people in Warsaw are in a coffin and waiting to die."

The line moved forward again. Annette's family was Polish. Gary thought he too would ask to go to Europe. He wondered if one could make that request.

"Yeah," Gary said. "Europe sounds like the right place to go. I don't like hot weather anyway."

Gary tried to be compassionate with Joel's plight as the wind threatened to steal his hat. Some of the people worked cups of coffee or hot chocolate. Others came out of the recruiter's office with the same steam they had entered.

"I ship out in two weeks," a beaming teen mentioned. "I'm going to take a bus to North Carolina. Fort Bragg in Fayetteville."

News that Roosevelt was addressing the House of Representatives and declaring war on Germany and Japan leaked down the enlistment line and received a hearty cheer. Gary stepped into the office. Posters of proud, superhuman army soldiers draped the walls. It was the same slick advertising that made hot dogs look so great. They never looked that good in real life.

"Son, step up and let me take a look at you." The sergeant circled Gary with a discerning eye. "I am sure you are not eighteen years old."

"Yes, sir. I am." Gary's voice cracked for the first time since he was fourteen. "I just turned this past Thanksgiving."

"So you want to fight for Uncle Sam." The recruiter spoke loudly. "You want to kill some Japs."

"Yes, sir. I do." Killing was a concept Gary hadn't thought through. Fighting the Japs. Beating the Japs. Revenge for Pearl Harbor against the Japs. Killing the Japs. It struck Gary suddenly that killing human beings came with the job.

"Fill this out, and make sure the birthday says you're eighteen. Otherwise I've got to send you home to your mama."

The recruiter wasn't fooled and let Gary slide. Gary wondered how many others got to slide. There were some questions about health, diseases, height, weight, city, and state. The next of kin line sent a chill through his torso. Gary signed his name. He had entered the army. Now he had to tell his girlfriend and parents.

He waited for Annette around the corner on the street where she walked home. He didn't want any teachers to spot him. Annette broke into a big smile when she saw Gary. Her long blond hair was pulled back with a pink bow, and her slender hips made the light blue skirt billow slightly.

"Where have you been? I thought you must be sick. You weren't in school." Annette Wisniewski could make any man's heart skip.

"I've got to tell you something, Annette." Gary breathed deeply. He was on the verge of hyperventilation.

"I've got something I've got to tell you too, Gary." She focused on Gary's green eyes and looked for warmth.

"Maybe you should go first. My news is pretty big." Gary felt his news would end all conversation for the afternoon.

"No, Gary. You go ahead. I'll tell you later." Annette shifted her notebooks from one hand to the other. Gary pulled them out from her arms and carried them.

"Annette." Gary took a deep breath. "I love you." Annette sensed he was stalling. Gary had something else on his mind. She already knew Gary loved her. "After everything that happened yesterday at Pearl Harbor, I feel Americans have to stand up and fight for our country's safety."

"I do too, Gary. Mr. Searens told me Roosevelt has already declared war. We're going to get those bastards." Annette seemed ready to enlist herself.

"I joined the army," Gary blurted out.

Annette spun on the balls of her feet. "Gary Alesse! Have you lost your cotton-pickin' mind? You are not going into the army. You are going to the University of Michigan to play football. You go right back to wherever you just came from, tell them you made a mistake, and rip up that piece of paper." Annette's eyes watered. "Gary, you're going to get killed. This is a war. Bullets and bombs. There are some really bad people out there doing really bad things to each other." She was distraught. He put his arm around her waist. She removed it and began pacing the sidewalk in a violent aerobic display. "You're book stupid, Gary—not life stupid." Gary was stunned to find Annette thought he was stupid at all. "This messes everything up, Gary. Please." She was howling. Neighbors started opening their drapes and nosing in on the histrionics. "Please go back and make this all stop."

Gary wouldn't. "I'm going to save your relatives in Poland." It sounded bad as it left his mouth.

"I don't care about the people in Poland. I'm an American. Our family has lived here for over a hundred years. I don't know anyone in Poland. My dad doesn't know anyone in Poland. My mom is American. We're from Chicago. We eat Polish sausage. Only my name is Polish."

"I'm sure it won't be that bad. I'll probably never even see any action. The United States will clean this mess up in no time." Gary wasn't sure if he was fibbing to Annette or himself.

"Gary, you don't understand. I need you alive." Annette was hyperventilating.

"Nothing is going to happen to me. I'll probably be loading boxes right here in the Chicago area at the train station."

"Gary." Annette paused and wiped the black mascara that was running down her cheek and mixing with the blush. "I'm five months pregnant. I'm starting to show."

It was the first bomb of the war for Gary Alesse.

December 9, Philippines

Minesweepers trawled in the night ahead of the six Japanese *Yugumo*-class destroyers and a single *Nagara*-class light cruiser. They looked for those thorny six-hundred-pound bombs that lay waiting a couple hundred feet below the ocean's surface. As the eastern sun peeked its first orange rays over the international date line, the warships unleashed the fury of twenty-four-inch guns on the beachheads of northern Luzon. Some of the cooks had already started preparations for the day's meals. This included *tinola*, a tangy soup with ginger, papaya, and chicken. Artillery shells ripped the sandy beaches and blasted trees and humans into the air. The Filipino regiment, under the observation of the

US Army, dug in deep for cover. Chet Skairny rallied the troops to seek refuge, but scores were caught in the open and fell victim to the multitude of deadly shells. Lieutenants warmed the high-powered SCR-399 mobile army phones and called in air strikes from the remaining B-17 bombers. They hoped there would be enough to help.

Norm Leymoita had been working throughout most of the night sorting out communications and preparing for another full day of activity in Manila. The distress calls sounded from the troops in north Luzon. He passed the communiqué up the chain of command.

The general alarm sounded at Iba Field. No one had slept in his or her own bed last night. The beds were all gone. Shaun had worked throughout the night salvaging the banged-up but repairable P-40 Warhawks—a job made more difficult because the supplies and tools had gone up in flames. The soldiers who remained readied for action. Crews began assembling near their craft and awaited instructions. Engineers worked all night doing a yeoman's job. They pieced together the pockmarked runway and enabled a few flights to launch and try to protect the air base and strategic points to Manila.

Manny spent the night in the dispensary. His burns were a little worse than he had imagined. The nurse assured him he would recover quickly. Not as fortunate were the poor souls screaming in agony as the nurses peeled the burned flesh and doused their raw, tender layers with running saline solution.

For the second day in a row, the German shepherds howled at the air-raid alarm. None of the dogs had slept well the previous night. They were testy and aware of their master's anguish. Rat had not slept well either. The images of dead bodies haunted his dreams, and screaming laced his memory. He was certain he could have done more. He thought of soldiers caught underneath the rubble who were still alive but perished while he and the dogs searched. He thanked God they had found the one soldier. Rat made a mental note to go visit him at the infirmary. Commander had gotten out of his kennel and was sitting beside him when he woke. He had protected Rat through the night.

Five B-17s were all Clark Field could muster. The crews were informed they were to make bombing runs to the Luzon Straight and repel the Japanese naval fire bombarding the beachheads of Luzon. The ten-man crew boarded the four-engine, 4,800-horse-power Boeing-made Flying Fortress. Loaded to the maximum, it lifted off with 17,600 pounds of bombs tucked beneath its 103-foot wingspan. As they climbed into the sunrise, Carl Broodend heard the roar of the jet engines. He was sore but alive.

"Transports! Transports on the water!"

It was difficult understanding the broken English of the Filipino regulars, but Chet knew exactly what this soldier was saying. The Japanese were on the water and heading their way. The Japanese bombs dropped incessantly. They gave the soldiers on the beachhead no maneuverability except backward. The bunkers took direct blows. The Filipinos looked as if they had been divided by the edges of a cookie cutter. Many of the dead were cut in half or had died after their entire sides had been blown off. Limbs fell on pillboxes like the branches of palms. Everybody was terrified. The Filipinos opened fire on the transports that were still too far out to sea. The waves were choppy, and the sea seemed to slow the transports' advance. Chet could hear the roar of bombers, but they were not coming from the strait. They were coming from behind their position. They were B-17s. Chet counted five very high in the sky. *Only five?* It felt as if the entire Japanese arsenal was just beyond the horizon. Five would not be enough.

The pilots identified the six destroyers through the morning clouds. There was one cruiser and three minesweepers. One of the crew spotted the six transports carrying Japanese infantry slowly to the shores. Bombing moving targets was no easy task, and the planes couldn't fly too low. They would get caught in the antiaircraft battery cannons of the warships. Each pilot communicated with the others and determined targets. The planes rumbled high overhead, and the Japanese vessels made evasive maneuvers. The ten ships and six transports began zigzagging through the strait in an unpredictable pattern. A pair of American B-17s let loose their ordnance, and the explosions created geysers of water fore and aft of the cruiser. Neither managed a hit. One of the flights made a pass at the transports scattered willy-nilly in the surf closer to shore. Smaller targets managed to stay clear of the American bombs falling from the pale blue Philippine sky. One Japanese minesweeper took a blow to the stern and erupted in flames and rich black smoke. The crews of the B-17s could see the Japanese sailors scurrying to smother the blaze and recover the dead and wounded. The final few passes over the Japanese fleet yielded no results other than to slow the war machine down. The minesweeper bowed to a watery grave, but the invasion fleet lurched forward.

Chet Skairny waited until the transport had run aground on the beachhead. As the gate swung open, he and the Filipino army opened fire. The tenacious and well-trained Japanese kept piling out of the transport and walking over the newly dead. Precise incoming fire kept the Filipinos from stretching out onto the beach to meet the enemy. Hundreds of Japanese troops returned fire in close quarters and gained valuable territory up the shore. Some Japanese transports experienced no resistance. The beachheads lacked sufficient bunkers, and the Japanese applied pressure to the wilting Filipinos, who retreated to the flatlands behind the beach and beyond. Chet moved quickly. He understood their forces were outnumbered. They needed a strong line with American regulars to help the Filipinos. *A few tanks would be nice,* he thought.

The first invading force of the Tanaka detachment secured the island of Luzon and moved quickly to their objective—capturing the vital airfield at Aparri and allowing the Japanese to fly air raids on the Philippines from the Philippines. The day wasn't an entire success for the Japanese landing forces, though. Rough seas had prevented a second landing party from stepping onto the soil of Vigan on the northwest coast. Chet was certain they would be back the following day.

Norm was going back to the barracks. Thirty-six hours in communications had taken its toll. A kind Filipino boy had offered to get him some *dinuguan,* but Norm really wasn't in the mood for pork cubes simmered in pig blood with a touch of garlic, onion, and laurel leaves. He craved shrimp sautéed in chili and garlic sauce—*gambas*—and he knew just the place to grab some on the way home. The Teletype rattled off more pages. The staff referred to the beige electronic wizard as "the little brown bitch that won't shut up." News clattered in from Malaya that the British had not fared well through the day's events. Roughly one hundred Japanese fighters and bombers had caught two grand battleships, *Prince of Wales* and *Repulse,* at sea. The Japanese had sunk both capital ships. Reports confirmed the destroyer *Express* managed, aside other ships, to rescue some 2,800 survivors. Eight hundred perished in the bowels of the two battleships when they capsized and raced to the bottom. With the Americans reeling from Pearl Harbor and the meager British contingent now mortally wounded in the Far East, Japan effectively controlled the oceans east of Africa to the western shores of America.

December 10, Philippines

General Homma directed the Eleventh Air Fleet, and it rumbled on the runways of Formosa—the Portuguese-named island. After the startling success in the previous day's devastation of Iba and Clark Fields, the Japanese bombers ventured farther south. They targeted the naval air base Cavite, which was north of Manila. Admiral Hart's naval fleet was tucked into the docks of Manila

Bay just eight miles southwest of Manila. They were exposed. Radar people informed General Brereton of the incoming bombers, and he scrambled together thirty-five P-40 Warhawks to engage the armada of Japanese fighters. Chet watched the Japanese bombers pass by high overhead while moving his troops' line farther and farther from the enemy's controlled beachheads. The dogs began to howl as the sirens wailed. Rat stepped out to see if Clark was under yet another attack. Commander barked angrily at the sky. Carl was lying in bed but feeling much better after the previous day's battering. He sat up in his bed and observed the clouds. Medics, doctors, and nurses scrambled and prepared for the worst. Shaun worked furiously to repair the few salvageable Warhawks, but Iba had been obliterated. He needed more time and supplies. Manny pieced together pots, pans, and spatulas and worked alongside his team to create a makeshift kitchen that could start producing food for the hungry, hardworking soldiers. The sirens shook Norm from his bed. He dressed quickly and headed for the communications center in the Marsman Building. He arrived on the rooftop in time to witness the antiaircraft guns firing in futility.

The Japanese Zeros engaged the slower Warhawks and punished them. The Zeros picked them off one by one. The amount of resistance slowly diminished, and the Japanese Betties and Kates unleashed their armaments from twenty thousand feet in the air. Without the fighters interrupting their paths and well beyond the range of the anti-aircraft fire, the Japanese bombers lined up their targets and took deadly aim. MacArthur and his family looked north as Cavite Air Base erupted. Norm stayed very clear of Admiral Hart, who paced like a hungry jaguar. The Japanese bombers had stretched south to Manila Bay. The smoke rose in steady new puffs. The Japanese were bombing his cache of warships in Manila Bay. An immense explosion ripped the ceiling off the storage warehouse for the entire fleet's torpedo stock. Two submarines docked in the bay received serious wounds. Others were fortunately patrolling the Philippine shores or monitoring the Japanese in the South China Sea. Admiral Hart evacuated the remaining ships of his small navy to the safety of the open sea and left the defense of the Philippine islands to his submarine fleet and a smattering of patrol boats. MacArthur observed his aircraft being whipped soundly too. He retreated his air fleet to save it for a later day. The Japanese attacks killed five hundred and left many more wounded.

Norm checked the Teletype and previous communications from the night. Wake Island had been attacked again, but the troops seemed to have held them off a bit better than they had in the Philippines. One report stated that a pair of shells had penetrated the side of a Japanese warship, and it retreated to sea. *One for the good guys,* Norm thought. It was a small victory in an ocean of defeat. The armies of Malaya were not faring well. General Yamishita's hardened forces had stormed the peninsula and parted the Indian Army under command of the British and Australians.

Chet and the Filipinos had withdrawn to the Luzon plains after quite a hump. They began digging a new line. The troops struggled to move the seventy-five-millimeter howitzers through the Philippine countryside. Mortars were placed, and bunkers were dug. Filipinos carefully laid mines in the approaching fields. Logistics remained an issue. The Japanese army approached from the north. Chet had learned that an additional Japanese landing force had secured the beaches to the west in Vigan. His soldiers were tired and quickly becoming surrounded. A forward scout had seen Japanese tanks unloaded from the transports. The unabated influx of Japanese soldiers made a foothold in the Philippines. They systematically worked their way toward the new Filipino line. The Japanese had a foothold and ruled the skies.

Shaun cannibalized pieces of doomed P-40 Warhawk fighters and pieced them together with the planes that had chances for survival. He took a windshield here and a tire there. Gaskets and screws that were useless on one plane could save lives on another. Deep in focus, he didn't notice Manny standing behind him.

"Hello, Shaun." Manny extended a brown paper bag. "I thought you might need something to eat. It's nothing fancy."

Covered in grease and oil, Shaun looked every bit the part of a mechanic. Shaun smiled, and his hunger kicked in. "Your timing is incredible. I'm starving." It was only a ham sandwich with a smear of mayonnaise, but Shaun ate it as if it were a Christmas roast. "How are your burns?" he asked as he munched a huge hunk from the sandwich.

"They're OK." Manny concealed the true pain and hid behind the comfort of a cigarette. Other people were worse off than he was, and he wanted to help—not hinder. "How about you?" Manny looked at the bandages that protected the gash on Shaun's arm and shoulder.

"Well, I won't be throwing the football for a while." Shaun looked melancholy.

"Are you a football player?" Manny's interest was piqued.

"I was a quarterback in high school." Shaun didn't embellish he was *the* high-school quarterback in Pennsylvania and had planned to attend the University of Pittsburgh before joining the army.

"I was a running back, but I loved playing defense. I was a safety. Hitting people was the best part of football." Shaun noticed the twinkle of a killer in Manny's eyes. "But I liked running the ball too. You could hit people that way as well." They both laughed.

"You're the guy who tried to put me on the sidelines," Shaun mumbled, and he took another bite of sandwich.

"Probably." A sinister grin crossed Manny's face, and Shaun knew he'd rather have Manny on his team than have to play against him.

"What do you think is going to happen, Manny?"

"I don't know. I hope the army can hold them off until Washington sends some help. We can't stay here very long. There's nothing left. Nobody has clothes or a place to sleep. I can't make food for everybody without equipment. And the food got blown up too. Man, it's a mess."

"The CO's been on us like crazy to get these planes fixed, but they're blown to hell. Anyway, we send 'em up, and they don't come back. It's a sad situation."

Both men realized they were dragging each other down. They headed back to work but appreciated each other's honesty.

Dogs were not allowed in the hospital, but in this case they made an exception. In a day of failure, Commander blossomed as one of the few bright spots on a dingy, dark day. Rat held him firmly on the leash so as not to betray the hospitality the ward afforded. Commander remained on his best behavior. He was humble but proud as he walked by Rat's side. Rat asked a nurse where he might be able to find Carl Broodend. She checked a clipboard that was overly stuffed with charts, diagrams, and patients' names. She looked drawn from the endless hours, but Rat found her quite pleasing to the eyes and promised to ask her out on a date as soon as this mess died down. She reached down and scratched Commander behind the ears. She obviously liked dogs. She would definitely be getting a phone call. The nurse directed Rat down the hall and to the right and cautioned that other patients didn't need a ruckus. *Like I'm going to bring a band,* he thought. He just figured this soldier might like to meet the dog that had saved his life. Rat rapped lightly on the door. He was not quite sure this was the room. Commander confirmed his notion by lolling out his big tongue and slobbering a quiet pant of excitement.

"Carl Broodend?" Rat whispered, and he entered the hospital room.

Rat's stomach turned slightly as the wounded in the room lay in bandages from head to toe. The glazed look of morphine emanated from their eyes. Some of the sufferings' extremities were swollen black from being crushed under debris. Others' wounds lay open with coverings of tannic acid jelly.

"I'm Carl Broodend." Carl slowly turned his head. He was still very sore, and his neck was weak.

"I'm Private Doovaine, and this is Commander—the dog that found you in the building."

Commander lifted his paw to shake Carl's hand.

"Well, hi, Commander. Thank you, sir, for saving my life."

Rat noticed Carl addressed Commander as "sir" and was immediately endeared to the young private. Carl didn't have a lot of strength, and he left his hand dangling off the bed. Commander proceeded to lick the wound. "And thank you, Private. I understand you're the brains behind this operation."

"I don't know about brains. The dogs seem to be a lot smarter than humans. I just help them do human things." Rat didn't handle compliments well, but he was serious about the dogs being smarter. "Thank you, though."

"I'm sorry. What was your name?" Carl bent to look at Rat.

"Doovaine. Everyone calls me Rat."

"Thank you, Rat. I thought I was a goner. Where did you come from? I've never seen any dogs at Clark."

"We're over at Fort Stotsenburg. I met all the puppies at Fort Benning in Georgia when I went to boot camp. They were starting a new program for the dogs to search mines and tunnels, and the program is still evolving to capture everything these amazing animals can do. Search and rescue is just the tip of the iceberg. These dogs can be trained after wartime to help civilian populations in time of need such as fires, earthquakes, or floods. They are truly astonishing."

"What's going on out there today, Rat?"

Rat had known the question was coming. "We took another big hit today. The Japs bypassed Clark and Iba and went straight for Cavite, and some intel says the navy took a big blow at the bay." New Yorkers always told it straight. "We're getting punched around pretty good."

"I gotta get back in the game." Carl made the supreme effort of tying to sit up, but his body would not allow such folly.

"You need to get some rest. Your time will come." Rat felt the emotions running through Carl's brain. They all wanted some payback. "How do you feel?" Rat could tell he was in some pain.

"I feel as if the entire Oklahoma defensive line ganged up on me for the entire game."

"Did you play some football in Oklahoma?"

"Yeah. Offensive and defensive line. But I was usually doling out the pain."

Rat chuckled. "I played the line myself. Sometimes it's tough down in the trenches. Us linemen have to stick together. Let someone else take care of you now, and then you can get back in the game. OK?"

"You talk funny. Where are you from?"

Rat was humorously incensed. "I talk funny? You talk funny, you hick."

They both laughed. It hurt Carl physically, but it was the best medicine he had received. They chatted a little more about New York City and the wide-open spaces of Oklahoma. Rat and Commander eventually bid him adieu and promised a return visit. Carl assured them he would visit them. He wasn't going to be recuperating very long.

Gary and Annette sat in the lobby of the justice of the peace. For the second time in the past few days, he wondered if being seventeen would pose a problem. The army had let him slide. He hoped the judge would do the same. Neither Gary nor Annette had slept well for the last few nights. They were tired, and now that Gary was aware, he could notice Annette showing. They did love each other, but this was real grown-up stuff—being married and having a baby. Gary was slightly relieved he had joined the army. At least he'd have a way to pay for groceries and diapers. The news of Gary joining the army had been equivalent to the sinking of the *Titanic* in the household. If Annette's fury wasn't enough for one day, Mama Donna could have electrified the entire Midwest. Larry understood better but counseled him on talking to his parents before making any more rash decisions. "For God's sake," he'd told him, "don't do anything stupid like volunteer for a dangerous mission." It was the second time he had been called stupid in thirty-six hours. Larry was going to make Donna look like a dim forty-watt bulb when he found out his son had gotten married and that he was going to be a grandfather.

Egan Paal played poker belowdecks on the *Enterprise*. He had nothing in his hand—a six-two off suit—but he doubled the pot with a twenty-cent raise. He stared down the sailor across the table, who sported a pair of ladies. Egan searched for a tell. Egan knew he was beaten, but his raise had flustered his opponent, and the sailor with the queens waffled. *Call? Fold? Call?* Egan knew he wouldn't call unless he grew a sack of clackers that Egan knew he did not have. He threw in his cards and relinquished the pot. There were only so many ways to pass the time trolling off the coast of Oahu and waiting for orders from CINCPAC.

Jason Cenode stuffed his laundry into the duffel bag and headed out into the wintry mix of snow and sleet. The crews were grounded for a couple days or at least until the storm sweeping across the Nebraska plains settled down. The squadrons had been practicing a new landing pattern over the last couple days. They said it was experimental and wanted the best flying crews to try it out. They had shortened the runway for landing and takeoff. At first the pilots missed both the takeoff and landing points, but they had started to hone in on the parameters. Their progress seemed to please the CO, but he was disappointed the weather had held up practice for at least a day. All the troops asked why the brass had shortened the takeoffs and runways, but nobody would give them an answer.

Christmas Eve 1941, United States

As the sun set over the Atlantic Ocean, lobster boats pulled into the docks of chilly Boston. Vincent and Carla Leymoita wrestled with the idea of heading down to the precinct and bailing out their youngest son for fighting in a bar on Christmas Eve. Dominic was going to have to learn a lesson one of these days. Hearts softened, though, and Vinnie went to get his son. Carla put the final touches on the tree and thought about the perils surrounding her son Norm. He was trapped in a much different, more dangerous jail than Dominic.

Madison, Wisconsin

Veronica Paal was getting sleepy, but she wanted to stay awake to catch Santa eating the cookies. Egan's ten-year-old sister and her magical thoughts about Santa would soon give way to lipstick and boys. Her father, Quincy Paal, breathed in the moments of her childhood. He held his finger on the ribbon as Veronica tied the bow on Egan's present. They had mailed a package weeks ago, but Veronica felt there should be something under the tree. She missed Egan. He was the impetus for a good time. Lois stirred her Beefeater slowly over six cubes of ice until it was nice and cold. She reached into the refrigerator, pinched an olive, and splashed it into her waiting birdbath. *How can Egan do this to his mother?* she thought.

Pittsbugh, Pennsylvania

Paige helped Sarah lift her polio-ridden legs onto her bed and covered her with a warm blanket. The Alleghenies provided a white blanket of snow for the holiday. Sarah followed big flakes tumbling through the streetlight. Paige opened "The Night Before Christmas" and read the memorable poem to Sarah. She fell fast asleep with visions of sugarplums in her mind. Paige kissed Gene and Cynthia Joint good night and headed home in the ankle-deep snow. She loved her home and parents but spent most of her time at the Joint residence. It reminded her of Shaun. Paige was despondent without Shaun. She put up a strong front, but she cried herself to sleep at night while looking at his picture in her half of the locket.

El Paso, Texas

Anna tucked the boys into bed. Miguel snuggled in his pajamas under the blanket, and Juan sucked his thumb. His eyes drooped heavily, and then he fell asleep. The excitement of Christmas had the children all revved up. Aunts and uncles had even arrived for the holidays. Anna couldn't sneak the bags of presents past the alert children sentries. Jaime was three and a half and asked for Daddy every day. Anna gave him the same answer every day. "Daddy is in a faraway land protecting us from danger. He is in the army. Your daddy is very brave—just like you."

The answer satisfied Jaime. Most of the time.

"Will Daddy be here for Christmas tomorrow, Mama?"

The question broke Anna's heart. "No, Jaime. Daddy won't be home tomorrow, but he sends his biggest hugs and kisses and says if you're not nice to Mommy, he's going to tickle you until you can't laugh anymore." That made Jaime laugh. Inside it made Anna cry.

New York, New York

"The lamb is beautiful, Daddy," Valerie's mouth watered at the prospect of roasted lamb for Christmas dinner.

Ronald Doovaine had slipped his butcher a little Christmas bonus and ensured a nice full roast.

"I got some fresh rosemary at the market and some really nice potatoes and carrots. Do you want the potatoes mashed or roasted?" Kay needed to know these details well in advance.

"Did you get the mint jelly? I can't eat lamb without mint jelly, Kay."

Kay had gotten the mint jelly. Kay was frantic with the holidays. The meal had to be prepped for cooking by morning. Family was arriving from Queens, and the presents weren't all wrapped. Plus Rat wouldn't be here.

"Daddy, I went to see *Citizen Kane* with Dolores today. Orson Welles is dreamy," fifteen-year-old Valerie gushed.

"You mind your studies, Valerie. You shouldn't be thinking about boys. Besides, Welles is a man. He's got to be twenty-three. You keep you mind on your studies."

Valerie loved it when Daddy was protective of her. Valerie eyed the faux mantle adorned with the stockings for the children. She was so glad the nickname "Rat" wasn't sewed onto his stocking.

Commerce, Oklahoma

Doyle and Ida milled around the lonely house. They didn't say much to each other, but they didn't fight anymore either. Doyle had given up drinking—at least for now. This was the second Christmas Carl hadn't been home since he had run off to the army. Carl would send any letters for his mother to her sister, Inez, for fear Doyle would rip them up or hide them from Ida. Ida never talked to Doyle about Carl. She could sense Doyle carried a lot of guilt about the whole thing. Ida knew Doyle was carrying a lot of things in that head of his—a lot of pain. She wanted to talk to him and find out what made him tick, but she was very afraid of the belt. "Merry Christmas, Carl. I hope you're safe," Ida wished before she fell asleep.

Chicago, Illinois

Mr. and Mrs. Gary Alesse attended Catholic Mass early Christmas Eve to avoid the inevitable stares that had found them recently. They chose a quiet pew accompanied by Lawrence and Donna Alesse. Everyone tried to make the best of the situation. Fast Gary had been baptized in this church. He had gone to elementary school in this parish. He had received his First Communion on this altar. All that had gone by so fast. Now Gary was going to be a daddy. Fast. Gary had also married. Fast. Too fast. Only weeks before Donna had looked like Gary's older sister. Now she looked like the grandmother she was going to be.

They knelt. All four buried their heads in their hands and began to pray. Larry prayed for his wife's sanity and hoped she would get through this trying time. Donna hoped Jesus would swoop in from the heavens, rip up the enlistment form from the army, and take Annette far away from Chicago. Gary prayed Annette truly loved him and that she would be in the mood to have sex one more time before he shipped out the day after Christmas to paratrooper school in Oklahoma City, Oklahoma. Annette prayed she would have the baby before May so she wouldn't look nine months pregnant at her high-school graduation. The Alesses painted on their smiles and made it through Christmas.

Saint Louis, Missouri

Lily Skairny wasn't going to make it home from Washington University in Saint Louis. Snow had locked down all the buses and trains from leaving the city. School officials had given her permission to stay in the dormitories. The halls were decked with silence and cold. She lit a candle to give warmth to the room. She curled up in a blanket and reread the most recent letter she had gotten from Chet. He didn't sound as scared or frustrated as she felt. He talked about the island and the weather. He wrote about their honeymoon but rarely mentioned the Japanese. Lily was certain Chet didn't want to frighten her. She missed him very much. He had given her something she had never had. She wanted some more as she lay down on her small dorm room bed and thought about Tiger. She knew he was going to come out of this fine. She just hoped he didn't get a tattoo.

Riverside, California

Aunt Julie Cenode lit a votive candle. She knelt and prayed for her "adopted" son, Jason. She had accepted the menace to the safety of the United States was grave. She saluted her son's courage to stand and fight. It was going to take a lot of brave people to slow the likes of Hitler and Hirohito. Jason had already sacrificed so much. The ultimate sacrifice would be too much for Julie to bear. She removed the thought from her brain and worked up the courage to step into the confessional. The panel door slid gently open, and the priest's solemn voice spoke a soft introductory prayer. She knew the priest, and he would know her voice. It made her more apprehensive.

"Bless me, Father, for I have sinned." She had said this part a thousand times but never the next part.

"Tell me, what are your sins?" There was no judgment in the priest's voice.

Julie tried to remain calm. "I have intercourse with men." It was off Julie's chest.

"Are you married?" The priest pressed to reveal below the surface.

"No. I've never been married. I've never found the right guy."

"So your sin is lust."

"No!" Julie barked at the priest. "I don't have sex for lust." She took a deep breath and reevaluated the confession. "It's not that I don't like the act. It's fine," she stammered. "I have intercourse so I can have a baby." It was all out in the open.

"Having a child out of wedlock is very trying for all parties involved. Shouldn't you reconsider taking a husband and trying to procreate with him?" It seemed a logical question from a person who had sworn off intimacy of any form.

"Father, I don't want a husband. I want a child."

"How long have you been trying to have a child?"

This was the one question she had been hoping would not come up. She paused. "Twelve years."

"So you've been having intercourse with men for twelve years trying to conceive a child?" It didn't sound so good when he said it out loud.

"Yes."

"Have you ever considered that maybe God did not intend for you to have children?" That was blasphemy, and Julie would hear nothing of it. She burst into tears. "Maybe your purpose on Earth is to help children in a different way."

For Julie Cenode the Christmas bells went off in her head.

Christmas Eve 1941, The Philippines

Norm Leymoita had never heard of War Plan Orange—until yesterday. *This has to be the final straw in a fortnight of abysmal news,* Norm thought. It was the most important communiqué he had ever sent. It was dispersed to every division, regiment, battalion, and platoon. It went to every general, admiral, colonel, major, sergeant, and grunt—every American and Filipino. Norm forwarded the news. All forces were retreating from the Japanese army to the natural defenses of the Bataan Peninsula and the fortress on the island of Corregidor. Corregidor was a small bastion guarding the entrance to the port of Manila. It was well equipped to handle a siege and protect some ten thousand men and women for half a year. Batteries on the high ground served as deterrents to naval vessels that tried to enter the harbor. The labyrinth of the Malinta Tunnel provided safety from artillery. Corregidor was an underground vault for humans.

MacArthur himself had journeyed to the front lines on Luzon and had quickly seen enough. The main Filipino fighting force was flummoxed and in disarray. Most didn't have helmets. Their rifles didn't work well. Many didn't have blankets or shovels to dig a line. MacArthur set his strategy. The troops were to commence digging a line at Abucay. Tens of thousands of Allied soldiers first needed to retreat through miles of Philippine countryside with only rudimentary roads and narrow bridges to travel. General Wainwright persuaded MacArthur to send up an American division to the existing line to buy time for the rest of the army to fall back and allow General Parker's southern Luzon forces to retreat, swing west of Manila, and join the others. Events would have to move quickly. In only days General Homma's Forty-Eighth Division left on transports from the speck-sized islands off Formosa called the Pescadores. Landing in three waves at Lingayen Gulf, they quickly overwhelmed any beachhead resistance and started unloading ten thousand soldiers, supplies, trucks, artillery, and tanks in an effort to rendezvous with the invasion fleet that had arrived the previous week at Vigan. Seven thousand soldiers landed in Lamon Bay south of Manila and squeezed MacArthur's troops in giant pincers. The great Philippine island of Mindanao lay overrun. It had been stormed at the city of Davao on the southernmost island of the grand chain. The Japanese swarmed the island except the Bataan Peninsula. Manila lay open for the taking. MacArthur declared Manila open and hoped the historic city would not be destroyed.

The Japanese took no heed of MacArthur's offer. Long-range artillery shells rained through the night like a typhoon on Manila from the newly formed position at Lamon Bay. The Marsman Building shook violently. Norm scrambled to gather the last of the communication equipment he could carry. The last ship for Corregidor left with staff, MacArthur and his family, and the president of the Philippines, Manuel Quezon. Crews worked night and day to shift supplies to Bataan, or they had them ferried to Corregidor across the bay from the rumbling docks of Cavite Naval Yard. Ammunition dumps at Cavite emptied and were destroyed in terrific self-inflicted explosions. The quartermaster mustered food, medical supplies, and clothing. General Brereton left on a transport to Australia along with the last of the P-40 Warhawks.

The Philippines
The argument escalated between General MacArthur and Admiral Hart. MacArthur contended the navy had abandoned Manila and the submarines had done a lousy job of knocking out Japanese transports and attending warships. The *Swordfish* had sunk one transport, but the main body of the fleet was sent out to sea. Hart countered with the inability of the US Army Air Force to provide cover for the navy, which put them in a deadly game of pickle with the Japanese bombing runs. Hart chided MacArthur for evacuating the bulk of the bombers and leaving only a token number of planes to defend the islands. Both sent reports to the principals in Washington. Washington sent MacArthur word that the long-awaited transports of supplies, ammunition, and warplanes were being sidetracked to Australia. Enraged the supplies were being diverted, MacArthur fumed that the transports were essential to his command's ability to fight back and survive. The generals in Washington, D.C. and MacArthur's old friend General Dwight Eisenhower already knew that. They just

couldn't help anyone in the Philippines. They'd have to go it on their own.

Making matters worse Secretary of the Navy Frank Knox was on a mission to provide a sacrificial lamb for the blunders at Pearl Harbor. In a preemptive strike against the inevitable congressional hearings and investigations of what went wrong at Pearl, Knox decided to chop off someone's head—Admiral Husband Kimmel's. In a time of utmost importance, with the world caving around the Pacific fleet, the Pacific fleet was assigned an interim leader. Admiral W. S. Pye had proven a very competent admiral. Kimmel left Pye with a sound, headstrong strategy, but Kimmel had just been relieved of his command. Pye studied the plans carefully. Kimmel had carrier task forces moving about in the Pacific. Task Force 11 steamed to Wake to relieve the combatants there. Task Force 14 headed toward the Marshall Islands. The *Enterprise* remained stuck on guard duty around the Hawaiian Islands with Task Force 8. Pye smelled traps throughout the vast Pacific. The last thing he wanted was to get another group of boats blown out of the water. Pye proceeded conservatively. He got nothing done. He rescinded assistance to the battlers at Wake Island. Norm received a communiqué. Admiral Chester Nimitz was due to arrive in Pearl Harbor that evening.

The brave marines repelling the Japanese force on Wake Island had finally succumbed to overwhelming numbers. Major Paul Putnam led his flyers in a valiant effort and kept the Japanese at bay on sheer guile. A daybreak beach assault eventually overwhelmed Major Devereux and his outnumbered garrison. The resplendent Admiral Kajioka arrived in an official ceremony. He renamed the island in honor of Emperor Hirohito and raised the Rising Sun Flag over the tiny atoll. One thousand five hundred military and civilian personnel were taken as prisoners of war.

Hong Kong fell despite a bold attempt by the natives and British to hold the royal city. Japanese forces cut through the lines and hounded British positions. South of Hong Kong, General Yamashita worked his way down the Malayan Peninsula with speed and brutality. He captured vital natural resources en route. On the other side of the world, the White House welcomed Prime Minister Winston Churchill for the holidays. He and President Franklin Roosevelt hammered out a strategy to win a world war. The plan made the Pacific and the Philippines a second priority.

Commander barked his happy bark. Rat looked over to see Carl Broodend walking his way. They shared the warm embrace of survival.

"What are you doing here?" Rat was happy to see Carl on his feet. Carl was a big boy and probably a good offensive tackle.

"I thought I'd bring the puppies some Christmas treats." Carl opened a bag full of steak bones.

"Where did you get that?" Rat wanted the steak that used to be around the bones.

"At the hospital. They were clearing out the freezers for the evacuation, and a couple doctors found them 'hidden,' so they fired them up. I missed the meal, but I got the bones."

Carl stared into Commander's eyes and held the bone by his fingertips. Commander looked at the bone as if it couldn't possibly be for him, and then he snatched it away before he lost his opportunity. Harlem, Hudson, Lexie, Madison, and Broadway all yelped with glee. Each shepherd received a treat and started gnawing.

"I've got something for you," Carl told the man who had saved his life. "It's not much, but it's still a little cold." Carl handed Rat a bottle of beer.

Rat was beside himself. It might have been the greatest Christmas present ever. Carl had brought himself one as well. "The doctors found these too."

"I haven't had a beer…" Rat started thinking. "Since the night before we shipped out to the Philippines back at Fort Benning."

"We got to Manila a few times when we first got here, but since the buildup we've been pretty busy."

Carl didn't mind a few beers, but when the other soldiers got into the liquor, he drew the line. He had seen what liquor did to a person. He was still Doyle's blood.

"What are you going to do now you're feeling better?" Rat already knew the answer.

"Doctors gave me a clean bill of health. I'm gonna lend a hand to the fellas at the line. I'm sure they could use a gunner." Carl swigged his brew. "Things are looking pretty bad up there."

The weakening front had moved mere miles north of Fort Stotsenburg and Clark Field.

"The CO says we've got to keep the Japs occupied while everybody makes it to the peninsula." Rat worried about the dogs. "If we could get a little bomber help from the outside, we could hold them off for a few weeks," said Rat optimistically.

"What are you going to do with the dogs?"

"I'm going to put them in the truck, take them to Bataan, and hope for the best. The cavalry should come pretty soon, if we can ride it out."

Carl and Rat each finished their one cold beer. Carl gave each dog a good scratching and got down on one knee to squeeze Commander tight. Commander looked sad as Carl lumbered into the jeep and headed back to Clark. Rat reflected on the new carols and hymns of Christmas—bullets and bombs.

Christmas Day 1941, The Philippines

Chet Skairny's Christmas present had arrived. It was US Army regulars posted on the newly formed line between the small cities of Tarlac and Cabanatuan. General Wainwright was personally filtering up and down the fortifications and inspecting foxholes and tank and artillery positions. The Filipinos snapped to attention and followed the drills of the American soldiers. Morale rose. Wainwright gave the troops confidence and reminded them they outnumbered the enemy. They believed they could not only hold the line but force the Japanese to withdraw. Wainwright and his staff continually evaluated the weakest part of the line. The Japanese looked to find holes and drive a wedge through the line or cave in the flanks and surround his army.

The shelling commenced. The Japanese mortars soared from advanced positions into diving teardrops, and they exploded around the bunkers. Aerial assaults created more havoc. The soldiers kept their heads down and their helmets on as they rode the initial wave of explosions. From the line Japanese seventy-five-millimeter M94 guns sent shells hurtling from eight thousand yards away. Earth fell from the skies like torrents of rain. White noise filled the air. Several positions took close hits. Injured fighters cried out. Medics retrieved the wounded, and fresh, wide-eyed soldiers replaced them. The Americans fired. That was music to Chet's ears—the sound of the seventy-five-millimeter howitzers blasting their ordnance across the front and preventing General Homma's advance. M3 tanks revved their engines. The twelve tons of armored machine lurched back and volleyed its thirty-seven-millimeter rounds. The American mortars searched for the enemy and worked their way through the sugarcane.

The front ran west to east from Tarlac to Cabanatuan. The hilly landscape provided many natural ridges and swales. Creeks, ponds, rivers, open fields, trees, and jungle created the playing field for the deadly chess match. Forward troops suffered from the growing accuracy of the artillery. The smallest barriers became key positions. The Japanese units crept forward by the inch to gain a stronghold behind any type of protection. Chet looked out of the foxhole at the sugarcane field in front of his position. The stalks were tall enough to hide the Nippon troops crouching and working slowly through the crop. American artillery exploded and killed and maimed the enemy. They cautiously kept coming and gaining valuable ground as their mortar fire became more precise. The trained, disciplined Japanese moved forward.

"Major," Chet said, "if we can take a couple groups and get them to that string of wells and troughs, we could push them back with small arms. I don't think they would be able to see the wells coming out from the sugarcane or from the rear positions."

The wells and troughs were easier to see from Chet'sosition on a small ridge slightly elevated from the Japanese position. The well was centrally located to the Japanese push and was situated on a narrow dirt path that divided the field. They agreed it was a superior vantage point with an element of surprise that could confuse the Japanese. Chet and his troops would have to get there quickly, or the swarm of Japanese lurking in the crops would execute them in the fields. They would be able to see Chet and his troops leave the bunker and submerge into the sugarcane, but a few suicidal crews of six soldiers in a field would not have much effect on the two hundred or so making their way through the valuable harvest. The major sent word down the line. He liked the idea. He sought a few volunteers, whom he found promptly. Chet waited for the signal.

"Go, Private."

Chet slithered out of the bunker on his chest, rose to his feet, scurried, and rolled down the small embankment to the edge of the sugarcane. Five other soldiers wilted in the hot Christmas Day sun and paused behind him.

"We gotta go fast. We gotta go straight and a little left in about three hundred yards. Then we'll be right behind the well." The wide-eyed soldiers had dirt smeared with sweat on their faces. They nodded. "You gotta stay low. We've got to beat them to the well, or it's over. Move."

Moving though the cane field was like swimming in a pond with hungry alligators. The soldiers couldn't see the enemy, but knew they were lurking. At first they went too slowly. Chet picked up the pace. The sugarcane leaves crackled like a symphony. Chet's heart pounded. Each sound was a beacon to their location. Every ten yards Chet screeched to a halt and took a deep breath. The crop was so dense it was possible to pass right by the enemy. Chet cursed the sluggish pace. He knew he could race four hundred meters around a track in under a minute. The pack and the gun caught the stalks, snapped them, and created sounds like distant gunfire that spooked everyone in the field. Seconds passed like minutes. Chet knew they were close. He crept forward. He found the sandy, white path—a simple access through the field. It was a swath the farmers used to pass the burrows through the acreage with haste. A mere four or five feet separated the Americans from the next field. They had beaten the Japanese to this point, but did the Japs have their own surprise?

Chet crouched down behind the well and checked the ammunition of his M1 carbine. He had two full clips and two cast-iron grenades. The other men took inventory and checked for other squads to join them at wells on the path. Chet found solace when another American crew scrambled for the trough's cover. Sweat poured down their faces. Chet whispered, "You have to be very quiet. Listen for the leaves to crack or the brush to crumble under their feet as they walk. Don't say anything, or they'll freeze."

Chet flashed hand signals to the other squad down the path to indicate they were in position and ready. The third party had not arrived. The assigned well was exposed.

Bottom lips trembled as silence became fear. Chet's urge to pop his head over the well was unyielding. Such imprudence could lead to a bayonet in the mouth. They waited for noise. Any sound. Any Japanese misstep, and they would throw the grenades. They held their breath and winced as they exhaled. Chet opened his mouth halfway so there would be silence as the oxygen entered his lungs. They waited. A barrage of shells flew over their heads and seemed part of a different world. The troops focused on the meters in the field—a pane of glass not yet shattered. Chet did not hear the crunch of a leaf or a branch. Chet didn't hear the enemy's boot stepping on a dry stalk. Chet heard the ting of a bayonet touching the helmet of a Japanese soldier. The enemy was just about to exit on the path. Chet guessed they were fifteen meters away. He signaled the second squad. All were ready with grenades.

Chet remained silent. He stood upright and heaved the first grenade into the sugarcane. Each of the Americans followed in synchronization and started an umbrella-shaped pattern of explosions. Gunfire returned through the sugarcane as the confused Japanese fired at the ghosts. The Americans fired back.

The major watched through his field glasses. He spotted the three wells. One was unmanned. The major eyed his lost unit. They were disoriented and flailing in circles among the giant plants. He shifted to the center well. It was secure, and explosions rocked the oncoming forces. The sugarcane swayed to the dance of the Japanese as they retreated for sanctuary. The well to the right had equal success and drove the forces back into the field. The major remained concerned about the well on the left. The Japanese approaching that area had not received any fire. The enemy still cautiously approached that position. A failure to maintain that position would put the other squads in harm's way. They would be flanked to one side, and the enemy would have cover from which to retaliate. He observed his lost unit swirl closer to the battle.

Chet felt they had the upper hand. He could hear the cries of the wounded and the alarmed cries of the panicked Japanese caught in the blind. He worried for the third group. *Where could they be?* He knew if the Japanese covered the third well, his lost unit would find trouble. Chet signaled, and his team hurled another set of grenades on the weakened enemy. They heaved them as far as they could in anticipation of the enemy having fallen back several yards. Chet was right. The shrapnel of the cast-iron steel splintered upon impact and sliced open the flesh of the enemy soldiers. Chet and his compatriots rained a hail of bullets into the field for good measure. Chet was fractions of a second away from smiling, but then he ducked as a bullet whistled by his ear and into the neck of his squad member. Blood sprayed like water from a garden hose with a pinprick in the tube. The soldier's eyes remained open while his punctured jugular drained him pale.

The unimpeded Japanese forces found the path and well. The exposed well was positioned to Chet's left. He intuitively instructed his people to swing behind the well and trough to their right. This exposed them to the reeling Japanese soldiers. They fired from behind the narrow barricade. The squad defending the well in the center remained in dire straits. The men at the center well were firing and diving back into the sugarcane for cover. The Japanese tossed a few grenades toward the center well. Chet screamed for them to get into the field or fall back to their well. He knew the ambushed and injured Japanese squads would regroup.

The lost third squad had gotten turned around in the field, but they emerged from the stalks. Like military scarecrows leaping off their perches, they popped out of the field and behind the newly formed Japanese position at the third well. The Americans decimated the attacking squad with machine-gun fire. A pair of US soldiers threw grenades into the field for effect. Japanese mortar fire had now recalibrated and honed in on the position of the wells. Chet knew the approaching squads had fallen back far enough to avoid friendly fire, and the third flank was reeling from the devastating surprise attack from the weeds. Chet signaled to bug out. He hoisted the body of the dead soldier over his shoulder and started the hump back to the ridge. Time lay trapped in quicksand. The evacuation moved slowly. Members of the squad provided fire to the rear as the Japanese mortar fire moved closer and closer. The Japanese gunners took out their anger on the retreating squads. Chet reached the edge of the field. The soldiers came to the bottom of the ridge and helped them to the confines of the bunker. Medics came for the dead and wounded. Chet knew the Japanese would be back, but for now they had stopped the advance on their front.

December 31, 1941, New Year's Eve
Norm hadn't taken a head count, but it felt as if Fenway Park had emptied civilians and soldiers and jammed them underground into the Malinta Tunnel. American and Filipino populations that passed each other on the streets with nary a smile now coexisted in the giant cave. The past week had tumbled at a furious pace as refugees from Homma's advance situated themselves into the tunnel with food and medical supplies and prepared for a long siege. Norm slogged through hundreds of communiqués every hour from the troops on the battlefield. He constantly battled the surface and sky wave antennae for better reception. American troops with the Filipino army faltered as the last of General Parker's south Luzon Force trudged through the ruins of Manila and reached the bridges at Calumpit. The last few American tanks provided cover as they crossed the Pampanga River and headed to San Fernando. The plan was to sweep back south to the Bataan Peninsula and join the other hundred thousand refugees digging in at Abucay and points farther south.

MacArthur took command of the situation room. Working over the thousands of maps littered around the desk, he conducted the evacuation like a maestro conducting an orchestra. General Homma's vanity helped MacArthur achieve his goals. The surging general and his forces seemed preoccupied with advancing victoriously into Manila and not with obliterating the fleeing army forces. Homma could have trapped them or annihilated them, but now the Japanese would have to fight them again.

A suspicious lack of air strikes allowed the greater portion of the Southern Luzon Force to cross the Calumpit bridges and escape Manila—the only crossing in or out in that direction. Army engineers raced against time and draped the bridge with explosives. They were ready to blow it sky-high on General Wainwright's order. Thousands still waited to cross. Armored vehicles, canvas-backed trucks, marching soldiers, and civilians carrying baskets jammed the narrow roads. Donkeys and oxen hauled the Filipinos' worldly possessions away from the juggernaut.

The fight in the north became tenuous. The line previously held between Tarlac and Cabanatuan crumbled. The eastern flank of the Forty-Eighth Division drove east around Mount Arayat and then south through Gapan and San Jose—a virtual straight line to Manila. It was a long road, but there was no resistance. The main northern front had fallen back past Camp O'Donnell to within a few miles of Clark Field at Bambang. It stretched a mere fifteen miles to the jungle-rich base of the western slopes of Mount Arayat. Thousands of Filipinos and a few Americans fled to the high jungles of the mountains. The Japanese war machine advanced, broke through the line, and created havoc and uncertainty within the units. It was time to be killed or flee. Many chose to flee, live, and become guerillas who would be thorns to the Japanese army for years to come.

"Scramble! Scramble! Scramble!" the sergeant screamed at the Filipino and American troops crossing the bridge at Bambang.

A Japanese tank rolled into sight, guarded by hordes of infantry brandishing their Type 99 7.7-millimeter rifles. The people scrambling across the bridge to safety became target practice as the gunners settled to their knees and blistered the bridge with bullets. Carl Broodend reached the south side of the bridge. His weapon had failed to fire. An American regular and Filipino failed to stay low enough and paid the price. The American took one just under the ear and collapsed a few feet from Carl. The

Filipino took several rounds to the torso. Blood seeped from his mouth, and the life escaped him. Carl crawled back out onto the bridge as bullets chipped away at the concrete around him. Quite a few more Filipinos sought cover behind the bridge. They were afraid to run through the gauntlet of bullets that would greet them. The US Army rigged the bridge to explode.

Carl worked his way to the dead soldier's Browning M1917 machine gun. The weapon weighed thirty pounds. Carl carried an extra magazine that guaranteed 250 rounds. He scraped the weapon along the ground and avoided fire. Two troops provided rifle fire and allowed him to position the gun. He engaged the rounds and opened fire. The hail of bullets sent the Japanese infantry to the ground for cover. He pressed the trigger and his advantage. Other friendly troops screamed at the people on the wrong side of the bridge. The last dozen or so ran with Olympic speed over the bridge to safety as Carl dispensed most of his ammunition. This left short, precious seconds to bug out when his rounds were gone. The Japanese would again take aim at the bridge. The Japanese tank was already beginning to train its sights on Carl's position.

The whirring of the machine gun indicated he had spent his allotment of bullets. Carl turned and ran with fury away from the bridgehead. He felt the fire on his heels but did not look back. He dived into a foxhole with the waiting demolition team. The Japanese pressed forward and brought the tank to the bridge's edge. They inched the tank cautiously forward and waited for resistance. Carl watched them take the bait. One imperial soldier waved his arm for the tank to proceed. The engineers waited until the tank and the troops were about a third of the way over the bridge. They detonated the explosives. Concrete blasted into the air along with the limbs of the Japanese infantry. The tank teetered and fell into the currents of the rushing creek. The Japanese wasted no time mourning the dead. They efficiently removed the injured and assessed how to cross the creek by foot or build a new bridgehead. Carl looked on and was stunned. The Japanese were machines. Carl and the demolition crew had no time to celebrate the small victory. General Wainwright ordered another fallback position just north of Guagua's Del Carmen Field. The Americans conceded Clark Field, the small city of Angeles, and the vital transfer junction of San Fernando.

The first few minutes of 1942 were peaceful. Manny beheld the stars in the Pacific sky with thoughts of Anna and his boys. He wanted to live and make it home to them. The convoy from Iba took them down the west coast of Luzon through San Antonio to Olongapo. The trucks moved slowly, but they were moving. They were receiving very little attention from the Japanese forces. They seemed to have Manila squarely on their minds. Manny looked at the moonlight shimmering on the waters of the bay and wondered how such unholiness had come to a place of such beauty.

Shaun sat in the back of the flatbed a few hundred yards from Manny but miles away. Supplies and equipment filled the truck, and there was little room to sit. Shaun thanked God he wasn't walking. He gently rubbed the locket Paige had given him and fawned over the silhouette of her picture in the moonlight. He imagined the touch of her hand, the smell of her neck, soft kisses by the fireplace, and the gentle brush of her hair. He hummed "Auld Lang Syne" to himself and imagined Paige's New Year's kiss on the dance floor, the orchestra, and the confetti falling from the rafters. He was sure someone was on the way to help them out of this mess.

Carl fell in line with the thousands of other soldiers and machinery retreating from the north. The columns grew full. Citizens mingled into the lines and headed for Mauben. It was west of the volcanic peaks of Mount Natib and on the west shores of the South China Sea. The chaos had altered seventeen million natural Filipinos' lives. Carl shared his canteen with another soldier. It surely was different from the cold beer he had shared with Rat. Carl shared his story about the attack on Clark Field. It was on-the-spot therapy. The ranks remained quiet as fatigue took its toll. A makeshift kitchen provided the marching infantry with a taste of vegetables cooked with coconut milk, soy sauce, vinegar, hot chilies, and bagoong. Carl noted it wasn't fried chicken, but it was better than nothing. The other soldier appreciated the humor and mentioned hot apple pie. They headed back into the march. Their uniforms were soaked and resoaked with days of sweat. The cloth started to chafe their thighs and ass cracks. Their socks were damp from perspiration and puddles. Some soldiers had been wearing wet socks for days, and their feet began to rot in the strangest ways. Other people started vomiting or possessed terrific fevers. This made the burden tougher on the medics, who were already bogged down with the wounded. The dead received no proper burials. They were left to rot where they had been killed.

Carl looked at the road. He watched each step forward one pace at a time. One of his boots was untied, but he didn't mind. His feet throbbed, and the loosened lace relieved the stranglehold. He reflected on his beloved mother, Ida, and wondered if she was as scared as he was. He wondered if World War I had raped Doyle's childhood. He wondered if the alcohol disguised the pain but invited the monster that refused to let the ones he cared for extend beyond his controlling circle. This was the control that prevented Ida from speaking to another man and the control that prevented Carl from blossoming into his own man. Was Doyle afraid they would leave him alone in a trench with his fears? Carl had seen things in a few weeks that would haunt him for a lifetime. He regretted not doing more to understand Doyle, but the situation had become dangerous. He would have gone to prison if he had killed Doyle. He had subtracted himself from the situation by joining the army.

His new marching partner stayed on his shoulder. They heard the sound of barking dogs in the night. It was Commander and the puppies in the back of a truck. Commander spotted Carl and became very animated. He started barking wildly and drew Rat's attention. Rat peered out from the back of the canvased truck and saw the smiling, waving Carl Broodend. A smile crossed Rat's face as he was reunited with his one-beer buddy. The convoy stalled as Carl approached the dogs. Commander leaped out of the truck and bounced around Carl's legs. Carl went to the ground and gave Commander a bear hug. The other dogs watched over the top of the gate. Their tails wagged at the sight of the bone bringer.

"How about a lift, Soldier?" Rat addressed Private Broodend happily.

"Don't mind if I do. My dogs are barking." Carl climbed in with the passel of German shepherds. "Can we handle one more?" He looked sympathetically toward his new marching partner.

"I don't see why not. If you don't mind a German shepherd sitting in your lap." He chuckled.

"No, sir, I do not," the soldier stated emphatically.

Carl and he had marched over a hundred miles in the previous weeks. He hoisted himself up and planted himself on the welcome wooden bench. Lexie nestled her chin snugly in his lap, and the two made instant friends.

"I'm Rat Doovaine. I'm in charge of the dogs." Rat extended his hand to Carl's unnamed marching partner.

Carl realized he had never introduced himself. "Carl Broodend."

"Hi. My name is Chet Skairny. Glad to meet you."

The convoy started rolling toward the next stop, and all grabbed some much-needed shut-eye on New Year's Eve.

At 6:15 a.m. General Wainwright gave the order to blow the vital bridges at Calumpit. The Southern Luzon Forces had made it safely through and were swinging south at San Fernando to populate the new line at Guagua's Del Carmen Field and the Bataan Peninsula's Abucay Line. The evacuation had created a consistent line across the peninsula. Ten thousand people swept west from Abucay across the face of Mount Natib to Mauben. The natural protection of the swamps, mountainous terrain, and dense jungles slowed the Japanese advance. The forces remained exhausted and hungry. The heat took its toll, and thousands of people became dehydrated. Quartermasters on Bataan took initial inventories of the food supply. The news was grim. In the rush to evacuate, the food supplies fell well short of the demand for an army of over eighty thousand plus additional civilian refugees. Medical supplies and antimalarial quinine were dangerously low. Similar shortages challenged the stores of Corregidor. More people flooded the tunnel than anticipated. By all accounts food estimates would last about forty-five days. MacArthur placed the troops and civilians on half rations. It was hardly a diet that could maintain a soldier fighting in the jungle heat of the Bataan Peninsula. Happy New Year!

January 9, 1942

Imperial soldiers hoisted the flag of the Rising Sun over the Manila Hotel. American blood curdled. General Homma organized a parade for the remaining Manila residents to witness his superior forces' arrival. The press documented the struggle of MacArthur's forces daily in the newspapers. The outraged American community yearned for Roosevelt's response and plan to rescue the tortured troops wedged onto the Bataan Peninsula. Promises of hope flooded over the wires to MacArthur's headquarters in the Malinta Tunnel from Washington. MacArthur pleaded with Washington to help as the desperate troops were introduced to the discouraging propaganda of Tokyo Rose. However, hope was the only thing they could send. America had just begun to generate the goods necessary to fight a two-pronged war around the globe. Despite concerted efforts the war-planning committee's consensus was the fighters on Bataan Peninsula were beyond rescue. MacArthur refused to believe nothing could be done. He refused to let his people believe help wasn't coming.

Homma's victory was not complete, despite his self-promoting and personal welcoming of himself to the capital city. A large army of Americans and Filipinos lurked on the Bataan Peninsula. Tokyo coveted the Manila Bay for the navy to make port for operations south in Borneo. Neither could happen until the forces on Bataan were suppressed and the defenses on Corregidor negated. Tokyo directed Homma to relinquish troops of the Forty-Eighth Infantry Division to assist the thrust into Borneo and Java. The seasoned veterans proved superior in every way to the American and Filipino forces protecting the Philippines and had achieved equal success in China. Homma was challenged with overwhelming the Bataan Peninsula with the underwhelming young soldiers of the Sixty-Fifth Infantry—the Summer Brigade. The Summer Brigade promptly displayed their inexperience and got bogged down for days while crossing through the thick jungles of Mount Natib. This personnel adjustment tilted Homma's calendar. Tokyo added that Homma had less than two months to achieve victory to maintain the emperor's ambitious agenda for the Southeast Pacific.

Boston, Massachussets

Vincent Leymoita held his wife, Carla. She trembled with the anxiety of not knowing whether her son Norm was dead or alive. Arguments with the delinquent Dominic raged. His random comings and goings frustrated a household on the brink of a nervous breakdown. Dominic rebelled from the stress by slipping deeper into the underground world of the New England Mafia. Carla agonized while reading the papers. She knew one son could already be dead in a war thousands of miles away and another wasted away before her very eyes.

Madison, Wisconsin

Veronica Paal pinned colored construction paper to the bulletin board with her busy fifth-grade classmates. Current events started making more sense. She grasped the meaning of the word "war." She understood the gravity of her brother Egan being a soldier. Veronica's childhood slipped away quickly. Her attorney father, Quincy, had become more involved in the politics of the war. He had also become an active member of the Republican Party with aspirations of a congressional seat. He felt he could make a difference in the way Washington worked. Lois, her mother, spent her days at the country club hobnobbing with Milwaukee's upper crust and sipping on dry gin. She knew perfectly well that Egan was safe and sound on that "cruise ship that circled around Hawaii," as she put it to her friends. She convinced them Egan had been especially chosen to be clear of harm's way.

Pittsburgh, Pennsylvania

Paige became physically drawn with worry over Shaun. She wore the locket like a bracelet so she could more readily clutch it when the wretched pangs gnawed her stomach. Sarah attempted role reversal and tried to cheer Paige by inviting her to play board games or twenty questions to relieve Paige's brain momentarily. Gene and Cynthia splurged and took the family to the movies to get away from the bad news on the radio. However, newsreels of the impending dangers faced by American soldiers only reminded them of the horror. Gene chased Paige as she raced from the theater in tears.

El Paso, Texas

Anna noticed her first gray hair and the crow's-feet around her eyes. The children exhausted her from dawn until dusk. Their needs were great. Her needs were neglected. She was lonely and scared. Her soul told her Manny was in trouble. She always had a sixth sense about those things. Today she had an especially bad feeling. What would she do with three little babies all by herself? She fell to her knees and kneaded her rosary. "Manny, please come home."

New York, New York
Ronald Doovaine joined Mayor Fiorello La Guardia's civil patrol to protect New York City. Valerie and Kay spent hours at the parish helping the nuns organize fund-raising drives for the Red Cross and Maryknoll. Kay felt the only way to stop thinking about Rat was to stay busy, and if they stayed busy doing positive things, positive things would happen for Rat. Denial was her survival technique. Sometimes accepting the truth was too much to bear. Ronald and Valerie both bought into Kay's system. It was an impossibility to think Rat could be dead. They both knew Kay was on the cusp of imploding.

Chicago, Illinois
Annette wrote to Gary and sent the letter to the airfield in Oklahoma. Gary still remained safely tucked away in the dead center of the United States. Annette had believed him when he said the war would be over before he got out of basic training. She mentioned she had felt the baby kick, and if it was a boy, she wanted to name him Peter. If it was a girl, she wanted to name her Ruth, which Gary immediately determined was not going to happen. She wrote that her breasts had gotten very large, and she wanted Gary to see them. She informed him her nipples were very sensitive as well when she touched them. Gary went to take a shower. Fast.

Commerce, Oklahoma
Commerce, Oklahoma, was a small town, but they got the news just like everybody else. Ida stared out the kitchen window at the

bleak winter sky. Sorrow crept around her like a poisonous vine around her spine. Doyle stepped slowly behind her. He put his arms around her waist and held her close. It was the first time he had touched her in years. She began to sob. Her husband had returned to her after so many years, but her son might have left her forever. For years she had fought the tears, but today she wept. Doyle held her until she stopped weeping with the sunrise.

Saint Louis, Missouri

Lily Skairny would never concede. She knew Chet was on the island with MacArthur. It was the only safe place to be, and Chet would be there. MacArthur got phone calls from the president. Chet could find a way to send a message to his wife.

"Operator, I'd like to make a person-to-person phone call to the Philippines. Specifically to the island of Corregidor. The call is from Lily Skairny to Chet Skairny. I'm his wife."

"I am sorry, ma'am. There's no signal. I believe all phone lines to the Philippines are in control of the US Army. Or the Japanese. I'm not sure."

"There's no way to patch me through?"

"I am sorry, ma'am."

"What if I call the army operator? Do you think the operator could get me a line?"

"Suit yourself." The operator was not unsympathetic to Lily Skairny, but people were trying to call all over the world, and it just wasn't working for anyone.

Lily picked up the phone and tried to call the army operator. She was sure the operator could get through to Chet.

Riverside, California

Aunt Julie Cenode returned from the lumberyard after emptying her savings account. Her modest Riverside home needed an addition. She had hammers, nails, gloves, and desire. Julie had decided to build a nursery for her babies. She didn't have them yet, but she would soon. She wanted babies, and she was going to give them a beautiful home to grow and thrive in—just as she had given Jason a home. It would be a home for the unwanted children whom she wanted so badly.

The Phillipines

Manny laid barbed wire around the perimeter to slow the impending Japanese assaults. He hoped as the Japanese traversed through the vegetation, they would get trapped in the prickly twine and become easy targets for the dug-in positions waiting for the invaders. Manny had not seen Shaun for days but found him throwing up bile on his boots. He was showing the first signs of malaria. Manny put his hand on Shaun's forehead. He was burning up. Shaun's eyes glazed as the fever gripped him. Manny laid Shaun down and covered him with a blanket. He prepared a mild soup of wild roots over an open flame. It was no wonder the poor kid had gotten sick. Everyone was starving and drinking filthy water. Rations were supposed to be halved, but they were fortunate to get that.

Manny worked one of the native Filipinos for information. They exchanged information in the crudest of communications. Manny used English, Spanish, and Tagalog in an effort to treat Shaun's illness. Translation was difficult, and Manny kept getting a poor rendition from the boy. The boy pantomimed chills, fever, and how mosquitoes bite. Manny started to get the picture. He knew that quinine would help and sent someone to find a nurse or doctor. He wrote it on a piece of paper so there would be no confusion with the language. What Manny did not know was that malaria was an infectious disease caused by anopheles mosquitoes and parasites that attack the liver and cause fatigue, headaches, high fever, rapid breathing, chills, sweating, anemia, and splenomegaly.

"Hey! Soldier! We want to talk to you."

Rat stayed at the line with the dogs. There really wasn't anywhere else to go except farther down the peninsula to the Mariveles Mountains—the final fallback of the retreat. Rat turned. The angry mob of Americans and Filipinos gathered in a daunting semicircle. The dogs sensed a threat and snapped to attention. Carl and Chet appeared by Rat's side.

"What do you want?" Rat said with no hospitality.

"We want that food in the back of the truck."

Everyone was hungry. Everyone was starving. Hundreds of soldiers and civilians felt the effects of malaria or worse. Supplies of canned meat and fish dwindled rapidly. The rations of rice weren't satisfying the human body's needs.

"The food in the back of the truck is for dogs. It's dog food. It's made of things humans shouldn't eat. They'll get sick."

"We're already sick. We're sick because we're starving to death, and you've got food. Now give us the food!" The mob rumbled in anger as they closed in around the truck. The dogs started barking.

Rat simply said, "No."

The mob leader, an American soldier, took a swing at Rat. Rat returned with a left to the jaw and pounced on the man. They rolled around on the ground and pounded each other. They wasted valuable energy for the fight against the Japanese. The dogs snarled and kept the mob at bay. A single shot rang through the air as Lientenant Colonel Rothschild holstered his Colt M1917 six-shooter.

"What in the blazes is going on here? Stand to attention!" Rat got to his feet and faced the senior officer with the other soldier. "Well, Private?" He looked at Rat. He was getting the better end of the tussle.

"These people came to steal the dogs' food, sir!"

"Is that true, Private?" The lieutenant colonel inquired and looked at the hungry mob over the private's shoulder.

"We're hungry, sir. The men are getting sick from starvation, sir. We felt any food could help the soldiers, sir."

The mob rallied in agreement. Others joined the confrontation after hearing the gunshot. Lieutenant Colonel Rothschild regarded the eyes of the people. Many were gaunt and quivered from fever. He looked at the German shepherds. They did not look well fed either. Their coats were mangy, and their torsos were thin. Rothschild found himself in a quandary. He paced while the soldiers remained at attention in the oppressive humidity. Rothschild felt his own hunger gnawing at his stomach. He couldn't fathom eating dog food and would stick it out on the rations provided. "Unload the food from the truck."

Rat was incensed. He shouted defiantly at the commanding officer. "The dogs will die."

Carl held him back from bumping the lieutenant colonel.

"So will the soldiers if they don't get anything to eat. Now back down, Private!"

Rat's eyes raged with fury. He would not back down. "What will we do with the dogs, sir?"

"Let them loose into the wild, Private. They are animals. They have instincts. Let them survive in the jungle."

"They won't survive in the jungle, sir! They are domesticated trained soldiers and need the same respect as the other troops."

"Private!" The CO went nose to nose with Rat. "They are dogs! Get that through your thick skull. Dogs will not supersede the needs of the fighting humans. Dogs are not soldiers. They are dogs!" Rothschild found the opportunity to unleash his pent-up frustration.

Carl spoke up. "Sir, these dogs saved lives at Clark Field when it was attacked. They deserve a better fate than to be left in the jungle." Carl spoke from his heart, but it only added fuel to Rothschild's raging fire.

"Do you want to get into this, Soldier? Do you? Can that dog pick up a machine gun? Can that dog stop a round of mortar fire or load an antitank weapon, Private? Can they, Private? Answer me now, goddamn it!"

"No, sir!"

"Then let them off their leashes and shoo them into the jungle before I remove my sidearm, shoot them myself, and throw them into a stew."

"No, sir. I cannot do that. They have no hunting instincts. They will die within a week."

Rothschild removed his pistol and shot Harlem in the head. The mob went silent. Rat pounced on the dead dog and wept. The soldier who had instigated the melee shrank inside himself. They were all just so very hungry. The well-trained dogs looked sadly at Rat and the dead Harlem but remained heeled. Chet reached for his firearm as Rothschild emptied another round into Madison. The crowd moved away. A green madness raced through Rothschild's eyes as if something unnatural had entered his soul. Rat's chest heaved in grief, and he shot a murderous glance at Rothschild from the ground. Rothschild took another step toward Lexie and blasted a bullet through the side of the female's head. Carl stepped toward Hudson to shield him, but it was too late. The fourth bullet in Rothschild's clip dropped the dog. Broadway barked and was silenced. He stepped toward Commander, and Rat flung himself in front of the dog. "Please! Please! Please stop! For the love of God. Please stop!" Rat's face had gone purple from rage and sadness.

"Step away, Private!" Rothschild made the order as Chet and Carl both stepped in front of Rat. Chet had his rifle loaded and ready and wouldn't hesitate to slay the mad colonel if he moved on Rat. "This is insubordination," screamed Rothschild.

"No, sir. Enough is enough. We're all in hell, sir. We'll all be dead in a week. Enough."

The evil green shade of Rothschild's eyes dissipated as he slowly holstered the empty pistol. Five German shepherds lay motionless on the ground, and the only sounds were the tears rolling down Rat's face and Commander's tongue licking his master's cheek in comfort.

"Take the animal food from the truck, and butcher the dogs. Share the food among yourselves and ration the meat. There is no end in sight in this dismal place."

Rothschild slunk away as the Filipinos unloaded what turned out to be very little food. A few civilians sheepishly slid the dogs away from the area to skin and cook them.

Rat held Commander closely throughout the night. He heard laughter from the scattered camps in the vicinity—laughter from people who had bellies of food for the first time in weeks. He hoped they had enjoyed their dinners. *Bastards.*

The aircraft carrier *Yorktown* arrived and paired with the *Enterprise.* Egan Paal made his paltry personal final preparations for leaving Hawaii. The *Yorktown* brought troops and aircraft for the garrison in Samoa—a strategic island for the Americans and their communications across the Pacific. The *Enterprise* was stocked and ready for an extended stay at sea, and it cut westward into the Pacific. Egan whiffed the fresh salt air of Hawaii and wondered how danger would smell.

Jason Cenode caught his first whiff of the changing winds. His B-17 airborne troops were being shipped east from Nebraska to board a new carrier called the *Hornet.* The *Hornet* would give them a lift across the infested waters of the North Atlantic to England, where his squadron would set up base with the British for air raids in France and Germany. How wrong Jason was.

The desk shook as little clouds of dust landed for the millionth time on Norm's paperwork. The Japanese shelling of Corregidor was incessant. He wondered how long the fortress could withstand such punishment. It had held up well to this point. Inside spirits were less fortified. Rations had been reduced again, and the children were starting to suffer. Very infrequently submarines and PT boats would sneak into the coves of Corregidor, bring small amounts of supplies, and evacuate women and children. They were dangerous, cloaked operations. Doctors and nurses worked around the clock tending to malnutrition, anemia, and the constant influx of the wounded. There was no release, and they suffered from the malady of cabin fever.

MacArthur planned a visit to the front the following day. His animated phone calls with Washington revealed the frustration. Gossip ran rampant in the tunnel that they had been abandoned. This was despite MacArthur's positive belief that reinforcements were on the way. The Japanese offensive at Abucay had stalled. The narrowing of the front helped the combined forces of the northern and southern armies belt the oncoming Japanese with artillery from tight positions. Japanese troops worked their way toward the western coast of Bataan but had taken many days to get there. This allowed the American forces at Mauben to establish strong lines. General Wainwright swore constantly at the sky as bombers continued to haunt his troops from the air—harbingers of the inevitable devastation. He prodded at the weak links in the line around the flanks of Mount Natib and could do nothing about the impending Japanese forays that were to arrive from the ports of the recently seized Olongapo except ready the last line of defense at Mariveles.

Norm could hear things others could not. He kept to himself the dichotomy of despair that fell on Corregidor and the news reports from the radio on the West Coast of the United States that cheered the rousing defense of the Philippines and purported the success of MacArthur's army. Norm was one of the few who knew the lies being enlisted in the battle against the Japanese.

January 26, 1942

The people of the US and Filipino forces fought with abandon, but the constant air strikes and the marauding Japanese tanks finally blasted a hole in the line at Abucay at the eastern base of the volcanic Mount Natib. The forces withdrew to the predetermined lines formed in the foothills of the Mariveles south of Orion. Air strikes hastened the march south and left people strewn on the roadside in the villages of Balanga and Pilar. Japanese Zeros razed the narrow road with cannon fire, and the heavy bombers loosed death from higher altitudes. General Parker had assumed command of the eastern front, and he watched his army fight valiantly, but disease and starvation depleted the ranks. Filipinos and American regulars openly mocked MacArthur's leadership as the general's promises went unmet.

Rat had barely eaten and looked frail. Chet and Carl both made him eat some rice. Rat grieved over the death of the shepherds and had been giving his rations to Commander. Commander stayed proud, but they all displayed the ill effects of poor diet.

"You've got to eat it, Rat. C'mon," Chet urged.

"Chet's right, Rat. You have to eat the rice. It'll feel good in your stomach. It will give you some strength," Carl said, and he patted Commander on the head.

Rat lifted the spoon and put the rice to his lips. He shoveled it in and then another bite. Rat acknowledged his hunger to his friends. Carl found him an additional bowl. Carl had an innate ability to get things. *Maybe it is that Oklahoman charm*, Rat thought.

Commander started barking wildly. Moments later the line erupted in gunfire. The soldiers reached for their firearms and sought safe locations in the fallback area. Rat picked up the bowl and devoured the rest of the rice in one bite. A firefight interrupted his first meal in days. They held their positions. The fight was ahead of them. As quickly as it had begun, it died down. Japanese scouts lurked in the night and poked for holes in the line. They occasionally charged wildly into the camps to assassinate the unsuspecting troops. Tonight it seemed as if the front line was on the ready. Chet, Rat, Carl, and Commander hiked up to see the results. The Japanese tripped on the barbed wire. Several Japanese threw themselves sacrificially onto the barbed wire as the firefight began. The other scouts walked over their backs and gained access through the thorny defenses. The quick exchange resulted in a few casualties on both sides, but the Japanese retreated back into the underbrush of the jungle. They had achieved the goal of scaring the bejesus out of the Americans and Filipinos.

General Wainwright didn't fare any better. After the crumpling of the line at Mauben, the troops fell back to cover the beachheads of Anyasan, Quinanuan, and Longoskawayan Points. Wainwright predicted they would come from the ocean. The jungle behind them was far too thick to traverse. Wainwright was right. On the night of January 23, two Japanese battalions separated in the South China Sea for detached attacks on Anyasan and Quinanuan Points and Longoskawayan Point farther south. In a furious firefight, the Americans and Filipinos staved off defeat again by soundly trouncing the two battalions. The bodies of Japanese troops littered the beaches. Wainwright knew they would return with more resolve as he inspected the welfare of his troops. They were becoming skeletons before his eyes.

"Surrender, and you will be treated with kindness. MacArthur is not coming to save you. He is eating chicken and pie and dancing with women on Corregidor. MacArthur is negotiating surrender. He will trade you for his own safety. Save yourself, or the superior Japanese forces will kill you."

The loudspeaker bludgeoned the night with repeated messages from Tokyo Rose and her tempting offers of food and decent treatment promised by the Geneva Convention. The Japanese were never very far away. The distance between the front line and the water's edge at the end of the Bataan Peninsula grew ever nearer.

"Do you hear that, Shaun? MacArthur's eating chicken and dancing with women." Manny had a knack for making Shaun smile with his wry wit.

"Who needs chicken? We've got Manny."

Shaun looked at Manny thankfully. Manny had nursed Shaun back from the brink of full-blown malaria. A small dose of quinine and some broth had built up Shaun's strength enough to carry him through tough days. Manny boiled water before putting it in his and Shaun's canteens. Manny had become quite the hunter, and he and Shaun were sharing a small bird Manny had caught and roasted on an open spit. Both had lost considerable weight, but they were surviving.

The people around them became bitter. Hundreds of Filipinos and Americans abandoned their posts and searched for refuge in the mountains. Starvation and aggravation had become parts of daily life. The troops chanted lyrics of being left to die and lampooned their own starvation to the tunes of famous battle songs. Those who had accepted the reality of dying by starvation or Japanese bullets heckled those who believed help was soon to arrive. Surrender was now a viable option to the soldiers. Hunger drove them to slay their own pack mules and horses for food.

The air raids and constant cacophony of Tokyo Rose made sleep impossible. Tracer fire illuminated the beachheads. The Japanese were back. Everyone dived into foxholes and manned the stationary Browning M2 machine guns that dispensed five hundred rounds a minute. Manny twisted the gun side to side as Shaun fed the bullets into it. Manny shot blindly. A severe lack of vitamin A had depleted his night vision. The Japanese advanced over their own dead, crawled up the beach, and hurled grenades that shook the embankments of the pillboxes. The Japanese suffered casualties, but the invaders grabbed a foothold. Manny and Shaun fought bravely through the night. As the sun rose, the Japanese remained. They battled for this valuable position for three deadly weeks.

February 1, 1942

The *Enterprise* ran quietly. Communications were silenced. At 5:15 a.m. the sailors prepared the US Navy's first assault in the war against Japan. They dropped the needed supplies at Samoa and returned for a rendezvous with the Japanese. Nimitz wanted Halsey to punch the Japanese in the jaw. The enemy harbor was the anchor to several transports and general quarters, and protected by anti-aircraft fire. The *Yorktown* was close by in the mist off Makin. It carried similar instructions. Tensions were tighter than a guitar string. The Americans entered the waters of the Marshall Islands and prepared to assault the world's largest atoll, Kwajalein. The Marshalls comprised a series of thirty-six volcanic peaks that poked their ridges just above the surface of the Pacific. Located directly south of Wake Island and north of the Gilberts, the Marshalls represented the extent of the vast perimeter the Japanese Empire controlled. Crews loaded the Grumman F4F Wildcats from the hangars below to the flight deck. Egan manned his turret and peered at the predawn sky as pilots began to board their planes for takeoff. The first rays of the rising eastern sun sprayed the atmosphere. Halsey set the *Enterprise* into the wind, and the Wildcats floated off the edge of the flight deck.

The first wave of Wildcats found their motionless targets waiting patiently. The pilots dropped their bombs, and the transports exploded. Black smoke poured from inside, and people scrambled to take cover. The Americans achieved a measure of surprise, but the Japanese reacted quickly. They filled the air with the puffy black flak of anti-aircraft fire. The Wildcats attacked the quarters and slew the commanding admiral. A pair of Wildcats dived to the sea after Japanese cannons peppered them. Forces on the island radioed the nearby carrier protecting the atoll and announced they were under attack. The carrier turned its bow into the wind, and Japanese Zeros were quickly in the air. They searched for the source of the American barrage. The Zeros found the Wildcats returning to the nest and zoomed in for the attack. The speed of the approaching Zeros mesmerized Egan and his fellow crew members. The Zeros came in quickly over the horizon and dived steeply through the sun. The Vals were not far behind, and their deadly torpedoes threatened the *Enterprise*. Egan spotted a Val coming in low and yanked his cannon low. He fired toward the menacing craft about to drop its torpedo in the water. The cannon fire blasted the Val's wing. It splashed into the ocean and drowned its pilot. A Zero raced from behind his position, and a cold chill ran down his spine. It was a swarm. The speedy Zeros outclassed the Wildcats, which exploded from the machine-gun fire and fell blazing into the ocean. There was an enormous roar followed by an explosion that rocked Egan from the turret. As they scrambled back into their seats, the sailors gulped. Fires raged aboard the *Enterprise*. Fire crews raced with hoses to douse the flames. Egan swung the chair to face the ocean as a Zero raced starboard past the flailing cannon fire. Egan swung violently and let loose a burst from his gun. The Zero splashed into the ocean. The Japanese retreated after downing thirteen Wildcats and superficially scorching the *Enterprise*. Halsey did not wait for their return. He radioed the *Yorktown* to bug out.

A Pacific squall tossed the ship around on the voyage back to the confines of Pearl. The troops roiled around in their bunks. Several vomited into their battle helmets. Egan looked at the riveted steel and reflected on the praise bestowed upon him after his fine performance that morning. He had shot down a Val and a Zero and was the talk of the floating community. There was no glory in this job, though. People had died today, and Egan had tasted real fear. He knew this was a game of survival, and for him to live, he and his crew would have to become better at their jobs. He chided the performances of the gunners and himself. He insisted on more practice and coordination between the turrets. He wanted them to dance like Fred Astaire and Ginger Rogers. He made sure everyone understood he was Fred Astaire.

February 2, 1942
Jason Cenode stood on the flight deck of the newly commissioned carrier USS *Hornet*. At 809½ feet and nineteen thousand tons, the carrier was being pegged for a top-secret mission. It was the last place in the world he expected to be. B-25s did not fly off aircraft carriers. He walked the deck, and the dimensions became very familiar to him. They were the same as the shortened runways he and the crew had been practicing on back in Nebraska. A crisp Atlantic breeze slapped him in the face as he thought back to all he had learned in such a short period of time. Hearing the news of Pearl Harbor on the radio. The never-ending practices at Fort Crook. The SAAB altitude chambers at basic. Having to work in the mess for punishment. It was going to be his turn to shine.

"Jason," said his buddy, "c'mon. We have to go."

Jason brought himself back to the ship. He and the crew were off to show Lieutenant Colonel James Doolittle they could do what he said couldn't be done. He checked to see if his picture of Bette Davis was in his pocket. It was. He was going to tape it up inside the machine-gun turret for good luck.

February 15, 1942
Norm Leymoita sipped on a glass of water and listened to the cries of the sick. There was no night or day inside the Malinta

Tunnel. The clocks belied the time. Six weeks had passed, and a growing sense of resentment pestered the morale of the captives. The Japanese refused to let up, and MacArthur refused to surrender. A nasty rumor spread that the Philippine president, Manuel Quezon, had brokered a deal with the Japanese to end the suffering. Somber news came to Corregidor over the wire that the British forces in Singapore had capitulated to General Yamashita. The British had been driven into their own Corregidor in Singapore. Their stand had been expected to last six months. General Percival had surrendered in less than two weeks. His battle-weary troops gave up the cause, ransacked the ravaged hotels' bars, drank liquor, and stumbled wasted through the streets. The Japanese filmed the surrender for posterity. Brutality began in earnest as thousands of Chinese citizens were slain and hordes of women were raped. Children were thrown into the Singapore jails.

Norm didn't know whether to be proud of the stand at Corregidor or petrified of the ending already played out in Singapore. Morale inflated with a small gust of good news. Central command verified that US attacks in the Marshalls had created havoc among the Japanese troops. That momentum quickly died, however, with news that the local troops on Bataan were struggling to maintain the line. In what was now labeled the Battle of the Pockets and the Battle of the Points, Wainwright's western troops folded and started retreating for the final showdown at Mariveles. The Japanese seemed to be taking a small breather while letting the Americans and Filipinos starve to death. They were waiting for surrender. The Japanese sweltered in the heat. Word from the front was that they too had fallen to many cases of malaria and other tropical diseases. This slowed the pace of fighting between the skeleton armies. Parker's forces only fared marginally better. They had been pushed back slightly to Limay. Submarine visits with supplies crept to a halt as the advance position of the Japanese troops on the western coast of Bataan made the missions ridiculously risky. Norm took another small sip of water from his cup. He had lost mass but was in far better shape than the poor souls on the peninsula.

Shaun and Manny played a stupid game as Manny shaved using the dregs of his tea. Starvation had driven them close to madness, and they chose to torture each other by naming foods they wished they could be eating.

Manny struck first. "Roasted chicken with mashed potatoes and corn on the cob."

"Spaghetti with meatballs and garlic bread with lots of butter."

They laughed as Manny pretended to be struck with a food bullet. He retaliated. "Roasted prime rib with a sour cream–stuffed baked potato and onion soup."

Shaun cackled, and his stomach growled. He went for the kill. "Beef and chicken fajitas with grilled green peppers, onions, rice, and beans."

Manny looked as if he was going to cry, and they laughed until it hurt. They stared each other down.

"A hot dog with chili and a chocolate shake." Manny countered.

It was simple but potent. Shaun looked wounded. They couldn't even get a hot dog with chili. A sadness cast over them. Disappointment was the prize for playing a stupid game. Shaun asked to be excused and moved into the jungle a few paces. He squatted down as the diarrhea squirted aimlessly from his body.

The pleas came from bunkers off the road in the thick of the jungle. Commander leaped through the vines in the darkness and followed the cries. He sensed someone was in danger, and he was going to find them. One of the constant bombing runs had scored a direct hit on the bunker. Chet, Carl, and Rat followed Commander through the dense foliage. Branches and leaves slapped them in the faces and shoulders. In a small clearing of a ridge that looked over the roadside, a mass of writhing bodies bled before them. A soldier strewn in front of the gasping regulars was missing the left side of his head. A Filipino moaned and wriggled. His leg had been shorn off below the knee. Chet removed his shirt and applied a tourniquet on the soldier's thigh. It did little to stop the massive flow of syrupy blood onto the jungle floor. His screams of pain rang through the night and across Manila Bay. They turned over the dead one by one. The exploding steel of the bombs had caused massive contusions and incisions. It exposed vital organs and entire cavities. Commander wagged his tail over the body of a dead soldier whose left eyeball had fallen out of its socket. It was a gruesome but familiar sight. Rat rolled the soldier over. Despite the enormous carnage to his face, he recognized Lieutenant Colonel Rothschild. He checked the tags to be certain. Rat coolly removed Rothschild's canteen and poured the water across Commander's tongue. The puppy lapped it up. He checked the pack for rations and found a single ration of canned meat—a commodity that had been lost for weeks. He pocketed the meat and continued to catalog the dead. For Rothschild what came around went around.

February 24, 1942
Egan and the *Enterprise* returned to hostile waters and provided cover for the task force launching a bombing strike of Wake Island. The Americans were confident no enemy carriers were in the immediate area, and the powerful guns of the US ships loosed their ordnance on the hunkered-down Japanese troops. There was only a smattering of resistance from the treacherous Zeros. Egan had drawn the long straw and felt fortunate to sit this one out. The hero of the Marshalls and Kwajalein wasn't all that excited about looking down the propeller of another Val. Egan thought of the brave marines who had held Wake for so long with so little. The idea that fifteen hundred had been taken prisoner of war numbed him. The *Enterprise* and its task force did little to

damage the Japanese garrison at Wake. Nimitz just wanted them to know they were there and would keep knocking on the door.

A US submarine slipped quietly into a cove on the seaside of the heavily guarded and besieged Corregidor. Norm watched as Filipino nationals saluted their soon-to-be-exiled president, Manuel Quezon. MacArthur's wife and son refused to leave the general's side, but the American governor of the Philippines did not. The next day Roosevelt ordered MacArthur to leave Corregidor south via Mindanao and head to Australia. He would then assume command of all US troops in the Far East. MacArthur postponed the order. His guilt reminded him of the people he would be abandoning in the Malinta Tunnel and on the Bataan Peninsula. The troops on Bataan suffered. They were backed into a corner but lashed back daily at the Japanese despite only eating a cup of rice a day each. MacArthur promised troops would come to give them salvation, and many still believed this would happen.

March 22, 1942

Norm peered at the big map of Southeast Asia MacArthur used to keep a tally of the Japanese juggernaut in the Pacific. On March 8 the British surrendered Java and left the enemy a stone's throw from the sanctity of Australia. Two thousand evacuating British troops had left the great city of Rangoon open, and the Japanese had waltzed in unattended. The Japanese stormed through Thailand and appeared ready to swing into upper Burma and create another flank opposing the Chinese and Chiang Kai-shek. Churchill's shuffling of generals equaled the arranging of desk chairs of the *Titanic*. Norm felt some satisfaction. The only troops to hold out against the Japanese were the embattled but brave people on Bataan and the refugees stuck in the damp Malinta Tunnel. Filipino nationals were giving the Japanese fits on the southern island of Mindanao, and MacArthur saw the daylight he needed to flee the crumpling Corregidor to his new presidential palace in Australia.

MacArthur's secret promotion and ultimate evacuation from the Philippines was a poorly kept fact of the dwellers in the Malinta Tunnel. Ravaged by hunger and stuck for weeks at a time in the claustrophobic confines of the constructed hole, the partisans quickly divided over MacArthur's motives. Many felt he had used his political influence with Roosevelt and Quezon to get away from the impending Japanese bulldozing. Others believed MacArthur would actually give the slobs in Washington a swift kick in the pants and bring them some badly needed help.

Norm took a deep breath of the fresh Pacific air. He had only been topside on Corregidor twice before. The Japanese followed no particular shelling schedule, and any and all times were dangerous. The perilous mission to remove MacArthur compounded the Japanese fury that Quezon had slithered from under their noses. Four PT boats had slipped up to the jetty, and the group had moved swiftly through the night seas over the uneven, pulverized rock formations. Norm assisted the crew with valuable communications equipment, and MacArthur passed his command to Wainwright. The rumble of the PT boats' engines gurgled the waters as they raced off into the pitch. Banging their way by starlight, the crew navigated through the night and hid in the coves and lagoons by day. Six hundred miles and almost three days later, the winded crew arrived safely at Mindanao for a moment's rest before the US Army Air Force dispatched a B-17 Flying Fortress to advance MacArthur, his wife and child, and select staff. They buzzed over the dangerous seas and avoided Japanese patrols, sneaky sea planes, and the Japanese navy, which controlled the seas. The news of MacArthur's safe arrival in Australia led to spontaneous cheers from detractors and supporters alike. Norm was glad to see smiles on the faces of the downtrodden cave dwellers. The press greeted the heroic MacArthur, and headlines across the world quoted the general as saying, "I have come through, and I shall return!"

Carl, Rat, Chet, and Commander sat in the shallow bunkers positioned in the tight jungle foliage. It was a good firing position high above the road. Carl mulled over their plight and felt it was time to reconsider the situation. "Fellas, I'm with you all the way, but I think it's time we think about getting out of here." He waited for his compatriots' reactions.

Chet slowly picked up the plan. "I don't understand. Where are we going to go? There's no place to go, Carl."

"He's talking about splitting ranks, heading down close to the docks, finding ourselves a boat, and taking it to Corregidor," Rat said.

"No," Carl corrected Rat. "We get a boat, and we sail south past Corregidor." Rat looked a touch surprised. "Corregidor is going to suffer the same fate as us. As soon as we're gone, the Japanese can expend all their might on Corregidor, and we'll be in the same situation we are here."

"So we're gonna hop in a boat and sail it past Corregidor where the Japs will be waiting for us with champagne and balloons. I don't think that's going to work, Carl. Our own gunners will probably sink us when we get close to Corregidor anyway." Chet wasn't mad. He was frustrated.

Rat reached into his dwindling pack and pulled out the Stars and Stripes. Commander barked joyfully at the flag. "I took Old Glory down when I left Stotsenburg. I didn't want the Japs to desecrate the flag."

"No. I'm not going to abandon General Parker. We've all been through too much. I'm not going to leave the troops." Chet couldn't believe the options. He didn't want to stay there and die either.

"Chet, you've fought enough battles in the last three months to last three lifetimes. So have I. I'm scared. I'd get in a foxhole with you any day, but I'm scared. It's time we thought about survival. It's time we thought about our families. Getting home, getting back to playing football, and getting married." Chet thought about Lily. "This is a nightmare. My pants don't stay up because I haven't eaten in weeks. Rat looks whipped. He has the fever. Chet, you smell like an outhouse. You've got the runs all the time, and you can't take good care of things without any toilet paper. I've killed people. I only ever wanted to kill one person, and now I've killed dozens. It doesn't feel good. My soul is in pain. We're all going to die right here in the jungle—either by bullets or wasting away."

"MacArthur's going to send some help. He's off the island, and help will be here soon. I know it." Chet hadn't really convinced himself, but Rat pounced.

"You think now MacArthur's off that bomb shelter, he's just going to give Roosevelt a call and say, 'Send over some planes?' You don't think Roosevelt could have done that himself? General Marshall couldn't send over some soldiers to help us. They would if they could, Chet. For some reason they can't. For all we know, the Japs are on top of the Golden Gate Bridge or raining mortar fire from Alcatraz. They might have carriers up and down the West Coast from Seattle to San Diego. We don't know. We're stuck here rotting in the jungle and waiting to be blown to pieces," Rat noted woefully.

"Nope," said Chet defiantly. "I refuse to believe it. MacArthur said he would return."

"Well, I just hope I'm still alive to shake his hand," said Rat. He pulled out the last piece of dried oxen tail and gave it to Commander.

New York, New York
Word of MacArthur's departure from Corregidor and the hardening siege of Bataan had Kay looking older than her years. It

was a beautiful spring day, and Valerie had coaxed Kay into some window-shopping on Park Avenue to get her mind off Rat. They stopped in front of a swanky jewelry boutique, and Valerie ogled a pair of dazzling pearl earrings. Valerie focused on the shiny white orbs and didn't notice the well-dressed Asian woman exiting the boutique with her shopping bag neatly slipped on her left arm. Kay noticed her and whirled her purse around. She clocked the startled woman upside the head. She scurried away in terror. Kay screamed, "Your people are killing my son! Your people are killing my son! Get out of America. Get out of America now!"

Oklahoma City, Oklahoma

The instructor slid the door open to the escalating roar of the propeller. They had practiced from the towers a hundred times, but nothing could prepare one for jumping into the brilliant Oklahoma sky from eight thousand feet. Gary was apprehensive but jumped into line. He watched as the others took large gulps. Their Adam's apples danced. The instructor screamed, "Go!"

The first duckling fell from the plane. A rhythm started as Gary inched toward the thin, high-altitude air. Gary wanted to take a moment of repose as he stepped to the door as if on a high dive with spectators waiting below for his next Olympic soar. The instructor's splintering voice shattered his daydream. "Go!"

Gary found himself rushing toward the plains. Fast. Gary liked fast and was going fast until the automatic jerk of the leash sent him floating earthbound with the other white-capped airborne mushrooms. Gary searched far across the horizon. He was on top of the world. It was almost as good as being on top of Annette.

Boston, Massachussets

Dominic Leymoita took the man's wrist and twisted it, and the man shrieked like a bird. The mechanic contorted, and Dominic grabbed the man by the back of the head and smashed it into the wheel jack. Blood squirted from a groove in the man's forehead and trickled down his nose. "Three hundred dollars, you idiot." He picked the man up by the scruff of his neck and slammed his head back into the wheel jack. It sliced him through his left brow. "Three hundred dollars by Friday, or I'm going to do the same thing to your wife's pretty face." He reached back and walloped the man with a wrench. It separated his mandible in three different places. "And I'm going to give you a tip because I'm a nice guy. When you pay me the three hundred dollars on Friday, don't bet the Red Sox this season. You always bet your heart."

Dominic hated the Yankees. The thought of the Yankees made his skin crawl, but they always beat the Red Sox. Dominic left the man weeping in a puddle of motor oil.

Pittsburgh, Pennsylvania

The trees were starting to bud, and the tulips blossomed in the Three Rivers area. The weather seemed balmy compared to the frigid winter, and Sarah and Paige went to the park. Paige pushed Sarah on the swings and wished they could climb a tree. The polio wouldn't let Sarah climb trees. Paige imagined herself monkeying up to the first branches, climbing limb by limb to the top of the canopy, and looking over the horizon. She imagined this taking her away from the pain and loneliness. She imagined looking west and seeing the plane bringing Shaun home to her safely. She rubbed her locket for good luck, looked at Sarah, and smiled a wry smile.

Panama

Jason Cenode stood on the deck of the USS *Hornet*. They had been dispatched to San Francisco. The engineering marvel known as the Panama Canal astounded him. Slowly they entered the locks and were raised gate by gate through the heat of central Panama. He thanked Jesus for not having to sail around the Cape. It was a funny thing. He didn't mind airplanes, but ships made him queasy. He had received word Aunt Julie discovered he was going to be in San Francisco. She was delighted and surprised. She had expected him to be in England. She assured him she would take a train up the coast to wish him well on his mission. Even Jason had no idea what his mission would be.

Madison, Wisconsin

Lois and the ladies of the club started their game of bridge when the colored boy brought Lois her Bloody Mess. The gin and spicy tomato juice concoction helped her focus on the cards. She shared the table with Rose, Henrietta, and Bea—all notorious blabbermouths. Lois didn't feel like idle chitchat. She was just fulfilling her busy social calendar and regretting making this date.

"Lois, I was talking to Frank Whitehead, and he said Quincy told him that Egan saw some action out in the Pacific Ocean, and he had received some type of commendation. That's wonderful, Lois!" Rose bubbled.

Lois responded with a conversation-halting thank-you.

Quincy shooting his mouth all over town really gnawed at Lois. He shouldn't have been praising the boy. He should have been doing something to get him off that awful ship with the common soldiers and back into school where he belonged. There were those who fought and those who ruled the fighters. The Paals didn't fight in wars. Lois played her hand. The subject of Egan was not revived again.

El Paso, Texas

Jaime, Miguel, and Juan ran like fools through the house. The noise level was outrageous, and Anna had a headache the size of Texas. Juan wasn't eating right. Miguel whined and cried at the drop of a hat. Jaime was having trouble being potty trained. He wouldn't let Miguel play with the fire truck, and Miguel was screaming unintelligible language that could be heard on Mars. The laundry piled up, and the groceries ran as low as the money. Jobs were becoming available as war created a whole new industry, but Anna had to watch the kids. The baby was wet, and Jaime finally punched Miguel in the ear.

"Silencio! Silencio! Por favor, silencio!" Anna rarely spoke in Spanish, and she fell to her knees in tears.

Her boys stopped screaming and gave their mother hugs and kisses.

Saint Louis, Missouri

Lily sat before the foreman, Durwood Shepholtzer, at the recently converted munitions plant. His comb-over and potbelly were indicators of endless missed promotions and a career spent on the lower rung of middle management. The factory was hiring, and the boys had all gone to war. Shepholtzer looked skeptical Lily could handle the physical labor of the job, despite her being what he considered a "big" girl. "Ms. Skairny..."

She quickly interrupted him. "It's Mrs. Chet Skairny. My husband's in the Philippines."

The foreman made an "ouch" face. *Those poor bastards in the Philippines,* he thought. He cleared his throat. "Mrs. Skairny, I have concerns about your ability to handle the physical part of this job. The hours are demanding, and I think it would just plain wear you out."

Lily got up from the table. "Mr. Durwood, do you mind standing?"

"Uh...no, ma'am. May I ask what the heck for?" Lily squatted before the supervisor, raised him up, and spun the man on her shoulders. His comb-over dangled off to one side of his balding head. "Put me down, Ms. Skairny."

"It's Mrs. Chet Skairny, and my husband's stuck in the Philippines. As long as I can't get to him, I'm going to make damn sure he has enough bullets to defend himself." Lily had both hands on the supervisor's desk. Her nose was violating his personal space.

"OK, Mrs. Skairny. You can have the job."

Lily smiled gratefully.

Commerce, Oklahoma

Ida idled. She was nervous of Doyle. He had been so good lately, and she didn't want to stop the momentum. She worried and need-ed something to take her mind off Carl. Inez had the thought of working for the phone company. Ida thought it was a good idea, but she had always stayed at home and made Doyle his breakfast, lunch, and dinner. She washed his clothes and made the bed. The house was small but cleaner than the Taj Mahal. Doyle arrived home from work, and she figured now was as good a time as any to broach the subject. He hadn't even removed his hat.

"Doyle, I can't stay in this house no more by myself. I need to do something, or I might just go off the deep end."

Doyle looked at her blankly. Ida could feel the temper starting to rise. Doyle removed his jacket and loosened his shirt. He took a deep breath, and Ida closed her eyes.

"Sure, Ida. Why don't you be a guard at that new Nisei intern-ment camp they're building down the road? You could help the war effort by watching them there Japanese spies."

Ida informed Doyle she didn't appreciate the sarcasm. She commenced working for the phone company the next week.

April 2, 1942

Jason watched the fog rolling in over the San Francisco Bay from the carrier's portside as tugs guided the great ship to open wa-ter. The great white sheet would soon envelop the massive USS *Hornet*. He waved to Aunt Julie until she became a tiny insect on the shore and he could see her no more. Aunt Julie had taken

Jason to dinner, and they had shared their recent stories. Jason recapped his letters with vivid tales of the pilots in Nebraska and the high jinks of basic training. Julie gave a belly laugh at each story and tried not to embarrass him, but she was so proud. As expected Jason was supportive of his aunt's wishes to open an orphanage. He was disappointed he wouldn't be there to help her finish nailing the addition together or see the first little baby under her tutelage. He couldn't have asked for a better person to raise him and was resolute to the idea of Julie raising children who needed her love. They dined on abalone and Dungeness crab at the wharf and shared a bottle of sweet wine. Julie had sworn to make the evening a happy affair and had done so until she broke down by the gangplank as Jason left. He was leaving for battle she was sure. Jason stretched both arms around her and held her tightly for many moments. He said softly, "I love you, Mom." It was the first time he had every called her that. Julie wept simultaneously with sadness and joy as she waved good-bye to her son.

April 9, 1942

The bloody, callous days leading up to April 9 started on Good Friday. Chaplains gave the service, and Manny urged the ailing Shaun to attend the Mass held in the open field. "Come on, Shaun. We can't just sit in this hole forever. We could use a little help from the Big Guy. You know what I'm saying."

"I can't make it." He lay crumpled on his pack with his rifle by his side. He was weak and found it a chore to put his helmet on his head.

"You can take Communion," Manny said with a gleam in his eye.

"I'm not Catholic, Manny. You know that." The guttural tones of Shaun's voice sounded gruesome.

"Yeah, but you could eat the wafer. They taste pretty good after all this rice."

Shaun laughed. Manny could always make him laugh. He wrenched his dying body to its feet and limped to the clearing next to Manny. The priest performed the Mass in Latin, and while Shaun didn't understand a word, it sounded like the most radiant opera ever performed. The dulcet tones emanated and personified the sadness of humanity's struggle against evil and the soaring hope of salvation. Shaun had been given the strength he would need to get through another day. Manny queued for Communion, and Shaun followed. He tried to understand the sacrament he was receiving. He understood the free wafer. The priest looked into Shaun's eyes as he held the body of Christ aloft, and after careful observation Shaun remembered to open his mouth. The priest placed the thin bread on Shaun's tongue, and he let it soak and stick to the roof of his mouth. It felt spiritual, and it stayed with him.

"It was nice of the Japs to let us have Mass on Good Friday," Manny mused.

Action on the front had come to a scary silence. Manny knew not that General Homma anguished over his troops' failure to capture Bataan, and Tokyo lagged behind schedule because of his lack of conquest. Homma felt the shame. His troops were ridden with the same maladies that haunted the Americans and Filipinos. They ran the Japanese aground. Homma brought in fifteen thousand fresh troops and 140 artillery pieces and readied to launch over seventy bombers in full advance at sunset.

Commander barked wildly. Japanese bombers started the first wave of attacks. Carl, Rat, and Chet struggled with exhaustion and malnutrition. They lay on the ground and tried to sleep away the pain. The torrential strike carried a bite that frightened Rat. He looked at Carl, and they all knew this was the time to implement their plan.

"Chet, we're leaving."

Chet looked into Carl's eyes and knew he was scared. Rat stuffed a paltry few belongings into his pack and grabbed his rifle and a sidearm he had requisitioned from a dead soldier floating in a swamp. He checked his magazines and wrangled Commander. Chet had not decided whether he was going all the way, but he wasn't sticking it out in the hail of bombs that ignited the brush under the heavy jungle.

They slipped down the mountainside. The din of the bombers exacted more pain from the embedded soldiers higher on the ridge. Carl and Rat did not look back. They felt compassion but not regret. Chet checked over his shoulder.

"This way." Carl waved as they paralleled the narrow road to Mariveles.

There was no shelter or escape. The Japanese had sworn to finish the fight tonight. Soldiers streamed from the mountain. They were unable to withstand the storm unleashed above. Gunfire crackled aimlessly at the sky and through the jungle. People reached their mental limits, went berserk, and shot at the night. Artillery fire failed to quell the advance. The Allies barely looked up from the bombardment. Adrenaline pumped through the soldiers' veins. A growing population of desperate Filipino and American soldiers retreated down the dusty path to the bay. Sixty thousand people hidden in the jungles at the base of Mount Natib scrambled like roaches under the boot of the Japanese Imperial Army. The going was slow. Zeros came in low and let loose their cannon fire in a killing spree of the soldiers. Bodies strewn on the side of the road and riddled with bullets impeded the retreat. Soldiers walked over humans like logs on a hike. Chet turned. The fires became infernos as if the volcano had come alive. Commander sniffed at the rotting carcass of Manhattan Mike. He had been dead for about a week, and even the flies didn't seem interested anymore.

The blaze snared Shaun and Manny. The flames surrounded them. Other soldiers smoldered in the inferno. They covered their faces as the smell of cooking flesh pervaded their olfactory senses. Manny's brow leaked perspiration as the heat roared in a circle around them. They had fought the fire before and survived. They would have to do it again. Dead soldiers killed from the concussions of the thousand-pound bombs lay piled in a heap. Manny grabbed Shaun, who looked resigned to death. He dragged the stunned soldier over to the pile of dead bodies and rummaged for the canteens of the perished. Manny gathered them into a pile, removed his knife, and sliced into the bowels of one of the dead. He removed the intestines and sliced it through. The fluids reeked, but Manny rubbed the digestive juices all over his face, neck, and body. Shaun thought Manny insane and laughed at the absurdity of the ending. He had wanted to marry Paige. He had wanted to be a football player. He had wanted to be the quarterback in the big game. The smoke from the fires made him gasp. Manny rubbed the guts of another dead soldier on his legs, boots, and all exposed areas. Manny lathered his hair with large intestine juices and then took the canteens one by one and doused Shaun with the infected water. Blood and water soaked Shaun and Manny from head to boot.

Shaun was close to death from starvation and exhaustion, but he understood. His eyes opened wide as if shocked by electricity. He regained the faintest glimpse of hope as he and Manny made a suicidal run through the flames. They lunged forward and dived headfirst into a roll. The brush attached itself to their clothing, but the flames did not burn. They rolled down the embankment into the lush, unburned jungle. Shaun came to rest in the thicket and sucked the clean air. He was still alive. He cried out, "Manny!" There was no reply. "Manny!" He could hear groans and breathing over the fires. "Manny!"

"Over here!" Shaun heard the weakened Manny cough.

"Are you OK?" Shaun searched for Manny.

"I'm all right."

Shaun found Manny scorched black again, as he had been the day they fought the fire at Iba. He dropped to his knees and pulled the soldier into a sitting position. Manny gave him an awful look of disdain. Shaun wondered if he had become too much of a burden for Manny. He had brought him food when he was hungry. Manny had nursed him when he had his initial bouts of malaria and had made him soup. Now he had literally pulled him out of the fire. He needed the truth. He had learned to care for Manny and was willing to go his own way for Manny to live. "What is it?" He didn't want to die alone.

"You smell terrible."

Manny could always make Shaun laugh. They regrouped and headed down the mountain to uncertainty.

Chaos ensued for days as some troops battled blindly against the plowing Japanese tanks. Others surrendered. Others schemed escape. Commander walked stiffly and suffered from the melting April heat. Carl, Chet, and Rat had found the sea. They had made it to the docks of Mariveles. They stopped and looked across the bay at Manila. Each remembered the gallant nights of hospitality that had entertained the young troops. Carl and Rat never looked back to see what chased them. They knew not to look at the nightmare. Chet looked back and saw the Rising Sun waving in the twilight breeze. It was fixed on top of Mount Samat. The Japanese had gained high ground, and the stench of defeat lingered rank in the air. Outnumbered or not the Japanese would apply the death grip soon.

Carl walked briskly toward the bay and the boats. He left his traveling mates to assess the emergent throngs. The area was a carnival from Hell—the dead end for the masses gathered for refuge to Corregidor. Rat guessed their idea wasn't so original. There were thousands upon thousands of soldiers. Disease had decimated and raked them all. They were clamoring for transport and seeking the attention of inundated medical staff on the verge of imploding. Grown soldiers cried in pain and stood in a line at the medical tent. Loose stool dripped down their legs. They were unable to control their bowels. The unsanitary smell of rotting human flesh, vomit, diarrhea, and the dead permeated the air. Chet fell to both knees and held his hands to his head in despair. They had marched from one hell to another. The sun was setting, and the Japanese would be back to drive a stake into the US hearts.

Carl found the group slumped against a tree. "I've got us a boat."

Carl could always get things, but Rat thought this was ridiculous. "How did you get a boat? Everyone here is ready to draw weapons for a boat," Rat said incredulously.

"A Filipino fisherman liked my idea of bypassing Corregidor and heading south." Carl paused and sheepishly added, "And the five hundred US dollars were persuasive."

"Where did you get five hundred bucks?" Rat didn't think he had ever seen five hundred greenbacks at one time.

"I've got no one to spend it on and was saving it for a special occasion." Carl winked at Rat and reminded him everything was going to be all right, and Rat believed him.

An unearthly explosion rocked the ground, and the masses scattered for cover. The Japanese were coming, but Chet knew this wasn't a bomb. His instincts were right. The Americans were starting to put the fuse to their own ammunition reserves. A small, elderly Filipino with white hair and a straw hat waved at Carl.

"It's now or never, fellas."

Rat wasted no time corralling Commander. Carl grabbed his pack and weapon. Chet didn't move a muscle.

"C'mon, Chet! Let's go!"

He was stoic. They stared each other down. Carl felt like giving him a right to the jaw and dragging him to the boat. He liked Chet and wasn't going to leave him there to die.

"I'm not going, Carl." Carl looked at him with complete disbelief. "I understand where you guys are coming from, and I respect you. You're good soldiers, and it was an honor to fight with you. But this is my duty, and I'm not going to abandon my post."

They gave each other quick hugs.

"See you down the line, Chet," Carl said. "We'll get together when this is all over and play a little football. What do ya say?"

"Sounds good to me," Chet said through tears.

Carl blinked. "You take care of yourself. Stay alive! I'd line up next to you any day, Soldier." Carl wanted to leave on a positive note.

Commander yelped, and the boat pulled into the night harbor. The raging inferno of the ammunition dump illuminated it. Commander turned his head in confused way and wondered why they were leaving Chet behind.

At night people couldn't see the death coming. The incinerating packages fell through the darkness like phantoms. Manny could hear everything. He could hear the bombers buzzing high overhead. Shaun could hear the whistling of the racing bombs. They could hear the rumble of the tanks growling through the jungle. They could hear the firefights and the screams of wounded and dying soldiers. The wind rustled and froze Manny and Shane into paralysis. They jumped and twitched. The vile smell Shaun and Manny carried on them permeated their skin. Mosquitoes and bird-sized flies swarmed their skin. There were no showers in the jungle. The Japanese lurked a few hundred yards behind them and quickly shrank a perimeter that would have them trapped against the South China Sea by morning. Manny brainstormed about his limited options. Fight, and he would surely die.

Surrender, and who knew the future as a captive? Escaping from this trap was a puzzle Manny had yet to piece together.

They marched through the darkness. Artillery fire, tracers, and high-altitude bombs sporadically illuminated the night. They checked around trees and bushes before moving forward. *Japs can be anywhere now,* Manny thought. Towering explosions reached for the stars as friendly soldiers dynamited the last of the fuel dumps. This was on the orders of Major General King, who had replaced Wainwright when MacArthur left for Australia. Wainwright watched from Corregidor.

The South China Sea was only yards away. Manny spied an abandoned craft. It was small—dinghy small. There was, however, enough room for two. The earth shook violently for about fifteen seconds, and the firing ceased. The earthquake rattled the Philippines. Manny knew God was swallowing the entire area for the atrocities being committed. He blessed himself and persuaded Shaun to get in the boat. The tides would carry them away from this place. Shaun collapsed into the boat. He was thin and gaunt, and he simply lay down against the small bench that crossed the wooden boat. Manny pushed the boat into the tides as the earthquake flummoxed the entire area. He sat down and let God take them. With a little luck, the tides would take them close to Corregidor. They could swim for the rock. Maybe they would float to sea. Maybe an American PBY floating plane or a PT boat would see them. Anything was better than here. Manny did not want to die.

The old, white-haired Filipino stayed fixed on a course across the bay. Carl and Rat finally observed Bataan. Mount Samat and Mount Natib still smoldered from the battle. People scrambled around the docks as the earthquake wreaked bedlam on the weary, confused troops. They must have felt they were in the eye of Armageddon. Nature's fury exacerbated the exploding fuel and ammunition dumps. Meteor-like projectiles launched high into the air, and the arching fireballs headed like flaming missiles for the bay. Boulders and rocks rained from the sky and splattered the armada of small crafts fleeing the devastation. Waterspouts heaved from the sea from the failing peninsula's depth charges. This swamped overloaded boats and sent the passengers into the dark waters of the bay. Blood and flesh from unfortunate souls caught in the blasts dusted Rat and Carl. Commander stayed low in the boat. It was the first time Rat had ever seen Commander uncomfortable.

Rat reached into his pack and removed the American flag. They would soon be crossing the eastern edge of Corregidor and weaving through the Japanese shelling of the bastion. The last thing they needed was friendly fire. They watched as round after round crumpled the rock like a sledgehammer. Their sympathy extended to all caught in the travesty. Rat thought of Chet and hoped he had found safety. Chet was a survivor. Rat shouted at Carl over the din. "What the hell are we really doing, Carl?"

Rat was surprised to even feel the gasp of freedom in the ocean air. He felt as if this might actually work.

"The captain says he knows an unguarded cove near Ternate. From there we hide in the jungles or wherever we feel is safe."

"We can't hide forever. We stick out like sore thumbs."

"No. You're right," Carl conceded. "We've got to keep moving. We've got to keep moving toward Mindanao. We can work our way south from there."

"Isn't Mindanao across more water?"

"Yes. It is." Carl knew the next question.

"How are we going to get another boat?"

"Ye of little faith." Carl winked at Rat.

Carl had pulled this rabbit out of his hat. Carl didn't doubt it could happen again.

"How do we even get to Mindanao?"

"We've got to head toward the Taal Volcano. It's about sixty-five miles south of Manila. We stay low. We scavenge food. We find papaya, pineapple, and bananas. There have got to be Filipinos along the way willing to help with food and water. We just have to stay away from the Japs."

"You make it sound like a safari," Rat teased Carl.

Carl even smiled a bit. "From Mindanao we get to Samar. From Samar we get to Leyte, which is going to be a trick. That area is not very wide and is crawling with Japs."

"I'm listening," Rat said as the boat clapped across the waves past Corregidor.

"Leyte leads us to Mindanao. It could take a month to get though Mindanao, but we've got to get to the Sulu Sea, which will take us to Borneo. The Japs are there too I understand."

"Great," Rat said wryly.

"Then it's across the Java Sea to Australia, and we're home free." Carl sounded like Magellan.

"So let me recap. We're going to travel by foot some eight hundred miles or so while avoiding the Japanese army, navy, and air force and not starving to death. While we are already sick with malaria, we are going to cross two seas and skip into Australia without a scratch."

"You got anything better to do?"

Rat smiled and looked over the bow. The shadowy coastline started to become defined as the old, white-haired Filipino stayed fixed on a course across the bay.

Manny and Shaun drifted fifty yards away from Bataan. The tides took them out to the South China Sea, and water accumulated slowly through the floorboards of the rotting vessel. Manny cursed himself for being so stupid. No one had used this boat because it wasn't seaworthy. He felt sorry he had dragged Shaun with him. They were sinking. Shaun sank fast as well. Fever racked his body. More water gathered in the boat as they drifted farther from the shore. Manny weakened. Neither had eaten much in days. Manny didn't want to drown. At least if he were shot, someone at the War Department would catalog his effects and send a flattering letter to Anna. He slid over the edge of the boat and pulled Shaun into the warm waters with him. He blocked out the thought of sharks—creatures that truly terrified him. He swung his arm over Shaun's chest, put his hand under his arm, and laid Shaun on his side. He scissors kicked toward the beach. Manny heard the gurgling of Shaun's mouth. His head bobbed in the water to the rhythm of Manny's kicks. "Stay with me, Soldier. Stay with me, Shaun." Manny talked to Shaun to keep him alert, but Shaun lay heavy on Manny. Manny kicked against the tides. "We're going to make it, Shaun. We're going to get home, and all this will be over, my friend. You can see Paige, and I can see Anna. You can play football again. You can pick up that ball and run with it. Maybe we can be in the same backfield. You could sweep around the end following my block." Manny kicked harder. He was starting to weigh down, and Shaun's chin and mouth went under and up. Manny could hear Shaun spitting the salt water away. He coughed as it leaked into his lungs. "Don't you want to see Paige again, Soldier? Don't you?" Manny screamed into the night. "I've got three little boys. I love you, Jaime. I love you, Miguel. I love you, little Juan. *Mi angels pequeños.*"

Manny rarely spoke Spanish. Manny hurt. His body was weighed down like a stone. He lost his grip on Shaun, reached instinctively, grabbed the soldier by his collar, and hauled him back above the surface. Shaun gagged wildly from the seawater and flailed his arms. This endangered both of them and could have sent them to watery graves. Manny held him tightly around the waist as they bounced in the waves like corks. "We're almost there, Shaun. Stay with me. Please," Manny begged.

His tears of despair merged with the ocean. Manny kicked. He heard something other than the whisper of death. He heard gunfire. They were close to the burning hell of Bataan. Manny pulled the water toward him, and his foot touched bottom as he kicked. He put his feet on the sandy bottom of the shoreline and dragged Shaun through the lapping waves of the beachhead. They both collapsed before they could exit the breakwater and they slept as the water rushed over them gently. They were still alive.

The boat pulled into the glassy lagoon. Reeds covered the shore. There was no dock to beach the boat. The old, white-haired Filipino slowed the boat and bumped into the shore-line. Carl looked around in the darkness. The storm of bombs exploding on Corregidor was in the distance. Commander barked violently. Rat whispered for him to heel and gave the hand signal for quiet. Commander was antsy and seemed frustrated by Rat's order. Carl stepped off the boat and put his foot on the dewy soil. Rat gathered his pack and joined him as Commander loped out of the boat. The old, white-haired Filipino let the boat drift silently from the shore. The untrammeled shoreline divided a small clearing before the thicket. There was no path or road to follow. The captain had chosen a good spot. Carl got his bearings and intimated to Rat he had chosen a direction.

A dozen Japanese rose from their prone positions in the reeds and emerged from the woods like zombies with guns. Rat and Carl raised their hands and surrendered. The Japanese encircled them. Their bayonets glistened in the moonlight. A soldier approached and smashed Rat in the back of the neck with a rifle butt. Another crushed Carl in the pit of the stomach. Commander growled viciously at the patrol. The leader shouted to one of the soldiers. On orders he raised his rifle and put a bullet down Commander's throat. Still groggy from the blow, Rat howled in agony. His companion had been murdered before his eyes. He struggled to fight, but the blow had been severe. Carl regained his breath while being jostled and searched. The soldiers scoffed at the two Americans. They laughed as they plundered their possessions and divided the meager spoils. Carl seethed in anger. The old, white-haired Filipino had ferried them across Manila Bay, past Corregidor, and to captivity.

The tide receded. Manny and Shaun lay warming in the morning sun. Manny checked Shaun. He was still alive. He opened his eyes and scoured the beach. *Everything looks so different in daylight,* thought Manny. He wondered how they had managed to survive the night. Manny looked at Shaun. He seemed in deep meditation. "We don't smell anymore."

Manny could always make Shaun laugh. Both realized the ocean had cleansed them of blood and perspiration. They were sticky from the salt water, but it sure beat being covered in another person's half-digested feces. They rose to their feet and turned to see the line of guns pointing at them over the sand. A soldier barked in Japanese through a bullhorn. Shaun lay back to the ground in surrender. As he moved to the ground, he removed his chain from his pocket, shoved his hand down the back of his pants in one deft movement, and inserted Paige's locket into his anal cavity for safekeeping. Shaun hoped it would stay put through the rivers of malarial diarrhea. Manny looked at the heavens and thought of Anna's soft mouth and the smiles of his three sons.

The soldiers beat the captives and led them to a road where thousands of Filipino and American soldiers filed. They were yoked into columns.

Chet surveyed the docks at Mariveles. Anything white was being held aloft in concession. Tanks rolled into the area, and loudspeakers announced in perfect English that Major General King had surrendered. "Bataan is now under the control of the Japanese. Move to the docks at Mariveles. You will be treated as prisoners of war."

Hordes of combatants shuffled to the docks to be invento-ried. Chet was astonished to see seventy thousand skeletons mov-ing about in a living cemetery. He put his rifle down and joined the flock.

Norm was not surprised but was deeply sorrowful for the peo-ple on Bataan. They had expected this day would come. They had fought to exhaustion, and the white flags surfaced like a parade of cotton balls from the vantage point of Corregidor. Norm faced the grim reality that he and the desperate residents of the Malinta Tunnel imminently faced the same destiny. He bowed his head in prayer and asked God for mercy for the heroic combatants who had defended the Bataan Peninsula until the crimson end.

April 18, 1942

It was the Pacific storm zone. Admiral Isoroku Yamamoto's bril-liant strategy to attack Pearl Harbor envisioned the Pacific storm zone as a cloak for his fleet as they crept across the great ocean undetected. The US Navy was about to return the favor. The USS *Hornet* departed San Francisco and rendezvoused with Admiral Halsey's flagship *Enterprise* in the storm-tossed seas seven hun-dred miles off the Japanese coast. Battened to the *Hornet*'s flattop landing zone were sixteen B-25s refitted with extra fuel storage. They were too large to fit below the flight deck, and their pres-ence prevented the *Hornet*'s preparedness for a quick strike with its complement of fighters. Cruisers joined the *Enterprise* and sailed to escort *Hornet*. They would provide air cover in the event of detection. Lieutenant Colonel Doolittle checked radar updates and averted patrols during the night.

They were still outside their flight zone, but initial prepara-tions began. Jason and the crews requisitioned the bombs for the B-25s and made final preparations for the long-range sortie in-tended to fly to the heart of Tokyo and set the city ablaze with in-cendiary bombing runs from the sixteen flights. Nerves jangled.

This crew had never flown off a carrier, despite their training in Nebraska. They would see if practice made perfect. There would be no landing attempts. It was predetermined the bombers would risk bringing the dangerous Zeros back home. They were to hit, run to the Chinese coast, and seek refuge on selected airfields. The cargo bay door opened, and the winch hoisted the bombs into position.

Egan manned the turret as humungous waves broke over the bow of the *Enterprise*. The carrier pitched and rolled in the high seas, and spray pelted him in the face. Dawn broke through the clouds, and Egan searched the sky for enemy patrols. The deck was wet and slippery, and the ship's lurching made it difficult for Egan to keep the field glasses firm against his eyes. He scanned the horizon and worked right to left. He jerked back left. He was sure he had seen a plane. He narrowed his search zone, and the bow of the ship dipped and crashed into the waves. He spotted the *Hornet* diving down out of sight and then rising up to the crest. It was as if the sea was going to heave it out of the water. Egan pleaded for a moment of stillness. He refocused. The clouds dolloped the sky and created glare. Then he found it—a Japanese patrol. He radioed his findings to the bridge. "Patrol plane. Nine o'clock," Egan reported confidently.

"Do you think he saw the fleet?" came the reply.

Egan strained to hear over the wind. "I saw him. I'm pretty sure he saw us."

Additional reports confirmed the patrol, and communications picked up the enemy's radio alarm. The cruisers opened fire and sent the patrol crashing into the sea. Halsey cursed. The damage had been done. The mission was in jeopardy. He radioed the *Hornet* for a status update. Doolittle's squad remained outside the perimeter, but he felt if the crews were to leave now, the Japanese would still not be expecting an immediate attack. They were currently far too deep for a carrier task force to have any impact. The Japanese would not be expecting the *Hornet* to carry long-range bombers. Fuel would be short he informed his crews. The extra distance might prevent them from making the Chinese coast. No one blinked. They prepared for takeoff.

Shortly before the mission commenced, Lieutenant Colonel Broward approached. "Jason."

"Yes, sir."

"You've worked hard for this, and we're proud of everyone involved."

"Yes, sir." Jason could sense bad news.

"With the extra fuel and now the increased mission distance, we've decided to drop a member of each crew to lighten the load in an effort to fly all the way to China." The lieutenant colonel saw disappointment in Jason's eyes. "The tail gun has been removed. You wouldn't even have a gun to man." Broward knew he didn't have to go through the litany of reasons. He understood how hard Jason had worked for this.

"I still think I can help the crew, sir."

Broward knew Jason was a winner as the young flyer choked back disappointment. "I know you do, son. You'll get your chance. There's a lot of war left."

"Yes, sir."

Jason took a deep breath, swallowed his pride, and went to work helping assist in the final stages of takeoff. He didn't sulk about being benched for this game. He cheered for his crew as if he had been born with pom-poms and provided inspirational chatter while they boarded the flight.

Egan sneaked a peak of the activity aboard the *Hornet*. His powerful binoculars honed in on a flyer receiving orders from his CO. The flyer didn't look pleased. He didn't look angry. He looked disappointed.

The twin engines of Doolittle's planes sparked. The propellers gathered speed and filled the wind with their signature buzz. Sailors overcrowded both flight decks in order to witness a first. They backed the B-25s to the bitter edge of the *Hornet*'s ramp. The crews of two carriers collectively held their breaths. The *Hornet* turned into the wind, and waves broke over her side. The B-25 rolled very slowly down the 809½-foot ramp. It picked up some speed. Egan didn't think it was going to make it. The plane was going too slowly. The fighters struggled in stark conditions. Doolittle's B-25 reached the end of the ramp. Its wings glided out over the edge. The tail dropped and hung just above the water. A large, rolling wave could have reached up and plucked it out of the sky. The plane started to rise foot by foot and gained altitude. Egan removed his cap, waved furiously at the *Hornet*, and celebrated with the crew. He spotted the disappointed flyer jumping up and down like a kangaroo. His smile was as long as the *Hornet*'s seaborne runway, which had been just long enough.

Chicago, Illinois

The plane touched down. Both Donna and Larry waited for their son. Donna seemed different—not as angry. Larry embraced his son. "You look thin."

Gary's frame had become lean and hard. He was not the cherubic child who had flown the nest so abruptly. "It's all the training, Dad. I broke the camp record for the obstacle course." Gary fished for approval.

"That's great, Son," Larry whispered in his son's ear. "We're going straight to the hospital. Annette's water broke."

Gary's face flushed. Donna, a new grandma, sat in the front seat. "Hey! Grandma, what have you been doing?" Gary couldn't resist needling his mom.

"I would appreciate it if you don't refer to me as 'Grandma.' It's unkind." Donna stared straight ahead at the road.

"You're going to be the youngest grandmother on the block."

"Gary Alesse, please don't torture your mother." Larry looked in the rearview mirror of his Packard and smirked. Donna fumed at the good-natured ribbing.

"Are you going to start putting your hair in a bun and wearing a shawl like Grandmom Alesse?"

Donna exploded, reached over the seat, and punched Gary in the leg. "Gary Alesse, you're going to put me in an early grave. Is that what you want? Is it? Do you want to be the death of me?"

Gary and Larry laughed, and the corner of Donna's mouth curled up. Larry pulled into the hospital parking lot and locked the doors.

The obstetrician prepped Annette in the delivery room. Gary hardly recognized her lying on the table with her legs up in the stirrups.

"You're looking good, Annette."

Annette spat a word he had only recently heard at boot camp. Her eyes bulged out of her head. She looked as if she was doing some type of sit-up.

"Is she OK, Nurse?"

"She's fine. She's having a contraction. They come and go while the baby moves down the birth canal. Take deep breaths, Annette," the nurse instructed.

"Annette, take deep breaths," Gary mimicked.

"Shut your goddamn mouth, Gary Alesse! You did this to me, you bastard!"

Gary's complexion changed. He became positive he had married Lucifer. "What do you want me to do?" Gary fumbled. He hadn't fumbled in three years of high school, and now he couldn't say a simple sentence.

"Do you want to be part of this, or do you want to wait in the lobby area?" The nurse was curt but professional.

"I'd like to be here." He paused. "For Annette." He looked at Lucifer fondly.

Annette burned a hole through Gary's forehead with her stare. *Yikes!* Gary thought.

"Then hold her leg up and open. Make her breathe so she can push."

"Yes, ma'am." Gary felt more tension than he did trying to shoot a target from a thousand yards.

"Don't you dare look down there, Gary Alesse. You look at me. You look at my eyes the whole time."

Her eyes looked as if they would pop out and roll on the floor like billiard balls. Gary sneaked a peek and got a clear view. A really clear view. Too clear a view. His head snapped back to Annette's protruding eyes.

"You peeked! You peeked! You lying son of a bitch! You peeked!" Lucifer gasped for breath after the full contraction.

"I didn't peek," Gary lied. He didn't want Annette to get any more riled up than she already was.

The doctor snuggled up between Annette's legs and studied the area. Gary managed to keep one eye on Annette and the other on the doctor.

Gary started to coach a little bit. "Push, Annette!"

She strained, and the sweat poured through her pretty, matted hair. Gary looked at the weight in his hands. *Boy, her legs have gotten big,* he thought. It was like holding a Browning machine gun. Those suckers were heavy. Annette kept pushing. Her face burst with red and purple.

"Push, Annette, push. Pretend you're taking a really big bowel movement."

"Goddamn it, Gary!"

The doctor and nurse both paused to look at Gary. *Oops.*

"We're starting to crown," said the doctor.

"What does that mean?" asked Gary.

"It means the baby's head is coming out, stupid!" Lucifer was back.

Gary sneaked another peek. *Boy, that sure can expand. A lot.* It looked as if a red bowling ball was coming out. The doctor instructed Annette to push one more time really hard. Gary held her enormous, hairy leg tight. His grip loosened. It was like trying to snare a wolverine.

"That's it, Annette. That's it," the doctor encouraged her.

What's it? Gary thought. Then he heard the tiniest yelp. He looked over, and the doctor held a little, teeny baby boy. He looked as if he was covered in Jell-O. Something was attached to him. It was gray and purple and nasty. The doctor cut the umbilical cord, and the nurse took the baby to clean him off and do birthing tests.

She returned with a swaddled, crying baby. She placed the child in Annette's arms, and she cried happy tears and looked at Gary with love. Thank God. Lucifer was gone.

"Say hello to little Peter, Daddy." Annette turned the baby so Gary could see.

"He sure does have a little peter," he quipped.

"Shut up, Gary."

Things were going to be just fine with the Alesses.

April 22, 1942

"Number six nine four three," blared the intercom in the mess.

Egan looked at his raffle ticket. The *Enterprise* had sailed all over the Pacific and had not returned to Pearl for supplies. The crew had been stuck with spaghetti and beans pulled from deep off the shelves of the ship's storage.

"Number two eight six four."

Egan thumbed his ticket again. He knew he didn't have a winner—not yet anyway. There were two thousand sailors on the carrier and about two hundred steaks left in the freezer. Odds were against him, but a steak sure would have tasted good right then. He pushed the beans around with his spoon. The news that Bob

Hope might entertain the troops at Pearl cheered him. Bob usually traveled with some pretty girls.

Upstairs on the bridge, communications officers were pleased to find Doolittle's raid on Tokyo had unsettled the hive of the Japanese navy. Radio listening posts from Alaska to Australia picked up valuable communiqués as the Japanese tried vainly to find the raiding task force at sea. The deciphering experts in Hawaii and Washington had won the "raffle" of coded enemy messages. Lieutenant Commander Joseph Rochefort and his relentless staff led the Americans, and they compiled a glossary of the coded language. The Japanese navy was everywhere and nowhere. It stretched across the globe from the Indian Ocean to the western reaches of the Pacific. Nimitz and his miniscule fleet couldn't afford a wild-goose chase. The Pacific Fleet Combat Intelligence Unit had decoded messages that indicated a strong surge into the Solomon Islands area. Nimitz and Admiral King had determined they could not afford to abandon this area. The code breakers deduced that the letters "MO" meant Port Moresby. A shift in Japanese forces down New Guinea to Port Moresby at the end of the Papuan Peninsula would give the enemy air cover over the Solomon Islands and the Coral Sea. A Japanese blockade of the Coral Sea would cut the shipping lanes to Australia and leave the continent to fend for itself. Nimitz would have to send the entire fleet in an all-or-nothing battle to the Coral Sea.

May 8, 1942

In early May a thousand marines of the Fourth Division dug into foxholes and barricades on the surface of Corregidor. General Homma gave Corregidor his full attention. He lobbed bomb after bomb onto the stubborn Filipino and American holdouts. The emperor's birthday marked a special occasion, and Homma sent the castaways a personal message to the tune of a 150-gun salute that turned Manila Harbor and Corregidor into a dust storm. Five months of habitual bombardment had reshaped the previously lush island's contour. Green plants were incinerated, defense guns were obliterated, and the shore road was obfuscated into the bay. General Wainwright stood fast to his conviction not to surrender, despite reports from the quartermaster that freshwater supplies had dwindled to less than a week. Wainwright knew it would be nearly impossible to gain a foothold onto the island. The amphibious assault troops who tried to cross the bay were either swept out of position by strong currents or blistered by the machine-gun fire of the First Marine Battalion and the three small forts in the bay that helped protect Corregidor. The guns chewed up the invaders, and Homma stewed.

Daring rescue missions by PBY floatplanes saved the lives of female nurses who had treated the Malinta dwellers suffering from rampant dysentery, malaria, and starvation. Norm had trouble breathing the putrid air. The wounded and dead piled up in the tunnel. Norm volunteered to man a gun on the moonlit surface. He embraced the helmet and abandoned the communications desk. He climbed to his position, dug in deep, and joined an array of soldiers from the marines, army, and navy as well as Filipino contingents. Noncommissioned civilians had joined the fracas for survival. Furious bombardment directed by General Homma himself rained ten thousand artillery shells on Corregidor. Norm dreaded the shaking of the bombs in the tunnel and wondered how anyone survived on the surface.

"Transports!" someone yelled.

They peered over the edge of the fortifications and saw the invasion fleet on the shimmering bay. Thousands were coming from straight away and the east. Some transports missed the island entirely and were swept away in the current. Norm fired the machine gun. A numb feeling ran through his arms and shoulders. The marines endured rounds from tanks and artillery as the transports moved closer to the east edge of the island. Machine-gun fire shredded the Japanese as they exited the transports. They just kept coming and eventually secured a landing force of over five hundred. It came at a cost three times. Firefights raged through the night. A marine next to Norm took a round to the belly and lay dying. The man slowly bled to death. His life seeped out onto his charred uniform, and Norm listened to the gurgling of his final breaths.

At dawn the enemy was firmly on Corregidor, and they advanced. The battery by the water tower teetered lifelessly from aerial attacks. It had been overrun. Major Williams gathered the brave troops for one last stand.

Norm stayed low and worked his way back to his foxhole after giving his group's status to Major Williams. "Fellas, we've got to buckle down and get that battery back. It's our only chance." Norm encouraged the soldiers.

Shells hollowed the earth deeply and formed craters the troops used for cover. Moving swiftly in black-and-white silhouettes of predawn, the reckless troops startled the weary Japanese and opened fire. A morning alarm of crackling gunfire surprised the Japanese. Norm rose up over a boulder and spied one of the infantry reaching for a grenade. He pulled the trigger and shot the soldier in the shoulder, but he did not die. He struggled forward and reached again for the deadly device. Norm took careful aim and drilled a bullet into his neck.

The enemy retreated. Williams and his crew requisitioned abandoned supplies. They stayed low and waited for a counterattack.

"That was scary," a naval enlistee said to Norm.

"Are you all right?" Norm looked at the blood oozing from the man's arm. The soldier hadn't seemed to notice.

"I'm fine. Just a little cut. Nothing to worry about," he said matter-of-factly.

"What happened?"

"I think the little Nip had just woken up. He reached for a pistol and fired, but he missed. I had him dead in my sights, and the gun jammed. Damn gun. He picked up his rifle, and we both charged." He took a swig of his canteen.

"Yeah?" Norm wanted to hear the rest.

"He stuck me with the edge of the bayonet. Those things are sharp. Well, when he didn't get me clean, his momentum lunged him forward, and I was able to get behind him."

Norm looked at the sailor. He had forsaken his firearm when it had locked up. "How did you kill him?"

"I snapped his neck. He was just a little guy."

Norm looked at him wide-eyed. "Can I stick with you?"

"Sure."

The counter did not come from the assault group. It came in the form of tank fire and precise battery fire from the Bataan shore. It pulverized the location the troops had just retaken. Earth and stone mixed with shrapnel whizzed violently through the air, and the protectors had no choice but to relinquish their hard-earned gain. They fell back through the same craters that had protected them before and dealt with the surging island forces that had now regrouped. Machine-gun fire and grenades pelted the retreating defenders as they returned valuable ground to the formidable enemy. Norm looked back and saw the sandbags that guarded the entrance to the tunnel. It wouldn't be long now. Norm said a prayer and apologized to God for not keeping in touch, but he needed a really big favor.

Inside the Malinta Tunnel, General Wainwright phoned Roosevelt. He told him he could not subject the unarmed wounded to execution. A cease-fire would commence midday. The code word "Pontiac" was radioed to commanding officers. Norm was on the top of the island of Corregidor. He removed his white T-shirt and put it over the muzzle of his rifle. They all held them aloft. Wainwright capitulated to General Homma that afternoon.

Norm and the residents of the Malinta Tunnel were systematically ferried back to Bataan and inventoried, and then they embarked on what the peninsula's soldiers referred to as the Bataan Death March.

Egan and the sailors anxiously awaited reports of battle in the Coral Sea. The *Lexington* and *Yorktown* had engaged the Japanese near Guadalcanal. The battle raged for days, and each side suffered tremendous losses. The chief petty officer sat before them. "Troops, the *Lexington* has been scuttled. It suffered a blow from a Japanese torpedo bomber. It fought to stay afloat, but they abandoned ship."

"What about the pilots?" Egan asked.

"They had to ditch in the ocean. They are looking for survivors." The sailors bowed their heads and prayed for the pilots. "The good news is the *Yorktown* held its own. We sank a Jap carrier. We prevented Japanese landing parties at Port Moresby and Tulagi from advancing. Despite the cost they stood their ground against the best the Japanese could offer."

Egan knew the *Enterprise* would soon find its way into the fight.

The Philippines

The Japanese tanks were tremendous motivators. They churned behind the prisoners and forced them to move toward the docks at Mariveles. Shaun and Manny struggled to keep pace. They were certain the tanks wouldn't hesitate to clip their heels, drag them under the huge tracks, and roll right over them. In long columns four abreast, thousands of soldiers marched toward the bayside docks to be inventoried by the Japanese. The locket made walking very unpleasant, but Shaun dared not divulge his secret. One man refused to relinquish his wedding ring and was clubbed with a rifle butt to the chin. Another sadly forsook his father's watch—a family heirloom. The exploration became ugly when one soldier emptied his pockets to reveal Japanese currency. Possession of Japanese currency could only mean he had killed a Japanese soldier and pilfered his belongings. Manny and Shaun looked away as two soldiers forced the confused man to his knees. Another removed his sword and beheaded him on the spot.

"Keep moving forward. If you do not move forward, you will not finish the trip. You are prisoners of war. We are your new masters. You will do what we tell you."

The loudspeaker blared the message in textbook English. It was repeated over and over to the starving POWs. The brutal soldiers lashed out wantonly against the American prisoners. One emaciated soldier struggled in the heat, and he began to cry in the column ahead of Manny and Shaun. The humid jungle pressed against him like an iron. The guards marched and sought out the weak. A young Japanese soldier followed closely behind the American. The prisoner shuffled along while relinquishing his diarrhea. It left a slimy trail of bile and mucus in the path. He stumbled and fell to the ground. A comrade slowed and helped the man retrieve his place in line. The Samaritan received a rifle butt to the back of the neck. The sick soldier doubled over in pain on the dirt carpet, and the guard punished him with a boot to the stomach. Suffering from the advanced effects of vascular malaria, the jaundiced soldier hurled blood from his malnourished stomach. The soldier kicked him repeatedly and screamed for the dying man to stand. Seeing he was physically unable to do so, the soldier kicked him over to his back and plunged his shiny bayonet into the man's sternum. He twisted the blade and released it from the prisoner's chest. The guard flaunted the thick blood at the end of his bayonet.

Manny checked on Shaun from the corner of his eye. Shaun managed. They cared for each other and were now keenly aware of the fate of a Samaritan. The docks were close. The two friends prayed for a sip of water.

Carl and Rat roasted in a field where they were forced to wait. Twine bound their hands behind their backs. The interned filled the overcrowded docks, and they smelled like the bottom of an outhouse. Sick soldiers vomited and lay in their own feces. The plague reached epidemic proportions. Carl vomited from the smell and had to sit next to his own puke. Rat looked yellow and clammy. Carl prayed he could withstand the heat. The number of prisoners overwhelmed the Japanese. Several groups of detainees had been sent to hike up the rocky road toward Manila. Rat overheard the intended destination was Camp O'Donnell or Cabanatuan. That was sixty miles away. A young Filipino addressed a Japanese soldier and tried to explain he was not part of the army. He was a civilian seeking shelter. The soldier gutted him with his bayonet and left his body to die in the hot Bataan sun.

Norm limped along the docks. The family he knew at Corregidor had melted into the tens of thousands of gaunt ghosts. The unshaven, thin troops looked far different from the muscled image of the Uncle Sam recruiting posters.

"Have you got any water?" a soldier begged.

Norm had some valuable water in his canteen and thought for a moment he should squirrel away his supply and just say no. His conscience got the better of him, and he opened the lid and extended it to the sick man. He took only a small, shy sip and returned it to Norm. Norm was embarrassed he had hesitated and gave it back to the man. "Have some more."

He took a larger swig and gave it back. "Thank you."

"You're welcome," responded Norm. He was saddened he couldn't do more for the man.

"What's your name?" the soldier asked.

"Leymoita. Norm Leymoita. I'm from Boston." Chet shook the feeble man's hand. "And you?"

"Chet Skairny. Missouri. Nice to meet you." Chet looked Norm up and down. "Are you from the rock?"

"Yeah. How'd you know?"

"You don't look nearly as bad as the other fellas."

It was true. The citizens of Corregidor had done plenty of suffering but nothing like the rough condition of the soldiers outdoors.

"Are you going to be OK?"

"I'm all right. I'm hungry." Chet cracked a smile. "It's funny. All these people here, and we're all from the same part of the world, but I feel so alone." Norm understood Chet's fear. "I was trooping with a couple nice fellas and a dog. They got a boat across the bay. I wonder if they made it." Chet looked out over the water and wished he had gone.

Norm looked at Chet. "Let's stick together and make it through this. What do you say?"

Chet appreciated the gesture. "That would be great, Norm."

A Japanese guard pounced on a group of Filipinos. Two other Japanese soldiers rushed over and commenced pummeling the men as they lay on the ground in the fetal position. They left one man's skull crushed near the temple.

Norm averted his eyes so as not to draw any attention to him or Chet. He whispered, "What's that all about?"

Chet whispered back. "Bushido."

"Bushido?"

"Back in ancient times, there were Japanese warriors called samurai. It's a strict religion. They deny themselves things to make them tougher. They claim to be able to put themselves in a trancelike state called Zen."

"What does that have to do with the beating?"

"The Japanese are trained as samurai. It brings very high honor upon the family. They are sworn to fight to the death for the honor of their emperor. They believe personal salvation is bestowed upon them if they uphold this ancient code."

"There was nothing honorable about that beating."

"Being captured is a fate worse than death for a samurai. It's a disgrace. The entire family lives in shame. They erase your complete memory in the town where you were born. The iniquity of capture erases all the good things you have done in life. Dying is better than surrendering."

"So they treat the prisoners like dogs."

"Worse than dogs. To the samurai prisoners are the very antithesis of what they believe. We have become mongrels to them, and they will treat us savagely."

A young Filipino girl wailed. Chet and Norm looked to see what agony had befallen her. Two Japanese men were by her side. One held her by the hair and dragged her bodily toward the woods. The other whacked her with his rifle. The men disappeared into the shallow depths of the woods, but Chet and Norm still heard the girl's cries. She stopped screeching in agony and now cried tears of shame. The soldiers raped her on the wooded underbrush within earshot of a thousand helpless men. *Samurai?* Norm thought.

Makeshift slings were created to carry the dead. That didn't last long. The added weight sapped the already-waning energy of the soldiers. The dead were placed at the side of the road for insects and rodents to feast on. The road wound up the mountain. Carl and Rat looked out over the bay. The water reflected the harsh sun that broiled them as they walked. Perspiration leaked out over their bodies, and on the few breaks they would employ the stagnant waters of the burrow pits to replenish their canteens. The burrow pits had become latrines for the soldiers fighting in the jungle, and urine and feces laced them. They prisoners were desperate for water, though, and filled their canteens with the filthy water. Rat looked around the bend. The column of people hiking the hillside road extended farther than he could see. He guessed twenty thousand people populated the rows. His guess was low.

The Filipinos took the brunt of the guard's fervor. They were made to carry heavy packs for long stints, and this crippled their ability to withstand the heat. If they didn't move fast enough, the guards would prod them with the edges of their swords or stick them with their bayonets. The procession sometimes halted as military personnel passed quickly by in either direction. These small breaks allowed some to catch their breath and regain their wits. Others collapsed. Fatigue forced one man to his knees, and he threw up on the road. Armored vehicles moved down the roadway and never paused for the man to remove himself from the road. They rolled over him and squished him flat. Carl and Rat looked at the ground and wondered what hell they were in.

Shaun hung in there. Manny now felt the effects. They pulled over to let a convoy pass and stood on the edge of the road. Shaun leaned against a tree and was startled to see the rotting remains of Americans and Filipinos buried in shallow graves. Manny blessed himself as they stepped away. Shaun opened his canteen and implored Manny to drink the unhealthy water. It was better than no water at all. A bespectacled soldier approached them. They prepared for the worst. Shaun flexed his degenerating muscles. He knew any confrontation was useless, but he wasn't going to let Manny suffer. They hadn't done anything wrong or out of the ordinary, but the randomness of the brutality had everyone on edge. The guard stepped closer and reached into his pack. He checked over his shoulders, secretively pulled out a rice cake, and handed it to Manny. He eyed both of them before turning and saying, "I'm sorry."

Manny split the rice cake with Shaun.

Chet and Norm found themselves in a special attention group. They were tied together. Ropes were around their necks, and they were herded like yaks. The guards were especially joyous driving this column. The prisoners were mocked as if subhuman. Laughter abounded among the guards. They whipped the animals and prisoners. The passing convoy took turns striking the prisoners with their rifles like baseball bats from the moving vehicles. Their comrades carried several prisoners who were concussed from the blows. If they fell they were slaughtered and left by the roadside. Chet and Norm walked for hours—even when the guards changed shifts. They kept the pace despite being driven faster and faster into oblivion. Spells were brief. There was no time to urinate or defecate. They relieved themselves as they walked, whether they could control their bowels or not. Human waste accumulated on their flesh. The rashes brought infections that bubbled on the people's loins and thighs.

The suffering created anarchy among the soldiers as the enlistees found the officers and blamed them for their plight. Mutinous threats filled the ranks. Norm and Chet lay low. They worked their way to the interior of the column. Odds were better they wouldn't get smashed in the face there. Beside the convoys plenty of Japanese infantry marched in the opposite direction. Japanese troops passed within inches of the shuffling prisoners. They prodded the captured as they marched by or provided an occasional elbow to the face of an already staggering soldier. Sometimes it was a quick fist to the face for good measure. Norm and Chet withstood the fury.

Shaun and Manny were sitting. They sat while the guards changed shifts and a convoy rolled through. One guard stood on an embankment and went over the rules of engagement for the hundredth time. "No obedience, and you will be killed. Do not try to escape, or you will be killed."

"Nobody's going to try to escape, you fool. We can hardly walk," Manny mumbled under his breath.

"Maybe when we get to the prisoner-of-war camp we can try." Manny saw the gleam in Shaun's eyes. "It's our duty."

"My duty is to stay alive for Anna and the kids. I'm alive... barely." Manny looked sick. "And you need to stay alive for Paige."

Shaun reached down his pants and removed the locket from his ass. "Oh, that feels better," he said, and he stuffed the mucus-covered chain into his pocket.

"Charlie! No!" someone yelled out.

Charlie had drifted away from the pack. Dementia brought on by exhaustion and lack of food and water had relieved him of his mind. Charlie looked at the sky and mumbled. A single rifle shot rang out and struck Charlie in the back. He fell face first into the dirt. Shaun and Manny looked at each other.

"At least Charlie is out of this hell," said Manny, and the soldiers threw Charlie to the side of the road.

Tempers flared among the guards on the fourth day. Violent beatings greeted the reluctant pace of the imprisoned. Carl and Rat glared as one guard leisurely sliced a man to pieces with his bayonet. The thunderclouds came in the afternoon and released cleansing rain. Carl and Rat turned their heads toward the heavens, opened their mouths wide, and drank in the freshwater. They held their loosened pants away from their bodies and let the rain wash away the waste from their loins. The rain came in torrents. The troops absorbed the moisture through their pores. Streams of water flash flooded down from the hills, and it pooled and puddled along the roadside. The people filled their canteens to the brim. They could not march. The storm was too heavy. The rest became a spiritual experience—a sign from on high they could endure.

Eventually the rains slowed to a trickle, and the lines reformed. A guard poked a captive who lay next to one of the gathering pools. He did not have enough energy left to stand and drowned in the rising waters. He floated helplessly in the rain that had saved the others.

The march continued. The dead heard no eulogies. The prisoners were slogging through the darkness and mud when a second miracle befell them. On a parallel course in the woods, Filipino citizens risked execution by laying pieces of sugarcane beside the roadside. Under the cover of night, the soldiers snatched the chunks from the edges and passed them to the starving prisoners in the columns. Carl and Rat bowed their heads and nibbling the natural candy like fiends sneaking a fix.

Norm and Chet slid to the roadside and let the rolling trucks of artillery pass. Chet's physical deprivation had reached critical stages, and after passing back through Balanga and the War Plan Orange front crushed at Abucay, Norm wasn't sure how much longer he could march. Norm's intuition said Chet wasn't going to make it much farther. He could only hope the nightmare would end at San Fernando. Norm gathered Chet's limp body. He glanced at the guards. A struggling convict begging for mercy on his frail knees preoccupied them. Two guards became bored with the weak man's pleas and gouged him with their bayonets in a deadly tag team. Norm swooped Chet into the flatbed truck and covered him with loose canvas sacks and corrugated boxes. He whispered in Chet's ear to stay quiet. "When a good opportunity comes, slip off the truck and mingle back in with the other prisoners."

The truck driver was unaware of the new passenger and motored away. Norm prayed he had saved Chet's life—not sent him to his death.

Norm could feel the ridges of ribs near his sternum, and his hips protruded. He felt the contour of his cheek and jawbones as if he was holding his own skull in his hands. He analyzed other people in far worse health. He calculated the larger soldiers had lost thirty to forty pounds from their frames. Smaller sorts slipped under one hundred pounds. He felt the prodding of a rifle butt and kept moving. He prayed to see Chet along the way.

Manny and Shaun reached the outskirts of San Fernando. The guards waited for orders from their commanding officers. A freshwater well attracted the full desire of the inmates. The guards blocked the well from access—a torturous move to squash the last iota of morale. The lust to quench their thirst was rabid. People shook like junkies as their focus for water became carnal. Some broke for the well only to find themselves impaled on the ends of sticks and bleeding—so close to the end of the nightmare. Manny and Shaun quivered for the fresh, clean water. In an act of desperation, they held each other's hands like teenage lovers and forged through the trauma.

There were no balloons or banners upon their arrival at the churchyard in San Fernando. The high walls of worship had been strung with razor-sharp barbed wire. This enclosed the courtyard of religious meditation. Blood-laden anal mucus covered the ground. There were no facilities, and the prisoners were leaking their waste spontaneously. The thousand who had passed through had generated a thick layer of filth. Manny and Shaun tiptoed through the noxious fumes toward a group of prisoners cooking paltry amounts of rice for the thousand. Manny and Shaun filed into the line and waited for their meals— a half cup of rice each. The chefs rationed a pinch of salt for flavor. The meager meal constituted double the portions they had received on the march. One soldier vomited promptly upon swallowing the starch. His body refused to accept the nourishment, and the disconsolate man meekly offered his portion to Shaun and Manny. They reluctantly accepted it. The man left and wandered in circles. Manny and Shaun knew his sad days were numbered. They relished the horrible meal and kept their noses plugged.

Carl and Rat shuffled from the staging areas at San Fernando—the junction of trains and transportation north and west of Manila. They had traveled through here in the retreat many months before. The onslaught of the Japanese advance had battered the area. Countless Filipinos had succumbed to the rule of the new "coprosperity sphere," and they worked diligently for the army's ends. They slaved away at the menial, backbreaking jobs the soldiers had selected.

Encouraged that the brutal march had ended, they waited on the platform. The trains chugged to a standstill on the tracks. Wooden cars opened their doors to the empty cargo spaces. Carl and Rat moved forward and hopped into the train. They extended their hands to assist the weak aboard. Living corpses packed the hold full. Carl held his hand up—a signal for the guard to load another car. The soldier menacingly pointed the blade at Carl as more refugees filled the space. Thirty people were crammed into the superheated wooden oven. It became nauseous from the stagnant air. Carl continued to load the startled prisoners aboard, and Rat assisted him. The men were filed like boxes against one another. Shoulder to shoulder and front to back, they squeezed into every square inch of the rolling coffin. People gasped for precious air. Carl heard his name shouted from the middle of the swarm of prisoners. He saw Chet in the far back on the platform. The guard stared at him. They locked eyes. Chet looked bad, but at least he was still alive. A hundred people filled a space for thirty. The guard pulled the door shut, and the mercury rose to deathly degrees.

Prisoners moaned, and fecal matter dripped on Rat's boot. Several panicked in the claustrophobic confines and struggled to get to the door. This caused others to tumble upon themselves into a skeletal pile. Horrific sounds of brittle bones snapping emerged over the roar of the surging engine. The proud prisoners screamed in agony. All pleaded to open the door and asked for wind. The train bounced along the tracks, and the still air held the putrid smell of urine and feces. The fluids ran across the deck of the boxcar. Vomit added to the odiferous mélange, and people reeled from the stench. Sweaty limbs were pressed together, and shallow breathing ran hot on their necks. Rat scratched his pubic region furiously, and the lice dug deeper into his skin. Carl told Rat he had seen Chet. Rat tried to smile. Mercifully the train came to a stop, and the guard slid open the cargo hold door. A warm breeze wafted into the hold, and the people held their chins high and gulped for air. Carl and Rat waited for the struggling passengers to lower themselves off the ledge of the boxcar. The guards poked and screamed for them to move faster. Carl stepped forward, and the soldier behind him slid down his sweaty back and crashed to the floor. Carl turned to help the struggling man to his feet, but he was dead—roasted in the oven of death. One hundred people got on. Only eighty-four reached the final destination. Carl, Rat, and a few other soldiers removed the bodies and laid them in the back of a Japanese truck for removal to a mass grave.

The survivors arrived at the prison camps. Chet and Norm were inside the despicable walls of Cabanatuan. Carl, Rat, Manny, and Shaun were situated at the horrific Camp O'Donnell. It was the final stop on the hellish Bataan Death March.

Satan laughed and laughed.

Boston, Massachussets

Vincent and Carla Leymoita sat in the pew of the Catholic church. They were slumped onto the kneeler with their heads in their hands and heavy hearts. The priest was giving a special Mass for the dead and wounded of the Philippines. He stepped to the lectern to deliver the homily. "'The people who sat in darkness saw great light; and to them that sit in the region of shadow and death light is sprung up.' This is from the book of Matthew. The world has become a place of much darkness and little light. The soldiers in the Philippines POW camps are in the hands of God. Through the prayers of the faithful the light will reach them. They do sit in the region of shadow. Theirs is a world of survival. You have prayed for them not to concede to the enemy, and they have not! They are the survivors. They still see more light than dark. They will see the light of your love. They will feel the light from your prayers. They will feed from this nourishment. They will drink from your cup. They do sit in the company of death but with the light from the lamp you burn. The prisoners will follow the light of your hearts home. Do not despair. It is time for you to show courage in the face of darkness. The brave soldiers in the Philippines are doing their parts in the war against death and shadow. It is time for us to do our parts. Your prayers light the way to their salvation."

Carla couldn't help but feel her son Norm was in the hands of the Japanese, and his salvation would come when the US Navy got off their butts and brought him home.

Pittsburg, Pennsylvania

The pain of not knowing whether Shaun was alive or dead made Paige ill. In bed for a week, she had collapsed under the daily stress of reading the papers and the fate of Corregidor. Upon reading the final report that Wainwright had surrendered, Paige fainted onto the Joints' living room floor. Sarah crawled to Paige and called for her mother. The doctor found nothing physically wrong with her. There was no fever, coughing, or sputum in her lungs. Her eyes were fixed and dilated. The doctor recommended tea and something easy to eat such as oatmeal or Cream of Wheat—something that would stick to her ribs. Sarah joined the doctor in the foyer before he departed.

"What do you think is wrong with her, Doctor?" Sarah asked.

Paige was the big sister she had never had.

"I think I know." The doctor studied Sarah's eyes. "She holds that chain tightly in her hands. What is that?" he inquired professionally.

"That's her half of the locket she and Shaun share," said Sarah.

"Shaun is on active duty in the Philippines?" he said. He tried not to rehash the recent tragedy that had befallen the war-torn island.

"Yes," Sarah quietly replied.

"You miss your brother, don't you?" The doctor squatted to Sarah's level. She nodded, and tears were in her eyes. "Well, that's what is making Paige sick. She has a broken heart. Do we know what happened to Shaun?" It was a tough question but helpful in his diagnosis.

"No," Sarah said.

Cynthia burst into tears, and Gene pulled them both close.

"We haven't heard anything from the army. We are praying he is alive. It's been very hard on all of us—especially Paige. They were..." Gene paused. "*Are* engaged to be married."

"Well, you just keep believing that. Shaun is alive, and there is no other way you can think. There is no medicine to cure Paige. You have to be strong for one another and pray. Can you do that, young lady?"

Sarah nodded with her head buried in her mother's apron.

Madison, Wisconsin

Lois slurred from the dry gin martinis. "Quincy, I am not going back to that psychiatrist. He's an overpaid quack. There's nothing wrong with me, and you know it."

Quincy tried to be patient. "I think you should go back. He's a very good doctor. He's good friends with Dr. Hergenradar." Status could sway Lois's opinion of anything.

"Do you want me to be crazy, Quincy? Is that what you're hoping for?" She swiped the pictures off the piano with a violent brush of her arm. "I can be crazy if you want me to be. Be a good wife, Lois. Go to the club, Lois. Play bridge with the girls, Lois. Make dinner reservations, Lois. Keep the maid in check, Lois. Make sure she picks up the dry cleaning, Lois. I am going crazy, Quincy!" The candleholder flew across the room as Lois's permed hair fell about her forehead.

"Lois, you're drunk. Just calm down." Quincy rarely raised his voice.

"Now I'm drunk and crazy! Go out and see that floozy secretary you spend all your time with. You're never here." Lois heaved a couch cushion, and it crashed to the floor. "I'm a drunk now. My husband sleeps around, but I'm a drunk. At least I can count on my booze, Quincy. Get out of my house, you bastard!"

Veronica listened from the top of the stairs.

El Paso, Texas

Anna filled every second of the day so she would be exhausted at night. The war brought a factory into the El Paso area, and with so many men gone to the war, women started to fill the positions. Anna couldn't do that because of the children, but she had taken on the added responsibility of watching some of the neighborhood children while the other mothers found positions at the factory. Four different mothers dropped off seven children between the ages of two and five. This made Anna responsible for ten holy terrors a day. She charged the families a nominal fee for the service. It was just enough to feed the extra members and put some loose change in her pocket. She spent the extra money on goods for the kitchen. Anna understood the new working mothers were too exhausted to cook, so she prepared meals for them to take home when they arrived to pick up the munchkins. She made burritos, tamales, and tacos. The mothers could take them right home to serve. The meals were inexpensive and delicious. Everyone was happy with the arrangement. The new income created a tidy profit for Anna, who could now buy the boys some desperately needed clothes. Six days a week she filled her days. On Sunday she could only think of Manny.

New York, New York
Ronald, Kay, and Valerie gathered outside St. Patrick's Cathedral in midtown New York. The Knights of Columbus were having a bazaar. Charities were represented. This included the Red Cross and Maryknoll, which Kay and Valerie sponsored. Doughnuts, cupcakes, and sweet-filled baked goods filled the long folding tables. Valerie bit into a powdered bite of heaven. She quickly reached for the corner of her mouth as some jam squirted there. Ronald found his friends wearing silly hats.

Sister Gertrude approached Kay with a smile. "How are you, Mrs. Doovaine?"

Kay turned. "Hello, Sister Gertrude. How are you?"

"I'm terrific." Sister Gertrude responded proudly. "With your and Valerie's help, we raised over seven hundred dollars."

"That's great, Sister Gertrude." She did feel proud of this accomplishment. "How is the money earmarked?"

"Earmarked?" Sister Gertrude was young.

"Yeah. How's the money going to be spent?"

"Oh," said Sister Gertrude, and that smile reappeared. This annoyed Kay. "We're sending it to the starving children of Africa and South America."

"Really?" Kay didn't sound too impressed.

"I just wanted to say thank you for all your help." She smiled and waved.

Valerie chomped a chocolate glazed doughnut. "Stop eating. You're going to get fat," Kay snapped at her daughter.

Kay found a bakery box and filled it with a variety of yummy goods—crullers, blueberry muffins, chocolate muffins, glazed and strawberry frosted doughnuts, almond-filled croissants piled up with ham, cheese-filled croissants on top of mascarpone cheese, and raspberry Danishes.

Valerie looked embarrassed. "Mom, what are you doing?"

Kay dared her daughter to challenge her. "The starving children of Africa and South America get seven hundred dollars of our hard-earned money, and what does Rat get? Nothing! You saw the papers. You saw how skinny those men looked. I'm sending this to Rat and the others in the Philippines."

Valerie knew Kay had gone off the deep end. Kay could not accept her son was dead.

Saint Louis, Missouri

Lily gathered old *National Geographic* magazines wherever she could find them—the library, doctors' offices, people's houses, drugstore trash bins, and newsstands. Some proved fruitful. She scoured each one for articles and maps of the Far East. She found maps of the Solomon Islands, New Guinea, and New Britain. She knew where Florida Island was and read articles on the atolls of the Gilbert and Marshall Islands. She had a map of China and Burma and literature outlining the natural resources of Java and Borneo. She studied them with fervor. She learned the oceans and seas, capitals, and surrounding cities. She pinned them up on her wall and marked the progression of the Japanese army with red pushpins. Lily knew the Flores Sea divided Celebes from Bali and that due east lay the Banda Sea south of the Moluccas. She studied crops and weather. She knew the rainy seasons of the Pacific Rim. She studied the exotic fish indigenous to the oceans. She became aware of the tropical jungles and their plant life. She saw how the Japanese worked from Okinawa to Formosa and then on to the Philippines. She paired the newspapers' reports to the movements of the American fleet and used blue pushpins to mark their locations. She wanted to know everything about Asia, the cultur*e, and the war. If Chet didn't come home soon, she was going to go get him.

Commerce, Oklahoma

Everyone knew Ida at the phone company. She was a natural and connected people on the switchboard with ease. Becoming head operator meant a raise and training responsibilities. Her supervisor whispered the promotion would be soon. Ida's confidence grew. Her sister, Inez, noticed the pride. The newly found equanimity helped her cope with the pain of her lost son, Carl. She hadn't heard from him in months and wondered if he was alive.

Inez picked her up from the phone company and took the short drive back to her house in the Ford flatbed. The hills rolled, the blades of the mills spun, and the arms of the oil fields pumped and searched for black gold. She smiled as she got out of the truck, waved, and adjusted her horn-rimmed glasses. She was surprised to see Doyle's truck in the driveway. She opened the door to the house, and a beautiful bouquet of spring flowers adorned the kitchen table. Her frozen heart warmed a little bit more. "Doyle?" she announced her presence across the living room. "Did you get these flowers for me?"

Doyle appeared from the bedroom. He had just cleaned up and looked as if he was going to go out. Ida's heart sank. He fixed the belt she knew too well and stared sadly at the floor. She said a silent prayer it wouldn't start all over again. She knew she could not survive another round of Doyle's drinking. He looked her in the eye. "No, Ida. Those flowers are from Carl." Ida looked up in shock. "He just wanted you to know he was doing just fine." It was the sweetest lie she had ever heard in her life. "But Doyle would like to take you to the diner. You've been working too hard to make dinner tonight."

Ida thought she would drop dead.

Riverside, California

When Julie Cenode read the papers, she almost had a stroke. Sixteen B-25s had flown to the heart of Tokyo and bombed the capital. She thought her son, Jason, had to have been on one of those planes. Subsequent news reports claimed there was a public execution. Others had been captured. Three had died in crashes, and the others had flown to China. The war had finally zapped Julie between the eyes. She sat in the unfinished nursery and cried among the wallpaper and glue. A knock at the door forced Julie to wipe the tears from her face—a futile effort to hide her pain. It was the postman. She didn't need a government servant. She needed a friend. She expected the first payment on the loan. Julie had gone into debt to give the unwanted children a loving home. She fluffed her hair around her bloodshot eyes and opened the door.

"I have a special delivery for a Julie Cenode."

The mailman butchered the name, but Julie didn't care. She just wanted him to leave. It was a cable from the US Army. Julie's heart plunged. Her hands trembled as she signed for the delivery, and the mailman took a second glance to make sure she was all right. She struggled with the paper. She thought of getting a knife to assist with the simple envelope, but she figured her trembling hands might endanger a limb. The cable peeled open. She stared at the words through the tears. "I'm OK. Stop. Stationed at Pearl for now. Stop. I love you. Stop."

The river turned to tears of joy, and her best friend in the whole world made her life better today—the mailman.

Oklahoma City, Oklahoma

The CO told Gary he was going places. Gary sat on his bunk and stared at his new orders. He was being shipped out to Pearl for a special training assignment. His expertise with a rifle combined with his record times on various speed courses had won him a trip right into the war. He sat frozen and thought he should have missed a few targets or pulled a hamstring. How would he break the news to Annette? How he was going to break the news to Donna? Oh, God! It would have to be a letter. Gary had just promised Annette he would be safe at the base in Oklahoma. He had told her the COs loved him and gave him special treatment. They had given him leave to see Peter's birth. Oh, goodness, little Peter. They had gotten him on a free flight to Chicago. His mind raced. He should have finished high school. He should have gone to Michigan and become a star running back. He shouldn't have joined the army. *What an idiot!* he screamed to himself. They told him he was stupid. *Maybe I am,* he thought.

Gary took a deep breath and calmed down. He'd get through this. He had been chosen because he was the best. He fired himself up. He was going to get the job done. He was going to go kill some Japs and get home to Annette and Peter. He had never gotten hit in high school. He wouldn't get hit by those Japs. He'd hit them first. Hit and run. Stick and move. Bob and weave. Gary Alesse was going places. *Gary Alesse is going to get himself killed,* he thought.

Hawaii, The *Enterprise*, May 1942

Egan was drunk. Really drunk. Rum made him break out in a strange red rash, but he didn't care. He danced with a group of really drunk nurses and pretended to play the ukulele. The drinks looked so innocent. They were just little umbrellas in some tropical juices. *Sure. I'll have another,* thought Egan. Another sailor came dancing into the group, and he was really, really drunk. He was wearing a grass skirt and holding his drink high above his head. It was a good idea to blow off steam, but the wheels were coming off the car. Both sailors danced and groped the girls, who didn't seem to mind all that much. Everyone was really drunk. Egan took a swig of his innocent rum concoction and asked the sailor, "What ship are you with?"

"I'm not navy. I'm army," he slurred.

"Army? Huh. I pegged you for a navy man."

"No. I sailed with the *Hornet* for a mission, but I don't like ships. They make me sick." He laughed and poured the sweet drink in the tiki cup down his throat.

"The *Hornet*. Are you a pilot?" Egan recognized this guy.

"No. I'm a gunner."

"A gunner?" Egan sported a broad smile. "I'm a gunner!" Egan hugged the soldier. "I think I saw you on the *Hornet* when Doolittle took the B-25s to Tokyo. Your CO was giving you some type of bad news."

"You saw that?" Egan shook his head as he danced and groped. "How did you see that?"

"Really big oculators," Egan said.

He had slaughtered the word "binoculars," but the flyer knew exactly what he was talking about. They both curled their fingers around their eyes and danced while wearing their oculators.

"Well, Army, what's your name?" Egan bypassed the hand-shake, told the stranger he loved him, and gave him a hug.

"Jason Cenode." Jason lifted him up and twirled him around.

Egan was inebriated but still realized it took a lot to swing him around. "You're a big boy. Did you play some football?" Egan asked.

"Defensive end and offensive tackle."

"Tight end and linebacker."

This consecrated their friendship. The two got back to drinking and dancing. By evening's end they stumbled down the pristine beaches of Oahu and decided it would be fun to punch each other as hard as they could. They laughed and laughed and wailed away at each other. The two behemoths blew off some steam until they collapsed in the gentle surf and passed out. The following morning Egan made it back on the *Enterprise* in time for the ceremony in which he received an honor for his role in the Marshall Islands. The marching band never sounded so loud.

The Philippines

Old friends were reunited and reinvigorated. Norm and Chet found each other. Chet explained how Norm had saved his life by stuffing him in the back of a truck. Norm's plan had worked perfectly. The truck didn't stop until San Fernando, and he had gotten just enough rest to slip off the truck and get lost in the crowd. He told Norm how he had seen his old buddy, Carl, at the train depot. Chet wondered if Rat was OK. Chet sized up the prison. "What a hellhole," he said to Norm.

Norm smiled for the first time in days. A circle formed the main mingling area, and thatch-roofed huts enclosed the circle. "It's got four walls. That's a start," Norm said dryly.

"What did you expect? The Manila Hotel?"

Norm looked strangely at Chet. Norm hadn't thought about the Manila Hotel in half a year—not since they evacuated. He remembered the good nights there a long, long time ago.

"What did I say?" Chet noticed Norm's mood change.

"Nothing. I spent a lot of time in the Manila Hotel. I worked in the Marsman Building manning the radios and phones in the communications office. I knew everybody by name. Nice people." Norm realized Chet didn't know much about him, but they would have plenty of time to catch up. "Oh! Look, Chet. Our cozy billet."

"What did you call them?" Chet inquired.

"For a man who knows so much about Bushido, it's surprising you don't know what a billet is."

"I tried to study my enemy's fighting capacity, telephone boy. Not his sleeping habits."

Norm laughed out loud. "Well, hillbilly, a billet is lodging for the troops. A place to sling their hammocks."

"I don't see any hammocks. I see some mats on the floor."

"Our billet is our hut. Those mats are our beds."

Chet looked dismayed at the woven cogon grass mats, but it beat sleeping in the jungle. The guards made a ruckus, and the prisoners moved to the dusty circle. Norm helped an ill man to his feet. Norm was thankful the infirmary would be able to help the troops regain their health. He assisted him over to the makeshift hospital. As he entered he saw the forlorn face of the overloaded physician. He was covering the body of a soldier who had died due to complications from malaria. The orderly set him beside several other dead. Norm learned that up to fifty men a day died in the camp.

"Excuse me, Doctor. I think this man needs help badly."

The doctor looked helplessly at the man—a withered skeleton. The doctor wondered what he could do with his primitive supplies and facilities. He had received hundreds like him. The doctor knew the man was going to die. The doctor's eyes welled with tears, but they receded just as quickly. He sat the man in a chair and gave it his best.

"Thanks, Doctor."

Norm gave him a friendly wave and decided now wasn't a great time to talk about his itchy skin and the burning sensations in his feet. Norm suffered from pellagra, a vitamin deficiency that caused dermatitis and the burning sensations in his feet, and intestinal ulcers.

Norm spotted Chet in the circle and picked up the monologue by the warden of the bastille. He wasted no time getting to the point. It was known as the "rule of ten." If anyone attempted escape, they would find and kill that person. After killing that person, they would kill ten random soldiers from the detention center. Norm and Chet knew it was technically their duty to try to escape, but they hoped nobody was insane enough to try. In their condition it was a preposterous notion. They had made it this far alive, and they didn't want to be part of the Cabanatuan ten.

Camp O'Donnell

The irony was that some of the prisoners had actually called this place home before. Camp O'Donnell was located near the small city of Tarlac. It had been turned into a concentration camp for the Bataan refugees. The camp already smelled of stale death and bodily functions. The prisoners were rampant with disease, and they sorted through the accommodations. Rat and Carl found a billet and settled in. They placed their lonesome packs by the mats. Rat's feet swelled.

"What do you think you've got?" Carl asked the anguished Rat.

"I don't know, but it hurts like hell." Rat's complaining had been insignificant until this point. Carl worried.

"He's got beriberi," said another soldier, and he joined the residents of the billet. "We call this place Rio," the soldier mocked.

Carl looked at the soldier in surprise. "How do you know this?"

"I've seen it before at Iba. His feet, legs, and ankles are all swollen badly. I bet if he removed his trousers, you would find his scrotum is swollen as well."

Carl said with horror, "Rat, take off your pants." Rat responded shyly. "Take them off. Let's take a look."

Rat removed his pants. His scrotum was larger than a grapefruit. The men huddled around him were stunned. "It just got like that in the last couple days of the hump."

"We're taking you to the doctor. Now," said Carl.

"You might want to have the doctor see if he has anything for the lice," another announced. "I'm not trying to point any fingers, but the lice will jump to all of us overnight if he doesn't fix it."

Carl looked lovingly at Rat. His buddy was getting whacked like so many thousands of other soldiers. "Come on, partner. Let's get going." He helped Rat to his feet. "Thank you, fellas. Looks like we're going to be in Rio for a while. What are your names?" He extended his hand in thanks.

"Shaun Joint. US Army. Pittsburgh," Shaun said and grasped his hand.

"Manny Droad. US Army. Texas," Manny said.

"I'm Carl Broodend. US Army. Oklahoma."

Rat winced as he rose to his feet. "Rat Doovaine. US Army. New York City."

Carl and Rat limped to the infirmary, and Shaun and Manny worked their way through the center of the camp—a courtyard of vomit and piss. Men stood in the midday sun and evacuated their bowels of bloody, mucus-laden feces and yellow-brown fluids. The only latrine in the compound was already so unsanitary that only the most desperate approached the area. It swarmed with giant, green-eyed flies.

On Sunday Shaun and Manny attended a service. The moans of the sick and the constant relief of intestinal disease interrupted it frequently. Shaun had become better acquainted with prayer, and salvation would be his release if he didn't survive this vexed, noxious site. His weight continued to drop. There were bad days and better days but never good days. His skin sagged and draped over his bony skeleton and revealed the outline of his sternum. The muscular legs that had once carried him through defensive lines for touchdowns were eroded to the width of baseball bats. Manny had fared no better.

They finished the standing Mass. No one could sit on the ground at O'Donnell. There was too much excrement.

The prisoners could walk within the camp if they had the energy. Hundreds of people lay on their mats immobilized. Others nursed them with bits of food and water and tried to nourish them back to health.

"They are looking for Americans who have certain skills to work outside the camp," Shaun said to Manny.

"I'm a cook," Manny curtly replied to Shaun. "I don't think they're looking for cooks."

"No, Manny. You're my assistant." Manny looked at Shaun in wonder. "I'm a whiz with engines, cars, and airplanes. There's a rumor the Japs might need help in the motor pools or with truck drivers. The Japanese don't all drive. Most ride bikes. They have a shortage. Can you drive a truck?"

"Yeah, sure. I don't really think I want to help the Japanese, though, even after all they've done for us."

Manny could always make Shaun laugh. "It would get us out of this place, Manny. This camp has death written all over it. Sitting here stagnant and wasting away like all the other corpses. People are dying every minute. Two an hour someone told me. Doing anything would help keep us alive."

"Are you thinking about trying to escape? They'll catch me and cut my head off. I don't want anyone else's death on my conscience when I die," Manny said, referring to the rule of ten.

"No. I promise."

Manny looked into Shaun's eyes and then to the fence that enclosed the compound. A soldier had collapsed by the base of the perimeter and was rotting in the weeds. Maggots and flies covered his body.

"Yeah, Shaun. Let's get out of here for a while."

They walked away from the decomposing soldier and listened to a pair of men singing the Carter Family's "Keep On the Sunny Side" and "Can the Circle Be Unbroken." Everyone did what they could to stay alive.

Carl and Rat sat near the infirmary and waited in a never-ending line of the exceedingly sick. A soldier behind them looked antsy. He was desperate, and Rat could sense it. "Are you OK, buddy?"

"I'm out of cigarettes. I really need a cigarette. Any of you guys got a cigarette?" He was really jumpy.

Rat had a cigarette and was going to give him one, but he too was in very short supply. "I'll trade you a banana for two cigarettes."

A banana. Carl's eyes lit up. Rat smelled a good deal. A banana among the starving could get more than two cigarettes. Rat reached for his pocket, and the man removed the gold-green nutrition from his pants. The two made the exchange. The black market of Rio was born.

The *Enterprise*

On June 3 an American pilot was flying in a PBY Catalina and saw a dozen ships approaching. They were seven hundred miles from Midway. His nerves frayed by the impending attack, the dedicated pilot reported he had found the main body of the Japanese forces. He had indeed found something. He had uncovered the invasion fleet from Guam and Saipan. Pilots jumped into the B-17's on Midway and headed west to repel the force. Their attempts were honorable but unsuccessful. The eastbound invasion force moved forward. The reports revealed to Admiral Yamamoto there would be no immediate surprise by his main body, and he anticipated his submarines would delay the rescuing fleet from Pearl. They prepared for the dawn strike the following morning—June 4.

Egan Paal and the other sailors kept their minds off the altercation by engaging in mundane chores, letter writing, and games of chance. The penny poker pot grew to twenty cents. Two guys folded and joined the other players on the sidelines. This left Egan heads up with a kid from North Dakota. Egan held a jack of hearts, a three of spades, a five of diamonds, a six of hearts, and a ten of hearts. He put his hearts together, hoped for a flush, and asked the dealer for three cards. He pulled the five of hearts. This made his ticker skip a beat. He turned the other two cards—a five of spades and an eight of clubs. He had thrown away a five, and that left him with the lowly pair of fives. A set of fives would have gone a long way to taking a big pot off the sailor, who was riding high with a pair of kings. Egan knew he was beaten and folded. He had won pots left and right before the Marshall Islands, and he hoped his losing streak didn't extend topside. They anted up.

"And two for the man from Wisconsin."

The dealer kept everyone's spirits high. The blinds—two and three cents—built the pot for the bettors. Egan turned over his cards. A queen of clubs and nine of diamonds off suit. He like the queen and nine and dumped the rest. A pimple-faced boy from Tennessee threw three cents into the pot on the initial round of betting. Egan felt his luck changing with the lady in his hand and matched the raise. Three other players got out of the way, and Egan asked for three. The hick wanted two cards. Egan stayed still and focused and didn't tip his hand. He turned over the cards. The nine of clubs gave him a pair. The next card was the nine of hearts. Egan had a set. His blood pressure bubbled when he turned over the queen of spades. Egan stayed cool but relished his full house.

"I'll raise the pot a nickel," the sailor from Tennessee drawled, and he placed what was probably the biggest bet of his life.

The kid looked a little nervous, and Egan felt the nickel was a message sent to scare him away. He knew the kid had something, but it was not enough to whip his full house. "I'll match the nickel and raise it a nickel," Egan said. He was sending the poor kid a message to get out and let him have the pot. The hick's fingertips trembled as he pondered his move. Egan didn't want the kid to get hurt. "Lay it down, kid. I don't want to take your money." Egan looked the kid in the eyes.

Not intimidated the hick raised the pot a quarter—the game limit. Egan felt bad for the kid. He was going to lose his money. A crowd gathered and watched the hand unfold. Egan fumbled the coins as the *Enterprise* rolled in the waves. "I'll see the quarter," he said with the full house tucked in his palm.

He laid the pair of queens and set of nines on the table as the party howled at the powerful hand. The kid looked dismal and ready to barf. He turned over a low-card straight flush and swept up the pot.

Egan smiled. "You pounded me, kid."

The hick smiled ear to ear to the roar of the crowd. Egan worried about the mission—and his losing streak.

The crew on the *Enterprise* woke in the dark hours before dawn to an elegant breakfast of steak and eggs. The superstitious Egan found the choice breakfast to be a bad omen. It was the fattening of the goose before breaking its neck for dinner.

"Steak and eggs," one man said in horror. "This means we're going to get murdered."

It was a ridiculous assumption but one many shared.

"We're going to be just fine," Egan said.

He checked his attitude and decided today was going to be a good day. The others followed Egan's lead.

Upstairs the bridge anticipated the pace of Nagumo's forces and accurately assessed them as being within a couple hundred miles off Midway and closing. Lying in wait northwest of Midway, Admiral Fletcher of the *Yorktown* correctly guessed the morning of June 4 would be the day the enemy attacked. He implored the general staff to be battle ready. Admiral Nagumo prepared to launch his strike force. Intelligence reports indicated the American carriers were still south near the Coral Sea. Nagumo failed to send out standard patrols to search the area. He launched the 128 planes off the decks of the *Akagi* and *Kaga* into the darkness. The deadly Zeros led the way for the Val bombers. They all headed into the magenta line of the sunrise.

The Japanese fended off the dregs of airpower the tiny Midway supplied. It was shooting fish in a barrel as the Kates and Vals outclassed the American Wildcats and Brewster F2A Buffalos. Nagumo waited for his second wave to be refitted with aerial bombs that could remove the Midway airstrip. The delay proved costly. Admiral Spruance was a virgin to the carrier wars, but he took his first gamble. He launched a full strike of bombers and fighters from the decks of both the *Enterprise* and *Hornet*. Egan watched the planes from his gun turret and waved his cap in admiration. The pilots knew the extreme range before takeoff and understood they might not make it back to the carriers. The idea of crash-landing in the ocean frightened Egan. Dauntless dive bombers, Devastator torpedo bombers, and escorting Wildcats took off into the wind and led Spruance away from the enemy fleet. Fletcher on the *Yorktown* sent half his planes to assist the *Hornet* and *Enterprise* flyers.

Nagumo received intelligence on the bridge of the *Akagi* that enemy ships had been spotted east of Midway. He was thunderstruck and ordered his staff to seek the American carriers. Their planes could be all over his backside at any moment. The refitting of the second-wave arsenal was taking too long. Planes were still below the flight deck. The returning flights from Midway were imminent. The news of an aircraft carrier made Nagumo furious. A hundred sorties would have to be ditched while he protected the ship.

Updates filtered to down the line to Egan. The *Enterprise* steamed outside the battle zone. Only the flyers received action. The *Yorktown* sank but not before fending off Yamamoto's surge with the assistance of the *Hornet* and the fearless fliers and brave sailors of the American carriers. Midway remained in American hands. Yamamoto's juggernaut was wounded. Egan Paal survived the most important naval engagement in US history without his ship ever being identified. *That is pretty good luck,* he thought.

June 15, 1942, Hawaii

Gary longed to bring Annette to Hawaii. He only saw segments of the beautiful island as he worked with a sniper team made up of the army's finest shooters. Combining speed, endurance, and accuracy with their weapons, the finalists hiked the volcanic mountains, worked up and down steep slopes, and learned to adapt to the jungle terrain. The exhausting climbing of narrow ledges and fighting through the vegetation hardened the fighters, who often spent days in the wilderness foraging for food. These survival skills played an important role in the mission. Drill coordinators purposely chose routes with no defined trails. They selected random points on a map, gave the soldiers coordinates and compasses, and left them to their own devices. The exercise challenged Gary, and he excelled in all facets of the program.

The Philippines

At Rio the prisoners tried to make the most of the wretched detention. The doctor had alleviated the swelling of Rat's scrotum, and Rat and Carl tossed a coconut they pretended was a football. They feigned real exercise, which exhausted their depleted frames. Shaun sat with Manny at the infirmary following a nasty bout with cholera. The ingestion of water laced with feces and vomit had induced his acute intestinal infection.

The hospital struggled with the number of sick soldiers. Located in a raised billet, the loosely laid wooden planks raised from the ground were supposed to provide an antiseptic environment for the doctors to field patients. The mortally sick were placed under the floor in makeshift beds to keep the dying out of the burning island sun. The human sewage dripped through the cracks in the floor and onto the dying people placed under the billet.

Carl and Rat had stopped their football game to lend a hand to soldiers burying the dead in a remote area of the compound. They carried the most decayed people in blankets to avoid the infestation of maggots and lice that ate the dead flesh. Without proper tools the prisoners did their best to provide shallow graves, and they said a few kind words for soldiers who hardly knew one another. Carl and Rat headed back to the billet for the meager portion of rice and some feces-and-vomit-laden water. Carl bumped squarely into a man who staggered through the colony.

He had gone blind from a lack of vitamins. As the death toll rose, morale eroded.

"I think they think I'm Filipino at the motor pool." Manny exposed his naturally dark arms.

"You're wearing a US Army uniform—that needs a good press by the way." Shaun smiled at Manny.

Most toured the camp in nothing but loincloths to beat the heat. Manny and Shaun held onto the smelly pants and shirts for service to the Japanese—and to smuggle black-market goods into the camp.

"It frightens me. For all they know, I could have stolen it off some poor dead guy." They chuckled at Manny's paranoia.

"What did you get today?" Rat inquired.

Rat handled the distribution of the goods and trades. He got top value. It was tough to squeeze their comrades, but the foursome was determined to survive.

"Our Filipino saviors brought us small quantities of salt." He tossed the squares onto a blanket. "There's a little coffee and some canned peas." Carl looked up excitedly. He loved peas. "And some sugarcane and cigarettes."

"That's it? That's unacceptable," Rat teased Shaun.

"It's tough getting this in. It depends on who's working the gate. The really young one never looks. He just keeps his eyes on our eyes."

"There are two guards I have to bribe to let us pass. They don't care. They get free cigarettes," Manny chimed in.

"How do you give the cigarettes to the guard?" Carl had to know. "You can't just walk right up to the gate and hand them over."

Manny laughed. "No. You can't. The guards from the motor pool pass us off to the guards at the gate. Once that transfer is done, the gate guards face us, and I have the cigarettes ready in my pocket. It's all in the handoff. It has to be smooth."

"What if you fumble?" countered Rat.

Manny answered proudly, "I never fumbled in high school, and I'm not going to fumble now."

Rat bet he never had.

A cool breeze rolled through the billet. They stepped outside to look at the night. A black sky hung the neon-white clouds. The rain would come tonight. It would come in torrents—even if just for a while. The prisoners never slept well. The gnawing pit of hunger kept them awake, and the nightmares rehashing the horrors of friends being blown to pieces and rotting before their very eyes made many insomniacs. If they woke in the morning, ornery guards handpicked by the cruel warden performed the daily head count. As they called roll the next morning, Carl and Rat looked at the shallow gravesite dug the previous day. The rain had washed away the topsoil, and the buried remains of the dead prisoners' limbs sprawled forth from the earth like mud-caked zombies rising from the grave. *There is no escape from this hell,* thought Rat and Carl.

Cabanatuan

It was like sitting in a sauna all day every day. The humidity sucked the fluids out of the body like a baster. Many men licked their own sweat to replace their fluids. Norm and Chet manufactured matching loincloths to try to beat the heat. They kidded themselves by saying the new look would someday be the fashion rage in the States, and they might even get their pictures in the Sears catalog. By the grace of God and the dedication of the worn-out doctors at the infirmary, Norm survived the devastating long-term effects of pellagra. Chet finally stabilized from the torturous march with a minuscule but steady diet. He didn't look like death. That was a victory at Cabanatuan. Now they combated two new enemies of the prison: boredom and flies. Every day was the same hideous, vulgar day—the whimpers of the dying, burials, and pain. Every day there was a long line at the infirmary of people with gangrenous sores on their bodies. Malaria ran rampant. Vascular malaria, cerebral malaria, dysentery, jungle rot, cholera, typhus, and schistosomiasis rambled through the camp. A wave of typhus stung Cabanatuan. The swarms of lice and fleas spread the bacterial disease. The insects became infected after feeding off the carcasses of dead rats, birds, cats, and humans. It began with a rash on the trunk of the human body, extended to the limbs, and drove the infected to delirium.

The flies were an unbeatable foe. Chet raged and attempted to slay each and every fly personally. Eating became annoying. Flies buzzed in large groups around Chet's face as he tried to hold his bowl in one hand and his spoon in the other. He was handcuffed with no way to rid himself of the pests. They would buzz around the bowl and spoon, land on the rice, and lay their eggs. They tried to nest in the corners of Chet's mouth. He jerked his head from side to side, but often they made their way into an orifice—the nostril, mouth, or ear canal. The back of the neck, chin, and eyes were sweet spots. Chet waited for his prey. He let them land on his shoulder, fingertip, or the back of his hand. He let the cigarette-sized demons get comfortable and secure. He watched the little bastards rub their two little arms together. Whop! Chet clobbered them with his other hand. It was a short-lived victory. Two flies always took the place of one. Chet hated this place. Movement provided no escape from the flies. Norm and Chet cut a switch from the tree and used it to fan the flies from their loin areas. They buzzed by the hundreds near their groins and unwashed contents.

Norm and Chet gathered for the unvarying speech from the institution's executive. He reminded them how lucky they were to be alive. They were alive because the emperor had shown them benevolence. The prisoners were cowards, dishonorable, and lower than dogs. This was all part of the boredom. Tiny moments graced the day, though. They talked football. They reflected on every play and every game in high school. They spoke of great plays and missed opportunities that stuck in their dreams. What had started as a joke became a habit. Norm would follow Chet around the compound like a running back following his tackle. Soldiers would see the tall Chet coming, and Norm would pop out from behind him. They would draw plays in the dirt, erase them, and make up new ones. They pretended to play for the Redskins or the Giants. When football sapped their interest for the day, they listened to the other prisoners hum gospel songs or think aloud about how the army was going to attack the Japanese and rescue them soon. Norm shared stories about his mother, Carla, and his father, Vincent. He rued the woeful path Dominic had chosen. Chet talked only of Lily. Chet and Norm retired for the night and headed back to the billet. To their shock they walked in to find a man hanging from the rafter of the hut. Strangled by his homemade noose.

Washington State

The clouds broke over the Pacific Northwest and unleashed a glorious day. The Kerichuck family hiked through the Cascade Mountains on their summer vacation—the last camping trip for a while. Ken Kerichuck and a team of aerodynamic engineers worked exhaustively designing the new B-29 Superfortress. The army hoped to have it in the air as soon as possible. It wasn't ready yet, but when it was the United States would have a special weapon. He hoped the war would end soon, and nobody would even need the Superfortress, but that didn't seem likely. Ken wrestled with his genius. He supported the American cause but had never envisioned himself designing flying death machines. Ken tried to enjoy his wife, Mary Pat, and their three children far away from the plant.

Mary Pat cooked some eggs over the open flame. Her oldest son, Dan, wrestled with his younger brother, Michael. Dan had caused some complications during his birth, and Mary Pat wasn't sure whether she would have any more children until she gave birth to Dan's sister, Dolores, in 1928 and then Michael in 1934. Dan B. Kerichuck had just graduated from high school and was headed to Stanford to play middle linebacker and study. Education was the most important thing in the Kerichuck family, and Dolores seemed to have Ken's special gift for science. She was precocious and wanted to become a doctor. Dan loved playing football. Michael wanted to be a firefighter.

Dan walked by Dolores. She was engrossed in a chemistry book, and he punched her in the leg. "Why'd you do that?" Dolores screamed in the wilderness and tried to smack Dan with the thick textbook.

"Because you deserved it."

Michael laughed. Dan was his hero.

"If you do it again, I'll put a frog in your pillow."

Michael stopped laughing. He knew she'd do it, and he wanted no part of the frog. Dan put Dolores in a headlock and tickled her while she screamed. Thrown prone by the tickling, she kicked like a bronco and tried to escape Dan's vise.

"Stop it! Stop it!" she yelped. Her shirt loosened, and her bra became exposed.

"I saw Dolores's underwear." Michael giggled.

Dolores turned as red as a crayon. She was still uncomfortable with her blossoming adolescent body.

"That's enough, Dan. Leave your sister alone."

"Hey, Dad." Dan acted as if nothing had happened while Dolores put herself back together like the scarecrow in *The Wizard of Oz*. "Where have you been?"

"Down by the river watching nature."

Dan knew "watching nature" was code for going poop.

"Daddy went poopy."

They laughed. Michael had learned the secret phrase.

"How's the river?" Mary Pat gave Ken a hug around the waist.

"It's moving quickly. The loggers covered the entire river with a float down to the mill."

This piqued Dan's curiosity. "I want to see that," he exclaimed, and he ran his fingers through his shock of red hair.

Ken looked at his son and nodded. "You can walk right down to the river and check it out, but then you come right back and help your mother pack up the gear."

"Yes, sir."

"We've got a big hike today, and I want to walk over that ridge and get to the mill by the early afternoon."

Dan gave a mock salute. Michael followed suit.

"I'll go with them," added Dolores, volunteering to babysit the boys.

Boys could become so distracted, and she didn't especially like camping. The sooner it was all over, the better.

Dan hauled ass down the hill toward the river. Michael struggled to keep up with his hero. Dolores sauntered down the hill. She was in no mood to run. Ken and Mary Pat watched their tribe working nature and wondered at how quickly the years had gone.

Dan had never seen anything like it. It was as if the loggers had created a giant dock across the river. The deceiving tide made the logs look still in the waters. The whole scene looked spectacular and gigantic to little Michael. It looked conquerable to Dan. Endowed with a solid six-foot frame and formidable chest, arms, and thighs, Dan felt it possible to grab one of the soaked trees and hurl it over his shoulder. He stepped out onto one of the logs by the shore gingerly and tested its durability. Soaked through the rings, the trees were heavy and stable in the water. They supported Dan's weight. The logs rolled, but Dan stabilized himself and found his stride. He bounced from log to log near the river's edge. Michael admired his hero.

Dolores wasn't nearly as enamored. "Dan B. Kerichuck, you get off those logs right now."

Dan thought she sounded just like Mary Pat. "C'mon, Sis. I'm just having a little bit of fun." His broad smile grew as he danced on the spinning wood. "I might even walk to the other side of the river."

"You will do no such thing. Get off there. You're scaring me." Dan didn't budge. "I'm going to get Dad." Michael looked at Dolores. She was going to get Dan in big trouble. "I'm serious."

"I dare you." Dan mocked his sister.

"All right."

She turned and huffed away. This left Michael and the clowning Dan by the river. Michael watched Dan work the logs in a tango that had taken him farther from the border of the flowing tributary. Michael watched his brother's feet spinning and moving the logs and jumping from one evasive log to the next. He spun its momentum until it whirled too fast, and then he slipped to another log. Dan's left arm went into the air as he stood on one foot. He tried to put his left foot down to regain his balance, but his heel missed the rolling log. He slipped through the logs like newspaper through the printing press. Dan was trapped in the river and boarded under the surface by the harvested pines. Michael screamed so loudly his parents heard it at the campsite.

Dolores's heart fell at the bloodcurdling scream. She loved her brother wholeheartedly, and if anything happened to him, her soul would be destitute. She was not very athletic, but she raced down the hill. Ken and Mary Pat tumbled behind. She retraced her steps and found Michael. His face was swollen with tears and worry. There was no Dan.

"Where's Dan?" Dolores looked at Michael.

Michael was distraught and couldn't speak.

"Michael, look at me. Take a deep breath. Where is Dan?"

"He fell through the logs," he said and burst into more tears.

"Where was the last place you saw him?"

Michael pointed to eleven o'clock. Dolores moved quickly down the river about twenty yards to her left and calculated the distance Dan would have moved in the river flow. Her eyes never blinked. She tried to find a sign of him in the area she computed he would most likely be. Ken and Mary Pat were out of breath and gasping for air. They found Dolores with Michael hot on her heels.

"What the hell is going on?" Ken was worried.

"Dan fell through the logs."

"Christ in Heaven." Mary Pat quivered, and she held Michael in her arms.

"Where do you think he is?" Ken shouted.

"I think he's around here…but I'm not sure." Dolores bawled, and the tears blurred her search.

Dolores and Ken scoured the pines. They all looked the same—giant matchsticks in a floating pile. Dolores moved downriver with the logs.

"Where are you going? I thought you said he was here," Ken said.

"The logs are moving. He could be caught in the current farther downstream."

"There!" Dolores screamed.

She saw Dan's bloody hands holding the very edge of a log and using it as a float. Across the river two Native Americans had heard Michael's scream and watched the tragedy unfold by the banks of the surging river. They crept out onto the wood and carefully following Dolores's pointing.

"There! There!"

Ken and Dolores shifted the rescuers position. They were mesmerized as the angels from the woods worked doggedly. They reached Dan and straddled one log. They stabilized it like a canoe and pushed the surrounding logs away with their feet. Their incredible patience and balance allowed them to get the proper angle to retrieve Dan. They pulled him to the surface and rested his limp body over the log.

July 1942

Admiral Yamamoto, after getting whipped at Midway, focused on the Solomon Islands. Thwarted by the American carriers in the Coral Sea, the general staff redoubled their efforts to take the Solomon Islands and isolate Australia. Port Moresby was on the southern side of New Guinea's Papuan Peninsula, and it was the key. The Japanese army would have to hack its way across the brutal jungles of the Owen Stanley Mountains and the natural Kokoda Trail. No American suspected General Horii would attempt to hike two thousand troops over the grueling trail to occupy the base at Kokoda.

A scout team of army paratroopers was sent to reconnoiter the northern coast of the Papuan Peninsula—specifically Lae and Salamaua. Gary Alesse had been in the Owen Stanley Mountains for two days with a superlative team of young soldiers gathering valuable intelligence for a possible invasion. The team of six sat perched on a ridge looking over Buna. They were camouflaged and patrolling the harbor after a night jump into the jungle. "Fellas," Gary said, and he held the binoculars still, "do you see what I see?"

They saw the fighters in the wind.

"You have a keen eye there, mate," said Snoad, the Aussie.

He watched the transports unload the first of thirteen thousand Japanese troops. Trunkey put down his canteen and grabbed his field glasses. "Well, I think HQ will get that valuable intelligence it was looking for."

"That's why the B 17's went over the other night when we dropped," said Parent in his Louisiana drawl.

"Doesn't look as if they did a whole lot of good," noted Jaffe.

"Fellas, we're the only thing standing between them and the garrison at Kokoda." Schwartz made the sterling observation that changed the dynamic of their mission.

The Aussie disagreed. "I'm not standing between anything, mate."

"Those are your countrymen up there holding that airfield, Snoad," countered Jaffe.

"That airfield is over fifty miles into the mountains. The Japs aren't going to cut through the jungle to get to Kokoda. It would take weeks," Parent said. He concurred with Snoad.

Trunkey spoke calmly. "Our orders are clear. We're to recon the area until twenty-four July. At oh three hundred of twenty-five July, we bug out to rendezvous point Brunette and brief the brass. What do you think, Alesse?"

"Orders are orders. But if the Japs head up the mountain toward Kokoda Field—and that's a big if—those troops will get slaughtered. Someone would need to warn them."

"They've got radios," said Parent. He was staring at Gary.

"They think Kokoda is only vulnerable by air. They would never expect a land crossing on the trail," added Schwartz.

"That's because it's not going to happen. It's too arduous—even for the Japanese," Snoad inserted snidely.

"We're gonna stick to the mission. Now let's get back to work." Trunkey refocused the team, and they evaluated the invading army's strength.

Snakes made sleeping in the jungle rough. A little snake could kill a soldier with one snap of its fangs. An elongated snake as thick as a thigh could squeeze the life out of a person, snack on the head, unhinge its jaws, and swallow the torso. There weren't snakes in Chicago—only Cubs and Bears. Animals and birds made creepy noises in the night. It seemed to rain every day. Snoad manned the watch. The sunrise erased the earliest morning shadows.

"Bugger me," whispered Snoad, and he roused the resting paratroopers.

"What is it, Snoad?" Trunkey wiped his eyes and grabbed the field glasses.

He saw the unfathomable—columns of Japanese whacking their way into the jungle and up the mountainside. A snake of soldiers curled back to the newly formed camp at Buna. The head of the serpent slithered in the jungle half a mile ahead. They had disassembled heavy machine guns for transportation through the vegetation. Hordes of soldiers and recruited locals piled into the great green ocean. They were there, but Kokoda wouldn't see them coming. Gary grabbed his glasses and observed the snake of soldiers slinking into the jungle.

"What do you think, Gary?"

"We're going to cover both bases. Three of us are going to head to the rendezvous and get this intelligence back to HQ. Three of us are going to haul ass over the mountain to Kokoda and warn the airfield."

"No way," stated Parent. "I'm not going up into those mountains with a garrison of Japs on my tail."

"I'm going to ask for volunteers. If we don't get enough…" Gary hesitated. "Then I'll go myself."

The group looked around at one another for volunteers. Parent stated, "I'm out."

Jaffe stared down Parent. "I'm in."

Trunkey looked at Schwartz and Snoad. "I'm going to follow my orders." Trunkey was out.

Snoad looked at Schwartz and then at Jaffe. "They're my people. Let's lend them a hand."

Jaffe smiled at Snoad. Schwartz was out by default. That was his slimy nature. He was smart enough to know everything but had no courage to follow through.

The men rehashed the new plan, studied the map, and marked certain spots for their mission. They were already behind the Japanese, so they chose a risky angle that would bring them close to the invading force. They stowed their gear, said their good-byes, and hoped to cash in on Snoad's promise of a cold beer in Sydney after the war. Schwartz sniveled. "Those suicidal bastards. They'll never make it off New Guinea alive. The Japs will find them, or the jungle will swallow them whole," he said.

To cut the angle the paratroopers had to ramble faster and farther than the Japanese serpent axing its way up the precipitous inclines of the Owen Stanley Range. Three could move quickly. It could be done. They plotted their way step by step through branches and over fallen trunks. They were always aware Japs had hidden eyes in the jungle. They ducked and weaved in and around tropical leaves that sliced their skin. Mud slipped under their feet. Grinding and grinding they climbed to surpass the enemy. Their well-tuned bodies leaked sweat, and they took several breaks to refill the canteens in the babbling brooks. They churned closer to the Japanese column and climbed through the foothills. The steepest segment was ahead. The mountains loomed, and its broad shoulders rose in front of the troopers like a wall.

A single Japanese scout sat in a tree and searched for American planes. The beautiful skies were clear. The young boy studied the jungle. Flocks of birds flushed suddenly from the trees. It happened every so often, but a pattern developed. He was sure it was a jaguar on the prowl. He would alert his commanding officer if it came too close.

"I need to stop." Jaffe put his hand on the tree and huffed.

Snoad didn't say a word. He knelt and gasped. He was secretly thanking Jaffe for stopping Alesse. Gary was relentless, but he took a swig from his canteen and let the guys breathe. He had done this before to Jaffe at Pearl—wore him out. Snoad was new to the fervent pace. Snoad admired him for taking the harder road up the mountain. They were going to save five hundred lives.

Gary reached for his glasses and found an expansive view searching for the Japs. *There!* They were farther than he had anticipated, and his team was too close. The Japanese were pushing the pace. They could conceivably make the Kumusi River near Kokoda by late afternoon the following day.

Gary decided to drive his crew harder. They could take it. They were the best at what they did. "Let's move out." Gary disappeared into the jungle.

The wiry Japanese scout saw the birds again. He was terrified of the big cats and called his hunch forward to the front of the line. "This is lookout number three. Over."

"I read you, lookout three. Go."

"Birds are flying from the trees in a pattern. I think it is a jungle cat. Over."

The leader couldn't believe his ears. He started laughing at the young boy. "Please say again, number three. Go."

The boy relaxed. "I have been watching the trees. Birds keep flying from the trees on a perfect line southwest. Ahead of our line. I think it is a jaguar or leopard scaring the birds. Over."

The leader listened more carefully this time. Jaguars didn't move in straight lines or near big noises. They were shy by nature. The specific route would lead them in the advance of their party. That unnerved the captain. They were being hunted, but not by a jaguar. Playing his instincts he sent ten scouts to forage in advance of the group, but he reminded them to move with stealth.

The vehemence of the equatorial sun of the Papuan Peninsula took its toll on the merging groups. Alesse, Snoad, and Jaffe tripped quietly through the morass, and Gary monitored his compass. They continued heading south-southeast on the last leg of the day's hump. They needed to set camp ahead of the Japanese. They sat for the first time that day, and Gary wondered how the original mission was going. Schwartz, Parent, and Trunkey were burdened with the task of finding the rendezvous point. In the middle of the night, a flashlight would beckon a waiting PT boat with Morse code, and it would whisk them around the peninsula to Port Moresby.

Gary worried his mission would be regarded as foolhardy. Dangers flashed through his flickering brain as the daylight waned. They proceeded to prowl toward the Japanese scouts and fanned out ahead of the driving troops.

Gary cleaned his rifle in the early-morning hours as the darkest night turned to gray. Trying to sleep was futile knowing the enemy was so close. They humped until the last tentacle of sunlight retracted from the western horizon. He thought about his journey and the voyage across the Pacific. He and the other paratroopers had rolled dice in the bowels of the boat and whooped it up. He recalled the flyer hitching a ride to Port Moresby to join MacArthur's Fifth Air Force and the young gunner benched for the daring mission over Tokyo. Gary recalled the gunner's name—Cenode. Jason Cenode. He remembered leaping into the black night skies over Papua with nothing to guide them into the quagmire except the glow of the moon. He thought of Annette and little Peter. He thought of Larry and Donna and made a personal vow not to give Grandma a hard time.

Gary roused the others from their slumber in the misty morning on the mountainside. Dense clouds covered the Owen Stanley Range. They were as wet as the soft earth under the blanket of eucalyptus trees. Snoad and Jaffe rummaged through their packs for some tasty B rations of nonperishable canned meat and vegetables for breakfast. Jaffe turned the sustenance with his spoon in disgust, but Snoad savored his as if dining with the queen in Buckingham Palace.

"That hit the spot, mates." Snoad released a hearty burp.

Gary snapped his fist in the air and signaled for silence. The two soldiers froze and reached quietly for their Carbine M1 .30 rifles. Gary had heard something other than the jungle. The tangled maze of wilderness dozed. Gary signaled for Jaffe to move east. Gary slid southeast. He set a triangular perimeter and secured the area. They had practiced this drill at Pearl. One soldier was at each point of the triangle fifty yards from each of the others at all times. Gary moved gently through the mist. Visibility was less than ten feet in the cloud and even less in the labyrinth of the jungle. Gary held his position and his breath. He heard the crackle of a twig snapping under the foot of...something. A boar? *That would be super,* thought Gary. Getting chased through the dark jungle by a wild boar with the Japanese less than two clicks away was not his idea of a wake-up call. He stood his ground. There was another crinkle on the jungle floor. The pace too slow for a boar. It was the same residual noise his steps made as he lurked in the dark. Gary froze. He saw the bill of the soldier's cap like a deadly shark fin. The soldier was concealed behind the leaves. He waited for the soldier to move. He smelled no fear in the soldier—just caution. Gary removed the long blade of his knife from his belt and gently unsnapped the holster's button. No glint reflected from the cold steel. Gary held his breath. The soldier took the fatal step. Gary reached around his neck, covered the startled soldier's mouth, and shoved the blade into his side. He sliced his lungs and kidneys. Gary gently lowered him to the ground to keep the noise to a minimum. Gary stood wide-eyed in the morning dew.

Snoad found himself in a similar quandary. He heard nothing, but his senses tingled. He stayed low and draped one foot over the other. *Lightly,* he reminded himself. The morning gray retreated and revealed the jungle's pastel colors. Nervous sweat carved a river down the wrinkles near his nostrils and hung off the falls of his upper lip. His tongue tasted his own fear. Soldiers whispered casual morning conversations. Snoad knew he had not been spotted. He needed to know how many. Should he avoid conflict with the enemy and stay hidden in the jungle or rendezvous with Jaffe and Alesse at the checkpoint? If he killed them, the Japanese would know they hadn't come back from patrol. He couldn't use his gun. He played it cool and guessed it was a routine patrol that would leave none the wiser. He sat like an icicle hanging on a ledge. One little drop hung from his nose. The Japanese resumed their trek and wove Snoad between them. Snoad grasped his knife. The snap popped. His eyes bulged, but he didn't move. *Damn!* The soldiers stopped. He assumed he had been identified. One soldier was three paces to his back, and the other was two paces to his front. Both inched toward his crouched position in the thick weeds. Snoad employed the advantage of surprise. He lunged through the weeds and gouged the soldier ahead of him in the stomach. He removed the shiv, swung at the soldier behind him, carved his neck, and released a fountain of blood. Snoad propped the dead soldier upright and used him as a shield. A third Japanese soldier raced in and tried to reach Snoad with his bayonet. He slashed through his blood-soaked partner. Snoad let the man charge like a bull and plunged him in the sternum with his bayonet. As the charging enemy fell, his rifle discharged. "Bugger!" Snoad crumpled to the ground.

He held his hand over the gunshot wound that had shattered his ribs just below his heart. His eyes never closed as his face slammed into the mud. Jaffe and Alesse heard the shot ring out like the bells of Notre Dame. Japanese heads snapped to the direction of the blast. The captain remained calm and waited for the scouts' reports. Maybe the kid was right. Maybe there was a big cat in the jungle. There had only been one shot. He waited for the reports but not patiently.

Jaffe found trouble of his own. The gunshot echoed through the valleys of the Owen Stanley Range and exposed the dead scout's position. Curiosity brought other scouts scurrying to the action. He worked his way to the checkpoint. Things were unraveling. He resisted the urge to double back and check on his partners. He leaped through the branches and thickets, endured terrible scratches to the face, and ate large chunks of foliage as the branches stuffed their arms in his mouth as he passed. His heart pounded. Feverish perspiration poured from his glands as he quickened the pace. He leaped over hollowed logs and puddles that nourished the jungle's appetite. He rose over the thicket and crashed to the ground. His ankle cracked like a twig. Jaffe held his knee and ankle in the air but refused to scream in agony and reveal his position. His ankle flopped at a right angle to his leg. Jaffe knew he was dead. He wasn't startled when the Japanese soldier came through the weeds. He looked helplessly at the soldier standing over him with a bayonet tip at his neck.

Their eyes met for a moment, and they discovered the differences of their cultures. The soldier was just a man, but they might as well have been from different planets. The soldier drove his bayonet through Jaffe's neck and went back to find his outfit. He was leery of other Americans on the Papuan Peninsula.

Whistles blew, and the snake coiled. The serpent's tongue searched for Gary in the lush forestation. Thirty or forty soldiers searched for three. Gary assumed it was three. He hoped to God it was three. *It is all a horrible dream,* he thought. It was no dream, though. The Japanese captain sent a hundred more of his finest soldiers to hunt down Gary. The captain reinforced his rear and flanks and searched for snipers. He had assumed correctly the Americans would be heading to Kokoda to warn the Papuans. The shortest distance between two points was a straight line, and he narrowed the hunting party's trajectory. The race to Kokoda began. Gary first had to meet the soldiers at the predetermined checkpoint. That was three miles in advance of their night position. Gary did the math. He was only an hour ahead of the hunting party. Snoad and Jaffe would have to hump it to the checkpoint. Fast.

The others never came. Gary waited and then swore under his breath. He didn't want to leave, but he didn't want to stay. What if they arrived, and he wasn't here? They would be confused. Gary pondered alone in the woods like Henry David Thoreau in a hellish nightmare. He took the last drops of his canteen. The search party was in the jungle but close. He checked his watch. He had fifteen minutes at best.

Slashing machetes chopping through the forest announced their arrival. The clever bastards knew where to look and where he was heading. Gary decided to leave without Jaffe and Snoad. He hoped they would try a desperate attempt to backtrack and reach Checkpoint Brunette. He looked at his watch. They'd never make it to Brunette. He decided to slow the hunters with a little taste of his rifle. Gary found a good line of sight and intended to blast the first soldier he saw. He figured that was about fifty yards, and it would slow their pace. He pulled the rifle to his eye and balanced it with his elbow and shoulder. One clean shot from this range was as easy for Gary as tying his shoes. *Wait for it. Wait for it.* The machete ripped through the jungle. He relaxed his finger on the trigger. The Japanese target stepped fatally through the weeds. The rifle cracked and the bullet bored through his brain at the same time. The Japanese hunters hit the ground, and Gary hit the road. He knew he had only distanced himself by a few more seconds. He had one thing to his advantage, though. He was really fast.

Gary pushed hard and was careful not to expose himself to any openings that would allow the Japanese snipers unimpeded sight. Portable mortars exploded randomly around him in fireballs. The soldiers shot blindly into the jungle and hoped for a lucky shot. Few shots were close, but a pair splintered the bases of trees near Gary's position. The heat bore down on him. His canteen was dry, and he needed water. Gary's body needed to stay cool. His thighs burned, and his feet were soaked to the socks. Blood ran down his face from the cuts on his forehead and cheeks. One reed had caught him on the eyelid. The sweat and blood stung his left eye. *Move and hide,* Gary thought. His determination carried him to the Kumusi River. Gary had only seen the river marked on the map and had never surveyed this quadrant closely. The original mission hadn't intended to head this way. He knew Kokoda was just across the river, and there had to be a bridge. He had also guessed the Kokoda Trail was actually a trail. There was no trail, though. *Maybe in the Jurassic period—when cave dwellers traveled over this godforsaken place,* he mused. Gary looked over his shoulder to make sure no pterodactyl screeched from the sky. He could hear the soldiers thrashing behind him but no mortar fire ahead of his position. That was good news. The bad news was they had made up some ground. He needed some water.

Gary shed his pack. It was a risky maneuver. If he were to get trapped in the jungle, he would have no food. Despite the survival skills learned at Pearl, he wanted to avoid groping for insects and edible berries. The jungle eased, and the foliage was not so dense. That was more good and bad for Gary. He could run faster, but the Japanese had a better chance of shooting him. A bullet whizzed by his ear. He sprinted in the afternoon heat. His legs felt as if they had sandbags tied to both knees. The Japanese surged, and more weapons fired. He tried to shift to another speed but couldn't. His overdrive was gone. He peeked back. The Japanese were a hundred yards behind him. The soldiers weren't closing, but the bullets were. Gary zigzagged his way around bushes and trees. There were plenty of obstacles to confuse the Japs, but he couldn't stay out in the open for more than a few seconds. He had to be getting close to the bridge or at least the river. Where was the river? He looked at his watch. Where was the river? The river and the occasional metal pellets searching for his brain frustrated Gary.

He slammed on the brakes. His toes curled in their boots. It was the Kumusi River. He looked over the edge at the raging rapids crashing over rocks and slamming their way through the canyon that had been carved through the Owen Stanley Range a million years before. He looked to his right and spotted the bridge. It was a mess of rope with a few wires strung through it. They had a better one at Gary's summer camp. The bridge flapped in the wind, and the small boards clacked together. Gary dropped to one knee and faced the rushing Japanese. He put his eye to the sight and waited a split second. Then he pulled the trigger. And then again. One soldier fell to the ground dead.

He sprinted to the bridge. Others rolled in pain, and this allowed Gary to sprint the eighty yards left to the bridge. His peripheral vision noticed Papuan infantry on the other side of the river. They lined up on the gorge's edge and fired at the startled Japanese, who splintered quickly into two groups. One group resisted the cover fire of the Papuan infantry, and the other headed for Gary. Gary prayed the Papuans could buy him enough time to traverse the bridge. He reminded himself he owned the records for this type of event in Pearl and Oklahoma.

Papuan sharpshooters retreated for cover. They were easy targets for the well-trained Japanese. Three brave Papuan soldiers remained at the far side as Gary came to the foot of the suspended bridge. He looked down and held his breath. He took his first step, and the bridge swayed hard to his left. He held the ropes tightly and regained his balance. He took his second step. It was better. He had to cross thirty yards of this swing set. He had to go faster. The Papuans fired a few shots. Gary didn't look back. He was getting the hang of it and moved ten yards quickly. Another bullet whizzed by his ear. They had a good bead on him. He took three more steps and wiggled. *Hold on,* he thought. He steadied, took three quick strides, and was halfway there.

He could see the eyes of the Papuan soldiers light up with excitement. They pleaded for Gary to move swiftly. Their arms waved like ribbons in the air. Gary felt a burning sensation in the small of his back. *A terrible time to pull a muscle,* he thought.

He looked at the Papuan soldiers. They were not so excited now. Gary wondered why. The second bullet drilled him in the shoulder, and the walking boards slipped from under his feet. Gary couldn't move his legs. He tried to swing like a monkey and get himself back on the bridge, but he couldn't swing his legs. He knew the Japs had gotten him in the shoulder. If only he could get his feet up.

Gunfire focused on the Papuans. They fired wildly at the Japanese, and the three Papuans who had been guarding the bridge revealed their machetes. They slashed the bridge's ropes one by one. The Japanese would not cross the Kumusi today. Gary screamed, "No!"

The Papuan soldier gave him a sorrowful look and then snapped the last cord with his razor-sharp blade. Gary closed his eyes and thought of Annette and his son, Peter. The torrents ripped his feet and sucked him into the mist of the raging water of the Kumusi River.

Washington State
"He's very lucky to be alive. Only time will tell if the collapsed lung will recover to full strength. It should improve along with the bruising and other contusions associated with the cracked ribs."

Doctor Morris had monitored Dan's condition since the accident. The Kerichucks worried mostly about significant injuries to the vital organs. Michael scribbled on a coloring book in the waiting room. Mary Pat was ashen from the turmoil of the last few weeks, and she prodded the doctor for a full analysis. "How is his face?"

"Bones in the face take a long time to heal, Mrs. Kerichuck. He's medicated to relieve the pain, and his head is stabilized for limited movement. Movement causes pain and tremendous headaches. The neurologists are continuing to check X-rays and charts for any type of brain damage." Mary Pat held Ken's hand tightly. "How about his extremities?"

Dan's pulverized hands, rolled through the heavy logs like flattened leather gloves, haunted her dreams.

"There is little reaction to stimulus. The bones in the fingers should heal, but the fingertips might be irreparably damaged. The recovery process would have to include intensive physical therapy."

Dolores found herself at home in the hospital. She knew this was where she wanted to spend the rest of her professional life. Ken asked the question Mary Pat could not. "Doctor, with the damage to the facial bones, is he ever going to be the handsome boy who went camping with us that day?"

Dr. Morris looked at the family. The family wasn't concerned about Dan's appearance. They were concerned about how others might perceive him. The doctor knew the Kerichucks were thrilled he was alive. "His nose was crushed, and we have little hope of a natural recovery of the septum. His nose has caved into the nasal cavity. His upper lip had to be sewn back together after his front canines pierced it. The thirty stitches are scheduled for removal in a couple days. There will be ample scarring around his mouth. There are severe depressions in both his cheeks. Our concerns have been the brain and Dan's ability to breathe with his nose."

Dr. Morris stopped short of saying Dan would look like a flat-faced, hideous freak who might as well join the circus.

August 1942

Jason Cenode liked the cockatoos of Port Moresby. The climate and terrain were different from California, but he liked the cockatoos. American forces were in the process of invading Guadalcanal, and the troops anticipated the blare of the Klaxon. Reports informed them the invasion of Guadalcanal had been going very well, and the marines coming ashore had received little or no opposition. Jason hoped the war might not go on for as long as everybody thought.

News of the American amphibious landings at Guadalcanal on August 6 made Admiral Yamamoto's skin crawl. Operation Watchtower never blipped on his radar, and Admiral Mikawa, who was leading the troops at Rabaul, had been caught with his pants down. Mikawa flushed more troops through Buna and Gona and over the Kokoda Trail to assault Port Moresby, but he failed to monitor the neighboring Solomon Islands. His air support was in disarray and spread thin. Planes needed maintenance for an attack on the American transports and accompanying naval vessels. The American carriers *Saratoga* and *Enterprise* repelled his mighty Zeros. Mikawa regrouped and sent the Zeros with the Kates to secure the landings. He steamed from Rabaul. This led to a night run down the slot between Florida Island and Guadalcanal to engage the US Navy.

Klaxons wailed, and the people scrambled from their bunks. Jason donned his flight jacket and cap and then forced his large frame into the glass-encased turret of the B-17. The machine gun felt comfortable in his hands. The new Fifth Air Force followed close behind the Australian Hudson fighter squadron. They plotted a course over the Solomon Islands in search of the Japanese naval convoy.

The *Enterprise*

Egan Paal was at his station aboard the *Enterprise*. He spotted the Zeros heading for the carrier, and his fear was instantly alive. Egan had witnessed the deadly capability of the flyers in the Marshall Islands. They buzzed the ship and rattled dangerous cannon fire from their twenty-millimeter guns. They flew so low Egan could see the color of the pilots' gloves. The Zeros plunged into the firing zone. They distracted the Wildcats, drew them away from the ship, and cleared the way for the Kates to drop their torpedoes. The *Enterprise* pilots bravely chased the Zeros in a dizzying dogfight. Egan fired at a Zero chasing a Wildcat, snapped its wing, and forced it to the ocean. The Wildcat was rewarded with two more Zeros. He screamed skyward, tilted the wings, and zigged through the sky until the Zeros' guns disintegrated the plane in midair. Egan watched the falling pilot. Flickering yellow flames enveloped his body.

"Twelve o'clock!" Shouted the lookout.

Egan saw a Val flying straight for him at a hundred feet above the ocean's surface. He fired his cannons. They plane dissolved in midair, but the torpedo dropped into the water. He felt the *Enterprise* lurch hard starboard and braced the turret. The carrier showed its stern and dodged the torpedo. Admiral Fletcher withdrew the *Enterprise* and *Saratoga* to safer waters after downing twenty-five planes. Egan's hands shook wildly. The nightmare of the Zeros and Vals haunted every thought.

"We've got company."

Jason heard the pilot. He was calm and steady through the headphones. He scoured the skies. The Zeros climbed high into the sun to engage the deadly but slow bombers. A pair of Japanese pilots eyeballed them on their return flight to Rabaul and decided to put another notch in their belts by downing the giant bird. The first plane whizzed by the B-17 and strafed the left wing with cannon fire. *So fast,* thought Jason. He swiveled to match their pace. He pulled the trigger, and the tracers flew weakly past the speeding plane. The Zeros worked into a cloud and reformed their attack. The pilot put the B-17 into a dive and tried to avoid the oncoming blitz. The Zeros raced in from behind them, and Jason could see the tracers whizzing by under his feet. The pilot banked hard to the left and exposed Jason to the Zeros. As the Zeros banked, he fired the cannon. The Zero pilot jerked in his seat as bullets riddled him. Jason sat frozen. The Zero with the dead pilot had not lost momentum and was flying on a collision course with the bottom of the B-17 and his turret. Jason's pilot banked drastically, and the Zero drifted to the sea. It carried the bloody pilot with it. The other pilot ceased his attack and headed to Rabaul. The pilot righted the B-17 and set a course for Australia. Jason exhaled and thanked his lucky picture of new Hollywood starlet Lana Turner.

Egan Paal walked the decks of the *Enterprise* as the crews polished the flight deck. Fire teams repaired their equipment, and the mechanics checked every screw on every plane. Egan thought the planes looked funny with their wings folded to make space. Maybe he would fly one day. He stretched his arms into the air and took a deep breath of salty air as the ship lurched in the waves. The warm night breeze suggested it would be another hot day on the equator. Radar fans circled, and the American flag rustled at the top of the mast. He thought about the admiral's overwhelming responsibilities. To destroy or be destroyed must weigh on his soul every night. He needed courage to send people into the air knowing many would die. He thought of the people around him. They were scared but found incredible courage during battle. They pulled together every day to make this floating city work. Egan marveled at the human spirit and chastised himself for being fatalistic at times. He made a vow to be more positive. He was a natural leader, and the others looked up to him. Egan bowed his head and said a quick prayer. He thought of his sister, Veronica, and her silly demeanor. He thought of his father and how wonderful a life they all shared. Egan thought of his tortured mother. She was too smart for her own good. If she'd just relax, she would be fine. She worried too much. She overanalyzed everything. *Calm down. Everything is going to be all right,* Egan thought.

The omnipresent Klaxons shrieked again. Jason was exhausted but hustled into his uniform and hit the tarmac for the tenth day in a row. The B-17 rose into the air, and Jason looked down through the turret at the familiar landmarks twenty-five thousand feet below. The brown edges of Australia contrasted with the cool blue waters of the Torres Strait. The lush green forests of New Guinea looked like a caterpillar from high in the air. The northern shores of New Guinea were near the banana-shaped island of New Britain. Jason knew these nooks and crannies from the air but not the horrors perpetrated in the jungles below.

Egan looked at the plain ham sandwich. They had enjoyed quite a few of these delicious plain ham sandwiches recently. He thought about his time alone on the deck and decided to relish the plain ham sandwich.

"Some of the boys are getting together a game tonight," said one of the sailors. He chewed with his mouth open.

"I'm in," Egan responded after an exaggerated attempt to speak after he had swallowed his food.

"Good. That makes almost two tables. Someone's going to make a little dough tonight."

The ham and bread slathered with mayonnaise moved in and out of the man's mouth as he worked his tongue around the food and his words. Egan wondered if the pimple-faced boy from Tennessee would be there. He wanted to get some of his money back.

Egan's CO walked by and looked at the young gunner. "We'll probably see some action today. Egan, you ready?"

"Yes, sir."

"We're ready for them. I can tell. There's a good atmosphere on the ship. The Japs better watch their step." He smiled and made Egan feel comfortable. "You'll probably be right back on that flight deck with a few more medals."

That made Egan proud.

"Fellas! I think I see fish in the water. Fellas! There are a whole lot of ships down there," Jason told the pilots. He was close to hyperventilating.

"Yes, sir! That's exactly what we're looking for," radioed the pilot. "Battle stations!"

The B-17s hovered over the Japanese fleet as the bomber focused his sight. The bomber calculated how long it would take the bombs to get there and where the ships would be when the bombs hit the water. He took into account the flying speed of the B-17. Moving targets just weren't any fun.

They loosed the bombs, and Jason watched as each giant black pill became smaller and smaller until invisible to the naked eye. Up so high Jason couldn't see the enormous geysers the bombs created on a miss. Hits, however, were easy to spot. The party of six B-17s blanketed the ocean with thousand-pound bombs. They released their full complement. The pilots veered and set return courses.

"Here come the Zeros," Jason said.

He had studied the pests and was starting to find the range. He downed a couple of the winged devils. The Zeros were in a particularly foul humor as they soared by the big bombers on their first strafing run. The Zeros focused on a single bomber and infested his airspace. The pilot put the plane in a dive. Jason unleashed cover fire to alleviate the pressure, but he had a terrible angle as his craft climbed. Black smoke poured out of the starboard number-two engine, and the Zeros raced out of the oily trail. It lacked climbing power and looked stalled in the rise. The Zeros stung its broadside. Jason watched his counterpart in the dying B-17 slump in the turret. His blood was splattered on the glass. The plane's port wing flew off into the sky like a berserk boomerang. The B-17 charged at five hundred miles an hour into the Bismarck Sea.

"Go! Go! Go!" the pilot yelled.

He tried to gain altitude as the Zeros swung their attention to Jason's craft. As Jason had studied the Zeros, the Japanese pilots had learned of the evasive techniques the American pilots used. The Japanese anticipated the dive and subsequent bank—taught as the corkscrew maneuver. The plane dived and twisted. Jason fought off the Zeros, and his finger cramped from squeezing the cannon trigger. The pilot rolled the plane back to starboard. Jason could see the smoke from their port number-one engine puffing by him. At first it was in whiffs and then in massive quantities that obstructed his view of the raging Zeros. Jason kept firing and hoped to get a lucky shot. Divine intervention arrived as four Avengers launched from the *Enterprise* raged into the assault. They caught one Zero by surprise and exploded it as it came in for the kill on Jason's B-17. Jason let out a triumphant yell as the Avengers drew the fire away from the staggered bomber. Jason watched the Zeros tangle with the Avengers for only a moment. Their frenzied fight took them out of view. Jason felt blessed and thankful he hadn't suffered the same fate as his brother's in arms. Smoke continued to billow from port engine number one. The pilot had shut it down. Jason climbed up from the turret to check the plane's status.

"That was close," Jason said to announce his presence in the cabin.

"A little too close."

Jason looked at the pilots going through their checklists. Lights flashed over the control panel. Jason returned to the fuselage. The rest of the crew attended to Colson. He had taken a bullet in the shoulder.

"You did some nice decorating," Jason said to the aching Colson, and he pointed out the bullet holes in the side of the plane that let the light stream in.

"You like that? I might open my own business when I get back to the States." Colson smiled at Jason. He was thankful he had cut the tension.

Pryor helped Colson to a seat and got him comfortable. "He's going to be fine. The bullet went right through. As long as he keeps pressure on the wound, he won't bleed too much."

"How are things up front?" Simpson asked Jason.

"They're pretty busy. One engine's out, and they're working on saving another." Jason tried to reassure the others.

"What other engine?" Johnson asked.

Jason had hoped to avoid this line of questioning, but he had to be straight with them. "Lee and Devane are working on port engine number two."

"We lost port number one," stated Rumbley. He was doing the math in his head.

"He's telling us we might lose both portside engines." Cooper had studied harder in high school.

Baglin slammed his hands against the metal walls of the faltering craft.

"They're doing their best, fellas. They've taken us here and back too many times to lose confidence now."

"They have to crash it in the ocean," said Baglin. He was getting ahead of himself.

"We're not going to crash in the ocean, Baglin. Lee and Devane will get it working." Simpson wanted everybody to remain calm. Colson looked concerned. His shoulder was killing him. He'd be lucky to survive a crash landing. They heard a dull silence. Lee emerged from the cabin. "I need everybody to strap themselves in. We've lost our portside engines. We're trying to keep even with the starboard engines. Fellas, we're going to hit the water pretty hard. Make sure you have your life jackets on."

They could hear Devane on the radio shouting, "Mayday. Mayday."

Lee shut the cabin door. Jason looked in the eyes of the others. They were scared. He was scared as well. He was terrified. He put the bright-yellow life jacket around his neck. It was known as a Mae West. Simpson made sure everyone was tied in. The plane seemed to be gliding.

"This flight is smooth. All the flights should be so relaxing." Jason's calming techniques weren't nearly as effective.

They couldn't see ahead of them. When they looked down through the turret, though, the ocean was coming nearer. Jason noticed the whitecaps of the waves. It wouldn't be long.

"Make sure you have access to your belts. You are going to need to remove them as quickly as possible once the plane settles in the ocean."

If the plane settles in the ocean, thought Rumbley. *It might just crack up and go down.*

Devane swung open the cabin door, and everyone winced into the bright light. The waves looked like the blue flames of an eternal fire. "Hold on."

Devane shut the door. The plane slammed into the waves. The impact jarred their heads and tailbones. Then there was a moment of complete calm as they skipped over the walls of water like a rock on a pond. The plane spun wildly as the starboard wing caught the tip of a wave. Jason heard the roaring engines sucking in the ocean and coughing it out with incredible speed. The fuselage split open and sucked Rumbley and Cooper into the air. Jason's face hit the water, and he struggled to catch his breath. Two halves of the plane drifted apart, and Jason could see the front end of the plane. The cabin stuck straight in the air. Devane slumped over the controls of the craft. He was dead. Lee struggled to remove his seat belt as the ocean gurgled into the cabin. Jason swam and helped Lee, but it was too late. The nose slipped under the surf and took the pilots with it. He looked toward the fuselage. Colson was having trouble with his belt. The tail was sinking fast. He swam to Colson. He reached the man's waist and unhinged the clasp. Colson couldn't move his arm, but he floated harmlessly away from the tail as it plunged to the bottom.

Jason took inventory. He looked for Pryor and couldn't see him. He saw Baglin kicking toward Colson to lend the injured man a hand. At least three of them were alive. He rose with a swell and saw the life jackets of Cooper and Rumbley in the distance.

The third yellow dot befuddled Jason. He swam to the flyer. He saw the jacket, but the soldier faced the water. Jason moved his arms and rose up and down in the rolling waves. He grabbed the man by the legs and pulled him toward him. *Be alive!* Jason screamed internally. He rolled Simpson over. His face had been bloodied on impact. He hadn't survived. Jason held him for a moment and then released him to the sea. The cumbersome life jacket had saved his life, but it made swimming against the tide a struggle. Jason kicked back to Colson and Baglin. He heard screaming from the top of the swells and saw Pryor waving his hands. There were four. They tossed about in the warm waters of the strait. Pryor released the dye marker into the water and prayed the floatplane would find them before the sun went down.

Egan watched the Avengers leave the decks of the *Enterprise*. He knew it wouldn't be long. He couldn't decide what was more agonizing. Staying below and listening to the action was terrifying. He couldn't do anything, and he didn't want to be caught below with a thousand-pound bomb ripping through the flight deck. On the other hand, being in the action was no picnic either. *Pick your poison,* thought Egan.

He waited with the other people in his crew for the call as the Zeros began their attack from the clouds. The enemy's ten fighters and twenty-seven Vals had launched from Admiral Nagumo's twin carriers *Shokaku* and *Zuikaku* in a desperate mood for revenge. The Americans had found the light carrier *Ryujo* and exploded it like a Roman candle. A small complement of fighters secured Admiral Fletcher, who committed the bulk of his air support to sinking the *Ryujo*. The *Enterprise* stood guard with the few Wildcats in the air and gun support from the battleship *North Carolina*. The Zeros flew straight into the waiting Wildcats, and the American pilots took the bait. Desperate to rid the *Enterprise* of the Zeros' threat, the Wildcats chased them away from the battle zone and opened the door for the dive bombers to enter.

The vulnerable *Enterprise* was naked in the water—an open target for the deadly Vals. The first bomb cut through the flight deck and rocked the ship. It hurled Egan to the metal deck and split his lip. Terror reigned as crews rushed to squelch the raging fires. Another explosion, however, blasted them off-balance. Egan worked to get out from the lower decks and help the gunners upstairs. He climbed the ladders, and a furnace of heat greeted him. Fires raged across the deck. He skirted the flames and made his way to the turrets. A sailor lay on the ground. Blood poured from his mouth, and crimson covered his chest from the cannon fire of the dive bombers. It was the pimple-faced boy from Tennessee. Fury shot through Egan's veins, and he hurled the new gunner out of the turret and started blasting the sky.

Egan looked at the giant clouds stretching their mushroom tips to the ends of the canopy. *They will come from there,* Egan thought. He waited and watched as the Vals dropped from the clouds, screamed to ten thousand feet, leveled off, and raced directly over the *Enterprise*. He loosed the cannon and hoped to catch the Vals before they positioned over the carrier. He raised the gun to the sky. A Val started its dive. Egan had to hit it before it dropped the bomb. He was too late. The bomb drifted from the plane, and the Val pulled out. Egan's world went into slow motion. He turned the gun and fired. The tracers of his cannon locked onto the Val's wing. The *Enterprise* rumbled from the weight of the erupting bomb. The fireball of the wing crashed upon his turret, and the thousand-degree metal of the wing seared his face and punctured his chest. The crew ran to extinguish the flames and remove Egan from the turret. They placed him next to the pimple-faced boy from Tennessee.

The sun set in the Torres Strait.

"I hear a plane." Jason looked upwards.

The other water-soaked survivors held up their weary heads and looked at the darkening sky. The PBY circled their position and began its landing approach on the calming seas.

"We made it!" screamed Jason as the adrenaline kicked in, and the men laughed at their luck.

The plane touched the waves and motored closer to the floating castaways.

"Johnson," Colson screamed at the sight of Johnson's face.

The pilots helped Colson into the plane, and Pryor took his turn to safety next. Jason helped Baglin onto the float. Jason grabbed Baglin's hand and crawled his way onto the rescue flight. The soaked life jacket and clothes weighed him down.

"Johnson, it's good to see you." Baglin smiled.

The men sighed relief as the captain welcomed them aboard. "What happened to Lee and Devane?" Johnson asked.

"They got trapped in the cockpit. They both went down with the plane." Jason spared him the details of Lee struggling with his belt and being sucked into the vortex alive.

"And Simpson?"

"Didn't make it. He died on impact."

There was a pause. "How about Rumbley and Cooper?"

Jason looked shaken. He relived the grotesque horror of finding the upper torso of each man floating in the water after being sheared in half by the B-17's propeller.

Egan's CO was right. Egan made it to the flight deck of the *Enterprise* to be honored again. An American flag draped over the casket as the sailors gathered with the carrier chaplain to perform the funeral service. The *Enterprise* stung from the Val's bites as crews repaired the massive damage to the ship. The *Saratoga* had suffered far worse. Torpedoes had entered its hull and forced it to retreat to the security of a dry dock and months of repair.

The *Enterprise* did not get the luxury of a dry dock. It maintained its patrol of the Solomon Islands with the *Wasp*, which had been struggling for months to protect Guadalcanal and the larger island of New Guinea. The chaplain gave his blessing to the dead sailor, Egan Paal, as his fellow sailors interred him to the brine.

September 1942, Washington State

Dan B. Kerichuck hated the aggravation of physical therapy. He became frustrated, and his temper flared. He never directed the anger at the nurse but was maddened he couldn't use his hands. He couldn't pick up a pencil or hold a glass of water. He couldn't tie his shoes or button his shirt. The doctors noted improvement, but Dan couldn't tell. He just wanted to be able to brush his teeth by himself.

"Hi, Boris."

Dan smiled. His brother, Michael, had started calling him Boris Karloff after his role in *Frankenstein*. Dan didn't mind. He didn't care what he looked like. He just wanted his fingers to work. Dolores walked in behind Michael as his mother, Mary Pat, chatted with Dr. Morris. Dolores had visited Dan every day since the accident. She had been arriving in the afternoon since the fall semester had started. Dan thought about Stanford and the guys on the practice field. He could have played as a freshman. Most freshmen didn't get the opportunity to play at all. Dan thought he could have started.

"Hi, Dan." Mary Pat fluffed the blanket. "Dr. Morris says you can go home soon."

She beamed and opened a brown bag filled with homemade Toll House cookies. Dan wondered if he could reach into the bag and grab one. Dolores observed the test. Dan reached his tender fingers toward the table. His fingertips trembled from the nerve damage. He had tremendous difficulty putting the thumb and index finger together. The thumb could reach all the weak fingers on his hand, but he couldn't feel what he touched. He nudged the cookie with his thumb and slid it toward his waiting forefinger. He felt like a monkey. He raised the cookie slightly off the table and weakly dropped it back. The cookie crumbled. Temper filled Dan's face.

"It's OK, Dan. You're getting better."

Dan began to cry. "I can't even pick up a cookie."

This was the first time his family had seen him cry. He had cried through the night plenty of times, though.

"You're going to be just fine. It's just going to take some more time…and work." She kissed his forehead.

"What am I going to do, Mom?" Dan sobbed in the chair.

"Dan B. Kerichuck, stop this whining." Insisted Dolores.

Dan thought Dolores sounded just like Mom. "What do you know, Dolores? You're not crippled. You can pick up anything you want. I can't!" Dan raised his voice and the brows of the hospital staff.

"You can do it, Dan. You can do anything you want. You just have to put your mind to it."

"Easy for you to say." Dan's look said he was tempted to punch the windowpane, but the extended hospital stay had shed weight from his tree trunk frame.

"You can do this or pout the rest of your life. This isn't the Dan I know." Dolores acted tough but couldn't hold the motherly facade. She cried into the palms of her hands.

Michael took the cookie off the table and took a big, delicious bite. This broke the tension.

Mary Pat brought the real mother back into the conversation. "Dan, you've come a long way, but it's going to take some more time. It's going to happen. It's just going to take more work. You're not a quitter. We haven't quit on you. Don't quit on yourself." Dan looked into his mother's eyes. "I'm going to leave this cookie on the table." She pulled another tempting Toll House treat from the bag. "You can use this to practice tonight. Maybe you'll get the prize."

Dan looked at his mother and smiled. She knew he'd never quit. Dan smiled at Dolores and was thankful for her love. Michael reached into the bag of cookies, and his mother smacked his hand gently. "Not before dinner."

Mississippi

Elroy E. Lemons wore number twenty-eight and did little more than shuffle the plays in and out to the quarterback. The five-foot-six 135-pounder was a human target. The Oak Vale Tigers needed four yards to beat the cross-county rival Prentiss Dragons. Four lousy yards would end three years of off-season verbal abuse by the high-and-mighty Dragons of the neighboring county. At the soda shop and movie theater, the Dragons wore their letter-man jackets with pride. They were the kings of high-school foot-ball. Raytel and Caleb Kigmenis, the twin brothers, manned the left side of the Tiger offensive line. Both breathed hard from ex-citement—not fatigue. All those hot, humid Mississippi August afternoons had turned to hot October afternoons. The two teams clashed in an mid-season rivalry game that would result in the Southern Mississippi Negro title. At six foot three and 240 pounds, both Caleb and Raytel were quiet giants. They thought the same thing at the same time. "Give the ball to Duncan. Let him follow us into the end zone," Raytel spoke in the huddle. "Three dive, left, on two."

It was the right play. Coach knew what he was doing. The backs lined up behind Cyrus, the quarterback, in the T formation. Duncan, the three back, would take the ball from Cyrus and follow Demetrius into the line behind Raytel and Caleb. Raytel was playing guard, and he instinctively felt quarterback Cyrus tuck his hands under center. He didn't need to look at his twin playing tackle. The defense shifted to the left side where the play was going. It didn't matter. *This is decided. Right here. Right now,* thought Raytel. The defense got low and prepared for the snap.

"Hut! Hut!" Cyrus called.

He handed the ball to Duncan, who scampered into the end zone untouched as time expired. The game was over. Raytel and Caleb had blown the hole wide-open and waited for Duncan in the end zone. The team rushed the field and mobbed Duncan. The Dragons' coach walked up to the twins and extended his hand. "Congratulations, boys."

"Thank you, Coach," they said in unison.

"It's too bad the big colleges only let white boys play football." Raytel and Caleb looked at the coach. They were slightly bewildered. "You boys would certainly show them a thing or two."

The twins smiled. "Thank you, Coach."

They appreciated the praise, but they would never play at Ole Miss.

Jeremiah and Mabel Kigmenis both were born in 1907. They married when they were eighteen and started a family right away. Caleb and Raytel surprised the Kigmenises by arriving together. Jeremiah carved out a piece of farmland with two more mouths to feed. *That's a lot more cotton and tobacco,* thought Jeremiah at the time. He and Mabel worked harder, and the children kept coming. Joe was born in 1928. Mabel wanted a girl, so Jeremiah gave her Teresa in 1929, Violet in 1930, and Angela in 1931. Mabel had more children than arms and legs. Then came June in the summer of 1933. Oscar followed in 1937, Celeste in 1938, and Carter in 1939. George joined the Kigmenis family in 1941, and Mabel knew she was pregnant with another girl. She was so excited. She had picked out the pretty name of Carmen. Jeremiah wished his farm were as fertile as his wife.

Raytel and Caleb could hear the fussing at the dinner table before they had even hit the porch.

"The black man does not have to fight in the white man's war. We've got our own war to fight right here."

"The black man should have a right to fight for his country," said Angela. She was wise beyond her ten years.

"The black man should have all the rights white people do," Violet added.

"That's right," confirmed Angela.

"You know Mama doesn't like all this talk at the dinner table." They welcomed the sweaty giants returning from the game.

"Did you win?" Oscar asked as he finished his chores.

Caleb and Raytel pursed their lips sadly but then broke into big, wide grins. "We beat the Dragons!"

The house shook as the boys received hugs from the family.

"What's all this racket?" Jeremiah entered the room and snagged the attention.

"The Tigers beat the Dragons today, Daddy." Oscar admired his big, big brothers. He hoped he could be that big someday.

"They did?" He picked up Oscar and gave him a bear hug. The pride gleamed in his eye. "I'm real proud of you boys. I know how hard you've worked for this." This was big praise from a farmer who didn't shovel big praise. "Well, what's for dinner? I'm hungry." Jeremiah tickled Oscar under the arm.

Mabel poked her head out of the kitchen. She spent most of her day cooking for the masses. "Well, since the Tigers beat the Dragons..." Another cheered filled the house. "We're having three-cheese macaroni with fresh ham and rosemary pear marinade." Mouths drooled as Raytel and Caleb hurried to clean up. Mabel further tempted the boys. "With pear chutney and cucumber salad, rutabaga and potato puree, and hotcakes on the side." She smiled at the children. "And if you help Mama with the dishes, there's citrus meringue pie for dessert."

Raytel and Caleb felt sore, but dinner was on the table, and they still had evening chores to do in the barn. Jeremiah still put them to work. The twins replayed the game. They knew they had accomplished something special in their senior year. No one could take this away from them.

"Good. You boys are here. Now we can eat," Jeremiah said.

He had been in the field since the sun had given him enough light to see where he was walking. It had been that way his whole life. Caleb and Raytel would be the first family members to graduate from high school, and they could help him expand his farm. The war had him supplying crops for the military. He struggled to keep pace. *That sure is different from a few years ago,* thought Jeremiah. A few years ago, he didn't think the Kigmenis family was going to make it. He was worried the bank would take the farm. Times were better now—at least on the farm anyway. The war put a couple extra coins in his pocket, but he was worried the draft would come after his twins. *What is everybody fighting over anyway?* Jeremiah wondered.

The Kigmenis family joined hands and prayed. Jeremiah thanked God for the beautiful ham and his beautiful, pregnant again wife. *Ham. That is the future of this farm,* he thought. If everybody tasted Mabel's fresh ham with rosemary pear marinade, they'd all eat pork, and he would be a rich man.

The Solomon Islands

The prickly Americans made a disaster of Yamamoto's well-laid plans. Guadalcanal was a mess, and he faced the difficult decision of whether to deplete his advancing forces in the Owen Stanley Range on New Guinea and move them down the Slot to fight the Americans at Guadalcanal. The Japanese had overwhelmed the Australians at the mountain town of Insurava like ants on a fallen picnic hot dog.

Upon hiking a few more miles to the crest, the Nippon forces split their attack down the mountain, crushed both Kapa Kapa and Ioribaiwa, and waited to sink their teeth into the capital, Port Moresby. Yamamoto knew action would have to be delayed. The losses had started to mount as the Australians had repelled an invasion at the tip of the Papuan Peninsula at Milne Bay, and the Americans made mincemeat of his supply line over the Owen Stanley Range. His soldiers were starving and sick in the jungle and running out of bullets. He radioed General Horii and told him to regroup at Buna and back over the torturous trail they had just spent weeks carving through the mountain. What had seemed an opportunity to punt the Americans out of the Solomon Islands had now turned into a multiple-month mud fight in the wilderness of Guadalcanal.

October 1942

Admiral William "Bull" Halsey returned from the disabled list and was put in charge of all the South Pacific forces. He transitioned right out of the frying pan and into the fire and had to react to the festering problem of the Solomon Islands. The *Hornet*, with the battleship *Washington* by its side, reunited with the *Enterprise* and its new companion, the battleship *South Dakota*.

Admiral Nagumo was at the helm of Yamamoto's grand fleet, and he engaged the Americans in a game of ghost fleet. Neither large group of naval vessels could find the other in the shrinking Coral Sea. Halsey ordered Admiral Thomas Kinkaid to launch a strike at dawn and find the enemy. They found them. Dive bomb-ers radioed they had uncovered three of the Japanese carriers. The sirens blared through the region as the *Enterprise* and *Hornet* set battle stations. The alarm sounded in faraway Port Moresby, and the B-17 crews of the Fifth Army jumped into the fray.

Jason Cenode was still shaken from his afternoon swim in the Torres Strait, but he climbed back into another plane headed into harm's way. The B-17s grouped together after takeoff and fell into standard flight formation. Jason looked at the other turret gun-ners through the glass and gave them a thumbs-up. He wondered who was going to die today. The pilot maintained his altitude, and Jason replaced his lucky picture of Lana Turner with the lovely Rita Hayworth.

The Dauntless dive bombers crashed through a cloud bank at the unwitting light carrier *Zuiho*. Zeros raced from the flight deck to greet the American messengers. Five-hundred-pound bombs were hitched under the planes. Dauntless bombers deliv-ered their payloads and punctured the *Zuiho*'s landing area. The blazing *Zuiho* retreated from the fight and left the Zeros to find the *Shokaku* or the *Zuikaku*.

Nagumo found the American carrier *Hornet*. The brave ship was under brutal assault from the Vals after the *Enterprise* hung it out to dry by slipping into the cover of a squall. Straight down from the sky the screaming Vals came. Antiaircraft fire from the *Hornet* peppered the sky as the crazed banzai warriors ripped through the flak. An alert gunner on the *Hornet* crippled a Val. The *Hornet* rumbled as the Val pilot turned his craft into a hur-tling bomb and sent it through the flight deck. Kates were com-ing low and took advantage of the commotion. They popped the *Hornet* with two torpedoes below and three bombs on the deck. The smoke from the *Hornet* rose for miles across the blue sky.

High in the air, Jason had a front-row seat to the spectacle waged over the *Shokaku* and *Zuikaku*. The small fighters were like hundreds of electrons as they chased one another around the carriers. The B-17s concentrated their armaments on the surrounding battleships and cruisers. The bombs created towering splashes until the trail landed on the end of a Japanese destroyer. The bombardiers celebrated after scoring this elusive hit. He watched a half-dozen thousand-pound bombs, courtesy of the *Hornet*'s planes, clobber the *Shokaku*. The pilots were unaware they now had no place to land. The battered *Shokaku* left the region for repairs.

The plane banked hard in return flight. Jason surveyed the fighters battling the Zeros. He was engrossed in the sadness of their plight. Little specks of orange popped in the sky. Each one meant more lives taken. He felt sorrow for the pilots but was thankful they had kept them off his tail. The plane flew unobstructed away from the conflict. Jason saw smoke rising on the faraway horizon. Their return path took them near the action over the American carriers. He was morbidly curious and wanted to see what was going on.

The B-17 raced closer to the fight. High in the clouds, battles raged over the American carriers. As one of the ships burned, the other swatted at the predators. The larger carrier was the *Enterprise*. The other carrier had to be the *Hornet*. Jason felt ill. He had come to know the fine crew on the *Hornet*. He recalled the blustery April morning off the coast of Japan and the energized crew cheering the squadron off to its mission. They were proud men. He sensed the ship had received a terrible blow and prayed the crew would make it off the crippled ship alive.

November 1942, Madison, Wisconsin

Friends and family celebrating the life of Egan Paal filled the church. Quincy's status brought out the city's elite. Lois suffered a breakdown and postponed the service for months. Doctors weaned her off the booze, but Lois became crafty at stowing away prescription sedatives. She saved them for the occasion and dipped heavily into her stash.

The colors of the church swirled in Lois's personal kaleidoscope. Veronica held her father's hand, and Quincy provided his arm to Lois, who used it as a crutch. There was no coffin. There was no body. A simple American flag adorned the altar. The pastor spoke of the sailor's bravery, and Egan's friend Grant tearfully recalled Egan's highlights from high-school football. Worshippers were invited to the Paal house for a reception. Before leaving the church, Quincy shook every hand and thanked them all for their support. Veronica stayed close to her father. Lois could only mumble thank you and offer a limp handshake. In the back pew, Gretchen could not bring herself to tell the Paals she had known Egan for one special night. They'd never believe her. She wasn't from their part of town.

Chicago, Illinois
Nothing changed the somber mood at the Alesse home. The US Army could not or would not share information about Gary. He was listed as missing in action. Donna and Annette found comfort in each other and sharing their love for Gary. Peter became a therapeutic distraction to Grandmom Donna. Peter looked just like Gary as a baby. Annette's world turned upside down. About to turn nineteen, she had forsaken college for motherhood. She had traded education for poopy diapers and the croup, and six months after high school, she was a widow. Larry consoled her and offered to let Annette stay at the Alesse house forever.

Boston, Massachusetts
Dominic sat in the front seat of the car while his boss received special attention from the female staff at the Beacon Club. He

checked his roll and noted there was plenty for the craps game in the basement. He removed the brown paper from around the neck of his pint of Jack Daniels and unscrewed the cap. He put the bottle to his mouth and took a healthy snort. It burned in a good way. The streets of Boston were cold at night, and the boss would be going home to his wife and kids after this stop. He knew he could crash at Dante's apartment, but his nag wife was tired of seeing him on the couch when she got up in the morning. He could hit up Irish Ian. He hadn't done that in a while. The dive hotels were cheap, but it added up night after night, and he didn't like dealing with the whores. They always wanted to move in on his room and stay warm for the night. Dominic knew he'd figure it out one way or the other. He just didn't want to sleep in the boss's car again. The Boston streets were cold at night.

New York City

Ronald and Kay watched the New York City crews put up the Christmas lights. Everybody in the States buckled down as inflation made things expensive and countrywide rationing was implemented. Kay could not believe it was already Thanksgiving—another one without Rat. Most likely it would be another Christmas too. It used to be the best time of the year. Now she felt the depression of the holidays. They window-shopped at Macy's. She darted in the door and told Ronald she would be right back. Ronald spied the towering Empire State Building rising into the darkness and the Chrysler Building racing it to the stars. Kay returned with a shopping bag on her arm.

"What did you get, Kay?" Ronald asked, and the wind whipped around the corner.

"I got Rat a scarf. It will keep him warm when he gets home for Christmas. I don't want him to catch a cold."

Ronald put his arm around his determined wife, and they walked the streets of New York City.

St. Louis, Missouri

Lily rang the bell as if her life depended on it. She shouted to the passersby to donate money to the Salvation Army.

"Lily? May I have a word with you?" asked Randall, the local coordinator for the Salvation Army.

"Hi, Randall. Would you like to donate some money to the Salvation Army?" Randall did not smile. "Might as well ask, huh?" said Lily. "Everybody's got to pitch in. Right?"

"Yes, Lily. It would be great if everyone pitched in," he said. "That's what I want to talk to you about."

"OK." Lily didn't know where this was going.

"The people who walk by on the street don't have to pitch in."

"Well, sure they do. Our troops need their help."

"Yes. They do, Lily." Randall struggled to broach the subject. She was vibrant to the point of being psychotic, and she was a big girl. "We've had complaints."

"Complaints about what?" Lily asked.

"Complaints you might be too aggressive with the shoppers."

"Aggressive. I thought that was why you put me out here. I've seen the other bell ringers. They sit on their butts and drink coffee. They're not trying very hard. In fact they're a little lazy, if you know what I mean." Lily winked at Randall.

"I would agree some are..." He searched for the word. "Passive." He was going to have to blurt it out. "Some people said they are scared of you. They feel as if you are forcing them to put money into the pot." Lily looked skyward to avoid eye contact. "Is this true?"

"I've nudged some people in the right direction." Lily smiled proudly.

"You can't do that, Lily." Randall finally looked her straight in the eyes.

"So you're telling me I can't ask people to do everything they can to help the American soldiers fighting for our safety.

You're telling me the few extra pennies in their pockets, which could send a lifesaving meal to a soldier abroad, I can't ask for that? My husband's over there somewhere, Randall. One of these care packages might make it to him. If you are telling me I can't do everything I can to help my husband's well-being, I can't do that."

Lily took off her Santa hat, shoved the bell into Randall's gut, and walked off down the streets of Saint Louis.

Mississippi

Raytel and Caleb were preoccupied with the entire family attending the game—their last high-school game. Raytel saw Joe sitting next to Jeremiah and Mabel. Mabel was holding the new baby. Carmen held little baby George. Caleb pointed out Teresa, Violet, Angela, and June. They looked for the little ones and found Oscar, Celeste, and Carter running around the end zone with other kids their age. The Tigers controlled the lopsided game 28–0 and had all but sewed up the title.

The Mavericks punted, and the Kigmenis boys grabbed their leather helmets and headed onto the field. They got to the huddle, and two junior offensive linemen came running into the huddle with them.

"What are you guys doing out here?" Raytel growled at the underclassmen.

One looked wide-eyed up at the hulking senior. "Coach told us to come in. You and Caleb are out."

Raytel and Caleb wondered how they had made Coach angry. They hadn't missed one play since they were freshmen. Maybe they had been looking in the crowd too much, and he was making an example of them.

The boys turned and hustled across the field. They kept their eyes to the ground and expected Coach's formidable snarl. The Kigmenis boys wondered why everyone cheered. They looked around the field and were surprised the crowd was applauding them on their last football game.

Pittsburgh, Pennsylvania

Paige walked down the street to the Joint household. She remembered the happy moments that kept her going. She had dressed Sarah up as a black cat on Halloween and taken her around in her chair trick-or-treating. She had dressed up like a scarecrow and had enjoyed not being herself for a while. She had learned to escape through reading, and she had finished *Gone with the Wind*. Scarlett troubled her. She could never reconcile how she wavered between her two lovers. For Paige there was only Shaun. She twisted the locket and slid it around her tender neck. If she had to love again, she wondered if it would be the same or like Scarlett's love for Ashley—safe. Paige started writing poetry. Sylvia Plath fascinated her. She aspired to her level but trashed the poems. Paige was unaccustomed to seeing her deep thoughts on paper. Paige walked down the street to the Joint household and struggled to find herself without Shaun.

Riverside, California

Julie Cenode held the three babies with no names. They hadn't come with diapers, food, or rattles. She had lobbied to care for one little baby, but it seemed the servicemen traveling in and out of the Riverside area had been in and out of a few of the young girls and left them with limited options. The regional hospital happily handed the adopted children to the well-recommended Julie. *Their loss, my gain,* thought Julie. She gave them names and hope.

She raised little Maureen's legs and wiped the icky green mess off her smelly butt. Tommy shot a rainbow across the crib and smiled as he did it. Now she had to change the sheets in the crib. *Great!* Ingrid sucked her thumb but played with a diaper pin in her other hand. *Let's get that out of there.* She couldn't wait for Jason to see her new brood. It was time to fix their bottles and rock the three to sleep. She had built a crib that held all three, and she could sit beside it and rock them at the same time. She wanted to do some drawings of silly giraffes and tigers on the wall and wondered if she'd start that project tonight.

Commerce, Oklahoma

Ida never thought of having company for Thanksgiving. In the past the holidays had been the worst time of year. Doyle would drink every night as the sun went down. Thanksgiving supper had been at Inez's house until the year Doyle got so drunk Jimmy told him he wasn't allowed in the house anymore. It had been the first time Carl tried to wrestle Doyle. Doyle beat Carl until he begged for mercy. Ida forgave but never forgot.

Jimmy Jr. and Bud ran around the house the way seven- and four-year-old boys did. Doyle's rifles fascinated them, and he took them out back and let Jimmy Jr. shoot a couple cans off a post. Inez couldn't figure the changes in Doyle. She had seen Ida take too many beatings. She would never trust the man again and was only cordial to him at best. Jimmy listened to the radio and the news of the war. Ida couldn't bear to listen to any more bad news. She took the cleaver and hacked off the drumstick. The skin was browned to perfection. That was Carl's favorite part of the turkey.

El Paso, Texas

Ernesto had been a friend of the Droad family for years. He got Anna a babysitter for the night and showed her some of the sights of El Paso. Anna knew the sights, but she was excited to get out of the house. They shared glasses of sangria and walked by the storefronts. "Anna, I had a wonderful time tonight." He looked at her fondly.

"Me too, Ernesto. Thanks for taking me out. I really needed that." She smiled. The comfort of a friend was good to have around the holidays.

"Maybe we could do this again next Friday. What do you think? There's a new restaurant I think you would like."

"I don't know, Ernesto. I've got to watch the boys."

"I'll get the babysitter again."

"Nobody's got that much money to spare, Ernesto. Bring your sister, Juanita, and I'll make you both dinner." She smiled, but Ernesto didn't seem all that interested. "What's the matter?"

"I don't want to bring my sister. I like being alone with you." The change of dynamics hit her as if she was a piñata.

"Ernesto, it's not that way. I love my husband." She averted her eyes.

"Anna, you have to accept your husband is dead."

Anna's eyes raged. "Manny is alive. Alive in my heart and soul. Until they bring his dead body to me and lay him at my feet."

Anna turned, walked away, and jumped into the first cab she saw.

Washington State

Mary Pat lumped an oversize portion of stuffing onto Dan's plate. Dan picked up the gravy and slathered the plate with the fatty delight. Michael thought Dan was going to try to eat all of Mount Rainer. Dan had mastered the use of utensils and was making the most of it. Dolores watched in glee as her brother replaced the weight he had lost at the hospital one scoop at a time.

Michael pleaded with his mother. "I don't like peas."

"You have to eat a few peas. They're good for you."

Mary Pat hated peas too and would eat exactly the portion required for Michael to eat. That was what good mothers did.

"The turkey's great, Mom." Dan lumped a huge combination serving into his mouth.

"Dr. Morris said he would help me get a spot as a candy striper at the hospital," Dolores announced proudly.

"That's because she is in love with Dr. Morris," Dan said through the dam of food in his mouth and the mangled lips.

Things were back to normal at the Kerichuck household. Dolores shot him a look that would slay an ordinary man.

"I don't want afternoons at the hospital to affect your school-work, young lady." Ken looked at his daughter and knew it wouldn't have the slightest effect on her schoolwork.

"It won't, Daddy. Dr. Morris…"

Michael made a kissy face, and everyone laughed.

Dolores's face looked like an apple. "Never mind!"

"I've got some news." Dan looked up long enough from chewing to address his parents.

His pronunciation suffered from the new shape of his mouth. The family paused to digest what Dan might have to say. He received the table's rapt attention. They were sure he was going to announce he would begin his studies at Stanford University in the second semester. Mary Pat looked proudly at her son. He had worked so hard to recover from the accident. The doctor said by next fall he would be strong enough to play football.

Dan swallowed his last bite and eyed the pumpkin pie. "I joined the US Navy."

Mary Pat wasn't sure she had heard correctly.

Christmas Day 1942, The Philippines, Camp O'Donnell

"Now, Rat, you're going to have to hold steady," Carl said.

He held Rat by the shoulders while Shaun held him around his waist. A makeshift fire was burning, and Manny held the pliers smuggled from the motor pool in the flames.

"You're going to cool those things off, aren't you?" Rat asked.

"Of course, Rat." Manny turned slowly and gave Rat his best Lon Chaney expression. Manny could always make Shaun laugh.

"Rat, you have to stop squirming." Carl looked at him sternly as the frail Rat summoned strength he thought long passed.

"You know, fellas, I'm just going to gut this one out. I'm sure the tooth will feel better tomorrow." Rat wanted no part of a tooth extracted by motor pool pliers.

"Rat," Shaun barked, "you have to lose the tooth. You have an infection, and it's going to spread."

Rat resigned himself to suffering the agony of prisoner-of-war dentistry.

"Besides," Carl added, "I'm sick and tired of hearing you complain about your tooth. You sound like my grandmother. 'My tooth aches. Oh, my tooth aches.'"

Rat hardly found it amusing. "Why can't the camp doctor do this?" He had asked this question about six hundred times, and the delay tactics were wearing thin.

"Because he doesn't know any more about dentistry than the man in the moon," Carl said. "He was too busy with the dying and diseased. He told us to find something to tweeze with. We checked. The pliers are fine."

"Well, who voted Manny to do it?"

"We did," they all shouted in unison.

"Now lay back." Manny instructed.

Manny removed the pliers from the fire and cooled them in the air. He waved them back and forth to speed the process, and he taunted Rat the whole time. He put his finger to the pliers and yanked it back—still too hot. They waited. Rat never moved his stare from the waving pliers. Manny touched them again. They were ready. He moved in to Rat's mouth.

"Carl, you have to slide over. You're in my light." Manny concentrated on the mouth. "This is my first tooth pull," Manny said for posterity. The men giggled as Rat squirmed. "Shaun, you're going to have to move so I can get the right angle." Manny pulled his knee up and over Rat's waist. He was now sitting in the patient's lap. "I think I have a good grip on it."

Rat screamed and pushed Manny back. "You've got the wrong one!" He glared at the first-day dentist. "It's the same molar but on the right side of my mouth."

"Your right or my right?"

"My right, you numskull."

Manny winked at Shaun. "You know, all these teeth kind of look alike."

Beads of sweat rolled down Rat's forehead.

"Towel." Manny looked at his newly deputized nurse, Carl. Carl looked. They didn't have any towels. They were prisoners of war. "Sponge?" Manny looked at Carl dead seriously, but Carl didn't fall for it this time.

Manny went in for the second time. He saw the very swollen and dark red area around the tooth. He poked at it gently with the pliers. "It's not very loose."

Rat heaved like a professional wrestler on a three count. They couldn't understand him because Manny's hands were in his mouth.

"Did you have to say that out loud?" Shaun said. He looked at Manny and told him to stop kidding around. They had tortured Rat enough. "Get it over with."

Manny didn't hesitate. He stuck the pliers in Rat's mouth and found a decent grip. He spun the tooth hard to the left and then swung it back forcefully to the right. The men gagged as they heard the cracking. He snapped it back left and then once again violently to the right. He yanked hard one time and held the tooth at eye level. "It's like opening a safe."

Rat held his mouth and screamed. Carl tried to shove some gauze into his bleeding jaw.

Manny went over to his pack after everybody had settled down. He reached in and pulled out six cans of verified US Army canned meat and vegetable rations. He tossed one to each of the men.

"I couldn't have made it this far without you guys. You have become my second family. Merry Christmas."

The men ate the meal as if it was prime rib roast and fresh green beans. It was the best meal they had eaten in eight months. Even Rat suffered joyously through every bite.

Cabanatuan

A crowd of people gathered in Chet and Norm's billet for an impromptu performance of *The Nutcracker*. It was terrible and excruciatingly funny, and everyone howled in approval at the clumsy dancers. The dancers were so painfully skinny their angular movements made them look more like marionettes. Nonetheless the entire group enjoyed the Christmas performance—even the soldier who literally died of laughter in the third row. There was no reprieve from the misery just because it was Christmas Day. A pair of soldiers removed the 105-pound man and took him to the infirmary for a burial in a mass grave located on the northern plains of Luzon. The prisoners resettled and mulled over their rice. The thought of more rice made them nauseated. A little variety on Christmas Day would have been nice.

"Ohio State is going to be the national champions in college football," Chet said.

He had been talking to a pair of soldiers working outside the camp on an engineering project for the Japanese. They had access to a radio and were able to pick up some armed forces news on the sly.

"Supposedly they have a heck of a new coach named Paul Brown," Chet continued.

"Really?" Norm asked. His interest was piqued. He hadn't thought of football in so long. Those were the days—the days when people could battle over their problems using strength, guile, and strategy without anyone dying. "How did Georgia Tech do?" he asked.

"The Ramblin' Wreck came in fifth in the final polls. Are you a big Georgia Tech fan? I thought you were from Boston."

"I am from Boston, but some coach from Georgia Tech wanted me to play football there."

"Why didn't you? You could have stayed out of this mess." Chet wondered why he hadn't. Running out onto a football field was the easiest, most fun thing in the whole world.

"I hung up my cleats after high school. I wanted to join the army and learn about communications." Norm rehashed his own past plans with doubt as they sat in the stench of Cabanatuan.

"Why communications? You didn't want to be in the field?" Chet asked. Norm had become his best friend, and he hoped he wasn't judging him.

"I think communications are going to be the next big thing in the business world." Chet looked curiously at Norm. "Do you ever go to the movies?"

"Sure."

"The newsreels they show before the films are going to be able to be sent into homes someday." Chet was baffled. "You are going to be able to sit in your living room and watch the news and other entertainment. It'll be just like radio but with moving pictures."

"So you're saying I'll be able to see Jack Benny?"

"Yes, sir."

"And Rochester?"

"That's right."

"In my own living room?"

"You got it."

Chet looked at him suspiciously. "That's just silly talk. Stop pulling my leg."

"I'm not pulling your leg, Chet. I think it will happen in the next ten years."

"I think you've got the fever or something. I've seen other people like this. Next thing you know, you'll be barking at the moon and saying we'll travel to the stars in a rocket ship like Buck Rodgers."

"We will. Someday."

Chet knelt in front of Norm and looked him in the eyes. "I didn't think it would happen to you. Let me take you to see the doctor." He tried to hoist Norm off the mat, but Norm just laughed.

Norm realized Chet wasn't ready to think about the future and let it go. Chet sighed in relief. Norm was talking about some crazy things. It was like thinking there was a bomb that could blow up the entire country of Japan. *Where do people get these nutty ideas?* thought Chet.

Norm walked over to Chet and handed him a pristine Hershey's chocolate bar. Norm had hidden his confirmation medallion of the Virgin Mary and traded it to a Filipino boy, who delivered on his promise of the chocolate bars.

"Merry Christmas." Norm looked at Chet.

They had been through eight months of hell together at Cabanatuan. They knew every day could be their last. The two naked men held each other tight in the furnace of the Philippine humidity.

February 1943

The Americans ground out the bloodiest battles of the Pacific War. The marines on Guadalcanal spent weeks destroying every fox-hole and dogged the Japanese soldiers one by one. The Japanese refused to budge, despite facing starvation and certain death by advancing American troops. True to the Bushido code, the Japanese army lost forty thousand men on the "Island of Death." Imperial general headquarters sent the last of the destroyers down the Slot to expedite the rescue of General Hyakutake and the last of his ten thousand soldiers, who were riddled with malaria and close to death from starvation. The American forces officially occupied Guadalcanal. Admiral Halsey began to leapfrog northwest through the the Solomon Islands and rendezvoused with MacArthur's troops in New Guinea.

The Australians and Americans pushed north over the Owen Stanley Range and recaptured Buna and Gona. Fierce battles left the Allied forces bewildered at the incredible determination of the Japanese soldiers to hold their positions. Single dugouts and foxholes took days for combined troops to flush out the stubborn Japanese. Some had even taken to eating their own dead to gather strength for the fight. MacArthur received news the final enemy element had been eliminated, and the focus could turn to Rabaul and the main body of the Japanese fleet. The Japanese reinforced their strongest positions at Lae in New Guinea in anticipation of MacArthur's drive up the northern coast. If MacArthur seized Lae, the Americans would have a stepping-stone to New Britain and a land path to the heavily guarded Rabaul.

The bombardier wouldn't tell Jason what the surprise was. He just told Jason to be ready for anything. Jason wasn't fond of surprises. The plane left the runway at Port Moresby and lifted into the air over the Papuan Peninsula. They crossed over the creeping green caterpillar of the Owen Stanley Range and headed north toward New Britain and Rabaul. Intelligence reports from Washington and Pearl indicated a surge in Japanese naval activity in the Bismarck Sea with possible transports heading to reinforce the Japanese troops at Lae and Salamaua. They flew above the heavy clouds that draped the coast of New Britain and the advancing convoy of Japanese troops.

"I think we found trouble." Jason heard the pilot's acknowledgment of the Japanese convoy. "Everybody, keep your eyes peeled."

Jason scanned the sky and looked for his old friends, the Zeros. He noticed the Wildcats on the prowl five thousand feet below and felt comfortable having the security blanket of fighters. Then something unusual happened. The B-25 did not gain altitude for a bombing run. They were diving toward the Bismarck Sea, and Jason swiveled to see if they had lost an engine. The nightmare of crashing into the ocean temporarily dazed him as he sought the cause of the plummet. "What's going on?" Jason said, and he looked at the smiling bombardier.

"This is my surprise," shouted the bomber over the roar of the engines.

"I don't like it." Jason looked at the blue waters quickly approaching.

"We haven't been effective at getting hits from the higher altitudes. We're going to fly in low and skip the bombs into the enemy ships."

Jason was sure he had misunderstood him in the cacophony of noise. The pilot wiggled his arm and pantomimed the act of swooping in low. *This is a really bad idea,* thought Jason. The B-25s were massive flying fighting machines but no match for the lightning-quick Zeros that lurked at five thousand feet. The Zeros would chew them up and spit them into the Bismarck Sea.

The B-25 kept dropping. The bombardier displayed a maniacal grin. Jason wanted to wipe it from his smug mug. The Wildcats splintered through the Zeros and led them on a chase. They swirled around the clouds and broken blue skies. They were slicing no more than two hundred feet off the surface of the waves, and the hatch doors opened. Jason could smell the sea. They were too close. The bombardier loosed the bombs, and they skipped like flat stones across the open waves at three hundred miles an hour. Jason opened fire on a transport. The screaming plane blew past him quickly. The other B-25s in the sortie executed the same attack, and the results were devastating. The pilot reared the plane back into the sky and gained altitude as the sinking transports and destroyers foundered in the Bismarck Sea.

"Son of a bitch." Jason sighed as the color came back into his cheeks.

The navigator plotted a course for Port Moresby and the relative safety of home.

The *Princeton*

Seaman Dan B. Kerichuck stepped onto the awesome new light carrier *Princeton*. He was a long way from Washington State, but that was what he wanted. He had grown tired of the pitiful looks friends and relatives had been giving him since the accident. His face was grotesque. His nose was flattened deeply into his skull, and his cheekbones had never fully regained their round form. His face was an even plane from his forehead to his chin. The logs had rolled his head flat. The scar that ran through his bottom and upper lip was hideous, and his speech was garbled. He shaped only the simplest words to sound intelligible. His hands had regained their strength, and his fingertips only lacked the lightest sensations. His frame had regained the atrophied muscles, and the fire crew specialists aboard the *Princeton* were elated to have him on their team. Dan was a horse—a powerful, determined mule who could take over for three people. Dan enjoyed the company. After seeing him once, they took their cheap shots about his scary looks, and then it was over. He had no such luck with the ladies. Several girls had screamed in horror when they turned to introduce themselves. This hurt Dan deeply. He learned to love the camaraderie of the men at sea.

The new light carrier USS *Princeton* (CVL-23) was newly christened to the waters of the Atlantic. Built at the shipyards of Camden, New Jersey, the appropriately named ship represented the fine Ivy League university and its hallowed members such as former President Woodrow Wilson. This ship suited Dan fine. He was newly acquainted with the waters of the Atlantic. He had gone through training on the beaches of Saint Lucie,

Florida. Dan had learned to respect fire—a living, breathing entity with a voracious and unpredictable appetite. Several team members had not been respectful to the fire and paid the price. The flames had lashed their searing tongues, licked the people, and reminded them fire ruled. The sailors returned from the sick bay with a newfound respect for the monster. Dan looked out over the choppy February surf and imagined Northern Africa. This was where General Eisenhower had led his troops through Casablanca during Operation Torch. He dreamed the *Princeton* would take him to the English Channel or into the Mediterranean Sea. He fretted about the gray and stormy North Atlantic and the grizzled sailors' sullen accounts of the wolf pack hunting U-boats the German used to terrorize the seas. He also hoped to meet a nice girl along the way who could overlook his rearranged features.

June 1943, the South Pacific

Admiral Yamamoto's failure to retake Guadalcanal resulted in the penultimate sacrifice. The secret world of code breaking uncovered a message the commander in chief and architect of the Japanese war movement was taking a trip to visit the fighting soldiers at Bougainville. Bougainville was the last in the chain of the Solomon Islands. It was east of Rabaul and within the reach of American fighter planes at Henderson Field. Outstanding Japanese punctuality worked against the admiral, who had come to visit the wounded and inspect the condition of the vital forward base. Acting on the tip from the code breakers, Admiral Nimitz gave Admiral Halsey permission to seek and destroy Yamamoto's convoy near Bougainville. Halsey sent seventeen P-38 Lightnings to search the airspace over Bougainville. They were loaded with extra fuel tanks that could be jettisoned upon attack. With Yamamoto's itinerary in hand, the P-38s found the timely admiral within minutes of his flight plan. The P-38s split into two groups and led the covering Zeros on a chase away from Yamamoto's bombers. The bombers were no match for the speedy Lightnings, and they blasted Yamamoto from the sky and into the dense jungle. The announcement of Yamamoto's death was publicly delayed, but American intelligence celebrated taking the Japanese queen off the chessboard.

Mississippi

Mabel opened the mail and handed it to Teresa. Mabel had never learned to read, and her two oldest children had recently become the first high-school graduates of the Kigmenis family. The letter looked official, and Teresa read the page. Her eyes opened wide, and Mabel started to worry. The letter bore some sort of emblem. She knew the boys were eligible for the draft.

"It says here Raytel Kigmenis is deferred from the draft for the following reasons. Mama, there's a box, and next to it, it says, '2-C. Deferred Critical Civilian Work—Farmers/Volunteers.' It sounds as if they don't have to go, but I want to check on that word 'deferred.'"

Raytel, Caleb, and Joe came into the house from the farm. Jeremiah was too far out to come and take a break. They had told him they'd bring him a cool cup of water. Their giant bodies glistened with sweat from plowing the fields. Joe worked the barn, milked the cows, and carried baskets full of eggs.

"Raytel, you got some mail. Caleb, you got some too."

The boys looked surprised. Mail didn't come their way that often. They both read the army correspondence intently. Neither smiled or looked relieved, and Mabel worried about the meaning of "deferred." Caleb and Raytel looked at each other. "We don't have to go to the war." Whispered Raytel.

Mabel and Teresa started jumping up and down. Caleb and Raytel had been sure they would be drafted. Mabel looked at her sons. They seemed disappointed.

"What's the matter with you two? This is a blessing. Now you don't have to go and get yourself killed like all the other young men of this country."

Raytel spoke first. They were twins, but Caleb always deferred to Raytel when it came to Mama. "We're going to enlist."

Mabel's hands went for her apron drawstrings. That meant a good whooping. It dawned on her she couldn't scare the boys anymore. They were men now. "Why would you do a foolish thing like that? You need to stay right here on the farm with your daddy." She stared them down with one hand on the frying pan.

"You said it yourself, Mama. Stay right here on the farm. That's where they want to keep black men. On the farm where we belong."

"I am not listening to this. You boys have been out in the sun too long. Let me fix you a cool drink." Mabel might have been in the kitchen too long.

Teresa picked up the ball for her mother. "Why do you want to go fight for the white man? They've never done anything for us."

Caleb countered. "That's why we want to go. We're never going to be able to share this country if we don't stand next to the white soldiers and fight for it. It's our country too. They'll praise all the white boys who went to war and keep all the black people on the farms."

"Are you saying you're not proud of your father? Don't tell me that's what you just said." The frying pan rose off the table.

"No, Mama. That's not what Caleb said. We're very proud of Daddy and the farm. That's what we're going to do when we get back. Right now we're going to help the country and ourselves. Caleb and I just want the opportunity to show them black people can fight. Then maybe we can show them black people can spell, read, and write—that we can become doctors or lawyers or generals or admirals."

"An admiral in the US Navy? Don't bet on it." Mabel now knew for certain a copperhead must have bitten her twins.

"What's all this commotion going on in here? Why aren't you boys back to work?" Jeremiah looked hot and exhausted.

"Your two oldest sons want to join the army."

"Marines," Caleb and Raytel said at the same time.

Jeremiah looked his sons up and down. He studied their faces and remembered holding the two little boys in his arms for the first time. It seemed like yesterday. That was a lot of cotton ago. He could remember the first time Raytel took a step, and Caleb followed him right away. He never let Raytel get too far ahead of him. There was the time the boys got stuck in the barn behind the mule. When the mule started kicking, he had to get them out. He had never seen them so scared. He remembered when they learned to read and write. Caleb was good at math—Raytel not so much. Raytel was a reader. He looked his boys in the eyes. "You men do what you have to do. But not until your chores are done for the day. After that you can work for the US Marine Corps." Jeremiah got himself the cool glass of water no one had brought him.

Mabel could not believe her ears. "Have you lost your cotton-pickin' mind? You give them your blessing to go and get themselves killed?"

"Mama, they're men now. They're not boys anymore. They can do what they want."

"You want them to get killed?" Mabel was close to putting her head in the wood-fired stove.

"Of course I don't want them to get killed. Maybe the boys want more out of life than the farm. Maybe they want some respect."

"What is the matter with the farm?" Mabel squealed. This was a telltale sign of her coming unhinged.

"There's nothing the matter with the farm, Mabel. The farm is my life. It's been good to the family, but maybe Raytel and Caleb want something different for themselves."

"Like what?"

"Maybe they want to go to the drugstore and shake hands with all the people on the street. Maybe they want to ride in the front of the bus. Maybe they want to drink from the same fountain or go to the same schools as white people. This might be one way to get those rights."

"Things aren't ever going to change, Jeremiah. You know that. They haven't changed hardly at all since Abraham Lincoln. It's not going to be any different for the boys."

"Maybe not for the boys, Mabel. But maybe for their children." Jeremiah went back out to the field to work the cotton.

August 1943

The US Marine Corps was under the command of the US Navy and would not allow brothers to serve in the same outfit. A disaster in the Solomon Islands had necessitated a new policy. The light cruiser *Juneau* was torpedoed and sank in Ironbottom Sound off Guadalcanal. The bulk of the crew drowned. Aboard were the five Sullivan boys from Waterloo, Iowa. All perished.

Raytel and Caleb walked into town to take the bus after tearful good-byes and the stunning news Mabel was again pregnant. Jeremiah held his sons tightly and slipped them each a hundred-dollar bill. Raytel tried to give the generous sum back, but he knew when to back down from his daddy. When Raytel and Caleb returned, they would have another sibling.

Raytel's bus pulled up. He was headed to Camp Pendleton in California. Caleb was headed to the new marine base in North Carolina called Camp Lejeune. The two boys would be apart for the first time.

"I'm going to miss you, Caleb." Raytel held back tears.

"I'm going to miss you too." Caleb couldn't hold them back. The two brothers hugged tightly. The bus driver blew the horn. Caleb shouted, "Last one back has to clean out the hog pen."

Raytel laughed. "I'll be sure to beat you home."

Caleb watched his brother head to the war as the white bus driver directed him to the back of the bus.

The bus ride to Jackson was lonely until a young black man named Darnell spoke to Raytel and broke his hypnotic stare. "Are you going in the service?" Darnell was a little man.

"I'm going into the Marine Corps." Raytel shook the man's hand.

"So am I." Darnell was happy to have a friend. "I can't believe I got drafted. My lucky nickel never failed me before. I threw that thing right into the pond. No-good nickel." Darnell wasn't crazy about dodging bullets for the US Marines. "Did you get drafted too?"

"No. I enlisted."

Darnell made a face that looked as if he had seen a bearded lady. "You mean to tell me you don't have to be here?"

"That's right." Raytel looked at Darnell. Raytel's eyes indicated he didn't want to have the sociopolitical conversation about a black man fighting in a white man's war.

"Well, as long as we're in this mess, we might as well stick together. Being a little guy, I was hoping to get some cover. You could be like my aircraft carrier. What do you say?"

"What are you going to be? A submarine just staying out of sight?"

They both laughed. The white people turned around and asked them to be quiet.

Raytel and Darnell watched as the pretty girls of Mississippi high society handed out gifts to soldiers boarding the train. The pair had not started their service yet, but Darnell managed to talk one of the young girls into a basket.

"Look, Raytel. There's coffee and candy." Darnell put the candy right into his lap. "And some fruit." He handed the fruit to Raytel. "And a deck of cards. I wonder if any of these boys know how to play poker. Raytel, do you know how to play poker?"

"No."

"Oh. Your family's religious. I see. No poker in the Raytel family. What did y'all play? Go fish?" Darnell cracked himself up as he unwrapped a butterscotch.

Raytel laughed. Darnell was so stupid. They got comfortable on the train. There was a special car for Negroes. Raytel made sure to get a window seat. He had never left his county. It was the first time he had been to Jackson. He wanted to see everything on the way. He wanted to see how big Texas really was. He wanted to see the oil fields and the plains. He wanted to see the deserts of New Mexico and Arizona. He wanted to see the Pacific Ocean in San Diego. Darnell was much more interested in playing cards and had roped a couple other fellas into a game of gin. It had already been a long, emotional day. Raytel leaned his head against the window and felt its vibration. It felt good. He settled into a long ride and let the rider's hypnosis carry him far away.

The train's whistle blew, and Raytel noticed most everybody in the car had fallen fast asleep. Darnell had curled up into a ball and looked so small. Raytel thought about asking the porter for a warm bottle of milk, but the porter ignored him and reminded them to hold onto their tickets. They were only going to stop in Little Rock for an hour and a half, and the train would leave without them. If they were in the service, they could get a warm meal at the local military base, and a USO-sponsored bus would shuttle them there and back.

Raytel was famished. He shook Darnell and told him to get up. He told Darnell about the dinner, and Darnell popped to his feet. They boarded the USO shuttle and were ordered to the back. The summer sun hadn't gone down yet, and Raytel looked at the hills surrounding Little Rock. They looked like mountains, and he imagined the size of the Rockies.

The ride to the mess was swift. Raytel didn't expect much from the food. Nothing was going to compare to Mabel's cooking, but he was hungry. The mess was divided into three sections.

A screen of some sort cordoned off one section. The dozen black soldiers were escorted to a section far away from the white soldiers. The white soldiers were told to get trays and work their way down the line in the cafeteria-style setting. The black soldiers were told to wait. A group of white people who were wearing some type of uniform now filled the empty cordoned off section. Raytel thought they looked like inmates from a local penitentiary. The inmates asked to get their trays and proceeded through the line. Raytel was hungry, and the allotted time was dissipating. The large group of inmates finally finished their procession and were all seated comfortably.

The black soldiers were given their turn. The food didn't look too bad, but the kitchen staff showed no interest in refilling some of the more popular items for the Negroes. The soldiers ate their meals and cleared their trays. On the way back to the bus, Raytel asked an attending sergeant who the people in the funny uniforms were. He looked at Raytel and begrudgingly told him, "They are German prisoners of war."

The train rode through the night nonstop. Raytel was disappointed about not being able to see Texas. New Mexico was next on the map. He was still excited about the prospect of seeing the desert. The brilliant red hues of the wind-carved mountain statues turned Raytel's head around. There were no trees or bushes and no water for miles. There were no rivers or streams. The train became insufferably hot, and people opened the windows, but that provided no relief from the soaring temperatures on the desert floor. All it did was make for a hot breeze.

The train stopped in Tucumcari for water and a quick stretch for the passengers. They reboarded, and the train started the slow rise up into the mountains. Raytel looked over the edges and stared at the desert below. He had come a long way from Mississippi. He tried to write a letter on the bumpy train. Teresa had promised to teach her mother to read. The train kept rolling.

Raytel and Darnell fell in line with the platoon. The drill sergeant walked up and down the line and looked at the new batch of fresh soldiers.

He screamed at the top of his lungs. "If the United States of America was not at war, I would quit this job. You are the biggest piles of dung I have ever seen in my twenty years as a drill sergeant." He got in one boy's face. "I can't make a soldier out of you. You still have your mama's tit in your mouth." The soldier smirked, and the sergeant promptly punched him in the chest. This left him on his butt and gasping for air. "Do you think I am funny, boy? Do I look like Bob Hope to you?"

The boy worked his way to his feet and sheepishly whispered, "No."

"Goddamn it, son!" The boy shuddered and pissed his pants. "You stand up straight and answer me like a man. Am I funny?"

"No, sir."

"Louder!"

"No, sir!"

"Oh my goodness, you wet your pants. Stick your thumb in your mouth." The boy looked confused. "Put your thumb in your mouth!" The boy put his thumb in his mouth. "Now suck it, you baby!" The boy started sucking. "What is your name, soldier?"

"Stiles."

"What?"

"Stiles!"

"Stiles what?"

The rattled boy screamed, "Drew Stiles!"

The sergeant went nose to nose with the boy sucking his thumb. "Stiles, you moron!" He glared at Stiles, who tried not to breathe or blink. "From now on this will be known as Baby Platoon. Stiles, you will be required to wear a diaper under your uniform. Is that clear?"

"Yes, sir!"

The sergeant walked down the line and sought a new victim. He stopped in front of Raytel, who fixed his eyes on a tree over the sergeant's head. He did not move a muscle.

"What are we going to do with the Niggras?"

"I don't know, sir!"

"Why are you here, boy? We're not fighting the Ku Klux Klan."

"I'm here to fight for my country, sir!"

Darnell was so happy he had chosen Raytel. So, so happy.

"You know what's gonna happen to you, boy?"

"No, sir!"

"You're going to get drunk and rowdy on a weekend pass and go AWOL with all the other niggras." He got right in Raytel's face and waited for Raytel to eyeball him. Raytel didn't move a muscle. "Then I'm going to hunt you down and put you in my brig—where you sorry niggras belong."

Raytel wanted to snap his neck but maintained his composure.

Then the sergeant fell back and addressed Baby Platoon. "You will fall out on my command and head straight for the barbershop. They will take all that hair off your baby heads. Then you will receive your government-issued gear and meet in the barracks at fourteen hundred hours."

"Yes, sir!"

Baby Platoon had learned its first lesson.

Camp Pendleton was located between the California cities of Oceanside and San Clemente. The drill sergeants punished the young recruits in the balmy weather and the summer sun. They practiced the simple things first. Marching became as routine as breathing. They would hike through the foothills for miles at a time. They learned to crawl under barbed wire on their bellies. They learned to fire rifles and mortars. They learned hand-to-hand combat, and Raytel became the undisputed champ of Camp Pendleton. The sergeant would lay down a log over a pit of mud and see if anyone could knock Raytel off. The double-ended poles were the equivalent of punching bags, and Raytel used his balance and strength to knock everyone off the log and into the mud. Raytel was a brute and a natural leader, and he carried Darnell through basic training. At the end of thirteen weeks, Raytel's massive frame had slimmed, and he carried the muscles of a Roman god around the base.

Raytel wouldn't let Darnell get out of line. A weekend pass allowed them to see the sights of San Diego, and in a black club Raytel heard the sultry sounds of Charlie Parker for the first time. Parker's music moved Raytel. The notes tied his emotions together.

Darnell drank too much and made time with a woman friend. He didn't want to leave the club. Raytel was determined not to bring any more attention to the black troops in the platoon. It was the first and last time Darnell ever challenged Raytel. Raytel put Darnell over his shoulder and bodily removed him from the club. Raytel would not suffer the punishments of someone going AWOL.

Upon graduation from boot camp, the drill sergeant shook Raytel's hand and told him he would share a foxhole with him anytime. Raytel looked at the first white man who had ever considered him just a man.

October 1943, the South Pacific
The race to Tokyo had begun, but the road would be arduous. The arguing chiefs of the army and navy still had to decide on the path. MacArthur wanted to shoot straight through Rabaul and head to a triumphant return and the people he had left in the Philippines. Nimitz and Admiral King in Washington wanted to neutralize the Central Pacific with missions to the Marshall and Caroline Islands. MacArthur had yet to prove his forces could advance as quickly as he predicted. The advance on Buna and Gona and the securing of the Papuan Peninsula had taken six months

and thousands more people than MacArthur had expected. Short on supplies and hesitant to push their small victories, the Allied forces in the Pacific stayed on their slow, steady, bloody path.

October 1943, Camp O'Donnell

The rainy season stretched from May to October. Shaun, Manny, Carl, and Rat braced as the powerful typhoon winds chipped away at the poorly constructed billet. It was only a matter of time before the roof collapsed and the prisoners would have to spend the rest of the night holding the pylons of the billet through the sheets of rain. There was only one good thing about the rains. It cleared the compound of the buildup of feces on the ground. The rain was no excuse for missing a day's work. Prime Minister Tojo implemented the "no work, no food" policy for all Allied prisoners throughout Southeast Asia. As if the epidemic of starvation hadn't already reached biblical proportions, the work camps sent the attrition rates of the dead soaring. Rain or shine the camps emptied, and the prisoners were sent to do the jobs of mules. Whipped by guards they carried buckets of dirt and slaved to construct the barriers the Japanese would use to defend Luzon.

Shaun and Manny had played their cards right at the beginning and landed plush jobs at the motor pool. Manny had become so disgusted with the food at the camp he almost refused to eat. He had grown terribly thin, and Shaun was worried. Manny's ire reached a boiling point while he was picking out white weevils crawling in the rice. He had become a master of the black market and the Filipino language of Tagalog. He used his savvy to garner treats and shared them with his friends. Peanuts provided desired proteins along with the rare duck egg, which they ate raw. They had so many bananas they became hard to hide from the guards. They shared the wealth with the starving inmates of Rio. Manny looked for things of value to trade and had a heated argument over Shaun's locket. Shaun refused to part with the keepsake, and

Manny challenged his loyalty to his friends and his desire to stay alive. Shaun told Manny he could have it when he died.

Cabanatuan
Today was the day the Japanese guards released Corporal Dogget from solitary confinement. The prison population had become a valuable, inexpensive workforce for the Japanese, and they preferred to work the prisoners to death than having the pleasure of stabbing them with their bayonets. Corporal Dogget had defied the guards in the field by refusing to pick up his dirt and move it any farther. The guards beat the already-malnourished and malaria-riddled Dogget and threw him 'the box'. Corporal Dogget became the example. Six weeks passed, and every day the guard took Dogget a plate of meager rations. Norm and Chet etched the days off on the billet stanchion. They procured a bevy of nourishments to revive the sick man. Only one other had entered the box, and he hadn't survived. The guard walked over to the box and pulled the nearly dead Dogget out of a hole no bigger than a doghouse. He made the man stand at attention as best he could. They could see Dogget was in dire need of medical attention. The officer demanded obedience from Dogget. Dogget spit in his face. They threw Dogget back in the box. He died two days later.

November 1943, Washington State
Dan would not shut up. Mary Pat was sky-high the Kerichucks were all sitting together at the family table, and Michael was engrossed as Dan told tales of the war. Dolores couldn't get a word in edgewise, but she didn't mind. Ken listened to the adventures of death and destruction, and his conscience churned inside. His flying armada would soon be rolling off the assembly line and adding to the carnage.

"So I was sure we were going across the Atlantic to fight Hitler." Michael chewed his mashed potatoes but never took his eyes off his older brother. "But our orders came in, and we started for the Panama Canal."

"The Panama Canal is one of the greatest engineering feats ever accomplished," noted the engineer. He sneaked a little pride for the profession into the conversation.

"It's amazing, Daddy. I'm telling you, these ships are big!" Dan ate the fried chicken and talked. Mary Pat noted the navy had not honed his eating etiquette. "And the locks raise the ships up, over, and through the hills and down into the Pacific Ocean. It saved us months of traveling." Dan picked up a thigh and chomped a big bite.

"When did you get to see the Japs?" Michael got to the nitty-gritty.

"We had to go through Pearl Harbor. It's beautiful. Dolores, maybe you and Dr. Morris can go there on your honeymoon." Dan went straight for the jugular.

"Shut up." Dolores looked at her father. He was snickering through some carrots. "Daddy! That was a cheap shot. Tell him to…shut up!"

The table hummed with laughter as Dolores stewed.

"We saw our first action in the Baker Islands. The *Princeton* provides air cover for the battleships and cruisers," Dan said to Michael. "Our fighters flew off the decks. The Wildcats are fast, and the pilots are brave. They flew through the air and provided cover for the bombers that dropped the bombs on Baker Island. The cruisers sent in their bombs from giant cannons on the ship."

Ken looked at his son. Dan knew this conversation was going a direction Michael could not follow. Dan cut it short. "Michael, we don't really see the Japs on the carrier, but we help the people who do."

Ken nodded approvingly, and Mary Pat cleared the air by announcing she had baked an apple pie. This diverted everyone's attention, and Dan added generous scoops of vanilla bean ice cream to his slices.

Ken had never had a drink with his son. Michael went to bed, and Dolores read a medical textbook by the fire. Ken poured a Scotch and handed a glass to Dan. They sat in the chairs close to the fire.

"Son." It was Ken's serious voice. "Why is the *Princeton* in Puget Sound? This was no routine overhaul. She was just commissioned in February."

"I didn't lie to you, Dad."

"I never said you did. I don't think you told me everything, though."

Dads are too clever, thought Dan. That was why they were dads. "We took a hit."

Ken looked at his son. Dolores gently put down the textbook and the fascinating chapter on cell structure. Mary Pat finished the dishes and eased her growing posterior into a chair. The flames Dan respected so much crackled in the hearth and provided an orange glow for the truth.

"I suspected as much," Ken said. He pursed his lips and let his son talk. He needed to share and hoped Dan was man enough to let out all his fears.

"We were off the coast of Bougainville, and Admiral Halsey commenced Operation Cherry Blossom."

"Oh, those are pretty." Everyone peered at the interrupting Dolores, who promptly went quiet.

"The Wildcats took off in front of the bombers. The battle-ships and cruisers fired on the beaches. The explosions could crack eardrums. Many have become hard of hearing. I couldn't see the land from the carrier, but I knew they were successful in their landings at Empress Augusta Bay. I think we caught the Japs by surprise because it seemed to take forever for the spotters to see the Zeros and Vals. We were attacking Bougainville. Aircraft from Guadalcanal and Henderson Field flew in for the mission to cover the transports of soldiers. There were planes everywhere. The Japs came in from the north—from Rabaul. The enemy pilots are crazy. They flew into the antiaircraft fire as if they were walking through a sprinkler. So many were shot down, but they kept coming. They terrorized the carrier and traded machine-gun fire. Our people were fighters. They held their positions and fought them off. You can't imagine the noise.

"Then one of the Vals got us with a bomb. My CO said later it was a minor hit, but I thought we were all going to die. We grabbed the hoses and worked our way into the fire. It was so hot I thought I was roasting. You can feel the heat searing deep under your skin and cooking your heart and lungs."

Dolores excused herself.

"I watched one of the pilots get caught in his cockpit. He struggled through the flames to get out. We sprayed down the plane, and a half dozen of us wanted to try to get him out, but it was too late."

Tears started rolling out of Dan's eyes, but Ken let him keep talking. Mary Pat moved in to console her son, but he shrugged her off. "People were screaming in pain, bloodied, and burned. We wrapped up several people in tarps, towels, or shirts to extinguish the fire that ate their bodies. The ones who survived were in so much agony I wished they had died." Dan sobbed. "There was nothing we could do to help them. They were in so much pain. The medics brought them morphine and rubbed jelly over their scalded flesh. They were cooked to a crisp." His chest started to heave. "And the CO called it minor damage. That son of a bitch."

Ken gave Mary Pat the palm of his hand as she went in again to hold her son. Mary Pat knew this was a different type of pain. This was the anguish of Dan's experiences—not the self-pity of the accident. It was compassion.

Dan wiped his eyes and regained a touch of composure. "We made it out of Bougainville, and the brass celebrated their success. They seemed so full of themselves and the victory, and the death didn't seem to bother them. They were more worried about the elevator shaft and how to fix it." He sniffled. "We sailed to the Central Pacific, and we joined a different task force. We left the *Saratoga* and the new *Independence* to guard the operation at Bougainville. We went to the Gilbert Islands. The marines were about to land at Tarawa and Makin." Dan looked at his father. He did not want to speak of the atrocities of Tarawa in front of his mother. "Then we came to the Puget Sound for repairs."

Mary Pat reached over his strong, broad shoulders and gave her son a sweet kiss. "I love you." She touched Ken's hand and retired to bed.

Both the Kerichuck men took sips of their Chivas, and Dan regurgitated the rest of his horror. "At Tarawa we were too far from the island, but the pilots told us the story. The bombing of the atoll started before dawn. It was merciless. I would never tell anyone on the ship, but I felt bad for the Japanese. I couldn't believe they didn't surrender. The pilot was sure everybody on the island was dead before the marines even left the transports. The *Maryland* led three battleships with seven destroyers and five cruisers, and they unleashed holy hell on the two-mile-long island. That went on for ninety minutes. We were close enough to see smoke rising from the burning palm trees. The marines are using a new transport weapon called an amphtrac. It has machine guns, and it's like a tank in the water. They headed to Betio at the tip of the island.

"Everything seemed to be going OK, but the sun came up, and the Japanese were still there. They were firing on the landing wave. The navy started bombing again for a long stretch. The Japanese were still there—dug in like moles. The LSTs were sent in. Dad, these are the craziest ships you can imagine. They're big, but they have flat bottoms that carry tanks, troops, and other assault vehicles, and they back up near to the shore. The people call them Large Slow Targets." It was funny but not funny. "There was something about the tides. The amphtracs were able to get across, but the next wave got stuck behind the coral at low tide, and the marines got hung out to dry. The Japanese slaughtered them. They made the marines wade in the water from a mile out in the lagoon. The pilot said there were more American soldiers on the beach than seashells." Dan started crying again. "They thought they would find nobody left after the one-day operation, but it cost thirteen hundred people their lives. They're all dead."

Dan broke down, and his father held him close. "Did the Japanese finally surrender?" His father rubbed his son's back.

"One officer and sixteen enlistees."

"Out of how many?"

"Four thousand." Dan finally looked up, and then he broke down again. "I've never been so happy to see you. I love you, Daddy." He blubbered. "I'm so scared."

Ken held his scared son the same way he had when he was three.

Port Moresby

Jason had been the recipient of a fine gift from one of the pilots. He found the picture of Rita Hayworth to be lovely and lucky, but he could not remove her from the window of the turret, so he added the stunning picture of Ava Gardner. Now he had Ava Gardner and Rita Hayworth watching over him. A beautiful pair of ladies was on his side. *It's usually good enough in poker,* Jason thought.

The Fifth Army Air Force was back in the air for another dangerous mission. The landing on Bougainville had been successful, but General Hyakutake was sure to challenge them heartily. Recently evacuated from Guadalcanal to resist the marines at

Empress Augusta Bay, he was the thorn in America's paw. The new Japanese commander in chief, Admiral Koga, was already pulling the end of an unsecured rope and had sent a powerful naval force to halt the American advance. As the deadly force arrived in Rabaul's Simpson Harbor, routine reconnaissance flights spotted them and reported to Admiral Halsey. A complicated quandary faced Halsey. Such a strong force could repel the advances they had just made on Bougainville. He had to neutralize the threat. However, the bulk of his fleet had been removed from the area and returned to Pearl Harbor for assignments elsewhere in the Pacific. This left him the unenviable option of sending in the newly repaired *Saratoga* and newcomer *Independence* to thwart the larger guns docked in Rabaul. Besides the supreme advantage in firepower on the water, Rabaul was the home to over four hundred land-based aircraft that could shred the carriers to pieces. Halsey sent the ships to do the improbable.

All the Fifth Army Aircraft were airborne. Jason had never seen so much firepower combined for one strike. The clouds were heavy, and they relied on the navigators to bring them into position over Rabaul. The clouds broke with providence, and the B-17s dropped their bombs over the stationary targets in Simpson Harbor. The Japanese had not seen the fighters coming from the *Saratoga* and *Independence*. They caught the Zeros at takeoff and blistered two dozen before the Japanese pilots' seats were warm. The fighters held the Zeros at bay while the B-17s did heavy damage to the mired fleet. Six Japanese cruisers and four destroyers received the brunt of the American sortie as the bombs set the fortress on fire. The Americans pressed the attack for almost a week. Nimitz released three more carriers of his growing fleet as they made a mad dash across the ocean to assist Halsey. The Japanese couldn't stand the heat, and Admiral Koga removed the naval presence from the kitchen of Rabaul. He left the abandoned Japanese army to fight the rest of the losing battle on the ground.

Cabanatuan

Chet looked for some grass to wipe his ass. Norm used a handful of dirt. They stood on the edge of the growing island of waste and excrement. The hundred-foot latrine was loaded as usual and unfit for the use of thousands of people. The flies and mosquitoes buzzed around the squatting, naked prisoners. Chet and Norm stood and walked back toward the center of the compound. They passed a billet filled with a dozen people incapacitated by malaria. Legions of lice infested their bodies. Some of the people ran temperatures of 110 degrees, and the fevers boiled their brains. The sounds of suffering became part of the background music at Cabanatuan. It was just a matter of time before they died. Chet and Norm observed the symptoms and watched each other carefully. A strange chill would freeze the torso, ignite the body temperature, and make it feel as if one had been doused with gasoline and torched. It was a thin line between recovery and death. Norm worried about a large, open, festering sore on Chet's crotch. Chet watched the barely visible lice crawl from his fingernail to the edge of his fingertip. He waited and pressed his thumb and index nails together to slice the organism in half.

Cabanatuan had been home for eighteen months. Chet had lost seventy-five pounds from his 220-pound frame. His height made him look like a cadaver. Norm had lost fifty. He weighed a paltry 125 pounds. Some of the smaller men were hitting ninety or eighty-five pounds. Many had halved their original body weights. Legs looked like sticks and arms like broom handles. No one carried strength or muscle. It was only the passion of living or the fear of dying that kept them alive.

Camp O'Donnell

The prisoners at Camp O'Donnell had not had real showers in ages. The rainy season had ended, so a natural cleansing was long overdue. The foul scent of stale urine and diarrhea consumed the smell of rank body odor mixed with the rotting flesh of the dying. Manny and Shaun watched one of the men of Rio analyze the dime-sized sore on his thigh as it grew to the size of a tennis ball within a matter of days. The gangrenous area filled with pus, and he scraped the wound out with a somewhat sterilized spoon. Rat and Carl looked on sympathetically. All of them realized the leg was going to have to be removed. They carried the man over to the infirmary, and the doctor prepared a butcher's saw. This made Rat's tooth removal seem like clipping toenails. With no anesthesia and few true surgical implements to perform the procedure properly, the soldier faced multiple treachery. He would certainly die of the infection that ravaged his leg. The pain would be excruciating. There was the strong possibility he would bleed to death during or after the operation. He could regain the infection and wait to die. The best possible scenario was to live without his leg. Shaun and Manny left the soldier in the hands of the young doctor. Rat and Carl paced away from the infirmary and blocked out the howling cries of the soldier as a meat saw sliced his femur. Carl knew the reaper would get all of them. It was just a matter of when and how.

He put his arm around Rat's naked shoulder and sensed that Rat cherished their friendship as much as he did. He realized there was one big thing he had never asked. "What's your real first name, Rat?"

Rat looked puzzled. He had never told anyone in the service his real name—except on his paperwork at Fort Benning. He thought it was a sissy name.

"I mean your birth certificate doesn't say 'Rat Doovaine.'" He paused. "Does it?"

"You're my best friend here. You're the best friend I've ever had." Carl felt the same way. "I'll tell you but only you. This is top-secret material." Rat was dead serious. Carl waited. "Donovan. Donovan Doovaine."

Carl couldn't understand the hubbub. Donovan was a fine name. "Nice to meet you, Rat."

Rat smiled. Carl loved breaking Rat's balls.

February 1944

The American worker made it possible for the soldiers to win the war. The fruits of their hard work had come to bear as carriers, battleships, destroyers, cruisers, airplanes, bombers, transports, and ammunition rolled speedily off the line by the ton. The Japanese fleet diminished through attrition, and the American naval forces grew by leaps and bounds. Nimitz could physically overwhelm his enemy, but the tenacious, stubborn fighting of the Japanese continued to haunt the admiral. Bloody fights at Makin and Tarawa had left the joint chiefs of staff with a sour taste. The press recounted the horrors of Tarawa to the American public. American dead started piling up.

The *Princeton*

"Look at all these ships," Dan marveled as Spruance's fleet organized for the attack on the Marshalls.

"I think the marines could walk ashore from Pearl Harbor if they lined the boats up end to end," observed Stew, another carrier fire specialist.

"All this for three little islands in the middle of nowhere," said Dan.

The greatest naval fighting force in US history floated at sea. Fifty-three thousand men waited to assault the islands, and 370 ships and 1,200 warplanes (carrier and land based) waited for their opportunity to strike Kwajalein. Some of the fleet was under the guidance of Admiral Mitscher and was tasked with fending off the strong Japanese naval forces from the Central Pacific headquarters at Truk. This was within striking distance of Operation Flintlock. Spruance wasted no time. In a three-day aerial extravaganza, the pilots punished the tiny atolls and re-moved all the planes in the Japanese inventory. With no threat of air support coming from the Marshalls, the big guns wailed away. Landing Ship Tanks worked in harmony with the amphtracs, and the marines stormed the three islands. Planning proved paramount. The Americans lost only four hundred people. Eight thousand Japanese surrendered or were killed or wounded.

The *Princeton* sailed for Eniwetok—the second phase of the operation. Admiral Mitscher went to pick a fight with the Japanese fortress of Truk in the Caroline Islands. Dismayed, the large Japanese naval presence had steamed a thousand miles away from the conflict to Palau. Mitscher took out his frustration on the facility at Truk. The key to the Japanese outer defenses of the Central Pacific was reduced to rubble. The Americans found equal success at Eniwetok, and Nimitz approved air strikes from carriers to destroy airfields on Guam, Tinian, and Saipan in the Marianas. The Americans had now penetrated the outer layer of the Japanese defenses. Spirits ran high among the sailors on the *Princeton*. Dan and his crew had avoided the fire.

The Japanese workers were busy as well creating the Greater East Asia Annihilation Fleet. The buildup of the fleet paled to the scale of the American forces at sea, but Admiral Koga felt the increase in carrier support would still present a formidable naval force. The Americans would have to come to them, and it would force Nimitz to deal with not only the combined fleet but the air-power on the largest islands under Japanese control such as the Philippines.

Prime Minister Tojo went on a rampage. He demoted Admiral Nagumo and General Sugiyama of the army and anointed him-self chief of staff of the army. Tojo had earned the nickname "Razor" as a general in the army and planned to execute some major changes in the following months. He drew a line on a map through the Pacific Ocean, and it went through the Marianas, the

Caroline Islands, and Palau. He determined it to be the last line the Americans would cross.

Port Moresby

Jason added to his collection of lucky pictures. He scored some pictures of the voluptuous Jane Russell and sexy Lauren Bacall. Jason took some money off the new people in Port Moresby in a card game and traded their money back for the pictures. He put them next to his other favorites.

The B-17 soared off the runway. Between the Fifth Army Air Force and the carrier attacks on Rabaul, twenty-nine thousand sorties bombed New Britain, and the Japanese still hadn't had enough. New Britain looked like a giant green crescent moon with the pretty blue ocean as a background. He had seen the island hundreds of times and imagined how peaceful it would have been before the war. He reread the most recent letter from Julie and was excited to get home to see her. Jason was scheduled for leave within the month and was antsy to help with the new babies.

The B-17s rumbled through the clear blue skies. Soon they would be over the target area. The eastern tip of the island contained the major Japanese naval base at Simpson Harbor. The ships were long abandoned. The air bases still posed serious threats. The Japanese army received resupplies of aircraft, and the current shipment contained the new version of the Zero. It was called the Zeke. The new A6M models were just as deadly as the Zeros but quicker and more agile.

Great, Jason thought ruefully. He looked down at the jungles. It looked as if someone had stirred a hive of bees. The Zeros and Zekes were everywhere. The Americans had upgraded their fighters as well and introduced the new Grumman F6F Hellcats to the skies. The two groups locked horns in a swirling display of flying skills. Two Zekes shot through the hollow and climbed to meet the B-17s. They were on Jason like stink on an ape. The pilots broke formation in evasive maneuvers. Jason pulled the trigger and screamed at the Zekes to come and get it. Tracer fire flew by like rocket-powered lightning bugs and blasted holes in the portside wing. There was no smoke yet, and Jason waited for the next surge. Two were on his tail, and he had to choose a target. He went starboard and blasted the Zeke into a fireball. It lost momentum and crashed. The glass of the turret started to shatter, and Jason could feel the rushing streams of air. Jane Russell came unglued and floated around the bubble like a butterfly leaving the cocoon. The suction grabbed Ava Gardner and freed her to the skies. The Zeke sprayed the turret with cannon fire, and fifty rounds a second riddled Jason. His dead body dangled below the turret and slammed into the hull of the B-17. The pilot could no longer control the mortally injured craft. The B-17 disappeared into the gorges of Finisterre Range. The flytrap of the New Britain jungle swallowed the plane whole.

July 1944, Saipan

Admiral Mitscher clobbered the air bases at Tinian and Guam with a two-hundred-bomber strike that devastated the airfields and removed a hundred Japanese planes. The news of the airstrip's destruction sent the morale of the marines soaring, but General Holland "Howlin' Mad" Smith warned there would be "a lot of dead marines." The craggy hills of Saipan provided the natural defenses of caves in which the belligerent Japanese were sure to hide.

"Saipan is a place we have not been before. It is not flat like an atoll. There are hills, mountains, and caves. The Japs will dig in deep. We must have the courage to keep stepping forward. There are twenty thousand Jap soldiers on the island. They won't leave alive. Civilians live on Saipan. It is possible you will see women and children. You must be cold. You are marines. You are killing machines," General Smith said to prepare the troops for the assault.

"Yes, sir!"

Darnell's eyes looked like two poached eggs bulging out his sockets. "Raytel, I'm scared, man. I'm really scared."

Darnell threw up on his boots. Raytel looked over the walls of the transports. The flotilla was forming in the bay. It was an incredible sight. Raytel couldn't believe the Japs hadn't surrendered on the spot. Shells raced high over their heads, and Darnell shook from head to toe. The USS *Powell*, USS *California*, USS *Monssen*, USS *Coghlan*, USS *Indianapolis*, and USS *Birmingham* unleashed an unimaginable barrage. Palm trees that had shaded the beaches of Saipan burned furiously and torched the foliage around them. Sand and coral flew hundreds of feet in the air. Dive bombers added fury to the white noise. Explosions erupted from the lagoon ahead and forced water to stream to the sky as navy demolition teams activated mines and cleared the coral obstacles. Like an enormous marching band, hundreds of ships moved into position. Landing Ship Docks, gargantuan 458-foot transports, backed into the beach, trimmed their ballast tanks to even the keels, and unloaded the upper deck, which Landing Craft Tanks occupied. Six hundred amphtracs hauling fifty men each fell into the procession. Landing Craft Infantry, protected by machine guns and mortar capability, fell in behind the troop carriers.

Darnell kept hearing the voice of Tokyo Rose whispering, "We're ready for you." Darnell wasn't ready for this.

They attacked west of Saipan. The flotillas divided into two attack groups. Raytel recalled the strategy sessions and studied the island. The north end of the island was Marpi Point. The landing stretched across four miles of beachhead. Tanapag Harbor ran to the tip of Mutcho Point. Farther south were the town of Garapan, a long stretch of beach, and coral reefs. That was where his platoon was to unload. Lying in the distance were the three volcanic tips of Mount Tapotchau, Mount Tipo Pale, and Mount Fina Susu. They seemed so far away. Gunfire from enemy embankments raced over their heads.

"Move! Move! Move!" the sergeant screamed.

The barge door lowered, and the infantry charged the beach. Raytel stepped over a screaming, wounded soldier in the shallows. Darnell followed right behind Raytel. They moved up to the beach and hit the ground. Mortar fire threw sand everywhere, but they dug into a makeshift bunker. Raytel rose and fired his weapon. Darnell dug in the sand like a badger. Thousands of marines scurried onto the beaches as the last of the air cover tried to dislodge the enemy. Tanks and artillery came ashore, and the enemy fire subsided as they retreated to the high ground over Garapan. From the base of Mount Tapotchau, mortars hurled down to the beach and slowed the American advance. Twenty thousand troops joined Raytel and Darnell on the four-mile beachfront.

"That wasn't that bad. Was it, Darnell?" Raytel laughed, but Darnell was still quaking.

"What do you mean? That was the worst thing imaginable. It was terrible. I want off this island now. They can throw me in the brig. It's a hell of a lot safer than here. I feel like walking over and punching the CO in the mouth. He'll have to throw me in the brig, right?"

"He sure would." Raytel moved around the bunker they had created for the machine gun.

"Wasn't that bad. What are you talking about? Did you see all those dead people? That one marine took a bullet in the eye. He's dead, Raytel! Dead! He's dead like I'm going to be dead. Man, they are trying to kill us! These people are crazy. I've got no business here. I've got to get out of this place."

"Just stay low."

"Low! I'm already low." The diminutive Darnell stayed low.

"You stay low, and I'll stay behind you." Raytel chuckled at Darnell.

"I'm not laughing. This is not funny. Do you see me laughing? No, sir. Not Darnell. Darnell is serious about leaving the US Marine Corps. Today! If something happens like this tomorrow, I might try to swim home."

Raytel couldn't stand it anymore and let loose a big belly laugh. Raytel was just as scared as Darnell but in a different way. Darnell could stay behind him all the way—as long as he made Raytel laugh.

The *Princeton*, Saipan

Dan B. Kerichuck knew the landings in Saipan had gone according to plan. Word had traveled quickly among the crew, but they knew something else was in the wind. They hadn't seen the last of the Japanese navy. He looked out across the Philippine Sea. They were out there somewhere.

Admiral Ozawa fumed over the loss of his land bases at Tinian, Guam, and Saipan. Now he had to inch closer and closer to the much larger American fleet, which outnumbered him two to one. His submarine fleet had failed miserably in terrorizing Spruance and his carriers. Ozawa had lost seventeen underwater assassins.

Saipan

Carter visited Raytel and Darnell. "How are you boys doing?"

"We're OK." Raytel gestured at the frightened Darnell. He was not sleeping a wink.

"It's not all right, Carter. We're sleeping at the edge of a jungle. The Japs could be right in those weeds, and we'd never know it." Darnell moved his head on a swivel.

"There are lots of things in those weeds, Darnell." Darnell's eyes got really big. "Like cobras, pythons, scorpions, and nasty bugs." Carter kept a straight face as the fear of natural elements overwhelmed Darnell's senses. "If a cobra bites you, you don't die right away. It will take some time. Your body becomes paralyzed, and you can't get out of the jungle. That's when the python comes and swallows you…"

"Banzai!"

Japanese tanks started blasted away at the soldiers on the beach. The Seabees had parked a bulldozer ahead of Raytel's bunker, and he could hear the gunfire ricochet off the metal. A thousand Japanese had slipped through the night jungle and rushed the beach. The startled marines fell back into the shallow waves of the bay. Raytel hoisted Darnell over his shoulder. He was frozen stiff with fear. Raytel rushed them to the water's edge. Raytel laid him down in the shallows and turned to fight. A Jap rushed him with a samurai sword that glistened in the moonlight. Raytel stepped out of the path, and the soldier thrust toward his abdomen. He grabbed the enemy's arm and freed the sword. Raytel punched the man in the face and shoved his head into the waters until he drowned. Gunfire abounded, and Raytel looked at the beach. People engaged in hand-to-hand combat littered the sand. The marines held their ground against the charging warriors. Perfectly aimed shells bombarded the beachhead. Destroyers found the tanks and immobilized the assault.

Outnumbered and beaten the sudden rush ended. The Japanese retreated back to the hills. They had left their calling card, though. *This will not be an easy fight,* Raytel thought, and he gathered Darnell from the bay where he had killed his first person.

Raytel and Darnell sloshed through the swamps of the lowland in the morning sun. They headed south toward Aslito Airfield.

"My feet are soaked, Raytel."

Raytel grabbed Darnell by the collar and pulled him close to his mouth. "You need to shut your mouth. There are snipers in the swamp."

He let him down back into the muddy water. Darnell straightened his collar, adjusted his helmet, and shut up.

The large trees that blocked the burning sun had large, buttressed trunks. The marines hid behind them to make their advance. Raytel spotted a bunker fifty yards ahead in the swamp, cleverly disguised by vines and earth. The enemy would wait for the bulk of the advancing force to move into slaughtering range. Raytel signaled Carter to move a unit around the left and flank the bunker. He signaled Dawson to head to the right and do the same. They had to move close enough to unload hell through the peephole. Raytel waited for everyone to crawl into position. They moved slowly but quietly and stayed clear of visual range from the moss-covered pillbox. There was an opening of swamp in front of the pillbox. The Japanese would use this spot for the kill zone— the clearing lined by large trees. Raytel needed to draw fire to the center so the flanks could advance. He looked at Darnell and communicated with his eyes and hands. Darnell knew he had to cover Raytel as he moved from tree to tree.

Raytel attempted to get into grenade range—about thirty yards. Darnell would have to follow Raytel and creep closer to the enemy machine guns. Raytel jumped through the swamp. He dived headfirst into the muck and landed at the base of a tree. The movement drew enemy fire. The two sides exchanged fire in a deadly tête-à-tête, and Raytel slipped forward through the trees. Darnell managed to cross the opening and was always a tree behind Raytel.

Raytel found Carter to his left. His helmet was barely visible among the green vines and bushes. Dawson moved closer to Raytel's right. Raytel needed three seconds to reach grenade range. Darnell stepped out from behind the buttress and held the trigger firm. He sprayed the pillbox at eye height and chipped away at the sodden embankment. Raytel was soaked to the bone in grimy, filmy swamp muck. He sucked the nasty fluid into his mouth as he dived safely behind the tree. Darnell ducked back to safety and gasped for air. His weapon burned in his hands. Raytel reached for the grenade. He counted to three and pulled the pin. He stepped into the oncoming fire, heaved the metal toward the bunker, and splashed down into the swamp.

The explosion ignited a furious firefight. Carter's left flank charged the Japanese position. They drew the fire of the pillbox, and bullets decimated them. The bodies splashed into the swamp as they gurgled the black waters with their last breaths. Carter's unit fell on the sword to open the door for Dawson. The enemy gunners couldn't kill everybody fast enough. Three grenades left the pillbox ablaze, but enemy fire still kept the marines at arm's length. Two more grenades rocked the stronghold and ruined the machine gun, and the dazed Japanese started firing with conventional rifles. The marines moved in for the kill. Their own machine guns forced the enemy low. Raytel waved the flamethrower into the fray. The soldier turned up the torch, blasted the inside of the fortress, and cremated those inside. Raytel looked inside the bunker to verify it was secure and confirmed the charred remains of the enemy. Raytel counted the dead—a tormenting process.

"We did good. We did good." Darnell finally sucked it up. "What is that smell?" Darnell plugged his nose.

"That's the smell of the dead." Raytel marched to the next bunker.

"A few more of those, and we're home free. Right, Raytel? How many more of those do we have to lick? Huh?"

"About a hundred."

Darnell's shoulders slumped. He had to get out of this place.

The *Princeton*

Dan cheered the planes as they roared off the flattops and gathered in the sky like a tightly woven flock of swallows swooping in formation. One Val bomber managed to score a hit on the *South Dakota*, but staunch antiaircraft fire and the swarm of Hellcats massacred the rest. It was the beginning of the Great Marianas Turkey Shoot.

Dan wrote to his parents. "I've never seen anything like it. The Hellcats jumped all over them, and you could see little orange flames spark the sky when a Val or Zero fell out of the air. Those that managed to get through the cover made mad dashes toward the battleships, and antiaircraft fire obliterated them. The *Princeton* never engaged, but we had front-row seats to the spectacular fireworks. I love all of you. Dan."

Saipan

Raytel connected with Dawson. Sniper fire splintered the tree trunk as Raytel heard the bullet whistle past. Darnell checked his ammunition, and they searched for the assassin's location. Raytel held up two fingers to Dawson to indicate a suspicion there were two snipers. They scoured the trees. They checked the tops of logs and searched for the toe of a boot or the tip of a fingernail. They couldn't find them. They were painted into the forest.

"Do you see that log flat on the ground?" Dawson whispered. Raytel and Darnell followed his finger. "We can't find this bastard. If I make a move to that log, it will draw his fire. Maybe then we can locate this SOB. Listen up."

Dawson checked his package. He had to make it four big steps. It would have to be a quick move. Dawson took a deep breath and one giant, swift step. Raytel expected him to drop and roll, but Dawson was halted in his tracks. The ground snapped, and a grid of razor-sharp spikes, hidden by the brush, gouged through his sternum and held him upright. His head turned, and Dawson looked at Raytel. He smiled a wry smile, closed his eyes, and died.

"What the hell was that, Raytel? What the hell was that?"

Raytel knew this was no time for Darnell to go berserk. "That's called a booby trap," he said.

Raytel was concerned he had walked into a minefield full of these nasty contraptions. He sensed the snipers' fire was corralling them into the deadly area.

"And Dawson was the boob. We're all going to die. That's it, Raytel. I'm done. I'm going to shoot myself in the thigh and go home."

Raytel put the palm of his hand on Darnell's helmet and swiveled his head back into the action.

"Sh." He put his finger to his mouth and pointed. The bush moved ever so slightly. Raytel had found his camouflaged foe. "He has branches attached to his helmet. He looks like the jungle."

"Where's the other one?"

"I'm not sure yet."

Raytel made a mental note of the conspicuous vine. He wouldn't go that way. Dawson's erect, dead body remained a few feet from them. Raytel signaled for Bowers to gently slide to his right. He showed Bowers where to look. Bowers had once clicked a nickel off a helmet at two hundred yards. The helmet had never moved. Bowers examined the area.

"What's taking him so long?" Darnell whispered to Raytel.

"He'll see him. Be patient."

Everybody remained extremely still. Someone had to make the next move. Crack! Bower's rifle exploded, and the branches of the bush rolled down from the higher position. The Japanese soldier was dead from Bowers's bullet through his left eye. Return fire came from the other sniper as he tried to get a bead on the well-covered Bowers.

A loud rustling indicated the sniper was bugging out and had bought himself a few precious moments. The field of booby traps provided the opportunity to gain plenty of distance from the marines. The marines poked at the earth in front of them with their rifle butts and sprang another half dozen deadly traps. Once in the clear, they headed farther south to Aslito. Raytel added more casualties to his list. The memories of the dead tortured him.

The marines humped it to Aslito. They dug foxholes and set up the heavy artillery of seventy-five-millimeter pack howitzers and Browning machine guns. The Japanese soldiers proved to be all the marines could handle. Casualty rates rose into the thousands. The American perimeter was set to the north, and the airfield continued to come under the fire of heavy air attacks. The howitzers blasted enemy posts with six-pound shells. Darnell spent the dusk hours tightening the barbed wire. The platoon decided he was the ideal soldier for the job. He was the least likely person on Saipan to want to see the enemy. He did a great job.

Lying in the foxhole, Raytel recounted the dead. Dead, dead, and more dead. Everywhere there were dead—Americans and Japanese alike. There were legs and arms blown off by mortar fire, scorched flesh from the flamethrowers, and gashes from the bayonets achieving their evil ends. Dawson had been skewered on the bamboo, and he had killed the young Japanese soldier with his bare hands. Both were dead just the same. The powers of humankind had devised many ways to destroy one another. There were bombs, bullets, planes, and ships—all for the purpose of killing others. What had become of Earth and God's message? He remembered Reverend Rucker and the one-room Baptist church in Mississippi. "Do unto others as you would have done unto yourselves." Were all the riches in the world worth the suffering and all the people who had perished in the most despicable ways? He thought of his brothers and sisters playing in the yard light-years away from the war, and he remembered the Japanese had thrown the first punch. *Why?* Raytel looked at the moon and wondered.

They came in waves through the night. They never quit. *Stop coming! Stop!* Raytel kept the machine gun humming, and Darnell fed belts and belts of ammunition into the heated killing machine.

They tangled in Darnell's barbed wire, and the marines' front line narrowed their fire at the stuck targets. They left them dead on the wire.

"Banzai!"

The Japanese charged over their dead brethren. They went over, under, and through the dead and steel, raced through the hail of bullets, and fell to the ground in agony and death. "Stop!" Raytel screamed into the blackness. *What possesses these soldiers? Is death really better than life?* Darnell kept feeding Raytel bullets until they were all dead.

The sun rose in the morning, and the dead Japanese littered the field like beer cups at a baseball game. Bulldozers came to scoop up the dead and unceremoniously dump them into mass graves. Aslito Field had been captured. This gave the US Army Air Force a landing strip close enough for the new B-29 Superfortress to rain death upon Tokyo. The survivors on Saipan raced north to the edge of the world at Morubi Bluffs.

Trapped on the edge of the eight-hundred-foot cliffs at Morubi, four thousand Japanese soldiers and hundreds of civilians dug in for a last stand for Emperor Hirohito. US forces suffered terrible losses as they climbed to pen in the enemy. The return fire against the Japanese was merciless, and the retreating Japanese were finally surrounded. The marines and army set a front line that had them trapped. The siege could be indefinite as the US forces waited for the Japanese to surrender. Loudspeakers spoke to the enemy in their own language and begged them to surrender. Army General Saito compelled his troops to make a final charge at the Americans, and he impaled himself on his own sword in shame. The once-proud Admiral Nagumo put a bullet through his temple. At dawn four thousand troops raged from their bunker in a mad dash to the American line. Armed with knives, swords, broomsticks, and handguns, infantry machine-gun fire mowed down the mass attack. The enemy soldiers stumbled through their own dead to break through the American lines. The surge stalled, and four thousand lay dead.

With tears in his eyes, Raytel surveyed the senseless death. His heart rose as he saw the civilians coming out of the caves. Many children and women were worn from the conflict, and they walked with their loved ones out of the caves and out of the war. They did not walk toward the line, though. They did not receive the extended hand of the Americans. They walked to the cliff edges and hurled themselves into the sea by the dozens. Others emerged from caves near the bottom of the cliffs and walked steadfastly into the sea. The pounding surf slammed them against the rocks and drowned parents and children alike.

Raytel held his hands to his temples in disbelief. His head pounded from the hate and the noise of death. He walked slowly toward the civilians as one by one they jumped to their deaths. Darnell screamed at him to stop, but Raytel was in a trance. He wanted someone to live. He walked toward the civilians. He came closer and saw a young Japanese woman wearing a yellow dress. It was filthy from bomb dust. She held a small child in her arms. The child was no more than six months old. A girl. A beautiful little girl. He looked in the woman's eyes. She was terrified. She looked at Raytel with unadulterated fear. Raytel knew the look. He had seen many white faces look at him the same way. He was different from her. She different from him. She was a person. A beautiful person with a beautiful baby. She had brown eyes, a slight curve in her nose, and a soft complexion hardened by the war. Raytel extended his hand and wished for her to come nearer. "The dying needs to stop here. This is not the business of children. They need not suffer." Raytel tried to disarm the woman with a gentle smile. He moved closer until he was almost within arm's reach. The baby smiled and showed the cutting of her first tooth. The mother pulled the pin on the grenade. Raytel tried to get the baby out of harm's way. He held the mother and daughter together as the grenade exploded between the three of them and drove them over the cliffs of the Morubi Bluffs. Darnell fell to his knees and wept. He wept for his friend Raytel and the other three thousand Americans who had died taking Saipan. He wept for the fifty thousand Japanese who had perished trying to defend it. Darnell just wanted to go home.

September 1944
Norm suffered mightily from fever, coughing, diarrhea, bloody stool, and excessive vomiting. Chet worried for his friend. The schistosomiasis came from freshwater—a flat-bodied worm carried by snails through the water and penetrated the skin. The infestation process caused the bleeding. Scar tissue had built on his bladder and intestines. Norm had the look of death, and Chet was nothing but skin and bones. He kept his friend cheered up as they watched some of the other prisoners dress up like showgirls and do an impromptu Broadway review. One soldier grabbed a shovel, pretended to strum the guitar, and did a fine rendition of Woody Guthrie's dust bowl anthem, "Do Re Mi." He brought the house down. Norm smiled to renditions of Tex Ritter's "Yellow Rose of Texas" and Gene Autry's "The Streets of Laredo." Norm impressed Chet with a nasally version of Ernest Tubb's "Walking the Floor Over You." It was just enough adrenaline to make Norm smile. Laughter was always the best medicine.

"Hey, Norm. What's going on here?"

Chet and Norm looked out of the billet as the show stopped to watch the commotion.

Norm saw the trucks pulling up to Cabanatuan. Hundreds of prisoners unloaded and checked into their new camp. "They look like our sorry selves. They're not new prisoners," Norm concluded.

They moved out of their billets to welcome the new people, who were suffering from the bumpy transfer. Norm grabbed the arm of one soldier and helped him to a seat in the billet. He was suffering badly from typhus. His rash had spread to his legs, and he was delirious.

"You'll fit right in here," said Norm bitterly under his breath.

The soldier gathered the strength to speak. "Where is here?"

"This is Cabanatuan."

"Where are you from?"

"Camp O'Donnell." The man coughed up some blood.

"O'Donnell. I heard that's a real hellhole."

"It is." The soldier's stark eyes revealed the horror. "I see this is quite the oasis."

Norm laughed. "Welcome to our island," he said mockingly. "What's your name, Soldier?"

"Broodend. Carl Broodend."

"Norm Leymoita. Nice to have you aboard."

"Thanks."

Rat found Carl receiving the hospitality of the prisoners of Cabanatuan. They all introduced one another with bony handshakes. Rat met Chet. Chet met Shaun and Manny. All met Norm.

"Why are you all here? Why did they transfer you from O'Donnell?"

Manny took the role of messenger. "The Americans are winning the war. MacArthur is a month away from returning to the Philippines, and the navy has blasted their way to the oceans east of Luzon."

"This is great!" Chet could see Lily's face. They were going to be rescued. Manny wasn't smiling. "What's the matter with that? That's great. Isn't it?"

"The Japanese are taking all the prisoners out of the Philippines and sending them to work camps in China." Manny bowed his head.

"They've turned luxury liners into transports. Thousands have been shipped from POW camps at Davao and Bilibid," Shaun added.

A soldier stumbled into the conversation. He was clumsy from parakinesia. He stumbled right through. No one even commented. They had all seen it a thousand times.

"How can we get out of it? Maybe we can make a run for it, if MacArthur's that close. We could hide in the hills." Chet's mind raced.

Norm looked around at the pitiful shape of the prisoners. "We wouldn't make it fifty yards. No one is healthy enough."

"They are only taking the healthiest soldiers," Rat noted.

"Nobody's healthy." Carl spat phlegm on the ground.

"That means everybody's going." Manny sounded defeated.

"Some of the sickest men are selling their stools. If you can pass it off, you might not have to go. That's a big if, though," Rat said.

"The price these people are charging on the black market for their stools is way too large. Even sharks like Rat can't make the trade."

Rat wondered about that.

"It's only a good trade if it works." Norm sat down. He was fatigued. "Besides, I can't leave Chet by himself."

They all looked at one another and felt the same way. There was no way out of this mess.

"Hurry up, MacArthur!" Chet said.

He made the others laugh as they tried to avoid a trip to Manila Harbor. They would wait for the cavalry while they all slowly died from cholera, malaria, dysentery, schistosomiasis, and starvation.

October 1944

MacArthur met President Franklin Roosevelt and Admiral Nimitz at Pearl Harbor and left the bloody remains of New Guinea for the Australians to clean up. Threatening to resign if the president didn't opt for his Philippines strategy, the politically popular Republican, MacArthur, got his way, and the politically shrewd

Democrat, Roosevelt, smoothed the way to his fourth consecutive term. In the end it turned out to be a sound military strategy. The Japanese had heavy ground and air forces on the Philippines that could endanger the alternative of capturing Formosa. Eliminating the Philippines kept the Japanese might in front of them rather than surrounding them. It was also a natural geographic location for the squeezing of the pincers of Spruance's fleet and MacArthur's army. Plans were made to start air strikes on Mindanao and Luzon by early October with an amphibious assault scheduled for October 20.

The Japanese folded under the weight of defeat. Prime Minister Tojo had assumed dictatorial powers but resigned to the emperor. He had failed to keep his promise of preserving Japan's Pacific perimeter. The Pacific had become a disaster, and the acceleration into China fueled a debate about whether the war should go on. The Japanese war council would not let the million lost Japanese soldiers die in vain. They voted to continue the war on all fronts under the watchful eye of Admiral Yonai. Yonai was handed the unenviable task of stopping the surging American juggernaut on two Pacific fronts as well as reinvigorated efforts by the British from Burma to Malaya.

The prisoners of Cabanatuan dressed for the first time in weeks. Chet was thinner than ever, and the clothes stuck to open sores on his body and crotch. The first stage of the prisoner transport was started, and the prisoners were loaded onto trucks for the ride south to Manila and the ghoulish Bilibid Prison. Bilibid had received its own share of notoriety as another of the hellish prisoner-of-war camps run by the Japanese military. Shaun and Manny sat in the back of the truck. Manny interpreted reports from local Filipinos that the Americans had started attacking bases in Mindanao. *It won't be long*, thought Carl and Rat. Norm prayed they could hold on just long enough for the Japanese to abandon the shipment of captives and flee from the advancing

American forces. The trucks rolled down the roads they had evacuated almost three years earlier.

After hard-fought victories at Peleliu, Ulithi, and Angaur in
the Palaus, the stage was set for the great offensive to retake the
Philippines. The American fleet made the Japanese naval forces
seem like a rubber duck navy. The Japanese admirals devised a
clever scheme to defeat the overwhelming odds. Admiral Halsey
led the Third Fleet north of the Philippines, and with the assistance of the new B-29 Superfortress, they undertook strikes at the
air bases of Formosa. They tangled with the inferior pilots guarding the island and made mincemeat of them during the attack. He
then retreated to help cover MacArthur's invasion force that had
set sail from New Guinea. A quarter of a million Japanese forces
lay in wait on the Philippines. More reserves were rushed south
to Mindanao to bulk up the garrison at Davao. Halsey solved the
problem of increased Japanese air support for the Philippines by
decimating the fleet at Formosa. Every warship the Japanese had
left concentrated on the Philippines in a do-or-die showdown.
The Japanese admirals engaged War Plan SHO-1.

The pounding of the guns started on the morning of October
20. It was right on schedule. The southern beaches of Leyte crawled
with transports and infantry. By midmorning the invasion had
received little resistance. MacArthur landed on the beaches in
early afternoon and announced to the staged microphones, the
people of the Philippines, and anyone else listening, "I have returned." The seventeen-mile commandeered beachhead became
the launching point for the drive through Leyte to Tacloban. The
Japanese army lay in wait.

The *Princeton* had plenty of warning of the incoming Japanese
fighters and bombers. Dan stood at the ready as the Zeros and
Vals bounced through heavy antiaircraft fire. *Princeton* planes
had been launched to find the Japanese surface forces, but they
still had the ample protection of Hellcats and destroyer fire. The

Japanese battled fiercely but were being mauled in the sky. A Val dipped into a cloud bank and disappeared. The Hellcats failed to relocate it, and it screamed out of the cloud at three hundred feet. It closed in on the *Princeton* with the Hellcats hot on its tail. They ignited the Zero into flames. Remarkably the pilot raised the craft's nose with its last bit of power and slammed into the flight deck of the *Princeton*. It brought along its hundred-pound bomb. The resulting kamikaze explosion knocked many overboard, and the fires raged.

Dan and his team swung into action. They worked the deck of the flattop around the gaping hole. Deep in the hole, the fire sucked in the oxygen. People fell off the hose. Dan held his ground, but his skin baked. They slowly made headway. The monster raged as Dan held the hose for almost an hour. Others worked below decks and tried to quench the flames, but the inferno was a beast about to roar. The bomb ignited a slow fuse in the magazine of the *Princeton*. The immense detonation crumpled the stern and separated the doomed ship. Dan was burned black from head to toe. His eyes were scorched and blind. He struggled to his feet. He was ablaze but attempting to tame the beast. Close to death and in agony, he screamed to the wind, "Tell my sister I love her." A second explosion from the magazine sucked Dan into the maelstrom of fire and incinerated him in the ship's bowels.

The *Princeton* blaze burned for hours and took hundreds more lives. The rescuing *Birmingham* received collateral damage. The *Princeton* was put out of its misery by friendly fire in the early-evening hours.

December 1944

The prisoners were herded through Manila like cattle. Norm looked at his old stomping grounds and hardly recognized the once-grand city. Hollowed from war's ravages, the once-teeming metropolis hummed only with the sounds of survival. They marched past the Manila Hotel and the Marsman Building. The Rising Sun did not blow as stiffly in the breeze as it once had. Chet noticed fear in the eyes of the Japanese soldiers. It was not the fear of the enemy. For them, dying was a form of release. It was the fear and shame and defeat.

They arrived on the steaming docks of pier seven and were forced into columns. Rat and Carl looked at the harbor with sadness. The once-busy bay filled with commerce and activity had become a marine graveyard. The hulls of great ships rose above the surface like whales grabbing breaths. The once-lush islands that dotted the harbor sat like cinder blocks in the blue waters, and the fortress of Corregidor evoked haunting memories of the half-year siege.

An unmarked ship sat still in the waters. It was docked securely to Pier Seven. The heat cooked the prisoners and proved to be the last breaths of some. Several slumped dead onto the dock. Shaun held Manny upright and encouraged him to live. They examined the ship taking them from the Philippines. A converted ocean liner, the *Oryoku Maru*, became their floating prison on a passage to China. The seventy-three-hundred-ton ship looked seaworthy. Shaun found the open decks refitted for machine gun turrets disturbing. Japanese nationals filed onto the pier. Thousands of men, women, and children walked past the living dead. Farmers, businesspeople, wives, teens, and infants were all transplanted civilians, and they slowly boarded the upper decks.

"I guess we got bumped from first class." Manny could always make Shaun laugh—even now.

Loading the civilians took hours, and the afternoon sun oppressed the prisoners. The wait unnerved them. Too much thinking on the hot pier led some to panic and try to break free of the columns. They were punished swiftly. Chet became shaky and restless. Norm held him close and assured him they were going to be OK. The line of prisoners started to move after the long wait, and this created spasms of fear. Japanese guards impelled the prisoners on with their bayonet tips. Sixteen hundred prisoners, a third with dysentery and countless others with malaria and cholera, walked up the ramp. They filed slowly down the narrow staircase of the *Oryoku Maru* and into the black cargo holds—the stomach of the ship. Guards smacked them with broom handles and screamed at them to move faster.

One by one they filled the three holds. They squeezed into the area meant for boxes and crates, and the air was dense and stifling. A large wooden bucket sat in the middle of the hold— the only latrine for sixteen hundred sick people on the weeklong voyage. Pressed against one another, back to back and shoulder to shoulder, the prisoners clung to one another as the *Oryoku Maru* rumbled. Urine and feces sloshed on the decks of the holds. People were unable to get to the wooden bucket through the mass of dying prisoners. Cries of fear sang as people vomited on the backs of others. The sun was setting on Manila as the *Oryoku Maru* left the harbor.

Carl gasped for air. He was suffocating before Rat's eyes. He slammed his fist against the closed hatch and demanded the attention of the guard. The bodily systems of dehydrated soldiers were shutting down in the furnace, and they licked the side of the ship for residual condensation. A guard opened the hatch, and Rat squinted into the last rays of the day. His eyes were dilated from the darkness of the holds. He demanded the hatch be left open for air and the latrine be raised and emptied so they wouldn't have to wallow in their own excrement.

The guard opened the hatch, and air seeped into the compartments. The soldiers snapped at it like a school of fish feeding in an aquarium. They lowered a rope. Rat and Carl attached it to the wooden bucket, which was overflowing with waste. The guards raised the bucket as it splashed the blend of feces, bloody mucus, vomit, and urine onto the heads and shoulders of the soldiers. The guards emptied the bucket and lowered it back into the hold. Then they closed the hatch.

Suffocation drove them to madness. Panic ensued, and Rat slammed on the dark hatch. The new guard was mildly sympathetic to their plight, and he agreed to bring up four people at a time and allow them a spot of fresh air. There were sixteen hundred in the hold. Rat took advantage and sent the most insane to the surface. For many it would be their last rays of sunlight.

The sun set as they passed the tip of Mariveles. They set a slow northern course that paralleled the western coast of Luzon. Soldiers dying of thirst drank their own urine. Fistfights broke out. Deranged prisoners clawed at one another and bit one another's flesh. Blood dripped from limbs as insanity raged. People licked and sucked the blood of others. Cries of pain and agony filled the hold as others wept in fear and loneliness. Howls and moans punctuated the claustrophobic terrors of others. The jostling continued through the nights as fits of fury came in sudden, shrieking waves.

The dawn light exposed the toll of the grisly night. Fifty soldiers lay dead at the hands of their comrades. Others had succumbed to heat prostration and suffocation. Skittish men cowered in the corners of the holds. Bearded and barely clothed, they were petrified of themselves and the malice they had wrought upon one another.

The *Oryoku Maru* cruised slowly with the morning sun. The guards lowered buckets of rice and water into the holds. This kindled a frenzy. Shaun and Manny were too weak to fight the scrum of people savagely scraping for food, and they sat meekly in the corner. Norm and Chet, bruised and battered from the pile, brought them a few morsels of rice. The hatch opened, and cool morning air refreshed the hold of the stale smells of blood and death. They raised the wooden bucket and showered the people and food with bile. Starving soldiers continued to eat the rice.

The unmistakable sounds of fighters roared above the ship. Chet pumped his fist as the Hellcats opened fire on the passenger ship. They strafed the upper cabins with machine-gun fire. The fighters made several passes over the ship, and the Japanese engaged the Hellcats from the turrets of the *Oryoku Maru*. The cries of wounded Japanese civilians and soldiers echoed in the ship's bowels. Morale grew in the hold. There was hope of imminent rescue. The skies went silent as the Hellcats left the air. The hatch remained closed for the rest of the day, and the Japanese sorted the dead from the wounded in a macabre cruise ship triage. The prisoners anxiously waited through another night. The possibility of freedom tomorrow encouraged them.

The *Oryoku Maru* was within a few hours of making the open waters of the South China Sea when the Hellcats returned. The prisoners cheered wildly in the dark storage holds below. The machine-gun fire from the *Oryoku Maru* was frantic as the fighters buzzed the ship.

"There are bombers in the sky," Shaun said. He recognized the sound of a different engine.

"They don't know we're on the ship. They don't know we're on the ship!" Carl started a huge chant as the prisoners futilely tried to communicate with the soaring planes above.

Shaun and Manny gave each other a chilled look. The Hellcats roared in and blistered the *Oryoku Maru* as the bombers dropped their torpedoes in the water. The tin fish swam to the luxury liner and blasted through the stern. A horrific rumble shuddered the ship. It veered off course and evaded the bombers. The grand ship ran aground. The captain was still close to the shoreline of Luzon and implored the Japanese soldiers to abandon ship. Some Japanese guards stayed to protect the emperor's cargo of human slaves. Another group took the lifeboats and their machine guns and headed for the beaches. The guards planned to make the prisoners swim to the beachheads. The machine guns would keep them in line.

The guards opened the hatch and individually brought the soldiers to the deck. Manny climbed weakly into the sunlight. Carl and Rat helped men up the steep stairs. Norm and Chet helped the very sick off the slippery, disgusting floors and toward the hatch. Shaun looked frantically for Manny. Now was not the time to lose his friend. They heard the bomber roaring overhead and the distinct whistling of a thousand-pound bomb. The bomb crushed into the midsection of the already-foundering ship and ripped through the vessel's innards. The concussion blasted the prisoners off their feet and disintegrated hundreds upon impact. Carl and Rat lay dead in the mangled hull of the *Oryoku Maru*. Norm and Chet evaporated in the fires that raged in the center of the explosion. The bomb had landed directly over where they were helping the sick to safety.

Shaun, disoriented by the concussion, climbed the ladder and choked from the smoke building in the hold. The sunlight topside blinded him for minutes. His vision returned, but the faded colors of the deck were only blurs. Thousands of people scurried along the decks and searched for any safe haven. Japanese survivors were being told to fill up the remaining lifeboats. Guards pointed guns at prisoners and told them to get in the water and swim. They pointed to the beach and the waiting machine guns. Prisoners waved at the navy pilots to stop their bombing runs. One Hellcat flew over and tipped its wings in acknowledgment. The pilots had no idea.

Shaun searched for Manny. A soldier struggled in the waters off the *Oryoku Maru*. It was Manny! His body was working on adrenaline, and Shaun jumped in to assist his friend. Manny's chin was barely above water. Shaun swam to him.

"What took you so long? I'm going to try to catch the next wave in." Manny sputtered.

Shaun grabbed Manny around the neck and hoisted him over his hip. He started to scissors kick into the shore. Manny gurgled the salt water in and out of his mouth.

"Stay with me, Soldier. We're going to make it. We're going to live. Don't you want to see Anna? Don't you want to see Jaime and Juan and Miguel? We're going to see Anna and Paige, and Anna's going to make us a fine dinner." Manny became heavy, and he started to cough violently as the water dripped into his lungs. "Come on, Soldier! Stay with me."

Manny's limp body was deadweight. Shaun started to sink. He began to cough water from his lungs as he encouraged his friend to stay alive. "We're going to play some football. Me and you. We're going to be in some big games, and your kids are going to get to see their father play. Stay with me, Manny."

Manny sank below the waves. Shaun grabbed at his collar and hoisted him up. Manny gasped for air and sank again. Shaun went to grab him and found his shoulder. He pulled, but his strength was gone. He embraced Manny closely as the sea covered their heads. Shaun watched peacefully as the locket around his neck floated before his eyes. He thought of Paige as the water rushed into his lungs. They sank into the waters of the South China Sea fifty yards from freedom.

Satan laughed and laughed until it hurt to laugh, and then he laughed some more.

Nimrod and the Barbershop

Jairus closed the book. "That's a very sad story. It's like what happened to me." Tears filled the child's eyes.

"Yes. It is. I suppose that's one of the reasons God assigned you to me. It hit close to home." Nimrod felt the weight of his failure.

"Are the men in Heaven now? I'd like to meet them."

"All the men were lost in war battles. Their bodies were never found. Their souls never crossed through the astral plane, and they are trapped in the abyss."

"Why did they take your wings? So many died in the war. How could you prevent it?"

"Every soul on Earth is provided an angel. The best angels watch over thousands and thousands of souls. None of the angels are expected to save everyone from the Darkness, but they are expected to save a lot. This was my first time guarding souls. I was inexperienced. Michael only assigned me those eleven names. As each died I showed him my face and apologized for my failure as his angel. I wanted them all to know I was accountable for my failures." Nimrod looked at the stacks of books in Basmilla Library. "I lost them all."

"It doesn't seem fair. Only eleven souls?"

"The angel Jegudiel saved six hundred thousand souls. He mourned his losses but saved so many. I failed to save one. Michael didn't think I had what it took to be a good angel. So he clipped my wings, and they made me an instructor." Nimrod needed some air. "Are you hungry?"

"Sure am." They headed out of the library. "You said you were an angel from Earth and an expert on Earth. I am not from Earth. Why am I with you?" Jairus asked.

"All angels study each culture from the galaxy so that when they are called to service, they can be prepared for all of God's souls."

"Am I the only soul in Heaven from the Behorrin Debartik Galaxy?" Jairus asked.

"Oh, no." Nimrod smiled. "Each galaxy has its own section of Heaven. It's all about organization and nothing about segregation."

Jairus and Nimrod sat at a picnic table in the park. They hailed a vendor. He handed them their lunches. They peeled back the paper, and before them were the most excellent bratwurst sandwiches—two thick links grilled and topped with sauerkraut, mustard, and horseradish sauce on a chewy whole-grain hearth-baked roll. "This is a favorite on Earth," Nimrod said.

He smiled, closed his eyes, and took a bite. It was the perfect meal for the moment. That was the way Heaven worked. Nimrod took a sip of the pale ale in the frosted glass next to the sandwich. A lady sat quietly at the other end of the table. She was enjoying fried flounder and hush puppies with a glass of sweet tea.

"Good afternoon," Nimrod addressed her kindly.

"Hello, Nimrod." The lady barely looked up from her meal.

"Who's that?" Jairus asked. He was enjoying his sausage.

"That's Sojourner Truth. She loves fish."

They walked on the path through the park and enjoyed the smell of the red and purple Queen Anne's lace that surrounded the base of the shagbark hickory trees lining the way. Wild-pink and darker-red dame's rockets were interspersed in a field of bulbous yellow buttercups. It created a stunning visual bouquet. White oaks danced with hundred-foot elms and chestnut trees. There was no unrest in the forest. There was no trouble with the trees in Heaven. Children ran from the steps of Escuela de Angels. They were anxious to be relieved of their studies. Kids were kids—even in Heaven.

Some kids carried book bags. Others toted scrolls and dusty books far too heavy for them to lift comfortably.

"This is your new school." Nimrod stood at the bottom of the stairs. His strong chin jutted out proudly, and his broad smile was evident in the light of the Divine Star Vetene. "I registered you yesterday, and you start tomorrow. You have an exciting set of classes."

"Exciting?" Jairus didn't look all that excited. School was school in any galaxy.

"You have Professor Einstein for math in first period and William Shakespeare for English literature in second period. Michelangelo teaches art, and Leonardo da Vinci teaches science."

"Where are we going?" Jairus didn't want to talk about school.

"You will be staying with me during your training. I live around the block." Nimrod escorted Jairus to his new home.

The red, white, and blue colors swirled inside the tube on the porch. "What's that?" asked Jairus.

"That is the sign for a barbershop." Nimrod would have to answer a lot of these questions. "A barbershop is a place where people on Earth get their hair cut. It's something you could use." Nimrod pulled at Jairus's tangled mess.

"Who cuts the hair?" wondered Jairus.

"Samson," Nimrod replied dryly.

Nimrod's living room was outfitted like a barbershop. It had bedrooms upstairs and a kitchen on the main floor, but it was a barbershop. "Why does it look like this?" Jairus asked.

"A barbershop is a very social place. After losing my wings, I wanted to have a place for souls to visit, hang out, and talk about Earth."

"What do you talk about?"

"In a barbershop we talk about nearly anything." Nimrod closed the door behind him. "We talk about sports and movies and music and people and politics."

"What are politics?" Jairus asked.

"We'll save that topic for later. Why don't we look around a bit?"

Heaven was the most wired place in the universe. It had complete reception of all broadcasting from all 38,387 galaxies in deep space. Radio, television, light imaging, subsolar transmission, octave beam, and phoenix array capability—Heaven had it all. Of course, there was cable but not in the normal cable way.

At Nimrod's barbershop, the social spot of Pyrub Cape, they usually watched three earthly things: ESPN, VH1, and MTV. All were worldly indulgences. Jairus was immediately obsessed with VH1.

Jairus eyed the platter of doughnuts from Child's placed between Mama Cass Elliot and Karen Carpenter. They were sharing a chocolate glazed.

"Would you like a doughnut?" Nimrod asked.

"Yes." Jairus grabbed a bear claw. "Scrumptious! Why are they so much better than regular doughnuts?" Jairus asked.

"Julia only uses ghulas dough. It comes from the galaxy Jouis Aneur. It is their interplanetary dough." Nimrod studied Jairus. He had all the tools to make a great angel, but Nimrod felt compelled to ask the hard question. "Why is your heart so sad?"

Jairus never looked up from the doughnut, and Mama Cass hummed "Monday, Monday" under her breath. "I miss my mother," he said.

"I figured as much." Nimrod looked at Jairus, who avoided eye contact. "It is important to share our feelings. Would you like to see your mother?"

Jairus raised his head from his shoulder and looked through his tears at Nimrod. "Can you do that?"

"Yes. But you will have to listen carefully to what I say. We have certain rules that must be followed. They are rules to keep us all safe from the Darkness."

Jairus's eyes grew three times in size. For the first time since their introduction, Nimrod had Jairus's full and undivided attention. He was going to make the most of it. "The Darkness is in constant battle with the light of Heaven and God. Heaven has angels, and the Darkness has rotten angels." Jairus looked as if he was going to speak, but Nimrod put his finger to his lips. "They are not like Heaven's angels. They are ghouls and cretins. They have abandoned their souls and crossed over the River Styx into the void of Hell. They receive their instructions from the evil generals that lurk in the fiery pit. The generals receive their orders from the Darkness itself. Across the universe they spread destruction and whittle away with fear at the souls God created. The demons despise souls. They embody the very ideal of life—the life they yearn to extinguish. The souls of the universe have been given the lessons they need to defend themselves against the ways of the Darkness. We have sent messengers through time to speak the Word of God. Yet even the righteous need help sometimes. That's when Heaven's angels come to their aid."

Nimrod still had the riveted attention of Jairus, and he continued. "The Darkness has succeeded in manifesting war throughout the universe. These are troubled times in Heaven. If the Darkness destroyed the light of the souls, then he would come to destroy the light of Heaven. Heaven's angels are in short supply and heavy demand. The Darkness is pounding away on many fronts. There is war in most of the galaxies, and thousands of civilizations are at risk. Our most profound messengers are in the line of fire. Jesus and Muhammad are in the Stounfad System fighting Geeshi Grub, the leader of the Hell Star Death Squad. Grub is expediting the swallowing of Blanco Trollien. Moses is in Jouis Aneur preparing for a direct attack from Gholar, and Buddha is in Behorrin Debartik—just like your mother. The Darkness sent the projectile through Yarrges Winch that killed millions. She was meant to live for a purpose, your mother. She was meant to stay and help the suffering. Just as you died for a purpose. You died so Michael could make you an angel." Nimrod stepped outside Michael's mission parameters. "When you become an angel, we can help your mother."

"How do we get to see her?"

"I will tell you. There are many steps to take before we can visit your mother. You cannot travel if you are not an angel. It is too dangerous for the untrained, righteous soul—especially one of a child. There is a bounty too grand for the demons to resist. There are places in Heaven that are connected with all the galaxies in the universe. Your mother is at the end of the Grazy Derlf Trail, which you will travel in time."

"Who are Vishnu, Shar, and Thomas? I saw their pictures on the wall."

"They are my best friends. You will get to know them well." Nimrod moved to the porch. Jimi Hendrix and Duane Allman sat in rocking chairs and picked out a terrific acoustic version of "Little Wing." Jimi played a catgut six-string and Duane a Dobro. Norwegian spruces and cottonwoods provided ample shade, and the needles of the balsam fir and rustling leaves of the sugar maple provided soft percussion for the masters. They had never sounded so good. This was how Nimrod lived at the barbershop. Anything could happen and usually did.

Delilah had done a nice job with the hanging baskets on the porch. Orange mushroom pimples and scattered aquamarine and goldenrod scarlet elf cups surrounded the deck. Nimrod opened the door and walked into his own personal tree house. He was determined to stave off the temptation of relaxation and conversation. Minutes could become hours quickly at the barbershop, and before he knew it, the shine of another day would be creeping through the window—another day wasted away. *No more!* he thought, and he jutted out his chin and looked around.

"I think there's plenty of lard in your hair, Mr. Presley." Sampson tried to soothe the singer.

"I don't know. I think this hair is sticking up just a little. Why don't you put in another handful?"

Samson rolled his eyes as Elvis took off his mulberry jacket, sat back down in the chair, and fixed his collar. Sampson squeamishly stuck his hands back into a bucket of animal fat and slathered it through the hair. Sampson pulled out his comb, and it slipped through the jet black mane.

"Perfect." The boy from Tupelo seemed pleased.

"I am glad you like it, Mr. Presley." Samson seemed just as happy.

"I know we don't use money here in Heaven, but I feel as if I owe you something."

"That's not necessary, Mr. Presley."

"How about I sing you all a song? How 'bout a little 'Don't Be Cruel?'" The King cocked his leg and seemed ready to belt it out.

The entire room in unison shouted, "No!"

"Aw, c'mon. How about 'Suspicious Minds?'" Elvis let loose a few bars. "We're caught in a trap…"

"No!"

Elvis straightened his collar and left the barbershop.

Groups of people loitered around the shop playing rummy, bridge, checkers, chess, and Scrabble. Mostly they were just talking and barely noticed Nimrod's bold entrance. Jairus followed him in.

"Who's that?" The crew had noticed the young man.

"This is Jairus. This lad is an angel academic. He is embarking on a colossal journey of acquirement. You dullards are lowering him to your level of imbecility. We are here only to claim our mines of information and retire forthwith to the sanctity of our quiet domicile. We will no longer wallow with the dim-witted and uninspired."

Jairus looked at Nimrod. He was acting like the biggest geek.

"Who is going to guide him on this colossal journey of acquirement, Nimrod?" Vishnu asked skeptically.

"I shall be the emeritus to his apprentice."

"The only thing you can teach him is how to bluff a six-two off suit." Thomas doubted Nimrod's emeritus status.

"I will admit I am handy with a deck of cards, but that is not my only talent, as you very well know."

"You can stuff your face like no one who has ever walked in this place," Delilah said, and the room erupted. Even Jairus couldn't help but laugh at his guru.

"Mock me if you will, but I see no other choice but to remove the child from this den of dim and focus on the task at hand. Michael has honored my new pupil and me."

"You can't do this alone, Nimrod." Thomas doubted his friend. "You'll need help."

"The angels are spread all over the universe fighting the Darkness. I am the only qualified faculty left." Nimrod accepted he was the last teacher picked. It hurt to think so little confidence had been bestowed upon him. "Who else will foster this child?"

"We will!" Shar, Vishnu, and Thomas all raised their hands.

"I don't think this is headed in the right direction. No. We need to stick to the original plan." Nimrod waffled—a steady trait when regarding serious matters.

Shar walked up to Nimrod, put her palms on his cheek, and comforted him. "These are trying times. We all want to do something to help. Our time is past, but our minds are fertile with wisdom and experience we can pass to the child. We are all old masters of battling the Darkness. Don't let us shrivel in the barbershop while the universe dwindles. Let us help. Let us feel the joy of being needed that you feel now." The copper jingle of her bracelets clanged home the point. "Success with a team is greater than failure as an individual."

Nimrod bowed his head and accepted he could not do this alone. "I have always counted you as my best friends. Your strength and love have shone here today. For Jairus and God, let us form Team Nimrod and exalt in the nurturing of this child."

"Why does it have to be Team Nimrod? Why can't it be Team Vishnu? Why do the people of India have to be second?" Vishnu liked watching Nimrod's blood pressure rise.

Nimrod looked at Vishnu—his foil and friend. "Are we going to be serious about this, or are we going to bicker and stomp around like spoiled brats? We're turning the television off and opening up the books."

"Hey, I wanted to watch *Oprah*. You can't turn it off now." Thomas whined.

Delilah emerged from the kitchen with chocolate chip cookies. She paraded them around Nimrod. They were his favorite. Delilah looked satisfied as she plunged a cookie into her mouth and plopped herself onto the couch. She was wearing nothing but blue-gray board shorts and a navy-blue tank top. Delilah was in her surfergirl phase, and Sampson really liked her long blond hair.

"Well, all right, but you have to turn the volume down so we can concentrate. Let's get to work."

"Nimrod?" Jairus gave Nimrod his best sad face. Nimrod looked at Jairus. "Can Sampson do my hair while we study?"

For the love of God himself, Nimrod blasphemed. This was never going to fly. Nimrod gave in. "Sure, but you have to focus."

"All right!" It was the happiest he had seen Jairus all day.

"How about a little Duran Duran action today?" Sampson was just as ecstatic as Jairus.

"Sure."

Shar, Thomas, Nimrod, and Vishnu circled their chairs around Jairus and Samson.

"I believe one of the best ways to study is in an open forum. I'll read about a few saints or deities, and we'll have a roundtable discussion about each one." Nimrod glowed at the challenge. He opened the sky blue textbook, thumbed through the pages, and analyzed where to begin. "I suppose we'll start at the very beginning." He chuckled at his lack of direction. He reminded himself a professor needed a well-planned lesson. Today he'd have to wing it. "Let's start with St. Alexis."

"Doesn't she live in the mountains near Jakeons Veer?" Vishnu recognized the name.

"No. She lives in the foothills of Mount Rabtik near Khaluarm Falls," called Delilah from the other room.

"No. I think that's Alphonsa who lives near the falls. Alexis lives in a farmhouse near Lherrey Land." Thomas was only pretty sure, though.

"I think I would know where Alexis lives, Thomas. Samson does her hair." Delilah was always sure.

"People, what does it matter where she lives? Jairus needs to learn what she did to help humankind on Earth." The room grew silent, and attention was refocused on the lesson. Nimrod cleared his throat. "As I was saying, St. Alexis was the patron saint of beggars, belt makers, earthquakes, lightning storms, and travelers." Nimrod mused over the information. He looked at the group. "Jairus, did you get all that?"

Jairus was in the middle of a shampoo. "I got most of it. St. Alexis likes belts."

The group giggled under their breaths.

"Not exactly." Nimrod exhibited patience. "She was the patron saint of belt makers."

"She likes to accessorize like any woman. Match up the belt with the slacks and shoes. Add a nice purse and blouse, and she gets a great outfit," Shar said.

Nimrod's eyes went bloodshot. "No, Jairus. Shar is just being silly." Nimrod smacked Shar's knee for the distasteful interruption. "Alexis watches over the hardworking belt makers on Earth."

"Why just belt makers? There are a lot of leather products. Why doesn't she care about all leatherworkers?" Nimrod smacked Vishnu on the knee this time. "It's just a question. Sorry."

"We'll adjust that to include all leatherworkers of all leather products." He stared at Vishnu. "She also prays for people in lightning storms, which can be very dangerous."

"I don't like lightning so much, but I love thunder," Thomas said.

He did his best thunder imitation, and then they all took shots at reproducing the unmatchable sound. Nimrod wiped his forehead. His pulse started pounding. The ruckus died down.

"Now, Jairus, let's stay focused on our lessons." Nimrod assumed a stern headmaster pose. "We'll move to the next one in the book. St. Albert is the patron saint of students, teachers, miners, and naturalists."

"Naturalists," Vishnu scoffed. "People at a nudist colony have a patron saint."

Nimrod was flustered. "I'm sure it's not that type of naturalist."

"What kind is it, Nimrod?" Jairus pressed the issue.

"I am sure they are just people who love nature." Nimrod grew a smidge red in the cheeks.

"Naked," Shar chimed in.

"Let's get away from this vulgar chitchat and proceed," Nimrod protested.

"Is being naked vulgar?" Jairus asked.

The question flummoxed Nimrod. "Well, no. God created beautiful bodies that should be glorified...in the right setting." Nimrod squirmed in his seat.

"Veronica Lake," shot Vishnu.

"Joan of Arc," said Thomas.

"She's not very feminine, Thomas," replied Shar.

"She's got great arms and a tight tummy."

"William the Conqueror—what a hottie," Shar said and swooned.

"I will continue despite your disdain for my student's education," Nimrod said. "St. Ambrose was known as the honey-tongued doctor."

"I've known a couple of those," snickered Shar.

Nimrod's voice raised. "He is the patron saint of bakers of honey bread, bees and beekeepers, geese..."

"Do geese really need a patron saint?" Thomas asked.

"How about the butcher, the baker, and the candlestick maker?" asked Vishnu with a smile.

"That is enough." Nimrod lost control, and Jairus giggled at how his friends had gotten under Nimrod's skin. "You will all kindly shut up while we finish this lesson." He eyed the room for someone to question his venom. "Saint Anne Matron is believed to be the mother of the Virgin Mary and the patron saint of"—Nimrod hesitated and eyed the room—"broom makers."

"Does that include whisk brooms and dustpans or just brooms?" Vishnu cackled, and the laughter became an epidemic.

Nimrod did not acknowledge him. "And cabinetmakers."

"Joseph was a carpenter, that old dog." Shar was cracking herself up.

Nimrod was undeterred. "And lace makers."

Everyone erupted in laughter—even Nimrod.

"Give to me your leather, take from me my lace." They sang the Stevie Nicks and Don Henley duet in unison.

Nimrod plowed forward. "Apollonia tore out her teeth with pincers after refusing to deny Jesus Christ."

"Wasn't she in *Purple Rain* with Prince?"

"Saint Augustine of Hippo." Nimrod continued to shout over the cacophony of laughter. "She was the patron saint of brewers." He bowed his head. He knew what was coming.

"When it's time to relax, one beer stands clear—Miller beer!" They all sang in unison.

Thomas, Vishnu, and Shar kicked like chorus girls to the Miller jingle as tears of laughter ran down Jairus's face.

"Hey, Delilah. These guys have a good idea. Why don't you go to the store and grab some beer?"

"I'm on it." Delilah liked a chilled stout while making dinner, and she had to pick up a few extra supplies for tonight's meal anyhow.

The lesson imploded, and his friends weakened Nimrod's defenses until he joined in on the fun. He finally accepted that some of the information had humorous value. Delilah returned from the grocery store with plenty of beer and wine and a cart full of what was to become dinner. Mandarin oranges and napoleons spilled onto the counter as she began to slice the russet potatoes into big wedges and marinate them in balsamic vinegar. Pots boiled on the stove for the whole-wheat spaghetti as Nimrod prepared the broccoli, chickpeas, and garlic to toss into the pasta. Shar worked on a batch of sticky rice with Chinese sausage and dried scallops. While she waited for the pot to boil, she deveined the plump shrimp and heated up a sauté pan with hot oil and garlic. Thomas opened a nice bottle of Syrah and set it on the counter to breathe while he worked on an appetizer of *acini di pepe* with spinach and feta. He had already started the roast chicken, and he could whip up the tahini sauce in a flash. They were utilizing the fresh asparagus with the chicken and to wrap the Dover sole. The shallots were chopped for the tangerine beurre blanc. Vishnu was making his favorite desserts—pumpkin brittle, sticky tofu pudding, and kiwi tarts with mascarpone. Jairus sat on the counter and watched how Team Nimrod really could work well together.

Nimrod poured himself a glass of the Syrah, swirled it in the crystal goblet, and opened up the aroma. It was grassy but not overly so. He let the grape rest on his palate. Notes of cherry and blackberry with hints of honey and caramel tickled his tongue. Shar made her own evaluation. She smelled blueberry and pear with the bite of green pepper. That was the beauty of wine. They did agree it was delectable.

They sat down to the feast after thanking God for the bounty. Nimrod looked fondly at his family of friends and mused about how lonely he would be without them. He could not imagine. He said a personal prayer to help him guide Jairus through the training. He knew he was part of something special.

"Pass the rice please," Shar said to Vishnu, who obliged with the added bonus of a plate of tender shrimp.

They dolloped their plates with little tastes. Someone rapped at the door. Confucius let himself in and placed a covered plate of *shumai* in the middle of the table. He removed the lid and released the savory smell of the dumplings stuffed with chicken and coconut through the kitchen.

"Confucius say, 'Don't invite yourself to dinner without *shumai.*'"

They all laughed as Confucius parodied himself.

"Hear, hear," the group toasted, and Jairus raised his glass of milk.

"Are we going to play poker tonight?" Confucius asked.

"I don't see why not," Thomas said. He was ready to ante up.

"I'm in," said Vishnu as he stared down Confucius with his cowboy eyes.

Confucius had licked Vishnu with a few bad beats the last go-around, and Vishnu was looking for some payback. Shar was always game, and the table looked at Nimrod—usually a staunch regular.

"No, folks. I'm out. I'm going to tuck Jairus into bed and get a good night's sleep. We've got things to do tomorrow."

Jairus felt sad he was distracting Nimrod from his routine. They mopped up dinner and snacked on pumpkin brittle while tidying up the kitchen. He showed Jairus his room and watched as Jairus brushed his teeth and made muscles in the mirror. He would be a man before he knew it, and Nimrod faced the uphill task of teaching a boy to be a man. *Teaching a boy to be an angel,* he corrected himself. He tucked Jairus into bed.

"Thanks, Nimrod."

Nimrod felt his heartstrings go pluck. "For what?" He was genuinely bewildered.

"For caring so much. It means a lot."

The whole harp went into a full concert. This was the closest thing to being a father. Jairus closed his eyes and dreamed of the grand day he would be able to traverse the Grazy Derlf Trail and find his mother.

Nimrod joined the poker table. He stayed up all night drinking wine and arguing who was better—Joe Louis or Muhammad Ali.

The light came through the window—and the voices. "Good morning, Nimrod." The chipper trio of voices rang like a sledgehammer to the temple.

"Gentlemen." Nimrod sat up and cleared his head. "And lady." Nimrod looked at Shar. Nimrod was counting on another hour of sleep. "What time is it? And why are you in my window?"

"It is six in the morning, and we have a message from Michael," Thomas said.

"Michael wants to see you at nine," Vishnu added.

"Sharp," Shar noted.

Nimrod threw on a robe. "Nine o'clock?"

"Sharp."

"Yes. I gathered that. Nine o'clock...sharp. Would you fine folks be heading that way?"

"No," they answered together.

"Where are you going?"

"We're off to the Wiyo Docks."

Nimrod knew it was going to be a long day. Jairus was still sleeping, so Nimrod left him a note and told him he would see him after school. Michael had called, and when Michael called, Nimrod listened. He was the boss after all. Nimrod selected a comfortable pair of walking slacks and his favorite pair of Birkenstocks. He walked out the front door after a cold glass of water. He headed for Judea, the main metropolis of Heaven.

Nimrod stopped and wiped his brow under the European alder. Lewis Carroll was sitting in the branch of an eastern sycamore. He just sat there smiling. It was warm early. Today would be a hot one. He continued on and watched John Lennon and George Harrison knock around the Hacky Sack under the beech tree in the park. They squished fresh strawberries as they kicked at the leather. It was a tad early for sports, but it was possible the two old friends had not gone to bed yet. He gave them a friendly wave and promised to catch them at the Canteen. The smell of the bay refreshed Nimrod's purpose, and he stepped up his pace along Haadad Marsh. John the Baptist was taking an early-morning swim. He spit the water out of his mouth in a mini geyser and let it land on his chest while he did the backstroke. Nimrod said, "How do you do?"

John the Baptist waved back, lost his momentum, and almost went under. That would have been regrettable.

Nimrod could see Iconadary Mall in the short distance. Busts of legendary prophets, saints, and heroes filled the grassy knoll He heard the squabbling of two old men.

"I was thinking robin's egg or periwinkle." Monet spoke with his hands and splashed the wall with his imaginary brush.

"You old buzzard. It demands an orange red or maybe red orange." Rembrandt held his fingers to the bridge of his nose in frustration.

Nimrod rolled his eyes at the savants and continued his journey. A living chessboard filled the courtyard of the Grand Hall of Judea. Today's match featured the Kingdom of Camelot versus the Egyptian dynasty of Cleopatra and Mark Antony. Nimrod moved to the upper level to see the action more clearly.

"What's going on in the match?" Nimrod asked another curious spectator.

"King Arthur sent Knight Lancelot into the fray with an inexplicable strategy, and Lancelot was slain forthwith."

"Surprise, surprise." Nimrod could smell that one from the Haadad Marsh.

"Cleopatra has been hounding Guinevere, and only Sir Dinidan is protecting her. He has come under the fire of Mark Antony's Arabian knights."

"Yes. It looks as if the Egyptians might have cornered Arthur this time."

"Brilliant!"

It was five minutes to nine. Nimrod had to go. There was a huge flight of marble stairs to climb.

The doors to the spatial war room were open, but Nimrod knocked nonetheless. He had only been here once before—to get his wings.

"Come in, Nimrod." The voice was not booming or abrasive, but Michael made his presence known.

His four wings fluttered in the breeze from the window, which looked out over Ghara Serpiana. Gabriel escorted Nimrod into the chamber as Raphael and Uriel sized Nimrod up. Saffron hairs, each of which had a million faces, covered Michael. Each face had a million eyes, and from each eye fell seven hundred thousand tears. Each tear became a cherub somewhere in the galaxy.

"Nimrod." Michael stared him down.

"Yes, sir?"

"Earth is on the verge of destruction. The Darkness is winning the war on several fronts. We believe we can strike at the heart of his plan, but we need time."

"Yes, sir."

"In an effort to spearhead resistance in Jouis Aneur, Behorrin Debartik, the Stounfad System, and several other galaxies, we have left the Milky Way exposed—specifically the colony of humans who inhabit Earth. Are you with me?" Nimrod nodded his head. The news was worse than he had thought. "Our sources have caught wind of a plot by Satan to destroy the planet. There are no concrete details, but if this is true and if he succeeds, it would tilt the scales of the universe dramatically to the Darkness."

"Yes. That would be very bad."

"As you well know, all angels are on assignment around the universe and under the commands of various leaders. Buddha is in the Behorrin Debartik galaxy. Moses is in Jouis Aneur, which is preparing for attacks from Gholar—the main planet of Hell. And Mohammed and Jesus are in the Stounfad System fighting against General Geeshi Grub and the Hell Star."

"What exactly is the Hell Star?"

Michael looked at Gabriel with worry. "The Hell Star is a synthetic black hole manufactured at the behest of the Darkness himself. It is capable of swallowing whole galaxies, bite by bite, and leaving nothing but a void." Michael showed the stress on his face.

"The Hell Star is not fully operational, but it's close. General Geeshi Grub had advanced through the Blanco Trollien Archipelago using only conventional weapons. Grub eliminated resistance on Oshu Land and is close to exterminating Maroed Rain. Foccod Knort is currently under heavy siege, and our forces received a blow when Grub captured the Sleoc Choiry."

"I'm sorry...the Sleoc Choiry?" Nimrod looked at the giant war map over Michael's desk.

"The Sleoc Choiry is mined for weapons-grade tritonon. Grub has more than enough ammunition to furnish his ground troops and supply his destroyers, battleships, and the fighters on his carriers. The Choiry also provides raw materials necessary to complete the Hell Star. It's only a matter of time before it's operational. Then they will systematically sail it through the universe and gobble up all that is light—including Heaven itself, if they find our location."

Nimrod's complexion went ghostly pale. "Isn't there anything we can do?"

"We are trying our best. King Fardorff and his scientists on Blanco Trollien are developing a Cannd Nova Bomb, which might destroy the Hell Star in its tracks. But it is unproven and untested. Grub has caught wind of the Cannd Nova Bomb and is searching the archipelago for its whereabouts. It is hidden in the Outacou Mines on Blanco Trollien under heavy security. It is a race against time to complete our weapon and destroy the Hell Star. The clock is already ticking."

"What can I do to help?" Nimrod waited for the answer.

"Nimrod." He paused. "You have to stop Satan on Earth."

"Me?"

"Yes, you, Nimrod. You are all we have left."

"I'm not experienced in these types of missions. I'm a teacher. And an ex-angel." Michael stared at Nimrod pathetically. "Can't we rearrange the bigger players here?" Nimrod looked at the big board. "Jesus has lots of experience with Satan."

"Jesus is on the front lines in the Stounfad System. We need him there." Michael was frank. Nimrod looked weak.

"How do I do this?"

"You first need to unlock his plan. Use guile and wit. Use a little espionage. Then you arrange a battle plan. With the limited means at your disposal, Guerilla warfare is a thought. But remember, our troops are numbered, and availability is limited on a need basis."

"Well, I need them," blustered Nimrod.

"Our need, Nimrod." Michael was not smiling.

"I don't know if I can do this." Nimrod looked at Michael for help.

"You have to do this, Nimrod. You're the only one left."

Nimrod was scared out of his mind. *Five billion souls. Five billion souls. Five billion souls.* Nimrod couldn't stop thinking about this overwhelming task that had been thrust upon him. The universe wasn't in his hands, but he could bring down the house of cards with one wrong pull. *Why me?* Nimrod thought. Who could he possibly find to help him defeat Satan?

Nimrod made one firm resolution. He was headed straight to the Canteen.

Jairus and Team Nimrod caught up to Nimrod in the Canteen. It was Heaven's watering hole, and it featured live music on a small stage. Hellen Keller brought a bottle of pinot noir to the table and shoved a bottle of sauvignon blanc in the ice bucket.

"Nimrod, where have you been?" Jairus asked his mentor. He was supposed to have seen him after school.

"I'm sorry, Jairus. I'm so very sorry. I have just possibly had the worst day of my life."

Team Nimrod noticed Captain Nimrod was talking more like Captain Morgan. "Sit down, Nimrod." Shar pulled his chair out and settled him safely back down. "Tell us what happened."

"Well, let's see. Three chirping birds woke me this morning. They brought a message I had to visit Michael. I almost caught one in the teeth from Claude Monet and almost drowned John the Baptist."

"Isn't he like two thousand years old?" Vishnu interrupted.

"Yeah, something like that." Nimrod continued. "I hiked all the way to Judeah only to have Michael inform me I have to face Satan mano a mano in a duel for five billion souls on Earth in a do-or-die Texas cage match. Then I had Hellen Keller as my server, and she wouldn't shut up. I had to repeat my order seven times, and she just looked at me with those big Coke-bottle glasses that make her look like she has giant fish eyes, and she wouldn't stop talking. Blah-blah-blah-blah." It was the second time Jairus had seen Nimrod agitated.

"Hey, Nimrod, can we have some of this food?" Vishnu eyed the spread.

Nimrod had ordered too much. Bib and tarragon salad and Sicilian cannelloni spread across the table. There was a huge plate of black bean–stuffed plantain croquettes with tomato sauce and pan-seared scallops with smoked tomato butter and warm spinach salad. Nimrod was finishing the lobster bisque, and Vishnu helped himself to the red curry duck with wonton napoleons. Jairus went straight for the caramel coffee meringues, and Shar had eaten, so she only spooned herself a small portion of cumin rice pilaf.

"Were you hungry, Nimrod?" Vishnu poked at Nimrod.

"No, Vishnu. I'm depressed. I can't do this. I'm simply not capable of whipping Satan in a battle for Earth."

"Down, down, down in a burning ring of fire," Johnny Cash sang to the audience in the background. Nimrod listened. It was that type of day.

"The souls on Earth are doomed," Nimrod said.

"So you're going to quit?" Thomas spoke through bites of black bean–stuffed plantains.

"Michael said there would be little or no support from the angels. What am I supposed to do? Sit down and ask him not to destroy Earth? I need some help."

Vishnu was the first to volunteer. "We'll help."

The others raised their hands in the affirmative. Jairus raised his hand too.

"What can the four of us do against Satan's legions?"

"We're Team Nimrod." Shar looked at Nimrod's eyes. "We can do anything."

They left the Canteen while Bon Scott sang "Highway to Hell" for the rockers in the crowd.

Team Nimrod returned to the barbershop and prepared to work—no televisions, MTV, VH1, or ESPN. They gathered around the table, and Shar made Nimrod a cup of black coffee. No one spoke. They all looked at Nimrod for an idea.

"What?" Nimrod returned their stares. "Why are you looking at me?"

"Where do we start?" Thomas poured himself a glass of ice tea.

Nimrod recapped his conversation with Michael in his mind. "Shar, find out from Heaven's communication center if we have any guardian angels on Earth who might have a little extra time. Ask for an old acquaintance of mine—Lily. Double-time! We have priority clearance, and if they need the password, it's 'ayej elf.'"

"Yes, sir!" Shar said.

She hopped up and called over to the communications office—a humungous operation that tracked the movements of all angels of Heaven and distributed the prayers of the living to corresponding saints. It was the largest switchboard in the universe. Jairus sat in the chair as Samson combed through his Duran Duran coif and devised a high-top fade look.

Nimrod was too focused to notice the new hairdo. "Michael said something about espionage." He looked straight at Vishnu. "If we can locate one of Satan's generals, then maybe, just maybe, we can find a clue about what the Darkness has in store for Earth."

"Communications says Lily can free herself. What do you want me to do?" Shar held the phone to her neck.

"Give me the phone." Nimrod took the receiver. "Hello, Lily. Go to New York City. Don't bother with the alleys and the red-light districts. Satan already rules those bastions and only uses lowly lieutenants to monitor those. Go to high society, nice restaurants, and hotels. His generals love the finer things in life." Nimrod placed the receiver on the hook. "There's not much more to do tonight except wait."

He looked around the room at Team Nimrod. Jairus's hair looked awful, but Jairus loved it, and the kid gave Samson a high five. Jairus's education would have to wait. Michael needed Nimrod to save Earth. "Let's get to bed. It's going to be a long day tomorrow."

They all stayed the night at the barbershop. They were strewn on couches and blankets on the floor. Nimrod cracked some fresh pecans they had gathered from the backyard and sat on the porch at the de facto headquarters of Team Nimrod.

Lan Orb Da Bann

The phone rang early in the morning. Delilah had Salt-N-Pepa's "Push It" programmed on the ringer. It was an inside joke between Samson and Delilah. Nimrod grabbed the phone. It was the communications office, as he had hoped. He listened carefully as the others stretched around him. Shar made coffee. Nimrod nodded on the phone and finally placed it on the base.

"Well?" Thomas hadn't rolled off the floor, and he spoke to Nimrod with his eyes closed.

"Lily got the tip we were looking for. She spotted Lucifer getting into a limousine on Park Avenue. She overheard them making dinner plans at a restaurant near Astor Place called Lan Orb Da Bonn. Six o'clock." The bell rang. "We need to get to Glengans Tiles, but who do we get?"

"Maybe we could get Anael. He's not much of a soldier, but he might be available."

"Who's Anael?" Jairus was going to get some lessons whether he knew it or not.

"Anael is the angel of Venus. He is also the angel that rules sexuality," Nimrod explained.

"What? Are we going to kiss the information out of Lucifer?" Vishnu was awake.

"Do you have a better idea?" Nimrod looked at Vishnu, who had really bad bedhead.

"I'll go," Vishnu volunteered. Every head turned.

"Vishnu, you haven't been on a mission in fifteen hundred years. You're rusty. What if you're spotted?"

"Then they'll take me to Hell, and you will come rescue me."

"I doubt that." Thomas still hadn't opened his eyes.

"What missions were you on before, Vishnu?" Jairus looked at the aged legend.

Vishnu got suddenly shy, and Nimrod stepped in like a good counselor. "Vishnu is a minor solar deity. He is associated with the movement of the sun. He successfully fought the evil Ravana with the aid of the monkey god, Hanuman, in order to save Krishna. Vishnu has the ability to incarnate himself as other beings. On separate occasions he has disguised himself as a fish, turtle, boar, man-lion, dwarf—not much of a trick for Vishnu—and a Rama holding an ax. He was present for the cosmic conflicts between God and the demons. There he is. The legend."

Vishnu's hair was all over the place.

"Wow!"

Nimrod sidled up to Vishnu. "Are you sure you want to do this, my old friend?"

"I'm sure. All I have to do is listen, right?"

"That's right."

"No fighting?"

"No fighting. I encourage you not to engage the enemy. I am brewing a plan that will strike fear into Satan's heart." Nimrod thrust his hand toward the Divine Star Vetene defiantly.

"I doubt that," Thomas mumbled. His sleepy eyes were still closed.

Shar packed Vishnu a sack lunch, and Nimrod gave Vishnu a map of Manhattan. The chariot pulled away and took Vishnu to the mission's launching point.

"What are the Glengans Tiles, Nimrod?"

"Glengans Tiles is a passage to Earth that will take Vishnu directly to New York City. Just like the Grazy Derlf Trail will take you to your mother in the Behorrin Debartik Galaxy." Nimrod put his hand on Jairus's neck.

"Why does it take you to New York City directly?"

"There are many passages to many places on Earth. We needed one that would take Vishnu to New York straightaway. There's always plenty of action in the Big Apple."

The chariot roared up to Lake Glengans, and Vishnu thanked the driver for the bumpy ride. He showed his clearance to the guard watching over the bewitching, opaque tiles that lay gently on the surface of Lake Glengans. Vishnu took a deep breath and stepped across the stones that led to the tiles. He tiptoed across several worn rocks and placed his foot tenderly down on the shimmering transport device. He stood still, and the guard pulled the lever. The lake did not rumble or wave. Everything remained perfectly still. The view from the mountain lake overlooking Lherrey Land was scintillating. A haze came over Vishnu, and he could see flashing lights. They were beautiful. Then he was gone.

The trip took only seconds, and Vishnu opened his eyes and checked to make sure all his body parts were where they belonged. The arrival point was in a remote section under Grand Central Station. Vishnu had the map, and he moved into the grand hall to look for the right train. He hopped on the subway and studied the eyes of the mortals on Earth. People scared of other people filled the busy car. They manifested their fear in different ways. Some stayed rigid and straight and put up fields so no one would touch them. Others curled toward the windows and away from their fellow humans. Others used magazines and books to say, "Don't talk to me." Fear was pungent in the air along with a whole group of other smells they didn't have in Heaven. Vishnu wanted to talk to the humans, but he reminded himself to stay invisible. Satan had soldiers everywhere.

The subway dropped him at Astor Place. It was a few minutes before six. He looked for Lan Orb Da Bonn. Looking through the forest of people made the search more difficult. *There!* He walked briskly across the street and entered the revolving door of the magnificent eatery. It looked like a museum rather than a restaurant. Businesspeople in fine suits filled the lobby in front of the host, and fifty-dollar handshakes garnered the vanity tables. Vishnu was underdressed and feared the maître d' would call him out. The main dining room was lush with deep mahogany and tropical shrubs. These camouflaged the open kitchen. Vishnu saw the end of an enormous fish tank that ran along the west wall of the establishment.

Vishnu melded into the crowd of suits and service staff and feigned interest in the marvelously large aquarium blessed with schools of rare, tropical poisson. As he looked over his shoulder to find Lucifer in the dining room, he sensed he was exposed. A server walked by with a martini and cosmopolitan. He looked back at the fish tank as she eyed him up and down. Through the clear waters, he noticed another dining room—a private room. It would be difficult to gain access to the private room. Instinct told Vishnu Lucifer was in that room. The aquarium bordered the private room and the main dining room.

He walked along the edges of the wall. There had to be a place where they had access to the tank. The glass was flush against the wall. He was getting dangerously close to the kitchen. A server's service station provided the opportunity. The tank ended there— out of view of the guests.

He slipped his hand to the top of the tank and removed the lid gently. He only had seconds. He dipped his index finger into the water. It absorbed him, and he metamorphosed into a tropical fish with a face and ears. The strange addition to the aquarium startled the schools of fish that swooped through the waters at first. Vishnu found his bearings and enjoyed the speed of the race as he became up close and personal with the fish. He looked into the private dining room from behind the shipwreck. This would be a fine vantage point.

People were mingling around the ornate room, sharing cocktails, and nibbling on gravlax with dill and sweet mustard sauce and blue, crab-filled mushroom caps the smart-looking staff passed around. The event wasn't solely for dinner, Vishnu surmised, as intense conversations combusted throughout the room. The water handicapped him. The sound was garbled. He smacked his ears with his fins to regulate the pressure. That was better. The audio was now resounding.

A gentleman called the group to his attention. "Ladies and gentlemen." He tried a little louder over the din. "Ladies and gentlemen, may I have your attention please?" The group muffled to silence, and all craned to look at the man speaking. "I am Sir Chad Mourrey, chancellor of the NCAA, and while you dine on the cuisine of Lan Orb Da Bonn, it would be my pleasure to unveil the new and improved status of NCAA college football. It is the result of countless hours of hard work and negotiating by selected representatives of the NCAA and university presidents. We think the direction we have chosen should put to rest the unresolved questions that have plagued this institution from its inception. So if you will kindly be seated, enjoy your meals while I go to work."

The crowd applauded politely, and the people searched for their assigned tables. As they dispersed the room became easier to reconnoiter. Some very beautiful women, resplendent in black evening dresses and pearls, reluctantly left the presence of one man. They peeled away and revealed Lucifer himself. He played the role of corporate titan, Mr. Stokes, with aplomb. He looked young and refreshed as if he had just returned from Saint Bart's. The temptation he possessed was palpable. Vanity, greed, lust, gluttony, and envy ran rampant through the room. Revenge was about, but Vishnu would have to look deeper to find it. *Not much sloth today,* Vishnu noted. Lucifer had these people in the palm of his hand. He was everything they aspired to be—handsome, rich, young, sexy, and worldly. The lights dimmed, and Lucifer took a seat in a booth just below the ridge of the aquarium. Vishnu stayed behind the shipwreck because Lucifer looked into the waters carefully as if he suspected something. Thank God the lights were dimmed very low.

Sir Chad Mourrey stood at the podium while the staff brought small plates of field greens with gorgonzola, diced Roma tomatoes, and cucumbers drizzled with balsamic vinaigrette laced with fennel seed. A screen illuminated behind him as he began his PowerPoint presentation. "The three main areas we addressed as a committee were the three main concerns you, as legislators of your respective universities, conveyed to us. The first concern was the crowning of an undisputed national champion. Well, ladies and gentlemen, college football now has a play-off system."

The crowd erupted and rose to their feet in approval. Mourrey pressed his hands to the podium and indicated for them to return to their seats. "The second concern was about the bowl games. Not one bowl game will be missed." The crowd once again roared in approval. "Not only will no bowl games be missed, but seven play-off games will be added."

The crowd was stunned momentarily but then rejoiced mightily. Dollar signs ran through their heads.

"The third facet of the new agreement is financial. It concerns how each university will get a piece of the pie. We have restructured every single Division One conference so profit sharing from television rights will enrich every school's athletic department."

The crowd was once again on its feet and forgoing the warm sourdough with honey butter.

"How did we do this? I'll explain, but we have to start from the top." Mourrey took a sip of what looked like water. "To better explain this, we will start with the third facet and work our way back to the national championship. In order for all schools to receive a larger share of the television rights, we have restructured all teams into six major conferences."

The diners gasped. Vishnu swam around in the bowl. He didn't know much about football but listened carefully.

"Tonight we will announce the divisions, and the executives of those leagues will announce the new names of the six conferences. We have worked out new television rights with multiple networks to market college football every night of the week—except Sundays but including Mondays." The crowd was giddy. "Ladies and gentlemen, there will be Monday night college football."

Lucifer rejoiced at the clapping, greedy sinners. There were so many ways to corrupt humanity and steal their souls.

"We think the ratings will be fantastic. We have the rights to select the Monday night game three weeks ahead of the schedule to ensure a terrific contest. We also will be broadcasting weekly competitions every Tuesday, Wednesday, Thursday, and Friday. And, of course, we will still rule Saturday's airwaves for America's favorite sport." He paused while they clapped. "Television rights this year alone have reached into the billions. Networks clamored to claim a stake in our game. We have affiliated ourselves with old partners such as ABC, NBC, CBS, and the multiple channels of cable giants ESPN, Fox, and TNT. But we have welcomed to our family new networks such as OLN, C-SPAN, Lifetime, Oxygen, A&E, National Geographic, and Spike TV. Telemundo will broadcast our new national pastime to Latino communities all around the globe. The Food Network has signed exclusive rights to cover the tailgating action around the country." Mourrey waited for the proper moment. "I am also very pleased to announce the creation of our own cable network, JFN. The Just Football Network cable channel debuts at the start of the season, and all the Division One schools will share all profits." The crowd was out of its skin. "The first title game will be aired on the JFN channel this season, and we plan to entertain fans all over the world with its insightful programming. During the season, besides a full slate of regular-season games, you'll have the interactive ability to scout your favorite team's next opponent or grade your team through living room film study. Twenty-four hours a day, you can submit your evaluations directly to the head coach. You can recreate games by substituting your own plays and change the outcome of tough losses. See how you would fare against other coaching master-minds around the country by using the interactive guide. In the off-season you'll be able to follow the strength and conditioning schedules of your favorite players and even vote by text message which cheerleader the quarterback should date. Our goal in the next three years is to put every game, coach, player, and personal activity on television every week." Mourrey slammed his fist to the podium with well-rehearsed histrionics. This brought the house down, and vinaigrette dribbled down the chins of the cheering and obsessed. "These changes will help provide the exposure each school needs to reap the benefits of our new contracts. Being associated with a powerful conference is another.

"We shift now to phase two of our new NCAA structure. Each team will be associated with one of the six divisions. Here to present the new alignment is Garth A. Moot, president of Florida Technology and Agriculture. A round of applause to the new speaker." Mourrey stepped aside and let Moot take the podium.

"Thank you very much. It's an honor to be here, and as president of Florida T&A, I couldn't be more excited that a play-off system will finally put to rest who the best in college football really is. As two-time national champs seeking an unprecedented third title in a row, I feel we can now shed the naysayers and prove to all this is one of the finest teams to ever run on the field."

There was a smattering of applause for the smug king of the hill.

"The first division we will reveal will be heretofore known as the Big South. This superconference will be host to Florida State, Clemson, Georgia Tech, Miami, Florida, Tennessee, Georgia, South Carolina, Kentucky, Vanderbilt, Arkansas, Alabama, Auburn, LSU, Mississippi, Mississippi State, Southern Mississippi, and Florida T&A."

A chorus of boos went up from the group. Nobody wanted to play Florida T&A. A single cheerleader from each team was in full cheering garb with pom-poms, and she made her way through the dining room as each team was announced. "Ladies and gentlemen, welcome to the eightteen-team Big South!"

"It sounds like the Confederate Conference to me," a heckler bellowed, and the crowd laughed.

"Conference President Eve St. Skater has deemed the next division the Heartland Conference. This conference will include Cincinnati, NE Louisiana, Memphis, North Texas, Tulane, Tulsa, Nebraska, Colorado, Kansas, Kansas State, Oklahoma, Oklahoma State, Iowa State, Missouri, Northern Illinois, Southwest Louisiana, Arkansas State, and Louisiana Tech. Welcome the Heartland Conference."

"Sounds like the Tornado Alley League to me."

"Must be a Nebraska fan. Eve, is it true the 'N' on the Nebraska helmet stands for knowledge?" Garth quipped.

"I don't know, Garth." Then she got the joke.

"The third division is made from teams from the east. The consensus was to call this league Big Beast. Seventeen teams comprise the Big Beast. They are Virginia, Maryland, North Carolina, North Carolina State, Virginia Tech, Syracuse, West Virginia, Boston College, Rutgers, Temple, the University of

Connecticut, Pittsburgh, East Carolina, Army, Navy, Duke, and Wake Forest. Ladies and gentlemen, welcome to the dance the Big Beast."

"Sounds like the Nor'easter Division." The heckler was wearing thin as the wine flowed freely in the private room.

"We go all the way out west for our next contingent. A sparkling group of seventeen teams comprise the El Niño Conference." Everyone laughed. Garth got into the act. "People are already calling it the Sand and Surf Division." That brought another round of guffaws. "The El Niño Conference is Pacific, San Jose State, USC, UCLA, California, Oregon, Oregon State, Washington, Washington State, Stanford, San Diego State, Hawaii, Fresno State, Utah State, Nevada, BYU, and Utah."

The men in the crowd started chanting, "Bring on the cheerleaders."

"Our fifth group includes the powerhouses of the Midwest. The group is our largest conference and totals a massive twenty-four teams divided into two divisions. Now I just opened the envelope revealing the new name of the conference, and I just want to ask Neal K. Pintelt, the president of the new conference, a quick question. Neal, come up here real fast."

Neal got up from the table and made his way through the maze of tables in the dark. He met Garth at the corner of the raised podium area.

"Neal, is this right?"

Neal looked at the envelope and its contents. "Yes, sir. That's right," he responded indignantly.

"Neal, there are twenty-four teams in the division. You can't call it the Big Ten. It doesn't add up." Garth had to question Neal's arithmetic.

"We felt strongly that tradition overrode change. We are going to stay with the Big Ten."

"How about the Big Twenty-Four? That has a nice ring to it."

"Don't mock me, Garth. One of our teams in the Big Ten is going to knock you off your high horse, and that will be the big hurt in the seat of your pants."

"Ladies and gentlemen, may I introduce to you the Big Ten. In no particular order, they are Ohio State, Michigan, Penn State, Notre Dame..." The crowd hushed. Notre Dame had joined a conference. "Michigan State, Iowa, Illinois, Wisconsin, Purdue, Minnesota, Indiana, Northwestern, Toledo, Miami Ohio, Ball State, Western Michigan, Eastern Michigan, Bowling Green, Central Michigan, Akron, Ohio, Marshall, Kent State, and Louisville. The committee was going to round it down, but they were convinced Indiana couldn't beat Ball State."

The crowd groaned at the bad joke.

"I think they should call it Farm Aid." The heckler was back, and so was the crowd.

"If you haven't heard your school mentioned, then they are here in the final group." Moot opened the envelope. "From the new Lewis and Clark Division..." The crowd roared. "This can't be serious." Garth got a nod from an official that it was legitimate. "I'm very sorry. There are seventeen fine schools here. The Lewis and Clark Division is Arizona, Arizona State, New Mexico State, New Mexico, UNLV, UTEP, Texas, Texas Tech, Texas A&M, Baylor, TCU, Houston, Rice, SMU, Colorado State, Air Force, and Wyoming. That rounds out the leagues. We're all excited for the competition this fall."

Moot received a cordial round of applause as he turned the podium back over to Mourrey. New York strips were served with Roquefort compound butter with horseradish, mashed potatoes, and flambéed haricot vert. Others had opted for grilled ahi done rare with lemon chive butter. The food came just in time as the drinks were kicking in.

"Good timing. Dinner is served as I prepare to address the meat of the program. I am sure you are all interested to know how the play-offs will work. Each of the conferences will determine its own champion. Each conference will be divided into two divisions. A championship game between the two division winners will determine the conference champion. These games act as play-off games themselves. The projected revenue for the conference championship games alone is staggering. All schools will receive a share of the revenue from the conference championship games with the lion's share going to the participating schools. The six winners of the conference championship games automatically qualify for the play-offs for the national title.

"That leaves two at-large bids. An NCAA-appointed panel similar to the one used in college basketball will determine the at-large bids. Criteria will be gauged on record, records of opponents, conference ranking, conference record against other conferences, margins of victory, and who has the better marching band. I was just teasing about that last one. It can be a little complicated, but I assure you the best eight teams will vie for a no-longer-mythical national title. I must inform you immediately that concessions had to be made with Notre Dame to join the Big Ten. Notre Dame must be considered for an at-large bid to the play-offs as long as their record is over a five hundred winning percentage."

The audience looked baffled and much more interested in dinner at this point. The wine flowed freely.

"Now to address the play-offs and the bowl games. It was going to be difficult to ask all the teams to travel to neutral sites. This would have been a financial burden for teams that advanced in the play-offs. Accordingly seeds will be assigned, and the higher seeds will play the first two rounds at home. This gives them an advantage they earned by the right of their seeding."

Grumbles rumbled through the crowd, and Vishnu finally tagged Nemo. "You're it!" exclaimed Vishnu, and he raced in the other direction.

"The play-offs will start the first Saturday after the conference championship games on November 22."

"You mean the season will be over on November 8?" The crowd digested this fact along with their steaks.

"I was anticipating that question. For teams that did not make their conference championship games or the play-offs, their regular—and I emphasize *regular*—seasons end. The outstanding response we got from our sponsorships will allow eighty teams to participate in forty bowl games this year. Almost seventy-five percent of college football teams will play in a bowl.. The bowl season starts on December 1, and we will televise all forty games nationally between December 1 and New Year's Day." The crowd loved the answer. "And that does not include the play-offs. You will be able to watch college games six days a week from late August through early November. You will then be treated to the highest levels of college football through the conference championships and the NCAA play-offs. The second round of play-offs will conclude on Thanksgiving weekend. Our ratings expectations are sky-high. Families home for the holidays will gather around televisions and watch as the back to back games reveal who will play in the title game." Mourrey had them right where he wanted them. "There will be a wait to build up suspense for the title game. Bowl games will kick off three days after the second round of play-offs to help add to the rising drama. In a new tradition, the national title game will be played on Christmas."

The crowd hushed in silence. "Christmas Day?" they whispered among themselves.

"Our projections are astronomical. Our corporate sponsor for the title game, the Angry Beaver Boot Company, paid one hundred million dollars for the rights to this single event."

The crowd forgot about Christmas as the vast amount of money floated through their brains.

"The title game will be rotated throughout the nation at its finest venues. Alternating the title game will be the Rose Bowl in Pasadena–Los Angeles, the Sugar Bowl in New Orleans, the Orange Bowl in Miami, and the Fiesta Bowl in Arizona. The Cotton Bowl is confirmed to be played in the Alamo Dome in San Antonio, Texas. It is with pride I announce the inaugural title game will be played right here in New York City at the new, state-of-the-art Big Apple Dome on Christmas Day."

The response was overwhelming. The people toasted with the champagne strategically poured before the announcement.

"The national title game will bring in almost half a billion dollars of revenue for a single event. The eighty-thousand-seat dome will be christened on Christmas Day. It will be its own advertisement and lure visitors from all over the world to New York."

The diners were frenzied at the thought of the riches. Gold paved the streets of New York. Lucifer smiled a sly grin as Sir Chad Mourrey found his way over to the table. This piqued Vishnu's interest as he swam behind the treasure chest.

"Well, Chad. Nice job selling the masses." Garth A. Moot said while eating the remainder of his wife's ample steak.

Gluttony, thought Vishnu.

"Now all we have to do is get the presidents of the universities to put their John Hancocks on the contracts, and we're all in the money."

Prepared documents had previously been sent for attorneys to review. The signing of the documents would be mere formality. Sir Chad Mourrey's signature carried more weight and could veto the whole plan if he didn't comply.

"Garth?" Mourrey looked at Moot. His conscience was stirring. "Would you excuse us for a moment? I must have a few words with Mr. Stokes."

"Sure. Go ahead." The beef entranced Moot. Lucifer and Mourrey stared at Moot and his obsession. "Oh, you want me to leave? I get it." Moot wiped his mouth with the fine linen, hoisted himself up from the table, and rattled the china as he left.

"What's on your mind, Sir Chad?" Lucifer looked at Mourrey with his black eyes.

"Mr. Stokes..." He chose his words carefully. "I'm not sure I can endorse this agenda."

"Please call me Samuel." Lucifer barely batted an eyelash, despite knowing the Darkness's plans hinged on things falling into line. "What's bothering you?"

Lucifer took a bite from a strawberry dipped lightly in chocolate. It was a personal request the chef had obliged.

"I think we have forgotten about the students. I think we are overlooking the families of these students." Mourrey drummed his fingers on the table in frustration. Vishnu listened carefully as he wagged his dorsal fin in the soft current. "To play football on Christmas Day seems to draw meaning away from what is supposed to be a special family day. It is a religious day. Children should be celebrating at home with their families, opening presents from under trees, and going to church—not chasing their classmates around the country to have people watch them play a game."

Lucifer did not move.

"I have concerns for the students who will be playing football all through their exam periods. That's not to mention the student fans. They will be distracted from their studies as well. Not one representative has yet mentioned academics, and as chancellor of the NCAA, I'm obligated to weigh the welfare of the entire student population over the welfare of the student athletes—or the endowment of the school. These people are lustful with greed, and they are forsaking what's at the very heart of an academic institution."

Lucifer dipped the strawberry into the melted chocolate.

Mourrey continued. "Mr. Stokes, your corporation has been a driving force behind these changes, and I know you are here to celebrate the finality of your hard work, but for all the billions involved, I don't think it will benefit the students or their educations. I believe the money will trickle down and line the pockets of the few, while many students will see no improvement in the quality of their respective universities." Mourrey took a deep breath. "Mr. Stokes, I don't believe I can commit to this travesty. I got swept up in all the hoopla and money, and I felt it could be utilized to help everyone, but I don't think that's going to happen. It has been weighing on my conscience."

Lucifer plucked the green leaf from the strawberry's crown. Every person had a price. It was just a matter of how much. "Sir Chad." Lucifer was very mellow. "How can I make it worthwhile for you to sign your name to that document?"

Mourrey looked at Lucifer in disgust. "Mr. Stokes, I will not be bribed. I am the chancellor of the NCAA and won't let you bully me around for a few dollars. I am not a slave to money like the other vultures in this room. I can assure you of that."

The server brought over two glasses of champagne that Lucifer had ordered to celebrate. She was a very sexy young Asian woman named Mai. Mourrey stammered ever so slightly as he made eye contact with the young server.

"What are you a slave to, Mr. Mourrey?"

"I will not be bought, Mr. Stokes. I am not a slave to anything," Mourrey lied.

Lies begat more lies. Lucifer would have what he desired. "You don't desire Mai?"

"Who is Mai?" Mourrey feigned ignorance. He knew perfectly well the server's name was Mai.

Lucifer had seen him chatting with her earlier and giving her his best Barry White sex voice.

"I can arrange for you to be with Mai, Mr. Mourrey."

"I can handle my own personal affairs, Mr. Stokes. Thank you very much indeed."

Mourrey was well beyond his prime, and his perversions cost a pretty penny. His were not the types of desire readily accessible back in Kansas City.

"Mai likes pain, Mr. Mourrey. And so do you." Lucifer placed the strawberry into his champagne. He was ready to celebrate his victory. Mourrey was visibly flushed. "Sweet pain, Mr. Mourrey. She can be yours tonight. In a few short hours. These are desires your wife doesn't know about. But she could find out." Lucifer showed Mourrey the compromising pictures. "And so could every president of every school."

Beads of sweat rolled down Mourrey's face. Mai tantalized his fantasy and fueled his shame. Lucifer put the pen on the table, and his lieutenant brought over the document. Mourrey's conscience had succumbed to his desire and fear. He scribbled his name on the paper. Lucifer sipped on his champagne. Mourrey had sold his soul for a piece of ass.

Lucifer whispered in his lieutenant's ear, but it was loud enough over the boiling crowd. Vishnu's ear was pressed against the glass. "Put things in motion. Armageddon will be nationally televised from New York City on Christmas Day."

Vishnu burst through the doors of the Canteen as the rest of Team Nimrod sat eating another fine meal.

"Everybody, stop. You have to listen to what I've heard." Vishnu was out of breath and panting like a dog.

Shar grabbed him a chair. "These are mushroom risotto cakes. You should try one." Shar gave him a small plate.

"The smoked salmon on dark pumpernickel with wasabi aioli is terrific," Thomas noted, and he savored the flavor.

"Maybe I'll try a…"

"Would you please tell us what happened?" Nimrod brought the table to order.

"Calm down, Nimrod. We can't do anything over dinner. Besides, Shar only sent me to New York with a tuna fish sandwich." He looked at Shar. "That was dolphin friendly, wasn't it? Because I made some new friends. Swimming sure does make you hungry."

Vishnu looked at Nimrod. He seemed very impatient. Vishnu spooned some of the baby carrots tossed with roasted fennel onto his plate. "I found the place, and our source was spot-on. Lucifer was there. Is that lamb?"

"It's rubbed with anchovy and rosemary," Thomas said as he stuffed his face.

"Continue, please." Nimrod needed to know.

"They were having a meeting about college football. I wasn't listening too closely to that part."

"Why not? Wasn't it important enough for Lucifer to be there?"

"Well, Nimrod, I was swimming around in a fish tank and was having it out with a nasty starfish. That's why."

Nimrod piped down, and Vishnu scooped up some of the artichokes braised with garlic and thyme. "As I was saying, it turns out they are going to have a really big game on Christmas Day. Supposedly everyone will watch it on television." Vishnu sampled the soufflé gnocchi. "These are great. Then the pervert went home with the cute Asian server." Vishnu plucked a lardoon off the dandelion and goat cheese salad.

"Perverts and Asian girls. Do tell." Shar was kinky. She liked to listen.

"We will refrain from any such talk in present company." Nimrod rolled his eyes toward Jairus.

"Aw, c'mon, Nimrod." Jairus was at that age.

"Vishnu, you need to fill in the blanks."

Vishnu stuck his fork into the tender Copper River salmon with pearl couscous, roasted tomatoes, and lemon oregano oil. "The last thing Lucifer said was 'Put things in motion. Armageddon will be nationally televised from New York City on Christmas Day.' And that was it."

Shar passed around the crunchy pecan cookies and blackberries with Chambord.

"No, Jairus, you can't have that," Nimrod said, and he removed the blackberries and Chambord from Jairus's hands. "You can have a cookie."

"Does any of this make sense to you, Nimrod?" Vishnu couldn't put it together.

"You said the meeting was about football, right?" Nimrod rubbed his chin.

"Yes. They are going to play a big game on Christmas."

"Big games are always televised, but New York doesn't have a stadium conducive to a big game in the winter."

"They mentioned something about the Big Apple Dome," Vishnu added between bites.

"New York City has a dome?"

"I think they said something about it being the first game or something like that." Vishnu had blackberry all over his face. He had finally found the sloth.

"It's starting to make sense. Satan is going to televise his attack on humanity from the one place the world will be watching, and their fate will unfold before their eyes. It will strike fear beyond comprehension around the world, and then he will send the demons in to attack."

"What do we do?" Jairus was petrified.

Satan is using football, Nimrod mused. "It's time to execute plan A. We need to meet with Satan. We kind of know his plan. Maybe we can shake his tree."

"I doubt it," said Thomas.

"How do we meet with Satan?" Jairus asked.

Nimrod knew he would have to ask Michael for a favor.

Michael was not keen on the plan, but he connected Nimrod with Balberith. The team prepared to travel to Jakeon's Veer.

"Shar, are the arrangements confirmed with Balberith?" Nimrod asked.

"Nimrod, who is Balberith?" Jairus was packing his lunch for the trip.

"Balberith notarizes pacts for the Devil—deals, appointments, wagers, contracts, and such. He's kind of like Satan's secretary and attorney." Nimrod toweled his hair. "Jairus, you know you can't go."

The disappointment was evident. "But why?"

"You're not an angel, and I expect things to get rather ugly. You'll be safer here."

"Can I at least travel to Jakeon's Veer?" Jairus made his sad face.

It was against his better judgment, but Nimrod agreed. Jairus smiled. He was excited for the journey.

Team Nimrod met in front of the barbershop. Samson and Delilah were there to wave them off. Michael had sent a special chariot to take them northwest of Judeah. Michael had sanctioned the rare meeting with Satan. He understood Nimrod was trying his best. He could promise Nimrod little to no support and hoped the meeting wouldn't turn into a slaughter. The souls of Heaven were extreme enticements to Satan. Balberith had certified there would be no attempt to harm the delegates from Judeah, but Satan had lied many times before.

Jairus enjoyed the bumpy ride. He had never explored the countryside, and he watched as the foothills approached. Sea green watercress and violet, blue, and yellow Solomon's seal adorned them. Nimrod pointed out the magenta spotted boletes and the red-orange angel trumpets tangled up in blue heirloom wheat. Shar's head kept turning from side to side as swaths of wood vetch turned from white to blue to peach before their eyes. A sea of rhododendron crashed into the hills and speckled the rise with yellow green, red orange, and midnight blue. Jairus noticed his arms were becoming tan and showed Thomas his growing muscles. The road slowed as they climbed into the mountain full of blue spruce and cedars of Lebanon. Pine truffles nestled against the roots of dawn redwoods, and the forest green shaded the chariot. They could smell food cooking on an open flame. Daniel Boone was camping under the four-thousand-year-old giant sequoias. The raw umber of the great trees rose 250 feet into the sky. Boone seemed to be having a good time trying to teach Bach how to play the country fiddle. Beethoven was wailing on a harmonica.

They had reached Jakeon's Veer, a giant wedge in the mountain divided the sequoias at a perfect right angle. Jairus looked sad as Nimrod took him aside.

"I'm worried you won't come back."

"I'll be fine. This is what I was trained to do." Thomas looked at Nimrod. He doubted that. "You just mind your studies, and I'll be back before you know it."

Jairus hugged Nimrod tightly. The centurion requested everyone stay in the chariot.

"Why?" asked Vishnu.

An Arabian with white wings galloped from the redwoods. It was Pegasus.

"I will return the boy to Judeah," said the centurion. "Michael wants you to travel in this."

Jairus stepped out of the vehicle. The centurion bridled Pegasus to the chariot but handed Nimrod no reins.

"What exactly are we going to do with a chariot?" Nimrod asked.

"It is Adam's chariot of light. It will protect you. And so will Pegasus." He slung Jairus up to the mount.

Jairus cried, "Where are you going?"

"To the Spirals of Cortez," Nimrod said, and he waved to Jairus. He was quite uncertain if they would meet again.

They steered the chariot to the corner of Jakeon's Veer. The leaves rustled, and the group stood close together. The haze came over the four of them, and they were gone. *Cool,* Jairus thought, and he craned to watch every last second.

The Spirals of Cortez

They had agreed to meet at the Spirals of Cortez—two remote pinnacles that jutted skyward from the flaming-hot magenta floor. These natural red lecterns had been selected many times before. They served as pulpits for not-so-sedentary debates. Whittled away by wind, water, and time, they stood proudly and alone. Face-to-face like fast-growing twins, they towered over the flat and fruitless landscape. It was an ideal place on Earth for immortals to meet and their armies to engage. Uninhabited over eons and with a vast canopy of cadet blue sky, solitude was assured. On the off chance lost Navajo scouts or adventurous campers stumbled upon this rare pyrotechnic caucus, they would hardly believe their own eyes much less make believable stories for others. It was a world in which many claimed to believe in God. However, rather than file a report that one had actually seen God, his angels, or even Satan, one would be better off confessing to the local Barney Fife about trying one's first hit of peyote and leaving it at that.

The Desert Floor

April loved the desert. April loved Rory. Rory was from back East. He had never seen the desert. They were alone at last and away from the city, their jobs, and the stress of traffic. They were free in the wilderness of the atomic tangerine desert. April hiked up the trail and stood on the copper rocks. "Rory, come see! It's a spectacular view of the brick-red twin rock formations called the Spirals of Cortez."

Rory couldn't have looked less thrilled. Sweat covered him, and his pack was killing him.

"Ancient rivers carved them from the desert floors millions of years ago—when dinosaurs called the land their own."

Rory gasped for air. He was used to taking the subway. Following April on the hike had been like chasing a jackrabbit while wearing cement shoes.

His tour guide continued. "The formations jut from the flat plane of the blazing burnt orange sands well over a thousand feet in air. They are wide at the base, but the twins narrow like the tips of pencils. You see how they scratch the sky?"

Rory thought April was completely out of her mind, but she had the body of a goddess, and her maroon hiking pants were soaked through.

"Only a few yards separate their points. Do you see?" Rory nodded his head. "Cortez traveled here after he destroyed the Aztec Empire and their king, Montezuma. Local Navajo tribes consider the Spirals of Cortez haunted and won't go near the sister rocks. Legend has it that this is where Cortez gave the Devil his soul for all the riches and gold he found to the north."

Rory looked out over the view. She could talk. Their goal was to make it to the base of the matching raw sienna peaks and set up camp. April had every intention of giving Rory the ride of his life, and she was in a hurry to get started. Their packs were heavy, and Rory had made the mistake of bringing his guitar. Singing to April in the desert under the red-and-violet sunset had sounded romantic at the time. Rory raised a small objection. A storm seemed to be brewing, and he recommended they set up camp here. April was one to stick to the plan. Rory knew what was good for him, and he continued to hike.

The clouds grew ominous and blotted out the sun. No rain had fallen, though, and they found plenty of time to set up their camp. The new tent from REI was nifty and more spacious than Rory could have imagined. April fried a few veggie patties in the pan and warmed some canned black beans.

"I know it's not great, but you need your energy tonight." April was giddy to get naked.

So was Rory, but he needed to chill. He finished his veggie patty, which was terrible. He would not tell April that. He pulled out a sandwich baggie and smelled the weed.

"Where'd you get that?" April asked.

They were on vacation, and making love to Rory in the desert while stoned seemed like the perfect release. Rory pulled out a bowl, and the two toked away. The hits were mellow, and the buzz kicked in right away. April took off her top and started rubbing Rory's shoulders. Rory pulled his guitar into his lap and started singing "Peaceful Easy Feeling." This always put April into overdrive.

The chariot came screaming down through the clouds. Pegasus flew hard into the wind. "Steer it, Nimrod," Vishnu cried in terror.

Shar held Thomas tightly, and Thomas shut his eyes.

"We're all going to die!" Thomas yelled as the chariot ripped through the Earth's turbulent upper atmosphere and left a flaming trail.

"Pegasus seems to have a mind of his own," Nimrod hollered through the wind.

"Well, talk to it. Do something!" Vishnu wished he could turn into a bird and fly away.

The chariot evened its flight path, but they still descended very rapidly. Mushroom cloud formations wallpapered the sky. The sun reflected an orange hue off the eastern billows.

"That's much better." Nimrod looked white.

"What did you do?"

"Nothing. He must be on autopilot or something."

Thomas opened his eyes ever so slightly. He looked around. It was amazing. It had been two thousand years since he had last breathed Earth's air. It was different from Heaven. Heavier.

"What is that?" Vishnu pointed at the small dots in the sky.

They were headed right for them. Team Nimrod looked at the dots become larger. There were dozens of them, and they were all winged.

"Incoming," Thomas shrieked at the top of his lungs.

A wolf with a serpent's head flew over the chariot and vomited fire. Hideous mongrels soared past as they lined up the chariot in their crosshairs. They were demons—agents of Hell with the sole purpose of ruining souls. They lived in Hell but prowled the world looking for souls to pervert. They swooped into a cloud bank and angled for their return. Pegasus kicked at the sky.

"We're all going to Hell." Thomas closed his eyes again.

"Nimrod, what was that?" Shar held her arms around Nimrod's waist as the chariot stayed the course.

"I believe that was Amon, the fallen angel, with his forty legions of gargoyles."

"Was it really a wolf?" Vishnu's eyes were popping.

"Yes. With a serpent's head. He can appear human but will have dog teeth."

"We're not going to make it." Thomas squeezed his eyelids tightly.

From over their shoulder, they heard the howling of Hell. It was not from the direction of Amon. His legions were still in the cloud bank. They ducked as a fallen angel riding a dragon with a viper in his right hand breathed the foulest stench over the chariot. Hordes of grotesque, salivating ghouls followed. Their wings rocked the vessel and swiped at Pegasus's wings.

"That wasn't Amon." Shar was petrified. Thomas passed out.

"No. That was Astaroth. That winged devil is a grand duke of hell. He too commands forty legions. He can appear as a foul or beautiful angel."

"I'd say he looked pretty foul," Shar was quick to point out.

"His breath is so bad you must use a magician's ring to prevent it from melting your face."

"I don't have a magic ring, Nimrod. How about some Tic Tacs?" Vishnu reached into his pocket.

The two groups combined forces and circled toward the four helpless souls of Heaven.

"Four against eighty-two. Yeah. This is a fair fight," Nimrod said.

He couldn't steer the chariot. It plowed dead ahead. The demons approached quickly as Amon and Astaroth pulled up in midair to watch the carnage. They waited to report to their master that the souls of Heaven's messengers could be forever tortured on Gholar—the slave planet of the Darkness.

"Hold on!" Nimrod shouted. The sky cracked with furious thunder as the four riders held their heads below the board. Nimrod suddenly remembered Jairus's lesson. "We'd better pray to St. Alexis to get us safely through this terrible lighting."

Which saint do we pray to not to get our asses kicked? Vishnu wondered.

Rory raised his head sharply. It was the loudest thunderclap he had ever heard, and the rain came down instantly. It was as if the heavens had opened a dam. April pulled him back on top of her. Rory felt the fear.

Angels from the fifth level of Heaven had flown in on winds from the east. Samax, with his brigade of Friagne, Guel, Damael, Calzas, and Arragon, arrived in time to smash into the legion. He drew the black blood of the beasts, and their veins rained over the desert. They had come to the rescue under the guidance of Mars, who was prepared to battle the underworld. Amon and Astaroth howled in agony as Samax snatched quick victory from their jaws. Balam joined the fray with his forty legions and snorted smoke with his head of a bull, body of a man, and tail of a ram. His tail sliced the air, and his eyes flamed. He rode naked on a steer into the battle. Samax and his warriors drew their swords. Guel and Damael split from the group to draw fire from the chariot. They rushed into the void. Their wings were straight behind them. They clashed their swords with the goblins of the sky, and their scraping weapons illuminated the night. More ear-piercing thunder shook the desert floor.

Rory rolled over, slipped on his boxers, and unzipped the front of the tent. April crawled naked over to Rory.

"What's the matter, Rory?" April was frustrated.

"Look at the sky, April. It's on fire."

April poked her head out of the tent. Over the tips of the Spirals of Cortez it looked as if the sky was burning. Brilliant flashes of light cascaded across the night in a dangerous display of nature, but Rory thought it looked like war. "Oh my God!" April was stunned, and Rory feared for their safety. The ground shook like during an earthquake.

Team Nimrod—minus the fainted Thomas—monitored the battle. Friagne and Calzas engaged the monsters but were being pushed to their limits. Outnumbered they began to give ground, and the legion fought toward the chariot. More help arrived from the west. Carmax and his fighters dived in from the sun and struck the enemy from the blind. Lama and Astagna slayed their marks, and Lobquin, Soneas, Jazel, Isael, and Irel drove a wedge into the mass and splintered the force of goblins to the wind. With the forces in disarray, the angels stabbed at the creatures freely. Terrible yelps of pain squealed over the thunder, and Heaven's swords dug deep into the rotting flesh of the demons. Their blood nurtured the landscape.

"Nimrod, what's that?" Shar exclaimed.

Botis, the president and earl of Hell, slithered from the underworld.

"All the celebrities are here tonight," quipped Nimrod.

The huge viper lay hissing on the clouds as his sixty-strong legion leaped into the quarrel.

"How can a snake be an angel of Hell?" Vishnu peered over the edges of the chariot.

"Botis will take human form but with horns and huge teeth. He's more intimidating this way."

The viper struck at Carmax, and the angels of Heaven swarmed around the giant cobra. Ismoli came from the north wind with Rhaumel, Hyniel, Rayel, Seraphiel, Fraciel, and Mathiel. They converged with the south wind, which brought forth Paffran, leader of Sacriel, Janiel, Galdel, Osael, Vianuel, and Zaliel. God's battalions were pulled from engagements across the universe and sent by Michael in desperation to save Nimrod's mission. They waited for the demons' line to reform and then smashed them in their pincers. The thunder's wave hurled the chariot through the sky. Lobquin and Rhaumel had come to escort Adam's chariot to a safe landing on top of the east spiral. The armies of Heaven and Hell dueled through the night, and the casualties started to mount. A blow from behind felled Arragon, and the demons gobbled him in midair. His soul would suffer in Hell for eternity. Irel fought bravely, but she became surrounded and was consumed in the fray. The legions were suffering massive losses as the swords of Friagne, Jazel, and Lama blazed in the night. The golden and gilded chariot landed safely on the hardened clay and red earth of the Spirals of Cortez. Pegasus pawed at the earth with his hoof.

Nimrod spoke to his fellow warriors. Their complexions were egg white. "I am going to open a dialogue with Satan. It will be a thunderous oration filled with our powers of goodness. I will intimidate him and throw him off-balance."

Thomas woke from his nightmare. Team Nimrod rolled their collective eyes. They were not sure whether Nimrod's roar could frighten a fawn in the forest.

"While he is reeling from my opening salvo, I will declare our mission statement."

"Mission statement? Are we opening a Dunkin' Donuts?" queried Vishnu.

Nimrod did not appreciate the sarcasm. "I am sure that after he hears our mission statement and understands we have the full forces of Heaven on our side, he will bow to us and our steadfast desire to quash his gambit."

"We don't have the full forces of Heaven on our side. I doubt he will listen." Thomas was realizing he was now awake in his nightmare.

Nimrod looked for their war faces. "Show me your war faces!" Nimrod was losing it. "Listen. I need your backup! When I finish my stern opening salvo, you need to reinforce my declarations with passionate resolve."

The battle of the angels continued in the billowing thunderclouds. The roars of pain electrified the flashing burnt orange sky. The sky dripped the blood of the good and evil, and the sorties of winged combatants circled and reformed their lines for another blistering aerial attack. The polished hooves of the demon Satan clacked on the dust. The warriors of the sky held at bay and hovered over their own. Abaddon, king of the abyss and prince of the seventh hierarchy of demons, walked by Satan's side. He who governed the furies and powers of evil, war, and destruction could only hold Satan's reins. He was referred to in Heaven as the Beast. Behind Abaddon stood Azrael. He had seven serpent heads with fourteen faces and twelve terrifying wings. The triumvirate behind Satan included Beelzebub, the Lord of the Flies and second to Satan among the fallen angels. Black flies with green eyes covered the prince of devils from head to toe. He smelled of the rotting flesh of the dead.

Satan convulsed. Worms and insects crawling in and out of his skin and fur riddled his body. The bugs laid eggs and feasted on his squalid flesh. Satan nipped at his skin for a nibble of the infestation. The Beast lovingly held his mater's reins. Pale and androgynous, the Beast opened his eyes to reveal a window to Hell. Rage beamed across the spirals with his glances. His soft, pallid skin suppressed the rage that seeped from every pore and camouflaged his hatred and desire to leap across the spirals and pound Nimrod and his crew with the axle of the chariot until their bones were powder and their souls surrendered to the Darkness.

"Satan!" Nimrod roared. "You've started a battle you cannot win. By the grace of God and the souls of humanity, we will repel you and send you weeping in disgrace to the Darkness." Nimrod felt pretty good about that.

Satan cackled, and he wrenched back his neck. His eyes floated in their sockets, and he hurled a wind of bile and stench across the spirals. His long, flicking tongue searched and found remnants of the sewage he had just spewed. He licked his own lips in gastronomic glee. He bellowed, "Your God has given up on humankind. He has disrespected me! He has not even sent a general of Heaven to challenge me. Where is Christ? Where is Muhammad? Where is Abraham? The people of Earth have been asking this question for thousands of years. Now I ask it too! Are things so awful they send me an unknown—an unworthy opponent to crush? Destroy you I will along with the souls of all humanity."

"Let's get out of here and get some help." Thomas was terrified, and he scooped the bile from around his collar with his bare hands.

"Absolutely not! There is no one but us. He's just trying to scare us," Nimrod said.

"Well, he's doing a heck of a job," said a petrified Shar.

"I need you to summon your courage now and face the demon." Nimrod squared his shoulders, looked across the spirals, and parried. "It is time for you to leave this place and take your rotting carcass with you. We will not waver." Nimrod looked toward his friends for a rally, and they stood tall.

Nimrod knew he was in over his head. The armies in the sky were growing restless for blood. The battle would end miserably for Heaven. Their brave warriors were sorely outnumbered. It was only a matter of time.

"We know your vile plan, Satan. It is flawed."

Satan looked at Nimrod the way a shark looks at bleeding flesh. "Then try to stop me. The souls on Earth are ripe for harvest. Our work is almost finished here. It is time for the Earth to die and deliver the souls to the mines of Gholar."

"The soul of humanity is alive!"

"Alive?" Satan's voiced boomed across the clouds. "Show me where it is alive." The clouds provided a backdrop as Satan force-fed scenes of Earth's misery to Team Nimrod. "Is it alive in the children of Africa, who starve while others feast? Is it alive in the heart of a five-year-old as a pedophile rapes and dismembers her? No! Where is your God? Where has he been? The human soul is weak. We have ruled this planet for ages. Despair rules here. Hordes of young stick needles in their arms to kill the pain of living. Whores sell their bodies for fixes. Junkies maim, rob, and steal to escape the pain of living. Drug dealers slaughter for greed and gluttony. People murder their own families for revenge and vanity. The rich live in castles, and the poor wallow in squalor. The rich, however, envy as much as the poor. The human libido is insatiable and grotesque. Jealousy and rage thrive within the carnal desire to satisfy the craving of human lust. The never-ending quest for pleasure has developed into a perversion we hadn't thought of in Hell. We own that! War rages in the Middle East, Bosnia, and South Africa. Hatchets and machetes slay other tribes for greed and power. The rivers run thick with blood. There is not a continent on the planet that hasn't seen the bloodlust of war. Modern masters such as Hitler and Pol Pot have exterminated the very lives your God claims to save.

"Where is your God? The planet is dying. The greed of the corporations is killing the Earth. Humans took the keys to the universe, made it into a bomb, and dropped it on their brethren." Satan laughed in exaltation, and his posse laughed behind him. "Fear rules this planet. I rule this planet! Races burn the homes of other races. Oppression of others has been a standard practice from day one here on Earth. There is slavery and the exploitation of the poor. How can you tell me their souls are alive? Wars are fought over religion. The good message is turned into massacre. That is my favorite. Fathers rape their own daughters and sons. Let me put these people out of their misery. Let my soldiers have the day they have longed for. I plan to personally dine on the flesh of every infant. They're delicacies, you know." Satan licked his lips in anticipation.

Nimrod had heard quite enough. "Why don't we lay a wager?"

"You have nothing with which to wager. Why would I entertain such folly?"

"I have something you desire very much."

"There is nothing on this planet I do not control. Be gone." Satan turned his back on Nimrod, and the armies in the air prepared to engage.

"I will wager the location of Heaven."

Team Nimrod couldn't believe their ears. Satan stopped in his tracks. He couldn't believe his either. "This information could put you in great favor of the Darkness," Nimrod said. "I know there are others in the night who seek to dethrone you." Satan's eyes glimmered with envy, greed, and pride. "Heaven is what the Darkness covets most. With Heaven removed from the equation, the Darkness would rule the universe."

Satan was curious to know the stakes. "What is your wager?"

"If I lose I will give you the location of Heaven and barter with the Darkness. If I win you let Earth live free of your torment forever."

The stakes were appealing to Satan. He kicked around in the dirt. "What is the game?"

"I hear you like college football and corrupted the game." Satan shot bolts at Nimrod. He was surprised Nimrod knew his passion. "You pick a team. If your team beats my team, you win." Nimrod prayed Satan would take the bait.

"What if they are not scheduled to play each other?"

"Then we will match them up—anyone, anytime, anyplace, anyhow. Agreed?" Nimrod added the fine print.

Satan struggled with the ploy. Heaven was too valuable. He had to have it. "I can choose any team I want? First?" Satan asked.

Nimrod confirmed. "And then I will choose my team. But there can be no interference in the teams' progress. It must be a fair game. Agreed?" Nimrod asked for transparency.

"Agreed."

"What team shall you pick?"

Satan did not struggle with the answer. He wanted the best college team to ever walk on the field. "Florida T&A."

Satan had handpicked the players personally. He had put them together like a de facto general manager. He had used this gambit before and robbed other cretins of the universe blind. They too had challenged his dynasty. They were a vile bunch. "And whom do you choose?"

Nimrod took a deep breath. There were several perennial teams that sported fine programs. Florida T&A had obliterated all of them. Florida T&A had all twenty-two starters coming back to secure the third title. He thought of Notre Dame. No. Tennessee. No. Ohio State. No. He went with his gut. "I'll choose…Navy."

Thomas passed out again, and Satan laughed.

"I'll have Balberith draw up the papers," Satan said.

He turned and extracted his legions from the sky. Team Nimrod boarded the chariot, and Pegasus leaped off the Spirals of Cortez. They waved gratefully to Carmax, Samax, Paffran, Ismoli, and all the battle-weary angels.

April and Rory vowed never to smoke pot again.

Nimrod was visibly shaken after his introduction to Satan at the Spirals of Cortez, and he frowned upon the full-on Afro Jairus had received from Samson while they were away. Team Nimrod worried as Nimrod exhibited all the telltale signs of depression. He refused to order food at the Canteen. He sat still as if in a trance.

Nicodemus, Heaven's attorney, excused himself from his guests and sauntered over to Team Nimrod. "I received an interuniversal e-mail from Balberith today." Nimrod put his head on the table. Word was out. "It seems you wagered the souls of the universe and the location of Heaven to spare the souls on Earth." There was a very uncomfortable pause. "The needs of the many outweigh the needs of the few, Nimrod." More stale silence lingered. "I am going to have to show this to Michael." Nimrod banged his head on the table. "You took Navy?" Nicodemus shook his head. He was flabbergasted. "You are a real nimrod."

Nicodemus walked away. He was disgusted, and he wondered about the fate of Heaven, which now rested with Nimrod's foolish bet.

"We need some help." Thomas had mastered the obvious.

"Let's go see Michael and see if he has any ideas," Shar insisted.

"The die is cast. I gave Satan my word." Nimrod looked miserable. "There is nothing even Michael can do about this besides berate me. We're must figure out a solution on our own. This is my responsibility. It's time for plan B."

"Plan A worked so well." Vishnu needled.

Nimrod searched the air for divine intervention. It wasn't coming. "I always told my students that when they needed help, they should ask for it. There are two people who know more about Satan's wiles than anyone in the universe." Team Nimrod looked at him for the answer. "Jesus and Muhammad."

"Jesus and Muhammad are in the Stounfad System, Nimrod," Thomas reminded their leader.

Nimrod gazed around. Vishnu spoke—the first to comprehend what Nimrod was thinking. "No, no, no. We are not going to the Stounfad System."

"They are in the middle of a war." Shar wanted no part of the plan.

"It's easy. We drop in, and we drop out. The Dunny Gate takes us straight to Vancil Hill, the holy capital of Blanco Trollien. We have a talk with Jesus and get a few pointers. Then we're back in Heaven to deal with Satan. Bada bing, bada boom."

"We need authorization for the Dunny Gate," Thomas reminded Nimrod.

"I've got clearance for all passages." Team Nimrod was skeptical. "It came with the mission." They were still unsure. Nimrod wasn't telling the whole truth. He looked at them sheepishly. "I am supposed to inform Michael of all my travels."

"Well, are you?" Shar wanted to know.

Nimrod held firm for a moment. "No." Nimrod planned to disobey a direct order from Michael the archangel. He could be expelled from Heaven.

"You've gone over the edge, Nimrod." Thomas was worried about his friend.

"I can't bear to face Michael and explain the predicament we're in. He'll be devastated. We have a few days before our next meeting and status update. I hope to return from Vancil Hill with a more tangible plan. I'll resolve this on my own."

Pride, thought Vishnu.

Trip to Dunny Gate

"Nimrod, the trip to Dunny Gate will take weeks on foot." Shar seemed uninterested in walking. "Is there no way to wrangle a chariot? It is at the summit of Mount Rabtik."

"Unfortunately not. Michael would be aware we are on the move." Nimrod packed his small bag with a change of clothes. "But, my dear Shahrazad…" He winked at Shar convincingly. "I have that all figured out."

"Nimrod, you never call me by my full name. Why now?" Shar was flattered but curious.

"Jairus has become very fond of you and all of us, and we chatted by the fire a little about Aunt Shar." Nimrod threw the pack over his shoulder.

"Aunt Shar," she said to herself. She felt so cozy.

"Are we ready?" Nimrod implored the team to embark.

"Aye, Captain Nimrod," Vishnu mocked his friend.

"Thomas?" Nimrod wanted all hands on deck.

"This is a bad idea, Nimrod." Thomas couldn't believe anything would go right.

"I'm ready!" Jairus yelled.

He had his bag packed and was ready for the journey. The tales of the last adventure were over the top. He was determined to tag along.

"Jairus." Nimrod looked sadly at the boy. Samson had done up his 'fro with some Jheri curl. "You may only go so far as the Dunny Gate." Jairus was not happy. "This is even more dangerous than the trip to the Spirals of Cortez."

"But you said you'd be in and out. Bada bing, bada boom."

Nimrod reminded himself to watch what he said in front of the impressionable boy. "That's just an expression, Jairus. Blanco Trollien is under siege. I don't believe we will find trouble. Vancil Hill is well protected. But there is no sense taking any unnecessary chances."

"Am I still allowed to go to the Dunny Gate?"

"Sure." Nimrod would teach on the journey.

Team Nimrod left the barbershop for the long hike to the top of Mount Rabtik. They came to the outskirts of Pyrub Cape, and Nimrod turned down a different path. They paced themselves through the two-hundred-foot white pines and were thankful for the shade. Nimrod looked at the sunlight twinkling through the black spruce. The brown false morels looked like brains on stems. They decorated the needles that had fallen from the chartreuse loblolly pines. They came to a ridge that overlooked a farmhouse and stable. The meadow lay before them filled with laser lemon blushed vinegar cups. They tapered at the bottom and then opened like vases. Wild strawberries ripened in unearthly shades of shocking pink and wild watermelon. Screaming green bishop caps surrounded them. Nimrod stopped to pick a blizzard-blue star-of-Bethlehem and handed it to Shar. The shape of stallions with sepia manes came into view, and Vishnu wondered where Nimrod had taken them on his excursion.

"Ah! Amelia, I'm glad I found you."

Amelia Earhart was cleaning the stables. She had a fine sweat on her brow and removed her gloves. "Nimrod!" She was happy to see her old friend and confidant.

Nimrod had always felt a responsibility to stay in touch with Amelia. He had been her apprentice guardian angel on Earth, and things had not worked out the way Nimrod had hoped.

"What brings you to Lherrey Land?" Amelia asked and invited everyone into the farmhouse.

Team Nimrod was thankful to be off their feet for at least a few minutes.

"Amelia." Nimrod was hesitant. "I need to ask you a favor."

Amelia brought a large platter of muffins with shaved almonds and cinnamon. Hands reached like desperate tentacles for the well-timed treat.

"Sure, Nimrod. What do you need?" Amelia was happy to have the company.

"I need to borrow some horses." Nimrod asked humbly.

Amelia almost choked on her muffin. "Nimrod, that's a huge favor."

"I'm in a bit of a bind."

"A bit?" Thomas said and bit the muffin. Shar smacked Thomas on the knee.

Amelia looked out the window at the ponies. They were her pride and joy—and responsibility. "How many do you need?" Nimrod looked at everyone at the table, and Amelia sighed. "Where are you going?"

Nimrod spoke into his hand and coughed at the same time. He hoped to baffle Amelia. "Mount Rabtik."

"Mount Rabtik!"

Didn't work, thought Nimrod.

"That's a heck of a climb," Amelia said.

She wanted to say no, but she had always felt sorry for Nimrod. He took a lot of heat when she died, and she knew it wasn't his fault. She shouldn't have tried to fly over the Pacific Ocean by herself. "Well, all right. But none of my babies had better get hurt."

Team Nimrod cheered Amelia. They headed out to the stables and prepared saddles and blankets.

"You make sure they get plenty of water, and don't drive them too hard." Amelia handed Nimrod a sack of carrots and sugar cubes.

Nimrod mounted his steed. "What is this horse's name?"

"That's Secretariat. He's the leader of this group. Shar, you're riding Sir Barton. He can be a little testy, but once you get to know him, he's very lovable." She helped Jairus into the saddle. "Young man, this is Gallant Fox. He's as smooth as Thelonious Monk playing the piano." She turned to Vishnu and his diminutive stature. "Maybe I can find a smaller horse for you. We have some miniature ponies."

Team Nimrod laughed at Vishnu.

"I'm fine, ma'am. Thank you. What is the horse's name?"

"You're on War Admiral. He likes to take off if you're not stern."

"Terrific," mumbled Vishnu under his breath.

"Thomas, this is Whirlaway. You should have an easy ride."

Amelia smacked the horse on its hindquarter and wished them good luck.

"Amelia," Nimrod said. He looked solemn. "I can't thank you enough."

"You can thank me by taking care of yourself…and the horses."

She waved as War Admiral tore off across the field and Vishnu held on for dear life.

They rode for hours, but stopped for lunch at Elorgis DD Ranch and snacked with St. Blaise. Vishnu looked crabby. War Admiral had gotten the best of him. They watered the horses and Blaise handed out some dashing ten-gallon hats. Nimrod got one with a feather and he pretended to be a pirate for Jairus. They forged on to Mt. Rabtik.

"Where are we going to stay the night, Nimrod?" Jairus had never camped out before.

"With the wind at our backs, matey, we should make the Darik Mill by supper. Argh." Everyone was getting a wee bit loopy, and Nimrod even sported a patch over his eye.

The climb into the foothills of Mount Rabtik slowed the pace. The monstrous face of the mountain took the brunt of the setting sun, and shadows cast down upon Team Nimrod. The up-and-down, deepening ravines were taking their toll on the sturdy equines' energy. They could smell the jerk seasoning in the air. They were close to the Darik Mill and Mother Alphonsa. Over the next ridge, they spotted the rising smoke coming from the small shack. The horses carried their riders through the Cloump Lemon Canal. They followed the odor to the front door, and then Nimrod rapped politely. The door was not latched, and it swung open slightly to Nimrod's touch. Alphonsa made her way to the door. The rotund Jamaican saint's face beamed as she hugged her old friend.

"Come in, mon."

She wiped her hands on her apron, grabbed her chef's knife, and continued slicing and dicing the Tyor leek and stirring the Glamora brine. She added the Tyor leek to the boiling water with tumbling pounds of rice. An open pit outside the kitchen door seared the jerk pork they had smelled over the mountains, and corn on the cob still nestled in their husks joined it. Hundreds of shrimp sizzled on the heat of the flattop. Stephen Biko worked diligently on crab dumplings and roti. He added the Glamora brine to the roti. Alphonsa turned to take the warm callaloo out of the oven and set them aside. Thomas neared the baking tray, and his hand reached for a tasty treat. Alphonsa almost took his hand off with her rolling pin.

"Not until everything's ready." She wasn't angry. It was just a rule. Alphonsa threw hot peppers onto the flattop and sprinkled a bounty of fresh garlic onto the pile. "Do you like callaloo, mon?" She looked at Thomas.

"I'm not sure what it is." Thomas held his hands in the fig leaf position—far away from the counter.

"Callaloo is a green leafy vegetable. You put it inside the turnover and bake it."

It sounded great. Multiple frying pans of grease smoldered on the stove. Biko put the snapper into the batter and then laid it into the iron skillet. The crackling intensified as the fish turned golden and flaky.

"What are you doing with the snapper?" Shar wanted to learn.

"The snapper is for the bammy, missy." Alphonsa looked at the skinny Shar. "Bammy is a flatbread. You stuff it with the snapper and fold it with onions and red and green hot peppers."

Vishnu was salivating, and Nimrod searched his pack for Tums. He didn't want to miss this meal.

"Did you know we were coming, Miss Alphonsa?" Jairus was very polite, and he took off his cowboy hat and set it aside.

"No. It is a very pleasant surprise. I have not seen Nimrod in many years." She smiled a hearty smile at Nimrod. "Why do you ask, little man?"

"Because this sure is a lot of food for two people." Jairus had never seen so much food in one place.

The soothing sounds of a bass guitar and steel drums began.

"There is never enough food for the children, little man. Children get hungry, and they have to be fed." Alphonsa rolled another batch of bammy and put it in the oven.

"Are your kids playing outside?" Jairus thought about playing with kids his own age.

"Yes, they are, Jairus." Alphonsa confirmed.

Biko pulled the jerk pork off the pit and laid it on the counter for Alphonsa. She hacked away at the meat and cleaved huge chunks onto several platters.

"How old are your children?" Jairus hoped one was his age, but it didn't really matter. Jairus liked kids.

"They are all ages, young mon. All ages." A guitar joined the bass and steel drums. "Would you all like to join us for dinner?"

"We'd be honored, Alphonsa," Nimrod said, speaking for the group.

Alphonsa turned and reached over the sink. She pushed open the heavy wooden shutters, and the fresh outside air poured in. Team Nimrod stared in awe. They moved closer to the window to confirm what they were seeing. Tens of thousands of children waited hungrily in the ravine for supper. They weren't impatient or rowdy. They were just thankful they would eat tonight.

"Where did all these children come from?" Vishnu could not believe his eyes.

"They come from all over the universe, mon. These are the children who died because they had nothing to eat. There are infants, toddlers, schoolchildren, and teens. Wherever they came from, no one found it important enough to give them enough food to live—much less be healthy. They are victims of starvation. The number of children grows every day." Alphonsa looked very weary from the sadness. "Their idea of Heaven is a little morsel of food. We try to give them more than that."

Bob Marley rang the dinner bell. He closed his eyes and sang "Three Little Birds," and the children knew everything was going to be all right. Wilhelm and Jacob Grimm entertained the children as they waited in line. They laughed at the marionettes as the Brothers Grimm performed "Sleeping Beauty."

Nimrod was the first to help Steven Biko make the children's plates. The others followed suit, and each child thanked them and smiled gratefully when he or she received the meal. They took to the hillside and listened to Marley's reggae, and the children ate as if these meals would be their last. That was the assumption they had made of their world. There was no guarantee of food tomorrow. Nimrod felt humbled and put his arm around Alphonsa. Alphonsa mentioned that breakfast would be upon them soon.

A cool breeze came over Mount Rabtik, and Team Nimrod lay inside their sleeping bags. Nimrod heard the sounds of whimpering and found Jairus crying under his covers. "Jairus, what's the matter?"

"I feel so bad for those kids."

"They are in a good place now. They are in Heaven. Alphonsa takes good care of them. She is the patron saint of sick and dead children."

Jairus wiped his eyes and then blubbered some more. "She is a really nice lady."

"She's a wonderful lady, but don't mess with her kids. I've seen her temper. She can do some damage with that rolling pin. Did you see Thomas's face?"

They both laughed through the tears.

"But they suffered so much while they were alive." The tears streamed down his face. He couldn't choose whether to laugh or cry.

"It is very sad. That is why we have angels—to help the suffering people." Nimrod had no real great answer.

"Well, the angels are doing lousy jobs," Jairus spat. "Did you see how many children starved to death? There were millions." He was inconsolable.

"We're trying our best, but we need help. We need help from the people in the universe. If they believed in God and heeded his Word, we could combat the Darkness. That's why we want you to be the best angel ever. I believe you can help us, Jairus."

"I wish there were more souls in the universe like Alphonsa. She's so nice."

"She is a wonderful person," agreed Nimrod. "The demons of the universe don't mess with her temper. She walks softly and carries a big voodoo stick. She is tenacious in the protection of the sick children."

"What can I do to help?" Jairus slumped his shoulders, and Nimrod pulled him close.

"It's not just you, Jairus. It's all of us. We all need to believe." *Easier said than done,* thought Nimrod.

Team Nimrod woke well before dawn to help Alphonsa make breakfast for the hordes. Nimrod had never seen so many eggs. He wondered from where they had all come. Heaven had its secrets. They saddled the horses, and Jairus sat on the porch swing talking to Alphonsa. Jairus was sporting his new dreadlock look courtesy of Mr. Marley. Jairus hugged Alphonsa and spoke into her ear as she helped him onto Gallant Fox. Alphonsa nodded to the boy, and they shook hands as agreement on their secret. The horses were rested and antsy to get going. They planned to reach the pinnacle of Mount Rabtik by nightfall by way of Khaluarm Falls.

Burnt sienna maples with smooth, gray bark shaded the trail. The horses nibbled on the anise funnel caps and false chanterelles, and Team Nimrod filled their pouches with the cool waters of the Khaluarm River. Climbing Prussian blue and spring green orchids scaled the nose of the rocks. The trail followed the turquoise river as wild salmon slammed their flesh through the rapids and searched for the tide pool where they could spawn their blue-green eggs. Lavender lilacs and psychedelic geraniums and daisies lined the banks. The smell of gardenias filled the air.

The horses continued as the sound of the raging waters of Khaluarm Falls thundered ahead. They came to the river edge and watched as the waters plunged from three mountain streams into the cyclone vortex that swirled a thousand feet straight through Mount Rabtik. Mist shot back through the eye of the waterfall and created a rainbow of all the colors of the universe. Team Nimrod had come to this special place of thought and prayer. They knelt and prayed for safe passage from Dunny Gate. The horses were spooked as they crossed Khaluarm Falls on the trunk of a single mahogany that stretched over the hundred-foot span. They all looked down through the eye of the gravity-pulled waterspout and tried to spy the bottom of the abyss.

Bittersweet flowering dogwood and violet-red juniper greeted them on the other side. The tips of quaking aspen gated the mountainside. White poplar with thistle leaves stood strong in the growing wind with the sturdy birch as the air grew thin.

They reached the summit, and Abraham Lincoln sat on a bench near a Japanese garden arrayed with the soft colors of melon and cornflower. The sixteenth president listened to the soprano of Maria Callas, and her voice filled the valleys below. She wore a silver crucifix around her neck. It trembled with the waves of her song. Lincoln looked peaceful and relaxed. The opera soothed the pain of his war. Underneath a hickory tree stood an easel. Salvador Dali painted the scene, and melted maize and olive green splashed the canvas. A white picket fence surrounded the Japanese garden. A single gate allowed entrance—Dunny Gate. Team Nimrod remained silent. They did not want to interrupt the opera or serenity. Nimrod whispered into Jairus's ear that they would be back soon. He was to return with the horses to Amelia. Secretariat knew the way.

They embraced, and Nimrod was the first to go. He opened the gate, walked into the garden and past the violas, and then disappeared. Thomas followed and then Shar. Vishnu turned and gave Jairus a thumbs-up. Vishnu walked into the garden but left the gate open. Jairus dropped the bags and rushed through the opening as it was swinging shut. The wormhole to the Stounfad System sucked him in.

THIRTEEN WEEKS

April 2004, Saint Paul, Minnesota

Mr. Tuby V. Gravenald sat in the folding chair long after everybody had left. How did one say good-bye to someone after thirty-five years? The soft spring air of Minnesota still blew cool as his daughter, Jane, and his granddaughter, Emily, sat patiently beside him. His love for them was unequivocal. His love for his wife had been thrilling and passionate. They had met in the summer of 1968—that turbulent year marred by protests against the Vietnam War and the assassinations of Martin Luther King Jr. and Robert Kennedy. Blacks fought whites, and cities burned but not for Tuby and Myra. He loved football, and she loved the outdoors. They kept to themselves and far away from the changing world around them. They fished in the ten thousand lakes in the summer, and he coached football in the fall. He had taken a position teaching history at a local Saint Paul high school and volunteered to coach the defense. The move paid off. He became assistant head coach and developed a reputation as a leader of young people. He was offered an assistant's job at the University of Minnesota in the summer of 1974 and never looked back.

He became the Gophers' head coach in 1983 and led the maroon and gold to three Rose Bowl victories. His squad was once ranked fourth in the final polls. Football had changed, though. He tired of the recruiting and constant struggle with the attitudes of the young players. Controversy surrounded the team, and the NCAA made accusations about falsified grades and booster payments to the athletes. Television and money ruled the game, and the pressure to win every single year grated on him. The entire Big Ten had changed. Teams were made to play almost any night of the week. Tuby informed the school the 2003 season would be his last. He told the press that he and Myra were goin' fishing— but not anymore. Myra died suddenly of a brain aneurysm, and Tuby was left alone. Jane touched his shoulder. The funeral attendants were ready to lower the casket into the ground. Tuby walked to Myra and kissed her one last time through the pine. Tuby was dry of tears, but anguish filled his heart. He turned and walked to the car. Jane and Emily were by his side.

Tuby sat in his study and pored over old photo albums filled with pictures of life. He turned the pages, watched Jane grow up, and watched himself grow old. Myra aged gracefully through the years and never appeared to change. Jane had broken the news softly that she and Emily would be leaving the following day. Jane Porote, aware her father would be alone, had encouraged him to think about moving to Annapolis, Maryland. She had a great job there and was putting her life back together. Her ex-husband had left her with a pile of credit card bills, and then he fled to Fiji with a nineteen-year-old. He had left a note that he needed to find himself. He also needed to find a safe haven from the prosecutors who had filed computer fraud and embezzlement charges against him. Tuby never considered that Jane would return to Minnesota.

Emily was starting to feel comfortable in preschool and was bringing over newly made friends. She was smiling for the first time he could remember. Two screaming parents had filled her toddler days. Tuby wasn't sure what he was going to do with himself—probably sit in his armchair and rot.

Tuby stood at the northwest gate and waited for the direct flight to Baltimore–Washington International. He gave Jane a warm hug and Emily a big squeeze. He treated Emily to a sunshine Care Bear and assured her the new friend would keep her safe through takeoff. They disappeared down the ramp, and he watched from the window to see if he could see them boarding the plane.

The plane taxied away from the gate, and Tuby watched it slide away past the terminal. He stayed glued to the observation window until he saw the flight lift into the air. It streamed exhaust into the blue Minnesota sky. It slowly vanished into the clouds, and he was officially alone. He got into his Cadillac and caught the expressway home. He pulled into the local shopping center and scored a bottle of Johnny Walker Blue. He might as well treat himself. It was going to be a long night. He swung the car out of the shopping center and into the forest of the neighborhood. The trees all had their leaves, that day of spring they became fully lush.

Tuby was surprised to see a uniformed man standing on his front porch. He was a naval admiral in full dress uniform. Tuby got out of the car and beeped the lock.

"Can I help you?" Tuby addressed his senior.

The admiral was very old but had a gleam in his eye. "Are you Mr. Tuby V. Gravenald?" He looked Tuby up and down and performed an inspection.

"I am. How can I help you?" Tuby extended his hand.

"I am Admiral T. 'Junk' Timple, US Navy." Timple grasped his hand. "Would you mind if I talked to you about football?"

Tuby had met fanatics before, and it was possible this guy was a nut. "What did you want to talk about?" Tuby worried it was an ancient Minnesota fan who wanted to condemn him for a tough loss.

"The US Naval Academy has authorized me to offer you the job as head football coach in Annapolis."

Tuby sensed he might not be a nut. "Please come in."

They entered the Gravenald foyer, and the admiral removed his hat. "Is that Johnny Walker Blue?"

Tuby had been trying to shield his brown paper bag. He wasn't ashamed. It just wasn't anyone else's business. He wondered how he knew it was Johnny Walker Blue. "Yes, sir. It is."

"I haven't tasted that in years. Two cubes please." The admiral sat down on the couch.

Two cubes only for the pushy old man, thought Tuby. He went to the wet bar and cracked open a tray of ice. He poured the admiral a generous portion. He didn't want to serve him again. He could still be a lunatic. Tuby got straight to the point. "So what's this all about, Admiral Timple?"

"Our outgoing head coach, Mr. Broamis, is a fine man. He left the Naval Academy with a little push. Seems he didn't have all his mid regs in order, so we showed him the hatch." Timple sipped his Scotch. "That's terrific."

"Mid regs?" Tuby asked. He was unclear with the terminology.

"Midshipman regulations, Mr. Gravenald. Conduct expectations."

"With all due respect, Admiral, the coach wasn't a midshipman." Tuby sipped his drink without ice.

"We all have conduct expectations, Mr. Gravenald."

"I suppose that is true."

"The situation has become FUBAR. We need someone to show these young men how to play football. We haven't beaten Army in four years. Those bastards." The hatred jetted through Timple's eyes.

"Sir, now is a difficult time for me. I buried my wife yesterday." Tuby looked into his Scotch.

"I know," Timple said curtly.

"I also retired after twenty years of coaching this past January."

"I know."

"Admiral Timple, quite honestly I don't think I have the desire left to coach a football team properly." It was the first time Tuby had admitted that to himself.

"That's why I've come to you, Mr. Gravenald. Our team wasn't being coached properly. I think you are the person for the job." Timple set down his empty glass.

Tuby stood with the admiral. "Sir, I'm really not in the market for a job. Myra and I had plans to do some fishing this summer. I sure that will be good medicine for me."

"Fishing." The admiral reached into his coat pocket. "Here's a round-trip ticket to BWI. Superintendent Gregory will provide transportation to the yard. He'll show you around. If you want the job, tell Superintendent Gregory. He'll draw up the contract." Timple grabbed his hat, and Tuby opened the door. "At the very least, it will be a freebie to see your family. I must return to the Naval Academy. I am scheduled to handle some very delicate papers in the admissions department."

"Delicate?" Tuby asked the kook.

"Yes. Eleven soldiers vital to the future of the navy and the safety of the world. My ship leaves port at eighteen hundred hours." Timple turned and walked briskly down the sidewalk.

That was strange, thought Tuby. *How does he know I have family in Annapolis?* He looked at the ticket. It was authentic. The flight left early on the third Monday of May.

Tuby watched the *Law and Order* marathon on A&E. He sure liked Lennie Briscoe. There was a little Stouffer's lasagna left, and he threw it in the microwave. The refrigerator contents looked thin. He was going to have to go to the grocery store. All the deli meat and cake from the funeral reception were gone. The grocery store was a smidgeon intimidating. Tuby hadn't really done any shopping in about twenty-five years. The laundry had piled up. That washing machine contraption was a real bear. *Why can't you just press a button and be done with it?* he thought, anguished. He had to sort out colors, whites, permanent press, and how much detergent to use. Who knew that stuff? Myra had taken care of all those things. He was going to have to call Emma, the maid. The bedsheets hadn't been changed since Myra passed. They still had her smell. Maybe that was why he hadn't washed them.

He grabbed another Heineken, popped the top, grabbed the lasagna, and went back to his tray table perched in front of the Sony. Maybe Claire Kincaid would be in this episode.

Tuby started to sleep later and later. He had already missed church. There was nothing in the fridge, so he went to a restaurant and ordered some nachos. He sat alone at the bar and enjoyed a Sierra Nevada. He watched some golf on the overhead television, and a few fans recognized him. They said he would be missed, and it made him feel good. The jalapeños churned in his stomach, and he hopped in the Caddy after leaving the barkeep a nice tip. He got home and turned on the television. John Candy starred in *Uncle Buck*. John Candy always made him laugh. He looked at the airline ticket that had slid under the empty fruit bowl among the mess on the kitchen counter. It sure would be nice to see Jane and Emily. Tuby decided to think about it. *Hard to Kill* with Steven Seagal was on after *Uncle Buck*.

The alarm worked. Tuby was surprised. He was just as surprised that he woke up. It was five thirty in the morning. "Jesus H. Christ on a popsicle stick," complained Tuby. "It's early." He sat on the edge of the bed and teetered between the pillow and the shower. That blanket sure was warm. He resisted and creaked toward the shower. The knees just weren't what they used to be. At least he had the originals, though. Everybody else seemed to have bionic parts these days. The shower steamed up, and he nicked himself shaving. It was a bleeder, and he dabbed some toilet paper to his chin and left it there. There was a nice blue suit in the closet with a solid shirt and a tie Jane had given him last Father's Day. He threw a few clothes in a small suitcase that could be carried on and zipped it shut. He felt good about finally taking his laundry to the cleaners. It was expensive but done. He double-checked to make sure he had his wallet, keys, and ticket. Jane and Emily sure would be surprised.

Tuby fastened his seat belt and put the tray in the upright and locked position. The very easy flight ended before it started as the pilot pulled up the nose on the 737, and he heard the tires skid on the runway. Landing worried Tuby more than takeoffs. The flight attendant wished them a nice day, and Tuby headed up the ramp. Timple had said there would be arrangements made to get him to Annapolis—a forty-five-minute drive. He expected to see a placard with his name inscribed on it and spelled incorrectly. There was no such driver, but there was a naval officer in dress uniform standing at the gate. They made eye contact and approached each other.

"Mr. Gravenald?" The officer smiled enthusiastically.

"I'm Tuby Gravenald," he confirmed.

"I am Captain Todd. What do you say we beat Army?" Todd's face filled with anxious fury at the thought. Tuby didn't know what to say. "Do you mind if I attach this badge to your coat button? It's your clearance."

"Clearance for what?" Tuby wondered what he had gotten himself into.

"We have a chopper waiting to take us to Farragut Field."

A chopper? Tuby had never been on a helicopter.

It was not a helicopter that covered the traffic for the local news. It was more like Marine One. The SH-608 had a flight crew and missiles. *An everyday commuting vehicle,* Tuby thought.

"How far is Annapolis by helicopter?" Tuby shouted over the rotor blades.

"About ten minutes." Captain Todd looked out over the hills and forests of the Maryland countryside.

It was a brilliant spring morning, and the pilot stayed just over the ocean of trees.

"Do you take this to work every morning, Captain Todd?" Tuby wondered where his tax dollars went.

"Negative. This is only used for special occasions and VIPs." The commander seemed genuinely happy to give the old coach a lift.

"I'm no VIP, Captain Todd. I'm just a football coach." Tuby watched the streams cutting liquid swaths through the green.

"But you're going to be Navy's football coach," Captain Todd said.

He smiled at Tuby like a dog that wanted to lick his master. The SH-60B glided over a ridge. Tuby was astounded. The shimmering Chesapeake Bay lay before him like a small ocean. Neatly tucked into the seawalls between the Severn River and Dorsey and Spa Creeks was the US Naval Academy. It even looked historic. The chopper took a vanity circle over the Navy–Marine Corps Memorial Stadium. The thirty-thousand-seat open stadium looked like a high-school facility compared to the Metrodome.

They flew over the main campus. The brick-lined streets and the neatly manicured grounds were home to many statues and monuments. A group of startled tourists looked skyward at the helicopter as if under attack. Tuby thought the pilot was going to land it in the bay, and then he realized they had touched the solid ground of Farragut Field on the edge of Spa Creek. Captain Todd opened the hatch, and the humidity blew into Tuby's face. An admiral held his cover on his head with his left hand and extended his right. This was either to help Tuby down or introduce himself. Either way it worked.

"Mr. Tuby V. Gravenald, I am Admiral James Gregory. I am the superintendent of the Naval Academy. Glad to have you on deck."

Tuby didn't understand all this "deck" and "mid regs" language. "Thank you for the help getting here. It sure is a beautiful campus."

Tuby and Gregory moved toward Compass Point and away from the helicopter. "It's a 'yard,' Mr. Gravenald. We don't call it a 'campus.'"

Well, la-di-da, thought Tuby. It was a free trip to see Jane and Emily. He could put up with this for a few hours, and then he'd give his darlings a call. He was sure they knew a fine place for dinner. Crab cakes were the regional delicacy.

They passed Ricketts Hall, and Superintendent Gregory babbled on about some history of the building, but Tuby couldn't take his eyes off the sailboats and cabin cruisers that dotted the bay and splashed the waters with colored sails, bikinis, and fishing rods. Myra would have loved fishing here—not so much the bikinis. Tuby got back in the game as tourists filed out of the Armel-Leftwich Visitor Center. They were armed with souvenirs and red visitors' passes that indicated they had paid for the tour and a personal guide wearing white socks and black walking shoes. They followed closely behind one of the groups around the corner.

"This is Halsey Field House. It's named after Admiral William 'Bull' Halsey of World War II fame. We'll come back here later."

Tuby knew him well. He had become a war buff.

Gregory stopped by the statue of a goat. "This is Bill. Bill is the Navy mascot. The US Navy used to have goats aboard to provide milk for the sailors on long cruises. Bill was the name of the goat on the warship USS *New York*. He became the ship's mascot and eventually ours. At the games Bill is always pointed in the direction of a Navy touchdown."

How quaint, thought Tuby. He had seen the goat on television but never knew the story. Minnesota had never played Navy in the thirty years he had been associated with the program.

Gregory took them up the ramp to Lejeune Hall. They walked past the indoor track and Olympic-sized swimming pool. Boxing, wrestling, and martial arts mats rounded out the corners.

"This is the ten-meter board all midshipmen have to jump from. It imitates the height of a burning ship. The fully clothed midshipmen must swim a half mile or else."

"Or else what?" Tuby wanted to know.

"Or else they don't graduate from the Naval Academy." Gregory was dead serious.

Most of Tuby's players had graduated if they could spell their names. They continued the tour, and Tuby saw gold footballs. "What are these?" Tuby's curiosity was piqued.

"The gold balls are dated with the score and dates of the years we beat Army." Tuby noticed the old balls from the 1940s were bigger than the modern ball. "It's a big deal to us, Mr. Gravenald. That's why we brought you here."

Gregory looked at Gravenald to take his temperature. Tuby could feel the heat.

"Is that the Heisman Trophy?" Tuby changed the subject.

"It is. Roger Staubach won that in 1963."

Tuby wished he could touch the Heisman Trophy. *Cool,* he thought.

"Let's take a walk, shall we?"

Tuby assumed the superintendent talked like this to everyone. His conversation sounded like giving orders. They stepped out into the humidity, and Tuby started to sweat. He took off his blazer. He thought about loosening his tie, but everybody was so tidy in the yard. He didn't want to look like a slob. He would suffer in this heat. "Is it always this hot?"

"Oh, it gets much hotter in July and August." *That isn't possible,* thought Tuby. "But our winters are fairly mild compared to Minnesota."

Tuby sensed the weather sell. A trade-off of the heat for the snow seemed like an even-stephen deal. Lose one bad. Gain one bad.

"This is Porter Road. It's more commonly known as Captain's Row."

The brick-lined street looked like Main Street, USA. The lawns were in immaculate conditions, and the sidewalks under the oaks were groomed nicer than a Beverly Hills poodle. Each window had a Beat Army poster or banner in the window. The American flag flew from every stoop. Tennis courts lined the opposite side of the street at the base of Ward Hall.

"You can live here if you beat Army." Gregory was half kidding and half serious. "We also have a six-thousand-two-hundred-seventeen-yard golf course to work on your short game."

Tuby didn't play tennis or golf, but the houses were nice. Tuby heard a roar from around the corner. "What was that?"

"That is Herndon. Come see."

They turned the corner between Ward Hall and Buchanan House. Tuby rubbed his eyes in amazement. A thousand teenagers were scaling a mini Washington Monument covered in Crisco. A mob of spectators crowded around the grassy, monument-filled park. They watched from near the trees and inside the gazebo and cheered rowdily at the madness. The young men and women assembled a human pyramid and tried to remove what looked like a paper cup from the tip of the obelisk.

"What the hell is going on?" Tuby had never seen anything like this.

"This is the plebe recognition ceremony—but no one calls it that. This monument is called Herndon. It is named after

Commander William Herndon, who perished in 1857 in the stormy waters off Cape Hatteras. The *Central America* foundered, and there were no survivors. They erected Herndon Monument two years later. The plebes…"

"What are plebes?"

Gregory looked at Gravenald. He didn't know the first thing about the US Navy. "We call our first-year midshipmen plebes. It is not an easy year for them. They are completely different animals from the children who began plebe summer last year. They were scared little mama's boys and girls. They've suffered the indignation of being young and stupid, and they've survived. Upperclassmen berated them. Professors pushed them to their academic limits, and they found the light after the dark ages of study in January and February. They've endured intense military and physical training. This is their coming-out ceremony. Now they become youngsters."

"Youngsters?"

"Sophomores to the civilian world."

"What are they trying to do?" Tuby watched the plebes try and fail and then try again to access the tip of Herndon.

"Herndon is rubbed with Crisco, lard, crankcase grease, motor oil, and anything else slippery to prevent them from getting the Dixie cup fixed to the top. When they work together as a team and snare the cup, legend says the mid who replaces the cup with a navy cover will become the first admiral of the class."

"How long does this take?"

One poor kid had gotten so close to the top and then slid all the way to the dirt over his greasy classmates. The crowd applauded the near miss.

"The record is an astonishing one minute and thirty seconds. The worst is an abysmal four hours, twelve minutes, and seventeen seconds, but we only started recording times in 1962."

"I don't have four hours, twelve minutes, and seventeen seconds." Tuby wanted to see victory, but Jane and Emily had a surprise coming.

"You're assuming the worst, Mr. Gravenald." Gregory seemed like an optimistic person but with little patience. "I would show you Bancroft Hall where all the midshipmen live, but it is quite a zoo at this point in time. Why don't we retreat backward to Halsey Field House, and I can show you where your office is."

Optimistic, thought Tuby. "Is that a church next to Herndon?" Tuby noticed the pretty dome.

"Yes. It's the Naval Academy Chapel. It is a marvelous setting. John Paul Jones is buried in the crypt below the chapel."

Tuby thought he might like to see that. They entered Halsey Field House and went to the offices upstairs.

"This is Lila W. Fromi, the secretary for the football coach. Hello, Lila. How have you been?"

"Fine, Mr. Superintendent. Is this Mr. Gravenald?" Lila beamed as she shook hands with Tuby.

Everyone looked so happy to meet him. It was unexpected.

"Nice to meet you, Lila." Tuby held her hand softly. He had been known to get a few ouches after handshakes.

"I am sorry to hear about your wife. I am sure she was a wonderful woman." Lila nodded sincerely.

"Thank you for your thoughts, Lila. She was." Tuby had gone a whole hour without thinking of Myra.

"We're going to slip into Mr. Broamis's old office and chat."

Lila opened the door for Gregory and Tuby. Tuby sat in a not overly comfortable chair while the superintendent sat behind the desk. "We have a saying here, Mr. Gravenald. Navy gets the job done above, on, or below the surface." Tuby had to think for a second. He got it. "We haven't been getting the job done on the surface—especially when it comes to beating Army. Matters have been complicated with this new league we are part of. The Big Beast. There are a lot of fine teams in this division, and the competition will be fierce. I agree it's good for exposure, but our academic and other requirements restrict the type of athlete who can play Navy football. Nobody wants to watch Navy lose on national television every week. The prospect of not being competitive can only hurt the Naval Academy. We desire the best student athletes to come to us if they choose. We don't desire their decisions to be based on the prospect of playing for a losing team. We want the opportunity to compete. We employ the finest military and civilian professors in the country and hold our students to the highest standards. I do not believe we made that same opportunity available to our football team. Mr. Broamis is a fine person. He just wasn't a fiery coach. That's why we want you to coach our team. You are the only option we considered." Gregory made his play.

"Superintendent Gregory, I am flattered, but I just retired. I also believe your school is held to stringent academic and moral standards. Articles in the press have tainted my reputation regarding running a college program, and I don't want to embarrass your institution," Tuby said and unloaded some of his baggage.

"You're clean. You have some filthy boosters, but we know you're clean."

"How can you be so sure?"

"Naval intelligence. Some believe it is an oxymoron. I believe Nimitz won the war with it."

"How about the press?"

"The simple fact the Naval Academy hired you out of retirement should put things to rest forever."

Tuby thought for a moment. It had been an awfully long time since he had been in a job interview. He didn't want to sound like a tease because he was certain he did not want to coach football again, but he should know all the facts. "What kind of financial package is being offered?" *There. I said it.*

"Mr. Gravenald, it's not a package to which you are accustomed. The salary is among the lowest in the country. You're looking at your office, and you have met your staff in Lila. You get a few assistant coaches, and I encourage you to retain the services of assistant coaches Edward Mashner and Murrey Scormir. They are fine men and excellent coaches. The team physician, Dr. Barry Money, has been with the team for twenty-five years. He's nonnegotiable. Recruiting topflight players is damn near impossible due to academics and rigid moral and ethical standards of the Naval Academy. Every midshipman will give you full effort, but his or her first obligation here is to the military and academics. Students here do not have the time to eat, drink, and sleep football.

"Yes, Mr. Gravenald. I want my cake, and I want to eat it. I think we can succeed at both, though. We feel the facilities are great, but they pale in comparison to the other schools in the Big Beast. There are no large athletic gear contracts or television shows. You can, however, get your teeth cleaned for free in the basement of Bancroft Hall anytime you want."

Gee. Sounds terrific, thought Tuby. "Why haven't you offered a current coach the position?"

"Nobody is ready. You can help groom your successor."

"Why would you offer me a job knowing I want to retire? I'm at the end of my rope."

"You're not at the end of your rope until your feet are on the deck. Minnesota gave you no choice but to abandon ship. We don't leave people behind at the Naval Academy, Mr. Gravenald. We want you aboard to navigate us on the right course. Why do you think we have so many old admirals? Wisdom comes with age."

"Superintendent Gregory, my daughter, Jane, and granddaughter, Emily, live in Annapolis," Tuby started.

"I know."

How do they know these things? Tuby thought. "I'd like to talk with them over dinner before I make any decisions."

"Where are you dining?" Gregory said. "I know three hundred good places."

"We haven't made plans. They don't even know I'm in town."

"Most places will be booked because of Commissioning Week. It's one of the busiest weeks of the year. Allow me to make reservations for you at the Drydock It's a wonderful restaurant in Dahlgren Hall." Gregory picked up the phone and buzzed Lila's extension.

"That isn't necessary."

"I insist. You've come all this way. Your bags have already been checked into the Hilton in Annapolis Harbor. It's a short walk from here. Room four nineteen." Gregory pulled out the electronic keycard and handed it to Tuby.

On Gregory's dime, thought Tuby. "Just to be fair, I will let you know my decision by tomorrow. I only think it proper you have a chance to search for another option if I decide not to take the position. Practice starts in a little over two months."

"You are assuming the worst, Mr. Gravenald." Gregory shook his hand. "The reservations are made for eighteen hundred hours. Thank you for coming."

Eighteen hundred hours. Tuby did the math. Six o'clock. That was a mere hour and fifteen minutes away. "You're welcome. May I use the phone?" He had to call Jane.

"Certainly."

Tuby was thrilled to see Jane and little Emily. It was the first time his heart had thumped happily in almost a month. He squeezed Emily tightly until she said he was hurting her, but she was giggling.

"Daddy, this is great news. Are you going to take the job?" Jane beamed at the prospect of her father moving to Annapolis.

"We'll talk about it over dinner."

He took Emily's hand, and the host took them straight to a table in the bustling dining room. The server brought a booster seat for Emily and ordered her a chocolate milk. Jane treated herself to a glass of Jekel Cabernet, and Tuby saw they had top-shelf Dalwhinnie and ordered the smoky, peat-flavored single malt. They opened the menu.

"So what's this all about?" Jane sipped her water while the server requisitioned the wine from the service bar.

"After you left Saint Paul, an admiral was waiting at the house. Old guy named Timple. I invited him in, and we had a drink. He told me Navy wanted to hire me as their football coach and gave me a ticket to Baltimore." Tuby thanked the server for the Scotch. He had been waiting for this all day. "Emily, Grandpa got to ride in a helicopter today!"

"Neat." Emily was more interested in the chocolate milk.

"A helicopter?" Jane was impressed.

"A real navy chopper. It was neat."

"So?"

"So, Miss Impatient, I met the superintendent, and he showed me around. The darndest thing I ever saw." Tuby watched his language around Emily like a good grandpa. "The cadets…"

"Midshipmen," Emily corrected.

Tuby was impressed. "You're right, young lady. Midshipmen were trying to climb this monument covered in grease."

"Herndon."

"Why do you all know these things and I don't?" Tuby felt lost outside Minnesota.

"Because, Daddy, we live here, and you've done nothing but worry about Gopher football for the last twenty years." Jane was right. It had been all consuming.

Jane ordered the cioppino—a seafood dish with saffron rice, mussels, clams, and shrimp in a broth. Emily got a hot dog without mustard. Tuby had been aching to try authentic Maryland crab cakes. They threw in some fried calamari marinara for good measure. Emily thought they tasted like rubber bands.

"Well, did the interview go well?"

"It was fine. I'm not sure about all the military stuff. Lids, hatches, decks, and ladders."

"I have Chutes and Ladders at home. Want to play?"

They both laughed at Emily.

"The campus is beautiful."

"The yard." Emily and Jane both corrected Tuby.

"You see, I'll never understand all this. It's like a whole different language. It's a different world. I don't think I can handle all that change." Tuby examined his Scotch.

"It's a different world close to us." Jane looked fondly at Emily as she stretched the calamari in her little teeth.

Jane had played her emotional card. He didn't know anybody here. He didn't know the roads. He didn't like hot weather. He just wasn't ready to coach again. He didn't have the energy. Losing Myra had taken a lot out of him. He ordered another Scotch.

"Daddy, you drank that pretty fast." Jane wasn't nagging—just observing. "What have you been doing in Minnesota?"

She already knew. A woman's intuition was a powerful thing. Tuby hemmed and hawed and lied. "I've been keeping up with the lawn and doing all those honey-do projects your mother left me." Tuby took a sip of Scotch.

Right, Jane thought skeptically. She looked in her daddy's eyes and knew he was lonely—and scared. He was also too proud to admit it. She wouldn't push him. Tuby was very difficult to push around. This was especially true when he had his mind set against something. They enjoyed a terrific dinner and made small chit-chat for the rest of the evening. Tuby brooded over the job. They shared a humungous fresh strawberry shortcake for dessert, and Emily got whipped cream all over her face.

He promised to call before he left. Jane insisted he stay at the house, and he explained that Gregory had already taken the liberty of checking the bags at the Hilton. Tuby declined the ride to the hotel. He wanted to walk back through the yard and think. They gave hugs and kisses and promised to get together soon.

Tuby felt awful about lying to Jane. He had never done that. What made a person lie? Many of his players had lied to him, and he had caught them all. Why did he always tell them they had lied? Because they were afraid of the truth. "Afraid" and "truth" were two big words in the English language he used to tell them. What was he afraid of? He stood in front of the magnificent Bancroft Hall. He looked at the statue of the Native American Tecumseh that overlooked the court of the same name. He saw the chapel lit through the gazebo and the string of monuments dedicated to past sailors. He especially liked the submarine monument. Its ghostlike faces were hidden in the granite waves, and hopeful dolphins quelled the sailors' superstitions. He walked toward Halsey Field House and saw two midshipmen squatting behind Bill, the goat mascot. He wondered what they were doing. The mids seemed startled, and Tuby asked the young men why they were shining the goat's balls. They had made them very shiny under the streetlamp. They explained they had lost a bet to an upperclassman, and their punishment was to "take good care of Bill's anatomy." Tuby chuckled and walked toward the water. He was not ready for the Hilton.

He found Compass Point and sat alone with his thoughts. The water reflected the lights of Annapolis as the sailboats and yachts slept on the calm. What were his fears? What was the truth? He admitted he was lonely. The first step was always the hardest. He felt that was normal and justified. Myra had only been gone a month. Was that fair, though? Would he not be lonely in six months or a year? He admitted he was unproductive and a by-product of loneliness and the D word—depression. He admitted maybe he had been drinking too much. That one was tough to admit. The mornings had gotten shorter, though, and the nights more blurry. He added up the sum of the truths. It wasn't the outcome he had hoped. He was not in good shape. He had no question about his coaching abilities. He remembered what Gregory had said about the situation at Minnesota. He had resigned but felt like a scapegoat. No one at the university shined his balls before he left. He extinguished his cigarette. That was another habit that had gotten worse. He stretched his legs while he sat on the bench. He worried about mentally handling the challenges of a new program. It took a hell of a lot of effort. All he had was time, though, and he really didn't want to clip the hedges. The conference was a bear, but all he had to do was beat Army, and he was ahead of the game. He could do that. It was Army. Tuby decided before his head hit the pillow. He would take the job.

Saint Paul, Minnesota

Tuby picked up the Cadillac at the airport and drove back to his house. He phoned Jane with the news. She was ecstatic. He called Gregory first thing in the morning and accepted the job. His head was swimming with the activity of the day, and he felt like a freshman quarterback being blitzed. He needed to slow the game down, but the play was already over. The deal was sealed.

When he saw his home, he realized he should have called a time-out. This was where he lived. He knew nothing but Minnesota. All the trips to other cities for games and bowls were just vacation junkets. There was never a question of moving until now. Tuby regretted his decision. He poured himself a Scotch and mulled over an escape plan. He ordered from Pizza Hut. He liked the cheesy crust and added pepperoni, sausage, mushrooms, and onions. He turned on the television and saw his picture on the local news. *What the hell?* thought Tuby, and he listened to the report of his signing with the Naval Academy. That was fast. Now any reneging on the contract, which was a serious part of his plan, would be flashed on the news. Combined with the NCAA investigation currently underway involving the scandals at Minnesota, any news of Tuby signing with and then resigning from Navy before coaching one down would have the local media hounds at his front door. He would be vilified as a cheater and a flake—a legacy that wasn't true on either account. That was what the public would remember, though.

Tuby loaded his suitcase into the back of the Caddy. He felt he was abandoning Myra. The local CBS affiliate's sports reporter, Merna Rhin, pulled up with the news truck looking for a scoop. "Coach Gravenald, why did you take the position at Navy?" She went right to work.

"I felt it was a good opportunity." Tuby really wanted to get in his car and leave.

"You said you wanted to leave football. Why the change of mind?"

This was a tough one. "Maybe I wanted a different ending than the one I had here." The truth kind of spilled out.

"Are you running away from the NCAA investigation of the University of Minnesota?"

"I'm not running away from anything. I have nothing to hide regarding the investigation." That one troubled Tuby.

"Does your wife's death have anything to do with your change of heart?"

"My personal and family life have always been off-limits. That will never change. You have one more question, and then I have to leave." Enough was enough.

"When do you take over the program at the Naval Academy?"

Tuby didn't hesitate. "Right now."

He got in the Cadillac and left the reporter behind. Tuby was annoyed at the questions, but it was her job. He was a public figure. *This society puts too much emphasis on a game,* thought Tuby.

It was a long drive to Annapolis. Satellite radio was a nice invention. It helped him on the journey. He piped in some news radio and listened to the world gone mad. Iraq, Iraq, Iraq. A young man wearing a ball cap, a Red Cross T-shirt, and a pair of blues jeans was thumbing a ride on the shoulder before the exit to the freeway. He had a single backpack and a well-groomed mustache. Tuby had hitched a few rides back in the sixties, but those were different times. It was most likely this person had a bagful of drugs or had cleaved a teen to death in North Dakota. Tuby was not sure why, but he stopped to give the man a ride. It must have been the Red Cross T-shirt.

"Where are you headed, young man?" Tuby electronically rolled down the window on the passenger side.

"Annapolis, Maryland."

The coincidence struck Tuby dumb. The young man was polite. His face was soft and hairless except for the mustache. He had pretty eyes for a man but was a big boy throughout he shoulders.

"Hop in."

"Thanks a lot!" He opened the door and set his pack in the well gently. "Where are you heading?"

Tuby looked at the boy. "Annapolis, Maryland."

"No way!" The boy looked at Tuby. "What takes you to Annapolis?"

"I am the Naval Academy's head football coach."

It was the first time Tuby had said it aloud. It felt good. The boy heaved a sigh of relief. He had been worried the coincidence meant he was stuck with a nut. He felt reasonably comfortable the head coach of Navy wouldn't slaughter him along the way and dump his body off the Ohio Turnpike.

"How about you?"

The boy snapped out of his daymare. "I have been working for the Red Cross." He pulled out his T-shirt. "We've been trying to bring medical attention to the rural communities of Malaysia and the Thai Peninsula. Typhoon victims mostly. I've been all over Southeast Asia. Some of the conditions on Borneo have become deplorable."

"What's your name?" Tuby might as well get to know him. It was going to be a long ride.

"I'm sorry. Vern. Vern Edaas."

"Tuby. Tuby Gravenald." They shook hands awkwardly while Tuby drove.

"Gravenald. Coach Gravenald?" Vern started to put the pieces together. "Aren't you the coach of Minnesota?"

Tuby rolled his eyes. More explaining was necessary. "I used to be. I just took the job at the Naval Academy, and today is moving day. Are you a football fan?"

"Yeah. I never played, but I used to be the team trainer in high school. I'm pretty handy with an Ace bandage and athletic tape."

Tuby laughed and pressed on the gas. "I can take you all the way, but I'm going to have to stop for the night at a hotel. It's too far for an old man to make it in a straight shot." Tuby didn't want to foot the bill for his new travel mate.

"That's cool." Vern sensed the direction of Tuby's comments. "I've got some money. I didn't plan on walking there in one day, either." Vern saw Tuby appreciated his sarcasm. "And I'll be glad to pitch in for some gas."

"That won't be necessary." Tuby was happy not to have a free-loader. "Why are you heading to Annapolis?"

Vern looked out the front windshield. "I just got back from Borneo, and I got a message that an old friend might be headed to Annapolis. We're going to try to catch up."

They settled in for the long ride. Tuby used Vern to get things off his chest, and Vern told Tuby stories about the sick and impoverished of Southeast Asia.

They stayed the night in Breezewood, Pennsylvania—a little trucker town on the Pennsylvania–Maryland border. The two chatted well into the night and left themselves with an easy drive the following morning.

Jane and Emily were waiting at Tuby's new town house. "Hi, Daddy." She gave Tuby a hug and looked oddly at Vern.

"Jane, this is Vern. We met along the way, and I gave him a ride." Jane looked wary. "Oddly enough he was headed to Annapolis."

"Oddly enough." Jane wasn't frightened—just concerned.

Vern showed Emily a magic trick, and Emily was astonished how he could make a scarf disappear into thin air.

"Well, Tuby, I thank you for the ride and company." Vern sensed the tension.

"Vern, it was a pleasure. That was the most fun I've had in a while. You're a fine young man." Tuby meant it and wrote down his number. "Give me a call. Maybe we'll head up to Gettysburg."

"I'd like that very much."

Vern and Tuby hugged like men who wanted to hug but weren't ready. Jane looked at her father's smile. He had really bonded with Vern.

"Where are you going to stay?" Tuby asked.

"I have the address of a hostel. It shouldn't be too hard to find." Vern pulled an egg out of his mouth, and Emily giggled.

Jane stared at her father. "Daddy, why doesn't Vern stay with you until he gets his feet on the ground?"

Tuby's eyes lit up. "That's a great idea. Vern, get your gear and come inside."

"I feel as if I'm imposing. You just got here and everything."

"I wouldn't have said it if I hadn't meant it."

Jane knew her father didn't want to be alone. Even though she was close, she couldn't occupy the times in the evening when he faced the solitude.

Everybody piled in to check out the new digs. It felt like home right away to Tuby. The end unit had a nice deck, and the kitchen had a bay window that faced the street and let in natural light. All the appliances were right out of the box. A professional interior designer seemed to have furnished them. The living room was spacious and had a nice mantle for Tuby's pictures of Myra. The master bedroom was grand, and there were two complete baths. The men would not have to share the facilities.

Vern helped Tuby carry in the luggage, and Jane had taken the liberty of filling the refrigerator with fruits, vegetables, deli meats, cheese, condiments, and bottled water. Cereals, grains, pastas, and sauces stocked the pantry. Things were off and running as Jane made the family some sandwiches. Tuby talked history with Vern as he depleted his repertoire of tricks on Emily. Jane reminded her father he had his first appointment with a Mrs. Rain Cutti first thing in the morning, July first. Tuby had about a month to rest before he went back to work.

July 2004, the Yard

Tuby and Vern made the trip to Gettysburg. It was well worth the drive. They followed the Shenandoah Mountains and the road-side Civil War historical plaques through the valleys of Virginia. It was Stonewall Jackson country. They saw Antietam and Bull Run. They saw how progress had turned the old battlefields into strip malls and apartment complexes. Gone were the haystacks and wooden fences. In were the drive-throughs and streetlamps.

Vern never made contact with his friend, but Tuby didn't mind. Vern was like the son Tuby never had. Tuby even offered Vern a job as team trainer. Tuby figured if Vern could help the starving and poor of Borneo, then he could tape a few ankles. Vern knew his football too. They talked about the good old players of days gone by.

"I'm here to see Mrs. Rain Cutti," Tuby said.

He had to fill out some forms and paperwork for his employment. He had his Minnesota driver's license and his Social Security card to complete the I-9 form.

"Good morning. I assume you are Coach Gravenald." Mrs. Rain Cutti looked at the clock on the wall. "Nine bells. You are very prompt."

Tuby expected people to be on time. It was only courtesy he adhere to his own rules. "Are you Mrs. Cutti?"

"I am. A pleasure to meet you. I have heard much about you." Mrs. Cutti extended her hand. It was soft and tan. "It's actually Ms. Cutti now. I'm recently divorced."

"What are we going to do today, Ms. Cutti?" Tuby was in full operational mode on his first day.

"We are going to tidy up your folder as a new hire, and then I am going to acquaint you with parts of the yard you might have missed." Ms. Cutti removed his file from the cabinet. "I understand you were shortchanged on the tour during your initial visit." She was referring to the chaos at Herndon.

"That was some celebration." Tuby signed his name to the withholding forms of the state and federal governments. He sadly checked the single deduction and thought of Myra.

"Mr. Gravenald?" Tuby looked up from the form. "I highly recommend you change your driver's license to Maryland. That way it will reflect your current residential status."

"Yeah. I keep meaning to do that. Have you changed your name on your driver's license to reflect your marital status?" *Quid pro quo.*

Rain gave him a sharp look. "Your I-nine will be incomplete until that matter is resolved." Ms. Cutti obviously was a stickler for details.

"I'll take care of that first thing tomorrow morning."

"This afternoon would be better." Her pretty face belied her stern manner. She closed the folder, placed it on the desk, and scribbled in big red ink "incomplete."

Tuby felt he was back in second grade. "Yes, ma'am."

"Let's take a walk to Halsey Field House, and I'll pass you off to Lila. I'm sure you are anxious to get to work. I'll show you a couple sights along the way."

Rain led the way. Tuby followed on her leash. They left Rickover Hall, and Tuby stared at the Severn River behind Dewey Field.

"You'll be spending a lot of time there, Coach Gravenald." Tuby looked at her quizzically. "That's where your team practices."

Tuby looked at the field adjacent to the Glenn Warner soccer facility. The synthetic field was perfect for practice during all types of weather.

"You share the field with the lacrosse and soccer teams," she said.

Share? Tuby thought.

"Behind the soccer facility is Santee Basin and the Vandergrift cutter shed. That is for the sailing and crew teams." Rain turned to the right. "That's Ingram Field—our outdoor track and field."

How much sharing? Tuby thought.

He heard the chant of "Beat Army," and scores of baby-faced children snapped around the corner wearing ice cream suits. "Who are the kids dressed up like the Cracker Jack guy?"

"Those are plebes, Coach Gravenald. They just started summer training." Rain was not amused. "They are enduring what is known as plebe summer. While other high-school seniors are going to the beach or flipping burgers at McDonald's, these first-year students are undergoing intense physical and military training. Last week was Induction Day, or I-Day. Their hair was shorn, and they relinquished most of their personal belongings. Most will only retain a watch, an alarm clock, a calculator, and toiletry items. They have few privileges and zero prestige. They are evaluated every minute of every day. That's seven days a week for six grueling weeks. Officers and select upperclassmen rate and rank all plebes on military aptitude, leadership potential, general behavior, and attitude. It can be almost twenty-five percent of their grades. More than a few have been sent home during plebe summer."

"That's a hell of a way to spend the summer before your freshman year." Tuby tried to take the edge off.

"Plebes, Mr. Gravenald. We do not call the fourth class freshmen. They are plebes. Just as we don't refer to the Naval Academy as Camp Tecumseh or the yard as the campus. Some of those plebes will be trying to make your football team, Mr. Gravenald."

Tuby decided to listen and not talk for a while, but he did have one question. "When will I get to meet the players?"

"Most upperclassmen are on their summer cruises," she explained. "All midshipmen have fleet duties at sea."

"So they're not home lifting weights?" He shouldn't have said it.

"No, Mr. Gravenald. They're not." Rain shot him a frightful look. "Most are exploring their career options. None of our graduates will turn professional." That was a cheap shot. "Some of the youngsters and upperclassmen will learn more about the US Navy and US Marine Corps by spending their summers on submarines or surface cruises. Some will be dealing with explosive ordnance disposal or working with SEAL units. Women are not allowed on submarines or in the SEAL outfits. That's something I'm lobbying hard to change."

I'll bet, Tuby thought as he looked at GI Jane. They passed Ward Hall, and Tuby noticed the aged nuclear fallout shelter sign pointing to the basement of Ward. He found this minutia of history fascinating. They walked through Tecumseh Court, up the stairs, and into massive Bancroft Hall.

"If you need to locate one of your players, Mr. Gravenald, he most likely will be found here. All four thousand five hundred midshipmen reside in Bancroft Hall in eight wings." She showed him a model of an actual room. It was a very simple cubicle with a shower and either two or three bunks. "We do sometimes refer to it as the Hall or Mother B, which I am not fond of." Tuby remembered his college days. It wasn't much different. "They are submitted to stringent white-glove inspections that check for grit and grime in the showers along with dust, filth, and general uncleanliness."

Tuby didn't remember that part of college. "What happens if the room is dirty?" Tuby wiped his finger across the table to double-check.

"Demerits, Mr. Gravenald. Demerits lead to punishment. Extra chow calls, rifle marching, extra duty, restriction of movement, and other similar punishments."

Tuby wondered if Ms. Rain Cutti assigned the punishment herself. He craned his neck and looked at the ornate artwork in the main lobby. The white marble floors with the pink-and-black inlay shone, despite the trouncing it received daily from 4,500 college kids.

They walked up the marble staircase and into Memorial Hall. Tuby immediately recognized the USS *Constitution* painted on the wall to his left and the USS *Constellation* painted on the wall to the right. A flag read, "Don't Give Up the Ship." The parquet floors made him want to dance the fox-trot with ol' Rain, but she really didn't seem game. She was quite a serious woman. He glanced straight up at the second dome in the structure. It was amazing.

Rain took him to King Hall, the mess, and Tuby tried to imagine the room filled with 4,500 hungry midshipmen three times a day. Rain hit him with some food statistics that blew his mind. They exited the way they had come—through Tecumseh Court. There were the victory bells from when Admiral Perry defeated

Japan. Tuby noticed another captured relic. It was an authentic Japanese Long Lance torpedo. Tuby recalled the people who had passed from its fury. He saw the submarine monument again but in the light. It was called Centennial, and it was his favorite monument in the yard.

"You said a phrase I didn't understand. What are chow calls?"

"Plebes perform chow calls. They are assigned as regular duty or as punishment. Plebes need to be on deck to provide the mids with six pieces of information. They tell them whether the meal that day will be inside or outside, the expected uniform for the meal, the menu for the meal, the attending midshipman or officer on duty for the day, the week's professional topics, and the day's main event in the yard." Rain seemed pleased Tuby was trying to learn.

"You have some pretty strict rules here, Ms. Cutti." Tuby tried to find more common ground. Rain seemed to like the disciplinary aspects of the yard.

"We have an eighty-seven-page book called *Midshipmen Regulations* that covers conduct guidelines for the men and women of the US Naval Academy." Tuby wondered if she ever stopped. "We have two types of infractions: major and minor. We deal with infractions through the administration. The book outlines everything from schedules and leave to dating and drinking."

Tuby interrupted so Rain could breathe. "What about drinking?" Tuby asked casually.

"We have an almost zero tolerance for alcohol and drugs. We highly discourage smoking. This is all listed in the mid regs. You might have to report a minor or major infraction. I suggest you get a copy and read it."

"Right after I get my driver's license." Tuby thought about the phrase "zero tolerance."

Another group of plebes marched down Stribling Walk by the Mexican Monument. They turned the corner, and an officer saluted. The plebes returned the salute and shouted either, "Beat Army" or "Go Navy."

"Why don't the plebes get to wear stripes?"

"Plebes don't wear stripes." Rain seemed unaffected by Tuby's wiseass comment. "Only firsties—seniors," Rain returned the smarmy comment, "have earned the right to wear horizontal stripes. Youngsters and second class have slanted gold stripes on their left sleeves. Firsties get a horizontal one on both sleeves. Depending on rank in class, firsties might have more than one stripe. A lieutenant junior grade has two stripes. A lieutenant has three. Those who have achieved the rank of lieutenant commander wear four, and midshipmen commanders wear five. Usually only the brigade commander has six stripes. Be nice to the brigade commanders, Mr. Gravenald. One could be your boss someday." Rain walked on. "We're coming to Halsey Field House, Mr. Gravenald. You will probably find yourself more comfortable here than in the yard." They walked into the field house, and Lila waited with a box on her desk. "Mr. Gravenald, I wish you the best of luck. Most coaches who pass through these doors share the common frustration that the Naval Academy is about academics, the military, and life training first. Football is just a game that helps midshipmen to their goals. It is not the be-all and end-all it has become at other universities. That has been the frustration of those who have come before you. Beat Army." Ms. Rain Cutti excused herself.

"Pretty lady but a bitch," mumbled Tuby under his breath.

"Did you say something, Coach Gravenald?" Lila had a dog's hearing. Tuby needed to know that.

"No, Lila. Just taking it all in."

"I got the things you requested." Tuby looked into the box. "All the Navy game films for the last three years, this season's schedule, and multiple game films on Duke, Pittsburgh, Temple, Maryland, Air Force—boo—Rutgers, West Virginia, Wake Forest,

Notre Dame, and Army—double boo." Lila looked for some reinforcement.

"Great job, Lila. I'm going to work." Tuby closed the door behind him and looked at game film of his team until the wee hours of the morning.

August 2004, The Yard

There was no breeze coming off the Severn River, and the practice field held the high temperatures. This made the turf hotter than the day. Vern taped up the players before the first practice of the 2004 season. Dr. Barry Money had completed the physicals of the seventy-five midshipmen who wanted to play varsity football. Coach Scormir and Coach Mashner said hello to those returning from the lousy 2–9 record the previous season. No one said much to the plebes.

"Coach Scormir, I think we should fly the black flag," said outside linebacker Barnett Prime, the returning firstie.

The black flag indicated a stoppage of events during plebe summer for fear of danger to the fourth class.

"You just pull your panties on tight, Prime, and we'll all get through the day," Scormir said back to Prime, and the team laughed and stretched.

Tuby walked on the field and saw that Scormir and Mashner had the team in the right lines for stretching. He went over some practice drills and schedules for the day. Tuby blew the whistle and addressed the team for the first time. "My name is Coach Gravenald. I care about football. That's all I'm paid to do. I'm not your mommy or your daddy. I'm not your sponsor family or your big brother. I don't give a crap about what you do in school or the crazy language you use here at the Naval Academy. I don't know what a scuttlebutt is or whether to cover or uncover. To me you put a ladder on the side of a house to paint. Understand my language.

If you don't want to play for a winner, then shove off." He looked at the sweat already pouring down their faces. "There's only one way I know how to play football. You win games on defense. Hard-nosed defense. Last year the Goats were terrible on defense." The midshipmen detested being called Goats, and Tuby knew that. "I'm here to beat Army." A cheer went up from the players. "But before we do that, you have to learn not to beat yourselves."

Tuby blew the whistle, and the players broke into offensive and defensive drills. The heat was painful. Tuby walked around evaluating the offensive players with a keen focus on the linemen. He recognized a few numbers from the game film but decided not to hold that against them. Mashner walked next to the coach and helped in the evaluation.

"Who's that fat ass there? Number sixty-two," Tuby asked Masher.

"Sixty-two?" Mashner looked over his clipboard. "He's a plebe. Name's Jason Emenith. We think he'll be an offensive guard. We recruited him out of Tennessee."

"You recruited him?" Tuby looked at Mashner as if he had lost his mind. Mashner knew not to answer. "He's all flab in the middle. No muscle tone."

"We'll take care of that, sir."

"Who's sixty-nine?" Tuby couldn't believe his eyes.

"That's another plebe, sir. His name is Bram Gareloin. He's out of West Virginia. We project him to be a guard."

"It looks like he's been guarding the local Burger King."

"Got it, sir."

"Goodness gracious. What is that?" Tuby looked at number seventy-eight. He was stuck on his back like a turtle.

"That's another plebe, sir. Raul 'Babe' Pantry. Babe is his nick-name. He's from Ohio."

"I gathered. What's with the glasses?"

"Those were issued to him during induction week. We found he needed corrective lenses. They're also referred to as birth control glasses."

"I see why. Do you want to help him up? He might miss the whole practice if you don't." Mashner lent the plebe a hand and sent the young man with the mouthpiece off and running. Tuby blew the whistle at the young man. He waved for him to come back. "Son, what's your name?"

"Pantry. Babe Pantry, sir!" The plebe slurred through the mouthpiece.

"Let me see that mouthpiece, Pantry."

Pantry reluctantly removed it from his mouth. It had about an inch of plastic on it.

"What is this?"

"My mouthpiece, sir!"

"I can see that, Pantry. Why is it so small?"

"I misunderstood the directions, sir!" Pantry was really loud.

"You misunderstood the directions to a mouthpiece?"

"Yes, sir!"

"How did you misunderstand the directions for a mouthpiece?"

"It said to boil the water, place the mouthpiece in the water for fifteen seconds, and then bite down." Tuby waited. "I thought it said fifteen minutes, sir!"

"So you let the plastic boil for fifteen minutes?"

"Yes, sir!"

"How many of your teeth does the mouthpiece cover, Pantry?"

"Two, sir!"

"Two whole teeth. Get back to your squad."

"Use your grape, Pantry." Mashner swatted him on his ample behind, and Pantry hustled his way back to the offensive line drills.

"What is he studying, Mashner?"

Mashner looked at the chart. "Aerospace engineering."

"Good. I thought it might be something important." Tuby walked through the rest of the field and evaluated talent. This was going to be tough.

The next day was hotter than the first. They worked on the kicking game. It was a lot of running in the heat. Tuby rubbed his eyes but not from the sweat. They didn't have a good kicker.

"Tug, get over here."

The quarterback and team's best all-around athlete, Tug Lerrin, hustled over to the coach. "What's up, Coach?" Lerrin said in his North Carolinian drawl.

"Who kicked for you last year?" Tuby asked the firstie.

"Last year was Evans. I used to be his holder."

"Well, who was his backup?"

"That was Jones. He graduated too."

"Does anyone on this team know how to kick a football?"

"I don't know, Coach. I don't think so." Tuby looked at Tug and hoped for a miracle. "No, Coach. I'll do anything to help the team. I just plain can't kick."

Tuby couldn't ask him to do everything. He sent him back out with the offense.

Tuby was using the football camp to act out the anger phase of his grief—much to the players' regret. He worked them hard and chided them for mistakes. He screamed at Pantry, Gareloin, and Emenith, the three giant plebes who were his only chance at having an offensive line. They were big boys, but they weren't tough or football savvy.

"Move, move, move," screamed Coach Scormir as he punished the linebackers with side-to-side drills.

"Low, low, low. Get under his pads, Pantry." Mashner lit into the offensive line. "Have you learned nothing from Mohney, Pantry?" Mashner was talking about firstie center Jack Mohney from Maryland. "Get out of line and watch him!"

Mashner threw Pantry aside and made him watch Mohney do the drill. Then he made him watch number seventy-three, offensive tackle Stan Markh. Markh was a second classman from Wisconsin. He pulled Gareloin and Emenith too and humiliated all three by making them watch tight end Elmo Linners, the firstie from New Jersey, do the drill to perfection. Mashner got in the plebes' grills and let them have it. Tuby had three offensive linemen but needed five.

He blew the whistle. Practice was over for the day. He gathered the men around. "I was doing some reading. There are twelve thousand applications a year sent to the US Naval Academy. Of those twelve thousand, about twelve hundred are accepted. Out of those twelve hundred, this is what I get! This is the best the navy has to offer? *The* US Navy? They must have used an aggressive outreach program to find this bunch. A bunch of student-body presidents and National Honor Society members. Castaways from the drama and debate clubs. Maybe your congresspeople nominated you. No wonder our nation's going down the drain. We are a terrible football team. I feel terrible for the seniors."

"Firsties." The voice sounded meek.

"Who said that? Damn it, who said that?" Gravenald was white-hot. There were a few moments of silence.

Finally Pantry stepped up. "I did, sir."

Cornerback Vern Stamcie, the second classman, whispered to number thirty-nine, strong safety Boots Morne, the youngster from Mississippi. "Pantry is about to get boned."

Gravenald got in his face and spit on Pantry's geek glasses as he yelled. "Haven't you listened to a word I've said? I don't give a goddamn about the special navy language. I'm here to win football games. Pantry, you'd better shape up, or I'm going to personally separate you from the navy and send you back to Indiana."

"Ohio, sir. I'm from Ohio."

"Pantry, from now on you will be eating next to me. Breakfast, lunch, and dinner. I'm going to work your bulbous Ohio ass into shape. I'm going to make you want to quit this place, Pantry. I am going to hound you. I will be with you when you sleep, when you piss, and when you shower. I'll be with you all on plebe parents' weekend at the end of this month. And you might as well drag those two other lard asses into the party. Gareloin and Emenith, you can thank Pantry for your new dining guest. You seniors will never beat Army with these clowns on the team." Tuby walked away from the team and let them slink off the field.

Pantry was close to tears. The team walked by him. "You're an idiot," said fullback Rob Wersnors, the youngster who lived near Tuby in Minnesota.

"We're all going to fry because of you, Pantry," leveled free safety Ronn Judge.

"Fire it up," said wide receiver Gerry Johnson sarcastically.

The players left the field and left Pantry all by himself.

"Another great day," Pantry said, adding his own sarcasm as he headed for the showers.

Tuby hadn't made it back to the field house. He had gotten stuck watching a young man kick the heck out of a soccer ball. It went fifty yards high and straight. He did it every time. He asked the soccer coach if he could have a word with the young man. He also signaled for Coach Scormir to come back with a football. "What's your name, son?"

"My name is Howdy Osaye."

"Where are you from, Howdy?"

"I am from Florida." Howdy struggled with his accent.

"You have a little accent, and it's not from Florida."

"No, sir. I was born in Nigeria." Howdy had a huge smile.

"Have you ever kicked a football?"

"No." Howdy shook his head.

"Do you want to give it a try?" Tuby spun the football in his hand.

Howdy looked at his coach. He nodded.

"OK," Howdy said, and he beamed a giant grin.

They walked over to the goalposts. Scormir placed the ball on the ground for an extra point. Howdy popped it straight up, and Scormir looked at Tuby. Scormir was afraid the experiment would not work. They tried it again. He hooked it but got it going in the air. One more time, and it went right down the middle with authority. They moved back ten yards. Howdy was getting the hang of it and yelled "touchdown" each time the ball went through the posts. They must have kicked the ball fifty times from all angles. Howdy missed a few, but he made a lot.

"I think we found ourselves a kicker." Tuby looked at Scormir, who had become a believer. "Now if I can get him to do it in pads with three-hundred-pound gorillas running at him, we'll be fine."

Scormir laughed, and the coaches retreated to talk more football.

"Gentlemen, thirty thousand people will be walking into that stadium in less than a month. We're behind the eight ball. Our offense is, for lack of a better word, horrible. We have some talent at the skill positions, but our offensive line is inexperienced. Our defense is going to have to keep us in games. If I can get Howdy to make a few field goals, at least we won't put up goose eggs." Tuby laid his cards on the table. "How do you see the defensive starters shaping up, Murrey?"

"Coach, we've got a couple real players at defensive tackle. They're undersized, but their motors run all day. I've got Timm Mettish going in one spot. He's a firstie with a lot of experience. I've got the youngster, Spike Himpp from Oregon, in the other spot. They feed off each other real well."

"How about defensive end, Ed?" Tuby looked at Mashner. He really wanted a cigarette.

"Coach, I like Earl Whitsche. He's quick on the corner, and I think he'll get to the quarterback. He's suspect on the run, but the linebackers should be able to give him a lot of help. Mettish and Himpp should eat up the middle and free the backers. Will Bocher's manned the strong side for three years straight and gotten better each year. He'll be more effective at stopping the run. He's beefed up nicely."

"He's a dedicated young man. I've been impressed. How about linebackers, Murrey?" Tuby sipped on a Diet Coke.

"Sal Geayser's got the middle spot. No one on the team tackles any better. He's a real stud and can get sideline to sideline as well as anyone in the conference. Prime brings first-class leadership, and Rich L. Chatters has that certain knack for being around the ball. He gets back in pass coverage, and I think he might pick off a couple balls this season."

"Gentlemen, the secondary scares me. That's not because they aren't good, but are they good enough to get the job done in this league? There are a lot of good arms and some athletic receivers." Tuby's forehead wrinkled. He had been at the office almost eighteen hours.

"Vern Stamcie's our best cover guy. We just have to make sure our scheme keeps him on the other team's best guy. Rolly Leaky is a quality corner, but he's not as talented as Stamcie. He's a proud firstie and will be disappointed not to be the number-one corner, but he's a team player. He'll be an asset to the D."

Ed felt good about his corners.

"Coach, Boots Morne is a youngster, but he hits like a freight train. It's going to be awfully tough to run the football with him in the lineup. I think Ronn Judge is our signal caller. He's a bright kid who doesn't get too amped up under pressure. He brings some experience to the free safety spot and is the type of natural leader we need on the field."

Tuby pinched his lip and agonized over the next phase of the conversation. "Good work, coaches. I agree on the assessment of the defense. It's going to have to keep us in a few games—especially early in the season. They could be a special unit if they continue to work hard." Tuby paused. "Now to the offense." Everybody kind of groaned. "I know what I think. I need you to tell me what you think."

Ed went first and snared the positives away from Murrey. "Well, Tug's our guy under center. No question. His arm strength has been terrific, and he has a good feel with both Gerry Johnson and Jason Drone. Especially Johnson. We've just got to give Tug time. I know you feel the team has to be pass oriented to win."

Murrey got in before all the upsides were taken. "Elmo Linners is going to be a standout at tight end. He's a hell of a blocker and finds the seams for Tug when he's in trouble. He has a good nose for the first down marker too."

"I know what you're doing, and I appreciate it." Tuby stopped the agony. "We all know the truth. Rob Wersnors is a great blocking fullback, and Johni Bronson will have an effective season if they can get some blocking up front. Jack Mohney is our center, and I thank God every day he is here. Stan Markh is an adequate strong-side tackle, but that leaves three spots unfilled on the offensive line. Two guards and a weak side tackle. This is the center of the line. We can't expect Mohney to block everybody. Tug can't get the ball off in practice. Bronson can't get across the line of scrimmage in practice. I know we have a solid defense, but what is the answer to the gaps?"

Nobody said a word until Murrey cracked. "We've got to go with the plebes."

This was not the answer Tuby wanted to hear. "Is there no one else? What about Hollins?"

"No. He's tough but too small. He'll get run over."

"James?"

"No. He can't block."

"Neither can those three blubber butts."

"He's worse. The plebes can at least hold their ground for a few moments. James can't do that. He gets blown up every day," Murrey said. He was shooting straight.

"So I'm starting the season with an offensive line that has two freshmen guards and a moron at tackle." Tuby looked at the desk. Fishing sounded great right then. "You better fit Tug for a body cast. Go on home. I've got to get some sleep. I've got breakfast with the three lard butts in the morning."

Tuby rose early and he walked into King's Hall, the giant mess, and found the team table. There was peanut butter on all the tables. *Odd,* thought Tuby. All midshipmen were required to eat with their squads unless part of a varsity team. Plebes were chopping their way up the stairs and filling in the mess.

"Johnson." The wide receiver stood when he saw the coach. "Where are my three fat boys?"

"Probably reading the *Cat V* again, sir."

"What the hell is *Cat V,* Johnson?" Tuby asked.

"It's the height and weight standards manual for midshipmen, sir."

Tuby appreciated the humor first thing in the morning. The galley was filling up, and the mids made room for the coach to get his chow ahead of the line. Tuby got back, and his three favorite plebes were sitting with piles of food. "Team." He addressed them loudly enough so surrounding tables could listen. "I have been reading again." They looked at the plebes. "Did you know twelve thousand hot meals are prepared here daily? In one hour the kitchen can fry a ton of shrimp or broil three thousand hamburgers. The hardworking cooks can simultaneously cook seven hundred fifty gallons of soup or three hundred turkeys weighing twelve to sixteen pounds. A typical day might serve a thousand gallons of milk, a ton of green vegetables, two tons of meat, and another two tons of potatoes. A remarkable seven hundred twenty pies, twelve hundred loaves of bread, and three hundred gallons of ice cream. All in one day. And that's just for Pantry, Gareloin, and Emenith." The entire section broke our laughing. "Pantry, you look fatter than when you left the practice field yesterday. Did you get a midnight snack last night?"

"No, sir. I did not, sir!" Pantry was not amused.

"Come on, Pantry. Don't lie to me. You had a pizza last night. Didn't you?" Tuby hounded.

Pantry stood. His face was furious and red. The galley paused as Pantry started barking. "Midshipmen are persons of integrity. They stand for what is right. They tell the truth and ensure the full truth is known. They do not lie. They embrace fairness in all actions. They ensure that work submitted as their own is their own and that assistance received from any source is authorized and properly documented. They do not cheat. They respect the property of others and ensure that others are able to benefit from the use of their own property. They do not steal."

Pantry walked out of King Hall without eating his breakfast. Gareloin and Emenith followed. Tuby ate his breakfast and wondered if he hadn't overdone it.

September 2004, Florida T&A

Head coach Merl Larrola hated these spaghetti dinner fundraisers. Dining on Styrofoam plates with a room full of Walmart hicks was not his idea of a good time. He reminded himself, though, he was there for a reason. Florida T&A needed a new tailback for the future. His star tailback, Worm Roanen, was a quicksilver with pistons for legs, but he would be going professional, and this small turd of a town had his replacement. He stared at the plate of lukewarm noodles covered in ketchup with a sprinkling of dried basil and expected the worst. His mother would have rolled over in her Italian grave. Her sauce had been rich in garlic, peppers, and herbs and steeped with pork sausage. This thought made him long for his younger days in Brooklyn. He removed his school baseball cap, rubbed his hand across his forehead, and placed the few hairs of his nonexistent coif back in place. He then placed the cap back on his dome. His Italian mother from Brooklyn would give him the backhand from the grave if she knew he was wearing his hat inside and at the dinner table. Head coach Merl Larrola hadn't learned all the lessons his mother had taught him, though.

Larrola faked a smile, picked up his spork, and charmingly told one of the host mothers of the school banquet how great the spaghetti smelled. Larrola could lie. He choked down the pasta and washed it away with a watered-down sweet tea, but he couldn't work up to taking a bite of the garlic bread, which had the texture of a garden wood chip. He told another mother he was just too full.

Larrola looked at assistant coach Seneca Tob from under the bill of his cap. The head coach wanted to get on with this, and Coach Tob was going to have to push things along. He had business with this kid and serious business to tend to back in Atlanta. Coach Tob brought the high-school senior over to shake the coach's hand. His mother never left his side.

"You know Florida T&A is going to win another championship this year." Larrola looked the boy in the eyes. "We're going to need you to win another four."

"Junior will probably go pro after his sophomore year." Junior's mother made the statement.

"He's an exceptional young talent, Mrs. Rose, but the NFL has age limits." Larrola adjusted his cap.

"We're filing a suit against the NFL to change that. And it is Miss Rose. Junior's daddy has nothing to do with this."

All righty then. "We'd love you to come take a look around the campus. You could meet the other incoming players during recruiting weekend. We have one of our biggest games of the year against Florida State, and you and your mother will have your own catered skybox to watch the game." Larrola put his arm around Junior in a fatherly way.

"We need ten tickets for the Florida State game." Mrs. Rose stood with her arms folded. "Junior, go find your brothers and sisters. I need to talk to Coach Larrola alone." Larrola hated this part. "Coach Larrola, you and I both know Junior is the best running back in the country. Flat out."

"Yes, ma'am. That's why I'm here." Larrola sized her up.

"The colleges all make a lot of money on these kids, and the kids don't get crap. If you want Junior to play for Florida T&A, there are some things we're going to need." Mrs. Rose breathed heavily through her nose.

"Mrs. Rose, being the star running back at Florida T&A is like winning the lottery. If Junior is as good as we all think he is..."

"He is."

"Then he will sign a large pro contract at the end of his college career, and Junior and your family will be set."

Mrs. Rose did not seem satisfied. "What if he blows out his knee? Then what do we do? Other schools have made assurances to Junior."

Larrola had heard it all before. "If there are any special requests for Junior or his family..." He looked Mrs. Rose in the eye. "I encourage you to talk to Coach Tob. He has a special way of making good things happen."

Mrs. Rose looked at Larrola with disappointment. Was he supposed to write her a check right then and there? Everybody wanted to get paid. Mrs. Rose realized Coach Larrola wasn't holding the keys to the car and marched over to Coach Tob. Plausible deniability was a terrific concept.

Larrola left Tob behind to negotiate with Mrs. Rose. The season started on Saturday, and he had a football team to coach. He called the home office to check on the team's progress. He was assured over the phone the team was focused and ready for the trip to Death Valley to meet new conference foe Clemson. He too was sure the Florida Technology and Agriculture Barbarians would pound the Clemson Tigers. His cell phone rang. "Head coach Merl Larrola." Larrola drove with one hand and held the phone with the other. "You got Junior to sign the letter of intent? Great!" The kid was almost home. "How badly did she hurt us? Another Escalade? Damn. And a cash stipend? And she wants a total of fifteen tickets to the Florida State game. Figures. No. It's not going to be a problem. No. That either. He'll be a done deal after recruiting weekend. I guarantee it."

Larrola hung up the cell phone. He wanted to make a stop before the hotel in Atlanta. His flight left early, but the night was still young. He rolled down the window and stuck his head over to the passenger side. She was young—really young. That was just the way he liked them. "What's your name, baby?"

"Tomika. Tomika Slett." She said it really sexy.

Larrola pulled out a roll of cash. "Do you want to take a ride?"

"Sure, baby. What do you want?" Tomika hopped in the passenger seat and rubbed Larrola's crotch.

"I want it all." Head coach Merl Larrola pulled away with the seventeen-year-old prostitute.

Week One, The Yard

Tuby and the midshipmen worked on the game plan for the opener at Duke. Majic Hommn, the Blue Devil quarterback, was a legitimate threat to pick them apart down the field with the pass or to scramble for big yardage. Scormir worked the defense on containment with ends Whitsche and Bocher, and he made Sal Geayser Hommn's personal spy. Majic wasn't going to beat them.

The offense was a different matter. Mashner sent Johni Bronson through drill after drill to get him to hold onto the football. Tug

Lerrin worked on short, quick passes to the flat that would give him the opportunity to release the ball. Draws and screens were thrown into the mix to try to keep the Blue Devils off-balance. Tuby spent extra time on the kicking game. He was convinced field position would win the game. Howdy had become automatic within forty-five yards and expanded his range daily. He learned to punt and soared high spirals up and down the field. He looked uncomfortable in a football uniform. It was a rarity that Tuby had a player who could kick a football between the uprights and quote how many electrons were in the shell of a cobalt atom.

The midshipmen worked hard and were in the best shape of their lives. It had been grueling, but they would have that extra zip in the fourth quarter. He walked through the yard. School had begun, and the midnight oil burned. He walked by Bancroft Hall and decided to check on his favorite plebes. He had been riding them hard, but he needed the plebes to play well in order to beat Army or anyone else on the schedule. He said hello to cornerback Rolly Leaky, the firstie from Montana, who didn't just study with fellow firstie Sherri Rastagon. Leaky had gone to the dark side and was dating a midshipman.

Tuby had never ventured through the passageways of Bancroft Hall. The labyrinth of corridors intimidated him. He knew he was close to Pantry's room, and then he heard commotion.

"Check your six!" Gareloin called to Pantry.

Pantry scrambled from the floor and stood to attention. Tuby saw the éclair.

"What are you doing on the floor, Pantry?"

"Hiding an éclair, sir!"

Tuby averted his eyes from Pantry's ample plumber's crack and dismissed himself. He was impressed Pantry really wouldn't lie—even about an éclair.

Vern was reading a book on World War I, and Tuby said hello. He was glad to have someone to talk to when he got home and was very pleased with the job Vern was doing as the trainer. Tonight he didn't feel like chitchat, and he went straight to bed. He tossed and turned in his sleep. He dreamed about Myra on their wedding day. She looked so pretty. She was dancing by herself and spinning round and round. Her face became worried and then anguished as her dress caught fire. She was falling and burning, and she thumped to the scorched sand. Demons surrounded her, and they punched and maimed her. The demons violated her, scratched her soft skin with their filthy paws, and humped his wife with relish. They looked into his eyes so Tuby could see their satisfaction. They kicked Myra when their pleasures were complete, roped her by the neck, and dragged her from place to place in Hell. They paraded her like a captured whore for sale. Myra sobbed and pleaded for God to save her. She cried Tuby's name. Tuby's eyes snapped open. The demon incubus was standing over him with a dagger and waiting to plunge it into the frightened man's heart.

The door opened, and Vern walked in. "Tuby, are you all right?"

Tuby's eyes were scared, and sweat covered his pajamas. His arms trembled as he held his weight up in bed. "I'm fine. I just had a bad dream," Tuby stuttered as Vern looked at his friend closely.

Friday afternoon came, and the team loaded onto the buses that would take them to Durham—home of Duke University. Pantry, Gareloin, and Emenith received the news that all three plebes would start. They eyed their midshipmen jerseys with pride. Tuby rallied the team around him. The gold Navy helmets bore no smudges from head-to-head clashes. Their pants were not stained with green turf smudges. Chalk from the first down lines or end zone did not cover their arms.

"We have to play good defense. We have to win in the kicking game. We cannot turn the ball over on offense. If we do those three things, we have a chance to win the game." Tuby held his hands high over his team.

Tackle Spike Himpp had been selected along with two others as team captains for the game. The plebes were anxious and ready to hit somebody. "We've worked hard for this. No one has worked harder than us. We've sweat and lay in the mud. We are a better football team than they are. We're in a hostile environment. That's when they call in the navy. Go Navy!"

Navy kicked off and gave Duke the ball.

"Stay in your lanes, and let's pin them back deep." Encouraged Tuby.

Leaky smacked his helmet and the other special teamers' shoulder pads. Howdy teed the football up as he had done so many times in the last month. He had butterflies and hoped he wouldn't miss the ball. Tuby put his hands on his knees and watched his team line up. Howdy ran up to the ball and pounded one deep into the end zone. Duke would start on the twenty-yard line.

Lanny L. Glower was the *Baltimore Sun* staff writer assigned to cover Navy football. He opened his laptop and began jotting down notes for his Sunday-morning article in the sports section. This was his first assignment to a Division One school and the inaugural game for the new Big Beast Conference. He was just as amped as the players.

Tuby hadn't gone to bed yet. He wrestled over the nightmares and played the Duke game over and over in his head. He heard the newspaper spank the front porch, and he went to the door, turned on the light, and picked up the Sunday edition. It was hot off the press.

The *Baltimore Sun*, Sunday, September 7, Osaye Sinks Duke
Wallace Wade Stadium in Durham, North Carolina, was filled to capacity on a sunny Saturday as the colors of college football were

on display again. The Duke Blue Devils hosted Navy's Midshipmen in the inaugural Big Beast matchup, and it was supposed to be a coming-out party for Duke's dangerous quarterback, Majic Hommn. The game turned into a defensive struggle as second classman and rookie placekicker Howdy Osaye's lone field goal in the third quarter proved to be the difference. It helped Navy to a 3–0 victory on the road.

Both offenses looked mired in the mud due to ineptness or outstanding defense. New Navy head coach Tuby Gravenald thought it was a little of both. "It's early in the season. Both offenses struggled, but they'll come around. We were awfully worried about Hommn. I thought our defense did a heck of a job keeping him bottled up. And I can't say enough about Howdy. He kept them backed up all day."

Howdy Osaye, the Nigerian-born former soccer player, made quite a debut. He boomed one long punt after another and kept Duke and Hommn inside their own twenty-yard line. The Blue Devils crossed midfield only twice but were snuffed before finding field-goal range. Coach Gravenald called a very conservative game that hardly pressured the Duke side of the field. Quarterback Tug Lerrin was sacked seven times. Running back Johni Bronson was knocked around as well and gained only thirty-nine yards on twenty-one carries.

The defense was the lone Navy bright spot. Sal Geayser made a team-high twelve tackles. Four were for losses. Ends Bocher and Whitsche kept Hommn in the pocket, sacked him twice, and forced him into several bad throws. Navy's break came late in the third when linebacker Rich Chatters pounced on a fumble at the Duke twenty-nine-yard line. The Duke defense responded by holding Navy to a three and out, but Osaye drilled a forty-two-yard field goal through the crossbars. The three points held up. Duke never got anything going, even after working the hurry-up offense early in the fourth.

The Navy defense came up big late in the fourth. Hommn misfired on fourth and seven from midfield. Navy went three and out again, but Osaye stuck the ball on the Duke four-yard line with a punt that couldn't have backed them up any nicer had he used a sand wedge. Navy moves to 1–0 in Conference A of the new Big Beast. They host Pittsburgh at Navy Marine Corps Memorial Stadium next Saturday in the home opener.

Tuby read the article twice. He really didn't want to be conservative. He just didn't have anybody who could block.

Florida T&A

"Coach Larrola," Jo Rose Wedom, Larrola's secretary, buzzed the coach on the intercom. "They are ready for the press conference."

Larrola open his desk drawer and took out a Tums. He knew press conferences were never easy at Florida T&A. He bustled down the hallway and met one of his handlers. Larrola took a deep breath and stepped into the bright lights of the media. He adjusted the microphone at the podium. "I thank you all for coming. Let's talk about Barbarian football." Larrola was not in the mood to tackle questions about his team's off-field behavior. "Let's start with Archi."

Larrola pointed to Archi W. Gazet, staff writer with the *Orlando Sentinel*. He was assigned to Florida T&A. "Coach, with a tough conference schedule, the conference championship, and the new play-off system in place before the national championship, how well do you think your team will hold up through what looks to be a grueling schedule?"

A softball question. Perfect, thought Larrola. "Well, Archi, this is easily the toughest schedule Florida T&A has ever had. I think it is the toughest conference in the country, and whoever survives and makes it to the NCAA play-offs, I think, has the inside track to the national title game in New York."

"Do you think you'll win your division?" The question came from the back of the room.

"I do," Larrola said confidently.

"How do you plan to neutralize Clemson's all-American linebacker, Ray L. Rocker?"

"I think our offensive line is ready to make some room for Roanen. Rocker is going to make some tackles. We just hope it's six or seven yards downfield."

"There have been reports one of your players assaulted an academic tutor named Johanna Detong during a study session. Is this true, and which player is it?"

It was too good to be true. Coach Larrola adjusted his cap. "I have heard a sexual assault complaint was filed with campus police. The university is investigating, but no charges have been filed, and no one has been arrested. To my knowledge none of our players are involved." Larrola hoped they bought that.

"There are more reports of payments to athletes in the form of goods, services, cars, and cash. Can you comment on that?"

"Being the two-time national champions, we've been under the microscope for two years. Not once has the NCAA found any irregularities in our football program. We run a clean program. Just because we're good doesn't mean we're dirty."

"Do you think the Barbarians can defend their championship for the third year in a row?" Archi got things back on the right track.

"This is a very special senior class. I think they want it more than ever. This is their swan song. But they know they have to beat Clemson first. This team is very focused."

Larrola thanked the press and worked his way back to the office. He hated the press.

Cornerback Cisco Deerrink wore a royal purple and vivid tangerine jogging suit. The Barbarian team colors had always suited

Cisco's style. He needed to see his girl, Skairy Beth. Skairy Beth was a freak. She had something good for him on the other side of town, but Cisco had no intention of taking the bus—even for some loving. He needed a car and some cash. He had taken some freshman's checkbook out of his book bag and knew a place he could cash one. Stupid kid should know better than to have his checkbook on his person. He needed to bring Skairy Beth some party favors to get her in the mood. That meant he needed a car. He had to get the check cashed, come back to the campus, and find the Sheik. He would be in the Oasis. He had to pick up some blow and bud and then get all the way to the other side of town. He almost forgot. He also had to stop and get some forties, and he had to meet with Shark Mulfalla, the campus bookie. The paper had the Barbarians listed at fourteen-point favorites. That was easy money.

He slid the T-bar down the driver's-side window and unlocked the new Mustang. He hot-wired the ride, and it purred. He might even let Skairy Beth take a ride. He left the parking lot and sported the ride by Hurl Stadium, the gargantuan 110,000-seat home field for the Barbarians. *Five hundred,* he thought. He would write the check for five hundred. That way he would have some extra Benjamins for the trip to Clemson.

Tackle Romans Steanen took the dare. His fellow linemen, Raul Zogo, the Mongrel, and Theo Drimend, the Mental Idiot, had made the challenge. If he did it, they would treat him to a bucket of wings and two pitchers of beer. Drimend and Zogo knew they were going to lose. Steanen lived for this type of stuff. He looked around. There were a few cute girls by the fountain. One of them was a cheerleader. Steanen was sure she wouldn't say anything. He rushed over to the school fountain in the night. The fountain was the centerpiece of the Florida T&A campus. It was a central place near the university library where people celebrated victory on the field.

The girls became frightened and ducked. They were unsure what madness lurked. Steanen pounced to the edge of the fountain and turned to face Zogo and Drimend. They were on the ground and rolling already. Steanen unbuckled his belt and unzipped his jeans. He squatted over the fountain's edge. The mist chilled his butt. He grunted, and a slow-moving chocolate substance oozed out of his bunghole. Steanen defecated not once but twice in the fountain, and the horrified, pretty girls fled the scene. Steanen pulled his jeans back up and raised the zipper. He locked his belt into place but never wiped his ass. He posed victoriously as Zogo and Drimend caught the repulsive action on their cell phone cameras.

Larrola had his team fired to the hilt as they took to defending their national title. The hostile Clemson crowd, which filled the stands with a sea of orange, did not intimidate them. The Clemson players rubbed 'the rock' for good luck and exited the home team tunnel. Captains Deerrink and Steanen headed to midfield for the coin toss. Steaned was an animal that would break fingers on the bottom of the pile. The other Barbarians loved that Steanen was on their side of the field.

Florida T&A lost the toss. It didn't matter. They planned on hurting Clemson.

Deerrink was still awake Sunday morning. They had partied all night and would continue to do so through the day. Skairy Beth read him the report filed by Archi W. Gazette.

The *Orlando Sentinel*, Sunday Morning, September 7, Barbarians Slay Tigers in Death Valley

Clemson University's Memorial Stadium was packed with more than eighty thousand faithful fans on a balmy September afternoon. They should have spent Labor Day at Hilton Head. Florida T&A welcomed them to the Big South in a big way. The lopsided 35–3 T&A victory ran their winning streak to thirty-five games.

The Barbarian seniors are now a gaudy 35–1 lifetime, and their quest to win an unprecedented third national title in a row is well under way.

All-American running back Worm Roanen, who rushed for three touchdowns and 210 yards on twenty-two carries, led the Barbarians. Quarterback B. Siemore Jett rushed for one touchdown and threw for another. He hit J. J. "Honey" Romans in the end zone in the fourth quarter for the nail in the coffin. The Barbarians running game was overwhelming, and senior Clemson all-American linebacker Ray L. Rocker was visibly frustrated. Head coach Merl Larrola removed most of his starters after the Romans touchdown. "Clemson is a proud football program," Larrola said. "There was no need to pile on the score. They just ran into a juggernaut today."

Animosity reigned from the start. Clemson players traditionally touch the Rock when leaving the home team tunnel. Florida T&A players incensed the Clemson players and fans by pretending to shine the rock with their posteriors. This caused the referees to step between the two squads and diffuse what could have been a game-marring episode.

Things settled down, and Roanen broke off right tackle and scampered thirty-five yards for his first touchdown of the day. Jett added to the margin with his own twenty-five-yard jaunt on third and two. This gave the Barbarians an early fourteen-point cushion. Roanen added his second in the second with a forty-yard burst straight up the middle. All-American Barbarian placekicker, Jacko Nobs, converted all five extra point opportunities. Clemson never found any momentum. Cornerback Wilson Dubink picked off two passes, and W. Jackson posted three sacks from his defensive end position.

The dominating performance gives Florida T&A a leg up in its title defense, although they face a monumental hurdle next week when they visit the Orange Bowl to play intrastate rival Miami on the road.

Seavisitsen Ark

Nimrod was surprised when the Dunny Gate did not leave them in the heart of Vancil Hill. He was more surprised when Jairus arrived on the Seavisitsen Ark.

"Jairus! What in Heaven's name are you doing here?" Nimrod was furious. "You disobeyed a direct command. This is much too dangerous a place."

"Where is this place?" Jairus looked around the ship.

The other members of Team Nimrod did as well.

"You are on the Seavisitsen Ark," a calm voice informed them.

"I'm sorry. The Seavisitsen Ark?" Nimrod questioned.

"We have been using the Seavisitsen Ark as a refuge for the population of Blanco Trollien and the faltering planet Foccod Knort. We are stationary in space and far from Blanco Trollien. Uranndas Exhale cloaks us."

Jairus looked at the beautiful array of gaseous clouds entering the galaxy.

"They are fleeing Blanco Trollien?" Thomas was concerned.

"I am afraid so. General Geeshi Grub and his syndicate have all but conquered Foccod Knort, and he has begun his initial assault on the home planet of Blanco Trollien. They have left Oshu Land and Maroed Rain in such ruin they are now using Foccod Knort as their forward base. Their main forces are amassed on the moon Zhoul Lot."

"Are there any survivors from Oshu Land or Maroed Rain?" Shar had visited the ocean planet of Maroed Rain once.

"None. The Delerdian population of Oshu Land is all but extinct. Nakaru time gas has poisoned the Mal Jon Sea of Maroed Rain. This has killed all life above or below the surface. Both planets are designated to be the first annihilated by the Hell Star. Some refugees were able to leapfrog from one conquered planet to the next but very few. They were either exterminated by Decrof X destroyers or trapped in the Rakwurr Net and made to work the mines on Zhoul Lot. Others died of brich rash. It became an epidemic when Maroed Rain was under siege. They were unable to produce the antidote, and the insects were able to reach through to the bones and saw right through. It left millions amputated and dead."

"How are King Fardorff and Princess Mytom Onaxa?" Vishnu knew them personally.

"King Fardorff refuses to leave Blanco Trollien or the holy city of Vancil Hill. Princess Mytom Onaxa refuses to leave her father's side."

"Are the Outacou Mines safe?" Nimrod asked.

The stranger looked at Nimrod warily. "You know of the Outacou Mines?"

"Michael, the archangel, informed me. He has sent us on a mission." Nimrod looked at the others. That wasn't 100 percent true.

"The Outacou Mines are secure. What is your mission on Blanco Trollien?" the stranger asked.

"I have no business with Blanco Trollien. I care for its safety and have come only to see a friend and mentor." Nimrod felt he was being interrogated.

"With whom do you wish to speak?" asked the stranger.

"I have come to seek the council of Muhammad and Jesus."

"I am afraid that won't be possible. Upon Muhammad and Jesus's orders, we have spliced the Dunny Gate to the Seavisitsen Ark. Regular transports are used to transport the civilian population from Blanco Trollien to the Ark. They await passage there through the Dunny Gate to a safe galaxy. I am saddened to say those are few. I understand Earth is at risk now as well."

If he only knew, thought Nimrod. "I am sure if we were able to contact either Jesus or Muhammad, he would invite us to speak with him on Blanco Trollien."

"We do not use Regall Code like a telephone, sir. We are at war. The safety of all life in the universe is at risk, and all life is leaving Blanco Trollien—not joining the destruction. Only the Kipren Army takes the transports back to the surface."

"This isn't working, Nimrod. What do we do now?" Thomas folded.

"I am not sure, Thomas." Nimrod was without hope.

"The first thing we shall do is take you to Tirrobe Deck and have the SKN doctor analyze you. Grub has tried to pass disease through the Dunny Gate before. It is required of all passengers." Team Nimrod followed the stranger. "Then we shall secure your space in line for a return trip though the Dunny Gate back to where you came from. The line for the Dunny Gate is long, and it could take awhile. I suggest getting something to eat after visiting the doctor."

Team Nimrod was being sent back to square one. All of Team Nimrod waited patiently on Tirrobe Deck for the SKN doctor, a computerized whiz that checked for disease, bacteria, alien abnormalities, brich rash, and other infections endangering the civilization living in the Ark, to electronically scan them. Jairus stepped up to the fluorescent scanner and stood still exactly as the Delerdian nurse had asked. He was clean. Vishnu followed and was subjected to some health jokes, but all came up clean. They were released to the general population. The conditions were overcrowded and chaotic. The refugees were peaceful and thankful, but there were so many of them. Hundreds of thousands had fled the terror of their home planets. They slept on the floors and in the sills. They made camps around chairs. The fortunate who garnered bunking facilities were smashed ten to a room.

Team Nimrod fell into the line for food. Feeding the masses was difficult, and getting food delivered to the Ark from Blanco Trollien was also difficult. The XJ Fhoon single-winged space engager fighters proved more than a match for the peaceful Trolliens, who had only recently come to possess a fleet of the ancient Eureck Rigger—a swift battleship that was serviceable but no match for the XJ Fhoon. The Fhoons blasted cargo ships from inside the gravity belts and took the Eureck Riggers and the valuable supplies with them.

All that was left for dinner tonight was ygyura, a gruel-like soup that had bits floating around in the bowl. Team Nimrod ate the meal. Everyone needed sustenance, but it was a far cry from their normal culinary feasts in Heaven. Nimrod and Jairus searched the Ark for a place to lay their heads. They would be stuck here for a week awaiting passage.

"I'm sorry, Nimrod. I shouldn't have disobeyed you."

"You're right. You shouldn't have." Nimrod was stern. "It is only for your safety I tell you what is right and wrong."

"Do you forgive me?" Jairus was on the verge of tears.

"Of course I forgive you. I love you." Nimrod held the boy close.

It was the first time he had heard "I love you" since his mother had passed in Behorrin Debartik. They walked around the Seavisitsen Ark. The humungous space station was larger than Pyrub Cape back in Heaven. Nimrod and Jairus looked at the Blanco Trollien Archipelago from the observatory window. They both found it hard to believe the planets were under such stress. They saw the Hell Star behind tiny Oshu Land and quivered in fear. Death itself sat in space and waited to be activated. Nimrod now looked into the eyes of his enemy. Nimrod envisioned the Darkness racing the Hell Star through the universe. It was destined for Heaven if Nimrod lost the bet.

Week Two, The Yard

Tuby never liked to look too far ahead on the schedule, but he couldn't help noticing they were scheduled to play Pittsburgh. Tuby's old friend and nemesis was the head coach of the Panthers. Greg E. Ashola—Greg E. Asshola to many of his friends—was an outstanding football coach and motivator. Coach Ashola also had a running back named Leman Drocane. He could take over a game. It was going to be another test of his defense. Pittsburgh's defense was steady. They would have opportunities if they did not make mistakes. It always came down to the offensive line.

Scormir worked the plebes. Mohney and Markh were giving them all the encouragement they could muster, but they were still missing assignments. Tuby got in the mix. "Pantry, get your ass down and your head up." Pantry, Gareloin, and Emenith all struggled with this. "Your ass is too high, and it forces your head to look straight into the ground. Try it again. That's better, but it has to be exaggerated."

Tuby got down in a three-point stance and showed the players. They looked awkward. They ran the play. All three plebes were late off the ball.

"Do you morons not know the snap count?" They all nodded. "Then when Tug says 'hut two,' go blast into somebody."

They tried the play again. All three plebes had their asses low, but now they were looking at the ball and hoping to get a jump on the count.

"No! No! No!" Tuby blew the play dead before Tug had even had a chance to get the snap. "Vern!" Vern popped out of nowhere. "Go find some cardboard. Five or six pieces from the lids."

Pantry, Gareloin, and Emenith worried about humiliation. They practiced the play. Tuby went after the plebes again. The rest of the offense was getting restless. Some of the mids complained about Tuby's conservative approach. They were supposed to be a pass-oriented team, but they never threw the ball. Tug was frustrated. Whenever they did throw the ball, it was in the flat or a screen. Bronson was hurting. He had gotten to the point where he didn't want the ball—a bad sign for a running back.

Vern came back with the cardboard Tuby had requested. Tuby put the cardboard over his knee and sliced it into even pieces. He called Gareloin, Emenith, and Pantry over. He shoved the cardboard into both sides of their helmets and covered their peripheral vision. The plebes could only see straight ahead. "This is something I learned here at the Naval Academy. You all need to keep your eyes in the boat. You need to look straight ahead. These are your eyes in the boat machines. They will help you to look straight ahead. You listen for the snap count. You fire off the ball when you hear the snap count. You keep your ass down and your eyes in the boat. The only people you will need to see will be right in front of you. Now focus!"

Tuby fell sound asleep. While Tuby slept Semyala, the fallen angel, unclipped his claws from the constellation Orion. Banished to Hell for seducing Eve's daughter, the watcher left his upside down perch and spread his evil wings. Under the cloak of night, he landed on Tuby's house. All the streetlights darkened, and electricity ceased. The shadow passed through the pane into Tuby's room and stood over the coach as Tuby writhed in agony. Semyala sent visions of Myra into Tuby's dreams. Myra was hanging inverted on a crucifix. Demons peeled her skin. Cockroaches filled her mouth and scurried from her nose and eyelids. She was desperate to be released. Ravens plucked at the loosened skin and squawked with hunks of Myra's rotting flesh in their beaks. Semyala entombed Tuby in his shadow as the man suffocated in the dark.

Vern opened the door with a candle in his hand. Tuby was lying in bed, kicking his feet violently, and holding a pillow to his mouth. Vern grabbed the pillow, and Tuby took a gasping breath. The lights went back on.

"Tuby, are you all right?" Vern was concerned.

"I think so." Tuby was visibly shaken.

"What's going on?" Vern sat on the edge of the bed and blew out the candle.

"Why do you have a candle?" Tuby looked at the smoldering wick.

"The electricity went out for a few minutes, and I heard you struggling. Man, you've got me a little spooked."

"I've been having these really bad dreams." Tuby had to tell his friend the truth—but not the whole truth. He didn't want Vern to think he had lost his mind.

Plebe Dahlia Werrch sat reading *Proceedings*, the monthly magazine of the Naval Academy, in Tecumseh Court. Cornerback Vern Stamcie sat down next to her and opened his electrical engineering textbook.

"EE?" Dahlia noticed the dandelion-colored book.

"Yeah. It's a tough load. I've got eighteen credit hours this semester." Stamcie looked at Dahlia. "How are you holding up?"

Dahlia knew he was talking about being a plebe. "It's been all right. There's a lot of studying." She giggled.

"Don't tell me. Leadership, chem one, calc one, English, and naval heritage."

"That's a pretty good memory."

Stamcie was proud of himself. "You never forget your plebe year." He looked at Dahlia. She was pretty. "I'm Vern Stamcie. Everybody calls me Stammy."

"Dahlia Werrch. Everybody calls me Plebe or Charlie Foxtrot." Navy code for big fat mess. They both laughed, knowing that the true meaning was innappropriate language.

"It's awfully busy around here, but maybe I can give you a hand with your calc." Stammy had to make practice.

"Sure. I'd like that." Dahlia smiled, and Stammy headed to practice.

Stammy was just laying the groundwork for next year. Dating plebes was off-limits.

Tuby didn't feel good about the practice. He thought the boys were lethargic and uninspired. Pitt would embarrass them in the home opener if they didn't start showing some spunk. He walked around the yard to clear his head. It was still balmy in what these easterners called an Indian summer. Back in Minnesota they might have already gotten a reminder from Old Man Winter. He looked at the naval chapel. Someday he'd have to go in there. The dome of the chapel could be seen for miles away as it illuminated the night. Legend had it youngsters didn't officially join the second class until they returned from their summer cruises and laid eyes on the chapel dome. Tuby couldn't keep up with all these traditions. He decided to swing by Bancroft and see what the plebes were up to.

No one was home, and it was lights-out. Tuby smelled a rat. Coach meandered through the hallways and down the stairs. Instinct took him to King Hall. He heard the sound of young men getting in trouble. Mohney and Markh had the plebes doing the cannonball run. Pantry, Gareloin, and Emenith were sitting at the team table. They were stuffing hard, dough-covered apples dipped in whipped sugar in their mouths. Emenith was vomiting on the floor with six apples in front of him. It had come down to a duel between Pantry and Gareloin. Each had polished off eight of the twelve. Gareloin was feisty, but Pantry was determined. Systematically Pantry kept at the dough-covered apples and gnawed them to the core. He had put some distance between himself and Gareloin and was going to coast to the win. Gareloin suddenly turned green and joined Emenith at the barf bucket. Pantry danced around the table like a heavyweight scoring a knockout. Mohney and Markh raised his hand in victory. *If only he were as determined to block,* Tuby thought and decided not to make his presence known. His linemen were bonding.

Tuby met Coach Ashola on the sidelines before the game. The electricity was phenomenal. The midshipmen marched over from the yard and filled the stands. All of them. It was an impressive sight. Tuby wished Ashola luck and headed toward his team. Tuby had decided to throw one of his plebes a bone and gave Emenith the nod to be a captain for the home opener with Stammy. Pitt won the toss and elected to receive. Tuby pulled the men to the sideline and reiterated the game philosophy. "Men, we've got to tackle Drocane. We're going to put eight in the box, and it's man-to-man on the corners." The band played "Anchors Aweigh," and Howdy drilled the kickoff to the two.

The *Baltimore Sun*, Sunday, September 14, Navy's New Destroyer: Osaye

Pittsburgh Panther head coach Greg E. Ashola thought he had Navy beaten. That was before Navy unleashed its not-so-secret new weapon, Howdy Osaye. Before a capacity crowd at the Navy Marine Corps Memorial Stadium, Navy matched last season's win total with a stunning display of placekicking. Navy was down early. The legs of Leman Drocane plowed through the Navy defense for two first-half touchdowns. The Panthers ground up the turf with Drocane and ground down the clock. They held the ball for a whopping 22:15 of the first half. Drocane carried the ball nineteen times and gained 120 yards as the bull ran roughshod through the midshipmen defense. The Navy offense looked just as impotent as it did the previous week and failed to make a first down until late in the first half. Only Osaye's remarkable punting, which forced Pittsburgh into long, punishing drives, prevented the score from being worse.

Head Coach Tuby Gravenald said he "had a nice chat" with the mids at halftime. Gravenald's troops responded with a drive of their own to begin the third quarter. Johni Bronson showed sparks and gained twenty-five yards on the drive. Tight end Elmo Linners picked up two crucial first downs to get Osaye into field-goal range. Osaye drilled a thirty-five yarder and then pinned the Panthers back on their own sixteen with a high, floating kickoff. The Navy defensive unit looked like a completely different team as they stacked up Drocane for losses on his first two carries and pressured the Panther quarterback to misfire on third and long. The Panthers punted from their own end zone and drilled a low, spiraling kick. The mids set up a return, and Boots Morne followed blockers to the fifteen. A late flag set the ball back at the thirty, and Lerrin failed to advance the ball. Osaye made the forty-seven yarder to make it 14–6.

With time winding down in the third, Osaye kicked off, and the special teams caused a fumble. Lerrin threw a lob to the corner of the end zone and missed wide receiver Gerry Johnson by a fingertip. Gravenald called for Bronson on second down, and he was stuffed for no gain. The alert Pitt linebackers also detected a third-down screen pass. This left Osaye to knock through his third field goal of the day to make it 14–9. The inspired midshipmen defense fed off the enthusiastic crowd. Drocane's trademark fourth-quarter pillaging of opponents never materialized. Free safety Ronn Judge, linebacker Barnett Prime, and stalwart Sal Geayser plugged the seams.

Lerrin led two fourth-quarter drives that were hardly things of beauty, but they got Osaye within firing range. He converted kicks of forty-three and forty-eight yards that put Navy up 15–14 with 1:56 on the clock. Pitt moved the ball briskly down the field and utilized the sidelines and two time-outs. Ashola used quick outs to set up the defense and then hit the go route to bring Pitt to the twelve-yard line with eighteen seconds on the clock. Pitt sent Drocane up the middle to either seal the game with a touchdown or center the football for kicker Linn Mainge. Geayser dropped Drocane at the ten, and Pitt called their last time-out. Mainge jogged onto the field. The snap was good. The hold was good. Mainge shanked it to the right.

Navy goes to 2–0 and heads to face new conference foe Temple in Philadelphia—the first of two visits to the City of Brotherly Love for the midshipmen.

Florida T&A

Free safety Wink Romance V joined offensive guard Randy Molt. They walked up the stairs of the athletic center to head coach Merl Larrola's luxurious office. Randy fancied himself a budding star in the world of rap music and was referred to around campus by his self-chosen moniker of the Suburban Gangsta. Randy sported blond cornrows and gold teeth. He was frequently in the company of large-butted white women. Wink's newest squeeze, Candy Ros RS, waited at the foot of the stairs. The self-promoting Candy liked to refer to the RS as "registered sexaholic." Her stage name was Candy Rocks. Her dancing partner, Bell Mount, was tagging along. The athletic department jiggled with all the booty. The quartet made their way to the coach's office.

Coach Larrola was on the phone. Wink knocked and let himself and Randy in to sit in the comfy leather recliners.

"Yeah. I'll give the ten and a half." The coach put down the phone.

Coach Tob joined the discussion. "Gentlemen, I've been hearing rumors."

Molt and Romance V made their not-guilty faces before hearing the coach out. Wink adjusted his wild strawberry collar and his razzle-dazzle rose bow tie. Wink was a legacy. His father, Blink Romance IV, had been a wide receiver with the Chiefs back in the early eighties. His son was a gifted free safety who was projected to go in the first round of the draft.

"There have been reports the two of you have amassed a cache of weapons."

Molt and Romance V shook their heads. "No. Not us, Coach."

"A theater major filed the report. He said an arrow from a crossbow struck him in the calf. He claims to have seen Randy running from the scene with the crossbow. Randy?"

"I haven't the first idea what you are talking about. I was home studying." Randy pursed his lips tightly.

"I haven't said when it happened. How could you be sure you were studying?" Larrola shifted in his seat, and Coach Tob shifted on the desk.

"I study all the time. I've got a lot of classes. I'm either at practice, studying, or taking a dump." Molt never batted an eyelash.

"Wink?" Romance V's head snapped up. "The campus police have a report from a pizza delivery person named Efrain. He claims you ordered two pizzas and breadsticks with extra garlic sauce…"

"Yeah. That was probably me. I like that garlic sauce." Wink winked at the coach. He knew the coach like garlic too.

"It also says that when he rang the door, you held a semi-automatic rifle to his nose and took the pizza, breadsticks, two two-liter Diet Cokes, and all his money, which totaled eighty-five dollars."

"No. No. That wasn't me. No way I ordered Diet Coke. Diet Pepsi, yes. No Diet Coke. Not a chance." Wink never blinked.

"So I can tell the campus police that neither of you are in the possession of handguns, automatic weapons…" Larrola raised his brow. "Semiautomatic weapons, assault rifles, grenade launchers, or crossbows?"

"That's right, Coach. I don't even own a pocketknife." Wink pulled out his pants pockets.

Randy got up to exit.

"Randy." Coach drew him back.

"Yes, sir?"

"I hear you want to be a rapper." Larrola needed no additional disruptive elements on campus.

"That's right. You want to hear me bust a rhyme? I got a lot of good cuts, and I want the public to hear."

"Are you accepting money for any of these recordings?"

"No, Coach. I wouldn't do that. Not until I graduate, and then the world will know about the Suburban Gangsta. Here are the latest tracks I've got going on: 'She Smoked It'; 'Whisker Biscuit'; 'Pimp My Ride'; 'Vanilla Shake'; 'Trailer Park Tornado'; the title track, 'Suburban Gangsta'; 'Notorious PIG'; and 'La Shaquita.' Girls, come in here. Coach wants to see us do our thing."

"Not really."

It was too late. Coach couldn't discourage the young man's dream.

"Coach, the girls are part of the act. It gives the performance a little effect. Ready? Hit it."

Wink started spitting a beat into his cupped hand, and Bell and Candy started gyrating their butts around Head Coach Merl Larrola's office. They added a few leg kicks and breast rubs for good measure.

"This one's called 'Big Fat White Ass.'" Randy started rapping.

The *Orlando Sentinel*, Sunday, September 14, Hurricanes Blown Away

The number-one-ranked Florida T&A Barbarians put together a masterful performance against the number-four-ranked Miami Hurricanes here at the Orange Bowl. In a well-balanced attack, six Barbarians scored touchdowns to hand Miami their most lopsided defeat at home in over twenty years. The final was 42–17. Head coach Merl Larrola called it "a clinic" and added, "When we play like this, there is not a team in the country that can beat us." Those strong words were evident from the opening kickoff.

Speedster Juice Chaistler took the opening kickoff ninety-nine yards and was pushed out of bounds at the Miami one-yard line. Seldom-used fullback Steer Reprivus plowed in for the touchdown on the Barbarians' first play from scrimmage. Jacko Nobs added the extra point, and the rout was on.

Miami fumbled the ensuing kickoff. B. Sizemore Jett, the Barbarian quarterback, found tight end Andrew Spore running free in the end zone. After Nob's kick Florida T&A was up fourteen with only fifty-eight seconds gone in the first. The deadened Miami faithful reflected Miami head coach Tad Narpick's sentiment. "We were down early to a good football team. We knew it was going to be an uphill battle. I'm proud of the boys. They never quit. Florida T&A is just a whale of a football team."

Miami found some success, hitting six-foot-six wide receiver Lanky Rheaf on consecutive plays to bring the ball to midfield. They went to Rheaf again, and free safety Wink Romance V pummeled him. Rheaf coughed up the football at the Florida T&A twenty-eight-yard line. Jett drove the Barbarians down the field. Worm Roanen went off tackle for fifteen. Jett found Spore again over the middle for another seventeen yards. It was back to Roanen for ten, and this set up a first down at the Miami thirty-yard line. Larrola called Toorleen's number on a wide receiver screen, and the ex–track star bolted down the sidelines for another first-quarter Barbarian touchdown. Up 21–0 the Barbarians added another touchdown late in the first half. Roanen scored his fourth of the season with a three-yard plunge and extended the lead to 28–0 as the bands marched onto the field. "It was all over but the crying," Larrola told reporters after the game. "We were on today."

Eliminating any second-half miracles, the Barbarians shut down the Hurricanes on their first possession of the second half, and then Jett added his own score. Jett was trapped behind the line of scrimmage on third and eight. He eluded the defensive end and headed toward the sideline. Jett cut back across the grain and found wide-open space. He trotted into the end zone with a sixty-four-yard touchdown.

Things got ugly from there on. Tempers flared, and both teams were penalized for unnecessary roughness. Guard Randy Molt should have been ejected. Replays showed he threw an uppercut to the chin of the Miami noseguard and bloodied his face. The refs called several intentional face masks and warned both coaches about excessive chop blocks to the linemen's knees. Miami got on the scoreboard late in the third on a field goal from the twenty-six, but Jett sealed the game with a fifty-four-yard strike to J. J. "Honey" Romans early in the fourth. Larrola substituted freely on both sides of the ball after Romans's score, and Miami scored two touchdowns in mop-up time before the thinning crowd. The final was 42–17, but the game was a worse rout than the score indicated.

Florida T&A heads back to Hurl Stadium for their home opener against Florida State next Saturday. Linebacker Music Roled brings the number-six Seminoles in to try to put a dent in the Barbarian machine.

Foccod Knort
It seemed a hundred Kwellew years Team Nimrod had to wait. The refugees were slowly evacuated through the galaxy as more and more were brought to the safety of the Seavisitsen Ark. King Fardorff made an address to the Trolliens on the Regall Code screen. The haggard king looked worn and thin, but he encouraged the civilization to keep the faith. He confirmed the fate of Oshu Land and Maroed Rain publicly for the first time. The status of Foccod Knort was uncertain, but the king hardly looked optimistic.

"I need to be fighting the syndicate," a soldier of the Kipren Army mumbled under his breath. "We all should be fighting Geeshi Grub." He looked at the disenfranchised about the Ark.

"We're all trying our best," Nimrod said to the angered soldier.

"I think I could be of more use with KS Teponik arms." He was referring to the ground weapons the Kipren Army on Trollien used. "Instead I get stuck manning the Derd Ferry."

Nimrod and he watched through the observation window as one of the Derd Ferries brought another set of homeless. The ferry slowly docked with the Ark.

"Saving lives is an honorable mission," Nimrod noted.

"You're right," the soldier conceded. "But I'd much rather blast some Sode gunfire into the caves of Gholar." The soldier looked longingly at Maroed Rain—his lost planet.

"You'll get your chance," Nimrod encouraged the young man.

"Froln, I found you." The soldier turned and saluted his commanding officer. "We must be leaving. The Derd Ferry is launching shortly, and we have to perform the checklist."

Team Nimrod gathered around the observatory window as another Derd Ferry approached though the cover of Uranndas Exhale.

"We wish you the best of luck," Nimrod said to the soldiers.

"Nimrod! Look!" Jairus sounded panicked as all turned to face the view of space.

The Derd Ferry's side panels were falling off to reveal the guns of a Decrof X. The two ships were about the same size, and the syndicate had broken through Uranndas Exhale and the Regall Code to find the hidden Ark. The camouflaged Decrof X opened fire. The XJ Fhoon fighters joined, and all riddled the side of the Ark with Sode gunfire. The Ark rumbled, and the rocking spacecraft sent everyone to the floor. The stage-five emergency lights flashed, and the ubiquitous voice of the Ark calmly called for battle stations. Fires broke out on all decks, and smoke began to fill the passageways. Team Nimrod looked helpless and sought to escape the exploding Ark.

"This way," the soldier yelled.

The travelers stayed low behind the two Kipren Army soldiers. Fire crews tried to extinguish the growing blaze. Shar tripped over a hose. Thomas helped her regain her footing. Vishnu and Nimrod both held Jairus's hands as they hurried.

"Where are we going?" Nimrod asked the soldiers.

He could sense no escape. Jairus was petrified.

"We need to find a Bevter raft," they screamed over the explosions.

They passed another window. The XJ Fhoons were everywhere, and several more Decrof X battleships had joined the attack.

"We're going to die," Thomas screamed.

"For once you might be right." Nimrod looked frightened.

He knew residents of Heaven couldn't die in Heaven. If they were killed outside of Heaven, though, the Darkness snatched their souls and sent them to the mines of Gholar to be eternally enslaved.

"What is a Bevter raft?" Vishnu asked the soldiers.

"It's like a lifeboat."

A direct hit from a Decrof X knocked them to the floor again. The Seavisitsen Ark returned fire from its starboard cannons, but it wasn't designed as a warship. It was a converted space cruiser that had taken vacationing Trolliens to Mal Jon Sea on Maroed Rain and to the paradise of Oshu Land. Refugees lay dead by the hatches as they had tried to escape from the smoldering ship. Cries for help raged as strongly as the fires. The Ark made terrible creaking noises.

"She's breaking up." The soldier sounded scared.

The soldiers hunted furiously. They climbed down a ladder and spotted an access to a Bevter raft. They loaded Team Nimrod into the small craft. Nimrod held Jairus on his lap to make room for the soldiers. The Kipren soldiers ran through a checklist. The explosions burst outward into space and sucked refugees into the void. The Bevter raft came to life and then fell. Team Nimrod's stomachs fell with it. Another blast of Sode gunfire hit close to the escape vessel. It shook everyone violently as they detached from the Ark. The pilots struggled to get the raft moving. They searched the panels of the pod and pressed buttons with abandon. The small windows allowed Team Nimrod to watch the Ark break apart section by section, and the lasers of Sode gunfire entered the ship's heart.

The pod stabilized, and they started moving forward. Everyone's heart skipped a beat. They were alive but heading into the cannons of the XJ Fhoon. The Bevter raft was no more equipped to fight a war than a canoe on a river. The pilot steered the craft toward Uranndas Exhale. The Bevter raft was not speedy, and they floated through the swarm of hornets. Team Nimrod watched as other Bevter rafts fled the Ark. Some were making headway. Cannon fire pulverized others. Some were caught in the explosions of the foundering Ark. Nimrod held Jairus close, and the young boy clung to his arms. Nimrod could see the Ark was burning fore and aft. A Decrof X roared by them and went directly to the ship's helm. The Decrof X released a salvo of intense light. The explosion rocked the raft as the great Ark broke into two pieces and incinerated the refugees. The raft hurtled forward into Uranndas Exhale.

"We lost the main engine," the pilot said to the soldier.

They worked furiously to revive the dead engine. Team Nimrod felt the heat rising from the stern of the raft. They were safe from the fighters. The nebulas of Uranndas Exhale cloaked them, but the gravitational field of Blanco Trollien pulled their drifting raft.

"I can't steer the raft." The pilot was frantic. "Our only hope is to survive a crash landing on one of the planets of the archipelago."

"Which one are we going to land on?" Vishnu saw the four planets become larger in view.

"I don't know. Fate will decide. The Bevter raft is designed to float in space until a rescue ship retrieves the survivors. We have no landing capabilities," the pilot warned them.

Nimrod peered through the front of the Bevter raft as the archipelago grew closer.

"How did the syndicate find the Ark?" the soldier asked the pilot.

"There is only one way. A spy alerted them to our position."

"Is there no way to shape a course to Maroed Rain? We could land in the ocean and not on ground," Nimrod thought aloud.

"Nakaru time gas poisoned the Mal Jon Sea. We would burn to death in the acid waters within seconds of landing."

"Let's not go there." Thomas closed his eyes and prayed.

"How about there?" Nimrod pointed to the Enen Rivers of Blanco Trollien.

"That would be fortunate, sir, but I have no ability to control the ship."

They watched as death came closer into view. Vishnu pointed to a lake on Foccod Knort. "What is that?"

They seemed to be heading straight for it.

"We would be fortunate to splash into Faynone West." Vishnu looked encouraged. "Unfortunately it is directly in the heart of Geeshi Grub's army. All survivors would wish they had died."

The Bevter raft became an oven. The lifeboat crashed into the atmosphere of Foccod Knort. Sweat poured off the passengers' brows as they held their arms over their eyes to protect themselves from the flames that had engulfed the craft. The ship rattled and bounced as gravity pulled the vessel faster and faster toward the surface. The flames dissipated. The oxygenated atmosphere revealed the orange and fuchsia sky.

"I am going to trim the flaps and try to help us maintain altitude."

The pilot pulled the lever. The raft planed slightly but still dropped like a stone. The pilot managed to ignite the engine. A desperate attempt to thrust them forward out of the dive worked. They would smack into the sands of Foccod Knort but not head-first. They slammed the hull of the raft onto a ridge and skipped like a stone. They pounded the sand again with a great thud, and lots of sand blasted into the air. The raft tumbled and rolled. Bodies were slapped around. The flailing stopped. The Bevter raft settled. The whine of the engine slowed as sand from the desert floor filled the raft.

Nimrod relaxed his grip on Jairus. Jairus was alive. Shar was alive. Vishnu had wet his pants but was alive. Thomas sat motion-less. His eyes were closed. Nimrod removed his flight restraint and crawled to his friend.

"Thomas! Thomas!" Nimrod shook his friend.

"Stop shaking me. Is it over?"

"Yes," Nimrod gasped. "I think it's over."

"Are we alive or dead?" Thomas wasn't quite sure.

"We're alive." Shar undid her buckle and crawled to the front.

The windows were blown out, and sand was pouring down the panel of instruments in the cockpit. She rummaged through the sand. The pilot was dead. The crumpled space shield had re-moved his head from his shoulders. She removed her shawl and laid it over his body. It was nothing Jairus should see.

They heard the soldier's moaning. Team Nimrod crawled to the cockpit. He had lost consciousness. Nimrod splashed his face with water. The soldier opened his eyes. He saw the shawl cover-ing his friend. He knew he was gone. The soldier moved slowly but went right to work. He shifted the wreckage around and looked for a communicator.

"Dragon B. Eagle, this is FR Seventeen. Do you copy?" The sol-dier shook the communicator. He tried again. "Dragon B. Eagle, this is FR Seventeen. Do you copy?" He typed "SOS" in Regall Code on the keypad. The communicator seemed to be getting a signal, but there was no response to his call or emergency signal.

"Dragon B. Eagle, this is FR Seventeen. Do you copy?" He typed the SOS again. The soldier became frustrated.

"Let's get out of the ship," Nimrod told the crying soldier. "Maybe we'll have better luck outside."

They banged the hatch open and crawled into the haze. The temperature was boiling. Everybody shook loose the sand and double-checked all body parts were operating. The soldier tried again to no avail.

"Thank you for saving our lives. I am sorry for the pilot."

"His name was Ragu Hulponn. He was my friend."

"We're all sorry." Shar put her arms around the anguished soldier. "What is your name?"

"My name is Froln Reem. I am a lieutenant in the Kipren Army."

"Where are we?" Jairus looked at the strange sky.

"I think we landed on Foccod Knort." Vishnu remembered the minutes before the heat.

"But where on Foccod Knort?" Shar asked.

They all looked at the soldier. "We landed in Gweer Chonds Barren Hell."

"Terrific." Thomas shook his hair, and the sand filtered out. "What do we do now? We're all going to die in this desert. We're going to roast, and then the vultures will circle our cooked carcasses and chip away for their Thanksgiving feast."

Nimrod looked glumly at his cohorts and their new friend, Froln. "It's time to go to plan C."

"Plan C? What is plan C? And why don't you tell us about any of these other plans?" Vishnu threw sand on his urine-soaked pants.

"Plan C is to get out of this alive, and I don't tell you my plans because I'm making it up as I go along."

"So much for our divine light mission to save Earth." Vishnu tied his shoe. He was sure walking would be in the future.

Froln reappeared from the Bevter raft. He had a map of Foccod Knort. "This is where I think we are." He pointed to the map. "This is where we want to go." He drew his finger to the other side of the map. "That's Jorrmy Erhe. That is the last stronghold of the Kipren Army. We might be able escape to Blanco Trollien from there." He paused and looked at the survivors. "Unless we bump into the syndicate."

Team Nimrod and Froln started the long walk through Gweer Chonds Barren Hell.

Week Three, The Yard

"Coach, some of the guys are getting frustrated." Tug had gone to see Tuby. "I know we won both games, but we're itching to throw the ball more—like we had planned from the beginning of the season."

Wide receiver Gerry Johnson seconded that opinion. "Coach, I know it's not all about me, but I've only caught a couple balls in two games. I'm ready to break out."

"We always run the same plays. We run Bronson down the middle and set up screens. The defense is waiting every time. We're not getting anywhere." Tug spun the football in his hand.

"Gentlemen, I understand your frustration. But until the line performs better, there is nothing I can do," said Tuby. He was firm in his conviction.

"But, Coach," Johnson tried to explain some more, "we're playing not to lose. We're not playing to win."

"Are you boys trying to tell me how to coach this football team?" Tuby raised his eyebrows. "I've won a few games in my career. I know what this team is capable of on offense. And it's not much."

"That's where you're wrong, Coach." Tug wasn't trying to be disrespectful. "That's the same way Mr. Broamis used to coach."

"I don't know how we'll beat Maryland in two weeks," Johnson added.

"Get out of here before I throw you out." Tuby slammed the desk with his fist. "Mr. Broamis." Tuby hit the desk again, and all his paperwork went flying.

Tuby got up the next morning and started the shower. He splashed some water on his face and brushed his teeth. The shower was too hot, so he turned it down. He soaped up and put his head under the shower. The water felt good. He opened his eyes, and blood filled the basin. Myra's skinless carcass lay at his feet. Tuby screamed and turned to flee the shower. A succubus, the sister of the incubi and countess of female demons, stood behind him and snarled. Her eyes were green with evil, and Myra's flesh hung from her fangs. The shower poured blood over them. Myra's corpse moaned in pain. The succubus picked Tuby up by the throat and slammed him into the shower wall tiles. His head split on the crown. He grabbed for the shower curtain and wrestled with the succubus. The two came crashing to the bathroom floor. Vern walked in, and Tuby was naked and swinging at the air. His head was bleeding from behind.

Vern got to one knee and tried to hold Tuby still. He was still flailing and kicking. Vern held the coach and pinned his arms. "Coach. Coach. It's going to be all right. Calm down. Take a deep breath." Vern used all his young strength to relax the sixtysomething coach.

Snot flushed from Tuby's nostrils as he hyperventilated. "Where's the blood? Where's the blood?"

"There's no blood. You've got a small cut on your head, and it's bleeding a little."

"It slammed me into the wall." Tuby curled his knees to his chest, and Vern laid a towel over him.

"What slammed you into a wall, Tuby?"

"I don't know. It was awful." Tuby could not speak of the demon or Myra.

He shook in terror. This had never happened while he was awake.

Strong safety Boots Morne was from Mississippi. Academics overwhelmed the youngster, and he didn't have time to fool around. The guys on the team were giving him a hard time about the number of textbooks he lugged.

"Boots, you don't even have to go to the weight room. Just tell Coach Gravenald you tote those around with you every day. He'll give you a chit that says you are excused from weight training today," said Rob Wersnors, and the mids laughed.

"Speaking of EI," Rolly Leaky said. He had spotted the plebes. "Here are three that could use a little extra instruction on how to block."

"Pantry, how do you think you'll do in physics?" Ronn Judge held up Morne's physics textbook.

"Former President Jimmy Carter was a physics major here at Canoe U." Pantry tried to change the subject and show a sense of humor.

"Pantry cracked a funny. How about that? Canoe U," said Judge. Pantry smiled along with the rest of the upperclassmen. "Pantry, that's the oldest joke in the book. You have to do better than that."

Pantry removed the smile from his face. There would be no bonding today.

"You know what day it is?" Judge said to Leaky.

"It's Friday." Wersnors overemphasized "Friday."

"Pantry, you do know what Friday means?" Leaky was excited.

"Yes." Pantry and the other plebes tried to look straight at their meal.

"You've got to tell the table a joke." Pantry was running out of material. "And if your joke is no good, we'll put you in joke jail," said the judge.

Pantry struggled to remember a joke. He liked jokes but could never remember them. "OK." Pantry stood. "We were just talking about Jimmy Carter, so I'll tell a Jimmy Carter joke." The upper-classmen waited patiently. "What do Jimmy Carter and the Key Bridge have in common?"

Even the plebes were worried about Pantry. The table looked around. Jimmy Carter had been twenty-five years ago. "I don't know," the upperclassmen conceded.

"They both go in and out of Rosslyn."

Nobody laughed.

"Joke jail."

Leaky was quick to imprison Pantry. Pantry now had to sit at the table and not eat. He was obligated to put his fork directly in front of his eyes to imitate the cell bars of a prison. He had to sit like that until he was released from joke jail. "If you come up with a better joke, Pantry, I'll let you out of joke jail. That other joke just wasn't funny."

The *Baltimore Sun*, Sunday, September 21, Osaye Scores Hat Trick; Navy Downs Temple

Who needs touchdowns when you have Howdy Osaye? The 9–7 victory over Temple in Philadelphia moved the Naval Academy to 3–0, but the midshipmen haven't scored a touchdown this season. The opportunistic Navy defense captured two first-half Temple fumbles, and Osaye turned them into six points. The midshipmen trailed at halftime 7–6 after Temple flanker Whiney Trob broke free on a short pass at the Owl twenty-five and slashed through the Navy defense for a seventy-five-yard touchdown.

Weather was a factor all game as Hurricane Jenna came ashore Thursday night. Big Beast officials were going to postpone the game, but the downgraded tropical storm swung back to the northeast. Several games on the slate were canceled in that region. The gusts made the kicking game an adventure. The forty-knot winds stopped punts in midair when teams kicked to the west, and the winds carried punts to the east for record distances. Both air attacks were grounded. It was impossible to throw into the breeze, and the ball sailed when it was behind the backs of the play callers. "It was like throwing shot put," said Navy's Tug Lerrin. "And when the wind was behind you, it was like throwing a javelin."

Only Osaye had the wind figured out. Cornerback Rolly Leaky recovered a fumble on the Owl thirty-five late in the first quarter after a vicious stick by Boots Morne. Lerrin drove the team for a first down, but the drive stalled there. Osaye drilled a low knuckleball into the wind that slipped over the crossbar by a hair. Lightning struck twice for the midshipmen. Early in the second, Ronn Judge stripped the Temple tailback and fell on the loose ball at the Owl forty-seven-yard line. With the wind at his back, Lerrin tried to find Gerry Johnson on a go route, but the ball took off through the end zone. Coach Gravenald tried to advance the ball to better field position, but the team failed to make the first down. Osaye came in to try the fifty-five-yard field goal with the wind. "Our defense had played well. If we missed, I felt they could hold Temple back. Howdy had the wind. It was a fifty-fifty shot," noted Gravenald. Osaye booted the ball. It started very wide to the left, but the wind caught it and pushed it through the uprights.

After Trob's touchdown in the second, the weather became miserable for the second half. The rain and gusts stymied both offenses. Temple punted late in the third, and the ball seemed to hit an invisible wall. The punt netted three yards, and Navy plowed Johni Bronson down to the Owl sixteen. Osaye clanged the upright with his final kick of the day, but it dropped over the bar to give Navy its 9–7 margin of victory.

Temple drops to 1–2 in the Big Beast, and Navy faces the 3–0 Maryland Terrapins at Navy Marine Corps Memorial Stadium next Saturday.

Florida T&A

Number fifty-two, Barbarian center Raul Zogo, was a known as the Mongrel. The ogre-like creature had the demeanor of one who would eat small babies with spicy wing sauce and a touch of ranch. He was an all-American. It was the Friday night before the Florida State Seminoles came into Hurl Stadium. The city was alive, and the Sheik was entertaining the high-school players on recruiting weekend at the Oasis. It was always one of the best parties of the year. Coach Larrola called it Sergeant Schultz weekend. He knew nothing.

Zogo waited for strong safety Scrum Laneal. He wasn't so much a footballer as an ex–rugby maimer. Scrum was a natural-born hitter. Zogo put on his new fox fur coat, even though the weather was still stiflingly hot in Florida. He was sure Laneal would be wearing his new alligator shoes. They had done some hunting, and with the help of school president Garth A. Moot, they had beaten a poaching rap. The two had been caught in the Everglades on an airboat with the dead gator and ten red foxes. Fortunately no one knew they had spearfished a manatee off Key West over the summer. That might have gotten them in some trouble. Still there was nothing Garth A. Moot couldn't do in Central Florida. He had the two-time defending NCAA football champions, and he wanted a third title.

Offensive tackle Ali Cherck was the Sheik. The Sheik lived in a five-bedroom mansion on a constructed lake near the professional golf course. Cherck didn't own it, and neither did his parents. He lived there as a housemate of the owner and paid rent—one hundred dollars a month. The people he shared the house with just happened to be on a two-year trip abroad. Cherck had the rule of the roost. The tiki torches were out, and the bar was set up. The high schoolers had been given rides to the party to meet the players. They mingled as the Barbarian team joshed with the youngsters from all over the nation. Handpicked female representatives had received invitations to the party. The Barbarian cheerleaders were dressed in heels and not much else. They laughed with the recruits.

Junior Rose, the prize running back from Georgia, was handed a beer and told it was fine. Everybody was just blowing off some steam. More Barbarian players started showing up, and things got rowdy. Beer bongs and drinking games went into full swing. The recruits were invited to the bar for shots of hard liquor and shooters. Others felt no issue with taking drags off the spliffs being passed around the edges of the party. A kid from Kansas took the nineteen points from the Sheik. He thought tomorrow's game would be tight. Girls were thrown into the pool and helped out. Their shirts clung to their perky nipples. The high schoolers went insane as the party gained momentum. Zogo had done a few bong hits and was scooping the hummus like a bear and smashing the dip into his mouth. Laneal challenged the high-school seniors to games of pain, and they saw who would cry uncle first.

Junior Rose thought the lights looked funny. He was catching trailers. His vision couldn't keep up with the light. They passed him the joint. He tried pot for the first time. The girls sure were pretty and friendly. He tried to talk to some of the college girls. He had the liquid courage he needed. The Sheik told him tonight he would get lucky. College girls were horny. The Sheik had guaranteed it. *What a night this is going to be,* thought Junior. The guarantee was just about to join the party.

They were known as the Fire Cherry Debs. They were all campus girls who had found a lucrative line of work with Dame Scorp. Tonight was a big payday for the girls. All they had to do was seduce a few high-school kids and remind them what a great place Florida T&A could be for them. The kids were easy. It was straight-up sex and nothing kinky. It was usually over in a few minutes, and then they could get back to the party and the real players. They walked down the stairs after powdering their noses and began to mingle with the boys. Raul Zogo looked at the Fire Cherry Debs as they worked their way down the stairs. There were three amazing black girls who all looked the same. Dame Scorp, who had been present when Zogo was a senior on recruiting weekend, reminded Zogo to wait, and he could have what he wanted. She told him they were triplets, and their names were Bea, Mary, and Jerry Rime. Zogo knew where he would be tonight. The pillow for the triplets. He smashed the cheese between the crackers and stuffed his face.

The Fire Cherry Debs fanned out and worked the living room, patio, pool, and bar. Brandy Serras matched up with a young buck from Iowa. The Latina El Nina promised to blow him away. Chloe B. Bremsche, the torrid nymph from Gainesville, snuggled up to a wide receiver from Alabama. Porcea Lando, the French exchange student, asked the tackle from South Carolina if he knew how to speak her language. All Karrie had to do was say her name to the youngster from Tennessee. Karrie Bones.

Certain targeted recruits were paired with special girls who had special talents. Dame Scorp thought the trophy quarterback from Washington State would like to be introduced to Wet Gigi Rhee and was delighted to find it was a perfect match. Linemen liked to stick together, so she sent Juani Rouse to talk to the guards from Tallahassee. She liked them two at a time. Michell Brinta was a petite little vixen with small, pouty breasts. She was wearing a tank top, and Coach Larrola had personally asked her to have a good talking-to with the receiver from Arkansas. Vivki Patatan and Tany Nobs, Jacko Nobs's sister, worked as a team with the shyer boys. They corralled themselves all into the same room. They saved the dynamo, Candy Ros RS, for Junior Rose. Wink Romance V, her boyfriend, understood it was just business, and he watched her seduce the pasted Rose.

Things had gone perfectly for Dame Scorp. Garth A. Moot, her personal client, would be delighted. She was sure a very large percentage of the recruits would be attending Florida T&A. She took the girls off the clock, and the recruits rejoined the party. Adrenaline shot through the crowd, and the high schoolers reveled in their moments of glory by diving into more alcohol and drugs.

It's good to be the king! thought each recruit. Some were too drunk to be disappointed when their conquests paired up with team members or regular students looking for trouble and willing to pay for it. Raul Zogo asked the Sheik to spot him a few bucks. He was going to party with the Rime triplets. Zogo was good for it, and the Sheik laughed as he handed over the Franklins. He walked arm in arm up to the master bedroom with his Amazon women.

The *Orlando Sentinel*, Sunday, September 21, Seminoles Buried with Hatchett

In a slaughter worse than Wounded Knee, the Seminole Nation reeled from the 56–0 shellacking at the hands of the Florida T&A Barbarians. In front of 110,000-plus at Hurl Stadium and a national television audience, the early-season Big South showdown turned into a Big South blowout. The game was delayed at the start after free safety Scrum Laneal attacked the Florida State Seminole mascot and knocked him off his horse. The two teams rushed to midfield, and a major brawl ensued. Helmets were flying, and punches were thrown as the eye of the fighting splintered off into several directions. Head coach Merl Larrola argued vociferously as several of his players were ejected. That included starter Laneal. The game finally started, but Barbarian taunting, which resulted in several more flare-ups, marred the event. The stands became a battleground as local law enforcement was called in for the safety of the visiting Florida State fans.

Once the game did start, the Barbarians rolled from the opening kickoff. The Seminoles looked shaken from the altercation and appeared intimidated the rest of the afternoon. Worm Roanen ran wild in the first half, gained 142 yards rushing on twelve carries, and scored three times. B. Siemore Jett hit eighteen of twenty-two passes for 308 yards and connected with four different receivers for touchdowns. Jett found tight end Andrew Spore crossing over the middle for twenty-two yards in the first. Late in the second, Jett hit Whiz Toorleen on a short slant from the Barbarian forty, and Toorleen took it to the house. Florida State was done by halftime. They went into the locker room down 35–0. The head coach for Florida State would not speak to the press.

Florida T&A has a chance to sweep Florida as they travel to the swamp to face the Florida Gators next Saturday. The 3–0 Barbarians will have a commanding lead in Division A of the Big South Conference if they return with a win from Gainesville.

Gweer Chonds Barren Hell

Froln searched the Bevter raft for necessary supplies. He found water and rations that would last only a few days. He handed out Plimter shoes, which would help the survivors adjust to the different gravity on Foccod Knort. Team Nimrod strapped on the Plimter shoes and found their balance. They filled the sacks with water, rations, and Tustori skins, which provided protection against the howling sandstorms of Gweer Chonds Barren Hell.

Froln and Team Nimrod charted their course. Froln unfolded the map on the wreckage of the Bevter raft. They looked over his shoulder. "We are here." He pointed to the map. "We will walk west through Gweer Chonds Barren Hell. Unfortunately the rocky desert provides very little cover if a Decrof X scouts the area. For all I know, we could be walking into Geeshi Grub's main army." Froln checked the energy of his tritonon clips. "If we bump into any trouble, we won't have much to defend ourselves with." Thomas swallowed hard. "We should be able to reach the Ynarroy

Pyramids by nightfall. We will follow the foothills by Depra Caves and head toward the Enen Rivers and Ursula Peak. We should be able to see the Acrir Marker from the desert."

"What is the Acrir Marker?" Jairus beat the others to the punch.

"The Acrir Marker is a light at the top of Ursula Peak. It is a directional marker for all lost travelers. It's like a lighthouse for the desert." Froln patted the boy on the head.

Jairus was easy to like. Although, he had funny hair.

"From there we head through Smurralley Lands to Sleoc Choiry." Froln waited for the question.

"What is Sleoc Choiry?" This time it was Vishnu.

"Sleoc Choiry is a quarry used for mining weapons-grade tritonon."

"I'm sorry. I was under the impression the Sleoc Choiry was already in the hands of the syndicate." Nimrod wondered why Froln would take them right into the enemy.

Froln showed Nimrod the map. "The land narrows at the base of Ursula Peak and into Smurralley Lands. Sleoc Choiry lies just past there. There is no other route to take us to Jorrmy Erhe." Nimrod took a deep breath. "We will take every precaution, but we will be in harm's way."

Thomas sat on the heated sand and put his head in his hands. Shar held Jairus close. She knew the child would be frightened. Nimrod had to trust Froln. He had saved their lives. The map truly showed no other way.

The storm broke. The tempest would be a daily occurrence. The desert was sheer from the storm, and the sand was pristine like new-fallen snow. The sun sank in the sky. In the distance they saw the Ynarroy Pyramids. The Decrof X destroyers ruined the view. Small villages smoldered next to the rubble. The great pyramids had been on Foccod Knort for fifteen thousand years. It had not been long since the syndicate had raided the site. They walked closer and saw the dead scattered among the dunes. The charred remains of the deceased were half buried in the sands of the storm. Their limbs stuck out like tree branches. Sand filled their mouths. Nimrod shielded Jairus's eyes, but he had already seen.

They were up before the sun. "Can you eat these plants?" Vishnu asked hungrily.

"They are called Rank Mulber. When they blossom, they flower. Those are quite edible and delicious," Froln said. Vishnu played with the bud. "But don't touch the plant before the bud blossoms." It was too late. Vishnu had his hands all over the Rank Mulber plant. "They have a pollen that infests the skin and germinates a seed inside the intestine."

Team Nimrod looked hopelessly at Vishnu. He jerked his hand away from the bush. "What happens when the pollen infests the skin and the seed germinates in the intestine?"

"Don't worry, Vishnu. You won't die. The seed has only one effect on the host." Froln stood far away from Vishnu.

"What's that?" Vishnu was happy to hear his skin wouldn't fall off.

"In about an hour, you will smell so bad that no living thing will want to be within twenty yards of you." Froln held his nose with his fingers. "The worst part about it is you can't get away from yourself. You will have to march in your own stench. Your skin also now carries the pollen. No one can touch you, or he or she too will become infested."

"Wait, wait, and wait. How do I get rid of this?" Vishnu wasn't sure how bad it would be, but he didn't want to find out.

"A magi can perform an Orligistic Choke." Froln tightened his Plimter shoes.

"Why can't you perform this Orligistic Choke?"

"Only the magi knows how to release the seed without infesting himself. I don't know the trick. I've seen it done. It's a painful maneuver where he inverts the body, squeezes near the neck, and…" Froln looked at Vishnu's groin area, and Vishnu checked his package.

About an hour into the walk toward the Depra Caves, Vishnu settled some fifty yards behind the group and downwind. He smelled so bad that even downwind most of the group was on the verge of vomiting.

Week Four, The Yard

Home football games gave the plebes the honor of painting Tecumseh, and they paused from their Friday joy to watch the colors. The flag came down for the day, and all in the yard stood and saluted Old Glory. The midshipmen folded the flag into a perfect triangle, and the plebes finished the artwork on the Indian. Plebe Jason Emenith had chosen to ring Tecumseh's head with a likeness of the golden Navy helmet for the week's contest versus Maryland. Tuby took his hand off his heart and watched the excitement of the plebes as they enjoyed one of the few privileges extended to them during the first year.

The vagrant broke the seal on the bottle of rum. The pint had cost him less than four dollars at the corner liquor store. Balam instructed the Watcher to send a message. Demons entered human form through the excess liqour. The rum dribbled from the corner of the vagrant's mouth and into his ratty beard. The Watcher became one with the alcohol. The vagrant ran his tongue through his beard and relished every drop. The Watcher entered the man's weakened soul. The vagrant's eyes glazed. They darkened to a greenish hue. The vagrant stood in the alley and hurled obscenities at the wall. He hoisted the bottle and slugged down giant swigs. The sweet sugarcane drink and the Watcher sent him into madness.

Tuby left gate C and turned to head up the hill by the Maryland state capitol. A vagrant staggered in the streets. Tuby slowed the

Cadillac. The vagrant wheeled, threw a bottle at the Cadillac, and hit the grill.

Tuby rolled down the window. "Hey! What do you think you're doing?" Tuby lit into the vagrant.

The vagrant lunged at the open window and growled. Tuby looked into the unearthly green eyes. They were menacing. He saw his daughter, Jane, and granddaughter, Emily, reflected in the evil green frost. The vagrant clenched his teeth and hissed, "Die!"

The *Baltimore Sun*, Sunday, September 28, Midshipmen Leave Terrapins Stationary

No one left Navy Marine Corps Memorial Stadium on the first fall Saturday of September. In a win for the ages, Navy held on to beat interstate rival Maryland with a desperate defensive stand on the last play of the game. The 12–7 victory moved the midshipmen to 4–0 for the first time in twenty years and left Maryland pondering how they didn't come away with a win.

Once again the Navy offense rode the leg of placekicker Howdy Osaye, who scored all the midshipmen's points on four field goals. The mids struck first. Tug Lerrin led the offense on a smart opening drive that stalled at the Terrapin seventeen. Osaye drilled the field goal after Navy had chewed up almost eight minutes of the clock. The swarming Navy defense rudely greeted Finger Chairif, the Maryland quarterback, on the Terrapins' opening drive. It took the Terps until late in the second to get things going. Rich L. Chatters and Sal Geayser lived in the Terp backfield, and Chairif wasn't able to stay in the pocket long enough to find his dangerous receivers downfield.

Osaye added another field goal early in the second following a dazzling punt return by cornerback Vern Stamcie. Stamcie's gallop to the Terrapin twenty-one gave the mids their best opportunity of the game. They couldn't capitalize for six and settled for Osaye's second of the game. Navy dominated the first half in time of possession and total yardage but trailed at halftime when Lerrin made a mistake in the flat. The Terrapin cornerback picked off a floating pass and returned it thirty-six yards for the touchdown. The 7–6 Maryland lead didn't sit well with Coach Gravenald. "It was a bad pass by Tug. He's a good decision maker, but this time he should have thrown it away."

The second half developed into a fierce defensive struggle. Navy found an opportunity after a Chairif fumble, but once again the struggling Navy offense couldn't muster the will to get it to the end zone. Navy went up 9–7 on Osaye's third, and Lerrin found tight end Elmo Linners down the seam early in the fourth for a big forty-five-yard gain that set up Osaye's fourth from the twenty-five. Osaye converted the forty-two yarder, and Navy held a not-so-commanding lead at 12–7. Chairif found his range with two minutes left in the fourth and the game on the line. An Osaye punt gave the Terrapins awful field position at their own sixteen. Chairif hit his flanker in the flat for a twelve-yard gain to move it to the twenty-eight. A draw to the tailback picked up another fifteen to bring the Terps to the forty-three. Maryland called their first time-out with 1:01 on the clock. Chairif misfired on his next attempt but scrambled on second and ten for twelve more yards. Chairif called the second time-out. The coaches screamed for him to spike the ball to stop the clock. Maryland had the ball on the Navy forty-five with forty-six seconds to play. Chairif hit the flanker again in the flat for thirteen yards, and the clock stopped with thirty-eight seconds. In a questionable call, Maryland ran a draw play. The play burst up the center, and middle linebacker Sal Geayser stopped the tailback at the twelve-yard line. Not wanting to call their last time-out, Chairif watched the clock tick as the offensive linemen prepared to stop the clock. Only seventeen seconds remained, but the Terps were at the twelve. They ran a wide sweep to the right on second down, but that didn't fool the Navy defense. The tailback only gained two but got out of bounds. With twelve seconds left, Chairif found his tight end over the middle, and he muffed the ball. The referee threw the flag for pass interference. The capacity crowd booed the questionable ruling, and Coach Gravenald ran willy-nilly up the sideline. Maryland lined up on the Navy half-yard line, and Chairif tried to go over the top. Sal Geayser popped him in midair, and Chairif tumbled backward. Maryland called their last time-out. With three seconds to play, they sent Chairif over the top again. Chatters, Geayser, and Prime all met him in midflight and drove the quarterback into the ground. He left his shoes in the pile. The midshipmen stormed the field, and Crabtown readied for a crazy Saturday night.

Maryland fell to 3–1 and a game behind Navy in Conference A of the Big Beast. The midshipmen travel to Colorado Springs next week to meet military rival Air Force in a quest for the Commander-in-Chief's Trophy.

Florida T&A

The second she left, Larrola dialed President Garth A. Moot. He requested she be reassigned or terminated. So what if Theo Drimend couldn't read? He was going to sign a professional contract for millions. It was true the coach didn't know that the history of video games was a class researching the origins of pioneer games such as Pong, Galaga, Centipede, and Ms. Pac-Man. He just didn't have time for tutors or teachers. His next scheduled appointment was much more important. His personal psychic, Starry Zbriew, was waiting in the lobby. She had brought her tarot cards, and head coach Merl Larrola was excited to see the future.

The *Orlando Sentinel*, Sunday, September 28, Barbarians Own Florida

In a three-week blitz, the Florida T&A Barbarians have left no doubt who rules the Sunshine State. After thumping Miami in

Miami and leveling the Florida State Seminoles at Hurl Stadium a week ago, the Barbarians completed the run of the state with a 33–7 drubbing of the Florida Gators at Florida Field. More than eighty-three thousand jammed the Swamp, which Barbarian players mocked as "the romp." Florida T&A fans were out in force. They were waving brooms in the stands and taunting the Gator faithful that a Florida sweep was imminent.

The day belonged to wide receiver J. J. "Honey" Romans. The swift wide receiver caught twelve balls from quarterback B. Siemore Jett and amassed a school record 245 yards receiving. The garish twenty yards per catch led to Romans's three first-quarter scores. Jacko Nobs remained perfect on PATs, and when the teams changed sides for the second quarter, the Barbarians boasted a 21–0 lead. The Barbarian defense keyed in on star Florida tailback EZ Pete Rolle. Middle linebacker Buster Chagora and teammates Bones Jetr and Marble Calple limited Rolle to thirty-six yards on twenty-three carries. The punishing Florida T&A defense was flagged for several late hits, and Cisco Deerrink was ejected for the second of two helmet-to-helmet collisions. One resulted in a Florida wide receiver being taken off the field on a stretcher. Deerrink could be seen on the field big screen reenacting the collision that sent the Florida receiver to the hospital.

Fights once again erupted in the stands as the home crowd engaged the Barbarian fans. The visiting section defended itself with their brooms and created a domino effect within the Barbarian band when the melee slammed into the tuba section. French horns and clarinets littered the sidelines, and law enforcement restrained those involved in the riot. Bloodied drum majors and drill team members were treated for minor injuries after the guardrail collapsed and they spilled onto the field. One band member was taken away by ambulance when an angry Gator fan clubbed him with a loose bass drum.

Koctfloub Howl

Froln checked the skies. Things looked clear, but it was well into the evening. They would travel in the morning. They would also sleep in the caves. It was safer.

Vishnu talked with Jairus of happier times. "In my seventh incarnation as Krishna, I fell in love with Lakshmi. She was beautiful. She would rise out of the water with a lotus in her palm. I would read her verses by Kabir, the Indian poet, and we would dangle our feet in the Ganges."

The story mesmerized Jairus. He knew nothing of love's power. "Is it true the river of Ganges flows from your toe?"

Vishnu laughed. "Ganges is the holy river of India. Its waters are sacred to all Hindus. People wash away evil in its waters, and the ashes of the dead are thrown into it. God created the river, as he created the beauty of the universe. I was only God's messenger. The people created that myth."

"Why do people believe in you more than God?" Jairus asked.

"Because civilizations only believe what they see, hear, or touch." Vishnu avoided the smell part. "Though we bring God's message to the people, they lack the faith to believe what they have not seen. They turn the messenger into the God."

"And they don't always listen to what God says." Jairus was picking it up.

"That's right. Sometimes they hear what they want to hear. Other times the Devil twists it all around and confuses everybody."

"What will happen to Satan, Vishnu?" Jairus was sleepy.

"Karma, little man. Karma." They fell asleep in the cool cave.

They were awoken to Shar's screams and the growl of the Koctfloub Howl. It was in the cave. The mangy beast snarled and roared. Its painful cry echoed through the cavern, and Froln instinctively reached for the tritonon clips. He slammed the empty cartridges down in frustration as the Howl showed its fangs. Hunger drooled from the creature's jaws. It charged toward Shar, and she dived out of its path. She rolled, and Thomas yanked her to her feet and pulled her into a nook. The beast searched for another victim. It spotted Nimrod. The massive creature rose on its hind legs. Its razor-sharp claws scratched through the cave's stone like putty. Nimrod was trapped against the wall. The Howl swiped at his belly. If not for the march and dropping a few pounds, his stomach would have been sliced open. The creature roared. Vishnu clapped to draw the beast away. Jairus darted to Froln, who hid behind a stalactite. The Howl turned its focus on Vishnu, but it didn't attack. Vishnu clapped again, and the hunter turned back to Nimrod. Vishnu tried to distract the Howl, but the vicious animal shied away from him. The Howl rose on its hind legs again and prepared to pounce on Nimrod. Vishnu charged the animal and struck it on the back. It slunk away from the diminutive man. Vishnu pressed his unknown advantage against the others' protests. The beast backed away. The Howl snarled at him, but it would not strike.

Froln had figured it out. "He can't stand your smell."

Vishnu charged the Koctfloub Howl. It shuffled away from him and deeper into the cave. Vishnu grabbed the torch and chased the animal deep into the dark. Down and down on the ledges of the cavern Vishnu drove the Koctfloub Howl. He pinned the beast deeper and deeper into the pit.

The group waited for Vishnu to return and heard the pained screech of a dying animal. Vishnu had driven the Howl over the edge and into a pool of pointed stalagmites. Nature's knives drove into the Howl's flesh. The Howl perished while suspended in the bed of doom. The stench of the Rank Mulber had spared Team Nimrod from the jaws of the Koctfloub Howl.

Week Five, The Yard
Vern took Tuby out for some wings. He felt the coach needed to get away from the town house and see Annapolis. Downtown was always charming as they stopped by Dunnigan's.

"Hello, Coach Gravenald. Do you remember me?"

It was Ms. Rain Cutti. *How could I forget?* thought Tuby. She was as pretty as ever and wearing a nice dress. Tuby wondered if she was still as crabby as ever. "Hello, Ms. Cutti. How have you been?" Tuby felt awkward ordering a beer. He wasn't sure if he was out of the no-tolerance zone. Tuby went for broke. "Can I buy you a beer?"

Rain paused. "I don't drink beer, Coach Gravenald." *Uh-oh.* "But I'll have a glass of wine." Tuby handed Vern his diet soda and Vern disappeared into the crowd. "Here you are, Mrs. Cutti."

Tuby handed her a crisp and light New Zealand sauvignon blanc.

"Please. We aren't in the yard. Call me Rain." She actually smiled.

"Well, hello, Rain." Tuby took a sip of the beer. It tasted good. It had been a while.

"I see you're winning your football games." Rain was setting Tuby up. He could sense it.

"Well, they're not my football games, Rain. The team wins the games."

"Do they, Coach Gravenald?"

Here it came—barroom sports psychology. He'd heard it a thousand times. "Yes. They do, Rain." There was a ring of disdain in Tuby's voice.

"Because I see a group of young men waiting to break free of the conservative reins holding them back."

"Ma'am, we're 4-0. I think we've got a pretty good thing going on right now." Tuby set his beer on the bar.

"A pretty good thing, huh?" Rain shifted on the barstool to approach Tuby directly. "It's not all about winning, Coach. It's about teaching. About letting the ropes out and seeing what these young men can and cannot do. That is what education is all about. Finding yourself and your limits. Failure is OK sometimes.

You won't let them try their best. You have won games despite hoping they wouldn't fail. Let them spread their wings. Let them fly. Show them how to dare to be great. If they don't win a football game, at least they lost giving it their best. You're holding the future of these young men in the palm of your hands. Don't hold them back. Set them free."

Tuby thought hard about ordering a Scotch.

"That's the way to do it, Pantry!" Tuby cheered his whipping boy along.

He had had the best week of practice of the year for the group of plebe linemen. He was crisp off the snap count. He made the right reads on blocks. He even got a compliment from end Will Bocher, whom Pantry pinned down a couple times.

"Pantry. Get over here!" Tuby never changed his tone. The burly tackle was heading to the showers after practice. "You had a great week. I'm making you a captain when we visit the Colorado Country Club."

A giant smile crossed Pantry's face. "Thank you, Coach. That's a great honor."

"How are you doing in school?"

This one caught Pantry off guard. He stumbled. "I'm doing all right. I'm worried about my QPE."

"Is that your grade point average?" Tuby wasn't sure what scale the midshipmen used.

"It's a little more complicated than that, Coach."

"Do you think I'm an imbecile, Pantry?" Tuby stepped in front of this week's captain.

"No. No, sir!" Pantry was wobbly. He had never meant to insult the coach.

"Well then, tell me what QPE is."

"Sir, for each course multiply the QPE by its credit value— usually the number of times the course meets per week. For example, if the midshipman has a C in calculus and calculus meets four times per week, then multiply two—a C is worth two points—by four for four hours per week. Add the resulting products for all courses taken. Divide that sum by the sum of the credits' values for all the courses taken. Round that number to two decimal places, and that is the QPR. The QPR is generally expressed for six, twelve, and sixteen weeks as a semester quality point ratio—SQPR—or overall as a cumulative quality point ratio, CQPR. The latter is often phonetically called a seekyooper. The CQPR is important, but it's only sixty-five percent of your grade. We're graded on class standing, conduct, military performance, physical education, athletics, and order of merit. From these we receive privileges. I want to be on the Superintendent's List."

"You see? That wasn't so hard. Hit the showers."

"Yes, sir!"

Pantry headed for the locker room, and Tuby's head was spinning.

The *Baltimore Sun*, Sunday, October 5, Navy Grounds Falcons
The first cold winds of autumn blew from the Colorado Rocky Mountains into Falcon Stadium as Navy and Air Force met in the first leg of the chase for the coveted Commander-in-Chief's Trophy. Navy's formula for success, a strong defense and manufactured points, were the difference today. Navy edged a tough Falcon team 14–10 in front of fifty-one thousand fans. Senior Air Force quarterback Air Myktona got the triple option for the Falcons going early. He engineered the opening drive down to the Navy twenty-three with a combination of masterful pitches and timely cutback keepers. The off-balance Navy defense, the strongest facet of the team, struggled to match Mytkona's clever deception with the pigskin. The ultimate surprise came on first and ten from the Navy twenty-three. Working out of the triple option, Myktona faked to the fullback and second man through.

The leery Navy squad stayed close to the line, and Myktona stepped back. He threw a strike to his wide-open tight end, who was standing all alone in the end zone. The drive covered eighty yards in 6:32.

Navy struggled mightily on offense again. Tug Lerrin was out of sync most of the first half. His throws were off, and he didn't seem to have a command of the offense. Navy punted seven times in the first half, and Howdy Osaye made each drive for the Air Force a long one. Navy's defense settled down, and most of the second quarter was played in the middle of the field. The bend but don't break philosophy worked. Air Force racked up rushing yards, but the midshipmen stiffened when they had to. Falcon punts put the mids in terrible field position. However, mini drives and Osaye's stellar punting bailed them out. Myktona moved Air Force into field-goal range just before the half, and the Falcons put three on the board to take momentum and a 10–0 lead into the locker room. Coach Gravenald promised to "change the tempo" when Navy came out for the second half.

The Navy offense looked worse than ever at the start of the second. Lerrin handed to Johni Bronson for a two-yard loss. Lerrin tried to hit wide receiver Gerry Johnson on a wide receiver screen, and he dropped seven more yards. On third and nineteen, the Falcons blitzed, and Lerrin went down in a heap. Staring at fourth and twenty-three, Navy pulled off the play of the game. Osaye set back to punt from his own seventeen and received the snap. He went to kick but pulled up and fired a strike to tight end Elmo Linners. It surprised the sleeping Falcons. Linners rumbled all the way to the Air Force thirty-three. The forty-six-yard play was the longest of the Navy season. Gravenald said after the game, "I wanted to let the players have a little fun." Inspired by the big play, Tug Lerrin came alive. He gained ten on a quarterback draw to take the mids to the twenty-three. On the next play from scrimmage, Navy scored its first touchdown of the season. Lerrin found possession receiver Jason Drone by the flagstick in paint.

Still working with a 10–7 advantage, Air Myktona patiently moved the ball down the field. A pitch to the tailback got them a first down. Myktona scrambled around the right end for another fifteen yards. Mytkona's mastery of the option had most of the crowd looking the other way, and he handed to the fullback and faked the keeper. The fullback shot through the belly of the midshipmen defense down to the Navy seventeen. Once again Navy denied the Falcons the end zone, and Air Force sent on the field-goal unit. The kick was blocked and nullified a beautiful drive.

With Air Force holding a slim three-point advantage, Myktona worked the clock. The Falcons were driving again and had the ball at the Navy forty-nine. With 3:15 to go, a touchdown would have iced the game, and a field goal would have put Navy in dire straits. Myktona worked the option to the short side of the field. Tackle Spike Himpp broke through the line and made Myktona pitch early. The ball fell behind the tailback, and the Falcon player slipped while reaching for the loose ball. Outside linebacker Barnett Prime scooped up the ball and raced forty-five yards down the sideline to give Navy the lead. Osaye drilled the all-important extra point, giving the Mids a 14–10 advantage. There was no dramatic comeback for the Falcons. The Navy defense was high from the game-winning play and stopped the Falcons on downs to end the game.

The Falcons dropped to 3–2, while the US Naval Academy moved into rarified territory. The 5–0 mids head to face Rutgers and the Scarlet Knights next Saturday.

Florida T&A
It was homecoming week on the campus of Florida T&A. The Sheik was going to have a big week. He and his protection, outside linebacker Bones Jetr, met Steve Skoallero behind the warehouse.

Everybody was gone for the day. Nobody would bother them. They had done this a million times. Steve opened the back hatch of his Hummer H2. Everything the Sheik had ordered was there. Three ounces of cocaine, split and ready for distribution. A sheet of LSD called Neon Carrot. Pig pink uppers and downers. A bag of Percocet—a favorite among the players. Lots and lots of pills of ecstasy—another popular choice among the weekend warriors. Crystal meth for the hard-core stooges in the crowd, and ten pounds of the ever-popular green bud.

"I threw in a bonus just for you, Sheik." Skoallero was happy to do business with the giant tackle. He always paid up front and never carried a weapon.

"What's that, Steve?" The Sheik liked a good surprise as much as the next person.

"This is a brick of Moroccan black hashish." Steve tossed it to the Sheik.

"Excellent!" The Sheik would keep it for himself.

The Sheik handed a folded wad of money in a rubber band to Steve. There was no need to count it. It would all be there. Jetr transferred the contraband into the back of the Sheik's Navigator, and the two headed to the liquor store to pick up a grocery cart full of booze and kegs.

Ali called bookie Shark Mulfalla. It would cut his cost dramatically if he offset his expenses with a weekend win. "We're minus thirty-four?" The Sheik turned the corner while he thought. "It is Southern Mississippi. Put three large on us." Ali clicked the cell phone shut. He was scheduled to pick up from Shark's mule, Bag Man Roue. He was ten thousand up with a lot of games to play. It was only money.

The *Orlando Sentinel*, Sunday, October 5, Barbarians Crush Southern Mess

If Southern Mississippi was expecting a letdown from Florida T&A after three weeks of big intrastate rivalry games, it didn't happen. If Southern Miss was hoping the Barbarians might be looking ahead to incoming Georgia next week, it didn't happen. In front of another sellout crowd at Hurl Stadium, the overmatched Golden Eagles fell victim to the machine that is Florida T&A 50–5.

The homecoming crowd filled the stands with royal purple and vivid tangerine on a picture-perfect Saturday afternoon. Southern Miss quickly assured the crowd it would not spoil any of the homecoming events planned for the day. The inept Golden Eagles fumbled on the second play from scrimmage, and linebacker Marble Calple picked it up and ran it in for the score. Jacko Nobs added the extra point to make it 7–0. Nobs kicked off again, and Southern Miss had a return set up as Sharrif Acorn found a seam on the left side. He was stripped of the ball with one man to beat. Florida T&A recovered, and B. Siemore Jett promptly found Whiz Toorleen streaking down the sidelines for six more. Three plays into the game, the Barbarians led 14–0.

"You don't spit into the wind, and you don't play Florida T&A at Hurl Stadium on homecoming," boasted head coach Merl Larrola.

For the first time in the season, incidents, on or off the field, did not mar the game. There were few if any Golden Eagle fans in attendance, and the play on the field was uncompetitive. Larrola pulled his starters again. "It's a long season," he said.

The second-stringers did their best to drive Southern Miss into the ground. A mishandled punt by the Barbarian second-string punter put Southern Miss on the board with a safety, and they added a field goal to give them five. Florida T&A scored two more touchdowns in the third and added seven more and a field goal in the fourth. Smiles abounded on the Barbarian sidelines as vendors slipped the starters snacks. Most of the defense was seen eating hot dogs and nachos.

The Barbarians rolled to 5–0, while the woeful Golden Eagles fell to 1–4. The Georgia Bulldogs bring their 4–1 record to Hurl Stadium next Saturday with a chance to tie the Barbarians at the top of the Big South.

Linoc's Torch Whirls

Shar tied Jairus's Jamaican dreadlocks into Mujaha knots. It felt good to have a little fun. Shar laughed at her handiwork, but Jairus liked them. It took their minds off the hunger and the walk. They had reached the limits of Gweer Chonds Barren Hell, but then they entered the climbing phase of the journey. It would now take more time to cover less ground. They had seen more death along the way. The Decrof X continued its extermination of the desert, and scores of burned and mutilated were strewn in their attempts to flee the syndicate. Team Nimrod and Froln relieved the dead of their rations. Others had died so they might live.

The terrain had become rocky. They climbed over ridges and stony hills. They could see the Acrir Marker flashing on top of Ursula Peak. It gave them hope but also teased them. It was still days away.

The volcano blasted into the arid sky. There was a huge wind and fire. The fires started swirling into the sky and rotating at immeasurable speeds. More of the fiery belches of the volcano spurred them on. One and then another of the fervent tempests wound its way down the face of the mountain. It twisted a thousand feet into the air, and the flames swirled around the superheated vortex. Two more vehement twisters vomited from the volcanic bowl and joined the parade.

"Froln!" Nimrod and the group watched.

They were paralyzed as the hotheaded tornado raged toward them.

"Linoc's Torch Whirls."

"What do we do?" Shar screamed.

The volcano had spewed forth two more of the whirling demons.

"There is nothing we can do. We are in God's hands now." Froln was right.

The massive, hellish twisters spread across the desert floor. They couldn't outrun the speeding fire torches. Six of the flaming beasts crisscrossed paths with random fury. There were no caves, ravines, ditches, or ponds in which to hide. They faced their deaths at the edges of Gweer Chonds Barren Hell. They were so close to escaping the clutches of the massive desert. The first of Linoc's Torch Whirls passed the group to their right. The heat was intense. They felt their skin recoil. They held one another so as not to be sucked into the vehemence. The winds pulled them. They knelt on the ground and clung to one another in desperation. Twin whirls zigzagged before them. They passed the anchored nomads. Shar's hair ignited from the intense heat. Nimrod removed his Tustori skins and snuffed the flames. The twins passed, and another went by their left.

"Now!" Froln leaped from the group and ran straight toward the fourth of the flaming serpents.

The group blindly followed. Froln seemed to be darting right into the eye of the Linoc's Torch Whirl, but the entity moved away from him on its random path. The sky sucked up the fifth column, and the sixth passed harmlessly to the north. They turned to watch the remaining whirls shred their way through Gweer Chonds Barren Hell. They danced and leaped across the desert floor and incinerated anything in their paths.

"God was with us today," he said, and the charred wanderers checked themselves for burns.

Week Six, The Yard

Tuby called Ms. Rain Cutti. Lila had gotten him the number. She sounded surprised when he asked her to join him at dinner. They would meet at the Chart House.

The Chart House floated right over the water, and Tuby had scouted a nice widow seat for the two of them. He felt odd asking a woman to dinner. He had always been faithful to Myra. Tuby had no expectations. She looked lovely in a plaid skirt and black turtleneck. She wore a golden brooch shaped like a goat.

Tuby complimented her. "I like your brooch."

"Thank you. This is a lovely table." Rain smiled more than usual.

The server came to get their drink orders. It was nippy outside, and the wind was blowing.

"I think I'll have an Irish coffee." Rain shivered.

"That sounds good. I'll join the lady. Bushmills, please."

The server jotted the order down and headed to the bar.

"I wanted to thank you for the conversation we had last week." Tuby looked for Rain's reaction.

"I thought your actions spoke louder." Rain winked at Tuby. In twenty years as a head coach, Tuby had never run a fake punt from deep in his own end. "The mids are capable of so much more. It was nice to see them gain some confidence."

"It really did work, although it was a very risky play. If it didn't work, the game might have been over right there." The server set the coffees down.

"There's that negativity. It's about believing." Rain had whipped cream on her upper lip. "The US Naval Academy is all about discipline and risk."

"Please explain."

"These kids are going to be flying jets and steering submarines. They're going to be docking aircraft carriers and destroyers. Some of them will lead troops into battle and be forced to make choices about who might live and die. They've been taught the disciplines of the job, but someone has to let them fly the jets for the first time. It takes a ton of courage to let a young pilot land a fifty-million-dollar jet on the deck of a carrier. There is risk in growth. Sometimes pilots crash and burn, but they died trying. It's a hard pill to swallow. For the ones who land, the world opens before their eyes. There is seemingly nothing they can't achieve."

Tuby fidgeted with the straw. "These kids are different from the ones I have had in the past." He didn't look up. "Don't get me wrong. Most of the kids I've coached were great. Most were more talented football players. Football ruled their lives. And mine. It was all about winning. Winning the Big Ten. Securing a bid to a major bowl. Anything but the Rose Bowl was a disappointment. I'd get nasty letters from the boosters if I didn't sign a star kid. They were disciplinary issues and academic issues." Rain let Tuby emote. "The midshipmen possess drives like I've never seen. Football is only a small slice of their days. Their academic workload is extensive. They study physics and engineering and chemistry. They spend their summers on battleships, for Christ's sake. They all live in the same hall. Their unity is special." Tuby let it out. "Football is just a game for them. It's fun. It's a great release from their day-to-day lives. They will all face the real world very soon. None of them will graduate and squander time trying to decide what to do with their lives. No one will pick up a job at Starbucks and wait for the right job to fall into his or her lap. A mid will stand behind the radar screen on a nuclear sub and track the movements of the North Korean navy while underwater for six months. Football is just a game. They all know they can't play forever. That's why they want to give it all they've got right now."

Tuby excused himself to use the lavatory. He washed and dried his hands. Rain was right.

He opened the door, and the Chart House was eerily empty. There was no one left in the bustling establishment. He had only been in the bathroom for a few minutes. *Where had everybody gone?* A black wolf jumped over one of the dining room tables. A raven-headed demon sat perched upon the growling animal. Andrab, the raven, waved a gleaming sword around his head. Tuby heard the snorting behind him. A hellish blood-smeared unicorn carried Anducias, the fallen angel. Myra was bruised and bleeding, and she lay on the back of the animal. Anducias reared the unicorn back on its hind legs. Myra crumpled to the floor. Rats came from all areas of the restaurant and gnawed at Myra's flesh. Her eyes reflected the millennium of torture she had suffered since her death. She begged for release. Tuby went to her side, but Anducias's sword fell on the table and blocked his path. Tuby stared into the demon's eyes.

"If your team wins another football game, Jane and Emily will die."

The voice was unearthly and terrible. Andrab heaved his sword at Tuby's chest. He heard Anducias laugh. Tuby saw light when he closed his eyes. When he opened them, the restaurant was the same as it had been when he went to the bathroom. Some patrons were looking at him. He felt weak and dizzy. Tuby fell to the floor. The last thing he remembered was Rain screaming for an ambulance.

The *Baltimore Sun*, Sunday, October 12, Scarlett Knights Say Howdy Do That

An impassioned Navy team played one for their hospitalized head coach, Tuby Gravenald. The absence of their coach overshadowed the improbable 9–6 win for Navy over Rutgers. Gravenald was admitted Thursday night after collapsing at a local restaurant. He expressed an interest in rejoining the team for the trip to New Jersey and the matchup with Rutgers. Naval doctors would not permit his release until they had finished tests. Navy's team physician, Dr. Barry Money, told the *Sun*, "Coach Gravenald is being held only as a precaution. He is feeling fine, and we expect him to return for next week's game, if all continues to go well. It is still undetermined why Coach Gravenald collapsed."

Florida T&A

"Let's talk about Andrew Spore." The president looked over some paperwork he had brought with him.

"Andrew Spore. Number eighty-five. Tight end. A handsome, talented young man with great hands. He leads the team in catches with thirty-four. I expect him to go in the top ten in the draft next year."

"He must have great hands, Merl. He also leads the team with kids. He's got five by five different mothers." Moot looked through his glasses at the document. "Coach, I think we've got a bit of a problem." Moot looked concerned, and so did Larrola. It was rare that Moot came to his office. "Some reporter has caught on to a paper trail and traced it all the way back to the university. She claims the university is supporting the families of the players by providing them with apartments and homes for the mothers of these children. She claims current team members are the fathers of twenty-eight children between them. Is that true?"

Larrola never lied to Moot. Moot could solve all the problems, but not if he didn't know about them. "It's very possible."

"Twenty-eight! I think we should make vasectomies mandatory for the football program." Moot was only half kidding.

"How did she get this information?"

"It seems one of the mothers of Buster Chagora's three children was miffed he had another baby by another woman. She felt the other woman got a better apartment and car, and she wanted an upgrade. When it didn't come to fruition, she called a reporter and started to sing. Now this reporter's on my ass. Twenty-eight!" Moot was amazed. "Does this mean we have twenty-eight different apartments and houses to cover?"

Larrola didn't have an answer to that.

"Coach, there are two more things."

"Yes, sir?"

"Johanna Detong's assault is still on the table. I wasn't able to quash the arrest. I'm going to be able to delay the player's arrest until after the title game, but after that I've got to give him up."

"That's OK, sir. He's a senior. It won't affect the program going forward."

"Good. The second thing is I want another national championship."

"Yes, sir."

The *Orlando Sentinel*, Sunday, October 12, Barbarians Dine on Georgia Peach Cobbler, Go 6–0

The Larrsen/Masolp Gorge

Team Nimrod followed the trail into the Ursula Peak Mountain Range. It was some of the steepest climbing in the galaxy. The ground slid from under their feet. They tied themselves together so one of the nomads of the group wouldn't cascade to the bottom of the slopes. Froln looked down from the heights at the Larrsen/Masolp Gorge. The Enen River flowed into the giant fissure and spilled its moisture over a half-mile-wide, 1,200-foot-tall waterfall. It was one of the great natural wonders of Foccod Knort. Billions of gallons of water flowed out of the north Eden Rivers, over the falls, deep into the Larrsen/Masolp Gorge, and into the southern side of the torrent by the A Hieble Vent. The billions of gallons settled and gathered in the gorge and waited for the vent to build up pressure. When the pressure grew, A Hieble Vent launched the billions of gallons into the air and sent the water on its winding journey to the Bophebo Sea. There was danger crossing the Larrsen/Masolp Gorge. There was no bridge. Timing the crossing was paramount. After A Hieble Vent exploded, the waters flowed down the crevasse and eventually exposed the rocks of the riverbed. While the gorge filled with fresh northern liquid from the waterfall, the A Hieble Vent built up pressure. There was a three-minute window to dash across the emptied Eden Rivers and reach safety. The expanse was only a hundred meters wide, but the riverbed was no racetrack. Uneven rocks and jagged stones layered it.

They neared the banks of the Eden Rivers and the gorge. The waterfall's massive resource filled the pit in about ten minutes. The A Hieble Vent exploded. The water ripped through the air, soared hundreds of feet, and then crashed into the waiting riverbed. The swirling rapids churned downstream. The riverbed fell dry for about three minutes after the last session's water drained. The sound of the water filling the gorge and waiting to erupt was intimidating.

"Were never going to make it," Thomas said.

"I agree with Thomas. Is there no other way?" complained Vishnu.

"What if we try farther downriver?" suggested Shar.

"I wish there were some other way. This was the way of the ancient explorers of Foccod Knort long before there were bridges and aircraft to pass over the great expanses," Froln told them.

"There must be a bridge somewhere," protested Nimrod. He was in agreement with his friends.

"No, Nimrod, they are gone. The syndicate destroyed them all to trap the Kipren Army."

Thomas had another good idea. "What if we went downriver where there is no A Hieble Vent?"

"The waters run too swift and deep. The current will swallow you, and you will drown."

"What if we follow the river to the sea and cross there?" Shar didn't want to do this.

"It would add another month to the journey. That direction also leads to Faynone West—the concentration of the syndicate. They have set up a base by the Bophebo Sea."

Team Nimrod stared glumly at one another. It was now or never. They tied themselves to one another with the rope they had used for climbing. It was a one-for-all venture. They watched two more cycles of the A Hieble Vent.

"We will move slowly," Froln stated.

"Not too slowly!" Thomas added.

"And surely," Froln continued. "If we go too quickly, one of us will get trapped in the rocks."

"If we go too slowly, we will all drown," Vishnu said.

"Maybe you should be in the rear, Vishnu. You could use the bath." Nimrod needled.

The gallows humor relaxed the group. They only cheated by seconds. They started while a few inches of water still covered the rocks. Their Plimter shoes filled with icy water. The tide was quick, even at the recessed level. All teetered on the rocks and tried to maintain their balance. They questioned the idea of tying themselves together. If one fell everyone would go. The water level dropped, but the sound of the gorge filling made them tense.

"One minute and thirty-one seconds," Froln said.

They were behind. The clock had ticked past halfway, but they had not attained the center. Froln increased the pace. In succession they followed in his footsteps as he hopscotched his way through the jagged stones. They had found a better rhythm.

"Forty-three seconds left."

Froln found the edge of the banks. They all needed to be at the top of the banks, or they would be swept away. Froln waited for all to step foot on the other side. First was Shar and then Jairus. Thomas came next and then Vishnu. Nimrod brought up the rear.

"Fifteen seconds."

They reversed the order of the chain. "Nimrod, you go."

There was no time to waste. Nimrod climbed to the top of the banks. The gorge swelled and began to roar. Vishnu pulled his foot onto the ledge. The ground rumbled beneath them. They pulled up Thomas and then Jairus by both hands.

"Two seconds."

Shar planted both feet firmly into the soil as the A Hieble Vent erupted. The energy was intense. Froln crawled up the side of the trench as the water crashed upon him from a thousand feet. Team Nimrod pulled in a giant tug-of-war against the natural wonder. The current pulled them toward the edge. Froln disappeared into the fury of the rapids. They dug their heels in. Thomas yanked with all his might, and the mist from the geyser drenched them cold. The initial surge dissipated, but the waters still raged down the Eden Rivers. They pulled Froln's limp body to the riverbank. They laid his blue skin on the wet bank. Shar reached to him and gave him the kiss of life. She kissed him again and breathed air into his lungs. She pounded his chest like a sledgehammer with both fists. She kissed him again. Froln coughed. He coughed again. Water spilled over his cheeks and down the side of his neck. He coughed one last time and sucked in air.

Week Seven, The Yard

Tuby had called Jane and Emily every day since the night at the Chart House. Ms. Rain Cutti had called Tuby every day since the night at the Chart House as well. The doctors gave Tuby clearance to go back to work. They found nothing physically wrong with him. His blood pressure was high but within reason. They chalked it up to stress. Tuby hadn't told anyone he had seen demons in his dreams and while awake. The last message the demon had sent scared Tuby. "Jane and Emily will die." The words haunted him. He decided to see a shrink.

He met Dr. Ginna Chairmen off the yard. It was not in her office or his office. It was just a cup of coffee and a chat. It was a professional visit, but Tuby wanted no insanity rumors circling. He thought he might be but decided to talk to the doctor.

"Are you Coach Gravenald?" Tuby stood to greet the doctor. "I'm Dr. Chairmen."

"I'm sorry to meet you away from your office, but I've learned there are eyes everywhere."

"You sound paranoid, Coach." Tuby was already being psychoanalyzed.

"I was referring to the press and my players, Dr. Chairmen."

"I was just kidding—a little psychiatric humor." *Defensive,* thought the doctor. "Tell me, what's really on your mind?" Chairmen pulled out a notepad and pen.

Tuby looked out the window and decided against leaving. It was now or never. Maybe he was crazy after all. "I've been having horrible nightmares."

"Nightmares are a normal sign of stress. What do you see in these nightmares?"

This was hard for Tuby to describe. It was and it wasn't. He knew exactly what he had seen. *Would telling the truth make him a wacko?* "I've been seeing demons. I've been seeing my wife with the demons." Tuby looked at his shoes.

"Are you still with your wife?"

"No. She passed this past April." Tuby tried to think of good times with Myra, but the images of her in pain still stuck like a sharp stick in his mind.

"You said you've seen your wife with the demons. In what way?"

"In every horrible way imaginable."

"Sexual?"

"Yes." Tears filled Tuby's eyes from the memory of his dreams. "And they were beating her. Skinning her alive. The worst parts of Hell you could imagine."

"Did these demons have names?" Tuby nodded. "Do you remember them?"

"Yes. I remember all of them. How can I forget? The demons names were Semyala, Succubus, Incubi, Andrab, and Anducias.'"

"Did they all appear in the same dream?" Chairmen jotted down the names.

"No. I've had the dreams over several weeks. They only came at night, and then one of them came when I was in the shower. Two appeared the night I collapsed at the restaurant."

"I need to ask you some questions, Coach Gravenald. If you tell me the truth, it might help me help you." Tuby nodded again. "Did you love your wife?"

"Dearly."

"Were you faithful to her?"

"Yes."

"Have you been seeing another woman since her death?"

"No. I met a friend for a drink."

"Do you have feelings for this woman?" Chairmen looked for the truth in Tuby's eyes.

"I don't know. I feel attracted to her. I like her company. But I don't think it's gotten to that point. I don't know if I want it to go beyond this point."

Chairmen chewed on the end of her pen. "Was your wife faithful to you?"

"Yes."

"Are you sure?"

"With all my heart I trusted Myra. I don't think she ever cheated on me."

"Are you a religious man, Coach Gravenald?"

"Not really. I believe in God. I go to church. Sometimes."

"Do you read the Bible?"

"No. Not very often."

"Have you ever studied the Bible?"

"No. Never."

"How did your father handle the passing of your mother?"

"I never knew my father. My mother raised me on her own."

"How did you handle the passing of your mother?"

"I cried. She was a tremendous influence on my life. Since I didn't have a father, she did a great job being both parents. But nothing like this happened."

"Have the demons ever tried to harm you?"

"Yes. In the shower. One tried to strangle me. In my bed one tried to suffocate me."

"Has anyone else in your family had similar dreams?"

"No." Tuby wasn't so sure about that one. "At least they haven't mentioned it to me. The demons did say they would kill my daughter and granddaughter."

Dr. Chairmen sipped on her coffee and settled her thoughts. "Coach, losing a loved one is one of the most traumatic things humans go through in life. It often takes years to accept death. Even the strongest people exhibit drastic behavioral swings. The time that has elapsed since your wife passed has been brief. Your emotions are still swirling inside your head. Grieving is a long process. Combining that with the added stress of living in a new environment and accepting the heavy burden of a new job might just be too much for your heart and brain to process. I'd like to do some research on some other aspects of the interview, and I would like to see you again if you feel comfortable with that."

"I'd like that very much."

She passed him her card. "In the meantime I know you are very driven. Professionally. Congratulations by the way on the exciting season your team is having."

"Thank you."

"If possible try to relax at work. When you have the opportunity, talk to your daughter about your wife. Tell her you miss her mother. She might be having the same feelings as well. It could help both of you with your grieving."

"So you don't think I'm insane?"

"No. You're not insane. Your brain is fighting on too many fronts. It needs to sort things out. I do want you to call me if you have another nightmare. That's why I gave you my card." Dr. Ginna Chairmen had to leave. "How about we plan to meet in two weeks?"

"That sounds great." Tuby put the card in his front pocket. He felt better already. Just being able to tell somebody the story was a relief. Tuby wondered whether he should have taken the job. Maybe the physicians and psychiatrists were all right. Maybe he was just really stressed and making himself mental. Tuby finished his mocha and headed back to the yard.

Abaddon, the pale white angel of death, sat in the booth in the corner. The king of the abyss watched the good doctor leave. It was going to be a thrill to drive a screwdriver through her neck.

Everybody was dressed to the nines. Homecoming was a special event. The midshipmen packed the hall with their dates. There were some really pretty girls, but it was mostly a big sausage fest. Pantry watched with Gareloin and Emenith as some of the players came in with dates. Here came Ronn Judge and Jane Thoma. They gave him a respectful right-hand salute. The photographer, Lynn Claiborne, took the arm of wide receiver Jason Drone. The hands went up for the lovely Sherri Rastagon and Rolly Leaky. They had already caught Stammy dancing with a plebe, Dahlia Werrch, but nobody got in trouble until they hooked up. Coach Gravenald received a humungous round of applause. Dressed in a suit and tie, Coach Gravenald escorted the lovely Ms. Rain Cutti. Jack Mohney was with the civilian knockout of homecoming, Mona Shuttarm. The boys gave their center a big salute. The plebes had waited for this part of the evening—slamming another firstie. Outside linebacker Barnett Prime held hands with Brenda V. Talp. The boys made their presence known and gave the upperclassmen a left-handed salute. They had just informed him he had the ugliest date of the dance. They ran.

The *Baltimore Sun*, Sunday, October 19, Navy Climbs over Mountaineers, Moves to 7–0
Rain only read the first paragraph. "Something happened to Navy football and Coach Gravenald while he was in the hospital. That something happened just in time. In front of a sellout homecoming crowd at Navy Marine Corps Memorial Stadium, Navy's offense came alive as the midshipmen outlasted the West Virginia Mountaineers in a triple-overtime extravaganza. Navy won 45–42, but the game had more twists and turns than the ski slopes of West Virginia."

Navy was 7–0. Rain smiled as she sipped her tea.

Florida T&A, The *Orlando Sentinel*, Sunday, October 19, Barbarians Sting Yellow Jackets, Move to 7–0
It's hard to imagine that Sherman torched Atlanta worse than the Florida T&A Barbarians torched the Georgia Tech Yellow Jackets this afternoon. In front of a capacity crowd that had dwindled by halftime, the Barbarians dismantled the Ramblin' Wreck and won 63–3. The Barbarians rolled up almost seven hundred yards of total offense and scored nine offensive touchdowns.

Tuby watched the highlights on ESPN. That was one hell of a football team.

Ursula Peak
The Acrir Marker, Team Nimrod's beacon for several weeks, sat directly above them on Ursula Peak. The trail would not lead them to the summit. The trail wound through the mountains five thousand feet below the craggy notch. They looked on the vales of Smurralley Lands to the west and north. They could see the Bophebo Sea to the south. Jairus looked back on the trudge

through Gweer Chonds Barren Hell to the east. The gulches and gorges looked impassable, yet they were there. The trail followed a thin cusp around the rim of the Ijolm Pit. A careless step, avalanche, or howling wind could send the travelers fifteen thousand meters down into the dark abyss. Shar was the first to see the ashrams at the base camp in a clearing at the lip of the Ijolm Pit. They moved forth to check for survivors.

"I'd stop right there if I were you." The Kipren Army soldier stuck the KS Teponik Arms into Froln's face.

Everybody froze, and the soldier held his nose from Vishnu's putrid odor.

"Easy, my friend. We're on the same side." Froln had his hands over his head and the gun in his face.

"Turn around."

All of them turned and put their hands on the sheer rock face. The soldier pulled up their shirts from the back. He was checking for the Mulcrew Neon Cachet. It was the symbol or mark of the Dark Army, and it was usually placed on the shoulder blades. "You're clean. Except this one." He pointed at Vishnu.

"He had a run-in with a Rank Mulber." Froln looked at Vishnu, who held his hands up hopelessly.

The soldier kept the gun pointed toward the strangers. Froln noticed he was gaunt and pale. His eyes were hollow, black, and desperate. "What business do you have here?"

Froln spoke for the group. "We are refugees from the Seavisitsen Ark. The syndicate attacked the Ark and destroyed it. We escaped on a Bevter raft, but enemy fire crumpled our engine. We crash-landed in Gweer Chonds Barren Hell. We are walking to Jorrmy Erhe to seek passage to Blanco Trollien."

"The Ark is gone?" Tears filled the soldier's hollow eyes. "My wife and children were on the Ark."

Shar saw the man's pain. "Maybe they were able to leave through the Dunny Gate."

Tears rolled down his face. "I told them to wait for me." Team Nimrod saw the love of his family reflected in his lifeless eyes. They saw the rage for the syndicate behind the love. "I was supposed to meet them there. I've been at war with the Dark Army for five years. We were stationed here on Foccod Knort to defend the planet. When Maroed Rain collapsed, they came in waves. The Decrof X were everywhere. They drove us through the desert and exterminated millions of soldiers. Those who didn't die were captured by the thousands in the Rakwurr Net and taken to the mines of Gholar and Zhoul Lot. Our battalion retreated across the Eden Rivers. We too were trying to reach Jorrmy Erhe and reform the lines on Blanco Trollien. I was to receive leave to send my family to Jouis Aneur, but they destroyed the bridges. We were trapped. I watched as Sode gunfire slaughtered my battalion. I ran. I left my battalion and fled to the mountains." The soldier dropped his weapon. "I should have died with the others."

"You are alive." Nimrod tried to uplift the soldier.

"And what now do I have to live for? My family is dead, and I am a deserter."

"You're not a deserter. You are a survivor." Froln stepped toward the aching soldier. He embraced him and understood his pain. "We all have suffered."

They walked toward the ashram. A shaman prayed at the base of the mountain.

"I am Froln Reem. These are my friends, Nimrod, Shar, Thomas, and Jairus. The smelly one's Vishnu."

"I am Lieutenant Gairwan Nolem. I think I can help your friend."

He walked over to the meditating shaman. A beast's fur shrouded the witch doctor. He stood before Vishnu and chanted. The others stepped away. The shaman danced around Vishnu, waved his hands, and spoke in an ancient tongue. Vishnu's eyes grew wide, but he held still. The shaman cartwheeled in a circle around his patient. He plucked a hair from Vishnu's neck. He grabbed Vishnu from behind, held him upside down, and squeezed his gonads and neck. Vishnu screamed as the vise grip crushed his scrotum. He couldn't breathe. The seed of the Rank Mulber leaked out of Vishnu's right nostril. Mucus covered it, and it fell harmlessly to the ground. The shaman put Vishnu on the ground. He held his nut sack in pain, but the smell was gone. The shaman laughed hideously.

Gairwan prepared a stew for Team Nimrod. Nobody knew what was in it. Nobody asked. They were starving and ate what was given to them. Gairwan smoked the leaves of the Deity Shrub. He was addicted. He smoked until he was out of his mind. He offered the Deity Shrub to his guests. They declined. The shaman took a toke. Team Nimrod watched as the two junkies lay wasted on the top of Ursula Peak. They were inside the ashram and comatose from the narcotic's effects.

"I have seen this before. It explains the fear behind his eyes." Froln looked sadly upon his fallen comrade.

"Maybe it is the Darkness he fears," Thomas said.

"It is the Darkness behind his eyes," Froln uttered.

As the sun of Foccod Knort rose over the eastern range of Ursula Peak, Team Nimrod filled their Dib sacks with food and water for their path down the mountain and into Smurralley Lands. Froln spoke in private with Gairwan. "You can travel with us. I won't leave you behind."

"There is nothing left for me. I have chosen my path. I know where I need to go."

"If not to Jorrmy Erhe, will you stay here?"

"It is my path to follow."

"You need help. You can't stay here. You've become a slave to the Deity Shrub. You have so much to offer. Please come with us."

Gairwan walked to the edge of Ijolm Pit. "My journey has come to an end. I only wish to be with my wife and children."

453

They saw a brief light shine in his black eyes as Gairwan lay back and fell into Ijolm Pit. Nimrod covered Jairus's eyes. Shar screamed in horror. Froln rushed to the edge just in time to see the body fall out of sight and into the void. The shaman wailed in agony. He would have no friend to share his isolation or addiction.

Week Eight, The Yard

Vern filled Coach Gravenald in on the injury report from the West Virginia game. The walking wounded packed Misery Hall, the trainer area in Halsey Field House. Elmo Linners had a deep thigh bruise. Will Bocher had a twisted knee. Ronn Judge was nursing a painful hip pointer. Vern set up the whirlpools baths and massage treatments for these and other players with nicks and contusions.

"Coach, I think I can get them ready by Saturday." Vern was optimistic.

"What's the alternative, Vern?" Coach needed these three starters.

"Palmer, the electrical engineer walk on, has been raring to see some action." Vern said it stone-faced, and it made Tuby smile.

"Work some miracles, Vern."

Tuby slapped his friend on the back and headed to the office to watch some film on Wake Forest.

Jane and Emily drove to the yard to meet Tuby. Jane visited her father a lot but more so after Tuby's stay at the hospital. Jane had asked Tuby to meet her at the midshipmen store. She wanted to get a head start on some Christmas shopping. She looked at the T-shirts and sweatshirts. There were so many styles and emblems. She was having a difficult time choosing the right one. Emily played with her grandpa. Tuby kept the four-year-old close and gravitated to a book about the aircraft carrier USS *Enterprise*. It was called the "Big E." He thumbed through the pages and tucked it under his arm. He wanted to know more about "Bull" Halsey and the great World War II ship.

"Are you Tuby Gravenald?" The voice sounded serious.

"I am. How can I help you?" Emily grabbed Tuby's hand and looked up at the strangers.

"I am Detective Ramos, and this is Detective Jeo. Would you mind if we talked to you for a few minutes?"

Tuby couldn't imagine what was wrong. It was unlikely one of his players had violated the law. "Sure." Tuby held Emily's hand. "Jane!" he called out across the shopping area.

Jane appeared through the racks of clothes, and she looked at the detectives. "Daddy, what's going on?"

"I'm not sure, Janie. These gentlemen just want to ask me some questions." Tuby passed Emily off to Jane.

"Is Grandpa in trouble, Mommy?" Emily asked aloud.

"No. They just want to talk to Grandpa." She scooped the child up and gave Tuby a concerned look.

The men stepped outside.

"What's this all about?"

Detective Jeo asked the first question. "We're from homicide, Mr. Gravenald." Tuby was shocked. "Do you know a Dr. Ginna Chairmen?" He held Ginna's appointment book in his hand.

Tuby stammered, "Yes. Yes, I do. Did something happen to Dr. Chairmen?" The detective said nothing. "We met last week for coffee."

"Do you have a personal relationship with Dr. Chairmen?" Ramos asked.

"No."

"Was it a professional relationship?"

Tuby didn't want to be profiled as a crazy patient. "I did meet her in a professional capacity. I recently collapsed and was admitted to the hospital. The doctors found nothing wrong with me. They said it was stress. I decided to speak to her about stress."

"Why did you choose to meet outside the office?" Jeo continued.

"I wanted a low-key environment. Informal and casual." Tuby could feel Jane watching him from the store window. "Tell me. What happened to Dr. Chairmen?"

"Where were you last night around nine o'clock, Mr. Gravenald?"

"I was with Coaches Mashner and Scormir. We were at Halsey Field House watching film of Wake Forest."

"We'll check that. We have to check all the bases, Coach Gravenald. We thank you for your time." The detectives started to leave.

"Wait! What happened to Dr. Chairmen?"

"Dr. Chairmen was found murdered."

Tuby felt the blood rush to his head. What they didn't mention was she had been dismembered and slit with a chain saw from her groin to her throat. Her heart had been removed from her chest cavity.

The *Baltimore Sun*, Sunday, October 26, Osaye's Kick Leaves Wake Demonized

Annapolis was the place to be Saturday afternoon. Traffic snarled for both the annual boat show and the Navy–Wake Forest match. When everybody finally settled in, they were treated to another Navy thriller. The midshipmen downed the Demon Deacons 31–30 at Navy Marine Corps Memorial Field. The back-and-forth game kept all attendees on the edges of their seats until the last play of the game. Howdy Osaye kicked a fifty-four-yard field goal to win as time expired.

Wake fell to 3–5, and Navy moved to 8–0 to stand at the top of Conference A of the Big Beast. Navy travels to rival Notre Dame in South Bend for a nonconference game with bowl implications.

Florida T&A

The cops clicked away on the camera unnoticed in the car on the street. They were looking through the grand window of Shark Mulfalla's new pad.

"Who's that?"

"That's quarterback B. Siemore Jett. He can't throw with a lot of accuracy, but his receivers are usually wide open, and he always has tons of time. He's got great breakaway speed, but he spends most of his afternoons handing the ball off to Worm."

"He can't escape from these pictures."

"No, sir. He can't. The NCAA will be excited to learn the quarterback for the country's number-one team is consorting with a known member of organized crime."

The players inside were already enjoying a night of gambling. They paired off with the Fire Cherry Debs and tried their hands at blackjack, poker, craps, and roulette. For any sports betting, they had to talk to Shark himself.

"Who's that?"

"That is W. Jackson. He's already got a sheet with us. We caught him scalping tickets to last year's games and the Orange Bowl National Championship Game. Florida T&A kept it out of the press, but he has already committed a parole violation."

Click went the camera. The other cop looked at W. Jackson's rap sheet. "He got pinched for assault as well?"

"Yeah. Here's the kicker. It was his own mother." Click.

"You're kidding."

"Nope." Click.

"What does the *W* stand for?"

"Nothing. It's just a *W*. The players say it stands for 'warhead.' He's quick around the corner and loves to hit the quarterback. This creep is a first team all-American. Can you believe that?"

"Yeah. So was O. J. Simpson."

The *Orlando Sentinel*, Sunday, October 26, Barbarians Cocked and Ready
In what amounted to a tune-up for the conference champion-ship game and the upcoming NCAA play-offs, the Florida T&A Barbarians drubbed the South Carolina Gamecocks here at Williams-Brice Stadium before eighty-two thousand fans. The Columbia faithful watched as the Barbarians dominated in every aspect of the game and completed a sweep of Conference A in the Big South. This secured the Barbarians a berth in the champion-ship game. Two games are left on the regular-season schedule, and both are against Conference B squads—Auburn and LSU. Florida T&A seems assured of at least an at-large bid to the inaugural NCAA play-offs, unless they stumble badly in their last two games.

Sleoc Choiry
Team Nimrod stayed low in the ravines and crevasses of the Smurralley Lands. Plant life again bloomed in the ground, and Ursula Peak looked long in the distance. Over the next ridge they would see the last of the Acrir Marker.

Shar walked and talked with Jairus. "This journey is longer than the hajj," Shar said aloud.

"What is the hajj?" Jairus looked at Shar's face. It reminded him of his mother's—not in looks but in warmth.

"The hajj is the pilgrimage to Mecca. It is one of the five pil-lars of Islam."

"Why do you go to Mecca?"

"In the religion of Islam, they believe Allah is God. They go to worship him in the holy city of Mecca."

"Why are there so many different religions in the universe?"

"God sends his Word with messengers around the universe. The messages are all the same. They are teachings about how to live a good, happy life. To do unto others as you would have done to yourself. The Darkness twists the minds of beings. They become vain and self-important. They believe only their religion comes from their true God. Instead of joining as one, they splinter into many."

"Is that why there is war?"

"Sometimes, Jairus. Sometimes." Shar looked sad. She had seen too much war.

They looked over the ridge at the Sleoc Choiry. The giant hole in the ground was ablaze with activity and illuminated as the syndicate flooded the hole with light. They worked night and day mining the deadly tritonon for their weapons and fuel. Decrof Xs were ubiquitous. Froln checked the KS Teponik Arms he had taken from Gairwan.

"I know we are tired." He looked at the group. "But we must travel through the night. It is our only chance to get beyond the quarry without being seen."

Nimrod looked at his charge. They seemed game. "Agreed."

They sipped some water and started their stealthy path around the quarry. The night grew long, but the manufacturing never stopped. The syndicate hauled and refined the tritonon on the spot. Soldiers refueled the Decrof Xs and XJ Fhoon fighters on the launching pads near the Sleoc Choiry.

"This is as close as we dare. Everyone must stay close and low," Froln said.

He brought the group to the edge of the light. He followed the ravines to stay low and undercover. The ridges had no place to hide. They would have been exposed.

"Who are those people?" Vishnu saw thousands of beings pulling and loading the tritonon onto movers. Sediment covered them, and they were close to starvation.

"Those are monks. They were captured and enslaved," Froln explained.

"Where did they come from?" Thomas hadn't seen any villages in weeks.

"They come from all over the universe," Froln said.

He watched Thomas gulp, and they moved through the night. They were edging away from the quarry. It would be light soon. They needed to be far away by sunrise. Froln suddenly felt the gun in his back.

"Be very still." The soldier was definitely in the syndicate.

Froln looked at Nimrod for help. The other soldiers in the platoon marched to the edge of the ravine. Team Nimrod heard the weapons arm. There would be no combat. They took Froln's KS Teponik Arms. They checked and confiscated the sacks. Froln managed to put the Regall Code radio in his pants. A soldier frisked them for weapons and other contraband. He was sloppy. He didn't find the Regall Code radio. He did find something of interest to the leader. He made Nimrod remove his shirt and reveal two ancient keys etched onto Nimrod's arm—the symbol of living in Heaven.

"Well, well, well. We've caught ourselves a bona fide resident of Heaven."

The soldier slammed Nimrod in the stomach with the KS Teponik Arms. Nimrod crumpled to the ground and heaved for breath. The others were forced to watch their friend suffer.

"The lieutenant will spoil us with extra rations for this prize." The soldier looked at Jairus. Shar pulled him close. "And a female!" The soldiers jumped up and down in sexual excitement. "It's our lucky day," exclaimed the soldier.

They marched the prisoners to the commanding officer, Lieutenant Amonz Agoogass.

"We have brought you a prize," the soldier said. "The Darkness will be pleased."

"Indeed." Agoogass looked at Nimrod. "A lovely prize." His sound was eerie.

"We want our reward," the soldier barked at Agoogass.

Agoogass grabbed the soldier by the neck and squashed his throat. The soldier struggled to breathe and began to choke. He ripped at Agoogass's wrist, but the lieutenant's grip was firm. The soldier turned bright yellow and then magenta. He was dying. The soldier's eyes shut, and Agoogass dropped him to the clay.

"The rest of you, take the boy. I will take the woman." Agoogass eyed Shar with lust.

"You will take no one." Nimrod stepped forward.

Agoogass turned to Nimrod. "You defy me?" Agoogass raised his fist.

"General Oleg will be disappointed if you kill me." Nimrod was bluffing.

Agoogass dropped his hands. "What do you know of General Oleg?"

"Gabriel has sent me to draw a truce with the Darkness." The captives looked angrily at Nimrod as he dug them deeper into a hole. "I alone can deliver the terms to General Oleg."

"Why have you not gone to General Oleg directly?"

"Michael, the archangel, learned of my plot. He sent angels to assassinate me. It was my information that led the syndicate to the Seavisitsen Ark. The death of the Ark would mean the death of me—and the assassins hunting me." Nimrod laid it on thick.

"How did you survive the Ark? I understood no one survived."

"There's a hero born every minute." Nimrod looked at Froln.

Agoogass started to believe Nimrod's claims. General Oleg had received a transmission from an unknown source indicating where the Ark was located. Only select members of the syndicate knew this information. Team Nimrod became confused and wondered if Nimrod had betrayed them.

"Who are these people?"

"These people are my gifts to General Oleg. This is Vishnu, the Hindu deity who battled and foiled the Darkness in millennia past. This is Shahrazad, a queen of Persia and prophet of Allah. This is Thomas, an apostle of Jesus Christ—Satan's enemy. Jairus is nothing. An angel in training, and a poor one at that. I plan to feast on him with the general when I complete our agreement. The mortal, Froln, is of no consequence. Though, General Oleg might want to torture him for information about the Kipren Army."

Froln was furious, and Jairus was heartbroken. Agoogass motioned to his assistant as they communicated with General Oleg. The assistant returned and whispered in Agoogass's ear.

Agoogass then turned and spoke to Team Nimrod. "You will all board a Decrof X and fly to Jorrmy Erhe. You will be imprisoned there. The syndicate has taken over the city and is setting up a forward base. General Oleg is on Gholar. He will board a light transport tomorrow, and he will meet with the angel upon his arrival."

The guards shuffled the captives toward the launching pad. Agoogass was pained at the thought of losing a night with Shar. She would have been a delight.

Week Nine, the Yard
Tuby and Rain stood beneath the Triton Light. The beacon blinked five times and then stopped. Then it blinked four times and stopped. Then it blinked five times and stopped. It was on the same cycle over and over.

"Why does it do that?" Tuby asked Rain.

"I don't know." Rain paused to think.

"Rain Cutti doesn't know a trivia question about the Naval Academy?" Tuby looked at her in disbelief. "I expect you to have that answer on my desk by noon tomorrow."

Rain punched Tuby playfully in the gut. "That's enough, Mr. Wise Guy." They looked out over the waters where the Severn

River and Spa Creek met. It was cold, but they were warm. "Are you doing OK, Tuby?"

"I'm going to be fine." Tuby put his chin into the breeze. "I am getting a lot of help. It's good to have Jane and Emily here." He looked at Rain. "It's good to have you here."

Rain put her head on Tuby's chest. "It's good to be around the players too. They keep you young."

Tuby paused and held Rain close. "It is a different set of problems I've never faced. Now I've got them asking me about thermodynamics instead of dynamic disco hits of the seventies." They both laughed and walked farther down the seawall. "Rain?" Rain turned to face Tuby. "Would you like to join me this weekend? We're going to play Notre Dame, if you haven't heard already." Rain gave Tuby another nudge to let him know he was being a wise guy. "Jane and Emily are invited. They've heard a lot about you. I think it would be great if we all spent some time together."

Rain didn't hesitate. "I'd love to go."

Tuby walked Rain to her car. He declined a ride back to Halsey Field House. He would walk over on his own. The elms and maples were releasing the last of their leaves. A cold, damp Halloween rain dripped across the yard. He cut the corner, and something hanging in the branches of one of the oaks startled him. A body swung from the tree in effigy. Tuby thought this took Halloween a bit too far. He spun the feet of the doll and tried to yank it from the branch. Emily's voice cried out from above. "Help me, Grandpa. Help me."

Tuby scampered to Halsey Field House. He returned with security, but no one was in the tree.

The *Baltimore Sun*, Sunday, November 2, Navy Steals Irish Luck
Notre Dame didn't think Gerry Johnson had caught it. Coach Tuby Gravenald didn't think Gerry Johnson had caught it. The

eighty-one thousand fans at Notre Dame Stadium didn't think he had caught it. Both Touchdown Jesus and the referees made the right call, though, when Navy wide receiver Gerry Johnson picked the four-leaf clover off the tip of the end-zone grass and gave the midshipmen a miracle win of 21–20 over the Fighting Irish.

Navy brought its 8–0 record to South Bend to vie with the 7–1 Irish. Both squads brought their defenses with them, and the first half was a slobber-knocker. Notre Dame linebacker Hi Noggins Jr. was all over the field and blew up the Navy offensive scheme time and time again. Navy fell behind 7–0 on a Nevin Goucy sixteen-yard run in the first. Then Navy hit the Irish hard as well. Linebacker Sal Geayser made key third-down stops, and ends Will Bocher and Earl Whitsche continued to meet at the quarterback. They sacked the Notre Dame signal caller four times. Coach Gravenald was pleased to see the return of his strong defense. "I think we had lost our identity a little in the last two weeks." Navy had only manufactured a pair of Howdy Osaye field goals by halftime, and they trailed 7–6 as both teams healed from the bruising first half.

Notre Dame put Navy in a hole in the third. Goucy found running room on the right side and sprinted to the midshipmen's eight-yard line. The Irish quarterback then found his big tight end in the flat for a touchdown and a 14–6 lead. Navy punted twice, and Notre Dame struck again. This time Goucy broke free through the middle. He avoided a tackle by Timm Mettish and sprinted to the goal line. Cornerback Vern Stamcie collared him at the Navy fifteen. The mids bowed their necks and held the Irish to a field goal, but the Irish took the 17–6 lead into the fourth. Navy then put together its most complete drive of the day. Lerrin moved the mids seventy-eight yards in twelve plays and capped the drive with a four-yard keeper. Coach Gravenald pulled Howdy Osaye off the field when the placekicker ran out for the extra point. The mids went for two, and Lerrin found wide receiver Jason Drone inches past the goal line.

With Navy down by three, 17–14, the Irish worked the clock. They sustained a 6:09 drive that resulted in an Irish field goal from thirty-two yards. Navy only had forty-four seconds when they got the ball back. Lerrin threw incomplete on his first attempt from his own thirty-four. He had to scramble on the next play and was sacked. Navy called time-out. Notre Dame went into a prevent defense. With twenty-four seconds on the clock, Lerrin found tight end Elmo Linners down the middle. The prevent defense worked to perfection. They caught Linners at their own forty-eight with eight seconds on the clock. Navy called their last time-out and came out of the huddle with three wide receivers to the right. "I just told him to throw it as far as he could," said Coach Gravenald after the game. Notre Dame set up a picket line across the goal line, and Lerrin asked for the ball. The three-man Notre Dame rush gave Lerrin plenty of time to set and fire. He heaved the football into the air. Players circled under the ball and waited for it to come down. Golden helmets were everywhere, and arms flailed to knock the ball down. An Irish defensive player did knock it toward the ground, but it went sideways. Navy receiver Gerry Johnson had fallen away from the jump ball. He was just getting back on his feet when the ball was spiked in his direction. He lunged for the ball and picked it off the grass with no time on the clock. The referee was standing right in front of the play and didn't hesitate to call the touchdown. Replays showed it was the right call. Osaye added the extra point, and Navy ran happily off the field. "That play works one in a million times. My hat's off to the Notre Dame squad. They played a heck of a football game," Coach Gravenald said and then went into the locker to celebrate with the players.

Notre Dame fell to 7–2. The 9–0 Navy midshipmen will next play a game in which records mean nothing. They head to

Philadelphia to face Army in the annual showdown for control of the Commander-in-Chief's Trophy.

Florida T&A

Head Coach Merl Larrola was back in front of the microphones at his weekly press conference. It was the part of the job he despised. He pointed to Archi W. Gazet. He usually got things off on the right foot.

"Coach, with Auburn coming into town and with the Conference A title sewn up, do you think you'll rest the starters for the game?"

"No, Archi. We've got bigger goals, as you well know. The starters will play, and we'll remain sharp." Larrola looked at a really pretty girl he had never seen before. He thought he'd give her a break.

"Coach Larrola…"

"Miss," Larrola interrupted, "I don't think we've been introduced."

"I'm sorry. Willow Dyheart of the Associated Press."

"Nice to meet you." Larrola wanted to be charming to the young lady.

"Pictures were circulated last week of your team entering a known gambling hall. Can you comment?" Dyheart had her pen ready.

Here come the dogs, thought Coach Larrola. "The players were attending a charity event, Miss Dyheart." Larrola tried to field the next question.

"Do you think it is appropriate for your team to be associating with organized crime—especially a felon like Shark Mulfalla?"

Larrola scratched his head. "The man paid his dues to society. I don't think it's fair to label him the rest of his life. He was just trying to do something good for a worthy cause."

"What cause was that?" Dyheart pounded away at the sweating coach.

"I don't know. You'll have to ask him. Next question." Larrola was agitated and wanted off the topic.

"Karen Evhy from UPI. Coach, there are numerous reports that professional agents have lavished tackle Shank W. Shonnejoy with trips, boats, dinners, and cars. Can you comment on that?"

"These rumors come up every year. No one has ever proven our players have accepted gifts from agents. That's a fact."

"Shonnejoy was photographed in Acapulco, Saint Martin, San Francisco, and Tahiti. All last summer. How does a college kid afford that?"

Larrola wiped his brow. "Miss Evhy, maybe his family paid for the trips, or he was part of an extensive exchange-student program."

The reporters laughed and bailed out Larrola. Evhy gave Larrola the evil eye and sat down. Dyheart jumped back in the fray. "Coach, J. J. 'Honey' Romans has come under criticism from women's groups about his end-zone celebrations. Can you comment?"

"Yes, ma'am. That's easy. It's just kids being kids."

"Each dance has a specific name. Do you know them?"

"No. I just try to let them express themselves." Larrola pointed elsewhere but couldn't shake Dyheart.

"One of them is called 'Dirty Dancing.' That's where two of your players shove the ball between their legs and grind on each other." Larrola had no comment. "There's 'Jailhouse Love.' The scoring player holds onto the goalpost, pretends the football is a penis, and imitates having sex from behind with another male inmate." Larrola did not comment. "This is a personal favorite—'My Bitch.' A teammate gets on his knees in front of the scoring player and imitates fellatio."

"Ms. Dyheart, we have freedom of speech in this country."

Dyheart dug in. "'Shower Time.' The scoring player puts the ball between his legs and pretends to shower. Other players group menacingly around and imitate a gang rape. 'Pigskin Movement.' The scoring player squats and pretends the ball is a giant turd released from the sphincter."

"Artistic expression," claimed Larrola.

"'Alone with My Sock.' The scoring player actually removes his shoe and sock, pretends to masturbate with the ball, and imitates wiping the semen off with his sock. 'The Vibrator.' The scoring player lies on his back, spreads his legs wide open, and uses the football like a vibrator on his crotch. These celebrations have been used throughout the season, Coach Larrola. Do you see no need to stop this?"

"Miss Dyheart, give them a break. Some of these kids were underprivileged growing up." Larrola left the news conference drenched with sweat.

The *Orlando Sentinel*, Sunday, November 2, Barbarians Tame Tigers

An angry Florida T&A team took to the turf at Hurl Stadium this Saturday afternoon and took it out on the Auburn Tigers. The Barbarians won 45–13. Fueled by rumors of NCAA violations and indecency during the game, the Barbarians played it straight and pounded the visiting Conference B hopefuls.

Auburn's chances of being Conference B champions were helped when Tennessee beat LSU. The Vols, however, can dictate their own destiny when the Alabama Crimson Tide visits Knoxville next weekend. Florida T&A visits LSU, who is now only eligible for a bowl, not the playoffs.

Jorrmy Erhe

No one talked to the traitor Nimrod as they sat handcuffed in the hull of the Decrof X. The daylight blinded them as they disembarked the warship. They looked around at the carnage that was Jorrmy Erhe. The city had been ransacked.

"We were going to catch a transport here?" Thomas questioned Froln.

"'Were' is the key word," Froln said.

He looked at the unbearable holocaust. The dead lay in the streets and on the steps of the pagodas. Bodies of the scribes hung in effigy atop the thousands of minarets that pointed to the sky. Flags of death hovered over the city. The holy Wormbid Bench, the seat in Jorrmy Erhe for God himself, had been reduced to rubble and painted with children's blood. Syndicate soldiers filled the streets and looted the stores for food and trinkets. They raped the survivors in the mosques and then executed them. They filled the Yolna Trollie with the dead and set it on fire. The captives heard the screams of some who had been left alive to burn. The guards had taken them to a makeshift prison. There were no jails in Jorrmy Erhe. It was a city of peace and prayer. War and the Darkness had defiled it. They called it Monvanath Jail. Monvanath was the cruel slave master of Gholar.

Week Ten, the Yard

"Gentlemen, were are nine and oh." A huge roar went up from the players on the practice field. "That doesn't mean crap to me." They looked at Tuby quizzically. "I was hired to win one game. Now let's get to work and beat Hudson High."

The players were on top of the world. Tuby had embraced the language and the players. The yard was ready for Army. The beaters and blowers banged their drums and tooted their bugles. The old admirals polished their antique brass. Joy Leorander interviewed Tuby for the *Washington Post*, and Bella Rogerrty flew in from Chicago and did a piece for *Sports Illustrated*. The midshipmen were getting heavy local and now some national attention. Tuby had been through it all before, but the picture was clearer now. The joy was in the ride. This team would play their hearts out. If they kept winning, so be it. If they lost one on the way, then they had tried their best. Only the secret of his own dreams bothered Tuby now.

The *Baltimore Sun*, Sunday, November 9, In Command: Navy Trounces Army 30–7

Navy must have played all its thrillers for the season. In what is perennially a close matchup between the two military institutions, Navy beat Army 30–7 before seventy-three thousand fans. It was the first contest played at Lincoln Financial Field in Philadelphia.

The midshipmen put their most complete performance together to oust the Army Black Knights. Coach Tuby Gravenald pulled out all the stops after Army won the coin toss and opted to receive. Navy opened the game with an onside kick and recovered the loose ball just before it hit the sidelines. Navy pounced on the opportunity as well. Quarterback Tub Lerrin, playing his final Army–Navy game, drove the midshipmen to the goal line. He sailed over fellow first classman Jack Mohney for the first score of the game. The Navy defense was a wall. Army produced no first downs on its first three possessions. Coach Gravenald then pulled out another trick play. Army lined up to punt, but none of the midshipmen challenged the punt. They all retreated backward and "formed a flying Brazilian wedge," said the coach after the game. The Army punter could have waltzed down the field, but he never picked up his head. He booted a high but short kick, and the well-protected recipient, Rolly Leaky, stayed behind the wedge until it had driven through the Black Knight defense. Leaky scampered in from sixty-eight yards out, and Navy led 14–0. Howdy Osaye added two field goals in the second quarter, and the two teams headed for the locker room with the score 20–0.

Navy got the ball to begin the second half. Lerrin drove the mids downfield behind the stellar running of tailback Johni Bronson. Bronson made a key first down to keep the drive alive when he bowled over two Army defenders and surged past the sticks. Lerrin found first classman Elmo Linners down the seam, and he scored to make the score 27–0. First classmen Timm Mettish and Will Bocher kept the Black Knights off-balance, and each recorded a sack. Gravenald was able to substitute liberally in the fourth. The Navy crowd cheered the first classmen as Gravenald gave the crowd a chance to personally thank them for four years by the bay. Howdy Osaye added a field goal to make the score 30–0. Army cornerback Chili B. Klebell scooped up a Navy fumble and returned it thirty-three yards to get the Black Knights on the board.

In a surprise season that saw two upstart teams win their conferences, Navy will host East Carolina next Saturday for the Big Beast Championship.

Florida T&A
Steer Reprivus watched the co-ed change into her nightgown She was fine. Steer liked soft, virginal women. He liked all women, but it was difficult to get the nice, young, clean ones. He had a face like a hammerhead shark, but he knew what he wanted. He had tried to rape that tutor bitch, Johanna Detong, but she had pressed the panic button on her car, and he had to take off. He was sure his attorneys would take care of that beef. Coach Larrola would see to that. Steer had decided the best way to do the bitches was to kill them afterward. That way they couldn't talk—the same way he had done to that little redhead over the summer. They would never find her freckled ass, and she damn sure wasn't going to talk. Steer watched as the co-ed talked on the phone and watched TV.

The *Orlando Sentinel*, Sunday, November 9, Blue Bayou: LSU Loses to Barbarians' Second Team

When the schedule came out for the 2004 season, pundits circled this game on their calendars. It had all the earmarks of a play-off game before the play-offs. This final regular-season tilt in the inaugural season of the Big South was stripped of any drama when Tennessee beat Alabama in Knoxville 16–10 Saturday afternoon. The night game in Baton Rouge in front of eighty thousand fans at Tiger Stadium was a solemn affair that saw Florida T&A head Coach Merl Larrola rest his starters for the entire game against the disappointed LSU Tigers. The Barbarians' second team disappointed the Tiger faithful even more when they licked LSU 27–14.

The conference championships are set for next Friday and Saturday. Navy will host East Carolina in the Big Beast Championship to determine who will head to the NCAA play-offs. The action swings out west at 8:00 p.m. for the El Niño Conference title game between the Oregon Ducks and Stanford Cardinal. Saturday promises to be football heaven for sports fans around the country. At noon Tennessee travels to visit the number-one-ranked Florida T&A Barbarians in the Big South matchup. At 3:00 p.m. the Big Ten determines its champion as the Michigan Wolverines host the Iowa Hawkeyes in Ann Arbor. Television fans will have just about an hour for dinner. Then in Boulder, Colorado faces Kansas State in the Heartland Conference Championship. Things wind up in the Lewis and Clark Division with Arizona hosting Colorado State to determine the final automatic bid. The NCAA selection committee will release the names of the two at-large bids on the JFN Network, which has exclusive rights to the announcement.

Monvanath Jail

Thomas etched the days on the wall of the Monvanath Jail. The scary guards lurked over them every second of every hour. There was no escape. General Oleg would arrive tomorrow to seal their doom. Thomas was certain he and Vishnu would be sent to the slave mines of Zhoul Lot to be tortured for eternity. Lieutenant Amonz Agoogass had visited Shar. She had been brokered as his reward for capturing Nimrod. Jairus had already been fore-warned he would be roasted on a spit and shared between the guards as they feasted on his flesh and drank Conzlie Ale. Froln expected to be executed on the spot. The syndicate had vowed to exterminate all who fought for the Kipren Army. No one spoke to Nimrod. He sat alone and stared through the bars of Monvanath Jail.

"We should all pray to Beatrix Da Silva," said Thomas with little conviction.

"Who is Beatrix Da Silva?" Jairus asked.

"She's the patron saint of prisoners, Jairus." Thomas never turned his head.

Jairus began to pray. He didn't want to be roasted. A pound-ing on the door of the makeshift jail startled them all. The Dark Army guards swung the door open and found nothing.

"What is it?" the leader asked.

The guard looked at his feet. "There is a box."

"Don't touch it!" The resistance had caused trouble in Jorrmy Erhe. The leader removed a wand from his utility belt. It vibrated, and magic mint light glowed around the thick shaft. The lights flashed. "It's safe. It's not a bomb."

The guard opened the box. "It's a case of Honeci Brand." The potent wine was a staple of the region. It had been grown in the fertile hills of the Smurralley Lands before the war.

"Maybe the resistance is trying to curry our favor." They ripped open the treat and quaffed down the wine in big gulps.

The hours crept well into the night. The guards had got-ten very drunk and rowdy. They threatened the prisoners and swiped at Shar. Their lewd gestures were repulsive. The Honeci

Brand finally wore them down. They became sluggish and sleepy and passed out in their chairs and on the table. One of the guards fell asleep in the closet. Another was next to the cell bars.

The Regall Code radio hummed inside Froln's pants. He stood in the corner and received the message.

"Stand back! Everybody into the corner!" The guards slept as Froln shouted.

Everyone, including Nimrod, huddled in the corner. The explosion was terrific. The stone of the Monvanath Jail crumbled around them. The blinding light of KS Teponik Arms fire filled the jail. The deadly attack pulverized the guards. The Royr Eagle hovered overhead. Kipren Army soldiers hung from ropes and rappelled into the jail from the allegiance battleship. Its bow portrayed the head of Anubis.

"We're here!" Froln screamed through the dust.

With alacrity they secured Shar and pulled her through the open hatch. They took Jairus next and then Vishnu.

"Hurry!" the rescuing soldier cried.

The battleship loosed it cannons on Jorrmy Erhe and the syndicate, whose sleep was disrupted by the night mission. Thomas went next and then Froln. Nimrod waited.

"Leave him. He deserves to rot in Hell," Thomas screamed over the engines of the Royr Eagle.

Froln, however, extended his hand and pulled him into the hull of the ship. The hatch closed. The Royr Eagle sped into the night as its shields deflected the Sode gunfire.

"Why did you save him?" Vishnu exclaimed.

"He has betrayed us." Shar wanted to push Nimrod out of the vessel and watch him fall to his death.

Froln and Nimrod started to laugh. They shared a good, hearty belly laugh. The Kipren Army soldiers as well as the members of Team Nimrod were confused.

"It was a bluff." Nimrod told his friends. The stunned team-mates looked at their friend in disbelief. "We were all going to die at Sleoc Choiry. I had to bluff to the syndicate."

"That story you told Agoogass was a lie?" Thomas didn't believe him.

Nimrod didn't like the term "lie." "It was a bluff."

"How could you know the syndicate received information about the Ark's location?" Shar wasn't sold on the traitor's story.

"It was a guess."

"A guess?" Vishnu screamed at Nimrod.

"A calculated guess," Nimrod added.

"How could you be so sure the syndicate would believe the story about Gabriel and the terms of surrender?" Jairus was confused.

Nimrod took the boy's hands. He was so young and had so much to learn. "The syndicate has many flaws, Jairus. One of them is greed. Another is vanity. The very thought one of the archangels would surrender was a boon for the syndicate. The Darkness would reward it with riches and power beyond belief. I was sure they would at least take a sniff of what I was selling."

"How could you be sure General Oleg wasn't in Jorrmy Erhe or on Zhoul Lot? How could you be so sure we were going to be rescued?" Shar was still confused.

"With General Oleg I got lucky."

"I received my first communication through Regall Code on Ursula Peak. The Acrir Marker is not just a beacon. It is a giant transmitter of Regall Code. The Kipren Army has been tracking us since we came off the mountain. All we had to do was stay together." Froln paused and looked at Nimrod. "And stay alive."

"You were in on this too?" Thomas was furious at being duped.

"I am sorry to keep you in the dark. The ruse had to look authentic. Your friend Nimrod did a great job. He saved your lives and mine."

They all breathed a sigh of relief. They were still angry, but they hugged their lost friend and sobbed. They were truly grateful to be alive. A soldier passed around Cinck pearls—the strongest antidote for Nakaru time gas. Each member of Team Nimrod took one pearl and swallowed it.

"Where are we heading, Froln?" Nimrod asked his accomplice.

"Blanco Trollien."

Week Eleven, the Yard

Tuby looked into the players' eyes. Helmets and Friday night lights shadowed them. They held their hands high in the team huddle before kickoff. The players quieted only to hear their coach speak.

"I didn't think you boys were players. You proved me wrong. I didn't think we would win three games. You proved me wrong. I thought I had made a mistake by coming here. You proved me wrong. I didn't think I wanted to be a coach anymore. You proved me wrong. I didn't think I would be proud to be part of college football anymore. You proved me wrong. Nobody said we would win the Big Beast. No one. Go prove them wrong! Lock and load, fellas!"

The *Baltimore Sun*, Saturday, November 15, Navy Blockades Pirates, Advances to Play-offs

The midshipmen's march over to Navy Marine Corps Memorial Stadium was especially crisp this chilly Friday evening. Navy's performance in the first annual Big Beast Conference Championship Game was even crisper. Before a US Naval Academy record of thirty-six thousand fans, many of whom had purchased standing-room-only tickets, the midshipmen thumped the visiting East Carolina Pirates 27–10, and Navy earned a right to vie for the NCAA college football title.

Firstie cocaptains quarterback Tug Lerrin and defensive tackle Timm Mettish were clear about wanting to receive the football after winning the opening coin toss. Navy set the pace for the game with a thirty-seven-yard kickoff return, and Lerrin fed the Pirates a steady dose of running back Johni Bronson. Bronson squirted off right tackle for a dozen to kick-start the festivities. Then he burst up the middle for twenty-three to bring the midshipmen to within kicker Howdy Osaye's range. Osaye wouldn't be necessary, though. Bronson started left and handed the ball on a reverse to speedy wide receiver Jason Drone, who scampered to the Pirate four-yard line. Fullback Rob Wersnors plowed it to the one, and Bronson did the honors by leaping over the top to put Navy on the board. The nifty five-play drive consumed only 3:25 of the clock, and Osaye gave ECU their first opportunity on offense.

Mettish and crew would be just as dramatic in their opening stand. He and middle linebacker Sal Geayser led a swarming midshipmen defense that corralled Pirate tailback Bobbie Corso twice in the backfield and then sacked quarterback Temo Atme for a six-yard loss on third and fourteen. ECU lined up to punt, and outside linebacker Rich L. Chatters split the guard and tackle and came untouched up the middle. Chatters caught the ball on his fingers and batted it up in the air. End Will Bocher covered the loose ball, and Navy was back in business at the ECU twenty-one.

Lerrin tossed the ball to Bronson on a sweep behind pulling guard Bram Gareloin. He plunged ahead to the Pirate thirteen for an eight-yard gain. Navy called Lerrin's number next, and he followed tight end Elmo Linners around the left end to the eight for a Navy first down. ECU stuffed Bronson once, but the second time he found a crease around the right side to punch it in for the score. Osaye added the extra point to give Navy a 14–0 advantage. "We couldn't have game-planned a better start," said Navy head coach Tuby Gravenald.

As the numbing November air swept in from the Chesapeake Bay, the offenses cooled off, but the defenses stayed warm. The second quarter was played to a virtual standstill. Navy outgained ECU one hundred yards to seventy-eight. ECU got on the board with a field goal with 4:20 left to play before the half, and Navy matched that trifecta with their own with just thirty-nine seconds to go before intermission. With a 17–3 lead, Coach Gravenald was taking nothing for granted. "ECU is a terrific second-half team. They did it all year long and earned the right to be here. I expect them to come out firing."

Come out firing they did. ECU received the second-half kick and marched down the field to the Navy thirty-two. ECU gambled on fourth and one to overtake the markers and was headed to the end zone. On first and ten from the Navy thirty-one, East Carolina threw the ball across the middle, and cornerback Vern Stamcie picked him off. Stamcie was tackled immediately at the Navy five. Lerrin and company spent most of the second half backed up with poor field position. Osaye punted them out of these holes as the ECU defense stiffened. ECU attacked again and again—only to shoot itself in the foot repeatedly. Atme brought the ECU offense to the Navy twenty-three on one drive, but the field-goal attempt sailed wide right. Another ECU attempt to score was foiled when Corso fumbled at the Navy nineteen. Midshipman Earl Whitsche recovered.

ECU, who held the ball 11:19 of the third quarter, finally broke the plane early in the fourth quarter when Corso dived to the flag. The referee threw his arms straight into the air, and the stage was set for a dramatic ECU comeback. They were down only 17–10. It wasn't to be. Lerrin and the offense hunkered down. Bronson and the offensive line burned the clock, and a frustrated ECU offense waited on the sidelines for the opportunity to tie the game. Linners and Bronson both picked up key first downs, and wide receiver Gerry Johnson made a sensational one-handed grab to keep the drive alive. With 3:12 on the clock, Lerrin tucked the ball under his arm after faking to Bronson and tiptoed into the end zone to make the score 24–10. Atme and ECU hurried down the field, but hope was lost when Atme threw his second pick of the day. Strong safety Boots Morne snatched that one.

ECU looks headed for the Cotton Bowl in San Antonio. Navy will have to wait to find out whom they face in the NCAA play-offs. The NCAA will select the at-large bids and announce them on JFN on Sunday. An ebullient Navy team didn't seem to care, though. "We are the Big Beast champs!" Lerrin screamed to the Annapolis fans as he held the new conference trophy. "No one thought we had a chance, but we believed in ourselves, and we believed in our coach." Lerrin held the trophy high over his head, and the midshipmen saluted their footballing classmates.

Florida T&A, The *Orlando Sentinel*, Sunday, November 16, Barbarians Volunteer Their Number One

Many experts believed the winner of the Big South Championship would be the favorite to wear the NCAA crown. None of the experts believed the hosting Florida T&A Barbarians would so thoroughly maul the visiting Big South Conference B champs, the Tennessee Volunteers. The Barbarians took it 52–3. Before a hungry capacity crowd of 110,000 at Hurl Stadium, the Barbarians clinched a berth in the NCAA play-offs and humiliated runner-up Tennessee in the process. The game cast doubt on whether the Big South would receive an at-large bid.

Sunday, November 16, JFN Cable Television Studios

"Welcome to JFN. College football fans everywhere are waiting to see the matchups for next week's opening round of the NCAA play-offs. I'm Greg Acrori. Let's start with the seeding. With the number-eight seed and an at-large bid, from the Big Ten, the Iowa Hawkeyes."

The director moved to a clip of the glum Hawkeye players as they threw down their burgers in disgust. They knew they would have to face Florida T&A.

"With the number-seven seed, the Lewis and Clark Division champs, the Arizona Wildcats. The sixth seed goes to the surprising Big Beast champs, Navy."

The picture cut to Tuby and the midshipmen gathered for the feed in Halsey Field House.

"Congratulations to the cadets at Navy." Acrori didn't seem to notice his error.

"The fifth seed goes to the El Niño Conference champion, the Oregon Ducks. They received the automatic bid with their twenty-four to twenty victory over Stanford. The Ducks must now travel to Ann Arbor to face Big Ten champs and number-four-seeded Michigan in the Big House. Surprisingly the number-three seed goes to the ten and one Tennessee Volunteers, who are coming off a fifty-two to three pasting at the hands of Big South rival Florida T&A. The eleven and oh US Naval Academy will visit Neyland Stadium and the sea of orange. Colorado takes the second seed, and the Heartland Conference champs will welcome Arizona to Boulder. The number-one seed was a foregone conclusion. The mighty Florida T&A Barbarians continue their dominance of college football and will host the Iowa Hawkeyes."

Blanco Trollien

The protective shield of the Zannyer Atom Dyke covered Blanco Trollien. The force field repelled the syndicate's repeated attacks. Team Nimrod climbed to the main levels of the Royr Eagle and peered from the windows of the flying battleship. Thousands of Mandric holes covered the agricultural landscape outside the metropolis. Soldiers and weapons of the Kipren Army filled them, and the battleship prepared for a landing. Flashes of light slammed into the Zannyer Atom Dyke. These were courtesy of the syndicate's Eureck Rigger stationed just outside Blanco Trollien's atmosphere. This softened the defenses, and the dyke was in peril. The daring pilot of the Royr Eagle, Rajo Mim, asked everyone to strap in. A panel in the dyke would open, and Mim would have only a few short seconds to pass through the hole that exposed Blanco Trollien. A lucky strike through the pane could kill hundreds of thousands waiting to evacuate.

Mim guided the Royr Eagle gracefully through the panel. It closed behind them, and for the first time in months, Team Nimrod felt safe. Nimrod did not share their enthusiasm. While happy to be alive, Nimrod felt he had failed in his larger mission of saving the souls of Earth. He now sought the counsel of Jesus and Muhammad. He knew precious little time remained to salvage the disaster that waited several thousands of galaxies away.

"Nimrod, why are you so sad?" Jairus asked his mentor.

"I have a lot to think about, my young friend."

"Such as what?"

Nimrod had requested the boy be persistent. Now he wished he would lay off. "I have to own up to some things I might have done wrong. That's why I came to Blanco Trollien. Never be too proud to ask for advice. Unfortunately I might be far too late."

"Is the Darkness winning, Nimrod?" Jairus floored Nimrod with the question.

Nimrod paused and thought about the right response. "Sometimes in a fight, a fight as long as God and the Darkness have been at war, one side gets in a few more punches than the other. Right now the Darkness is punching us pretty good. This is the time we have to buckle down and be more clever and stronger than the Darkness. We're going to be fine. We'll bounce back." Nimrod felt he had done well with his answer, although he wasn't quite convinced himself.

"What is the Hell Star?" Jairus asked.

"The Hell Star is the scariest weapon ever created in the universe. Quasars and black holes fill the universe. They are part of the natural life and death of a star. When a star collapses, it is under tremendous gravitation and forced into a single point. This collapse creates a field in which anything that falls into the field is trapped into infinity—even light. Black holes and quasars take billions of years to capture things that come within their gravitational pull. The Hell Star is a synthetic version of nature. It can be moved through the universe at the Darkness's will, and it can swallow all that comes into its path."

Jairus's eyes got big. Nimrod rehashed the consequences in his own mind. Rajo Mim set the Royr Eagle down deftly. They were safely under the Zannyer Atom Dyke, but neither Nimrod nor Jairus felt safe from the Hell Star.

Team Nimrod passed the mihrab—the semicircular recess in the wall of the mosque pointing the direction to the Rupick Church. They paused to watch the mullahs perform the ancient thread ceremony. They placed the thread around the boys' necks to indicate they were twice born and entering the first stage of their new lives. They were destined to new lives of survival in the war for the planet. The city walls were etched with the sacraments of life. Vishnu rubbed his fingers over the timeless engravings. If the Zannyer Atom Dyke failed, the light missiles from the Eureck Rigger would smash the ten-millennium-old testaments to life's lessons and endurance. The etching of the message "enlightenment" was worn thin from wind and rain.

Rajo Mim approached the group. A dour expression drew the life from his face. "Muhammad and Jesus are returning from the Outacou Mines to greet you with King Fardorff."

"We thank you for all your help, Rajo." Nimrod bowed his head to the brave pilot. "I can't help but feel you have not shared all your news." Nimrod read Rajo's tell.

"No. I have not." He looked high into the dyke as fire continued to pummel it. "The syndicate has captured Moses, the prophet. He was taken to Zhoul Lot."

Play-offs, Week Twelve, The Yard

Satan called Abaddon to his throne in Hell. He lashed the servant with a serpent, and Abaddon slunk through the mire in agony. "You have failed me." Satan drew back the viper whip and slashed Abaddon across the face. "You shall be banished from my kingdom for your incompetence, you fool." Satan drew back the lash again and struck the quivering king of the abyss. "I shall hang you from the yardarm and let the ravens eat your eyes. Then you can negotiate the mines of Gholar in your blindness and feel the true sting of the Darkness's fury. You will curse your existence and breathe my name in hatred for letting you live."

Abaddon whimpered at his merciless lord. "I will not fail you again, Master."

Satan belted Abaddon in the mouth. The serpent's fangs ripped open the demon's cheeks. Leeches fell from the rotten branches and latched onto Abaddon's flesh. They sunk their teeth into the bloody flesh.

"Do not fail me again, Abaddon." The raven cawed on Satan's shoulder and picked the ticks out of his rancid fur.

Tuby sat in the chair at the head of the table. Emily wore a crown and fancy princess shoes. She was celebrating her fourth birthday. They all got to wear tiaras and be princesses with Emily. They opened presents. Hi Ho Cherry-O got Emily's adrenaline pumping. A Barbie phone and makeup kit sent Emily around the moon. Emily loved the new puzzles and Scooby-Doo DVD Grandpa had picked up on the way over. She thought Shaggy was funny and Daphne pretty. Emily loved her sunflower the most. It was always the $2.95 gift that pleased a child the most.

They lowered the lights and brought out the cake. One big candle shaped like the number four burned bright over the pink frosting and amateurish stenciling of "Happy Birthday, Emily" in purple confection. Emily closed her eyes to make a wish and took a deep breath to blow out the candle. With one huge gust, the candle flickered out. Tuby and Jane clapped, and the proud Emily handed out Barbie napkins. Jane stood to turn up the lights, and Tuby looked at the cake. It read "Emily Will Die."

He looked through the windowpane to see Abaddon's pale, slashed face looking in on the party. Tuby's body seized in fear and anger. The girls noticed nothing. He looked back at the cake. "Happy Birthday, Emily" was all it said.

Tuby insisted Jane and Emily travel to Knoxville for the game. Taking another Friday off was not conducive to Jane's work schedule. She had already taken a Friday off to travel to Notre Dame, and Thanksgiving was the following weekend. Jane had lots of work to get done before Wednesday afternoon, but Tuby wouldn't let the issue go. They obliged and never asked Tuby why he was so persistent.

The team boarded the short flight to Tennessee. The players were in tremendous spirits, and Emily had fun with them on the flight. Vern did some magic tricks, and she really liked the peanuts. Mommy even let her drink some ginger ale. Tuby watched the leafless trees of the Appalachians down below. He was almost happy to be on the road. One hundred five thousand hostile fans awaited him at Neyland Stadium. The nightmares awaited him at home.

The *Baltimore Sun*, Sunday, November 23, Big South Swallowed by Big Beast of the East

The US Navy has traveled around the globe from the North Atlantic to the Indian Ocean. The academy, however, had never sailed the sea of orange in Knoxville, Tennessee. Before a Volunteer school record 107,000 fans, the US Naval Academy midshipmen tamed the roiling fans, stifled the Tennessee offense, and returned home with a remarkable 17–3 win. Navy head coach Tuby Gravenald called it "the biggest win of my career."

The checkered Tennessee end zones saw little of the home team today. The Navy defense loaded the line of scrimmage and dared the Volunteers to throw the ball. Tennessee tailback Cary Terrock returned to the Volunteer lineup after a jarring hit last week at Florida T&A that sidelined him with a mild concussion. Navy keyed in on Terrock with middle linebacker Sal Geayser. Defensive tackles Timm Mettish and Spike Himpp gave Geayser plenty of room to patrol sideline to sideline and catch Terrock before turning upfield. Geayser made a team-high nineteen tackles—most of them on Terrock.

The Tennessee defense was sturdy all afternoon. Navy signal caller Tug Lerrin struggled to move the resurgent offense and was forced into several three and outs. The first quarter passed with no score, and both coaches played it very close to the chest. Punter Howdy Osaye kept the Volunteers pinned deep in their own territory. Tennessee finally picked up some momentum on a pass-interference call on cornerback Rolly Leaky. The assisted third-down conversion put the ball at the Navy forty-eight. Terrock bludgeoned his way to another first down, and quarterback Ricki Meveld hit his wide receiver on a slant to bring the ball to the midshipmen's twenty-four. The drive stalled, and Tennessee booted a field goal with 4:06 left to play in the first half.

Lerrin and crew swung into action. Running back Johni Bronson, who had been shut down all day, was the recipient of a middle screen, and he scurried down to his own forty-two. Lerrin hit wide receiver Gerry Johnson in the right flat for fifteen and then turned to the left flat and found Jason Drone for another sizable gain. Lerrin avoided catastrophe when the Tennessee safety dropped a sure interception, but the Navy QB loaded up on third down and found tight end Elmo Linners over the middle for an eight-yard gain. The ball rested at the Tennessee twelve-yard line. Lerrin handed off to Bronson off left tackle for four yards and then again to Bronson off the right side for another four. Faced with third and two from the Volunteer four-yard line, Navy spread the field. Bronson went in motion and left an empty backfield. With the defense spread, Lerrin was able to find a nice seam on the quarterback draw and stick it in the end zone for a touchdown. Navy went into the tunnel ahead 7–3.

Tennessee adjusted its strategy to start the third. They still went to Terrock, but Meveld started to throw the ball. Navy stayed in single coverage on the outside, and cornerbacks Vern Stamcie and Rolly Leakey stayed glued to the Volunteer wideouts. The first-down passing attempts left Tennessee in second and long. They invariably tried Terrock on second down to reduce the yardage on third, but Geayser lay waiting for the Volunteer tailback. Several third and longs resulted in Navy ends Will Bocher and Earl Whitsche both garnering sacks. Gravenald sent well-timed blitzes from the outside and safeties to keep Meveld off-balance.

Lerrin led a ball-control drive late in the third that led to an Osaye field goal. Tennessee received the ball to start the fourth quarter, and the hordes of Volunteer fans rose to their feet to encourage their team. Meveld and Terrock both responded with Tennessee's best drive of the day. Starting at his own twenty-one, Terrock found some space between the guard and tackle. The omnipresent Geayser was blocked, and Terrock smashed his way to the forty. Meveld hit his tight end in the flat, and he stomped out to the Navy forty-nine. Terrock again burst through the middle and brought the pigskin to the Navy thirty-seven. Meveld threw incomplete on first down but then found his wide receiver streaking down the sidelines. He lofted the ball into the air, and the speedster grabbed it and was pushed out at the two. Navy brought in its goal-line defense as Tennessee attempted to tie the score. Geayser stuffed Terrock on first and goal. Tennessee tried the jump-ball pass into the end zone on second down, and strong safety Boots Morne broke it up. The Volunteers went over the top again with Terrock on third and goal. Outside linebacker

Barnett Prime and Himpp met Terrock in midair and forced the tailback to the ground. The fans rose to their feet and shouted for the coach to go for it on fourth and goal. Tennessee had already eaten 5:46 off the clock and needed the score. They ran Terrock wide, and Geayser pulled him down by his shirttail at the one-yard line. Navy took over on downs.

A Tennessee stop would have kept the Volunteers in the game. Gravenald and company had no intentions of leaving the back door open, though. Navy executed a 7:13 drive that culminated in a Johni Bronson touchdown with just over two minutes left in the game. Game, set, and match went to the visiting midshipmen as 107,000 fans headed quietly to the parking lot. "Individually these guys aren't great players, but they're one heck of a team." Coach Gravenald smiled as Tennessee state troopers escorted him from the field.

Colorado beat Arizona 38–17 in Boulder and will host the red-hot Naval Academy next Saturday.

Florida T&A
Number eight, placekicker and punter, Jacko Nobs, took off his shirt and sat down on the sandy beach for the photo shoot. Nobs was ditching his Tuesday classes. The oceanography major felt very comfortable by the water. The six-foot-three, 225-pounder from Wanneroo, Western Australia, spent most of his childhood swimming in the Indian Ocean just north of Perth. However, his strong right leg that was capable of bombing sixty-yard spirals with a nice touch of backspin had gotten him all the way to Florida. The senior didn't get a lot of field-goal attempts due to the proficiency of the offense, but he hasn't missed an extra point. He was sixty-five for sixty-five. His leg helped the defense too. He was very effective on kickoffs with thirty-six touchbacks and a net starting line at the eighteen. His great range on field goals had NFL scouts salivating. His longest was fifty-eight yards. With a sterling field-goal percentage—fourteen of fifteen attempts—he

was a potential top-ten pick. His lone miss was a sixty-five-yard-er at the half of the Florida game. Nobs was also a favorite with women. His sturdy frame, sandy-blond hair, and accent made him a natural selection as the male counterpart for the upcoming *The Women About Town* swimsuit issue. TWAT photographers set up the shoot, and Nobs fed himself a steady diet of Fosters and cray-fish, lobsters, oysters, shrimps, and clams.

A sexy redhead interviewed him for the article. "You're not like regular kickers, are you? You like to mix it up."

"That makes me a favorite on special teams with the other players. I learned to tackle playing rugby back home. It's quite a different game."

"How do you catch the ball with only seven fingers?"

"Practice makes perfect, missy." Nobs smiled and touched her knee with the two fingers on his right hand.

"How did you lose the fingers?"

"A great white shark attacked me in the waters near Perth. Big rascal. Had my whole arm in his mouth. I was lucky to lose only the three fingers. That's why they call me 'Lucky Seven' at the AKG fraternity."

"Our female readers will be dying to know if you are currently dating someone. Are you?"

"I am currently dating Miss October of *Penthouse*, Wendy Raith. Here she is right now."

Raith sat on Jacko's lap, and the two mugged for the cam-eras. The photographer was ready, and the interview ended. Nobs smuggled his grapes over to the set. Wendy, who wore a whole lot of nothing, followed.

The *Orlando Sentinel*, Sunday, November 23, Barbarians Leave Hawkeyes Cockeyed
Head coach Merl Larrola said what everybody else was thinking. "Look out, New York City. Here we come!" That was the mood at

Hurl Stadium as 105,000 rabid fans started calling their travel agents during halftime of Florida T&A's 49–0 drubbing of the Big Ten representative, Iowa Hawkeyes.

The Barbarians still have one hurdle left to leap. They face another Big Ten opponent to make the championship game for the third consecutive year. Michigan stopped Oregon 27–13 to earn the right—or punishment—to play the Barbarians on their home turf over Thanksgiving weekend. The Wolverines face a monumental task. Florida T&A looked brutally sharp as they destroyed the 10–1 Hawkeyes. The offensive juggernaut of Worm Roanen and B. Siemore Jett clicked on all cylinders. Both seniors had a hand in all seven Barbarian touchdowns, and Roanen completed the first touchdown pass of his career on a halfback option pass in the second. Roanen rushed for 176 yards on nineteen carries with three touchdowns, and he was finished by the middle of the third. Jett threw for two of his own and rushed for another, and the Barbarians were just faster than the laboring farm fellows from corn country.

The Barbarians torched Iowa early. By the middle of the second quarter, they led 35–0. What had been a festive atmosphere at Hurl Stadium turned into a downright party. The Jumbotron flashed pictures of the Empire State Building and pictures of the Barbarian players. They superimposed linebacker Buster Chagora's face on the Statue of Liberty and edited in Bones Jetr ringing the opening bell on Wall Street. Speedy wide receiver Whiz Toorleen was pictured racing the New York City subway. He won. The crowd was overly hyped and overly served. One half of the stadium started singing, "Start spreading the news," and the other half returned with, "We're leaving today." Everybody wanted to be a part of it. Fans kicked like the Rockettes throughout the stadium.

Larrola summed up his feelings for the game and his critics when leaving the field. "There are a lot of people around the country who believe we run a dirty program. I'm tired of hearing it on television and radio. I'm tired of reading about it in the newspapers and magazines. These kids are just great players. I'm doing it my way for the fans and the players, and nobody better stand in our way." Nobody has, and it doesn't look likely anybody will.

Rupick Church

Team Nimrod climbed the last few steps up Vancil Hill. It overlooked Blanco Trollien. The shining domes of the cathedrals floated in the morning mist. They walked the path to Rupick Church to meet King Fardorff and his beautiful daughter, Mytom Onaxa. Centuries of travel and trade had worn the cobblestoned streets. Rabbis and priests walked with the children to the mosques. The smell of incense filled the air. Pedestrians stopped and whispered, *"Bhagavan,"* as Vishnu walked past. The legend of the Hindu deity had grown through the millennia, and many followers worshipped the galactic saint. Natives performed the Ghost Dance in the park in prayer for their fallen brethren. They turned the corner to war cries of "jihad" as the caliphs raised the ire of twenty thousand civilians. The mothers and fathers of this peaceful civilization would have to bear the arms if the Kipren Army failed.

They passed over the Igige Lochs. These lakes surrounded the castle of King Fardorff, but they had grown putrid and still. Froln opened the massive teak door. The church was dark and solemn, and the monks were deep in Omainge prayer. Neond laws required all who entered the Ka'ba, the holy sanctuary, to kneel and pray to Trollien's Yunnty god for safe passage. Shar stood and lit the menorah. Thomas removed a scriptural text written on parchment from the phylacteries, knelt, and read the history of the ancient holiday of Rynroya. Five hundred score years ago that day, Rynroya had stopped the rising Bophebo Sea from drowning

Blanco Trollien. Rynroya had sacrificed herself by walking into the raging ocean with a single handful of dirt. The waves swallowed her, but the tides ebbed. Blanco Trollien was never threatened again.

Nimrod excused himself and walked the aisles of Rupick Church. The mosaics carved the past into the stone wall. He found the altar. The Morjinz Chalice glinted in the light of stained glass. Exquisite tapestries stretched across the entire altar. King Fardorff was praying with Jesus and Muhammad on the Kink Broona rugs. The mystics sat cross-legged and staring through the temple. Vishnu, Shar, Thomas, Jairus, and Froln sat silent at the altar's edge in the presence of God's chosen children.

Muhammad spoke with his eyes closed. "You have come far and passed through dangerous lands."

"I have indeed. My friends and I have seen the Darkness and his destruction." Nimrod bowed to Muhammad.

"There is fear in your heart, Nimrod," Jesus said softly.

"It is true, my Lord. It has been my charge to save Earth from Satan's fires."

"Satan is a liar." Jesus drank from the Morjinz.

"Have you entered a covenant with the immoral?" Muhammad spoke once more.

"I have."

Jesus opened his eyes. Fury electrified him, but he held his temper. "You have decided to play Satan's game. Satan will send all his legions to their deaths to secure victory."

"That is why I seek both your counsel."

"What does Heaven gain with your victory, Nimrod?" Muhammad remained placid.

"The Darkness and Satan shall flee Earth forever."

"That is a lie," Jesus reminded Nimrod.

"And what shall we pay?"

Nimrod swallowed hard. "The location of Heaven."

King Fardorff stood immediately and glared at Nimrod. "What gives you the right to barter with our final refuge? That is not for you to decide."

"Michael, the archangel, granted me the power. I was given the authority to do whatever I could to save Earth."

"With a modicum of prudence," Fardorff protested. "The security of many in the hands of so few. How does Michael feel about this?"

"I am sure he is not pleased."

"Have you not spoken personally with Michael about this predicament?" Jesus leered at Nimrod.

"No. I have not. I planned to seek your wisdom before returning to Judeah. Nicodemus verified the agreement. We were fortunate to survive the attack on the Seavisitsen Ark. We have journeyed for far too long. I am certain Michael will expel me from Heaven. I came to seek your help. Not your judgment."

"I should hand you to General Oleg myself." Mytom Onaxa appeared with a votive. "Our eternity bartered like coins on a card table."

"I am sorry for my stupidity. I should have sought the elders' advice sooner."

"Yes," Muhammad agreed. "Much sooner."

The mystics passed the hand-cut crystal decanters. Armagnac and brandy from the grapes of the Jouis Aneur galaxy filled them. Nimrod passed, but Vishnu took a huge swig for himself and his friend. Thomas doubled up as well. Everyone was in a heap of trouble. Soldiers from the Kipren Army stormed through the teak doors of Rupick Church.

"King Fardorff," they major yelled through the hallowed sanctuary. "It's the Hell Star."

Everyone retreated to the balcony of Rupick Church. The Hell Star eclipsed the sunny sky. Oshu Land, the last planet in the archipelago of Blanco Trollien, could be seen on the western horizon. It was breaking into pieces and being sucked into the gravitational field. Street artists captured the surreal scene on parchment. Chunk by chunk the orb blasted apart. No debris escaped into space. Everything funneled into the black hole of the Darkness—never again to see light. Nothing of Oshu Land would remain by sunrise. No longer would it sit gracefully over the Bophebo Sea. The syndicate would head the Hell Star to Maroed Rain next. Within two months the archipelago of Blanco Trollien would become only a memory of the holy in the universe.

King Fardorff left at once with Mytom Onaxa for the Outacou Mines. The completion of the Cannd Nova Bomb had truly become a life-and-death matter. Jairus spoke in solitude with Jesus. The Nazarene whispered encouragement into the young angel's ear. Nimrod walked the balcony with Muhammad. "You have seen the danger that awaits firsthand, Nimrod."

"It is a horrible fate for the universe. Share your thoughts with me." Nimrod bowed his head.

"There is only one truth about Satan. He is a notorious liar and a murderer. You can count only on his immorality. He will twist the game to his advantage. It lies with you to outthink the evil of his genius." Muhammad placed his hand on Nimrod's shoulder. "It is time for you to leave this place. The wrath of the Darkness is upon us. It will take all your faith and wit to defeat Satan and save Earth. It might be the only place for believers to seek refuge. Go now."

Team Nimrod gathered. Nimrod led them down the tower's narrow stone stairs. He swung open the doors and took one last look at the Hell Star. Then he paused.

"What's the matter, Nimrod?" Shar asked her fearless leader.

"I don't know where to go. How do we get back to Heaven?"

"I don't know." Thomas kicked at the dirt.

"Don't look at me." Vishnu had no idea.

"We go to the Acorn Wall," Jairus said. "I asked Jesus to guide us. He said the Acorn Wall would transport us to Judeah."

Play-offs: Week Thirteen, Boulder, Colorado, Saturday, November 29
Del Dave Wralls drove a large Mack truck hauling gasoline all over the country. Exhausted from driving Wralls swung northwest to Interstate 25 and hit stops in Pueblo and Colorado Springs. He had finished this leg of the route outside Boulder, Colorado, and planned to have some fun. Del Dave knew a little strip bar called the Swimming Pole with dancing girls twenty-four hours a day. Del Dave was ahead of schedule and had plenty more gas to pump tomorrow.

A trucker had a lot of time to think. Del Dave was angry his ex-wife had changed her name back to her original name. She was no longer Hannah Wralls. She was Hannah Siemka again. The straw that snapped Del Dave's back was that Hannah was going to have his son's name legally changed too. Hannah couldn't have turned out to be more of a bitch.

Del Dave remembered the bartender's name. Pearl. Pearl Shersting. Pearl had put down a few Budweisers in her day. She sure didn't look like the girls dancing on the pole at two thirty in the afternoon.

Folsom Field, 4:45 p.m.
Tuby held Emily in his arms and gave her a kiss. Emily was scared when the home team charged the live buffalo onto the field. He passed her back into the stands with Jane. Tuby had made sure they would be in Colorado for the big game. They had flown into Denver the Friday morning after Thanksgiving. Jane didn't have to worry about asking for time off this week. She had made a turkey, and they invited Vern to join them for the special occasion. Tuby couldn't have been happier. He had wolfed down two

helpings and disguised the dryness with lots of gravy. Tuby promised to go on a diet and rubbed his tummy—much to the delight of the giggling Emily.

The flight had proved uneventful. They touched down at Denver International Airport and boarded two state-of-the-art buses to Boulder. Each seat had a video monitor, and the bus raised and lowered to board the passengers. Tuby was just happy it had heat. The forecast called for dry and cold with lots of wind. The bus driver had some fun with Pantry. Pantry stepped onto the bus, and the driver pretended it wouldn't rise. He made him get off, and the hydraulics worked fine. He stepped back on, and they didn't work again. Fat jokes at Pantry's expense had become a team sport.

Tuby paced the sidelines. It was time to coach his team. "Howdy. How's the wind?" Tuby asked his kicker.

"It's blowing across the field. Sometimes it is very strong," said the Nigerian. He was wrapped tightly in thermal underwear, gloves, two pair of socks, a hoodie, and a Navy turtleneck.

"It's going to be hard to kick field goals today, huh?" The coach looked for the truth.

"It might be, Coach."

Tuby sent Will Bocher and Barnett Prime out for the coin toss. If they won the toss, Tuby wanted the ball to start the second half. Bocher called tails, and it came up heads. Colorado obliged and elected to receive the ball. Howdy kicked a fluttering duck into the wind, and the Colorado receiver watched it bounce around on the ground. He thought it was going to go out of bounds and had to dive on it at the end as the Navy special teams came charging. Colorado started with miserable field position.

"Let's keep them pinned back, Murrey." Gravenald encouraged his defensive coach.

Scormir called the defense to middle linebacker Sal Geayser. "Split, fire right, cobra."

Colorado handed the ball to sophomore sensation Briney Maceie. Geayser introduced himself and rung Maceie's bell. The Buffalo lost two yards.

The Swimming Pole, 5:30 p.m.

Del Dave was half in the bag but figured that was the plan. He bought some shots of Rumple Minze for the other people at the bar and cashed in another twenty-dollar bill. He asked Pearl for singles. He planned to spend a lot of time in front of the new girl, Lil Lobby. A trucker buddy, Doug Jack Loobney, pulled in just in time. Doug Jack was the man with the plan. He had all the goodies to keep Del Dave awake through the night. Del Dave pulled up a barstool for Doug Jack just as Navy free safety Ronn Judge picked off a pass and returned it for a touchdown.

Folsom Field, 6:10 p.m.

Tuby signaled Tug to call time-out. "Tug, the half is winding down. We need to get this right."

The score was tied at fourteen.

"Coach, we've got third and nine from our own forty-five," Mashner reminded his coach.

"Well, I sure as hell don't want to give the ball back to the Buffalo. They ran wild over us the last two possessions," Tuby said.

Tug tried to call the play. "I think I can catch Elmo down the seam, Coach."

"Nah, Tug. They've been stacking him up on the line of scrimmage all day." The referee pointed to his watch. Tuby had to hurry. "This crowd is awfully fired up. That defense is foaming at the mouth. Let's see how aggressive they really are. Forty-five left dive bingo. And tell those fat asses to give you some time."

Tub ran to the huddle. "Forty-five left dive bingo, and Coach says to give me some time. Break."

Wide receivers Gerry Johnson and Jason Drone both lined up far to the left. Drone hugged the sidelines. Johnson was five steps inside. Tight end Elmo Linners lined up wide to the right. Tug called the signals, and Linners went in motion to the left. He set up in the slot, and then fullback Rob Wersnors went in motion to the right and planted himself on the line of scrimmage. This spread the defense out. Tug snapped the ball and faked the hand-off to Bronson to freeze the linebackers. Johnson hesitated while Drone angled hard across the middle. Linners took the same angle from closer to the line and pulled the defense into the middle of the field. Johnson squared his ten-yard out route perfectly. The Colorado corner bit on Lerrin's pump, and Johnson hustled down the sidelines. The ball seemed to float in the air forever. It cradled gently into Johnson's hands, and he galloped into the end zone. Navy had a 21–14 lead going into the half.

The Swimming Pole, 6:40 p.m.

Del Dave chain-smoked Marlboro Reds and imbibed Bud after Bud. "Funny Dale Frew, how the hell have you been?"

Funny Dale Frew had just driven in from Missouri and had the same idea as Del Dave and Doug Jack. "Pearl, I'll have what these boys are having, and make it a double. I've got some catching up to do." Pearl popped the tops and slid a pair down the bar to Funny Dale. "Any new girls in this toilet?"

Del Dave slurred, "They've got this brunette." Del Dave burped. "Her name is Jilian O'Cherre. She sure does have a tasty pie."

The truckers cracked up. Funny Dale whispered into Doug Jack's ear. Doug Jack reached into his jacket pocket and slipped Funny Dale a vial of crystal meth.

"I want some of that." Del Dave got boisterous.

"Man, you have to be cool."

Doug Jack slipped Del Dave the same amount. It was more than enough to rack his brain. Del Dave passed Doug Jack back some cash and headed to his truck cab to get high. Doug Jack joined him. Abaddon and the demon Belial watched the stripper Meghin Lomker. She couldn't have been more than fifteen and a junkie. They also kept a close eye on Del Dave Wralls. He might just come in handy if Navy beat Colorado.

Folsom Field, 7:30 p.m.

Colorado tied the score at twenty-one late in the third quarter on a pass to Buffalo wide receiver Skinne Wasad. Tuby called time-out early in the fourth quarter. Navy had the ball on the Colorado seventeen. It was fourth and five—no reason not to kick a field goal. Tug headed to the sideline.

"Tug. Bring the whole goddamn team!"

Lerrin turned and shouted to the offense. They sprinted to the sideline and huddled around Coach Gravenald. He looked into his players' eyes. "The rest of your lives lie ahead of you. You're all winners, and nothing is ever going to change that. Football is just a moment in the game of life. It's not as important as being there to watch the birth of your child. It's not as crucial as the love of your parents or your wife. It's not like the curing of a disease. I've watched this team grow up through the fall. I've watched boys become men." Tuby looked at Pantry. "These opportunities don't come along that often. What do you say we not kick the field goal, shove it down their throats, and head for the end zone?"

The players erupted. "Pantry!"

The big boy turned back to face the coach. "We're going right behind you." Tuby thumped Pantry in the chest.

Pantry charged onto the field and didn't even huddle. He squatted on the line in his three-point stance and waited for his teammates. "Thirty-six Ohio bump." Tug called a play they had run a thousand times.

Nobody was going to fool anyone. They were just going to see who had more heart. Tug snapped the ball and stuck it into Johni Bronson's gut. Bronson followed Wersnors into the six-hole behind Pantry. No one touched Bronson for ten yards. Lerrin followed Pantry into the end zone on the next play. Navy led 28–21 with 6:30 left in the game.

The Swimming Pole, 8:30 p.m.

Del Dave Wralls was flying. Colorado had just lost the game, but he didn't care. He was high, high, high. He picked up his Marlboros and stuck another one in his mouth.

Belial relaxed his eyes and became translucent. Belial walked across the poorly ventilated strip club. He was invisible to the drunken patrons, and he stood in front of Del Dave Wralls. Del Dave took a long drag of the cigarette. Del Dave sucked Belial in through the tip of his tobacco. Belial was in his lungs, and then he entered Del Dave's soul.

Del Dave's eyes turned a vicious green. Del Dave tried to fight the madness running through him. He ran to his truck cab, but the fury raged inside him. Del Dave reached for his gun. He wanted to blast the demons out of his head. He had never had the courage before, but this time it was worse. Insanity ran through his brain. Vile thoughts pervaded his mind.

Del Dave put the gun in his pocket as Belial gained control. Del Dave got out of the cab and saw the young stripper behind the club hitting the crack pipe. Del Dave hit her on the head from behind with his gun. Belial laughed as he sodomized the woozy teen in the alley next to the Dumpster. He threw her body into the trash and fired up the rig. Flammable cargo still filled the Mack truck. It rolled onto two wheels as it careened out of the Swimming Pole.

Folsom Field, 9:30 p.m.

Tuby regretted making the appointment in Cheyenne, Wyoming. Recruiting was the bane of the job. A chopper waited to zip him up to see the star athlete. He planned to visit with the youngster briefly and then rejoin the team at Denver International Airport. Tuby kissed Jane and Emily and ushered them onto the team bus. Everyone was out of their minds excited. The US Naval Academy had earned the right to compete for the championship against the powerful Florida T&A Barbarians, who had squashed Michigan in the Sunshine State 45–9. Tuby wished he could celebrate with the team. The bus driver, Chet "Pinto" Japel, closed the door. Tuby waved at Jane. She held Emily up to the window, and Emily's nose smashed against the glass like a piggy's. Jane mouthed, "I love you." Tuby blew them both a kiss. He would celebrate with them in a few hours.

Chet "Pinto" Japel was not a small man. He had earned the nickname Pinto as a youth when his fat ass had become stuck in the compact car model. Chet radioed the other driver and informed him they were taking a shortcut through the mountains.

Getting to Route 119 actually took them away from Denver at first. The players celebrated the big win and rehashed every play of the memorable victory in order. Each took a turn telling his version of the story. Howdy was still cold in the Rocky Mountain air, but he warmed the bus with his glowing smile. He had never imagined being part of something this huge as a child. Pantry engrossed all the players—even the upperclassmen—with details about how he had blown back the defense of the Colorado Buffalo. The team sang choruses of "Anchors Aweigh," and laughter filled the bus as it climbed the narrow roadway. Steep, snow-covered inclines lush with evergreens bordered the dark two-lane road. The buses strained in the climb as they hugged the outside guardrail.

Belial felt the truck become a missile. He took his foot off the brake and let gravity pull the moving bomb faster and faster down the mountain. It wobbled around the bends and swerved madly across the double yellow lines. Belial only tried to keep the weapon on the track. It would be approaching...soon. Del Dave vomited on himself trying to expel the toxins in his system. Belial left Del Dave in the puke and disappeared through a crack in the window. Del Dave was still out of his mind when he saw the headlights of the buses.

Pinto Japel tried to swerve, but the Mack truck caught the bus broadside and drove it back into the second bus. It sent them both over the embankment. Jane lay on top of Emily. The fireball erupted into the night sky and ignited the fuel on the buses. They exploded one after the other as they toppled down the hill. Midshipmen flew through the cabins of the buses. Searing flames engulfed the trapped men and women. The buses smacked the evergreens and broke them in half. Sheared metal gouged into their flesh and severed all that came into its path. Bodies flew from the wreckage. Tumbling debris crushed those inside. The cascading inferno scorched many to death. The razors mangled and sliced into the passengers. None had time to react to the disaster. Second and third explosions fed the beast on the mountainside. Thumbs, arms, feet, and heads littered the slopes. It was a trail of blood, char, and smoke. The buses finally came to rest in the bottom of the ravine. The smoldering remains were now hollow shells. Very few moans could be heard in the silence. The fuel-soaked branches of the evergreens burned in the night like sadistic Christmas trees in Hell.

American soldiers fell again—victims of the universal war with the Darkness.

Satan laughed and laughed.

Tuby and Superintendent Gregory waited impatiently at DIA. Tuby started to worry. It was almost midnight, and there was no sign of the buses. There had been no word from the drivers and no cell phone calls from Jane or any of the players. Tuby's heart sank when he saw the Denver chief of police approaching the terminal.

"Are you Coach Gravenald?" the police officer asked.

"Yes, I am Coach Gravenald. This is the superintendent of the US Naval Academy, Admiral Gregory. What's going on?"

"There's been a terrible accident."

Gravenald and Gregory couldn't imagine how terrible.

A Denver police chopper took them over the accident site. The trees still flickered like candles from the air. The flashing lights of fire and rescue vehicles covered the mountain road. It was impossible to see into the ravine where the buses had ended their deadly slide. The pilot landed the helicopter dangerously close to the rocks. Paramedics and firefighters rushed everywhere. Body bags filled with the dead lined the road.

"What happened here? Where is Jane? Where is Emily?" Tuby screamed over the radios of the rescue teams. Gregory was equally stunned but tried to restrain Tuby. "Jane!" Tuby cried out. "Emily!" The tears poured down Tuby's face.

The firefighter rappelled into the dark. Each time he returned with more dead. Coach Mashner's skull was crushed, and his body was charred. The lifeless body of center Jack Mohney lay crumpled and uncovered in the road. Gregory found a survivor. The physician, Dr. Barry Money, had miraculously suffered only a concussion.

"Barry, can you tell us what happened?" Gregory checked to see if the shocked Money had the energy to relay the events.

"We were just driving up the mountain. The driver said he knew a quicker way. Everybody was having fun, and then there was fire, and we were sliding down the mountain…"

A paramedic screamed, "We have a survivor!"

Gravenald and Gregory ran helter-skelter through the blinding strobes of the rescue vehicles. A little girl lay on a stretcher.

She was unconscious and in serious condition but alive. It was Emily. The medics worked frantically to save the little girl.

Tuby looked for Jane. She couldn't be far from Emily. He ran up to a firefighter. "The little girl. Did you find the little girl?"

The firefighter shook his head. They were all exhausted. Tuby ran to others. They all had no idea. Most bodies were men. Tuby turned to see his friend Vern standing behind him. Tears streamed down his face. Vern held Jane in his arms. Her face had been peeled away, and it revealed her bloody skull. Vern had found them both. Jane had covered Emily through the accident. She'd saved Emily's life by sacrificing her own.

Tuby held Jane close and wept over his only child. He petted her hair and kissed her face. The blood stained Tuby's cheek and chin.

Gregory tapped him on the shoulder as Tuby grieved over Jane. "Tuby, they're going to take Emily to the hospital with a chopper. Do you want to go with them?"

Tuby wasn't sure of anything. Horror overloaded his heart and soul. He forced himself away from his daughter. The tears blurred his vision as he looked back into the blinking red-and-white flashing emergency lights. Gregory guided Tuby to the chopper. He sat and looked at the sweet four-year-old. The blades of the helicopter roared, and they lifted into the night. Tuby remembered the words Gregory had spoken when they first met. "We don't leave people behind at the US Naval Academy, Mr. Gravenald." Tuby felt he had left them all behind.

Neurosurgeon Dr. Marci Bodathe received Emily off the chopper. Tuby waited all night for Emily to come out of surgery. She had massive contusions to her skull. Dr. Bodathe said her chances of survival were 10 percent. The bleeding had already smothered parts of her brain. If she didn't die, it was likely she would be in a coma. Tuby had become Emily's legal guardian in a matter of hours. He gave Dr. Bodathe permission to do anything she could to save Emily's life. She was all he had left.

The surgery team appeared after five hours of operating. Tuby sat with Dr. Bodathe. "Emily is still alive, Mr. Gravenald." Tuby closed his eyes and thanked God. "She is in a coma, though."

Tuby closed his eyes and started to pray. Dr. Bodathe rubbed his tired shoulders. It was not easy carrying the weight of the world.

"Is the damage irreparable?" Tuby asked the doctor.

Dr. Bodathe despised this part of her job. "In my experience the damage is irreversible. It would be a miracle if Emily ever opened her eyes again. If she wakes from the coma, your granddaughter will be paralyzed from the chest down. She will most likely be blind and deaf. The contusion from the accident was immense. I am surprised she made it here alive."

Very few others arrived at the hospital alive. Admiral Gregory spent the next day confirming the identities of the dead. Vern found Tuby in a chair near Emily's room. They held hands and prayed.

Judeah

"Raphael!" Nimrod turned quickly. He was surprised to see the angel. "I must speak to Michael immediately."

"I'm sorry, Nimrod. I received orders from Michael to take you directly to the Metant Trail for passage to Manchock Refou. God is waiting for you there."

God trained his opaque stare at Nimrod and summoned him to come forward. They walked down a chiseled path of ice. "Nimrod." His voice was stern.

"Yes, sir?"

"I gave Michael my confidence in you. Was I wrong?"

Nimrod felt the heat. He shook at his core. "No," he answered humbly. "Our mission was sidetracked. We have just returned from Blanco Trollien and need to be briefed about Earth. We are woefully behind."

"Unbelievably," God said, "your team made the championship game against Florida T&A."

"That's great!" Nimrod exclaimed. "We're alive!"

"Not so fast." God turned Nimrod to him. "You can't trust Satan to keep his word. He is a liar. He has destroyed the Navy football team and paved the way for him to win the bet."

"He cheated!"

"What did you expect?"

"What I am going to do now?" Nimrod looked into the void.

"Show a little confidence in yourself, Nimrod. There are still three weeks before the game. You are battling with Satan. What are you going to do about it?" Nimrod didn't know. "There's a lot riding on this."

Nimrod did know that. Nimrod looked God straight in the eyes. "Can you help me with Anytime?"

God's eyes sparkled, and he smiled at the idea. "Yes. I can."

THE GAME

Monday, December 1

Nurse Linda Finnety brought Tuby a cup of black Maxwell House coffee and rubbed his shoulders. Tuby opened his eyes. It had not been a horrible nightmare. The last thirty-six hours had been a heinous reality. He thanked Linda for the coffee. "How long have I been asleep?"

"You've been sitting upright in that chair for twelve hours."

Tuby's hair was askew. He had visibly aged from the Thanksgiving weekend tragedy. "Has there been any improvement in Emily's condition?"

Tuby stood over his granddaughter. The intubation tube filled her trachea, and the respirator chugged on breath after breath. Wires and tubes tracked her heart rate, fed her intravenously, and noted blood pressure. The sticky tabs of the EEG monitored Emily's weak brain waves. Her head was shaved for surgery, and a gastric tube was inserted into her stomach to provide the nourishment to sustain life. Nurse Terese Gifforgs changed Emily's intravenous tubes and supplied medicine and fluids.

"No, Mr. Gravenald. I am afraid there has been no change in Emily's condition." Nurse Finnety's eyes spoke the truth. "The chances of Emily recovering are extraordinarily slim."

Even recovery was no picnic basket. Dr. Bodathe had explained the harrowing condition of Emily's future. Tuby closed his eyes and prayed to God. He tried to reconcile his anger with the Lord. Tuby still battled over the loss of Myra. Her death had been sudden and cruel. He felt abandoned. Thoughts raged inside his head. *Why does God make me suffer so much loss and pain? Why has he taken Myra and Jane so quickly from me? Jane, my beautiful daughter, is gone.* Tuby was unaccepting of his reality. *The players. Those wonderful young boys. Why, God? Why?* Tuby wept beside Emily's bed. He buried his hands deep in his pockets. *Why didn't I have a chance to say good-bye? How could you be so powerful and benevolent, God, yet impotent to save the good and innocent of the world? Jane never hurt anyone. Myra was kind and considerate.* Tuby wallowed in self-pity. *Why me? Why do I bear this heavy cross? Why didn't you take me? Why was I spared and left to agonize over the dead? Why do these torturous dreams of demons and pain fill my head? Why have you hurt little Emily? She is just a child. She has committed no sin.* He wrestled with his own beliefs. *Do I truly believe in you, God? I don't know. It used to be so easy. We'd go to church. We'd say our prayers, and things seemed to always work out. It's easy to believe in God when things are going fine. But where are you now? Do I not pray enough? Have I not led a life that pleases you? I don't know if I can believe in you anymore, Lord. Are you just a symbol we worship? Are you a trick of our imaginations? Are you an opiate passed down from generation to generation to quell the masses into obedience? Like good sheep we follow you, but others control our lives and the way we think. Are you really out there? I don't know anymore.*

The knock sounded gently. Admiral Gregory looked haggard and fatigued after speaking to the victims' parents. Some of the families had been at Folsom Field to watch the glorious victory over Colorado. He personally delivered the news of deaths. Gregory stared into the vacant eyes of the disbelievers. Family by family the admiral suffered each death anew as he watched the anguish surge from the depths of the parents' souls and erupt out of their bodies in tangible wails of grief. Fathers' eyes went hollow. Their lips quivered, and they tried to restrain the tears. They clung to their wives. Mothers sobbed uncontrollably. Their faces contorted in sorrow. They clung to their husbands. Gregory held them together, and they formed tripods of agony. The phone calls were no better. Gregory tried to reach through the phone to soothe the pain. He heard more than one receiver hit the floor. There was never a way to console the inconsolable.

"Tuby, may I speak with you?" Gregory prepared to catalog the tragedy for the coach.

Tuby lifted his face from deep meditation. He did not want to leave Emily's side, but he understood he owed it to the players and their families. He accepted more weight to his cross. Tuby gingerly rose from the rigid chair and stepped into the hallway. Nurses Finnety and Gifforgs continued their chores for Emily in the ICU. "Hello, James." Tuby never referred to the superintendent by his first name.

"Do you mind if I chat with you for a minute?" Gregory looked at the lifeless Emily lying in the antiseptic room.

"No." Tears still filled Tuby's eyes.

Both grown men let the emotions run, and they held each other in the hallway. Their chests heaved with sorrow, and fatigue buckled their knees. The horrible reality set upon them. Gregory, the responsible school official, now accepted the tragedy on a personal level. Tuby had only been able to focus on Jane and Emily.

He needed to hear the fate of the team. "Tell me some of them survived."

"Yes, Tuby. Some of them survived." There was little joy in the positive news, though. "Even the survivors are in pretty bad shape." Tuby sat silently. "E. Brian Palmer, the engineer, walked away without a scratch. Jason Emenith has two broken legs. Palmer, Emenith, and Tug are the most fortunate of the group. Tug's got a broken arm, collarbone, and shoulder. They will make full recoveries. Gareloin has a broken neck. He faces a long recovery, and the doctors are unsure whether he will have lingering paralysis. He will be forced to wear a halo for a while." Tuby sat dazed but listened. "Sal's got a broken back, hips, and legs. He has tremendous facial lacerations and is in traction. He could be in traction for several months. Once again the doctors are unsure about paralysis or recovery time—if at all. He's pretty beat up but alive." Gregory gathered his thoughts. "Rolly Leaky is in the room right down the hall. He's near Emily. His head was crushed severely. He has brain damage and is in and out of consciousness."

There was a long pause.

"Don't tell me that's it." Tuby looked out of the corner of his eye at Gregory.

Gregory couldn't look over to Tuby. There was no other good news. "That's it."

"Spike Himpp?"

"Dead. Lacerations severed the artery in his leg, and he bled to death," Gregory responded.

"Jack?"

"Jack Mohney's dead. Burned in the fire."

"Johnson?"

"Gerry Johnson's dead."

"Wersnors?"

"Dead."

"Bronson?"

"Johni Bronson is dead. Crushed to death."

"Jason?"

"Jason Drone is dead."

"Pantry?"

"Pantry is dead."

Tuby choked up. The weight crushed him. He couldn't believe big fat Pantry, his whipping boy who had come of age, was gone. Tuby sucked it up. "Timm Mettish?"

"Dead." Gregory finally looked at Tuby. "You don't have to do this to yourself."

"I want to say their names aloud. Each one of them." Tuby rubbed his eyes. "Stan?"

"Stan Markh is dead."

"Bocher?"

"Will is dead."

"Earl Whitsche?"

"Dead."

"Chatters?"

"Rich L. Chatters died on the operating table yesterday morning. He was one of the few who made it out of the ravine."

"Prime?" Gregory hesitated. "What happened to Prime?" Tuby asked again.

"Tuby…" Gregory swallowed hard. "Prime was incinerated so badly we had to fax dental records from the yard to identify him."

"Ronn Judge?"

"Ronn died in the fire."

"Boots?"

"Dead."

"Stammy?"

"Stammy's dead, Tuby." Gregory was spent. "Coaches Mashner and Scormir didn't make it either."

"How about Howdy?" Tuby thought of the smile that rivaled the sunrise. He remembered that hot August afternoon when he called him over to take a few shots at the goal. He remembered how Howdy had asked permission from his soccer coach. Gregory didn't have to say a thing. Tuby knew he was dead. Tuby sat glumly and in shock. "I left them behind, James. I should have been there with them. I should have been with Jane and Emily."

"You gave them your heart and soul. No one left anyone behind. Nobody could have done anything about this."

"How did this all happen?" Tuby had not watched the news or read the paper. He had only sat beside Emily's bed in the ICU.

"It seems some drunken, doped-up trucker went on a rampage. Police have tied him to the rape of a dancer at a local strip club. Bartender says she had seen him before, but he had never gone berserk like this. Other witnesses say he tore out of the club in his gasoline truck. He was a rolling bomb just waiting to happen, and it happened to us."

"What do we do from here?" Tuby asked.

"It's an international tragedy. I addressed the press yesterday and again today. I spoke to the president and the secretary of defense. They both assured me they would do everything in their powers to help us bring everybody home. The air force has volunteered a C5A Galaxy to fly the dead back to Annapolis. That happens Friday. There are plans to hold the funeral service at the chapel on Sunday."

"How are we going to have a funeral for more than seventy people?" Tuby asked. He was behind on the funeral logistics.

"It will just be a service. We will help the families get the bodies home Monday. They can take the boys to their hometowns for burial."

"What about Emily and Jane?"

"Jane will be flown home with the team, if you so desire. It will be up to you and the doctors to decide whether Emily can survive the flight."

Tuby pondered Emily's fragile state. He knew he wanted to be at the service, but he had no intention of leaving Emily behind. Responsibility anchored the burden of grieving. "Sunday, December seventh." Tuby noted the date. "Ironic. Isn't it?"

The Canteen

Nimrod sat in the Canteen and sulked about his situation. A great sadness engulfed him, and Karen Carpenter sang "Rainy Days and Mondays." Jairus sidled up to his crestfallen mentor. "Hey, Nimrod. What are you doing?"

"Jairus. How are you, young man?"

"I'm fine. I brought my lesson books." Jairus tried to sound positive. "Do you want to teach me about some saints?"

Nimrod looked at himself in disgust in the barroom mirror. The chips were down, and he was holding a beer. The picture told Nimrod's story. He decided to tell Jairus the whole story about himself. "Sit down, Jairus. We need to have a talk. There are some things I need to tell you." Nimrod took a long sip of the malty beverage. He knew this wouldn't be easy on Jairus or himself. "When we first met, I was immeasurably excited to have been chosen to be your instructor. It had been some time since Michael had shown any faith in my abilities, but I failed you and myself almost immediately."

"What do you mean?" Jairus looked confused and concerned.

"Jairus, I've been a fraud my whole life." It was tough for Nimrod to say it aloud.

"I don't understand."

"I'm not who I said. I lied to you." Jairus looked close to crying. "We had a discussion on the school steps about my name. I wanted to impress you. I told you I was Nimrod, the Hebrew-famed war hero and hunter. I told you I was a pre- and postbiblical legend. I embellished. I lied and told you I was classified as a Mesopotamian god or Egyptian king."

"You name isn't Nimrod?" Jairus felt betrayed.

"My name is Nimrod. But I'm hardly the famous Nimrod of legend. I feel like Nimrod the Nobody. I am a distant relative of Noah by way of his son Shem. I am but a legacy of those who pleased God before me. I carry no true legend of my own." Nimrod felt ashamed of his life.

"But you are a saint." Jairus couldn't correct the contradiction.

"That I am." Nimrod asked for another beer.

"How can you be a saint and a nobody?"

"I waited at the gates for a long time, Jairus. Only attrition and the favor of my family opened those doors. I don't believe I earned my entrance into Heaven. My ancestors felt I could redeem the family's virtue, which my human life had tarnished, by becoming an angel. I led a decadent life on Earth. A life of wine, women, and song. Noah encouraged Michael to accept me to the School of Angels." Nimrod looked past the mirror and back fondly to those heady days.

Jim Croce sang "Time in a Bottle" on the Canteen stage.

"But you graduated from the School of Angels. I've seen pictures of your wings."

"I can fool the best of them, Jairus. That's what I am best at." Nimrod placed the glass to his lips. He knew he was terrific at fooling himself. "I was always an exceptional student and a nice guy, but I was never very good at getting anything important done. I was a terrible guardian angel. I was honest about that. I tried, but I failed miserably with my assignments. I could never understand the Darkness. Even now the depths of his hatred are still a shadow to me. It never made any sense. What was there to be gained from harm and sadness? I've never been sure of the game. There's always one sucker at the poker table, and if you can't figure out who it is, it's probably you. The Darkness could see me coming from a mile away." Nimrod shook his head in pitiful self-realization. "I have always been more comfortable with leisure, pleasure, and the joy of life than with trying to outwit the Darkness. Eventually my failures led to Michael losing his confidence in me, and he would no longer let me guard the souls on Earth."

Jairus had heard enough. "Nimrod, you can sit here all afternoon and drink beer if you want, but you've taught me a lot of things. You've taught me about saints and religion. You've taught me about kindness and compassion. You've shown me your heart. You've shown me the universe. You protected me and all your friends from danger. You were willing to sacrifice yourself before letting them into harm's way. You showed me love when I needed it most. Maybe you're not the best angel to ever graduate from the School of Angels. Your name might never be famous like Jesus, Muhammad, or Buddha. You might not have a bumper sticker that says 'Nimrod Saves.' But it's the most important name I know." Jairus hugged Nimrod and kissed him on the cheek. "And you're the best poker player in the universe."

Jairus left Nimrod alone with his thoughts. John Lennon and George Harrison joined Buddy Holly on the Canteen stage and sang "I'm a Loser" in three-part harmony. Nimrod listened closely.

Tuesday, December 2

Tuby sat across from Dr. Marci Bodathe in the hospital conference room. They talked about pulling the plug.

"Mr. Gravenald, it has only been two days, but Emily's condition has not improved." Dr. Bodathe tried to be gentle. "And I don't expect her condition to make any appreciable progress. It is not and never will be the hospital's policy to recommend to the legal guardian that a family member be taken off life support. Is it also not our policy to condemn the decision to do so. I can only give you my professional opinion."

Tuby never looked up from the chair. "How long can she live on life support?"

Bodathe had heard this question before. "Almost indefinitely. Science can sustain her for a very long period of time. There are documented cases of people staying on life support for almost two decades."

Tuby sighed. "Two decades. Emily would be twenty-four." It was impossible to fathom the future. "And she would just lie there like that for twenty years?"

"More than likely. She would grow, but there would be restrictions to her growth because of her state. It is difficult for the human body to gain the nutrients necessary for proper, sustained growth. Her muscles will atrophy, but she would have a therapist to exercise her muscles." Bodathe tried to skirt the gruesome details. She avoided discussions concerning bedsores, infection, and bodily functions. She did not address the long-term biological changes of puberty.

"Could she make the flight to Annapolis?" asked Tuby as he tore open the Sweet'N Low and put it into his coffee.

"It is very risky."

"How risky?"

"Fifty-fifty chance she makes it all the way to your chosen hospital alive."

"My other choice is to move to Denver."

Dr. Bodathe felt like being the chamber of commerce representative but knew this was not the time to toot the city's horn. "That's correct."

Tuby had a lot to think about in a few short days.

Wednesday, December 3

Shar became concerned. She had not seen Nimrod all day. Vishnu and Thomas played dominoes at the barbershop, and Jairus was in school. She started calling around the neighborhood. She phoned the Canteen. They had not seen him all day. He called Judeah on the off chance he had gone to see Michael. No dice. She finally saw the note on the refrigerator. Nimrod had gone to see Ba, the breath of life—a giving force of ancient Egyptian belief. He hoped Ba would perform the ritual ceremony of breathing into the mummified corpses and bring his Navy team back to life.

Nimrod stood at the mouth of the cave. He was somewhere between Heaven and the underworld. The mist was dense. A small bluish glow allowed him to see. It was a dangerous place, and Nimrod sensed demons lurked inside the cave and waited for him to take an untrue step. Wolves snarled inside the cave. The cavernous walls amplified the howling. The gnashing of bloody fangs ripped through the mist and came toward him quickly. Ba held the reins of the wolves tightly in his ghostly left hand. He was nothing more than a vaporous apparition. Rotten teeth filled his bulbous head. His vile breath reeked in the cave. Nimrod found himself again in a place he probably shouldn't be.

"It is only the desperate who come to the underworld to visit Ba." The voice thundered in the cave.

The demons crawled and hissing behind the rocks. Closer and closer they came to Nimrod. Their red eyes filled the night. The wolves snarled at Nimrod's feet.

"I am desperate, Ba. I have come to seek your help." Nimrod tried to sound steady.

"What can a relic such as Ba do for a soldier of Judeah?" Ba studied Nimrod warily.

"Satan has cheated me. He has taken lives entwined in an agreement between us."

Ba's laugh rumbled in the chambers of the cavern and mocked Nimrod outwardly. "Cheated by Satan, the crown prince of Hell? That is no surprise. What kind of fool are you?"

"I am a desperate fool," admitted Nimrod. Nimrod passed the names of the Navy players to Ba.

"I cannot deliver these souls back to life. They have already passed through the astral plane into death."

"Can't they just pass right back through?" Nimrod wasn't trying to be cute.

"They are gone! I cannot help you." Ba turned the wolves back into the cave.

"Cannot or will not?" Nimrod challenged Ba, and he turned angrily back to the fool from Heaven. "When the light shines bright into this cave once again, its beacon will be searching for you, Ba."

"The light will never shine again. You have seen to that, loser. To seek favor with Judeah is a waste of time. It is all but certain the Darkness will rule the universe." Ba floated behind the wolves and back deep into the cave.

"What about souls that have not passed through the astral plane?" Nimrod shouted at the retreating Ba and regained his attention. Nimrod handed him eleven new names.

Ba studied the names. "Clever, angel of Heaven. With this I can help you. Consider this a favor I will seek returned when the Darkness comes to destroy my world."

"Consider it done."

Satan had taken his team. Now he had Anyone. The bet was still alive.

Thursday, December 4

Tuby filled out the paperwork. He wasn't sure if he was making the right decision, but everyone supported whatever decision he would make. God had not given him any wisdom through his prayer. Tuby felt lost. Emily's condition had not improved. He couldn't pull the plug, though. He signed his name on the bottom of the legal document. Admiral Gregory and he had made all the arrangements for the transfer back to Annapolis. Tuby insisted on flying with the four-year-old. Tuby also signed the paperwork for Jane. Her casket would travel with the team members. He handed the pen to Vern, who had been at his side the whole week. Tomorrow they were all going home.

Friday, December 5

Tuby asked the funeral home director to open Jane's casket one more time. It looked like Jane, but it wasn't Jane. Tuby pressed his lips on her cold, lifeless cheek. His tears dripped on her nose, and he let them roll down the side of her face. He recalled the day she was born. She had come out screaming and ready. She peed all over him the first time he held her. He remembered how she was always a stiff-legged baby. They used to call her the ski jumper after the way she would tilt and never bend her little legs. Jane had been a fussy eater as a kid, and Tuby had taken her to task about eating more vegetables and fruit. Jane always challenged him back about his diet. She had never been easily fooled. He recalled the first time she won a ribbon. Jane had won first place in the two-hundred-meter freestyle as a sophomore. Tuby had picked her out of the pool, squeezed her tight, and drenched his own clothes in glee. All he wanted now was the chance to look her once more in the eyes—a chance to say good-bye. Tuby closed the casket.

It was the first time Tuby had been outside the hospital since Sunday. He winced at the sun. Tuby followed Jane's casket to the hearse and watched them close the black door and pull away. Now it was time to move Emily. He and Vern had kept the vigil by Emily's bedside for 124 hours. An army of doctors and nurses prepared to transport the comatose patient. Dr. Marci Bodathe supervised the transfer with the help of Emily's dedicated nurses, Linda Finnety and Terese Gifforgs. Both loved the little girl and were sad to see her go. No one knew how she would survive the flight. They loaded Emily into the back of the ambulance and took both Tuby and Vern to a specialized navy hospital plane waiting on standby.

The press surrounded the airfield. They kept their distance but the cameras rolling. Fortunately no one asked Tuby any questions. The press footage would look the same at both ends of the trip. Seventy-five pine caskets shrouded in American flags boarded the C5A Galaxy in Denver, and seventy-five pine caskets adorned in American flags disembarked in Maryland.

Emily survived the flight. So did additional passengers Tug Lerrin, Sal Geayser, Rolly Leaky, Brian Palmer, Jason Emenith, and Bram Gareloin. No one said much on the ride home. There wasn't much to say. They all dreaded Sunday, December 7. The difference between this Sunday and the Sunday sixty-three years before was they all knew it was coming.

Sunday, December 7

Rain Cutti refused to leave Tuby's side for the next two days. She brought both Tuby and Vern food and encouraged them to get a good night's sleep. It was a request neither could oblige. Tuby gave her the keys to his house, and she made sure Tuby's suit was dry-cleaned. She took Vern's measurements at the hospital and had a black suit tailored immediately. People reacted differently to grief. Rain needed to stay busy.

Tuby and Vern woke before the sunrise on the particularly cool Sunday morning. They watched with dread as the first rays of dawn broke the night sky. Tuby had asked Rain to stay the night. He wanted her to accompany him to the service at the naval chapel—the one he had never entered. He rued that this would be the first occasion. The long black limousine arrived, and Rain slipped between Vern and Tuby in the backseat. No one wanted to be very far away from the other. Tuby had called the car early so he could stop and say good morning to Emily, and he brought a nicely framed picture of her mother to put on the table in the hospital room. Tuby knew Jane would always look over her sweet baby.

The driver pulled into the yard and turned down Porter Street behind the chapel. Tuby recalled the madness of Herndon Monument on his first visit. The pallor of death and sorrow now replaced that enthusiasm of life. Thousands dressed in black had come to say good-bye. The president of the United States was to give the eulogy. Admiral Gregory greeted them and led them to a receiving line. Tuby requested to meet the parents of his players as they filed into the house of worship. He stood by the 10,500-pound anchors of the USS *New York*. He held the hand of Boots Morne's mother. Her eyes were soft and red from crying. Tuby shook the hand of Stan Markh's father, a Vietnam veteran. The atrocities and death of war could still not prepare a father to bury his son. Tuby wept openly when introduced to Thelma Pantry, Babe's mother. Tuby wanted to share so much about her son with the woman. Tuby met them all, and all seemed to have pass through the anger phase. All that was left for today was sorrow. Tuby still felt both.

He walked into the naval chapel. His sensed the hallowed ground. A shiver ran through his body like someone walking over his grave. The organ played from the balcony. A magnificent model of a tall ship floated in suspension over the organ. The pale blue walls mimicked the sea. The nondenominational chapel was built in the shape of a cross, and the balconies on the wings swung low and provided unity among the worshippers. The dome above them rose to the heavens and filled with stars. Tuby was seated in front of the altar in front of a single burning candle. Rain informed him the candle burned in perpetuity for the prisoners of war. Tuby never removed his eyes from the flickering flame. It warmed and comforted his soul.

The navy chaplain addressed the numb congregation. Polite and succinct he said nice things about the midshipmen, but he had not known many of them personally. His words and prayers, he knew, were only part of the healing process. The gathering of so many who loved them was the biggest comfort of all. President George Bush performed the eulogy. He somehow tied the accident, the football team, and the US Naval Academy to the bungled operations in the Middle East, terrorism, Saddam Hussein, and Osama Bin Laden. The service ended with a loud "amen."

Tuby held Rain's arm as they walked down the center aisle of the chapel. Glancing back at the prisoner-of-war candle, he caught the faces of the anguished families he had just met. The cold December wind whipped into the church vestibule, and Tuby slipped on his sunglasses to protect from the glare and light of the public's eye. The press once again kept their distance, but they were getting antsy for interviews with Tuby. It was the last thing in the world he wanted to do.

Admiral Gregory pulled him aside, but he obviously didn't want to broach the topic. "I am calling a press conference tomorrow at noon. The NCAA wants to substitute another team into the championship game, and we haven't addressed the sporting aspect of this tragedy."

"What is there to address, Admiral?" Tuby responded. He was annoyed—not by the admiral but the public. "I don't even know why they would play the game."

"Money, Tuby." It was sad but true.

"So what are you going to tell the NCAA? We've got no players, so we can't play?"

Gregory sympathized with Tuby's angst. "In essence. Yes. Technically we still have the right to field a team of qualified midshipmen from the academy. We could suit up anybody registered or with amateur eligibility and send them out onto the field."

Tuby rolled his eyes. "We could field a team and challenge the Florida T&A Barbarians on two and a half weeks' notice with players who might not have played a down in years?"

"Technically. Yes." Gregory knew the rules. "But I have no intention of doing that. The NCAA is asking us to forfeit so they can put on a competitive game for Christmas Day." Gregory fumbled with the funeral program in the wind. "I just wanted to let you know my decision before you saw it on television tomorrow. You're the head coach. It is really your call."

"Yeah. Go ahead and forfeit."

It sure would have been a fun game to play, Tuby thought. He got in the car and went to bury Jane.

Monday, December 8

Tuby woke early Monday morning. He and Vern decided to go back to the naval chapel. He wanted to see the candle. It had stayed with him through his dreams. They drove cautiously through the gate and heavy fog. He pulled in next to the chapel and saw the guards walking around the tomb of John Paul Jones in the chapel crypt. The young midshipmen recognized the coach and let him access the crypt. Tuby walked around the circular path. The ornate green marble in the center held the remains of America's greatest naval hero. Tuby read the inscription on the sarcophagus. "I Have Not Yet Begun to Fight." He read the words over and over.

Tuby snapped out of his trance and followed the staircase up to the main level. He wanted to see if the light was still burning. It was. He stood next to the candle in the gray morning light. It captivated him again. He watched the flame dance and the small stream of black smoke disappear into the dome. Tuby thought of Jane and Myra and remembered the players. He thought of Emily. He thought of God. He wondered when God was going to cut him a break.

Tuby left the candle and headed to the church's doors. He opened them into the soupy fog. The rich, dense moisture covered Herndon. Tuby could see the shape of a person heading toward the stairs.

"I've been waiting for you, Coach Gravenald." It was Admiral T. "Junk" Timple.

"Admiral Timple, it's been a long time." Tuby wondered why the admiral always showed up after a funeral. "How did you know I would be here?"

"Good people always turn to God in times of trouble. I thought this would be the most obvious place."

"What can I do for you, Admiral?" Tuby zipped his jacket.

"I thought you might want to go win a football game."

Tuby had had just about enough of this crazy old coot. "Admiral, we're forfeiting the game today at noon. Admiral Gregory has called a press conference. If you haven't heard, there's been a catastrophe here at the yard."

"It's not the first tragedy." Tuby snapped his eyes toward the codger. "We have never quit before."

Tuby was hot. "Now listen, you artifact! Nobody here quit. The players died. My daughter died. My granddaughter might as well be dead. There is no team."

The admiral was unfazed. "I'm sorry to hear about your daughter and granddaughter. The innocent are always part of the casualties of war."

"War? What war?" Tuby started toward the Cadillac.

"We're always at war, Coach Gravenald." The admiral never moved from Herndon. "Just as you are at war with the demons in your head." Tuby froze. "Those midshipmen died in battle. They will be missed, but there is no time to mourn our loss. Others need to fill the void of the battlefield. The war is not over."

"Isn't the goal of a war to win, Admiral? Am I supposed to take some mids out of the pool and turn them into football players?"

"The goal is to win. The goal is to never quit fighting the enemy. Ever. We must meet him head on wherever and whenever we can with whomever we can."

"And I suppose you have a group of men who are willing to play for the national title."

"I do."

They appeared one by one from the fog. Their forms filled with human flesh as they stepped forward. Carl Broodend stepped forward first. The bomb that had struck the *Oryoku Maru* had torn his chest apart. Gary Alesse moved out of the shadows. Bullet holes provided by the Japanese soldiers of New Guinea filled his back. Jason Cenode, riddled with cannon fire from the Zeros, touched Herndon. The gaunt and thin Manny Droad held his comrade Shaun Joint by the arm. Chet Skairny and Rat Doovaine stepped into the circle around Tuby and Admiral Timple. The giant Raytel Kigmenis held his right leg in his hands and hobbled up the walk with help from Egan Paal, whose wounds had not healed from his adventure with the crashing Val bomber. A charred and unidentifiable Dan B. Kerichuck balanced himself on the thin legs of Norm Leymoita.

Tuby cried out. He was petrified. "What the hell kind of mutant show is this? What kind of stunt are you trying to pull?" Tuby was freaking out.

"This is no stunt, Coach Gravenald. These soldiers have already made one sacrifice for their country and have waited a long time to play this football game. They are the most highly coveted players from a time gone by. I recruited them all myself. Trust me. They will serve you well."

"These men are sickly and wounded. They need a hospital— not a football field."

"You will provide that for them, Coach Gravenald. You have an excellent trainer," Timple eyeballed Vern. "I am sure it is nothing a good meal in King Hall won't cure."

Tuby looked at the seared Dan Kerichuck and begged to differ. "There's only eleven, Admiral."

Carl Broodend chimed in. "We all play both ways, Coach."

Sure you do, thought Tuby. "Are these guys even legal?" Gravenald didn't want to be a stickler. He was unsure these guys were even alive. He was certain this was just another of his bad dreams.

"Tell Admiral Gregory to look in the top-secret file named 'Lt. Earl Leron.' He'll find all their paperwork to be exactly in order. These men are part of a special missions program and have taken time out of their busy schedules to help the US Naval Academy win the national championship." Timple paused. "And they just might make those bad dreams go away." Tuby and Vern were dazed. "I must leave you now. My ship leaves port at oh nine hundred."

The new Navy football team saluted the admiral as he slipped into the fog. Tuby put his hand on a tree. He was dazed. Vern moved the men through the mist to Halsey Field House. Egan Paal looked at the sign on the athletic field. "Is that the same Halsey who commanded the USS *Enterprise?*" he asked Tuby when they entered the doors to the training room.

"It is. Admiral William 'Bull' Halsey."

"I served under him in the Second World War," Paal stated proudly.

Tuby knew instantly the young man was insane. Timple had probably recruited them all from his own asylum.

Tuby watched as Vern went to work on the eleven ghosts who had walked into his life. Vern bandaged, taped, scrubbed, scraped, and gauzed the wounded. He called a plebe over, handed him a hundred-dollar bill out of his own pocket, and sent him to get as many subs as the money would buy. The plebe returned with cold cuts, and steak and cheese footlongs. There were meatball subs and chicken teriyaki delights. Tuby watched the new midshipmen devour the subs with lightning speed. Tuby couldn't believe his eyes, but he was certain some of the very skinny men gained weight right in front of him.

Tuby's first phone call of the day was to Admiral Gregory. Norm Leymoita kept trying to hold Tuby's cell phone. Norm had always told Chet these would be big someday. Tuby thought he was losing his mind. "James, I need you to do me a favor." Tuby knew Gregory was still very busy coordinating the funerals around the country.

"Slow down, Tuby. What is it?"

"I just had the most bizarre meeting with Admiral Timple."

"Admiral who?" Gregory worried for his coach.

"Admiral Timple. The officer you sent to Minnesota when you first wanted to hire me."

"I sent Admiral Taylor to talk to you, Tuby." Gregory became more concerned. "What is this all about?"

"You didn't send Admiral Timple to Minnesota?"

"No."

"Well, I just talked to him not an hour ago, and…"

"Tuby, that's impossible. Admiral Timple has been dead for fifteen years." Gregory heard the receiver fall, and Tuby screamed.

Tuby called Gregory back and tried to regroup. "James…" Tuby had started to hyperventilate ever so slightly. "Do you have a top-secret file named 'Lt. Earl Leron?'"

"Tuby, you're acting crazy. What's this all about?"

"Just check for me please," Tuby insisted.

"I know all our files. There is no file for a Lieutenant Earl Leron."

"Please check!" Tuby had never screamed at the superintendent before.

Tuby waited for what seemed an eternity. Gregory read the names of eleven registered men in the top-secret file. All were listed as missing in action. Gregory got back on the line. "Tuby, where did this file come from?"

"I don't know. Why are you asking me? I'm the one talking to the dead admiral."

"Where are you?" Gregory sounded just as spooked as Tuby looked.

"Halsey Field House."

Gregory was on his way. He eventually showed up and watched with fascination. Naval intelligence had always impressed him, but they had never been able to pull off a gag like this. The players' paperwork was spot-on. They were all students at the US Naval Academy, and he didn't even know they existed. He had the midshipmen fingerprinted, and they were a ten-point match. Each of them.

"What do we do now, Tuby?"

"Tell them at the press conference we're going to play ball."

"Tuby..." Gregory hesitated. "This is way beyond me, and I've got to make a lot of inquiries. These guys are legit, but they're also more than half dead. You can't put them on the field."

"I've got a good feeling about this, James."

Tuby watched Chet Skairny slug down a twelve-inch turkey sub with the works. Tuby swore his calves got bigger after each bite.

"Do you think they can play?" Gregory's head was swirling.

"I don't care if they can play or not. Something magical is happening right in front of me."

Admiral James Gregory appeared promptly at noon before a bank of microphones and cameras. He read his statement to the press. "The last week has been a time of extraordinary suffering for the family that is the US Naval Academy. Under these trying circumstances, there would be no dishonor for us not to field a team in the upcoming national championship game. Yet, despite the heartache felt around the yard, eleven midshipmen have decided to step into the shoes of their fallen comrades and attempt to complete the path of the players before them. They paraphrased Admiral Farragut when I asked them if they were sure about playing in the game. They said, 'Damn the torpedoes. We're going to New York.'"

Tuesday, December 9

Tuby called in a favor from some of the kitchen staff at King Hall. The cooks came in and started making food for the new players. Tuby had never seen a group of people, any people, eat the way these guys could eat. Steaks, turkey, hamburgers, grilled chicken, roasted chicken, ham, sausage, mashed, boiled, and fried potatoes—they sucked it all down. They scavenged green beans, broccoli, cauliflower, brussels sprouts, carrots, squash, and zucchini. They poured ice-cold milk down their gullets and drenched themselves in freshwater. They ate ice cream, pound cake, strawberries, peaches, oranges, and chocolate bars. They sliced huge pieces of apple, cherry, and pumpkin pie and smothered them in whipped cream. They never tired of eating. They were human bottomless pits. Tuby watched as Kigmenis limped into the dining hall. On Monday morning he had had one leg. Now he limped on two, but the wounded leg was heavily bandaged. Tuby kept the players away from the public. He was sure they wouldn't believe their eyes. He couldn't believe his. Gregory told the press the players had been on a top-secret mission and maintained full eligibility. He didn't know what else to say.

The following morning Manny and Shaun went to the training room. Vern put together more supplies for the wounded men. Manny sat down on the trainer's bench while Vern inspected his frail but improving frame.

Egan, Rat, Chet, and Dan watched a rerun of *Baywatch* on the television. They looked at the device the way a dog looks at a snake. The linemen were a little frightened. They wondered why all the women were running around in their underwear. They watched as Pamela Anderson raced across the ocean on a Jet Ski. They thought a Jet Ski sure would be cool to ride. Norm played with the phones, and the computer mesmerized him. Vern went through the desktop's capability and used terms very unfamiliar to Norm. RAM, megabytes, downloads, and the Internet were terms he would have to solve. He did recognize the standard grid of letters on the keyboard. Jason listened to the radio and found the heavy-metal station. He turned it off. He was positive the radio was broken. Gary Alesse heard two F-14 fighters scream overhead and ducked outside in time to see the taillights blink away in the low clouds. They were fast. Gary loved fast things. Carl read a report in the *Time* magazine on the desk. American soldiers were at war in the Middle East. *Times haven't changed all that much,* he thought. Raytel looked outside the window and watched a Negro naval officer stride past. The African American wore the boards of an admiral. "Times sure have changed," Raytel mumbled under his breath.

Tuby gathered the men in the locker room. He listened to many of the amazing and horrific stories from World War II. Tuby remained in awe of the magic and mystery in the locker room. Tuby knew football and was still trying to wrap his head around the spirits that had rushed into his world. It was a world far larger than his imagination, but he knew God had heard his prayers.

He wanted to get to know them and find out their football capabilities. "Gentlemen, the players on this year's team were special boys. I've learned quickly you are very special men as well. We have the chance to do something special. Something good has to come from all this bad. Hopefully for you and maybe for me. My granddaughter is still lying in the hospital in a coma. I ask you pray for her every day." The men nodded at their new coach. "We don't have a lot of time to prepare. The team we are preparing to play is simply the best college football team ever assembled."

"What team is it, Coach?" Kigmenis asked, and he stretched his right leg.

"It is the Florida T&A Barbarians." It sounded so natural to Tuby.

"Never heard of them." Shaun looked at the men, and they all shook their heads.

"Florida T&A. Two-time NCAA champs. They're seeking their third in a row. Worm Roanen. B. Siemore Jett. Bones Jetr. All-Americans, the lot of them."

"Nope. Never," Norm confirmed. "What kind of name is 'Worm,' anyway?"

"We've got a 'Rat,'" Broodend kidded his partner, and the group enjoyed their first chuckle together.

"Is Jett fast?" Alesse wanted to race him.

"Yes. He is." Tuby was sure this was all a bad joke, but just in this short meeting, he had watched a small laceration over Egan Paal's eyebrow disappear. "What is your name?" He pointed to Jason Cenode.

"Jason Cenode, US Army Air Force."

"You're in the navy now."

Jason and his mates looked at one another incredulously. Tuby closed his eyes and prayed for patience. *Admiral Timple did a really good job with the paperwork,* thought Tuby.

"What position do you play?"

"Offensive tackle and defensive end."

Tuby sized Cenode up. He certainly was tall enough and had the right frame. He needed to put on a few pounds, but he wasn't nearly as thin as some of the others.

"How about you?"

"Raytel Kigmenis, US Marine Corps."

"You're in the Navy now, but that's not far off. What happened to your leg, Kigmenis?" It was disturbing knowing the marine only had one leg.

"I bumped into a grenade in Saipan."

Tuby sat down on a bench. This was all just too crazy. "What position do you play?"

"Offensive guard and defensive tackle."

Tuby figured. The man was massive. Tuby just wanted to make sure he wasn't a running back. After all Kigmenis was limping on one leg.

"How about you?"

"I am Gary Alesse. US Army. I play running back and cornerback."

"You?" Tuby looked at the incinerated carcass of Kerichuck and winced.

"Dan B. Kerichuck, seaman, US Navy."

Tuby had to ask. "What the hell happened to you, son?"

"A Val came in low out of the clouds. Hit us with a bomb dead center on the flattop. I and the rest of the fire crew specialists tried to control the blaze. The bowels of the *Princeton* erupted, and the beast swallowed me."

"Did you say the *Princeton*?"

"Yes, sir."

Tuby rubbed his eyes. "What position do you play?"

"Center and middle linebacker."

"And you're the guy who served on the USS *Enterprise*. Right?"

"Yes, sir. Seamen Egan Paal. I play tight end and outside linebacker." Egan's face lit up.

Tuby pinched his lips together with his fingers. He knew that name—Paal. He just couldn't place it.

Carl stood and spoke for the group. "Sir, this is Chet Skairny, US Army." Chet saluted to both Tuby and Vern. Vern studied Chet's gaunt face closely. He looked so weak. "Chet is an offensive tackle and a defensive end. That's Norm Leymoita. He's a running back and a strong safety. This is Rat Doovaine. He's regular army, and he plays tight end and outside linebacker. That skinny pile of bones is Shaun Joint. He's the quarterback. I'm Carl Broodend, and I play offensive guard and defensive tackle."

Tuby sensed from the beginning that Carl was the leader. "Thank you, Carl. You're all navy now. I suppose the rest of you were just on diets?"

"No, sir. The rest of us were prisoners of war in the Philippines."

Tuby stopped cold. The flickering light of the candle from the naval chapel twinkled in Carl's brown eyes.

Wednesday, December 10

Head coach Merl Larrola walked to the podium for the press conference. He hated press conferences. "I'd like to open the press conference with a statement." Larrola adjusted his ball cap. "It is with our deepest condolences we salute the members of the Navy football team who passed in the tragic accident of November 29. Our hearts and prayers go to their families in this time of tragedy. They would have posed a tremendous challenge at the first-ever NCAA title game. It is a shame we won't have a chance to compete against them."

Archi W. Gazet of the *Orlando Sentinel* started the questioning. "Coach, in light of Superintendent Gregory's statements Monday that they plan to play the game, do you think Navy can field a competitive team?"

"The US Naval Academy is a fine institution. Fit and ready young men and women fill their ranks. I don't know if they can field a competitive team in this short a time, though. I doubt it."

"Would you rather play a team the NCAA chose?" The question came from the back of the room.

"I would rather play the team that earned the right to meet us. Obviously that will not be the case. I think the fans deserve the best game possible. I think in this instance it would have been more prudent for the US Naval Academy to recover from the tragedy and not play the game."

"So you're saying you would rather the NCAA pick another team?"

"I never said that. I said I think the fans deserve a competitive contest."

"Which team would you have rather played among the play-off teams?"

"It doesn't matter. We would have beaten them all."

"So, are you making a guarantee to beat Navy in the title game?"

"I am pretty sure we can whip a bunch of intramural flag footballers."

"Do you have any concerns Navy has brought in a group of ringers?"

"No, Archi, I don't. Navy is an honorable institution, and the NCAA has certified these players. My only question is, if these players are good enough to compete against Florida T&A, why weren't they already on football scholarships?"

"Coach Larrola, nobody at Navy is on a scholarship."

Thursday, December 11

Tuby wasn't going to change his style. If he was going to coach, he was going to coach. He pinned the quote from head coach Merl Larrola on the bulletin board in the weight room. "I am pretty sure we can whip a bunch of intramural flag footballers." The players read it and got fired up. Even in a few short days, the players had started to become much healthier. Color came back into their faces. The prisoners started to bulk up and re-gain their muscle mass. Tuby was able to see parts of Kerichuck's skin around his eyes, mouth, nose, hands, and feet. The burns were going away. The scars on Alesse's back were all but healed. Kigmenis wasn't close to 100 percent, but he had started to jog on both legs. Egan Paal and the rest of the team sat in the film room with Tuby for hours going over film and remembering how the game of football was played. It was so much faster. The ball was thrown so much more. There was new equipment. Tuby ran them through some walking drills and basic plays wearing just helmets, shoulder pads, and shorts.

"Dan," Tuby said, working with his center, "snap it crisply to Shaun."

They worked on the basics. Shaun opened his hands under Kerichuck's crotch and felt the ball slap into his open hands. The ball was much smaller than he was used to. "Let's see if we can get everybody to come off the ball together."

Shaun got under the center. "Down. Set. Hut one. Hut two."

The line moved forward and into the dummies on the field.

"Not bad. Keep your butt low." Tuby motioned to Skairny.

"Coach, I can't see out of these plastic bars. Can I take them off?"

"No, you can't take them off." Tuby didn't have time for fun and games. "Vern!"

"Yes, Coach?" Vern was always close.

"Get Skairny a face mask that will allow him to see better."

"Yes, Coach."

Vern went with Chet to the sidelines and fixed his helmet.

"Let's line up in some different formations." Tuby clapped his hands.

The men stood still. "What kind of formations?" Shaun questioned.

"Wide receivers split. Single backfield. Split I. We might work the wide receiver in motion or shift the fullback and the tight end. Things like that."

"We don't know what that means, Coach."

Carl moved into the huddle with Tuby and Shaun. "Coach, the way we play football is simple. We line up and push them back. On defense we tackle the runner. We really don't have plays on offense or defense. Shaun runs the wishbone, and we block. He makes the reads and either keeps the ball or hands it or pitches it to Manny, Norm, or Gary. We've seen some of these formations but never used them."

"That seems a little simple. Don't you think?"

"It's a pretty simple game, Coach. It's our toughest eleven guys against their toughest eleven guys."

"So you don't know any plays?" Tuby was at a loss and headed for embarrassment.

"Other than right or left, no. The quarterback feels the game. He prods the defense for weaknesses, and then we attack. We all use our intuition."

"Well, Mr. Broodend, this is my team, and we run plays. It's the way we do things now." Tuby slapped the playbook onto the turf. "I recommend you learn these before practice tomorrow."

Friday, December 12

Emily lay frozen in the bed. Her nurse, Clare Rell, looked over her pitifully. Clare didn't look too hot herself. She had dark rings around her eyes and always seemed cold. Tuby gave her a cordial smile as they passed in the doorway. Tuby pulled the chair beside the bed and gently stroked Emily's hair. He caressed her skin and then closed his eyes to pray. Vern stood over them and watched the beeping monitors. Nothing had changed. Nothing ever changed.

Vern went to pull the car around, and Tuby waited in the lobby. They had gotten a terrible spot. Tuby slipped into the bathroom to pee. He stood before the urinal and never noticed the demon sitting on the sink counter.

"Good morning, Coach Gravenald." Abaddon sat crosslegged. His deathly pale skin made him even more ghastly by the fluorescent lights.

Tuby pissed down the leg of his pants. "Goddamn! You..." Tuby lunged for the evil angel of death.

Abaddon cackled while Tuby choked on his own tongue. Tuby reached for his neck and tried to breathe. His teeth pierced his fingers as he stuffed his fist into his mouth and tried to remove the gag. Blood ran down and over his lips and down his chin. The servant of the netherworld never raised a finger. "You shouldn't swear, old man." Abaddon ran his long fingernails through his platinum-blond hair. His black eyes watched the suffocating man struggling on the floor. "You escaped me once, but not again." Tuby turned royal purple. "It was a pleasure to watch your daughter burn." Tuby's bulging eyes revealed his hatred for the demon. "I should have killed you in the beginning, but I crave your soul. Now you can have the pleasure of joining your whores in Hell." Abaddon reached high over his head, and his palm revealed a dagger made from a vulture's claw.

The door of the bathroom swung open, and Vern found Tuby lying in his own blood on the floor and gasping violently for air. Abaddon had been foiled again, but Tuby had seen his message— loud and clear. The cockroaches scurried through her eye sockets and feasted on Emily's decaying skull. Lose the game, and Emily would live.

Saturday, December 13

Admiral Gregory protected the new team the way the government guards the truth about UFOs. Gregory created dossiers for the men and released them to the press. He bent the truth just a little. The press bought that they were all just a group of dedicated midshipmen doing their duty.

The incredible medical recovery of the players continued. Carl Broodend had gained a team-high thirty-five pounds and was up to 145 pounds. The others had put on weight, and they continued to eat at an unbelievable rate. The scars continued to heal. Tuby started to see some flashes of talent. Everyone's speed, strength, and endurance increased threefold in five days. They noted that Gary Alesse was fast—really fast. Jason Cenode found the weight room to his liking and roped Doovaine, Leymoita, Droad, and Skairny into training sessions. Raytel had started to run. Dan Kerichuck's burns receded to the point where his disfigured face was discernible. He was one hideous son of a gun. Tuby had never seen men work as hard as these players. They rarely slept and worked night and day on football. Tuby and Vern were exhausted from teaching. Egan Paal seemed to flourish in the new environment and constantly stayed at Tuby's side. He wanted to make sure the coach was all right.

Tuby invited Rain to meet them at the hospital. Tuby numbed when he saw Sal Geayser. The middle linebacker lay in traction. He was looking at the ceiling and trying to read a book on the desk via an orbiting mirror. He could only rotate his eyes and move his mouth. He could speak very softly. A slew of bandages covered the facial lacerations.

"Sal, it's Coach Gravenald." Tuby tried not to tear up. He wasn't sure what else to say. "How have you been?" wouldn't work. "You look good, Sal," wasn't appropriate or true.

Sal broke the uncomfortable silence. "Coach Gravenald, it's good to see you."

"It's good to see you too, Sal."

"I hear we have some mids who want to play in the big game."

"Yeah, Sal. We have some guys who are trying to fill some awfully big shoes. We sure could use you out there."

They both tried to smile, and then tears welled in Sal's eyes.

"I think my playing days are over, Coach." The tears fell gently down his cheeks.

"The doctor says you've got a great chance for recovery." Tuby tried to spin it in a positive way.

"I'll live. I just won't be able to walk." Sal closed his eyes, and the pain ran free. There was no sense in reminding him he was still alive.

It didn't surprise Tuby to find plebes Emenith and Gareloin hanging out in the same room.

"I think we've got a mutiny here. Attention on deck!" Tuby startled the plebes.

Huge smiles covered their faces. Emenith waved as he lay prone with his two broken legs, and Gareloin stood slowly and balanced the gangly halo that secured his neck. "I thought a mutiny was four plebes." Gareloin hugged Lerrin and then Coach Gravenald.

"That's four in Bancroft Hall. It's only two at a hospital." Tuby laughed. "How have you boys been doing?"

Tuby watched as Emenith hid the *Playboy* under the *Southern Living*. "We've been doing just fine. The doctor says I'll make a full recovery and be ready for practice in August."

Tuby rubbed the young man's shoulder. He seemed to be doing just fine.

"I don't know if I'll be ready for practice, Coach." Gareloin hammed it up with the halo. "But I might be looking for a job as offensive coordinator."

Everyone laughed. Gareloin's rigid movements were not funny, but they all knew it was funny.

"What are you reading there, Jason?" Tuby busted Emenith in front of Rain.

Emenith grew very red in the face and fibbed to his coach. "It's *Southern Living*, Coach."

"That's Ms. Cutti's favorite. Rain…" Tuby turned to the administrative executive. "Why don't you sit down next to Emenith and see if you can't find a good recipe for dinner?"

Gareloin moved his fat ass and halo directly into the path.

"What's the matter, Bram?"

"Jason doesn't like people on that side of the bed." Gareloin was making it up as he went along.

Tuby watched him sweat. Bram whispered in Ms. Cutti's ear, "He can't stand, so he has to pee in a bag. He gets embarrassed when people see it."

Rain promptly turned right back around. Tuby admired Gareloin. That was pretty quick thinking. Pantry had had an effect on all of them, it seemed.

Tuby and Rain went to see Rolly Leaky in the ICU. Tuby thought of Emily's hospital. They seemed to all have the same smell. They shared the same types of bulletin boards and family pictures. The nurses always seemed to be dressed the same but different. They checked in at the nurse's desk.

"We are here to visit Rolly Leaky. I am his coach at Navy." Tuby didn't like to throw his name around, but he wasn't immediate family. They could be sticklers about these things.

The nurse looked very confused and ran her finger up and down a chart. She picked up the phone and turned her back to Tuby and the other visitors.

"Ma'am." Tuby disliked waiting. "Is everything all right?"

"Coach Gravenald…" The nurse couldn't look Tuby in the eye. "Mr. Leaky passed away." The group fell mute. "The Leaky family removed Rolly from life support this morning."

Vern didn't know where the box of mail came from, but he handed out the stacks of letters. "Broodend." Carl stepped forward and took the bundle. "Doovaine." Each recipient looked more surprised than the last. "Kigmenis. Cenode. Paal. Alesse. Joint. Droad. Kerichuck. Leymoita."

They all held the documents in their hands. Each of them was holding a treasure.

Paal asked Vern, "Where did these come from?"

Vern quipped, "Probably the same place as you."

Paal conceded the point. All of them were part of the cosmic mystery.

Chet looked very sad. "Sir, did I receive any letters?"

"I'm sorry, Chet. The box is empty."

Chet looked at the floor. He was dismayed.

Each settled in to read each word of each letter countless times. Their hearts pounded with love as they tracked their family histories. They laughed with joyous news of grandchildren and swooned with the sorrow of lost loved ones. The players rode the emotional roller coaster of their families' lives in a few short hours. It warmed the soldiers to know their families had missed them. They had never been able to say good-bye. Chet tried emulate the glow of the others, but he could not. He still felt so very alone.

Shaun Joint opened the pouch and felt the soft leather of Paige's diary in his hands. Tears streamed down his face as he opened the book that revealed Paige's handwriting. The diary started on September 12, 1945. He read the notes and poems and the sacred thoughts in her mind. Paige wrote of his parents' death in 1962 and Sarah's passing in 1973. She wrote of her service to the victims of Typhoon Nora and an earthquake in Nicaragua. She mourned the loss of her friend, Roberto Clemente, who died in a plane crash on his mission to help. Paige sat before the US Congress emoting her passion to build a monument for the Vietnam soldiers. She wrote of her continued aid to victims of natural disasters around the world. Shaun read the pages of Paige's diary, reading about her growing concern for the environment in the late 1990s and her disgust at the lack of response by the United States for the victims in Rwanda and the Kurds in Iraq. There was also something about Monica's dress, but he didn't understand that. Shaun read the final lines of a poem in Paige's diary written the night before she passed in 2003.

From around my neck please take the locket.

Place it deep inside your pocket.

For it carries the other half of my soul

And needs to be joined so we can be whole.

Cherish the locket and comfort it,

For destiny says that Shaun will come for it.

Paige Shaun curled into the corner of the room holding the letters and the memory of Paige tightly.

Carl Broodend thumbed through the Christmas letters sent to family and friends from his mother, Ida. His family and the world had changed so much. He was amazed that Ida had held hope he would return and that his father had ached at the loss of his son. Churchill had visited Oklahoma. Carl wrestled with his emotions for his father, Doyle, who had sobered up and become a good husband to Ida. He passed in 1951. Ida worked for AT&T while Bud and Jimmy Jr. worked hard at the mill. The family grew. Inez kept getting grandkids. Carl's heart fell when he read Ida's note from 1987. "My hands don't work so well anymore. I live here at Saddle Brook Retirement Home. I am lonely. I guess Jimmy and Inez didn't want me around anymore. I had become too much of a burden. They visit once a week and keep me up on the kids and the news. The kids hardly ever show up until around this time, Christmas, and they come for an hour and leave. I hardly recognize them anymore." Carl reread the last letter in his hand with thoughts of Ida alone in a home.

Rat Doovaine read the letters of his sister, Valerie, and her correspondence with their Aunt Mary. In 1947 his mom and dad celebrated the creation of a country called Israel after the world learned of the extermination of the Jews in Europe. Valerie expounded on her love of Broadway and the new actor Marlon Brando. Valerie mentioned Rat in every letter as if he was still alive. She had loved him very much. Rat raised an eyebrow when Valerie decided to become a nun in 1954. She found her calling teaching children and becoming Sister Val. Rat held the letters to his heart after reading that his father died in 1975. The last letter noted the passing of his mother, Kay, in 1982. Sister Val had no immediate family.

Egan Paal talked back to the letters from his sister, Veronica. Her loneliness outlined the dysfunctional mother he had left behind and Veronica's struggle to deal with the loss of her brother and the presence of her mother. "I keep sending out these letters to Santa every year, and I'm getting a little impatient with both you and him. I never get the present I want for Christmas. I still miss you after all these years and probably write these letters as a form of therapy." Egan yearned to hold his sister close. Egan read he was an uncle to Angelina. Veronica had a child out of wedlock in 1960. The last piece of paper in Egan's pile was cut out from the newspaper.

October 1, 2001, Obituary, *Milwaukee Times Journal*

Angelina Paal, age thirty-one, has now been counted as one of the three thousand victims of the terrorist attack on the World Trade Centers of September 11. Angelina is the granddaughter of Quincy Paal, an eight-term congressman from Milwaukee who held office from 1956 to 1971. He vacated his seat upon the death of his daughter in 1971. His daughter and Angelina's mother, Veronica, was a victim of breast cancer. Quincy Paal died in 1983, and his wife, Lois, a Milwaukee socialite, died in 1985. They raised Angelina after the death of her mother. Angelina was a popular activist in the Gay and Lesbian Alliance and did extensive fund-raising for the AIDS Awareness Foundation. She was in a private meeting with her broker when the World Trade Centers collapsed. She is survived by her life partner, Carole Sutherland.

It dawned on Egan there was no one left.

Dan B. Kerichuck pulled one of the letters and shredded it open.

December 14, 1985

Dear Friends and Family,

For many years my mother wrote the annual family Christmas letter. My mother passed away in May of this year. She died of pancreatic cancer. She was eighty-two. She lived a full and wonderful life. Besides her children she had two great loves in her life. Her first husband, Ken, died tragically in a car accident in 1949. My mother desperately loved my father, and we worried she would never recover from this loss and the loss of her son, Dan, in the war a few years prior. It was a blessing to all of us she met William Keel and married in 1953. They lived the full and rich life my mother deserved. William died in 1977 of lung cancer. He was a darling companion and faithful husband. We will miss Mary Pat, our mother, and thank her for all she did for her children and grandchildren.

Michael's children are doing well. Michael's son, Matthew, is sixteen and his daughter, Gail, is thirteen. Gail is prone to dressing like Madonna, and Matthew is interested in racecars. They live with their mother, Jennifer. Michael has become a very successful real-estate developer and is working now with a company called Microsoft to find them headquarters in the Seattle area.

Our research at Duke for a cure for cancer took several steps in the right direction. I wrote an article on breast cancer that was published in the *New England Journal of Medicine*, and experiments were launched on the space shuttle for testing in the void of gravity. Johns Hopkins has discovered a treatment for liver cancer. We hope these efforts can help future generations to live longer and healthier lives free of cancer. Not much has happened to me personally. However, we had to evacuate the laboratories due to Hurricane Gloria, which came inland and caused quite a scene.

To all, a merry Christmas and happy New Year. God bless.
Love,
Dolores and Michael Kerichuck

Dan shredded open the other letters, put them in chronological order, and pieced together his family's past—or future.

Dolores and Michael both signed the last Christmas letter in 1999.

Manny read about Anna and his beloved boys, Jaime, Miguel, and Juan. He was so proud of all of them. Jaime had a son and named him Hector. Anna said the baby looked like Manny. Anna opened a restaurant to support the family called Tejas. Manny read furiously. There were so many grandchildren—Gabriella, Carlos, Benjamin, Maria, Sonja, Mauricio, Felix, and Alphonso.

Manny prayed when he read his first grandson, Hector, died of a disease called AIDS. He rejoiced at the prosperity and work ethic of his family. He opened the last letter.

December 6, 2002

I am eighty-two. My legs are weak, and I can hardly stand. My hair is gray, and my skin sags. But my eyes still cry, and my heart can still ache. I have lost another grandson to the sands of Iraq. Felix Droad, the son of my oldest child, Jaime, was killed in the second Gulf War.

In my life I have loved greatly. I have felt the joy of my Manny's warm arms and the elation of holding my grandchildren while they slept. I have felt pride in my heart as my sons have succeeded in a world of poverty and despair. Yet as the holiday season approaches again, there will be one less present under the tree—a gift removed from the death of war. I beg Almighty God to send us a miracle. Make the pain and suffering of the mothers of the world stop. *Feliz navidad.* Love, Anna Droad.

Manny longed to hold Anna and relieve her of her sadness.

Gary read through the letters. Fast. Like his comrades he mourned the passing of his parents, Larry and Donna. Annette took Donna in, as they had done for her, after Larry died in 1979.

Annette dedicated her life to their son, Peter. She became a news reporter and moved to Los Angeles to be close to Peter. Gary did not know what "rock and roll star" meant, but Peter was one of them. Gary read some bits of the letters over again. "Peter has also asked me to address his personal problems to family and friends. He says he doesn't want to hide and says sharing can help others. Peter hasn't had much success in the music business lately. His last album did not fare well on the charts, and the band was struggling to release new material. Infighting between the bandmates resulted in the group splitting apart. Peter seemed very depressed and recently checked himself into rehabilitation for alcohol and drugs. Peter had become dependent on cocaine and was drinking way too much. He has been there for nine weeks." *Uh-oh!* Gary thought. Peter must have gone too fast. He wondered whom he had gotten that from.

In 1986 "Peter got married in Malibu to a very young Eastern European swimsuit model named Nadia. She is very sweet and pretty, although she is rail thin. I don't know how she is going to bear my grandchildren." Gary smiled. Annette hadn't changed much after all. Gary marveled at the success and resiliency of Annette and his son as he flowed through the words. "Peter won an Oscar for his score of the film *The Sculpture of David*. It's a thriller about the statue of David's missing arm that held the map to Heaven. It was the proudest moment of my life seeing him holding the statue and dedicating it to me. I cried, and my mascara went all over the place." Gary started to cry too. He hadn't screwed up after all. The last of the letters was dated in 2000. Gary didn't know how to fill in the blanks.

Raytel read Teresa's speech from the family reunion in 1997.

"We have suffered our share of tragedy through the years. We lost Raytel, Violet, Angela, Carter, and Bruce along the way. It is the heavy price you pay to live in this world of ours. Some of us lost faith along the way. I was one of those. We all were.

But the strength of the family and the Lord God kept us all together."

Raytel worried how high the price had been. He tracked back to 1959.

"For the first time in many years, the entire Kigmenis family will all be together. Caleb has returned from Korea. Teresa has had another baby—this one a little girl. She looks just like her mama. Violet and Angela have been all over the South helping the civil rights movement. June was married this year, and she is as happy as a lark. I can't keep Carter out of those juke joints. George is about to graduate from high school, and Bruce likes to run track and field. Daddy's still working the farm, but he gets a lot of help these days from Carmen, Oscar, and Joe. Celeste is really enjoying college life at Grambling and says she wants to be a doctor someday. Daddy is going to build Mabel a new house. It's going to have indoor plumbing and full-on electricity in every room."

Things changed so quickly, thought Raytel.

In 1963, "Violet and Angela were murdered in a church bombing in Alabama...Uncle Carter, whom they idolized, died of a heroin overdose in a Chicago flophouse with a bunch of junkies and whores...Oscar, George, Bruce, Joe, and I all took the walk from Selma to Montgomery, Alabama." The words raced by him like the bullets in Saipan.

"The Kigmenis farm is now the largest and most profitable family-owned farm in the state of Mississippi. It took seventy-five years of hard work through four generations to achieve this goal. That little farm feeds thirteen children, twenty-seven grandchildren, and nineteen great-grandchildren so far." *Holy cow. The world had changed.* Raytel wondered about his twin, Caleb, and why he went back to war in Korea.

Jason Cenode read the statement voraciously. He had never heard the full story of his birth and his real mother.

August 14, 1974

Official statement at the opening of the Cenode Center

In 1924 my sister, Hillary, had a baby at the age of seventeen. Greed infected America in the 1920s, and my sister ran away with the father to chase more money and champagne. They left a swaddled baby on the family's doorstep, and we weren't to hear from them again—at least not for a few more years. Finally the stock market crashed, and they found Hillary and the man dead in a hotel room in San Francisco. Apparently they had committed suicide together after finding out they had no more money.

We named the child Jason, and I loved him as if he was my own. Jason was a beautiful child with dark hair and blue eyes. As angry as I was with my sister, I secretly rejoiced at the opportunity to be Jason's mother. I felt it had become my destiny. As I later learned, I could not have children of my own, and I was more than ever resolved that this fate was a blessing from God. As Jason grew he became more and more athletic and found himself a natural student. He brought home excellent report cards, one after another. He was very popular in school. Many girls were interested in him, and he loved to listen to the radio. It was Roosevelt's address to the country after Pearl Harbor that changed everything. From that day forward, Jason wanted to help America's cause against Germany and Japan. He wanted to leave promptly, but I would have no part of it. He was far under the age limit, and we fought incessantly about this until he turned eighteen and joined the US Army Air Force.

The rest as they say is history. They never found Jason's body, but we know his B-17 crashed into the mountains of New Britain. I was never able to say good-bye. I have struggled with that frustration ever since. I poured my frustration into raising two adopted children who had been orphaned. Over the years I adopted many more and developed a standing with California. With the help of volunteers, generous state grants, and private donations, we became the family to thirty-five children over the past thirty-odd years. I decided to put the memory of Jason to good use. I am proud to announce the opening of the Jason Cenode Center, Home for the Orphaned and Abandoned. This is a place where the children will continue to be safe, well fed, taught, and loved. I envision this as a community, state, and national program to save these children from certain poverty or a life without love. We are going to continue giving these children a home.

I will strive with all my energy to personally staff, oversee, and fund this project, or I will die trying. We've done it unofficially for thirty years. I hope to do it officially for one hundred years. I am already an old woman, but I have so much left to do. The children are our future, and I won't let the past hold them back.

Love to all,

Julie Cenode

December 2, 1976

Letter to the Community,

It has been an extraordinary year as the Cenode Center has expanded beyond its initial walls. A state grant allowed us to construct a new wing and add ten new beds to the facilities. We were able to upgrade the bathroom facilities and do much-needed work on the grounds. There is still much work to do, but we are taking large strides in the right direction. We unfortunately are spending an inordinate amount of time fighting the construction of a too-close nuclear power

plant. Nuclear power seems to be the flavor of the month for countries, but I believe the dangers outweigh the rewards—especially when it comes to the children's health. The plants frighten me. Governor Jerry Brown will be hearing my voice loud and clear. If he doesn't listen, then we'll take our fight to the new president, Jimmy Carter.
Julie Cenode

December 3, 1981
Speech at the Chamber of Commerce:

What an exceptional, fun, and busy year for everyone here at the Cenode Center. The Cenode Center was cited for excellence in a state program and will be considered for federal funding within the next fiscal budget. We also have been granted a scholarship that will help send some of our family to college. This is outstanding news, and it greatly benefits the continuing growth of the children. I owe a debt of gratitude to a new member of the Cenode family, Commander Patrick Hart. Commander Hart came to us as a simple volunteer. He quickly adapted himself to the environment and became an integral part of the children's lives. Besides his regular responsibilities with the US Navy, he has become an invaluable counselor and administrator at the Cenode Center. His tireless efforts have spawned numerous new educational ventures for the children. To him we all owe a debt of gratitude. As I grow older, Commander Hart has been taking over some of the more serious responsibilities of running the orphanage. His bilingual talents have been instrumental in teaching a second language as well as helping the growing number of Latino children find our orphanage as a safe harbor.
Merry Christmas and happy New Year,
Julie Cenode

December 5, 1991
Annual Holiday Letter

A happy holiday season to all. This yule season holds so much promise and hope as the Cenode Center prospers by the growing love and prayers that come from around the world. Our family members extend across the United States—from Maine to Alaska and Florida to Hawaii. They have made names for themselves in London, Beijing, Brisbane, and Quito. Our love has no international boundaries. Despite this love the world continues to be a haunting place of hatred. The United States has once again been drawn to the battlefield as mothers anguish over the loss of their children—as I languished over the loss of mine almost fifty years ago. We continue to fight around the world and closer to home. The violence has struck the hearts of the Cenode Center. One of our own, June Drantes, an innocent eight-year-old girl, was struck by a stray bullet in a drive-by shooting. She died upon arrival at the local hospital. This senseless killing has become the ugly tattoo of humankind. It will take all our prayers and hope to overcome and rectify the hate in the eyes of humankind.

It is with this heavy heart I leave my position as director of the Cenode Center. It will always be my joy to visit, and I will never be able to stay away for long. My strength is waning, although my passion thrives. I have handed over the reins and the future to the hands of the able Commander Patrick Hart, who has been my friend and professional confidant for ten years of loyal service. He will assume the position upon his return from the Grand Canyon, where he is visiting Biosphere II with some of the science-oriented children of the Cenode Center. I thank you for allowing me to live my dream and for all the love that has filled my lungs with every breath. Merry Christmas and happy New Year.
Julie Cenode

December 7, 1993

Dear Family and Friends,

For all of us, it has been a sorrowful year at the Cenode Center. Our mother and founder passed away of a blood infection on July 4. It is no surprise Julie passed on such an important date in American history. She was one of the true great Americans. She sought neither fame nor fortune. She aspired neither for power nor glory. She gave of herself out of love—love for children. She bankrupted herself to raise two adopted children but never bankrupted her soul. The love of hundreds of her children rewarded her. They flew from around the world to say good-bye to their mother. Four thousand people of all races, religions, and creeds came to pay their final respects to Julie Cenode. I insisted before her death we change the name of the center to the Julie Cenode Center. She would have no part of it. Destined to be the home for the unwanted, it remains dedicated to the first son she raised, her nephew, Jason Cenode, who was killed in World War II. It is my privilege to announce that a new national fellowship will be named in her honor. It is also her legacy that a new television rating system has been installed to better help parents understand the content of television shows children watch. Never an advocate of television and always a staunch believer in the imagination of the written word, it was still Julie's desire to help children and parents avoid the pitfalls of sex and violence of the modern medium.

Her legacy will live with the grandchildren of her institution. It was a privilege to have known her as closely as I did. I will miss her. Merry Christmas and happy New Year.

Commander Patrick Hart

Jason read with awe about the life of Julie Cenode, his mother.

Norm didn't know quite what to expect from the collection of letters written by his wayward brother, Dominic. Dominic had made a bunch of pen pals after spending a few years in the penitentiary. *Figures,* thought Norm. Dominic had wasted such a promising life.

Norm's father passed in '69 and his mom in '72. Dominic connected with these mobsters in prison and offered to "bring them things for the joint." He still gambled and ran numbers. He went on about a lost relationship with a woman named Rose. He said he loved her. *That's a giant step for Dominic,* thought Norm. He even said he was sorry for the things he had done and felt guilty for doing them. *That's another giant step,* thought Norm. Norm knew his brother would never change, though. Dominic moved to Las Vegas in 1986. That was putting a match to dynamite. Norm sat with his back against the wall. He wanted to see Dominic but wouldn't have a whole lot to say. Norm just looked away. He felt disappointed and alone.

Chet worked around the room. He shared stories with the players and consoled them when the emotions became overwhelming. He put his arm around them and felt their loneliness. They in turn returned the hugs. Chet was sad. He hadn't gotten any letters.

Monday, December 15, Oklahoma

The obese, inattentive nurse slung the mail on Ida Broodend's nightstand. The aged mother struggled with the glue that sealed the letter. The nurse didn't help. Ida read the contents, and a sparkle glistened in her eye. She asked the nurse if she could use the phone. Ida hadn't dialed the number in years. She was amazed her arthritic fingers pressed all the right buttons on the first try.

"This is Jimmy. How can I help you?"

"Jimmy, this is Aunt Ida." Ida struggled to hold the phone to her ear. She was very weak and old. "You need to come get me."

"Why, Aunt Ida? What's the matter?"

"You and Bud are taking me to New York." Ida held the three tickets to the NCAA Championship Game tightly in her feeble hands.

Las Vegas

None of them ever saw the mail carrier. Dominic Leymoita opened the envelope and assumed one of his friends was paying off a long-past-due debt. He had nothing else planned for Christmas and booked a flight from McCarron Airport in Las Vegas to LaGuardia.

New York City

Sister Valerie Doovaine thought she must have won a raffle at the church when the envelope slipped under her apartment door. Inside was one ticket to the opening of the Big Apple Dome. Sister Val had watched the structure rise from the West Side ashes. All she needed was to take the subway.

Pittsburgh

Paige Delaney's lifelong friend, Diana, read the letter and subconsciously clutched at Paige's locket. She wasn't sure why, but she would take the bus to New York. She was too old to drive.

Mississippi

Teresa Simmons slit open the manila envelope. Thirty-five tickets for the NCAA Championship Game fell to the floor. Teresa fell with them. Her daughter helped her up, and she called Caleb Kigmenis. Caleb knew a guy who chartered buses in Jackson. Caleb needed to give him a call.

Los Angeles

Annette Alesse figured her son, Peter, wanted to surprise her on Christmas with a trip to New York. She couldn't care less about the football game. She wanted to skate at Rockefeller Center one more time, though. She called her travel agent and booked two first-class round-trip tickets to La Guardia.

El Paso

Anna Droad shopped and then picked up the mail. She was surprised to see the large manila envelope slipped under her door. She sat down and stared at the contents. *How in the world?* Anna thought. She called an old business friend and chartered a plane. Loaded from a lifetime of work and with thirty-two tickets to the biggest game of the year, Anna decided to take everyone.

Durham

Dolores Kerichuck snuggled in the chair reading the *Journal of American Medicine.* She heard the envelope slide onto the wooden floor but never noticed anyone on the porch. She opened the piece of mail simply marked "Dolores" and called her brother, Michael, immediately. They would rendezvous in New York on Christmas Eve.

Riverside, California

Commander Patrick Hart found the package on his desk. He hadn't signed for any packages. He removed the tape from the box and sat down slowly in his seat. It was not possible what he was seeing. He counted the 415 tickets. Each had the name of a child—everyone who was or had ever been a part of the Jason Cenode Center. There were instructions to meet in New York City and $100,000 in cash to help with lodging and food for the trip. It was simply signed, "A Friend." Commander Hart started calling all around the world and booking flights.

Tuby got a postcard with a stamp marked from Heaven. It simply said, "Win the game, and save Emily. Save the world." Tuby turned the postcard over. The rays of the sun burst through the clouds. "In addition to all this, take up the shield of faith with which you can extinguish all the flaming arrows of the evil one."

He had seen the demons and lost faith in God. It seemed God still had faith in him and knew the demon would lie.

Wednesday, December 17

After nine days of practice, the players were starting to look like a team. They were not a very good team, but they were a team Tuby could put on the field. He was sure Florida T&A would slaughter them, but Florida T&A had done that to everybody else. Tuby put the players in full pads for the first time. He had been granted permission from the NCAA to hold a scrimmage with players from another university. The Division II James Madison Dukes agreed to visit the US Naval Academy. The new Navy squad held its own.

Tuby circled the players around him after the scrimmage with purpose and newfound energy. "You boys have come a long way. There's still a long way to go, and I just don't know if we'll have enough time to get there. But you work hard and are tough. You showed me a lot today. We're going to have to run the ball and play solid defense. We don't have much of a passing game. Hell, we don't even have any wide receivers. Tomorrow we'll work on some special sets with the tight ends to spread the defense out. We'll also work more on special teams."

Thursday, December 18

Nimrod plotted the trip to New York and vowed to protect Navy from another ambush by Satan. Delilah prepared earthly wardrobes and covers for espionage. This included naval officer uniforms, maintenance overalls, and casual wear for restaurants and clubs. New York crawled with demons, and Team Nimrod needed to stay incognito. Nimrod planned to come out from the shadows to meet with Satan one last time.

Monday, December 22

Head coach Merl Larrola and the team arrived by charter at La Guardia Airport, and the New York press met Larrola. Hordes of lights, cameras, and action besieged Larrola and company.

"I understand arrests will be made after the New Year in the sexual assault of Johanna Detong. Can you comment?" Willow Dyheart shoved the microphone in his face.

"I don't know the first thing about any arrests." Larrola moved along with his bag.

"Karen Evhy, Coach. Florida detectives have tied the recent rape of another co-ed to a murder on campus. Is there a serial rapist and murderer on your team, Coach Larrola?"

"Absolutely not."

"Is it true a group of campus girls known as the Fire Cherry Debs were arrested in a recreational vehicle outside Hurl Stadium and charged with prostitution?"

"I don't know anything about that."

"Sources say there is a paper trail that leads through your office all the way to the desk of University President Garth A. Moot. How can you deny payments to players and their families?" Dyheart speared Larrola with questions.

"I can deny them, and I will." Larrola's brow furrowed, and the sweat beaded on his forehead. Larrola swatted at a photographer with his ball cap.

"State investigators have sought an injunction to review all the cell phone calls of Ali Cherck. Will those calls link him to felon Shark Mulfalla?"

Larrola never answered. He got in the limousine, and it sped away. The flashes of the camera caught it all.

The front page of the *New York Post* showed Larrola giving the New York press the finger as he escaped in the limousine. The headlines read, "T&A Coach Thinks New York Is Number One."

Tuesday, December 23

Team Nimrod stepped onto Glengans Tiles. Against his better judgment Nimrod allowed Jairus to come. The guard pulled the lever, and in seconds they were gone. They returned to Earth deep in the bowels of Grand Central Station. Team Nimrod arrived clad for a night on the town. Nimrod was in a banana-yellow suit with a matching fedora. He found a cane in his right hand. Interlocking gold and diamond rings that spelled "Bling" adorned his left hand. A heavily braided gold chain that spelled "MOFO" hung from his neck. Shar sported a black trilby hat with a gathered, mellow brown rose that matched her headband and sculpted feathers. The black patent-leather skirt accompanied fishnet stockings and six-inch metallic spiked heels. Her low-cut blouse exposed her chest, but a roughed-up biker's jacket warmed her. Thomas's outfit mirrored Nimrod's, but it was pink. They made a terrific pair of matching pimps with Shar walking beside them. A nineteenth-century dark-paisley smoking cap and a hippie-style poncho crowned Vishnu. They made him look as if he dealt opium on Forty-Second Street. Jairus was unexpected on the journey and sported only a pair of blue jeans, black Dr. Martens, a Shania Twain T-shirt, and the biggest mullet the Big Apple had seen since Billy Ray Cyrus. Jairus's hair said business in the front and party in the back. Only in New York did this quintet blend into the crowd.

"Delilah!" screamed Nimrod.

"Where to now, Big Daddy?" Vishnu poked.

"To the Grand Hyatt, Midnight Express," Nimrod said, returning the favor. "Come on, Shar, and don't shake it too much."

The group slipped right down the street to the old Commodore Hotel. At the check-in counter, they met a Southern belle. The young lady brought up Nimrod's reservation and checked his identification closely. Management had been on the lookout for hookers and pimps moving in on the Grand Hyatt's turf. The NCAA Championship Game had brought all the freaks out of the shadows.

Everything checked out, and Nimrod handed her his American Express card to pay for the $275-per-night rooms. Jairus looked at the soaring atrium and the cascading waterfalls that decorated the lobby. Patrons dined at the elegant Sun Garden and smoked big cigars at Trumpets. Just outside the door, several homeless people begged for food. Nimrod called room service, and they sent a heavenly spread.

It was still early in the afternoon, and Team Nimrod decided to walk down to Thirty-Fourth Street and visit Macy's. Jairus had never met St. Nicholas. It was something he had always wanted to do. Jairus sat on St. Nick's lap and whispered in his ear his wish for Christmas. St. Nick's cheeks blushed, and he smiled at Jairus as he left his knee. Thomas doubted it was the real St. Nick and approached the imposter. He grabbed his hair and wig and tried to pull them from the fraud's face. Thomas was embarrassed when they did not slide off his head.

They slipped into D'Agostino's Grocery and filled four bags of goodies. They passed them out to the vagrants along the way and wished them a merry Christmas. They entered a historic department store and were agog at all the material things. People clambered over one another to purchase the most unessential items at astronomical prices. Beautiful women hiding their faces from the world hawked perfumes and makeup. Customers bought expensive shoes by the dozens at prices that would feed the starving in Africa for a month. Parents spoiled children with drivable miniature Hummers and train sets that needed assembly by an electrical engineer. Bags stuffed with jewelry, toys, clothing, and electronics were hauled out to Broadway and into cabs, stuffed under family trees for Christmas or Hanukkah, and discarded in a few short days.

Tuby kissed Emily on the forehead. His body was going to be in New York, but his heart and mind would be with his little girl. Tuby felt guilty for leaving. He was feeling guilty about a lot of things these days.

Wednesday, December 24

It was difficult moving Ida in and out of airports and taxicabs, but she was a trooper. Jimmy Jr. and Bud checked themselves into adjoining rooms at the Crown Plaza, and both agreed they couldn't take Ida out sightseeing, although both wanted to see the pit that was the World Trade Centers. Ida napped on the queen-sized bed while Jimmy Jr. went to find them something to eat.

Dominic stayed at the St. Moritz on Central Park South. He liked the suite that overlooked Seventh Avenue. He called Elaine's and made reservations for two. It had been a while since he had had good spaghetti Bolognese. He called his old bookie from back in the day. They would meet at 7:00 p.m. for dinner.

Sister Valerie looked at the sky. She smelled snow in the air. It hadn't started, but her nose was rarely wrong. The shepherd poked its head out of the alley. It was a big dog but friendly. Valerie stood still and let the dog smell her hand. She petted him behind the ears. He looked underfed and had no tags. She checked his full coat. He was free of fleas and mange. She gave the dog a cracker from her purse and tried to slip away, but the dog followed her. She frowned. The shepherd frowned back. Valerie thought he was cute. She didn't want him to stay the night in the snow. She decided to take the dog to the pound after the holiday. It would be her good deed for Christmas.

Diana got lost coming out of Port Authority. She wanted to head to the West Side and find the Milburn Hotel. A bicycle-riding hood tried to snatch her purse. She struggled with the cloaked youth, and a local woman who sprayed mace in his direction finally scared him away. The Samaritan gave Diana directions to the hotel and helped flag down a cab.

The Kigmenis clan gathered in the lobby of the Hotel Elysee while Teresa checked them in. The kids in the group kept hollering, "Mississippi's in the house." Caleb slept in the same room Tennessee Williams did back in the 1940s.

Annette and Peter met in the hallway of the Melrose Hotel. They were off to try the seafood at the Atlantic Grill. Peter talked about the mouthwatering Chilean sea bass with the porcini crust and tamarind glaze.

Anna enjoyed the flight into LaGuardia with the tribe. She had never been to New York and wanted to do it right. She booked rooms at the Plaza for the entire group and headed to Tavern on the Green. Anna marveled at Central Park and the big buildings.

Commander Hart watched as the final buses rolled up to the Chelsea Savoy Hotel on West Twenty-Third. Logistically it was like moving an army, but all 415 Cenode Center graduates were now checked in. Now all he had to do was get them dressed and ready for dinner. He had reserved the entire dining room at Carmine's on West Forty-Fourth.

Dolores found Michael walking aimlessly around Penn Station. The Knicks were scheduled to play a Christmas afternoon match-up against the Heat at Madison Square Garden, and Michael wondered if he could talk Dolores into two sporting events in the same day. They headed off to Le Madeline but swung by the Paramount Hotel so Michael could drop off his bags.

On Christmas Eve Nimrod knew where to find Satan. Delectably sacrilegious Satan would be at the club called the Church. Team Nimrod piled into the cab. The taxicab driver pulled up right in front of the renovated house of worship. The sidewalks thumped from the bass and heavy-metal guitars. Vamps and vixens lined the sidewalks dressed in black. The street reeked of drugs and cheap sex. Condoms and hypodermic needles littered the gutters. Money exchanged hands openly for pills and small bags of lost hope. A young girl performed fellatio on a man in the dark near the leafless shrubs. They sauntered into the church under the gaze of the bewildered metal heads.

A sea of evil faces parted, and the king of evil slapped his tongue at the ants that crawled on his hoof. Abaddon caressed his master's fur. Satan chortled about their impending victory. Christmas would be remembered as the day of death.

Nimrod strutted down the alley proudly and confidently. "You've lost your bet, Satan."

"I've lost nothing." Satan bellowed a laugh that caused the crowd to turn. "To the contrary, fool, it is you and your flailing army of angels on the cusp of destruction."

"Your squad is outmaneuvered and outmatched. I will grant this single opportunity for you to call off the demon army. I will spare you the humiliation of tomorrow's defeat and disgrace."

Satan moved to the edge of his throne. Fury and rage filled his face. He barked, "Disgrace? It is your disgrace that has neatly secured the fate of wretched humanity and this filthy planet. The annihilation of this entire soulless galaxy is at hand."

The desolate crowd roared in approval. Death, for them, was a better alternative to life.

"It is with compassion I ask you to fold your hand. I shall not ask again. This is your last chance." Nimrod stared down the throat of the gargoyle.

"Dismiss yourself from my sight. You are a desperate angel who tries to bluff me. I will not lay down my hand on the eve of my greatest triumph. I shall not sleep tonight because I yearn to watch them die tomorrow."

Nimrod stayed calm. "If you feel so strongly, then you won't mind if I raise the stakes."

Team Nimrod couldn't believe their ears.

"Silence, you fool! You have nothing left with which to barter." Satan mused for a moment, and his predatory eyes met the tender pupils of Jairus. "Except the nubile soul of the child." Satan's serpentine tongue slithered near Jairus's mouth.

"No! Jairus is off the table. He is just my student—one of the very souls I seek to save."

"Then leave here in shame. Witness the carnage firsthand. The world will witness the power of the Darkness, and the gullets of my demons will feast on the flesh of puny humans."

"You can have my soul." Nimrod felt the hardening in his throat and could not swallow.

"The soul of a heavenly angel." Satan pondered the satisfaction. It was a first-rate prize.

"And the souls of my three comrades."

"What?" Vishnu had never agreed to these terms. Team Nimrod turned ashen.

Satan leered at Team Nimrod with hunger. "The snakes in the pit haven't had such spoils in years." The knees of Team Nimrod quivered in their corduroys. They had to quash the overwhelming urge to run. "Four souls of Heaven." Satan craned his neck in an unnatural way. "Intriguing." He jerked and convulsed. "What is my price, oh jester of Heaven?" Satan mocked.

"You destroy the Hell Star forever in the Stounfad System and cease all hostilities in the universe."

Satan released a belly laugh. "Your price is steep, loser. You have not heard of the demise of Maroed Rain?" Nimrod closed his eyes and prayed for the lost planet. "You bet in desperation, but you have nothing in your hand. Foolish, foolish man who tries to frighten me away." The king of nightmares breathed deeply. "I am Satan. You do not scare me! You bluff. I will use your scrotum as a cloth to wipe away the tears of my laughter."

That unnerved Nimrod. "So it is agreed."

"It is agreed. By this time tomorrow, you will be on your knees pleading for mercy, and I will mock you. Then I will jam this cane into your chest, pull out you heart, and eat it like a candied apple."

Team Nimrod punched Nimrod in the arm on the cab ride back. Their lives were now in the balance.

"Have you completely lost your mind?" Thomas said.

"I tried to bluff him out of the bet." Nimrod looked at nothing out the window.

"Well, he called you. Now we're all going to spend the rest of our lives in Gholar. If we're lucky."

"You're supposed to be saving our souls, Nimrod. Not gambling with them." Shar got out of the cab.

Jairus looked pitifully at his mentor. He didn't know what to say. Jairus felt fooled. Shar grabbed his arm and pulled him into the hotel. Nimrod walked up and down Park Avenue all night thinking.

Thursday, December 25, Christmas Day and Game Day

The rarest of sights hung over the Hudson River—a winter rainbow. Snow would fall on Christmas Day, but it spawned little hope in Nimrod's heart. There were only a few hours left until Armageddon. The first flakes fell. Nimrod thought how horrible the demon-spilled blood would look on the fresh layer of white. There was no hope the game would be canceled. The stadium had a retractable roof. *Besides,* Nimrod thought, *they never cancel football games because of snow.* He decided to go back to the hotel and rally the troops one more time. At least they had good seats for the end of the world.

Already in makeup telecaster Greg Goutiner wanted to make sure his eyes looked just right. Greg was ready to broadcast the biggest game of his career. Color commentator Greg Acori joined him in the booth. The charming, average ex-player had a terrific look and had tried on a couple different blazers to find the one that accentuated his lats. Sande Sirren was inept but gorgeous. She was assigned to prowl the sidelines, and she practiced her questions with the crew.

"Coach Larrola, are you happy you get to wear your home colors today? Coach Gravenald, it has been a tough few weeks. Hasn't it? Coach Larrola, do you think you're going to win the game? Coach Gravenald, did your team make it to the stadium all right with all the snow?"

Sandy really liked that last question. It broadcast her strengths to the media moguls as a weather personality as well as a sportscaster. The production crew and director pored over final preparations for the event and the billion people viewing worldwide.

The Navy players walked around the Big Apple Dome in awe. They had never seen a structure so massive. None of them had ever seen artificial turf. They felt the painted concrete—the hard-and-fast surface—was a definite Florida T&A advantage. Tuby informed them they would have to wear tennis shoes on the turf. Cleats would not be necessary. It really didn't seem like football to them. They watched as the roadies assembled the stage for the pregame entertainment.

The Florida T&A players got their first look at their opponents. They guffawed in the tunnel and videotaped themselves yukking it up with little handheld portable cameras. They filmed themselves from head to toe. Fans yelled for autographs, but all had headphones stuffed into their ears. They couldn't hear a cannon fire as they worked multiple devices. Larrola gave them five more minutes, and then it was going to be time to suit up and start pregame drills.

The crowds outside the Big Apple Dome accumulated like the snow. The subways jammed, and taxis slowed in the streets.

Smashed Florida T&A fans entered the stadium ready to rumble. They filled their seats, hung signs over the railings, and tried to find the television cameras to make *SportsCenter* in the evening. Hundreds of fans shoved pints of booze into their pants to avoid the outrageous prices at the concession stands. Once inside they bought Worm Roanen and B. Siemore Jett jerseys and stuffed the Barbarian coffers. Attendants filled the luxury boxes with racks of deli meat, cheese, sandwich rolls, sausages, and wings. Managers unloaded cases of premium alcohol. A full hour before game time, the stadium filled to capacity, and the noise reverberated in the constructed cavern.

Jimmy Jr. and Bud asked the usher if Ida could sit on the edge near the rail because of the wheelchair. He politely obliged and gave the two boys seats right next to her in the handicap spots. They were right on the Navy fifty-yard line. Anna Droad and family sat in three rows right above Ida. The loud and raucous Kigmenis family filled in rows one section over. The families started making friends right away. Diana was all alone and wondered why she had come. It was so loud. *But it is colorful,* she thought. She sat alone below two large families and introduced herself to Dolores and Michael Kerichuck. They had just grabbed a couple hot dogs and beers for thirty bucks. Annette and Peter Alesse settled into the excellent seats. Dominic Leymoita struggled with his damn cell phone. He thought thirty-five and a half points was too much for any championship game—even under the circumstances. He figured Florida T&A would call off the dogs after the first half, and Navy would cover the spread. Sister Valerie felt very awkward about bringing the German shepherd. The dog just wouldn't let her leave without Valerie taking him. She wore dark glasses and pretended she was blind. The dog behaved perfectly and took her right to her seat. The usher sighed and shook the cramp from his arm as he checked in the group of 415 from the Cenode Center. The stands behind the Navy fifty-yard line were full. The obnoxious hoots of the Barbarian faithful surrounded them.

Larrola huddled his team around him. The team was quiet and focused—more so than at any point that year. Larrola knew he didn't have to give them a pregame pep talk. "You're the best team that's ever played college football. You're the two-time defending NCAA champs. You're about to win your third. Most of you will be playing in the pros next year. I might have to join you." The players laughed. "Make your last college football game something to remember. The bigger the score, the bigger the payday on draft day. Take no prisoners. Show no mercy. Let the world witness how good you really are. Kill 'em!"

The team responded with their repeat of the coach's request. "Kill 'em."

Tuby surrounded himself with his eleven guys. It was twelve counting Palmer, the electrical engineer, who suited up in case of an injury. Tug Lerrin joined the sidelines after being released from the hospital. Tuby fueled their faith. "Gentlemen, if there was ever a team of destiny, this is it. Your bravery has never been in question. I'm really proud of you for sticking your necks out. We're going to give them one hell of a fight!" The men carried Tuby's hope into the tunnel.

Given the lack of players, the Navy squad followed the entire entourage of 4,400 midshipmen from the tunnel. They marched in unison and made crisp turns onto the sidelines and into the stands. They surrounded their brethren as if protecting them before the battle. Highlights of the Navy season replayed on the Jumbotron. They seemed out of place and inappropriate. There was military footage of jets screaming and carriers and nuclear submarines diving. Despite the escort Tuby and the team still felt small in the giant Big Apple Dome.

The fireworks exploded, and dry ice covered the field. Piggie Paul, the Notorious PIG, rapped his big hit "Bacon" for the pumped-up crowd. A delirious Florida T&A Barbarian team sprinted onto the field. Each player removed his helmet, mugged for the field camera, and tried to get a little airtime. The Barbarian hordes screamed for blood. They smelled the title three hours away. They flaunted pseudo animal-skin headwear complete with snouts, and they waved plastic spears and spun medieval weapons. Many wore imitation breastplates and faux spiked boots. The highlight reels rolled on the Jumbotron, and the players piled on top of one another in front of their own bench. Head coach Merl Larrola grabbed his headset and waited for the referee to call for the team captains.

"What do you think about all that hype?" Tug asked Tuby.

"I was going to get Admiral Gregory to send a battleship up the Hudson and shell the stadium. That might have gotten the fans' attention."

Tug laughed and noted Tuby hadn't completely lost his sense of humor.

Greg Goutiner read the advertisement for the sponsor before starting the JFN broadcast. "The Big Apple Bowl is sponsored by the Angry Beaver Boot Company. You'll stay warm if you stick it in an Angry Beaver and snap it shut." Goutiner paused as the cameras focused on his new green contacts. "Ladies and gentlemen, merry Christmas. We're here in New York City for the inaugural title game for the outright NCAA football championship. Despite the tragedy that befell the US Naval Academy, they're here, the fans are here, and of course the Florida T&A Barbarians are here. My partner, Greg Acori, joins me in the booth. Greg, does Navy stand a chance at winning tonight's game?"

"Unfortunately, Greg, they don't. Now saying that you're still going to see some exciting football played by the most explosive team to step onto the gridiron—the Florida T&A Barbarians. They are locked, cocked, and ready to rock. Everybody will be witness to the coronation of history's greatest team."

"Sande Sirren is down of the field with head coach Merl Larrola. Sandy."

"Hi, Greg. I'm standing on the sidelines with head coach Merl Larrola. Coach, are you happy to be wearing your home colors today?" Sandy smiled her perky smile and shoved the mike into Larrola's grill.

"We sure are, Sande. New York has been a wonderful host. They've made us feel right at home. The stands are full of the greatest fans in the world." Larrola waved at the drunks.

"Coach Larrola, do you think your team is going to win the game?" Sande seemed serious and thoughtful. She pensively waited for Larrola's answer.

"I do, Sande. I think you're going to see a little bit of everything tonight, and no disrespect to the Navy players, but we've just got more talent, dadgummit."

"Back to you in the booth, Greg." Sande smiled, and a plastic beer bottle from a rowdy Barbarian fan pegged her in the cranium before the camera switched back to the booth.

The public address announcer spoke. "Let us all rise for the singing of our national anthem. Please welcome Usher."

The crowd stood, and Usher wailed away at the nation's theme song. The midshipmen stood still and saluted the flag. The general public failed to remove their caps or snouts or hold their hands over their hearts.

Team Nimrod got into the stadium after much coercing from their leader. They had seats near the midshipmen and needed to change into their military costumes. They all slipped into the bathroom stalls. Jairus waited by the sink.

"Nimrod!" Thomas screamed from the filthy stall.

"You have to be kidding me," Vishnu complained.

"I'm not leaving here until you fix this. Why did we trust you again?"

"Trust me? I trusted Delilah." Nimrod looked hopelessly at his costume. "I told her. Uniforms from the USS *Enterprise*. Not the *Star Trek: Enterprise*."

Thomas looked in the mirror. He was wearing the pale blue Spock top with tapered black pants and black boots. It came with pointy ears, bad bowl cut, phaser, and communicator. Shar wore the sultry red miniskirt of Uhura, the communications officer. Nimrod got Captain Kirk's gold jersey, and in an unfortunate mix-up, Vishnu became Worf, the converted Klingon. He was resplendent with rippled forehead and shaggy hair.

"We can't go traipsing around the stadium like this," Thomas said.

"No. We can't."

"Well, what are we going to do? Just sit in the bathroom? The first half is about to start. I don't want to spend the last few hours of my life siting on a toilet bowl dressed like a Klingon!" Vishnu added.

"Just let me think." Nimrod sat on the toilet. It was always a good place to gather one's thoughts.

Roman Steanen walked out to the giant red apple painted at midfield. Cocaptains Jacko Nobs, Theo Drimend, Worm Roanen, B. Siemore Jett, and Bones Jetr joined him. In a display of unity, all eleven members of the Navy team walked to the core of the apple. They were about to play their first game in over sixty years, and each had butterflies. The referee explained the rules of the coin toss, which Drimend had trouble understanding. Navy's Carl Broodend called heads. It came up tails. Florida T&A elected to receive. Roman Steanen hissed insults at the Navy players. The Navy players stared at him. They weren't daunted.

Dominic Leymoita leafed through the program. Poor Navy had endured that terrible accident. He had no clue what players represented Navy. He didn't recognize any of the names until he came across Norm Leymoita. Dominic sat straight up in his seat. A similar quiet rippled through the stands behind the Navy bench right before kickoff when the public address announcer blasted the starting lineups over the PA system.

Carl Broodend placed the ball on the tee and went to the huddle. "We've been called to duty once again. We all dreamed of playing one more game. Well, here's our chance to show them what the old men have got."

There was a gleam in each and every eye as he called the break. The adjusted their helmets and slapped their armor. The referee blew the whistle, and Broodend wasted no time heading for the ball.

Broodend booted a low liner to the fifteen. Chaistler fielded it. Chaistler followed the center wedge and veered left to the thirty, thirty-five, forty. Chaistler had one man to beat, but number fifty, Rat Doovaine, shoved him out of bounds. *Damn it!* Tuby didn't need the Barbarians starting with tremendous field position on the fifty-yard line.

"They are quick," Norm said when he gathered in the huddle. "I felt as if I was running in sand."

Jett lined the offense up in the I formation. J. J. "Honey" Romans went in motion. Jett handed the ball to Worm Roanen, who worked his way off right tackle, behind the Sheik, and through a big hole. Norm Leymoita dragged him down in the secondary. It was a Barbarian first down at the Navy thirty-seven. A haze fell over the stadium. Time seemed to stand still as the families of the World War II soldiers tried to make sense of the miracle happening before them.

"Florida T&A is too powerful and quick." Tuby grabbed Tug's arm. "The Sheik just drove Cenode off the ball and out of the play. That was a gaping hole for Roanen."

Jett snuggled under center. The Barbarians were in the I formation. Fullback Steer Reprivus shuffled in motion to the right.

Jett got the ball to Roanen. This time he went right. He squirted around the corner for a gain of seven before Egan Paal and Gary Alesse pushed him out of bounds.

Tuby yelled at Tug. "Watch how wide receiver Whiz Toorleen and Andrew Spore crack back on Cenode and then the Sheik takes care of Kerichuck and gets Roanen to the outside."

Dan got everybody in the huddle. The fiery middle linebacker chastised the defense.

"C'mon, guys. We're getting blown off the ball." Dan sounded garbled. He was not used to the mouthpiece.

"They're big, Dan." Jason Cenode was panting.

"And fast," added Raytel.

"Hit them then. Make them feel it," Dan implored.

"They can't feel anything. There's so much padding in these uniforms. You could get hit by a bullet, and it would bounce right off." Carl was frustrated.

The Barbarians came to the line. On second down and three, Jett put them in the I formation again. Toorleen was wide right. Toorleen motioned into the formation, and Jett faked the pitch left to Roanen. Jett headed right behind Reprivus and the Sheik and then flipped the ball to Toorleen on the reverse. Romans cracked back on Skairny and allowed Toorleen the corner and a wide-open field. Navy free safety Manny Droad made an ankle tackle at the Navy fifteen and saved a touchdown.

"Beautiful execution, everybody." Larrola cheered on his team. "That was a great effort by the free safety to stop the score."

The scoreboard flashed the first down. Jett put the offense in the I formation again. Tight end Spore moved into the H-back. Toorleen and Romans moved up to the line of scrimmage. Manny wondered why they moved around so much. He saw Zogo snap the ball to Jett. Kerichuck and Broodend snuffed the quick trap to the fullback Reprivus for a three-yard gain. The Navy players helped one another up and gained a little confidence.

Tuby put his hands on his knees. They lined up for second down and seven from the Navy twelve. T&A split the backfield. Spore lined up in the slot left next to Toorleen. Romans split wide right. Reprivus went in motion and left a single back deep. Zogo snapped to Jett, and Jett took a seven-step drop. The receivers streaked to the end zone, and Jett tucked the ball under on a quarterback draw. Kerichuck smashed him at the two. Jett adjusted his helmet after taking a good lick.

Annette saw Gary in the goal-line formation and didn't believe her eyes. Jett faked the handoff to Roanen and rolled out to the right. Andrew Spore was wide open for the touchdown. Annette couldn't care less that T&A scored. The magic of Gary on the field was mesmerizing.

Spore waited for his teammates and then performed a vulgar end-zone celebration.

"You got to see a little bit of everything that makes Florida T&A a great team on that drive. The speed, the power, the finesse," Larrola told sideline reported Sandy Sirren in a midgame interview. "Chaistler's return started it all. Florida T&A is nearly invincible with a short field."

Nobs added the extra point for a 7–0 Barbarian lead. The drive lasting 2:50 and covered fifty yards in six plays.

Team Nimrod hid in the bathroom stalls. Many fans had broken the seal, and the lines in the bathroom started to back up. Angry patrons pounded on the doors. Nimrod had to think of something.

"Nimrod, no more of your ideas. We need to find Satan and beg for our lives. We've failed." Thomas was pleading.

"It's not over yet."

"It's been over," Vishnu lamented.

"We're only down one touchdown. It's time to implement plan E."

"Plan E?" Shar said.

"Yes. Plan E. This one's going to work," Nimrod said none too confidently.

"Just like plans A, B, C, and D?"

"Put on the maintenance costumes," Nimrod said.

The fan banged on the door. "Come on, man. I have to take a dump. These nachos are going to make me poop my pants."

"Just a moment. We're maintenance, and the toilets were acting up. We're just a few seconds from having them fixed." Nimrod had bought some time for the group. "Ready?" Nimrod questioned his team.

They stepped into the lavatory.

"Where's Jairus?" Nimrod looked for the teenager.

"Jairus?" Vishnu called for his little friend.

Shar searched around the urinals and towel dispensers.

"Jairus?" Thomas cried out.

"He's not here," Shar confirmed.

They stepped to the concourse and spied the concession area. Jairus wasn't in the food lines or getting a T-shirt. "We have to find him." Nimrod looked ashen.

"Nimrod." Vishnu looked deep into Nimrod's eyes. "If you really have a plan E, now is the time to execute it."

"There are demons everywhere. Jairus could be in danger."

"We're all in danger, Nimrod." Shar didn't want to leave the boy behind, but time was running out.

"I was charged with his safety. I can't leave him alone." Nimrod craned his neck and searched the crowd.

"It is the safety of the many versus the safety of one. You were charged with the responsibility of saving the people of Earth. Jairus will be fine," Shar rationalized.

No one in the group felt that was true. They all fretted for his well-being. Nimrod thought of the terrified boy sitting in Satan's lap. Nimrod let out a tremendous sigh. It was the most difficult decision he had ever been forced to make. "Execute plan E."

Jairus was in God's hands now.

"Welcome back. As Jacko Nobs prepares to kickoff, I wanted to remind our viewers to tune in for the new Monistat Seven Bowl being played this Saturday, December 27, between the Alabama Crimson Tide and the Texas Longhorns in Seattle, Washington, on JFN." Goutiner filled the few seconds before the kick. "Greg, what does Navy do to counter the Barbarians onslaught?"

"Well, Greg, they've got to try to slow this game down. They need to get a first down and establish some offense. This Navy squad is unique in that every player plays on both offense and defense. At this rate those guys will be exhausted from chasing the Barbarians around the field."

Nobs booted it deep. Gary Alesse fielded the ball and headed up the field. Linebacker Marble Calple drilled him. The crowd stood as the ball came loose. A wild melee ensued, and the referees tried to sort it out.

"This will be costly to Navy," said the master-of-the-obvious color commentator.

"The referee signals Navy ball. It will be first and ten on their own eighteen-yard line. It looks as if Carl Broodend came up with that loose ball."

Jimmy kept shaking Ida. A calming smile had appeared on her face.

The Navy players gathered in the offensive huddle. Rat and Chet looked at Gary. "Sorry, guys. It won't happen again."

Alesse wiped the blood from his mouth.

"It better not," warned center Dan B. Kerichuck.

Quarterback Shaun Joint took control of the offense. "All right, guys. Settle down." Shaun batted his helmet. He couldn't hear the play being called in from the sidelines. The receiver in his helmet was malfunctioning, and the time on the play clock was running down. He looked hopelessly at Tug on the sidelines and held his hands in the air in confusion. Tug tried to relay the play to the quarterback with hand signals. The play clock ticked down to eight, seven, six. Shaun called time-out. Tuby and Tug groaned as Shaun headed to the sidelines.

"I don't know what all these signals mean."

Vern squirted some water through Shaun's face mask.

"We've worked on them over and over." Tuby was fuming.

"Listen, we'll simplify everything. Your wristband is numbered," Tug said. Shaun looked at the cumbersome wrap around his forearm. "My right hand will give you the first number, and my left hand will indicate the second." Tug gave Shaun an example of play twelve. Shaun could manage that.

"Why can't we just run the wishbone? Then there would be no plays to call."

"Because the wishbone doesn't work in modern football. Now get out there and run the offense."

"Yes, sir." Shaun went back and called the play in the huddle.

"Navy seems to have gotten things sorted out on the sidelines," stated Goutiner.

"I think you are seeing the nerves of some very young players," mentioned Acori.

Joint lined them up in a pro set. Alesse spread to the right, and Leymoita was to the left. Manny Droad was at tailback, and Egan Paal was in front of him at fullback. Joint took the snap from Kerichuck and handed the ball to Paal up the middle. Defensive tackle Harry Tearnytt stopped him right away for no gain.

"That is football 101, Coach. That's not going to work against the bigger Barbarian front four," Tug reminded his coach. "The Barbarian front four outweighs the entire Navy offensive line by over three hundred twenty pounds. That's a tremendous advantage. They are huge, but they are also quick."

Tuby glared at Tug. On second down and ten, Joint squatted under center and handed it to Droad. Middle linebacker Buster Chagora smacked him in the backfield for a two-yard loss.

Tuby spit on the ground. "Paal just missed the block. He was out of position." Tug glared at Tuby.

It was third and twelve, and Navy was moving in the wrong direction. Joint went into the shotgun. Droad and Paal protected him. The snap was high, but Joint handled it. He looked to hand the ball off to Droad, but he wasn't there. Joint scrambled toward the sideline and looked for a receiver. Joint tossed the ball out of bounds. The crowd groaned. Bones Jetr knocked Joint to the ground. Penalty flags went flying, and the Navy players surrounded Jetr. Jetr took a swing at Broodend. Doovaine tackled Jetr, and the Navy players jumped into the pile. Both teams tangled in the scrum while the referees tried to break it up. The referee threw his hat because they were out of flags. Dominic Leymoita laughed in the stands. He knew not to mix it up with his brother, Norm.

Referee B. K. Ascanni addressed the crowd. "There are multiple fouls on the play. The first flag was for roughing the passer on the defense. That fifteen-yard penalty will be enforced from the previous line of scrimmage. There were also flags for unsportsmanlike conduct on the defense." The Barbarian fans booed. "And unsportsmanlike conduct on the offense. Those penalties offset. First down."

Shaun lined up under Kerichuck. He took the snap on first and ten and pitched the ball to Droad on the old student-body right play. Florida T&A got pressure upfield, and free safety Wink Romance V came up strong to make the play. The players jostled at the bottom of the pile. Romance V stuck his hand under Droad's mask and raked his face. Anna screamed her husband's name from the stands, and Manny came up bleeding from the scratches.

"We gained one on the play." Tuby tried to be optimistic.

"That brings up second down and nine." Tug added pessimistically.

Joint broke the huddle, and Alesse went wide right. Leymoita went wide left. "Coach, should we pass the ball?" Tug asked. "Our biggest play so far has been the fifteen-yard penalty."

Joint took the snap and handed it to Paal again. He went straight into the teeth of the Barbarian front four. Tackle Barney Steern leaped up from the pile and paraded around the Navy backfield as if he had just won the lottery. He put on a show and flexed his muscles. The Barbarian fans loved it.

"Third and long again," Tuby muttered to himself. "Call a pass."

Joint went into the shotgun. He stayed in the pocket and looked for a receiver. The pocket collapsed around him. Shaun tried to duck under Shank W. Shonnejoy, but the big defensive end leveled him for a sack. That brought fourth down.

"He never had a chance." Tuby scratched his head.

Broodend belted the punt high into the air and deep. It was a great kick that drove Chaistler all the way back to the eleven, and Gary Alesse was right there to meet him.

"Alesse could have fielded that one on the fly. That kid is fast." Vern said to Palmer.

Ida told anyone who would listen it was her boy, Carl. She had always known in her heart she would get to see her son play again. Ida was very old, but she could see clearly now.

"So with seven twenty-eight on the clock, the Barbarians take over at their own eleven-yard line," Goutiner reminded the viewing audience.

"I expect the Barbarians will open it up here," said Acori.

"Jett steps under Zogo and takes the snap. He tosses the pitch to Roanen, who sweeps left around tackle Romans Steanen. Roanen squirts to the seventeen, where Rat Doovaine takes him down."

"Once again a nice job by Florida T&A of moving the Navy front four off the line. Doovaine made a good tackle to stop Roanen from a big gainer."

"Jett lines up in the shotgun with Romans to his left and Toorleen to his right. Reprivus goes in motion and leaves Roanen alone in the backfield with Jett. Jett takes the snap and fakes to Roanen. Jett flings the ball out to Toorleen on a wide-receiver screen. Toorleen has a team of blockers out in front, but Paal knifes through and drags Toorleen down for no gain."

"That's how you contain these Barbarian wide receivers. You can't let them get going, or they will run right by you."

"That brings up third and four from the Barbarian seventeen-yard line. Jett gets under center this time, and it looks as if he is changing the play at the line. Reprivus shifts to the offset I, and Jett hands the ball to Roanen. He heads right behind Reprivus and the Sheik, Ali Cherck. Roanen turns upfield, and Raytel Kigmenis and middle linebacker Dan Kerichuck tackle him."

"It looks as if Roanen got enough for the first down."

"Roanen did. The referee is pointing downfield. It will be first and ten for the Barbarians from the twenty-two-yard line."

"T&A went back to their bread and butter. Right behind Cherck and Drimend."

"Jett brings the offense to the line and surveys the Navy defense."

"Navy is playing a very vanilla brand of defense right now. They have single coverage on the wideouts. I expect Jett to take a shot downfield very soon."

"Reprivus comes out, and Juice Chaistler comes in. That gives T&A a three-wide-receiver set. Navy shifts around to match up with Chaistler. Jett takes the snap and fires to Romans slanting over the middle. Romans catches the ball for a short gain, but free safety Manny Droad drills him."

"Romans took a shot, but he gets up and waves a finger in Droad's face."

"Droad swats the finger away, and the referees get between the players. They don't need another fracas like earlier in the period." Goutiner paused to catch his breath. "That will bring up a second down and six from the Barbarian twenty-six. Jett takes the snap and hands to Roanen. This time Roanen moves left with the ball. He fakes the reverse to Romans and keeps it himself. He follows Molt and Steanen. There's a huge collision, and Chet Skairny helps Roanen up from the pile."

"Skairny really laid a lick on Roanen. That was the first time the Navy defense got any type of penetration."

"It was not enough for a first down. Roanen gained about two, and that will bring up third and four from the twenty-eight. Jett lines up in the shotgun and takes the snap. Jett looks and tries to find a man. Jett slings the ball over the middle, and Andrew Spore makes the grab at the thirty-four. Strong safety Norm Leymoita promptly tackles him. First down for Florida T&A."

"Navy is doing a good job keeping the Barbarians in front of them, but Jett is doing a good job of taking what the defense is giving him."

"The Barbarians continue to work their way out of the shadow of their own end zone. This drive started at their own eleven. Jett lines up with first and ten on his own thirty-four. Reprivus is back in, and the Barbarians set up in the power I. Reprivus goes in motion to the left, and Jett takes the snap. He stretches and hands it to Roanen, who goes off tackle. Doovaine drops Roanen at the thirty-nine after a gain of five."

"That's the counter trey. Steanen and Molt crash down into the middle, and Theo Drimend and Ali Cherck pull from the right side and get ahead of Roanen."

"Second and five from the thirty-nine. Jett takes a deep drop and is looking down the right sideline for the speedster, Toorleen. Jett launches the ball, and it's a footrace. The ball drops to the turf. Alesse met Toorleen stride for stride."

"That was really great defense. Alesse knew where Toorleen was the whole time and kept his eye on the ball."

"That will bring up a third and five. Jett lines up in the shotgun with Roanen to his right. He takes the snap and fakes to Roanen. Roanen picks up the charging Doovaine coming hard from the left side on a blitz. Jett tucks the ball and runs up the middle. Kerichuck meets him right at the forty-four-yard line. This one will be close."

"They'll have to measure."

"Jett looks woozy from the tackle. Ascanni brings out the chains. The Barbarians are going to get the first down by the nose of the ball."

"T&A got a very good spot. You can see Jett's knee touch down at the forty-three on the replay."

"Jett will bring the Barbarians to the line. It's first and ten at their own forty-four. Jett calls the play. He has Romans to the left and Toorleen to the right. Tight end Spore goes in motion and makes it strong-side right. Jett takes the snap and hands it to Roanen. Roanen follows Cherck and Spore. Roanen plows ahead for a few. Kerichuck makes the tackle."

"Navy has clamped down on the run. T&A is still moving the ball, but they are not getting the huge holes they got on the first drive."

"Second and seven. Jett drops back to pass. Roanen swings into the flat, but Doovaine is on him. Jett looks downfield but can't seem to find anyone. Jett moves out of the pocket, dances away from Kigmenis, and rambles toward the sidelines. Jett fires the ball back across the middle. Romans goes high in the air to make the catch and comes down at the Navy forty-three-yard line. What a catch by Romans!"

"Jett finds a way on this play. Navy had things covered pretty well, but Romans comes back to the ball like all good receivers do and just makes a great catch using his athletic abilities."

"Navy looks frustrated as the Barbarians keep the drive alive. Zogo lines up over the ball, and Jett stays back in the shotgun."

"They've crossed midfield. This is where the Barbarians excel."

"Jett takes the snap and throws a quick out to Romans in the left flat. Cornerback Shaun Joint meets him, and Romans steps out of bounds. Romans flips Joint the ball, and Joint flips it right back. Once again the two sides jaw at each other, and I'm getting the impression the Navy players just plain don't like the Florida T&A guys."

"I think they're just a little frustrated, Greg. The T&A players are flamboyant, but they are great football players as well."

"That was a gain of six, and it brings the ball to the Navy thirty-seven. T&A has used up some time on the clock, and with three thirty-four left in the first, they line up for second down and five. Jett goes under center and sends Romans in motion to the right. Jett takes the snap and hands the ball off to Roanen. Huge hole up the middle, and Roanen tries to bend it outside to the right. Paal is there to make the stop but not until Roanen picks up twelve yards to take it to the Navy twenty-five."

"Watch Zogo pin Kerichuck and seal him. That opens the lane for Roanen, and he does a nice job following his blocks. Good interior running by Roanen on that play."

"The Barbarians are well within kicker Jacko Nobs's range, but I'm sure head coach Merl Larrola is thinking six at this point in the game."

"I would think so, Greg."

"Jett lines up in the shotgun. He looks to Romans and touches his helmet. Romans is one-on-one with Joint on the left side. Jett takes the snap. He lofts the ball to the corner of the end zone. Joint is step for step with Romans. Romans makes a brilliant catch in the end zone, but the referee waves it off! Romans was out of bounds."

"Romans and Joint are moving down the field. There's a little hand fighting, but no one gains the advantage. Right there. Romans has both feet out of bounds. Good call by the back judge."

"That will bring up second and ten. Reprivus comes out again, and the Barbarians spread the field with Toorleen, Romans, and Chaistler. Roanen goes in motion and leaves the backfield empty. Jett takes the snap and fakes the quick throw to Romans. Jett tucks it under and heads straight up the middle. Jett veers to the left, and again Manny Droad meets him hard."

"Droad makes a picture-perfect tackle on Jett, but it's not until the senior picked up eight yards. Jett's ribs might be hurting after that stick."

"He does seem to be messing with his shoulder pads, but he stays in the huddle and calls the play. A big third and two for the Navy defense."

"A Navy stop here will give them a lot of needed confidence."

"Jett takes the snap and hands to Roanen. Roanen follows Reprivus and Cherck. Roanen will pick up the first down and more as he takes it all the way to the Navy nine-yard line. First and goal Barbarians."

The Barbarian fans began to chant, "Worm! Worm!"

"Whenever T&A needs three or four yards, they go behind Cherck. Everyone knows that, and no one is able to stop it."

"Jett quiets the partisan Barbarian crowd and snuggles under Zogo. Roanen is lined up behind Reprivus in the power I. Romans is split wide to the left, and Toorleen comes in motion from the right hash. Jett takes a three-step drop and fires over the middle. Romans makes the grab—but no! Leymoita jars the ball loose with a scathing hit on Romans. Romans pops back up and pleads his case that he had possession of the football, but the back judge is definitive in his call. No touchdown."

"That saved the Navy six points."

"That will bring up second and goal from the nine on a drive that started way back at the Barbarian eleven. One fourteen remains in the first quarter. Jett lines up over center and points in the direction of Leymoita and Alesse. T&A has dominated this opening frame and wants to see the fruits of their labor on the scoreboard. Jett drops back to pass and fires again to the end zone. Toorleen beats Alesse to the inside. Touchdown, Florida T&A."

Toorleen lay on his back and did the "Vibrator" end-zone dance. The band started blasting the Florida T&A fight song, and the fans joined in the singing.

"Nobs on to add the extra point, and Florida T&A streaks out to a fourteen to nothing advantage over the US Naval Academy midshipmen."

"That's just how they do it, Greg. They've got so many weapons."

Diana didn't watch football and wasn't quite sure what was going on in the game. She knew her section was quiet, and she kept hearing the public address announcer calling the name of Shaun Joint. *That isn't possible,* she thought.

"Welcome back to the amazing Big Apple Dome in New York City. I'm Greg Goutiner, and this is my partner, Greg Acori." Goutiner opened his eyes very wide so the viewing public would notice his sexy green contacts. "Greg, it all seems to be going according to plan for the Florida T&A Barbarians."

"It's exactly the way they draw it up in the locker room. No one has stopped them in three years, and the undermanned Navy team is in danger of letting this one get out of hand."

"I want to remind our viewers there is plenty of great football action through the New Year on JFN. Join us Monday night for the Like a Rock Viagra Bowl featuring Clemson and Northwestern at eight o'clock, Eastern time."

"That should be a great matchup."

"Nobs sets up to kick off with just under a minute remaining in the first quarter of the NCAA title game. Nobs kicks it deep, and Alesse moves under the ball. Alesse at the ten, the fifteen. Alesse tries to move upfield, but Cisco Deerrink drops him at the twenty-two-yard line. Deerrink is tenacious on special teams."

"Joint huddles up the midshipmen. This is only their second possession of the game."

"That's right, Greg. T&A has held the ball for most of the quarter and have racked up one hundred forty-one yards on two drives."

"Joint brings Navy to the line. They line up in the power I. Joint takes the snap and hands to Droad. Droad bulls his way for a couple, and Buster Chagora stacks him up at the twenty-four-yard line."

"Navy has no confidence on offense. They're going to have to do something dramatic to get back into this game."

"Joint takes the snap and turns and pitches it to Droad. The pitch is behind him, and the ball is loose. Droad reaches to recover the live ball. Harry Tearnytt blasts Joint out of the way, and W. Jackson picks up the ball. He might score. He does! Touchdown, Florida T&A."

W. Jackson gathered the defense and did a little "Jailhouse Love" dance for the crowd.

"Twenty to nothing, Greg. This one might be over."

"It sure seems like an awfully big hole for the midshipmen. Jacko Nobs makes it twenty-one nothing."

"This is what Florida T&A has done for three years—and especially this season. They pounce on you in the first quarter and remove you from your game plan. You might as well pass them the crown right now."

In the luxury box of Mr. Samuel Stokes, Satan salivated. He called Abaddon over, and his slave lay at his feet like a well-trained Rottweiler. "It looks as if the Navy coach finally got the message," Satan said. "Fear will subjugate any person's soul." Satan nipped at the microscopic worms that wriggled beneath his flesh. "Abaddon, go kill the girl and bring her heart to me. I want to watch this man suffer while I squeeze the blood into his mouth."

"Then you would be breaking your agreement," Balberith pointed out to Satan.

"That's what I do," Satan reminded his subject. Abaddon smiled slyly at his king. "And bring me that boy who travels with Nimrod. I want to roast him on a spit and watch him cook to death on the Jumbotron."

Abaddon left immediately to serve his master's desire. It would be his pleasure to disembowel the little child.

Security had to restrain Caleb. He kept trying to get on the sidelines to talk to his twin brother. He knew it was Raytel. He shouted at him from the stands, but the players never came off the field. He finally sat back down in his seat. It was the craziest thing he had ever seen, and Caleb had seen some crazy stuff.

Team Nimrod sneaked around the seamy underbelly of the Big Apple Dome. They searched and avoided security and real maintenance personnel.

"What exactly are we looking for?" Thomas wondered.

"We are looking for electrical panels. They should be near the engineering room." Nimrod held the map and studied the grid with little prowess.

"Are you planning to turn out the lights?" wondered Shar.

"I'm going to turn out his lights," fumed Vishnu.

"No, I'm not going to turn out the lights. I'm going to do something better than that." Nimrod stayed focused on the map.

Navy managed not to turn the ball over on its next possession and actually got a first down. The mini drive stalled at their own thirty-five, and they were forced to punt. Florida T&A marched down the field again and put seven more points on the board. Worm Roanen finally hit pay dirt from six yards out. Team Nimrod heard the thumping of the stands and knew their mission had come down to its last breath. They scrambled to find the right panels, and they were incensed when Nimrod realized he was holding the map upside down.

"It's all Florida T&A. It's twenty-eight to nothing as we return to the Big Apple Dome. Don't forget, next Tuesday on JFN, we encourage everyone to 'go with the flow' as we present the first annual Tampax Bowl in Tempe, Arizona. Greg, that should be a good matchup when the Miami Hurricanes face the Washington Huskies."

"It will be a lot better than this one. I guarantee that."

"Navy lines up with first and ten from their own twenty-six-yard line with six twelve to go in the half. Quarterback Shaun Joint hands to fullback Egan Paal, and he stumbles to the line of scrimmage for maybe a couple."

"The Navy offense has the imagination of a cashew. I don't know if Coach Gravenald is just trying to get this one over with or if he just doesn't trust the talent of his players."

"Could be a little of both. Navy lines up for second and nine. Joint drops back to pass, and the rush is all over him. Bones Jetr drops Joint in the backfield. Jetr is standing over Joint and doing the robot. Jason Cenode pushes Jetr in the chest, and the two teams are once again at each other's throats. The referees separate the two units, but no flags are thrown. What do you think of all the animosity, Greg?"

"Well, Navy is getting their butt handed to them on the field. They are proud, but if they responded with their play, maybe some of the showboating would stop."

"Navy is mired in third and long again. Joint lines the midshipmen up and hands the ball to Droad. Droad goes nowhere, and linebacker Marble Calple blankets him. Navy will be forced to punt, facing fourth and fourteen."

"Fortunately the leg of Carl Broodend has made Florida T&A drive the length of the field. Unfortunately the defense hasn't been able to stop the Barbarian offense."

"Broodend drives another high, high kick into the stratosphere of the Big Apple Dome. Chaistler tracks it down. He takes the ball at his own seventeen-yard line and moves to the right. Chaistler avoids the arm tackle by Leymoita and turns upfield. Chaistler only has Broodend to beat. What a move by Chaistler. Chaistler at the twenty, fifteen, five. Touchdown! Juice Chaistler."

"That is the speed we've been talking about all day. Player for player the Barbarians are faster and stronger than any team in the country."

"Jacko Nobs has been perfect on his first four attempts in the first half, and he converts his fifth. Florida T&A is routing the US Naval Academy thirty-five to zero."

Dolores and Michael Kerichuck kept looking at the Jumbotron to see if they could see number fifty-one's face. They would know for sure if they could just see his face. They just wanted to see that big, ugly, beautiful face.

"We hope everybody stays with JFN for the ultimate halftime show, which features a Christmas performance by the death-metal band Disturbed. Florida T&A prepares to kick off."

"I am certain Coach Gravenald just wants this half to be over. I wouldn't be surprised to see head coach Merl Larrola call off the dogs at halftime."

"Alesse takes the ball out to the twenty-three-yard line, and Navy will start there with just over three minutes to go in the half. Joint lines up over Kerichuck. Joint pitches to Droad, who sticks his nose into the line and pushes forward for three."

"Where do you want to go to dinner tonight, Greg?"

"I know what you're saying, Greg, but we still have a whole half to play."

"This one's over. Tell Mama to slice the pie."

"Joint hands to Paal, and the burly fullback bulls his way forward for two more yards."

"My mother makes the best mincemeat pie."

"The clock is ticking, and Florida T&A calls a time-out."

"Florida T&A wants the ball back one more time. They are going to go for the jugular and put this game far out of reach."

"Joint leans over center and takes the snap with one fifty-eight on the clock. He keeps it himself and dives for the first down, but Joint will be short, and T&A calls another time-out."

"This is the killer instinct that head coach Merl Larrola instills into the psyches of his players."

"Broodend is back to punt, and folks, this is a rocket. This one is driving Chaistler all the way back to his own five-yard line. Chaistler takes the kick, and ow! Gary Alesse levels Chaistler."

"Is that Chaistler's head rolling around on the field?"

"No, Greg, that's just his helmet. Chaistler took some kind of hit after fielding that punt."

Training staff helped Chaistler off the field, and the Barbarian offense took the field.

"The Florida T&A Barbarians have ninety-five yards to go with a one forty-four on the clock."

"With this field position, Larrola just wants to give Nobs an opportunity."

"Jett drops back to pass from his own end zone and swings the ball out to Roanen in the flat. Ouch! Linebacker Egan Paal strikes Roanen. It was all Worm could do to get out of the end zone."

"Paal just read that play from the beginning."

"The clock is running and down to one ten. The Barbarians hurry to the line. Jett drops back to pass and drills a strike to tight end Andrew Spore over the middle. It's well short of a first down, and the clock is still ticking. T&A will want to save their last time-out for the field-goal try. Forty-nine seconds left in the half. Jett falls back to pass and throws it to Toorleen in the flat. Alesse tips the ball away at the last second."

"T&A will have to punt, and Larrola is upset with his team's inability to move the ball despite being up thirty-five to nothing."

Jacko Nobs stepped back into his own end zone to punt. Out of the corner of his eye, he saw his girlfriend, *Penthouse* Pet of the Month, Wendy Raith, flash her tits to the crowd. The crowd roared in approval, and the cameras put it on the Jumbotron. Nobs never saw the snap whiz by his ear. He could only see Wendy's nipples on the big screen. They were larger than flying saucers. The football rolled harmlessly out of the end zone for a safety. The Barbarians went into the half leading 35–2.

A throng of handpicked losers gathered around the stage and thrashed like idiots to the earsplitting death-chamber music vomited by Disturbed. Satan enjoyed the show from Mr. Stokes's luxury box.

There was no fighting in the Navy locker room. They were getting pounded, and the soldiers knew it. Tuby and Tug knew it. Vern knew it. Dr. Barry Money knew it. Tuby sat alone on the bench in front of the lockers. The stress of the previous eight months crashed down around him. He started to cry. Tuby let it all out and sobbed uncontrollably. He sobbed for Myra. He wept for Jane. He cursed himself for his own selfishness. Egan Paal walked over to the distraught coach and put his arm around him.

"Coach, we're all here for you," the young man said.

The other players took a knee beside Paal and Tuby.

"I really don't know why. I haven't done a thing for you players. I've cheated you. I've cheated everyone here."

"I don't understand, Coach." Paal stayed with the heaving coach.

"I don't know what miracle brought you here. I don't know what or why, but all I could think about was using you and the way you healed so quickly. I figured that if I stuck with you, some of that miracle would rub off on Emily and heal her. It hasn't. I haven't had enough faith. I only wanted what you had. I gave up on this freaking game long before I ever laid eyes on any of you. I never believed we had a chance to win. I guess I don't don't really believe in very much."

"We've always believed in you," Raytel said, speaking for the group. "You're a great coach and a better man."

"Am I a good man? Is it a good man who dreams his wife is in hell? Is it a good man who has forsaken his god and bartered with the devil? Is it a good man who has abandoned his daughter and grandchild? I never even had the chance to say good-bye. God, what am I doing here?" Tuby buried his face in his hands.

"None of us know what we're doing here, but we must be here for a reason. Something good has got to come of all this, Coach. It's a mystery to us too. Life was a mystery, and so was death. There has been more pain and suffering on the trip than you can imagine, but we're all here together. We never got to say good-bye to our loved ones, yet we still carry that hope— the hope that only love can bring. I know we'll keep searching for answers. Meanwhile we'll clutch tightly to one another and faith. We're in God's hands now. We always have been." Egan made Tuby look into his eyes, and then Egan hugged him and held him close.

The lights went black inside the locker room.

"That's the wrong panel, moron." Vishnu held the flashlight after the lights went out. The stadium had gone dark.

"Why don't we try the one that says 'Retractable Roof'?" Shar held open the electrical panel.

"That's what we've been looking for," Nimrod said.

He shifted his tools and map over to the gray box. He unscrewed the cover plate and sifted through the miles of high-voltage wiring.

"Security will be here any second," Thomas said, warning of the inevitable.

The sweat poured off Nimrod's brow as he searched for the right combination of wires to cross. He shaved off the plastic coatings of the green and black wires and melded them together.

They heard the screws of the retractable roof start to turn and open to the snowy skies above.

"That's it! We did it! I owe Mother Nature a huge favor. Shar, remind me when I get back to Pyrub Cape to send her a case of Conzlie Ale."

"I'll remind you that we've got to get out of here right now!"

"What about the lights?" Thomas wondered.

"Leave them off. It will take security thirty seconds to fix that problem, and we can slip away in the dark."

"If it takes thirty seconds to solve the lights, won't they be able to close the roof?"

Nimrod looked at Thomas as he trashed the electrical box. He pulled wires out from everywhere, and sparks lit up the utility room. It would take a crew most of a week to repair the circuits.

Nimrod shared the plan with his team. "When I made the bet with Satan, we confirmed the game would be played with anyone, anytime, anyhow, and anywhere. I asked God for some help—something I have been ashamed to do in the past. He is helping us with the 'anytime.' Ba helped with the 'anyone,' and we just fixed the 'anywhere.' The second half is going to be played on our terms. In the snow. In the great outdoors and in the 1940s."

The Navy team left the dark, claustrophobic confines of the locker room and headed for the tunnel that led to the field. The stadium was still dark and a cold wind swirled around the field. Fans reached for the winter coats, gloves, and knit hats they had worn to the stadium. Tuby swore he felt a snowflake land on his cheek.

The lights went back on, and a hush fell over the capacity crowd. The roof was wide open, and the snow was pouring down onto the field. The field was no longer Astroturf. It was lush green grass. The towering yellow goalposts had been moved from the back of the end zone and replaced near the goal line with twin-posted, wooden-framed goals at each end. The field was still the same length and width. The goalposts were just as wide as before. It would be the same for both teams.

Navy stepped onto the turf, and Carl Broodend noticed his shoes. Gone were the Nike Air pump athletic sneakers used for the Astroturf. His foot felt very natural in the black patent-leather, high-top cleats with the sharp steel spikes. Gone were the scientific dual-layered shells, impenetrable plastic-alloy face masks, and tinted visors. Raytel felt the thin padding of the leather on his head and looked unobstructed around the field. He tied the chin strap in place so the aged helmet was tight around his ears. Gone were the arm pads, elbow pads, shin guards, and mouthpieces. There was no more radio inside the quarterback's helmet. There was no more playbook wristband on the quarterback's forearm or cumbersome flak jacket rib padding. All the players reached inside their jerseys and pulled the strings tight on their shoulder pads. There were no more buckles, latches, or Velcro. It was just tie them up tight and play. Jason loved the bulky thigh pads and kneepads. The Florida T&A coaches and players cried foul.

Satan smelled a humongous rat and sent Stokes down to the field to find out what the hell was going on. Mr. Stokes, as a premier investor of this event, charged onto the Florida T&A sideline with NCAA President Sir Chad Mourrey, University President Garth A. Moot, and head coach Merl Larrola. They called over referee B. K. Ascanni, who donned his gloves and winter hat. He adjusted his whistle and moved to the irate group of executives.

"You're not seriously thinking of playing this game?" Garth Moot railed on the ref.

"Why not? It's a little snow." Ascanni put the whistle between his teeth. "Are your players going to melt?"

"Most certainly not."

Sir Chad Mourrey brushed Moot aside. "Something untoward is going on here, sir. As president of the NCAA, I think it would be best if we halt the game until some type of investigation can be arranged."

"Please define 'untoward.' That's a little fancy for a boy from Kentucky." Ascanni was a prominent member of St. George's parish. He was the patron saint of fair play in Louisville when he wasn't being the best referee in football.

It was Mr. Stokes's turn. "The field has changed from turf to grass. The players are now adorned in getups from who knows when."

"1943," Ascanni stated. His grandfather had been a tackle at Army.

"The parameters of the field have changed." Mr. Stokes noted the goalposts.

"Same game. Different rules, Mr. Stokes. You know about playing by different rules. Don't you, Mr. Stokes?" Ascanni winked.

"Well, we didn't sign on to play by any other rules, Mr. Ascanni. That's why we want you to halt the game."

"That's not true, Mr. Stokes. If you read the contract for the NCAA title game like I have, it says on page one hundred forty-three, section six, paragraph C, the game will be played by anybody, anywhere, anytime, anyhow. I believe one of your own people signed, Mr. Stokes. Someone named Balberith. Something strange like that. This clearly falls under the category of 'anyhow.'"

"This is ludicrous."

"I'll tell you what's ludicrous, Coach Larrola. You've got a thirty-three-point lead and thirty minutes to play to win your third national championship, and I'm about to blow this whistle. If your team doesn't get on that field, Florida T&A will forfeit the game."

The snow accumulated on the bill of Larrola's ball cap. Stokes called up to the luxury box, and Balberith confirmed the deal. Satan seethed and bucked his hooves around the suite. He smashed the mirrors and liquor bottles.

The program director moved into the booth. Play-by-play man Greg Goutiner and his partner, Greg Acori, waited for the people in the truck to solve the technical difficulties.

"Gentlemen, all we have now is audio. We're going to go with that until we get the picture back."

Goutiner was pissed. No one was going to see his brand-new green contacts. "There's no picture?"

"Yes, Greg. That's what only audio means."

"Well, what the hell am I supposed to do?"

"Pretend you're on the radio. Like the old days of Jack Buck and Vin Scully."

"Who?"

"Never mind." Goutiner was a nervous wreck the rest of the evening. The thought of having to actually describe the action made him ill.

Sande Sirren found head coach Merl Larrola on the sidelines. "Coach Larrola, it looks as if we have a nor'easter blowing into the dome. Did your team practice in the snow?" Sande just knew the studio executives would love she had said "nor'easter."

"No, Sande. We never practice in the snow. We haven't had any snow in Orlando, Florida, in about fifty years. If we had we would have moved inside."

"Do you feel comfortable with a thirty-three-point lead?"

"Well, it's been one weird halftime with the uniform adjustments, the changing of the turf, and the weather. Weird things happen in inclement weather."

"Uniform adjustments? What are you talking about?"

Larrola left and headed to the team on the sidelines. Sande looked around. She had just noticed the players didn't have those thingies around their helmets.

Larrola called the team over. The equipment manager had not brought any winter gear. The game was supposed to be played indoors. The Florida T&A players were freezing and had gone to family members in the stands and taken their coats. Most of the skill position players were covered on the sidelines in full-length mink and fox furs. Larrola tried to ready the team. "Thirty minutes to our third championship."

"I ain't playing like this. There's nothing covering my face. This face is worth a fortune in endorsements." J. J. "Honey" Romans smiled sarcastically at Larrola.

"Coach, my helmet doesn't fit."

Wilson Dubink was having technical difficulties with his faux dreadlocks. He couldn't stuff the woven nest into his leather crown. Half a dozen other players had the same problem.

Ascanni blew the whistle. Larrola grabbed Romans by the jersey. "Now, you listen to me, you prima donna. Each and every one of you is going out on that field and playing football, or so help me I will blackball you from the NFL. You'll only be able to show you face around Germany with the Rhein Fire, where those Nazis don't give a rat's ass what you look like."

Romans piped down. He knew the coach would do it. Romans had seen it done before.

Tuby remembered what Ms. Rain Cutti had told him months ago. He passed the word on to his players before the second-half kickoff. "I'm a stubborn old man. I always think I know best, and it's hard to admit when I'm wrong. I'm sorry I let you down. A dear friend once told me it's not all about winning. It's about teaching. It's about letting the ropes out and seeing what young people can and cannot do. That is what love is all about. It's about finding yourself and your limits. Failure is OK sometimes. I want to let you try your best. I've been holding you back. I'm going to set you free. Spread your wings. Fly. Dare to be great. Shaun, run your offense."

"No hand signals?"

"Nope. You call the game. Let's play some football!"

Tuby released the team to the field. He also released Emily to the care of God. She was in his hands now. She always had been.

Jacko Nobs teed up the ball and readied to kick off. With virtually no wind, the snow fell steadily and gently covered the grass. Gary Alesse waited for the kickoff. Nobs wasn't used to the heavier kicking shoe or the slightly larger ball and shot a line drive down the middle of the field. Norm Leymoita grasped the squib kick and followed the wedge straight up the middle. The two teams collided in the snow. The Florida T&A Barbarian special teams learned that the second half would be full of pain. Safety Wilson Dubink tried to break up the wedge and took a forearm to the nose. It shattered on contact and left him bloodied and crying on the field. The trainers hauled him off the field. It was first and ten Navy from their own thirty-five-yard line, and quarterback Shaun Joint huddled up the antsy offense.

"Egan, you move back to tight end. Norm and Gary, no more wide receivers. We're going to the wishbone." They broke the huddle.

They noticed the difference in the Barbarian defensive line right away. They were exposed. They were scared. They had also failed to make adjustments to the clear run formation.

"Once again we apologize for the technical difficulties. It's beginning to look a lot like Christmas here in the Big Apple Dome. The snow is falling, and Navy begins the opening drive of the second half on their own thirty-five. They are moving from right to left. Joint lines up under Kerichuck and takes the snap. Shaun veers to the left and pushes the ball into the belly of Manny Droad, who smashes into defensive tackle Barney Steern and middle linebacker Buster Chagora. Outside linebacker Bones Jetr caves in on Droad as well. No! Leymoita has the ball. Joint removed the ball from Droad's stomach and instead handed it to the second man through, Norm Leymoita. Norm has space and bends it to the outside. Cornerback Cisco Deerrink bowls Leymoita to the ground after a fifteen-yard gain. The mids are in business in the center of the field."

"That was a heck of a fake, Greg. It had the Barbarian defense completely hoodwinked."

"It had me hoodwinked, too," Goutiner confessed. "Navy lines it up again with Joint under center. This time they veer it to the right. Joint fakes the handoff to Droad and swings it outside. Joint fakes the pitch to Leymoita and keeps it himself. Joint's got running room. Joint crosses the forty, and Wink Romance V tackles him deep in the secondary."

"Tackle Chet Skairny and tight end Egan Paal just manhandled W. Jackson. It also looks as if Marble Calple is bleeding. We can't bring you the replay for obvious reasons, but while Calple was on the ground, I think he took a cleat to the forearm. He's in a lot of pain."

"Head coach Merl Larrola does replace Calple for the time being, and Navy is waiting at the line for the discombobulated Barbarian defense to get organized. First and ten Navy at the Barbarian thirty-seven. B. K. Ascanni has placed the ball on the right hash. That makes the left side of the field the wide side. Joint moves to wishbone to the wide side and fakes to Droad. He fakes to Leymoita. Joint stares at Bones Jetr in the hole and pitches the ball to the trailer, Gary Alesse. Alesse has open field. Alesse to the twenty, the ten. Touchdown, Navy!"

Color commentator Acori recapped the play. "Tight end Rat Doovaine and tackle Cenode break Shank W. Shonnejoy down. Guard Raytel Kigmenis pulls to the left and just pulverizes Buster Chagora. They knock heads, and Chagora is going to feel that one for the rest of the game."

"Probably for the rest of his life. He went down like a sack of potatoes. The midshipmen in the stands are going berserk, and

Joint lines the mids up for a two-point conversion. Joint takes the snap and hands it to Droad. Nothing fancy here, and Droad walks into the end zone. He lays the ball in the snow, and Scrum Laneal picks up the ball and kicks it into the stands.

"The ref throws the flag, and the Barbarians will be penalized on the kickoff. It's Florida T&A thirty-five and US Naval Academy ten. We'll be right back after this station identification."

Team Nimrod had changed back into the pimp clothes and had taken their first glimpse of the field. They arrived in time to see Manny Droad cross the goal line for the two-point conversion. The ball that Laneal punted into the stands landed right in Nimrod's hands. Nimrod smelled the epidermis of the swine. The leather felt good in his hands. He handed the ball to a kid, and Team Nimrod moved toward their seats. They still faced a long, uphill battle, and Nimrod had yet to locate Jairus. Nimrod stressed as the Barbarian fans heckled him in his flesh-peddling getup.

Carl Broodend huddled the team for the kickoff. "We were terrible on defense in the first half. We can win this game if we play defense. We've found this team's weakness. They have no heart."

"Welcome back to the Big Apple Dome. We want to remind all our viewers—who aren't viewing anything right now—that at nine o'clock in the morning on Tuesday, December 30, JFN will bring you the Depends Senior Bowl live from Mobile, Alabama. Greg, that's always one of my favorite games of the year."

"You know it, Greg. It's always fun to watch halfhearted players bloated from Christmas dinner competing in a game where no one wants to get hurt."

"Navy showed some pride on that last drive. They went sixty-five yards and only took a few minutes off the clock."

"Joint executed the wishbone to perfection, but it was the offensive line that really got the job done. During the break many of the Barbarian defensive players were protesting to head coach Merl Larrola about the lack of a face mask. Several players are being looked at for shiners and scrapes."

"Broodend kicks off from the fifty-yard line because of Laneal's unsportsmanlike conduct penalty. He chooses not to boot it out of the end zone. Instead he squibs it down the middle, and Chaistler is having a hard time getting a grip on it. The ball is squirting around the five-yard line, and Alesse and Chaistler dive for it. Both men dig in the snow, and the referee signals Barbarian ball."

"That was close. Florida T&A got lucky."

"The Barbarians still have an awfully big lead. It's thirty-five to ten, and Navy had no answers to stopping them in the first half. Let's see if B. Siemore Jett and company can quell the new-found enthusiasm of the Navy unit. T&A lines up at their own seven with twelve fifteen to play in the third. The Barbarians are moving left to right in the snow, which is starting to cover the grass. Jett hands to Roanen, and they move behind the Sheik. The Sheik slips, and Jason Cenode and Egan Paal hammer Roanen at the six."

"Greg, the Sheik didn't slip. Cenode gave him one heck of a head slap, and the big man just couldn't keep his balance."

"Cherck is protesting to referee B. K. Ascanni, but to no avail."

"The bizarre circumstances of the second half lend themselves to numerous questions, but I'm guessing that because the head slap wasn't outlawed until the 1970s, Ascanni is considering it a legal move." Goutiner whispered to his producer. "What the hell is happening here? This is crazy."

"The Barbarians line up for second and eleven. Jett takes the snap, rises up, and fires to Romans on his right. The ball floats a little, and—oh, goodness! Manny Droad clotheslines Romans. Romans is clutching his neck, and the two teams square off on the sidelines. There's a lot of pushing and shoving, but the Florida

T&A players back off. Navy returns to the huddle, and T&A faces third and long."

"Either Jett couldn't get a grip on the ball because of the snow, or the slightly bigger ball gave him trouble. Romans got hung out to dry."

"Jett steps back into the shotgun with Toorleen on his left and Romans, who stayed in the game, on his right. Reprivus goes into motion. Jett takes the snap, and the Navy defense pours into the backfield. Jett flips the ball to Roanen. They've got the screen set up. Kerichuck shoots through the lumbering offensive line and stuffs Roanen at the line of scrimmage. Navy will get the ball with tremendous field position."

"Great read by Kerichuck. The offensive line saw him coming. It looks as if no one on the Barbarian team wants to hit anyone. That's the Barbarians' first three and out today."

"Jacko Nobs steps into his own end zone to kick. Here's the snap. Nobs fields it and gets it away. It's a beauty, snow or no snow. It drives Alesse back to midfield. Deerrink and Romance V are there to meet him, and Alesse wisely calls for a fair catch."

Jaime, Miguel, and Juan covered their mother with their coats. She had wonderful sons but needed no additional warmth. She could feel Manny's presence, and that warmed her soul.

"Navy has another terrific opportunity here with the ball at midfield."

"They sure do, Greg. If Navy can stick it in, we might have ourselves a ball game."

"Sande Sirren is on the sidelines with Coach Tuby Gravenald. Sandy."

"Coach, you looked so bad in the first half. What adjustments did you make at the half?"

"We prayed for divine intervention, and we got some. The players have a lot of faith in themselves and me. They are really strong. I told Shaun to run the offense he's most comfortable with. The new offense looks very effective."

"Back to you, Greg." Sande looked out onto the field. *What new offense is he talking about?* she wondered.

"Joint lines up under Kerichuck."

"Greg, T&A has moved eight men into the box and brought their safeties and corners closer to the line of scrimmage."

"Navy has the wide side of the field to the right. Joint veers to the short side of the field. He fakes the handoff to Droad and then Leymoita. Alesse follows behind Joint and waits for the pitch. Joint turns it upfield and squirts for five—let's call it six—yards."

"Again Joint finds the seam Kigmenis created. The big fella just tees off on Bones Jetr and creates a crease for Joint. I think Jetr might have lost a tooth."

"It's second and four from the Barbarian forty-six. Joint takes the snap and fakes the handoff to Droad. Joint veers right. No! Droad has the ball. He's heading straight up the field! Laneal pulls Droad down at the T&A thirty-two-yard line. A gain of fourteen for Manny Droad."

"It's a simple trap play, and Florida T&A is showing the inexperience of playing against an option quarterback. Center Dan Kerichuck catches Chagora moving to his left and pins him away from the play. Kigmenis blocks down on Harry Tearnytt, and the other guard, Carl Broodend, sweeps Barney Steern out of the play. That allows Droad to get into the secondary fast. Great read by Joint."

"First and ten Navy from the Barbarian thirty-two. You can sense the Barbarian fans becoming restless. Joint takes the snap. He hands to Leymoita, and the second man through goes off tackle to the left for four yards. Chagora makes the stop."

"T&A buckled down that time, but Navy still got positive yardage on the play."

"Second and six from the T&A twenty-eight. Navy is moving from right to left with nine twenty-seven to play in the third. Joint takes the snap. He veers to the right. Joint moves down the line. He hands to Alesse, the second man through, and Alesse meets Marble Calple. Calple takes a hit from Alesse."

"Alesse just buries his head into Calple's sternum and is fortunate to hold on. Alesse bowled him over."

"Ascanni marks the ball. It will be third and a short two. T&A brings almost everybody into the box. Joint crouches under center. Joint fakes the handoff to Droad, and then Joint follows Droad through the hole on a quarterback keeper up the middle."

"T&A is confused, Greg. They just don't know where Joint is going with the ball, and they are very tentative defensively. That was another great surge by the offensive line. Kigmenis and Kerichuck pushed back the T&A middle two."

"Navy gets the first down and starts fresh from the Barbarian twenty-yard line. Navy lines up in the wishbone. They haven't varied from this formation in the second half. Joint takes the snap and veers to the left. Joint fakes to Droad and then to Leymoita. Joint works his way down the line and pitches to Alesse. Cisco Deerrink dogs Alesse, but Alesse beats him to the corner and picks up six before running out of room on the T&A sidelines. One of the T&A players gave Alesse a shove, and the two teams mix it up on the sidelines again. Alesse headbutts the Barbarian player, and the reserve is holding his mouth. Blood is pouring from his fingers."

"I don't think the refs saw the headbutt. That was a cheap shot by the T&A player, and I can understand why Alesse retaliated. There's no flag, and head coach Merl Larrola is incensed."

"Both teams regroup, and Navy will have it with second and four from the Barbarian fourteen. Joint brings Navy to the line. Joint takes the snap. He moves right and fakes to Droad and then Alesse. Joint flips the ball to the trailer, Leymoita.

Leymoita barrels his way inside the T&A ten and down to the seven."

"Do you remember a few plays ago when Alesse ran over linebacker Marble Calple? Watch him execute some matador defense on Leymoita here. He wanted nothing to do with the running back on that play."

"Navy is threatening with seven forty-nine to play in the third. Joint is under center. The partisan Barbarian crowd is on their feet. All the spectators are on their feet. The snow continues to fall. The field is holding up well. Joint veers to his left. It's Droad down the gut of the defense for three."

"T&A has everyone up at the line of scrimmage, and they still can't get a push."

"Navy with second and goal from the four. The Barbarians are in their goal-line defense. Joint surveys the field. Joint turns to his left. Droad goes through on the left side, and Alesse follows Droad. But it's Leymoita coming back to the right. He storms into the end zone, and Navy has stormed back into the game."

"Greg, that's the old cross buck. They catch everyone on T&A's defense moving to his right, and the misdirection allows Leymoita to walk untouched into the end zone. Great play call by Joint."

"Navy lines up for another two-point conversion. This would bring them to within seventeen points. Joint moves the option to the right and works down the line. Joint cuts upfield and is in for the two points. Navy trails thirty-five to eighteen. We have ourselves a ball game."

"This is unbelievable, Greg. The Barbarian fans are booing their own team."

Sister Valerie sat with the German shepherd in her lap. The dog was very well behaved and very warm. She sensed it was watching the game as closely as she was.

Satan thrashed around in the luxury suite like a severed high-pressure steam hose.

Nimrod scanned the crowd and corporate boxes. He was hoping to catch a glimpse of Jairus. Thomas and Vishnu fended away offers from the Barbarian fans to take Shar to the stall for a quickie.

"Six oh two remains in the third, and the Barbarian offense sure could give their team a lift with a good drive."

"That's right, Greg. They don't even need to score. They just need to eat up some clock and let this Navy offense cool down. The Navy players have to be exhausted. All of them have played every snap this game."

"Broodend sends the kick high into the snow. Juice Chaistler squares his feet and makes a sure catch this time. Chaistler takes it right up the middle, and ouch! Dan Kerichuck levels Chaistler."

"What a beatdown by Kerichuck. The guy has a face like a frying pan, he met Chaistler in the hole, and whap!"

"Chaistler is woozy and is being helped off the field. Jett brings the offense on and gets them huddled up as they watch the speedster struggle off the field. JFN wants to invite everyone to watch the new show where Sande Sirren goes undercover and inside Pop Warner Football, where she reveals the truth about Scooby-Doo vitamins and their effect on the players."

"There has been a ton of controversy about the orange Velma tablets, Greg."

"It has to be better than the food in the greenroom. Florida T&A lines it up on their own twenty-five with five fifty-two left in the third. Jett hands to Roanen, and the all-American takes it off tackle for five to the thirty-yard line."

"T&A followed Cherck, and that is more what they are used to."

"The US Naval Academy digs in on defense. Jett comes to the line and crouches under Zogo. Jett takes the snap, rises straight up, and dumps a quick pass to tight end Andrew Spore. Spore is out past the forty, and Manny Droad brings him down at the forty-two-yard line. First down, Florida T&A."

"Great play call by Larrola and his staff. I think they talked about the snow, and they are trying not to let the weather take them out of their game plan."

"Jett brings the Barbarians out of the huddle, and Romans goes wide to the left and Whiz Toorleen wide to the right. Reprivus lines up in front of Roanen, and Jett hands the ball to Worm. Worm works it left and finds a sliver of room behind Romans Steanen. He takes the ball out to the forty-six."

"The T&A fans are back in the game, and you can sense the urgency by the Barbarian offense."

"Jett works the clock. There is under four minutes in the third. Play clock down to three. Jett takes the snap. He tosses the ball to Roanen again. Roanen sweeps right. Roanen is shoved out of bounds at the fifty-yard line, and that will bring up third and two."

"This is the drive T&A needed. We mentioned it moments ago."

"Larrola takes a lot of time sending in the play. Jett hurries them out of the huddle and brings the Barbarians to the line. Jett takes the snap, and it's Roanen to the right again behind the Sheik. Roanen surges forward for the first down."

"Not by much. Paal and Kerichuck met Roanen with a vengeance. Roanen did that on his own."

"That will move the chains. T&A has the first down on the Navy forty-seven. Jett breaks the huddle and waits for the clock to wind down. Zogo snaps the ball, and Reprivus gets a rare opportunity. He crashes forward for three yards."

"Roanen needed a breather, and Steer got them positive yardage. That's a bonus for T&A."

"Second and seven from the Navy forty-four. Jett moves into the shotgun. Jett takes the snap. He fakes the handoff to Roanen and spins away from Skairny. Skairny's giving Jett some chase, and Jett has some room to run on the right. Jett takes it past the forty to the thirty-five, and the senior steps out of bounds in front of Gary Alesse."

"Nice improvisation by Jett. Jett was looking for Romans on a slant, but Skairny blew the play up with his pressure. Jett caught the defense retreating and ran to the open space."

"That gives Florida T&A another first down. The clock winds down in the third. There is one fifty-seven to play before the fourth."

"If T&A scores a touchdown, this game is over."

"You already said the game was over in the first half."

"It will really be over. Navy needs to hold them to a field goal to have any chance."

"Jett lines up under center. Jett takes the snap and pitches the ball to Roanen. Roanen sweeps left. Roanen follows Randy Molt to the Navy twenty-nine, where Rat Doovaine brings him down."

"This is why Roanen will be the first player in the NFL draft. He shows great athleticism on this play, but he also shows patience. If he doesn't wait for Molt, that's a two-yard gain."

"It's now second and four. Jett surveys the defense. Roanen stands behind Reprivus in the power I. Jett takes the snap and fumbles it. Jett pounces on it, but it is a loss of one on the play."

"The fundamentals. It was a good snap, and Jett stayed with the ball. I think it was just too slippery to handle."

"B. K. Ascanni does ask for another ball, and the snow continues to fall. Time is ticking away in the third, and Florida T&A faces a third down and five here."

"This is a huge play in the ball game."

"Jett lines up under Zogo. The play clock is at five. Jett takes the snap. He tosses the ball to Roanen on a sweep to the right. Roanen sticks his head into the line, but he will be well short of the first down."

"Raytel Kigmenis just moved Theo Drimend out of the way. Kigmenis used a strong swim move, got under Drimend's pads, and forced Roanen to snake into the teeth of the defense. Big stop by Navy."

"All-American Jacko Nobs is on the field to try a forty-seven-yard field goal."

"No, Greg. It's a thirty-seven yarder. Remember the goalposts are just on the other side of the goal line."

"That is true. Nobs from thirty-seven yards. There is no wind. Here's the snap. The kick is up, and it is good. Nobs makes it thirty-eight to eighteen, Florida T&A. Time expires in the third quarter, and Florida T&A will kick it off to start the fourth after scoring the field goal."

"That score also forces Navy to score three touchdowns in the fourth quarter. That is an awfully tall order."

The 415 freezing members of the Cenode Center did the wave every time the public address announcer mentioned the big tackle's name. Captain Hart led the way.

"Nobs tees it up, and Florida T&A starts the fourth quarter with a twenty-point lead. The kick is in the air and starts to fall right around the eight-yard line. Alesse settles under the ball and heads straight up the middle. There's a wall there, but Alesse shoots through a gap! Alesse is in the open field. Alesse crosses midfield. He's only got Nobs to beat. Alesse runs right over the former rugby player with a stiff-arm. Alesse is at the forty."

"No one's going to catch him!" Acori stood in the booth.

"Alesse to the twenty, the ten. Touchdown, Gary Alesse!" The entire Navy side of the field was going bonkers. Tuby held his hands to his head. Tug had run up the sidelines to keep pace with Alesse and urge him into the end zone. Vern watched with a twinkle in his eye. Chet Skairny had thrown the key block that had sprung Alesse. It was a shuddering forearm shiver to the neck of Bones Jetr, and the huge linebacker was still rolling in the snow in agony.

"A ninety-two-yard kickoff return by Gary Alesse has ignited this crowd and stunned the Florida T&A Barbarians."

"The shortest distance between two points is a straight line, and that's what Alesse does. He follows his blockers right up the middle, and on the snowy turf, he was never forced to zig or zag. He was able to build up some steam and take it to the house."

"Navy lines up for two again."

"I don't like this call, Greg. They need three touchdowns, but they don't need the two-point conversion."

"Quarterback Shaun Joint lines up under center Dan Kerichuck and takes the snap. It's a quick pitch to Norm Leymoita, and Leymoita scoots in from three yards out and makes the score thirty-eight to twenty-six, Florida T&A."

"Navy went right to the spot where Bones Jetr plays. The linebacker was removed after the kickoff, and Navy found the weakness."

"Navy is only down twelve with fourteen forty-five to play in the game. We'll be right back after a word from our sponsors."

Annette Alesse was still hopping up and down on the sidelines and screaming, "Gary! Gary!" Peter thought his mother might have had one too many Irish coffees. Annette knew it was her husband and Peter's father. He ran so fast.

Sal Geayser listened in the hospital with Jason Emenith and Bram Gareloin. Gareloin swiveled around the room with his halo on and threw popcorn on the stationary Geayser and the immobile Emenith. The nurses and doctors peeked in from the hallway to hear the game. Everyone in America huddled around and listened to the action. They were mesmerized.

Head coach Merl Larrola was as cold as his team. He stared at the snow-covered sidelines and cursed his players and the T&A fans. They continued to jeer his team's performance.

Shark Mulfalla threw his hands in the air and glared at his flunky, Bag Man Roue. He had bet the farm on this game. There wasn't a chance in the world he would cover the spread. Mulfalla had bet the entire stack on T&A, and that included the new house.

Abaddon the Beast lurked about in the ICU ward and waited for the right moment. Emily's nurse, Clare Rell, would be coming back from her break. The king of the abyss held Rell's soul and exploited her weakness. Satan fed his servant's need and promised her the eyes. The hunger grew deep inside Abaddon's loins. The Beast stalked his prey and yearned for the feast.

"We hope everyone has stayed with us despite the technical difficulties. What looked like another Florida T&A blowout at halftime has turned into a very exciting football game."

"Navy has stormed back with a combination of heart, toughness, explosive playmaking, and offensive prowess. It is no longer a question of can Navy make it all the way back, but will they?"

"Carl Broodend is set to kick off for the US Naval Academy. The mids in the stands are apoplectic. Broodend kicks it high and deep, and Chaistler settles under the ball. Chaistler surveys the onrushing midshipmen and decides to take a knee."

"What a mistake, Greg! Chaistler thought he was in the end zone. But the snow has buried the lines, and Chaistler knelt down at the five-yard line. Oh, goodness."

"The mistake by Chaistler gives T&A horrible field position."

"T&A has to get the ball out of their end."

"That would seem to be the plan. B. Siemore Jett brings T&A's offense to the line of scrimmage. You can see the Navy players' breaths steaming at the line of scrimmage. Jett snaps the ball and hands to Roanen. Roanen follows Steanen and Molt on the left side and picks up three yards."

"Good safe play by T&A to get something positive and get out from the shadow of the goalposts."

"The Barbarians have second and seven from the eight-yard line. Jett stays under center and receives the snap. Jett fakes this time to Roanen and steps back to pass. Jett finds Toorleen on a slant, and Manny Droad meets Toorleen hard."

"Droad delivers a huge shot, but Toorleen holds onto the ball. Toorleen has great hands—even without the receiving gloves."

"It was not enough for a first down, and Ascanni holds up the call for third and a yard. The center of the field has become quite muddied. Jett brings the Barbarians to the line. "Where do you think they'll go, Greg?"

"Right behind the Sheik."

The Sheik pouted about his wager. He had dropped a bundle on this game himself.

"Jett crouches under Zogo and points to Leymoita. Zogo calls the signals for the offensive line. Jett takes the snap. Florida T&A is moving from right to left. Jett hands to Roanen. Indeed! Roanen carries behind the big tackle, Ali Cherck, and picks up the first down."

"Every time. That was huge for Florida T&A. They just want to keep making first downs and chewing up the clock. Time is Navy's worst enemy right now."

"Twelve oh one remains in the fourth, and T&A starts again with first and ten on their own seventeen-yard line. Jett takes the snap and pitches to Roanen. Roanen moves left this time and tries to break it to the outside, but Rat Doovaine drags him down by the collar."

"One thing that has truly impressed me about this Navy squad—they are sure tacklers. They put a good lick on you, and they don't let go."

"Roanen does pick up a couple on the play to make it second and eight. Jett takes his time in the huddle, and the Barbarian linemen look winded."

"Their hands are on their hips and knees, but the Navy players just keep getting stronger."

"Jett comes to the line. Five on the play clock. Jett drops back. Play-action. Jett looks to the left for Romans. Watch out! Jason Cenode hits Jett high, and Raytel Kigmenis drills him low. He is sacked back at the twelve-yard line."

"Great penetration from the Navy left side. Cenode hits Cherck with an open palm to the chin and just drives the tackle out of the way. Kigmenis bowls Drimend into the backfield, and the pocket caves in. Jett had no place to escape."

"That brings up third and fifteen. Jett brings the Barbarians to the line promptly this time. Jett lines up in the shotgun. Chaistler is in for Reprivus, and Roanen is next to Jett in the backfield. Jett takes the snap. Jett looks left and lets the ball fly toward the sidelines. Joint is on Romans. The ball hangs in the air. Romans goes up and snares the ball, and Manny Droad belts him immediately."

"Romans has to be seeing stars after that hit. What a great effort to just hold onto the ball."

"B. K. Ascanni is going to ask for a measurement. It is very close to a first down."

"It's going to be tough to get a good spot in the snow."

"Here come the chains. They pull the chains tight, and it looks like T&A will be short by the nose of the football. Ascanni holds up his fingers and indicates just inches to go for a first down. The Barbarian faithful are urging Larrola to go for it."

"With nine forty-eight to go and a twelve-point lead, it would be foolish to not punt the ball."

"And Larrola listens to Greg's advice and sends on the punting unit."

"It's the right call, Greg. No doubt about it."

"Jacko Nobs steps back to punt. The kicking game has been an adventure for the Barbarians today. Nobs receives the snap at his own seventeen-yard line. Here's the kick, and it's very short."

"Nobs's left foot slipped in the snow."

"Alesse will not be able to field the kick, and it comes to rest at the Navy forty-eight-yard line. A twenty-five-yard punt by all-American Jacko Nobs. Navy will be back on offense with nine thirty-five when we return."

Abaddon watched the nurse go about her duties. She was a weak and detestable human. The staff in the hospital diminished at 11:00 p.m. Clare Rell would be looking for the morphine. She needed the fix. It helped her get through the night. Abaddon knew it would not be long now. He would enter the nurse's veins through the hypodermic needle and slay little Emily. The hospital administration would have to explain to the public how a junkie nurse slaughtered the head football coach's comatose granddaughter.

"We are back at the Big Apple Dome in New York City. Greg, do you notice anything different about me this evening?"

"Yes, Greg. I noticed how bold your new green contacts look."

"Navy picks it up with nine thirty-five to go in the game. Shaun Joint brings the midshipmen to the line. They stay in the wishbone attack. It is Droad at fullback and Alesse and Leymoita at the two tailback spots. Joint takes the snap and works his way down the line behind Broodend and Skairny. Alesse takes the ball and slides forward in the snow for about five."

"W. Jackson just catches Alesse by the ankle and trips him up. Good gain on first down for Navy."

"It is now second and five, and Joint takes the first snap of the drive in T&A territory. Navy is moving left to right, and Joint veers to his right again. This time he pulls the ball and fakes the pitch to Leymoita and turns upfield. Joint busts across the forty-three to the forty-one-yard line, and Navy has a first down."

"That was great interior blocking by Broodend, Skairny, and tight end Egan Paal. Joint flat out used linebacker Marble Calple on the pitch. Calple has got to stick to the quarterback and make him pitch. He's got plenty of help from Wilson Dubink. Playing defense against the option is about assignments and trust. It's all about teamwork."

"Joint hurries to the line as the clock ticks past eight thirty to go in the ball game. Joint snuggles under Kerichuck at the Barbarian forty-one. Joint veers to the left this time. He fakes to Droad and moves. No! Droad has the ball again and is stomping through the secondary. Manny Droad is all the way down to the T&A twenty-five-yard line. That is a sixteen-yard gain."

"Just great blocking and another nice read by Joint. Kerichuck blocks down on Tearnytt, and Kigmenis flattens Buster Chagora. Broodend pulls and traps Barney Steern, and Droad is into the secondary in a flash."

"Navy has owned the time of possession in the second half and is running all over the vaunted Florida T&A defense. Joint breaks the huddle."

"It is a very basic alignment. There are no tricks. There's no motion. There's no shifting. The quarterback doesn't have to change the play at the line of scrimmage. It is a simple matter of true smashmouth football."

"Joint takes the snap and moves left again. This time he does hand it to Leymoita, and the second man through takes it to the twenty-one-yard line."

"T&A just can't get pressure up the field. The defense was in the right position, but Kigmenis, Cenode, and Doovaine just pushed them back."

"It's second and six from the twenty-one. Joint lines the midshipmen up and takes the snap. They run the counter to Alesse, and Alesse breaks it outside. Jetr and Deerrink and giving chase.

Alesse lowers his shoulder and drives the ball to the Barbarian twelve-yard line."

"The T&A defense gets too aggressive at the wrong time, and Joint reads them perfectly. Everybody on the defense crashes hard to the left. They follow their keys and commit. Only Alesse brings it back the other way for a gain of nine."

"Navy can get a first down. There are just under seven minutes to play. Joint takes the snap and veers to the right. He fakes to Droad and then to Leymoita. Alesse is trailing. Chagora hits Joint hard, and Joint flips the ball to Alesse. Alesse crashes to the five, and Navy can smell the goal line."

"Alesse pops up and heads straight to the huddle. He never gave up on Joint, and Joint delivered the pitch as Chagora pummeled him."

"It's second and three from the five. Joint lines it up, and everyone goes straight ahead. Droad drives down to the two. Navy has a first down, and it is goal to go!"

"This crowd has gone completely bonkers. I even see Barbarian fans rooting for the underdogs now."

"Navy hurries to the line. The clock is still their nemesis. Joint lines up under Kerichuck. Joint takes the snap and fakes to Droad, and Joint follows the fullback into the end zone. Touchdown, Navy!"

The midshipmen on the sidelines hugged one another and screamed.

Shar had never been to a football game. She thought it was a lot of fun. Thomas still doubted Navy would win, and Vishnu passed out hot chocolate to the Barbarian cheerleaders. He thought some were quite cute.

"Navy lines up for two."

"This just doesn't make any sense, Greg. They don't need two."

"Joint takes the snap. He veers to his right. Droad collides with Tearnytt, and Joint slips through Broodend and Droad and into the end zone. Navy now only trails by four, thirty-eight to thirty-four, with six twenty-two on the clock."

Nimrod was frantic about Jairus, and he isolated where Satan was viewing the game. Strange flashes of light emanated from the private suite's window as the evil master went ballistic. Nimrod just hoped Jairus wasn't in the luxury box with that rotting hellion.

Sande Sirren was in the middle of the midshipmen who filled the stands. "Are you guys having fun?"

No one said a word. They just screamed into the camera.

"Navy prepares to kick off. Greg, does Navy try anything tricky here?"

"I don't think so, Greg. There is still plenty of time on the clock. They just need to hold the T&A offense."

"That is easier said than done, but the Barbarians have slowed to a crawl in the second-half snow. Broodend does kick it deep, and Chaistler checks carefully his position on the field. Chaistler takes the ball at the two and brings it to the right side. Chaistler is forced out of bounds at the twenty-three-yard line, and Jett will take over there with six eleven on the clock."

"I would expect a lot of Worm Roanen and Ali Cherck on this drive, Greg."

"That's what has carried them to two consecutive NCAA football titles. Can they make it a third? This Navy team has given them all they can handle. Jett crouches under Zogo. They sweep the ball to the left behind Steanen. Romans cracks back on Doovaine, and Doovaine goes down. Manny Droad comes up from his safety spot and drops Roanen for a two-yard gain. Droad pops up and gets right in Romans's face. The two players are nose to nose, and Doovaine is on the ground and in a lot of pain."

"Romans cracked back on Doovaine and went straight for the knees. There is no question that Romans tried to take Doovaine out of the game."

"Navy only suited twelve players for the game. The only reserve is a youngster by the name of Brian Palmer, and the scouting report indicates Navy would be better off with him on the math team."

"That was just plain dirty football."

"Ascanni settles the troops down, and Jett brings them to the line for second and eight. Navy did bring Doovaine off the field, and Gravenald has decided to go with ten players on defense."

"That's just crazy. The kid has got a uniform on. Let him stand in someone's way."

"Jett looks for the hole in the Navy D. He hands the ball to Roanen. There is a big hole on the right side behind Cherck. Roanen passes the thirty, and Dan Kerichuck, the middle linebacker, clobbers him."

"What a hit! Kerichuck saved the first down. That was another fierce tackle."

"Doovaine limps back on the field. Florida T&A faces third down and a long two. The clock has ticked down to just over four minutes. A first down here, and Navy is in a lot of trouble."

"You can say that again, Greg."

"A first down here, and Navy is in a lot of trouble. Jett brings them to the line and watches the play clock wind down. Four on the clock. Jett takes the snap and hands to Roanen. Navy strings out the play going left. Roanen tries to head upfield, but Droad, Doovaine, and Shaun Joint meet him. Roanen does not get the first down."

"Doesn't it figure Rat Doovaine would be part of that play? That's karma, Greg."

"Larrola is going to need some karma from his punter, Jacko Nobs. The punting unit does come onto the field, and Larrola has the defense huddled around him. Larrola is lighting them up on the sidelines."

"I've never seen a coach get so mad at his players. He is smacking them and kicking snow at them."

"Nobs takes the snap, and this is a beauty. Alesse is driven all the way back to his fifteen-yard line. Alesse makes the catch but loses his footing in the snow. He maintains his balance and scoots to the sidelines, where he is shoved out of bounds at the twenty-four-yard line. Navy will start there with three forty-seven to play."

Nurse Clare Rell looked over both shoulders and then opened the medicine cabinet. She stuck the hypodermic needle into the jar of morphine and pulled the plunger back. She filled the plastic tube with the sweet painkiller on which she thrived. Abaddon felt the pull of the suction. He was drawn into the syringe. She stuck the needle back into the pocket of her uniform and headed to the ladies' room.

All the fans in the stadium were on the edges of their seats. Some of the Barbarian fans were close to throwing themselves out of the four hundred level and onto the field. Some considered death a better alternative to losing.

Vishnu offered Nimrod a hot dog with mustard and relish. Nimrod declined. Vishnu knew stress was pulverizing Nimrod. He never turned down a hot dog.

"Navy starts this drive with three forty-seven to play, and they have to go seventy-six yards. A field goal will not help, but they do have all their time-outs. Joint brings the midshipmen to the line. There has been no variation on the Navy offensive set in the second half. Navy is moving left to right. Joint veers down the left side. He hands it to Leymoita, the second man through. Leymoita barrels up to the twenty-eight-yard line for a gain of five."

"Nice play, but the mids are going to need more than five yards at a time if they plan on getting to the end zone."

"Joint huddles them up quickly. Three seventeen to play. Joint calls the signals. Kerichuck points to Chagora, who shifted to the right side of Navy's line. Joint takes the snap and moves right. Chagora is in the backfield and has Joint by the legs. Joint pitches the ball to Leymoita. His knee was not down. W. Jackson tackles Leymoita after picking up three."

"Chagora makes a great play. He wasn't able to stop Joint for a loss, but he disrupted the offense, and Jackson was able to make the tackle. That brings up a huge third down."

"It is third and two, and Navy does not call a time-out to talk this one over."

"That is a big surprise. The game is on the line. You don't want to get into a fourth-down situation."

"Joint crouches under Kerichuck. Two forty-seven remains on the clock, and it is ticking. Navy is in the wishbone. Joint takes the snap and turns to his right. He hands the ball to Droad. No! Joint rises up and fires to tight end Egan Paal, who has slipped past the charging Barbarian defense. Paal is all alone and heading for the end zone. Cisco Deerrink is giving chase. Deerrink is closing on Paal. Paal is at the Barbarian thirty. Paal stiff-arms Deerrink, who won't let go. Deerrink has Paal around the neck, and Paal is dragging him past the twenty to the fifteen. Paal wraps the ball with both hands. Wink Romance V hits Paal from behind and tries to strip the runner. Romance V doesn't wrap him up. Romance V has fallen to the wayside as Paal drags Deerrink to the five. Touchdown! Touchdown! Touchdown! Navy has taken the lead!"

It was pandemonium.

"I can't believe it. I just can't believe it."

"The US Naval Academy has taken the lead on a seventy-two-yard pass from Shaun Joint to tight end Egan Paal. What a spectacular run by Paal!"

"That was Navy's first pass attempt of the game."

"Navy lines up for the two-point conversion."

"This is insanity. Navy only needs one point, and it is a three-point game. If they do not make this attempt, then the Barbarians can win the game on a field goal. What is Gravenald thinking?"

"He's probably thinking about Paal's run. Joint takes the snap and hands it to Droad. Droad smashes it right up the gut, and Navy is on top, forty-two to thirty-eight. Now Florida T&A must get a touchdown to win the game. There will be no tie."

Nurse Clare Rell sat on the john and stuck the needle into her arm. She closed her eyes and let it release through her veins. Abaddon slipped into Clare's bloodstream. The nurse would not receive the same comfort from this evening's fix. Rell rolled down her sleeves and felt the jolt in her heart. Something was different. Something awful was happening.

It was Larrola's turn to berate the offense. He lit into them with both barrels. He called them weak and insignificant. He called them losers. Cherck gave his own coach the finger on the sidelines. Romans spit in his face. T&A was coming apart at the seams. However, the entire offensive unit took the field for the final series. They didn't care about Larrola. They didn't care about Moot. Deep down they really wanted to win the game.

"Just an unbelievable turn of events in the second half."

"Do not count Florida T&A out. They are still the champs, and they have two eleven on the clock. This team only needs one play to score."

"Broodend boots the ball high and deep. Chaistler settles under the ball at the ten. He takes it up the middle and is brought down at the Barbarian twenty-six-yard line. We stand right at two minutes to play as B. Siemore Jett brings the offense on the field."

"T&A has all three time-outs. In the passing game, the advantage goes to the offense. T&A hasn't thrown the ball much in the second half. They went into their version of the prevent offense and tried to chew up the clock. They kind of forgot about the pass."

"Jett lines up in the shotgun. Jett takes the snap. He looks down the field to Romans. Jett flips the ball to Roanen in the flat. Roanen has some room to run on the left side. Roanen is past the thirty-five to the thirty-eight, and Droad brings him down."

"Great setup of the screen. The first down stops the clock."

"Larrola sends in the play. Ascanni winds the clock. Jett brings the offense to the line. T&A is moving right to left. Jett is under the center, Zogo. Jett takes the snap and drops back. He fires quickly to Toorleen, whom Norm Leymoita meets savagely. Toorleen picks up six, and Florida T&A hustles to the forty-four-yard line. One forty-eight to play. Jett is in the shotgun and takes the snap. He hands the ball to Roanen on a delay. Roanen squirts through the center of the line and dives for the first down. Snow covers Roanen's face."

"Nice idea, but I don't think they have enough for the first."

"They do not, and T&A takes their first time-out. There is one thirty-eight to play in the ball game."

Nurse Clare Rell felt sick. She vomited in the sink and felt weak. She looked in the mirror. Her eyes had turned an evil shade of green. She felt bugs crawling in her skin. She scratched at her flesh with rage. She pulled the hair from her head and slammed her wrists onto the edge of the sink. The thoughts running through her head made her want to die. Abaddon seized control of Rell's body and pulled himself off the floor. He knew exactly where to look for the bone saw.

"Florida T&A now faces third and one at their own forty-seven. Greg, does T&A pull a page out of Navy's book and go for the whole ball of wax?"

"No, Greg. Navy has seen the T&A sets. T&A is at midfield with plenty of time. They just need to get this first down."

"Jett lines up under Zogo. Jett takes the snap and hands the ball to Worm Roanen, who moves right and behind the Sheik.

Roanen bursts through for a first down, and Egan Paal takes him down."

"Everyone in America knew it was coming. It is a hard play to stop."

"T&A is now in Navy territory, and Jett lines up at the Navy forty-six-yard line. Jett takes the snap and hands to Roanen, who moves left. Roanen turns upfield, and Rat Doovaine upends him at the Navy forty-two. It's a gain of four."

"T&A should think about throwing the ball. The clock is starting to run."

"I thought you said they had plenty of time."

"If they throw the ball and get it down the field, yeah."

"There's one minute to play. It's second and six. Jett lines up in the shotgun. Jett takes the snap. Jett is in trouble. Navy has a full-on blitz, and Dan Kerichuck drags Jett down back at the forty-eight. That is a loss of six to bring up third and twelve. T&A calls their second time-out."

Abaddon found the bone saw. He moved the device down the hallway and slinked past the other nurses, who were reading *People* and *Us Weekly*. One of the nurses ogled over the handsome kicker from Florida T&A in the new *TWAT* edition.

He closed the door quietly behind him and entered Emily's room.

"Greg, with forty-eight seconds to play, Florida T&A is letting this one slip away."

"They have two plays to get twelve yards. T&A is more than capable. Don't count them out."

"Jett lines up under center. There is not a person in this stadium who is not standing. Jett takes the snap. Jett looks downfield. Jett gets pressure from his right. Jason Cenode misses Jett. Jett ducks and heads to his left. Romans is wide open in the flat, but Jett can't find him. Jett tucks the ball and scrambles. He avoids a tackle by Doovaine and is heading upfield. Droad zeros in on Jett.

Jett dives for the first down. It is going to be awfully close. B. K. Ascanni breaks up the pile and spots the ball. Ascanni calls in the chain gang. They are going to measure."

"What an individual effort by Jett. He did this all on his own. He had a great sense of Cenode coming from his right and great presence of mind to tuck it and run when the play broke down. He got a great block from Roanen to get him close to the marker."

"Ascanni holds his hands about two feet apart, and T&A calls its last time-out."

"Fourth and a foot. This is the ball game for T&A."

"Larrola and Jett talk it over on the sidelines, and Larrola looks sick, Greg."

"It's probably the cold weather."

"Probably. Jett heads back onto the field."

The unique group of strangers sat in the snow behind the Navy bench. Ethereal bonds wrapped them. For one moment in a lifetime, the families of the long-lost players became one in hope. Not one of them blinked.

The drool poured from Clare Rell's mouth and down her chin. The possessed nurse plugged in the bone saw and felt the quiet whirring of the motor. Abaddon coveted the soul of the child. It would be his in just a few gruesome moments.

"Seventy-eight thousand strong are on their feet in the Big Apple Dome. Thirty-eight seconds remain, and Florida T&A is in danger of having its forty-seven-game winning streak snapped. Jett lines the team up in the I formation. Shank W. Shonnejoy is in for Whiz Toorleen, and this gives the Barbarians a two-tight-end attack."

"This is a goal-line situation for Florida T&A."

"Romans goes in motion to the right. Romans taps Jett to let him know he has gone by. Zogo snaps the ball. Jett turns and hands the ball to Roanen. Roanen jumps high over the middle. No! Jett still has the ball. Romans is streaking down the center of the field on a post pattern. Alesse has slipped in the snow. Romans is wide open, and Jett lets the ball fly."

"Just what in the hell do you think you are doing?" Mother Alphonsa was pissed.

Jairus stood beside the hefty Jamaican and glared at Abaddon.

Abaddon was shocked, and he turned to look at his enemy. He began to snicker in the Devil's tongue. The gurgling bile regurgitated from Nurse Clare Rell's mouth. "You are too late to save the child. She is mine, and so is her soul." Abaddon moved the bone saw closer to Emily's neck.

"Why don't you leave that poor nurse and show us your face, you coward?" Alphonsa was not impressed or amused.

Abaddon left the nurse, and she collapsed to the floor. His meely flesh crawled around his bones. The Beast's eyes revealed the hunger of an animal denied. "A child and a black bitch. Which of you will halt me? I am Abaddon, and I have come to claim this soul as my own to rape in the fires of Hell."

"Well, if we're making introductions, mon, my name is Mother Alphonsa, and I'm going to introduce you to my big, bad voodoo stick." Alphonsa pulled the rolling pin from her hip and started whaling on Satan's pet. The light from Jairus's eyes created a shadow on the wall over Emily's bed. Abaddon whimpered and shielded himself from Alphonsa's beating. Jairus laid his hand on the sick girl's temple and closed his eyes.

J. J. "Honey" Romans was all by himself. He was running in stride with the advancing football. The pass was directly on target and floating softly in the snowflakes. Romans stretched out his hands, let the ball settle onto his fingertips, and wham! Romans collided with the goalposts, and the ball tumbled out of his hands. Romans forgot where he was on the field, and it had cost Florida T&A their third NCAA title. B. K. Ascanni signaled incomplete.

Quarterback Shaun Joint took a knee, and the Navy players surrounded him. The Barbarian players attempted no high jinks.

Some Barbarian players ran from the field into the locker room. The starters knew they had been beaten and shook the hands of the opposing team. The US Navy midshipmen in the stands rushed the field. The Big Apple Dome was complete bedlam.

A giant shadow emerged from the luxury box of Mr. Samuel Stokes. Satan's wings spread over much of the field and covered the crowd. They drowned out the banks of light. The vulture-shaped mystery hovered only for a moment and then slipped through the open roof of the Big Apple Dome. Satan would lick his wounds, and the Darkness would punish him severely. Satan had been the fool's fool.

The Hell Star erupted in the space over Foccod Knort, and the syndicate of Geeshi Grub began to retreat. King Fardorff watched with Jesus and Muhammad from the balcony of the Rupick Church as the ultimate weapon of the Darkness fell obliterated into the orbit. Mytom Onaxa, the princess of Trollien, delivered the news to her father. The captive Moses would be delivered to the Larrsen/Malsop Gorge by nightfall.

Coach Tuby Gravenald shook the hand of head coach Merl Larrola at midfield and then gathered his players and took them to the sidelines.

"When I first met you, I told you you were different from the players who started the season. They were very special boys. I was right. You are different from them. You are special men. It was the greatest football game I have ever seen. Thank you for letting me share in your miracle. Thank you for teaching me so much."

Each player hugged Coach Gravenald and thanked him for believing. Tuby would never stop believing. Ever.

The families of the players gathered on the railing and screamed their names. Team Nimrod made their way onto the field, and Nimrod whispered in Carl Broodend's ear. Broodend and the team called things to order. Nimrod addressed the gathering crowd.

"Merry Christmas!" The families returned a hearty "Merry Christmas" to Nimrod and crew. "Tonight you witnessed the greatness of God and the power of love. We have all traveled from many places to be here tonight—and none farther than the players in tonight's game. I was your guardian angel long ago. I was the guardian angel for all you. I was a young angel at the time, and I failed you. Redemption is my gift on this holy day. It is my opportunity to give a gift to you, for Christmas is for giving. Gentlemen, thank you for saving the world…twice! As a long-overdue Christmas present and as my way of saying thank you for being so patient, I'd like you to reunite with your families. Norm Leymoita, step up here."

A numb Norm stepped to Nimrod. Dominic went to his brother as if he had walked out the door sixty years ago. Norm noticed the changes in Dominic—the wrinkles in his face and the sadness in his expression. Dominic had grown heavy over the years. The eyes did not lie, though. The two brothers embraced and joined together, and the moments of their separate lives filled each other's hearts.

"I haven't always been a good son or brother. It could be a long, long time until I see you again." A lifetime of confession streamed from Dominic's eyes.

"Well, I'll be there waiting for you when you get there—just like you waited for me," said Norm. He imparted a lifetime of forgiveness to his lost brother.

Dominic felt the spirit of Christmas for the first time since 1940. He wept like a child.

Nimrod took Annette Alesse by the hand and helped her down the slippery stairs. "Gary Alesse, this is your wife, Annette." Gary looked into Annette's teary eyes and pulled her close. "And this is your son, Peter."

Peter joined Annette and Gary, and they embraced as a family for the first time. "That was a great kickoff return, Dad."

"Did you like that one, Son? I just saw the hole and took off. I felt as if I was playing for the Chicago Bears."

Gary saw himself in Peter. He understood mortality for the first time.

"Were you a big Bears fan?" Peter just wanted to hear his father talk. He absorbed every breath and word.

"You mother didn't tell you? I'm going to have to have a talk with her about that."

Gary put his arm around Annette. The Alesses laughed together and found the window of their lives open to a beautiful view.

The German shepherd barked uncontrollably. Valerie struggled to handle the excited dog.

"Rat." Doovaine stepped up to Nimrod. "Someone is very excited to see you." Commander rushed to Rat and jumped into his trainer's arms. Commander licked him all over his face. Rat looked up to see his sister, Valerie, take off her glasses. Tears streamed down her face, and Commander heeled by his side. Rat pulled his sister into his arms, and she wept. Sister Val, oddly enough, had never believed a miracle was possible. Now she knew her prayers had always been heard.

Dan B. Kerichuck twisted his little sister's arm. The three brothers and sisters fell to the ground and mobbed one another. The normally sedate scientist gushed with laughter, and her childhood returned in a moment. They threw snowballs at one another and wrestled. Michael watched his older brother tease his sister, and the trio laughed until it hurt. It was unadulterated joy. The only thing missing were the jammies with feet. The Kerichucks felt as if they were six again, and a lifetime of sorrowful waiting was whisked away in the snow. Dolores admitted to herself no amount of science could ever recreate an honest-to-goodness miracle. She reconciled her battle with God and freed her soul.

Manny Droad wept with happiness. For Manny it had always been Anna. For Anna it had always been Manny. They kissed like young lovers and held each other tight. Jaime, Miguel, and Juan felt the inner strength of their father. They felt Manny's courage and love. Manny felt the same strength in Anna. They had always been together in their hearts. Manny stared at his boys. They were older than he was to the eyes, but he saw the babies he had left behind so long ago. He knew their names without being told. They had been the fuel that kept his soul alive.

Nimrod directed Jason Cenode to the stands. "Your aunt could not be with us today. You will see her very soon. Julie loved you very much and turned her sorrow into joy. Her joy created a place where children could find love. Her love for you founded the Jason Cenode Center for Orphaned and Abandoned Children. In the stands are the four hundred fifteen men, women, and children who call or have called the Cenode Center home. They have gone to all directions on the globe, but they came here to give you a message."

The 415 members of the Cenode Center stood. In unison they shouted, "We love you, Jason! Merry Christmas!" They flooded out of the stands to embrace their inspiration.

Jason looked at Nimrod. "I want to thank you for this wonderful present." The tears streamed down his face. "Julie might have been my aunt, but she will always be my mother."

Jason hugged all 415 graduates of the Cenode Center and remembered each and every person's name.

Raytel Kigmenis stared into the face of his twin brother. Neither knew what to say. Caleb broke the silence. "You're a little late. I beat you home."

"You won. I got held up."

The brothers embraced, and the generations of the Kigmenis family formed a ring around their lost brother. Raytel saw his brothers and sisters had swindled life's attrition. He also noticed the family tree had grown tall and proud. His family had continued to fight the good fight, and they were winning. The giant cried in his sister Teresa's arms. He held his brother Joe with all his might. The Kigmenis family knelt in the snow, thanked God, and remembered their mother and father, Mabel and Jeremiah. For no tree could grow strong with deep roots without the seed of love.

Jimmy Jr. and Bud wheeled Ida down the ramp. Carl Broodend watched as his frail mother looked into his eyes. She stood from the wheelchair and walked through the snow. She never moved her eyes. "I knew you would come back for me." Ida held her son.

"I am sorry I left." Carl wept and combed her white hair.

"You should be," Ida said, and Carl laughed. "But I am not leaving you again. This time you are taking me with you."

Carl knew Ida was close to death. She had waited long enough. He looked at Nimrod, and the angel nodded. "I'll never leave you again. I am taking you with me."

Jimmy Jr. and Bud kissed Ida on the head and said good-bye. She was safe now.

"Where is Shaun Joint?"

"I am right here, sir." Shaun stepped up to Nimrod.

"Diana?" Nimrod said.

The events surrounding her bewildered Diana. It was the most beautiful dream she had ever had.

"Shaun, a young woman loved you and was lost without you," Nimrod said. "You have half of her heart. Diana has the other half."

Diana pulled the locket from her purse. Shaun looked at the other half. Shaun kicked off his shoe and sock and stood barefoot in the snow. He pulled his locket from the sock and held them both in his hands. He placed them together gently, and Paige's apparition appeared before him. She was more beautiful and happy than ever. The two lovers kissed, and the stardust swirled around their heads. Shaun and Paige twisted into the heavens together and slowly dissipated into the night and eternity. They would spend the rest of time walking the sunny beaches of Ghara Serpiana together and in love.

"Chet Skairny." Nimrod found the big tackle from Missouri. "Chet, there is a letter for you."

Chet rushed to Nimrod. He was still smarting from not getting mail at Bancroft Hall. He ripped open the letter and started to read.

December 24, 2004
Dear Chet,

    I wasn't sure I would ever find you. Or that you would find me. Or if you were even looking. I didn't know if you were alive or dead. So I came looking for you. At the end of the war, nobody could tell me where you were or if you were alive. The army said you were assumed dead. I saved up what I could, and I flew to Manila. It took a lot of courage with the war being over and the world still in chaos. From what I could find, you were in a prison camp located somewhere near Manila called Cabanatuan. I researched the records, and local Filipinos said prisoners were taken by ship to Japan, Malaya, and China. Others told me about the nightmare of the prison camps and the mass graves that consumed the dead. Still others believed American soldiers were hiding in the jungles of Mount Arayat. A guide took me through the jungles, but there was too much to search. I refused to believe you were dead. I went to Japan and searched for you.

    I was with the Red Cross, and we worked with radiation victims from the atomic bomb in Nagasaki. It was a horrible, frightening scene. It is always the innocent who suffer the most in war. Children were scarred for the rest of their short lives as the radiation ate away at their bodies.

I cried myself to sleep every night. China had become a Communist state, and I couldn't go there. I could only pray you were on the Malayan Peninsula and had survived the prison camps there. I searched the jungle villages from upper Burma south through French Indochina. The beginnings of unrest broiled north in Korea as the United States and China fought for Korea. French Indochina was a place of turmoil as postwar politics begat more violence. The poor suffered as we tried to save the starving and malaria-ridden victims of a world bent on destructing itself. We struggled to bring them food and medical supplies as thousands died of neglect. I eventually contracted malaria and died in the fall of 1947. I've been waiting ever since. I've finally found you.

I love you. Your wife,
Lily Skairny

Chet looked around for Lily. Everyone else had someone to hold onto.

"Coach Gravenald," Nimrod said. Tuby looked surprised. This was Chet's moment. "You both share a special person. Lily has finished her first assignment as your guardian angel."

Vern removed the mustache and coat, and Lily was revealed. Her brand-new wings flapped proudly in the snow, and her smile illuminated the sky. Lily was an angel. She picked up Chet and flew him around the stadium. They went swooping, diving, and gliding in the dome. Lily kissed her husband's face, and Chet relished every moment of the ride.

Tuby was confused. "Vern is really a girl?"

"That's right, Coach. And one heck of a guardian angel. She bailed us both out of some tough spots."

Tuby remembered all the nightmares. Vern—Lily—had always come to his rescue.

"Lily fixed the players."

"Now you're starting to catch on." Nimrod was proud of his student.

Egan Paal was delighted to see the joy on his teammates' faces. Egan had read the letters. He knew no one was here for him. He was satisfied to be happy for everyone else.

"Egan." Egan looked at Nimrod. "I want you to meet your son."

"There must be a mistake. I don't have any children."

"Coach Gravenald, I want you to meet your father." Egan and Tuby looked at each other. "Egan, there was a special Thanksgiving night in 1940. Do you remember that?"

Egan would never forget. "You are my son?"

"You are my father?"

Tuby had never met his father. The two men had become close over the last few weeks. Now they were closer than ever. Tuby's heart sang. Egan's heart sang louder. Nimrod smiled an unrestrained smile. His friends watched him share his moment with others. Nimrod had bluffed them all, and they knew it.

No one could see the sleigh, but they could hear the faint jingles. Then they grew louder. Then they saw the red light. St. Nicholas pulled the sleigh to a stop in the middle of the field, got out, and helped his precious cargo to the ground. Jairus fluttered his little wings and stood next to Emily. Emily walked toward Tuby and held the doll Santa had given to her for Christmas. Tuby ran to Emily, and she smiled. He held the little girl in his arms and cried. Emily wondered what all the fuss was about.

Tuby looked at Egan and then at Emily. "Would you like to meet my dad?"

"Sure," Emily replied. "Santa sure is a nice guy."

"He sure is, sweetie."

Tuby looked at St. Nicholas and winked. There was a twinkle in Santa's eye. Then he released a belly laugh and celebrated the best Christmas in a long time. Thomas tried to hide behind Vishnu. Santa spotted him and changed his expression. He pointed to the doubter and signaled him to approach. "We've got some issues we have to discuss. First, the beard tugging hurt. Second…"

Santa lectured Thomas. He had been a bad boy. Vishnu got a kick out of an elf berating his buddy.

Nimrod held his student closely. "Jairus, you scared me. I thought you had been captured."

"I was just trying to help." Jairus cried on Nimrod's shoulder.

"You did more than help. You did a great job, Jairus." Nimrod rubbed the top of the boy's mullet.

It was always a mixture of joy and sadness when a boy started to become a man.

It was time to say good-bye. The soldiers had not had that opportunity before. They seized every second, and then it was time to go. Jason Cenode waved good-bye to his family and walked with Carl Broodend. Carl picked up Ida and carried her into the tunnel. She died in his arms and woke moments later on her way to see St. Peter. Raytel kissed all his family. It wouldn't be too long before he saw all them again. He told Caleb how proud he was of him. Caleb shook his twin's hand. Shaun had already left with Paige, and Chet was hitching a ride with Lily. Dan looked into the windows that were Dolores's eyes. He thanked her for helping others. He slugged Michael in the arm and followed Rat and Commander into the mist. Manny kissed Anna and held his three boys. He had never been so proud. Manny rarely spoke in Spanish, but he whispered, *"Adios, mi amor."*

Anna's heart sang the song of the angels. Dominic watched his brother leave—again. This time around Dominic promised to do it right with what time he had left. Gary teased Annette that she needed to join him fast. Annette hoped it wouldn't be too fast. Peter had grown up well. They made plans for the future.

Tuby looked at his dad, Egan. "Thanks for the good advice."

"You're doing great. Keep up the good work, and take good care of Emily."

Emily liked Egan. Egan rubbed his son on the head.

"Yes, sir." Tuby held his father close. It soothed his soul.

Egan walked into the tunnel, and the players—and soldiers—were left to rest in peace.

St. Nicholas bid Shar, Vishnu, Thomas, and Jairus adieu. He handed Nimrod a wrapped present, and Nimrod thanked him for the favor. He turned the sleigh into the wind and took off toward the North Pole. Santa had a bumper sticker on the back of the sleigh. It said "Nimrod Saves." Nimrod held back the tears.

Vishnu walked over to Nimrod. "How did you do it?"

Nimrod didn't want to talk about it, but Vishnu had stuck with him the whole way. "I got Satan to walk into a wall."

"I don't understand." Vishnu gave Nimrod a blank stare.

"It's just like poker, Vishnu. There are no guarantees in a bet, but I felt I had Satan whipped the whole time. I also knew he would cheat. I felt I had a better hand than he did from the beginning. I had eleven aces. The trick was to make him believe I had nothing and keep getting him to raise the stakes." Nimrod paused. "And I had to make you and the team believe I had nothing. You don't bluff well."

"You did a great job of that."

Nimrod thanked him for the backhanded compliment.

"How did you know the soldiers would win the game?"

Nimrod looked at his buddy. "Because they had more heart."

"Well, what are we going to do now?" Vishnu was tired.

"I don't know about you, but I am going to Avalon to take a little vacation."

Vishnu thought a month on the mystical Celtic island of immortality would do him good, so he invited himself along.

Nimrod pulled the present from under his arm. He opened the card. It read, "Merry Christmas—Michael." Nimrod opened the box. Michael had given him his wings back.

January 1, 2005, New Year's Day

Dominic Leymoita knew he was going to die. He would have never believed it would be in Nevada. He had thought maybe a hole in upstate New York, a swamp in Florida, or a car trunk back home in Boston—not in Nevada. He called his driver, Nevin, and told him to pick him up at 10:00 a.m. Dominic went to his closet and removed a shelf that revealed a panel. Behind the panel was the dial on a safe. He spun the dial. Six for Bill Russell, thirty-three for Larry Bird, and back to seventeen for John Havlicek. The door swung open silently.

The driver showed up a few minutes before ten. Hobbled from years of obesity and hacking from more than a half century of Pall Malls, Camel no filters, and Marlboro Reds, Dominic let Nevin in his pressed black suit help him into the car. Nevin offered to take the briefcase and put it in the trunk, but Dominic politely declined.

"Where shall I take you today, Mr. Leymoita?" Nevin asked quietly.

"Riverside, California."

Nevin didn't even flinch. Riverside was not in his usual zone or state, and he did have to consult his onboard computer for directions. They headed west and watched the baking desert landscape rise before them.

A few minutes past 2:00 p.m., the sedan pulled up in front of the Cenode Center for Abandoned and Orphaned Children. Nevin helped Dominic from the car, and they worked their way up the few stairs to the front office.

"Is Commander Patrick Hart available?" Dominic said without a smile.

"I am Commander Hart. How can I help you?" he replied and extended his hand in greeting.

"I would like to make a donation to the Cenode Center. I think what you do here is wonderful."

He passed Patrick the briefcase and coughed wretchedly into his other hand.

"Thank you," Patrick stammered. He tried to place the face that looked so familiar. "May I ask who you are with?"

"Let's just say I'm with a group of made guys who aren't as bad as we're made out to be." Dominic gave him the don't-ask-any-more-questions eye.

"I understand," said Patrick. He was very clearly confused.

There was a wisp of silence.

"I'm going to have Nevin take me home now. You take care of those kids." He turned and headed back to the car.

"I will." And he would.

The Lincoln pulled away, and Patrick opened the briefcase. It was an impossible amount of money. There were bundles and bundles of hundred-dollar bills. Dominic had left $3.2 million, to be exact. Hart was certain another saint must have visited him.

Dominic wasn't trying to buy any favors or cut in line. There were only a couple things he could do with the money. He could put it all on black, double up, and throw himself one whale of a going-away party with the guys and girls. However, Dominic knew he could lose, and he wanted his last play to be a winner. He wanted a sure thing. He had found it. He felt better than when the Red Sox won the World Series. Finally.

Dominic passed away in the limo somewhere between Barstow and the sunset.

www.ingramcontent.com/pod-product-compliance
Lightning Source LLC
Chambersburg PA
CBHW051927020726
47501CB00001B/13